THE SUNSTONE BROOCH

The Celtic Brooch Series, Book 11

Katherine Lowry Logan

COPYRIGHT PAGE

An original work by Katherine Lowry Logan. *The Sunstone Brooch* copyright © 2021 by Katherine Lowry Logan

Print Edition

Website: www.katherinellogan.com

IT TAKES A VILLAGE:
Chief Editor and Content Editor: Faith Freewoman
Virtual Assistant, Fact Checker, Researcher, and Keeper of the MacKlenna Clan Series Bible: Annette Glahn
Freelance Proofreader: Elaini Caruso
Beta Readers: Lori Seiderman, Paula Retelsdorf, and Jen Coleman
Marine Advisor: John Retelsdorf
Medical Advisor: Dr. Ken Muse
Historical / Theodore Roosevelt Expert: Dr. Tom Appleton
Cover Design by Damonza
Interior Design by BB eBooks
Cover image by Jerry Blank

THE CELTIC BROOCH SERIES

CAST OF CHARACTERS

1. **Baird, Philippe:** husband of Rhona (first appeared in *The Topaz Brooch*)
2. **Baird, Rhona:** wife of Philippe (first appeared in *The Topaz Brooch*)
3. **Becky:** JC's office manager
4. **Benoit, Remy:** Elliott's bodyguard, former Army medic (first appeared in *The Topaz Brooch*)
5. **Brodie, Paul:** assistant and friend of James Cullen Fraser, Columbia graduate
6. **Dow, Wilmot:** Teddy Roosevelt's partner
7. **Duffy, Emily:** goddaughter of Kit MacKlenna Montgomery, daughter of Frances Barrett Duffy (first appeared in *The Three Brooches*)
8. **Erik:** chief of Viking warrior council
9. **Ferris, Sylvane:** ranch hand at Teddy Roosevelt's Maltese Cross Ranch
10. **Fraser, Blane and Lance:** sons of Kevin and JL O'Grady-Fraser (first appeared in *The Pearl Brooch*)
11. **Fraser, Elliott:** husband of Meredith Montgomery, father of James Cullen Fraser and Kevin Allen Fraser, Chairman of the Board of the MacKlenna Corporation, retired equine vet (appears in all *Brooch* books)
12. **Fraser, James "JC" Cullen:** son of Elliott Fraser and Meredith Montgomery, Harvard graduate, lawyer
13. **Fraser, Kevin:** husband of JL O'Grady-Fraser, father of Blane and Lance, son of Elliott Fraser, half brother of James Cullen Fraser, MacKlenna Corporation CFO (appears in all *Brooch* books except *The Ruby Brooch*)
14. **Grant, Amber:** wife of Daniel Grant, stepmom of Noah, mother of Heather
15. **Grant, Daniel:** husband of Amber Grant, father of Noah (first appeared in *The Amber Brooch*)

16. **Grant, Noah:** son of Daniel and stepson of Amber Grant

17. **Kelly, Elizabeth:** wife of Matt Kelly, mother of Amber and Olivia, lawyer (first appeared in *The Amber Brooch*)

18. **Kelly, Matt:** husband of Elizabeth Kelly, father of Amber and Olivia, lawyer (first appeared in *The Amber Brooch*)

19. **MacAndrew Williams, Ensley:** heroine, Harvard graduate, editor, friend of James Cullen Fraser

20. **Mallory, Amy:** wife of Jack Mallory, mother of Patrick and Margaret Ann, ESPN baseball analyst (first mentioned in *The Broken Brooch*)

21. **Mallory, Jack:** husband of Amy Spalding Mallory, father of Patrick and Margaret Ann, brother of Charlotte Mallory, *New York Times* best-selling author (first appeared in *The Sapphire Brooch*)

22. **Mallory, Charlotte:** wife of Braham McCabe and mother of Lincoln, Kitherina, and Amelia Rose, sister of Jack Mallory, surgeon (first appeared in *The Sapphire Brooch*)

23. **Mallory, Patrick:** adopted son of Jack and Amy Mallory

24. **Malone-O'Grady, Wilhelmina "Billie" Penelope "Penny":** wife of Rick O'Grady, mother of Jean, West Point graduate (first mentioned in *The Pearl Brooch*)

25. **MacKlenna, Sean:** husband of Lyle Ann MacKlenna, Kit MacKlenna Montgomery's uncle

26. **MacKlenna, Lyle Ann:** wife of Sean MacKlenna, Kit MacKlenna Montgomery's aunt

27. **McBain, Alicyn and Rebecca:** twin daughters of David and Kenzie McBain (first appeared in *The Pearl Brooch*)

28. **McBain, David:** husband of Kenzie McBain, father of Henry, Robbie, Laurie Wallis, Alicyn, and Rebecca, President of MacKlenna Corporation, veteran, author (appears in all *Brooch* books except *The Ruby Brooch*)

29. **McBain, Henry and Robbie:** twin sons of David and Kenzie McBain (first appeared in *The Broken Brooch*)

30. **McBain, Kenzie:** wife of David McBain, mother of Henry, Robbie, Laurie Wallis, Alicyn, and Rebecca, veteran, West Point graduate, MacKlenna Corporation attorney (first appeared in *The Emerald Brooch*)

31. **McBain, Laurie Wallis:** daughter of David and Kenzie McBain (first appeared in *The Three Brooches*)

32. **McCabe, Braham:** husband of Charlotte Mallory and father of Lincoln, Kitherina, and Amelia Rose; Jack Mallory's brother-in-law, Kit MacKlenna Montgomery's first cousin, former Union cavalry officer, lawyer, senator (appears in all *Brooch* books except *The Last MacKlenna*)

33. **McCabe, Donald:** father of Kit MacKlenna Montgomery, Captain

34. **Merrifield, Bill:** ranch hand at Teddy Roosevelt's Maltese Cross Ranch

35. **Montgomery, Cullen:** husband of Kit MacKlenna Montgomery, lawyer, author, founder of Montgomery Winery (first appeared in *The Ruby Brooch*)

36. **Montgomery, Kit MacKlenna:** wife of Cullen Montgomery, goddaughter of Elliott Fraser, guardian of Emily Duffy, founder of Montgomery Winery (first appeared in *The Ruby Brooch*)

37. **Montgomery, Kristen:** deceased younger sister of Cullen Montgomery (first appeared in *The Ruby Brooch*)

38. **Montgomery, Meredith:** wife of Elliott Fraser and mother of James Cullen Fraser, grandmother of Blane and Lawrence Fraser, owner of Montgomery Winery (appears in all *Brooch* books except *The Ruby Brooch*)

39. **Montgomery, Thomas:** son of Kit and Cullen Montgomery

40. **Norman:** Teddy Roosevelt's cook on roundup

41. **O'Grady, Austin:** son of JL O'Grady-Fraser and Chris Dalton, half brother of Blane and Lawrence Fraser, University of Kentucky graduate, point guard for the Cleveland Cavaliers (first appeared in *The Broken Brooch*)

42. **O'Grady, Connor:** husband of Olivia Kelly O'Grady, father of Betsy, brother of JL O'Grady-Fraser, Shane, Rick, and Jeff O'Grady, son of Retired Deputy Chief Lawrence "Pops" O'Grady, former NYPD detective, VP of Global Security for MacKlenna Corporation (first appeared in *The Broken Brooch*)

43. **O'Grady-Fraser, Jenny "JL" Lynn:** wife of Kevin Allen Fraser, mother of Austin O'Grady, Blane and Lawrence Fraser, sister of Connor, Rick, Shane, and Jeff O'Grady, daughter of Retired Deputy Chief Lawrence "Pops" O'Grady, former NYPD detective, VP of Development and Operations MacKlenna Corporation (first appeared in *The Broken Brooch*)

44. **O'Grady, Lawrence "Pops":** husband of Maria Ricci, father of Connor, Rick, Shane, Jeff, and JL, Retired NYPD Deputy Chief (first appeared in *The Broken Brooch*)

45. **O'Grady, Patrick "Rick":** husband of Billie, father of Jean, Marine, former NYPD detective, brother of JL, Connor, Shane, and Jeff, president of Montgomery Winery in Napa, son of Retired Deputy Chief Lawrence "Pops" O'Grady (first appeared in *The Broken Brooch*)

46. **O'Grady, Shane:** VP of Global Security for MacKlenna Corporation, brother of JL, Connor, Rick, and Jeff O'Grady, son of Retired Deputy Chief Lawrence "Pops" O'Grady (first appeared in *The Broken Brooch*)

47. **Orsini, Sophia:** wife of Pete Parrino, mother of Lukas and Churchill Parrino, painter, artist, entrepreneur, granddaughter of Seamus Digby (first appeared in *The Pearl Brooch*)

48. **Parrino, James Churchill:** Pete and Sophia's adopted son (first appeared in *The Topaz Brooch*)

49. **Parrino, Pete:** husband of Sophia Orsini, father of Lukas and Churchill, former NYPD detective, former Marine, VP for Global Security for MacKlenna Corporation, JL O'Grady-Fraser's former NYPD partner (first appeared in *The Broken Brooch*)

50. **Ricci-O'Grady, Maria:** wife of Lawrence "Pops" O'Grady (first appeared in *The Diamond Brooch*)

51. **Roosevelt, Theodore "Teddy":** New York State Assemblyman, future 26th US president

52. **Rowe, Mr.:** Teddy Roosevelt's partner

53. **Russell, Barb:** Ensley's best friend in NYC

54. **Sewall, Bill:** Teddy Roosevelt's partner

55. **Sewall, Lucretia "Kitty":** daughter of Bill and Mrs. Sewall

56. **Sewall, Mrs.:** wife of Bill Sewall, Teddy Roosevelt's cook

57. **Sten:** Erik's brother

58. **Stuart, Joseph:** son of Tavis Stuart

59. **Stuart, Tavis:** VP of Global Security MacCorp, Naval Academy graduate (first appeared in *The Topaz Brooch*)

60. **Stuart, Mark:** brother of Tavis Stuart, the ex-boyfriend of Penny Malone while she was at West Point (first mentioned in *The Topaz Brooch*)

61. **Viking warriors:** Erik, Arne, Forde, Bjørn, Birger

62. **Williams, George:** Ensley's cousin, a friend of James Cullen Fraser

1

Medora, ND—Ensley, Age 16

This book contains violence, sexually explicit scenes, and adult language and may be considered offensive to some readers.

SIXTEEN-YEAR-OLD ENSLEY MACANDREW Williams practiced a kind of bull-riding air guitar several times, circling in the dirt, clutching invisible bull ropes while her free hand waved above her head. Girls close in age watched from their folding chairs, cradling puppies and talking on their cell phones.

They weren't there to watch Ensley ride. Nope, not at all. They were there for the guys wearing clean button-down shirts, cowboy hats, and crisp 20X Wrangler jeans with colossal belt buckles.

They all looked good in clean clothes with shirts tucked into waistbands. But like her, when it came time to ride, they all traded crisp blue jeans for old, dirty ones.

Except for when she rode bulls, she wouldn't be caught dead in dirty, stretched-out jeans. And hers were so hopelessly gross that even a spritz of lemon juice and water couldn't take away the stench.

Randy Myers, a former bull rider who managed Ensley's parents' ranch in North Dakota, stopped chugging a can of Rockstar energy drink long enough to applaud. "You look ready to go!"

"If I can go ninety seconds on a mock bull, I can go ninety on a real one."

"That's what they say, monkey."

Randy had called her monkey since she climbed her first fence as a toddler, and while it embarrassed her as a preteen, she'd gotten over it. Now the affectionate term always made her smile.

"Will you tape me up, please?"

"Let me see you stretch."

"I've already done it."

He chugged the Rockstar again then tossed the empty can into the trash. "Do it again."

"Grrr." She kicked a denim leg onto the uppermost fence railing (it was a short fence) and stretched like a dancer on the ballet barre. Then switched legs. "Good enough?"

"Nope. Do it again." He got up off a hay bale stacked against a barn piled with old tires and dusty mechanical equipment. "Other leg, too." He removed his gray Stetson, wiped his forehead, and donned his hat again.

She stretched out the other leg, sweating in the North Dakota summer heat, which people from the South called a warm winter day. "Anything else you want me to do?"

"Yep! Go home."

"Not gonna happen."

She waved to a group of cowboys who smiled and winked when they strutted by. But they were more interested in the other girls—the ones sitting in folding chairs. The ones not wearing dirty jeans. The ones who didn't smell like shit. And the ones who gave out Snapchat handles as quickly as flirtatious glances.

They were the buckle bunnies.

Ensley wasn't a buckle bunny, and the only handle she had was attached to her bull rope. She was a rodeo gal who didn't date her competition.

"Will you tape my wrist, please?" She always asked nicely, or he'd snap at her for acting like a princess. She didn't want to be a princess. Hell, no. She wanted to be a rodeo queen. She was smart and pretty enough to be a queen, but she was a little conflicted about her long-term goals. When she couldn't ride anymore, she wanted to do something with books. Whether that meant she'd be a librarian or an editor or—in her dream of all dreams—a writer, only time would tell.

Randy whipped out a roll of tape from the back pocket of his jeans. "Got it right here."

She pulled up her sleeve and held out her arm. He started about four inches above her wrist and layered it down and over her wrist bone and across her palm. Then he started over again. The only time she'd broken her wrist was when she did the taping herself. Since then, he always wrapped her wrist. She could do her ankles just fine, but getting her wrist wrapped the way she liked was impossible.

Cowboys had often asked why she wanted to ride bulls. If she was in a ballbuster mood, she'd say, "Because I like sweaty flesh between my legs." Then she'd give the obnoxious cowboy a once-over and say, "And you'll never be big enough. So go away."

She'd fallen in love with the sport dominated by men years before her parents allowed her to get on a bull. First, she had to prove she was serious about it. And the way to do that was to attend a three-day session at Sankey Rodeo School and pay for it with her own money. The first time she got bucked off, the cowboys said she wouldn't get back on.

They were wrong.

Randy finished taping and held out her vest. "Here you go, monkey."

She zipped it up, adjusted the neckroll, and then collected her mouthguard and helmet with its attached face mask.

"I like your new girl-bull-rider patch. The colors even match the fringe on your chaps."

"It came in the mail the other day, but I don't know who sent it. It's cool, though, isn't it? But it makes me wonder if I have a stalker." She brushed off her custom-made leather chaps with their coordinating long, flowing fringe—the same dusty orange as her granny's favorite piece of jewelry, a sunstone brooch.

"Well, if any man dares to mess with a girl bull rider, it just goes to show you what a dumbass he is."

"Ha, ha."

"Be extra careful on this ride." He checked her chin strap and tightened it. "No broken bones today."

"Wrist, arm, ankle, and ribs are enough for me."

"And one concussion."

She wiggled the helmet to check the stability for herself. "Only one?"

"If you get another one, I won't stick around to pick you up again."

Randy didn't have to remind her that a bull rider usually got an injury in one out of every fifteen rides, and this was the fifteenth since she broke a rib.

She threaded the bells through the end of the bull rope, made a large loop, and secured it with a big knot. "Mom and Dad won't stick around, either. It's hard enough watching from the bleachers."

"Your dad wants to be your barrelman."

She tested the strength of the knot. "No way. Only one of us needs to be out here."

Randy laughed. "When I told him no, he said he'd fire me so he could be your flankman."

"Good luck with that. He'd make me too nervous."

How many times had her dad told her that bull riding was a macho pastime on par with race car driving and the most dangerous eight seconds in sports? Dozens. No, maybe hundreds. Riders got stepped on, landed on their heads, dislocated joints, pulled groins, and broke bones. But she enjoyed participating in a sport rooted in the mystique of the Wild West, and riding was in her soul. She was born to be a fighter, and right now, riding a fifteen-hundred-pound bull that weighed as much as the truck she drove was her form of fighting.

She played the game, took the pain, and was willing to pay for what she loved with sore muscles and occasional broken bones. It had to be the biggest adrenaline rush in the world. And unless she broke both legs, she'd always get up and walk, hop, or hobble out of the arena.

Tonight, though, would make it all worthwhile. This event was the last one before she had to either quit or step up to the next level, where the competition would get much stiffer. If she won, it would make moving up easier, although there wasn't much opportunity for her to become a professional bull rider.

The announcer called, "Williams 511, let's go. Put your rope on."

Randy rapped on the top of her helmet again. "Time to cowboy up."

Adrenaline was surging now as she climbed up into the bucking chute, carrying her bull rope and bells. Slowly she eased down on the bull's back. Her pinky toes lined up with the bottom rungs on the gates, so her spurs faced north-south, not east-west.

From here on out, it was all muscle memory. Her mind had to go blank. If she thought about what she was doing, she'd be a second behind, and she had to be in the correct mindset to react instantly.

She dropped the bull rope with the attached bells—jingling against the rungs of the chute—down the right side of the bull.

"I need a hook."

Randy stood on the left side of the pen, his rubber boots sinking into the stinking muck and excrement. He used the flank hook to grab the knot tied at the end of the bull rope. After running it underneath the bull, he handed her the loop. She ran the rope tail through it and pulled, tightening it around the belly of the bull, and continued tightening and adjusting it until she positioned the handle on the rope just right.

Then she ran her gloved hand through the handle and adjusted the position once more. Satisfied, she took the tail of the rope and wrapped it over the top of the handle, and closed her hand over the rope, tightening the grip.

Adrenaline was pouring into her veins now.

She wrapped the rope tail around her wrist again, across her palm, and finished with weaving the rope through her fourth and fifth gloved fingers, forming a tight fist. Then she punched down on it.

The rest of the tail she pulled over her right leg.

It was time.

She reached way up on the railing and pulled her lady gooch to her pinkie—slide and ride. She sat slightly cocked to one side to avoid smashing her face on the slide gate when the bull pitched in the chute.

Then she grinned, winked, and gave a calm verbal command to Randy and the gateman. "Okay, boys."

The gate flew open, and the clock started when the bull exploded from the chute. The clock would stop when Ensley's hand came out of the rope, her feet touched the ground, or her free arm touched the bull.

The bull bucked with an explosive upward movement that forced her body to rock back like she was sitting in a rocking chair tipped back as far as it would go, while the front end dropped when the animal hit the ground, jolting her.

One, two, three bucks as the bull spun in a circle.

She flung her legs high to spur the bull, hoping to earn bonus points.

The bull went into another spin while bucking, and she struggled to get into the bull's rhythm. The bull then kicked out to the side and twisted its torso, tilting her to the opposite side, putting pressure on her arm.

Then the bull bucked her off, and the ride turned into a complete shit show.

Ensley was on her feet, but her hand was caught in the bull rope. She flopped against the bull like a rag doll. With all her weight pulling down on her arm, it forced her hand to clamp shut when she needed it to open so she could break loose.

The bull tried to hook her with his horns, determined to get her off and away from him. She was stuck, trying to hang close until the bullfighters came out to help her break free. Seconds ticked off the clock. The snorting bull beat her up as he twisted and bucked.

"Damn," she screamed, struggling with the rope.

The bull twisted so hard that her hand finally came loose. The force, though, knocked her to the ground, where the bull kicked her in the hip, sending her flying. When she landed in the dirt, the impact knocked her out.

She floated above her body without any pain, disconnected from the injured girl on the ground and the aghast spectators whispering their fears.

Men ran toward the body while others ran after the bull. And she watched all the action from her perch high above the arena where there was no pain.

You must go back, Ensley.

I'm too broken.

You must be the warrior you were born to be. The Keeper will need you for the coming war.

What war?

You will discover that in time. But always remember you carry the handprints of your ancestors on your heart. And when you are ready, your true love will find you.

Then the voice blew a breath of warm air across her face. When she looked again at the injured girl, the image of an ash tree supporting the universe with its roots extended into the underworld appeared on her forehead.

What's that?

You are marked. Never forget.

And then the warm air blew it away.

2

Napa, CA (1881)—James Cullen, Age 13

T HE LIGHT WENT out.

His head throbbed, and blood trickled down his face.

He was scared and tired and hungry, and he wanted to go home. And now he was in total darkness.

Don't be scared, wee laddie. Ye come from a long line of Highland warriors. Don't ye give up. Not today. Not ever.

His heart pounded in his chest, his throat, even in his ears, and he almost pissed his pants—again. "Who's there? Who are you? I can't see you."

He plastered himself against the wall as soon as he realized he didn't actually hear the voice. It wasn't as if a woman stood next to him. He sensed her voice, like mental telepathy. He shook his head hard, just like Tater Tot shook when he came out of the lake.

"Who are you?" he asked again.

The disembodied woman said, *A guardian.*

Anxiety still gripped him, but he wasn't afraid of her. "Like an angel?"

Nay, not an angel.

"A Jedi Knight?"

I've never met one.

"A see-through person, then. A ghost, like Uncle Cullen?"

Aye, a see-through person. I'm Kristen.

"Uncle Cullen had a sister named Kristen. I've seen her name on my family tree. She drowned."

Aye.

"I heard she saved Uncle Cullen from drowning after he was shot."

I've always watched over him.

"Are you watching over me?"

I'm watching over ye both.

"Is Uncle Cullen in trouble, too?"

That's why I'm here. Ye have to go back.

"What do you think I'm trying to do?" he said in a frustrated singsong voice, waving his arms for emphasis. "I lost my light." A touch, soft as a feather, brushed James Cullen's cheek, sending shivers up and down his spine.

Before ye were born, young Cullen, ye were given the gift of sight. Ye're blessed.

"What's the gift of sight?"

The ability to see what others cannot.

"Like Superman's X-ray vision?"

Ah, wee laddie. The gift is limitless, but it doesn't all come at once.

Okay, this was getting too weird for even a campfire ghost story. "Do you have the gift?"

Aye.

"But you're dead."

I don't have an earthly body.

He was hallucinating. That had to be the answer. The moldy smell he'd been smelling must be those hallucinogenic mushrooms.

It's time for ye to use yer gift.

"How can I use it? I don't even understand what it is."

Understanding will come.

"When? Why can't I understand now?"

What ye seek will be revealed.

"You're talking in circles."

Clarity will come, too, young Cullen.

"The only thing coming my way are the men with butterfly nets. See, I don't believe you, and what I seek, you're not capable of giving me. I want to go home."

It's not my purpose to give ye anything.

A faint breeze washed over him, and his hair fluttered. He jumped to his feet, turning in circles. "Hey, wait, Lady Yoda. Don't go. I didn't mean to be rude. Tell me more about the gift." The air grew still, and in his heart, he knew he was alone again.

3

Cleveland, OH (2 years ago)—Austin

AUSTIN O'GRADY WOKE up to the morning sun hovering over Lake Erie. The view from his contemporary waterfront home was spectacular. He'd found the gated community in Bratenahl, Ohio, when he signed with the Cleveland Cavaliers and purchased the five-million-dollar estate with his basketball earnings.

Austin forced himself out of bed and stood naked in front of the floor-to-ceiling window in the master bedroom, stretching as he gazed out over the lake. But he didn't have time to stand there. He'd committed to a workout at the practice facility with his teammates.

And he was ready to test the coach's prediction that if he worked hard enough, he could dominate the league next season and be the first player in basketball history to have a perfect game—five points, five rebounds, five assists, five steals, and five blocked shots in a single game.

He had a goal. He had a plan. He had the motivation. Nothing was going to stop him.

A few hours later, after a perfect workout, his legs felt great, better than they had all year. Everything for him was clicking except his love life, which always seemed more exciting to his family than it was. But he couldn't complain. He had no trouble finding a date to attend a party or share his bed, but no real sparks.

And he'd yet to meet a woman worthy of the MacKlenna badass moniker. He wasn't even sure another woman like JL and his aunts existed. So for now, as long as the women he dated liked sports, he'd keep asking them out and measuring them against an impossible standard.

He was running on zero energy when he made the trip back

home, but at least he had time to take a nap before meeting with his writing instructor to review the latest chapter of his book, *How to Play Basketball and Win.*

But when he woke up, he was still exhausted and considered canceling the meeting. But Pops had raised him to keep appointments, so Austin dragged himself out again.

The meeting with his writing instructor was only a couple of miles away, and since it was such a beautiful day, what better way to enjoy the sun on his face than from the back of his Yamaha?

The session was productive, and at the end of it, Willie walked him to the door. "What have you got scheduled for the rest of the day?"

"Well, Shakespeare, I plan to go home, eat, take a nap, and review my notes." Austin walked out and climbed back on his bike.

Willie watched from his doorway, frowning a bit. "Where's your Corvette? You shouldn't be riding a motorcycle."

"I shouldn't be doing a lot of things I do." Austin pulled the clutch toward him and revved the engine without moving forward.

"And where's your helmet, man? You shouldn't be riding a bike, and you shouldn't be riding one without a helmet."

"You already told me." Austin put the bike in gear, released the clutch, and cruised down the street, revving the cycle again just to bug Willie. Then, in the middle of a third rev, the motorcycle popped up and shot off with the front tire hovering above the pavement.

Let go, Austin. Let go!

But he couldn't. His grip tightened as he struggled to hold on. When the back wheel spun out of control, his heart leaped into his throat, and he was terrified he might slide off the back. He used all his strength to shift his weight forward, over the handlebars, hoping it would force the front wheel back onto the pavement.

But the bike was heading straight toward a telephone pole. And he couldn't do a damn thing about it except tense up and prepare for impact.

The crash was explosive, metal crunching all around him. He couldn't turn his body out of the way, so he ended up swiping his entire left side and spun above the ground like a horizontal pinwheel before hitting the lawn facedown.

The pain was so intense he screamed, and he couldn't move from his waist down, which terrified him even more.

Willie ran toward him, and as he got closer, his jaw dropped, his face turned pasty white, and his eyes flooded with tears. At that moment, Willie confirmed what Austin already knew.

He was fucked up.

Willie squatted beside him and called 9-1-1. "Motorcycle accident a block from City Hall on Bratenahl Road. Cavaliers star player Austin O'Grady is seriously injured. Hurry."

It felt like someone was skinning Austin alive, starting with his lower body, and he was beginning to lose consciousness.

Willie squeezed his hand. "It's going to be all right. Help's on the way. Hang in there."

But Austin knew he would never be all right again.

His life was draining away.

Then everything went black, and he found himself looking down at his own body.

Go back, Austin. It's not your time.

It hurts, Mom. It hurts real bad.

It won't always hurt. Go back for Pops. Go back for JL. They need you. You're not a quitter. Stay alive. The love of your life is coming.

4

Cambridge, MA—Ensley

THE UBER DRIVER parked his Ford at the curb on tree-lined Channing Street in Cambridge, and Ensley MacAndrew Williams thanked and paid him. Then she climbed out, grabbing her computer bag.

The driver opened the trunk and removed her wheeled weekender. She slung the computer bag over her shoulder and accepted the luggage, wheeling it up the walkway to the front door of the Williams family's Dutch Colonial house. Her ancestor built the residence in 1890, and a long line of family members, including her, had lived here rent-free while attending Harvard University.

She had hundreds of warm memories of living in the house during her four years as an undergrad and two years while at Boston College working on her master's.

As she punched in the familiar security code to open the front door, her cell phone rang, and her boss's ID popped up. She pushed open the door before answering the call.

"This is Ensley."

"Hey, it's Susan. I've got some news to share."

Ensley's antenna shot straight up at the sound of her boss's voice, and she paused on the doorstep. Susan's terseness wasn't normal, but Ensley couldn't imagine what was wrong.

"It's not good news, is it?" Ensley asked.

Susan let out a long sigh. "No, it's not, and I can't do anything to soften it. So here it is—"

Ensley held her breath.

Don't let it be the Roosevelt book, please.

"I just got word that Simon & Sandler has purchased our publishing house, and they're laying off most of our editorial staff. I'm sorry."

Ensley took a quick breath. "But what about my client, Professor Whiteside, and his Roosevelt book?"

"That's just like you, Ensley, to worry about your client and not the loss of your job. They assigned the professor to another editor."

She'd tied all her hopes and aspirations to the tail of that book. "I've waited for this manuscript, this client to come along. It's a perfect fit with my skill set." She wasn't a crier, but damn, this hurt. "So you're saying I've lost my client and my job?"

"I'm sorry."

"Is there anything I can do? Anyone I can call? I'll even work for free just to edit his manuscript." And she would, too, but no one would agree to that. "It took forever to set up an appointment with the professor. I'll call him at home tonight."

"That's not necessary." Susan sighed again. "They canceled your appointment and set up another one with the new editor."

"Already?" Just like that—one phone call—and it was all taken away from her.

"The new editor has already contacted him and scheduled a Zoom meeting for next week."

"Zoom meeting? Really? I took the train up here, traveled on my dime and my time, to meet him in person. His new editor won't give him the time he needs to develop his manuscript, and you know it."

"You always go the extra mile, Ensley. But in this case, it's out of my hands and out of yours, too."

They were letting her go and giving away her dream client. In a daze, she rolled her suitcase to the bottom of the staircase, dropped her purse and computer bag, and left them there as a wave of hot, stuffy air nearly wilted her on the spot.

"When does this all go down?" She dragged herself to the Nest thermostat to turn on the air conditioner. There was another long sigh on the other end of the phone, and it was beginning to annoy her. Ensley deserved to be the one sighing.

She set her goal to become an editor at a New York City publishing house at the beginning of her senior year in high school. She'd worked her ass off, gotten her dream job, and now a nameless person at the top of an org chart yanked it away. Just like that!

"It's all done, Ensley. I'm sorry. You can come in tomorrow and clean out your desk."

Her lips quivered, and she could barely speak, but she managed to say, "I'm in Cambridge. Can it wait until Monday?"

"Sure…but Ensley, they won't pay your food and hotel expenses."

Well, why don't you just kick me when I'm down?

They had approved her meeting with Professor Whiteside at his office in the history department at Harvard, and now they weren't paying for her hotel. She wasn't staying in one, but still, it was the principle of the thing.

And it sucked.

"I'll just submit my transportation expenses. No hotel. No food."

"Look, I feel so bad about this."

"It's not your fault. I don't blame you. It would have been better, though, if you told me before I took the train up here."

"I just got off the phone with the president of the publishing house and decided to call you first so you could turn around and come back to New York."

That's big of you.

Ensley sat down in a spoon-back hall chair in the foyer. "Is your job safe?"

"For right now, but who knows what will happen tomorrow. If you need a letter of recommendation, let me know."

"That will help. Thanks."

"I'll do it right now so I can sign it as senior editor," Susan said. "In case…well…in case things change."

"I hope you keep your job. The house would be stupid to let you go."

"That's the way I feel about you. You're an excellent editor, and I wish you the best. If you ever write the next Great American Novel, I hope you'll give me a chance to read it—wherever I am."

"Sure thing." Ensley couldn't even say goodbye. She just disconnected the call.

Her phone rang again. She didn't want to talk to anyone else, but she checked the caller ID anyway. Her BFF's name—Barb—flashed on the screen. If she didn't take the call, Barb would call back in a few minutes.

Ensley needed a moment to regroup, so she let the call go unanswered and took several deep breaths until she got herself under control. When Barb called back, Ensley answered. Barb's sweaty face appeared on the screen, with Central Park's Dene Slope filling the screen's background.

"Hey, girl. It looks like you're in the park. How far did you run?"

"The full loop," Barb said. "All six-point-one miles. I thought you'd be here for the group run. Where are you?"

"Cambridge. I told you last week. Have you forgotten already?"

"You know I don't remember anything if I don't write it down," Barb reminded her.

"Look at the calendar on your phone, girlfriend. Today is Thursday, and you did write it down."

"Okay, I believe you." Barb sat down on the rustic bench overlooking a wildflower meadow—one of their favorite places in the park—and she wiped her forehead with the bottom of her tech shirt. "I was hoping you were free for dinner. I guess that's a no."

"I'll be here until Saturday afternoon. If you want to have dinner when I get back, let's make it late."

Barb removed her ball cap and used it to fan her face. "That might work. Although I have a date Friday, and if it goes according to plan, I might not be free until Sunday."

Ensley was calm enough now to venture into the light. She picked up her computer bag and purse and hauled them to the eat-in chef's kitchen, which was hot as a whore's doorknob on nickel night. She managed a smile. That was one of Randy's favorite sayings, along with sweating like a whore in church. Thinking about him reminded her that his birthday was in two weeks, and she never missed FaceTiming with him.

She switched on the ceiling fan and stood beneath it while the blades dispersed the cold air blowing from the ceiling vents. Then she remembered what Barb just said.

"Wait a minute. Did you say a date?"

"I did."

"Does that mean my cousin George got the message and asked you out?"

Barb's face lit up. "Yep, he did, and you could have picked me up off the floor."

Ensley dropped her purse and computer bag on the counter before finding a water glass and filling it from the tap. At least she could be happy for her best friend. And it truly did make her happy. Barb had wanted a date with George ever since she recovered from breaking up with the asshat who cheated on her.

"What'd you say to him?" Barb asked.

Ensley gulped water before she answered. "Nothing. You told me not to." She set down the phone and opened the wine cooler to find two bottles—a chardonnay and a sauvignon blanc. She grabbed the Montgomery Winery chardonnay.

"Hey, I can't see you. Prop up the phone," Barb said. "The ceiling fan blades are making me dizzy."

Ensley leaned over the counter so Barb could see her face. "Until last night, George and I hadn't talked in weeks. I guess he finally picked up on all the hints you've been dropping."

"Maybe your old flame Wyatt talked to him."

"God, I'm glad that fire burned out." Ensley filled the empty water glass with wine. "I haven't talked to Wyatt in eight months, and I hope I never have to talk to him again. He's a frigging sports nut. Nothing comes between him and a basketball or football game. I could have handled the games if he'd only been willing to do something I wanted to do once in a while."

"He isn't into your high-adrenaline activities. Next time you meet a guy, find out right off the bat if he'd rather be a participant or an observer. Wyatt is happiest drinking beer with his buddies and betting on games."

Ensley carried her wine over to the kitchen table, where she leaned the phone against the empty bowl she used to keep full of fruit when she lived here. "It was easier to put up with him than to break up and jump back into the dating pool."

"Wyatt was light-years outside your dating pool. Why don't you ask George to fix you up? At least he knows what kind of guy you're looking for."

"We're meeting for dinner in about an hour. I'll ask him."

Barb's jaw dropped. "He's in Cambridge?"

Ensley flopped down into a chair and adjusted the phone a bit so she could see Barb's face better. "Don't get your panties in a wad. He'll be back in the city in time for your date."

"He better come back. He got reservations at The Polo Bar."

"Holy cow!" Ensley sat bolt upright. "How'd he do that? I want to go. That restaurant is supposed to have the best ambiance in New York City." Ensley wasn't the jealous type, but she had to admit a dinner date at The Polo Bar was droolworthy.

"I'll let you know. I plan to order pigs in a blanket and take in the ambiance."

"Sounds like you're more excited about where you're going than who you're going with."

"George could take me to his local pub, and I'd be just as excited. But I'm extra-impressed that he's taking me to The Polo Bar."

Ensley relaxed a bit, but the loss of her job lay heavy on her disappointed heart. "Well, my cousin's a classy dude." And he was. All her cousins were classy guys, but George was the only one still single.

"So, what kind of guy are you going to tell George to hook you up with?"

"All his friends are in finance, and I find them boring."

"I'm in finance, and you don't think I'm boring."

"I'm not dating you, and besides, we rarely talk about work."

"You want a man who can cook and discuss literature, but I'm going to tell George to fix you up with a six-five athlete from his gym who squeaked through an SEC school."

Ensley rolled her eyes. "I'm going to get a puppy instead."

"No, you're not."

"Miniature Goldendoodles are so cute, but I wouldn't want to leave a puppy alone all day."

"Then it's a guy you're looking for."

"I don't want one more than a foot taller than I am. Hugging a guy when you only reach his navel is sort of disgusting. And as far as schools in the Southeastern Conference, I'm working with two talented authors from the South. One went to Vanderbilt, the other to Ole Miss."

"Ole Miss is one of the top twenty party schools in the nation."

Ensley sipped her wine. "Inquiring minds want to know where you heard that."

Barb laughed. "You don't care anything about sports, do you? If you did, you'd know that tailgating before a football game in Ole Miss's Grove tops the list of the ten coolest college football experiences."

"And you know that be...cause...?" Ensley dragged out the word.

"Because," Barb said, "unlike you, I enjoy college football and basketball."

"Then *you* should date Wyatt."

"No way! But don't be such a snob. You might find a manuscript from an athlete in your slush pile that's well written and entertaining."

"I got one recently from an NBA player whose injury ended his professional career, and I passed on it."

"What's his name?"

"I can't tell you," Ensley said.

"I bet it's a very uplifting story."

"Yeah, right. This franchise pays a player millions of dollars to throw a ball into a basket. Then he does a dumb stunt on a motorcycle and injures himself so badly he can't play ball again. Why would anyone buy a story like that?"

Barb gasped. "You're talking about Austin O'Grady, aren't you? How could you turn down a manuscript from him? Please tell me you didn't."

Ensley lifted her glass of wine, cheering herself on. "I certainly did."

"Didn't you google him? Weren't you curious about his story? O'Grady graduated at the top of his class with a degree in accounting, was the Naismith College Player of the Year, and a first-round draft pick. And you turned him down? I can't believe it."

"I wasn't impressed."

"Damn, girl. He's a stud. Look at his picture."

"I'm not in the habit of acquiring a book based on the author's looks or rewarding anyone for doing something stupid."

"Or forgiving them." Barb sighed and gave Ensley a sad smile. "You're not talking about a basketball-player-wannabe-writer, but the drunk driver who killed your dad."

Ensley white-knuckled her glass and gulped her wine. "People who do stupid things and end up hurting themselves or others don't deserve sympathy or forgiveness. And just so you know, I didn't turn it down because the author was a ballplayer. The guy knows how to write, and I like his writing style."

"So why'd you turn it down?"

"He hasn't finished the story. I told his agent that her client needs to work on the ending. When he figures out what he wants to do with his life and does it, the book will have a point. Right now, it's just languishing between the accident and his desire to return to the NBA. I would buy a motivational book. But that's not what he's written."

Barb smirked. "That was big of you."

Ensley cringed at hearing the words she'd wanted to fling at

Susan thrown back at her. "Well, I didn't want to destroy his second dream."

"As I said, that was big of you."

It hurt to send out rejection letters, but it went with the job—or went with the job she used to have. "Don't be mean, Barb. I can't accept everything that's submitted."

"I know you can't. So how's your recent release doing? It was a historical romance. Right?"

"It was the fifth book in a series, and the author added hot sex scenes to further character development. It wasn't filler. It was important to their relationship."

Barb laughed, rolling her eyes. "Don't tell me readers complained about the sex?"

"Okay, I won't." Ensley laughed too, which gave her a rush of warm fuzzies that evaporated quickly. "Well, some readers thought it was vulgar. But here's the deal. *New York Times* best-selling romantic suspense authors write the same level of heat."

"So, what are you saying? It's all about readers' expectations?"

"I think so. More readers liked it than didn't. And the ones who liked it *really* liked it. What I found interesting was the violence depicted in the battle scenes didn't bother anybody, but the sex had them slinging one-star reviews."

"You read one-star reviews, make a note of them, and move on. If it were me, I'd hide in a corner and cry."

Ensley dismissed the idea with a wave of her hand. "If I did that, I'd have to switch careers or live in a corner crying all day."

"And you'd never switch careers. You love it too much. Now… Changing the subject… What's George doing in Cambridge?"

Ensley kicked off her slip-on Allbirds, stretched her legs out on the neighboring chair, and rubbed her tight hip, a reminder of her rodeo days. "He has a meeting with a client in the morning. Then he'll take the train back to the city."

"So you both had to go to Cambridge to see each other."

"Okay, it's time to start this conversation over. You think it's awful that I sent O'Grady a rejection letter and pitiful that George and I can't work out a time to meet in the city. And you're disappointed I didn't run with the group. So what the hell is going on with you?"

Barb dropped her head back, then slowly lifted it. "You don't miss much, do you?"

Ensley reached for the bottle of wine and refilled her glass. "In your case, griping is out of character. So what's wrong? Is it your mom?"

"She didn't get the promotion she was up for at work, and we're both convinced it's age discrimination. I want her to hire a lawyer, but she doesn't want to rock the boat."

"I'm so sorry. I know your mom had her heart set on that job." Ensley had her heart set on her editing job but couldn't think about that right now. So she focused on Barb's mom instead, but every time Barb mentioned her mom, Ensley's gut squeezed into knots.

It was only a year ago that Ensley's mom had a heart attack and died just two years after her dad, and she missed both of them every day, every hour. They had been her number-one fans, but at least they weren't around to see her disappointment.

After a fortifying sip of wine, Ensley said, "Have you met Chris? She runs with our group occasionally."

"The skinny blonde? Sure."

"She's an employment lawyer. You should make an appointment for your mom. It's worth a meeting. She might have a case against her employer."

"Damn. Why didn't I think of that?" Barb said. "Maybe Chris will be at tomorrow's run. If she is, I'll get her contact info and set up an appointment. I feel better already just knowing there's something I can do. Mom might not have a case, but at least I can find out. Right?"

"Right."

Barb blew out a breath. "So, what are you doing in Cambridge?"

Ensley hated lying, but she wasn't ready to share her news. "I'm meeting with a new author tomorrow. He wrote a book about Teddy Roosevelt, my favorite president, and I love the manuscript. I think it'll make the NYT best-seller list. It's that good."

Barb propped her phone against the back of the bench while she did a few quad stretches. "Just as long as I don't have to read it."

"You've never read any of the books I recommend, so I'm not holding out hope that you'll read one about Roosevelt."

"Doesn't he have his face on that mountain?"

"Geez. Tell me you didn't just ask that." Ensley rolled her eyes. "He's on Mount Rushmore with Lincoln, Washington, and Jefferson. And he's widely regarded as the first modern president of the United States. He was a fascinating man."

And now I'm no longer editing a book about him.

"Right. I knew it was somewhere out there where you used to live and play Junior Ranger."

"I lived in North Dakota. Mount Rushmore is in the Black Hills of *South* Dakota."

"I'm in finance, sweetie. History isn't my thing."

"Neither is geography," Ensley said with a snicker.

Barb switched legs and stretched her other quad. "Hey, don't be cruel."

"You know… It's time we both broadened our horizons. I'll talk to George about fixing me up with someone, and you can read the Roosevelt book when it's released."

Barb picked up her phone and started walking down the trail, passing the wildflower meadow. "Since that book won't be out until next year, I can safely agree to broaden my horizons. I doubt either one of us will remember this conversation. Well, maybe you will. You have one of those eidetic memories."

"Not quite."

"Close enough. Hey, you know what?" Barb said. "When your Roosevelt guy was in the White House, modern sports emerged in America, and the athletic paradigm still reigns today."

"How in the world do you know that?"

"It was a question on Jeopardy."

"I should have known."

"Okay, I've got to put my phone away and pay attention to where I am. I'll call you soon."

"Stay safe." Ensley put the phone down and carried her wine and suitcase upstairs. She couldn't stay out late tonight because tomorrow was her first face-to-face meeting with her new client.

What the hell was she thinking? She didn't have a client meeting tomorrow. She didn't even have a job.

Don't cry. George will know something is wrong. And I don't want my disappointment to interfere with dinner.

She hefted her suitcase onto the luggage rack, noting that she had just enough time to rinse, dry, dress, and add a touch of makeup. If she wasn't wearing a cowboy hat, she'd pull her long hair up in a messy bun, but tonight it would hang down her back.

She finished her wine, then jumped in the shower.

Fifteen minutes later, she zipped up her jeans, shoved her feet into her cowboy boots, slipped on a denim jacket, and tied a red-checkered scarf around her neck. She'd dug it out of a trunk full of clothes and memorabilia she moved from the ranch. The scarf was a high school 4-H project made from an old tablecloth, and it even had a built-in face mask. Yeehaw!

George was due any minute now, and she had to set aside all thoughts of her job loss.

She posed in front of the mirror. Except for the hurt in her eyes, she looked spectacular, if she did say so herself. But the jacket could use some bling to pull everyone's attention away from her sad face.

She picked through the several pieces of her mother's jewelry she brought with her to wear with this weekend's outfits. The antique Celtic brooch originally belonged to her four-times-great-grandmother, and it would look gorgeous with the denim jacket. The center stone glowed like the sun at sunset, plus it was big and bright with plenty of bling—a showstopper piece.

Her mother once said that the stone restored the enjoyment of life to the wearer.

We'll see about that.

She held it up to the light and noticed a small crack around the stone. Had the jeweler damaged it while cleaning it recently? Noticing a tiny clasp at the edge of the stone, she flicked it with her fingernail. The stone popped open and revealed an inscription.

Ensley ran her finger over the words engraved on the inside, thinking they looked Gaelic. She'd edited a series of Scottish romances that used similar words.

She sounded them out. *"Chan ann le tìm no àite a bhios sinn a' tomhais an' gaol ach 's ann le neart anama."*

As soon as she spoke the last word, a misty substance spread out around her feet. "Christ!"

She jumped out of the way, but the mist followed her, stinking up the room with an earthy smell. She grabbed her hat and fanned the fog, but it only grew and thickened around her.

The brooch heated, burning her hand, and, heart racing and adrenaline pumping, she threw the damn thing and ran out of the room, but the mist followed her.

She couldn't outrun it or fan it away.

Go outside!

But by the time she hit the bottom step, the mist completely engulfed her. "Help!" she screamed, frantically waving her hat and arms, but she was stuck in the thick of it now.

And that was the last she knew.

5

Cambridge, MA—James Cullen

J AMES CULLEN FRASER relaxed in the billiard hall of the exclusive undergraduate Porcellian Club in Cambridge, sipping whisky. At the same time, he stared up at Teddy Roosevelt's portrait, one of a long line of famous members of the centuries-old club.

JC had spent countless hours in this four-story stone and brick building during his undergraduate studies and law school. But this was the first time he'd entered one of Harvard's most secretive, men-only social clubs since graduating four years ago.

And nothing in the club had changed. It still had the same smell of cigar smoke, the same buttery softness of cowhide leather chairs, and the same mustiness created by the hundreds of old leather-bound books in the library.

The purpose of his Cambridge visit was to meet with the Manager of Donor Services for the law school. The appointment was at nine tomorrow morning, but instead of taking an early flight, he came up from DC late this afternoon.

Since he was here alone, he stopped by the club, hoping to find a friend to join him for dinner. But so far, no luck. He'd give it another few minutes. If no one he knew showed up, he didn't mind eating alone. He did it often enough since his niche law practice required him to travel light—and travel often.

He continually scanned the room, careful to appear disinterested. Scattered around the room were ten men, all in their early twenties, grouped in twos and threes, mostly talking about women. He wasn't interested in talking about tits and asses. He preferred discussions about literature, politics, international relations, or sports. It wasn't that he didn't enjoy women's company. He did—often—but he was resisting the pull of a long-term commitment. Being tied down wouldn't fit into his lifestyle or life plan for at least another decade.

An old story had floated around the club for years that if a member hadn't made his first million by the time he was thirty, the club would give it to him. JC made his first million before he turned sixteen. Since then, as his portfolio expanded enough to put him on the Forbes list of under-thirty multimillionaire philanthropists, he looked for more ways to give it away. That's why he was meeting with the Manager of Donor Services. He wanted to underwrite another scholarship.

"JC!" a familiar baritone voice called out to him.

"George!" JC pushed to his feet and greeted George with a fist bump/hug combo. He and George met their freshman year, and while their friendship continued through undergrad and law school, they lived in different cities now and only saw each other once or twice a year. But their bond was still strong enough that he would be a groomsman at George's wedding and vice versa. "Nice surprise."

"What brings you up here from the hotbed of political discourse?"

JC laughed. "You've got that right. I have a meeting on campus first thing in the morning. What about you?"

"I just got out of one meeting and have another one in the morning." George signaled to a waiter, who glided over and took his order for a beer. "I'm glad I ran into you. I rented a condo in Vail for early December, so block out a few days. I'm trying to get the old crowd together for a ski weekend."

"I'll put a hold on the first two weeks of December. Let me know as soon as you have a date."

"Sure thing." The waiter returned with the beer and set it on the side table next to George.

"Put it on my tab," JC said with a nod to the waiter.

"Thanks. I owe you one."

"Hell, George, we stopped keeping track years ago." JC tapped his hardball glass against George's bottle. "Cheers."

George took a long pull. "Hey, I'm meeting Ensley in an hour. Unless you already have dinner plans, why don't you join us?"

"Ensley? God, I haven't seen her since"—he shrugged—"I don't know when." George's drop-dead-gorgeous cousin had been a temptation at one time, but JC never crossed the line with her. Guys never dated their best friend's sister—or, in this case, cousin.

"Thanks, but I don't want to intrude."

George gestured with his beer bottle. "Intrude? Come on. Didn't we eat together almost every night? You won't be intruding now any more than you were then."

"It's different now. We don't see each other every day. So what's she doing? Is she still working in New York City?"

"Yeah, but she's still struggling with losing her mom. It's been hard on her."

"I should have called her before now. When you lose your parents, it's gotta put cracks in your world."

George nodded. "Dr. Fraser's in his late seventies. That has to concern you."

"Dad's timeless. He beat cancer, recovered from a mini-stroke, and looks younger today than he did when I first came to Cambridge." Discussing his family's health with anyone outside the immediate family was off-limits, even with someone as close as George. JC turned the subject back to Ensley. "So what's she doing about the ranch?"

George rolled the bottle between his palms, looking at JC with sad eyes. "She sold it last week."

JC hissed air through clenched teeth as the news swept over him. "Damn. That sucks. Why'd she do that? Was it an inheritance tax issue?"

"No, she would have qualified for an extension, but she knew she'd never move back there, and worrying about it would have driven her nuts."

A memory of Ensley racing across the Badlands, blond hair streaming out behind her, reminded him of the stories he'd heard about Aunt Kit, galloping her Thoroughbred, Stormy, across MacKlenna Farm's rolling hills. Aunt Kit was as much a part of the farm as the farm was part of her. And it was the same with Ensley and her ranch.

Although she still had lingering issues with her hip replacement following the bull-riding accident she had as a teenager, she loved the ranch. But it was that accident and months of rehab that forced her to reconsider her future. She hung up her spurs for good when Harvard accepted her into its freshman class.

He sipped his drink, aching for the choice Ensley was forced to make, and knowing it hadn't been an easy one. He stopped reflecting and laughed. "I'll never forget the campouts and heading to the hunting grounds at five thirty in the morning to duck hunt. Neither one of us could keep up with her."

"That's because she returned to the ranch every vacation and kept doing what she'd always done while we traveled abroad."

"That makes me question her decision to sell even more. She loved that place." JC took another sip, savoring the whisky's spicy notes of cloves, ginger, and cinnamon while he thought about the ranch and the joy of riding through the Badlands. "I wish I'd known it was for sale."

"What the hell would you do with a North Dakota ranch?"

JC shrugged. "I don't know, but I think there'd be a business opportunity to market a working ranch as a family vacation destination. Maybe even offer seven- to fourteen-day cattle or horse drive adventures."

"Like the movie *City Slickers*, where men go to learn how to be real cowboys?"

"Or women looking for empowerment by playing in a typically male environment. Something like that—rough and rugged. Look at Ensley. She looks like a Barbie doll, but as soon as you see her compete in the rodeo, you see her power and grit."

"Before you notice her other attributes?" George asked.

"I wouldn't go that far."

"Well, if she ever heard you say she looks like a Barbie doll, she'd kick you in the balls."

"Yeah, I know. She heard me once, and that's what she tried to do."

"I think selling was a mistake," George said. "I don't believe a job will ever give her the satisfaction and personal challenge she found in ranching."

"It's a shame she had to sell the ranch to find that out."

"I don't know that she has—yet. But she wouldn't take my calls before the closing. She probably figured I'd try to talk her out of selling."

"Would you have done that? I know I would have tried. Couldn't she live in North Dakota and do her job remotely?"

"She'd hate it. She's always wanted to live and work in New York City."

"With both parents gone, I guess it makes sense." JC finished his drink. "So, dinner tonight is a celebration?"

"That was the plan, but now I don't know if she'll be laughing or crying in her beer."

JC hoped she wouldn't be crying and regretting her decision since she couldn't undo it. It was like selling stock one day and watching it double in value the next. You had to live with your mistake.

"Why'd she come to Cambridge for dinner? With you both in the city, you can do that anytime."

"One of her clients is a professor of American history here. He wrote a book about Teddy Roosevelt's time in North Dakota, so she came up to meet with him. I told her I'd pick her up at seven thirty. If you want to come along, we should leave soon."

"I think I will after all. Do you have a car?"

"No, I'll schedule an Uber."

JC paid the bar tab while George tapped on his phone. "Done. The driver should be here by the time we get downstairs."

JC had come to the club hoping to find a dinner companion and found George. After the past three weeks, he'd been looking forward to a relaxing evening with good friends. What he'd discovered in Asia needed to simmer on his mind's back burner for several days before he tried to unravel the implications and decide on his next steps. In the past, being with friends had always helped him clear his mind. He hoped it still would.

"I saw a picture of you with a hot blonde in *The Washington Post*," George said. "You were at a black-tie charity auction. You got something going on with her?"

JC shook his head, trying to dislodge the uneasy memory of his date that night. The woman had been more interested in other men at the event than in him. Or maybe he'd shown such little interest in her that she looked elsewhere.

"I needed a date. A friend fixed us up. It worked for the night. That's all."

"Sounds like you're living up to your reputation," George said. "But I don't believe any of the bad-boy rumors. You have more respect for women than any man I know."

"Yeah, well." JC shrugged. "I don't have time for a relationship, and it's less complicated if women know upfront that I'm not interested or looking for anything permanent."

George clapped JC on the shoulder. "Maybe not right now, but you're a born family man. You'll settle down eventually."

Except for Uncle Cullen, the men in the clan hadn't settled

down until their late thirties, early forties, and JC intended to follow suit.

But it was about more than age.

He'd asked his mom when he was a teenager how she knew she was in love with his dad, and she said, "When you love someone, you love their journey." So far, he'd never met a woman whose journey even interested him. Well, that wasn't exactly true. He'd always been interested in his cousin Emily's journey and how she'd transitioned from a child of the mid-1800s to a twenty-first-century physician.

But even though he was interested in her journey, she wasn't his soul mate, and he wasn't sure he'd ever find one.

He followed George out of the Porcellian Club, and the Uber driver was there by the time they reached the curb.

They settled in the backseat of an SUV, and George asked, "How's Austin? I followed his rehab early on but haven't seen any press reports in months. How long has it been? Two years. Right?"

"Yeah. It was touch and go for a long time." JC would never forget his brother, Kevin, calling to let him know that Austin, Kevin's stepson, was in the hospital. JC hopped on a plane and flew to Cleveland to be with the rest of the family. The medical reports were horrible.

Austin had severed the femoral artery in his left leg and cracked his sacrum. The cartilage connecting his right and left pubic bones pried apart about ten inches, causing nerve damage. It was a coin toss whether he'd be impotent for the rest of his life. The dislocation of his knee tore every ligament in the joint, and it severed the peroneal nerve, which carried the signal from his brain to lift his foot. The specialists didn't think he'd ever have full control of his foot again.

Afterward, JC spent months seesawing between blaming Austin for his reckless behavior and worrying he might not survive. The accident pulled the rug out from under every member of the family, and while they'd all returned to their pre-accident lives—except for Austin—the rug remained uneven and twisted.

"The pain had to have been horrible."

JC flinched as Austin's screams replayed in his memory in surround sound. "It was constant and unbearable. The morphine drip never trickled down fast enough."

"Has it let up? I mean, he's not in constant pain now, is he?"

"Not like he was, but Dad's afraid Austin's addicted to painkillers."

"He should know, right?"

JC's head shot up, and he glared at George, momentarily forgetting that he'd shared his dad's addiction with his friend.

"That was twenty-eight years ago, but I guess the fear of it happening again never goes away. Thank God for my mom. Dad wanted her more than he wanted the painkillers. But in his case, everyone knew about it, so it was easier to get help. It's not like that with Austin. He cut off his mom's access to his doctors and medical reports, so no one knows what drugs he's taking."

JC had overheard his dad talking to Uncle David about finding a back door to access Austin's medical records. Uncle David had no qualms about venturing into the gray zone and had taught JC just about everything he knew about the dark web. Although now, JC was pretty sure his knowledge far exceeded his uncle's.

"Is the pain only in his foot or everywhere he was injured?" George asked.

"I don't know, but it hasn't stopped him from working out every day. Dad had a training facility built on the ranch in Colorado with a regulation-size basketball court and an Olympic-size pool. Then he hired a full-time trainer, massage therapist, physical therapist, nutritionist, and coach to work with Austin. I heard he asked his agent to get him a tryout this summer."

"Is he ready?"

"He won't know for sure until he gets out there and performs under pressure. He's trying out a new shoe with straps that wrap around his ankle and lift the toe portion of the shoe about six inches off the ground. Now he doesn't have to hike his hip with every step. The raised toe box allows him to clear his gait."

"What about his dad? Is he helping out?"

"If anyone understands what Austin is going through, it's Chris Dalton since an injury forced him to retire early. He goes out to the ranch several times a month to work out with Austin. I just hope Chris isn't encouraging him to believe in the impossible."

"You don't think he'll have a comeback?"

"I'm not a doctor, but based on the extent of his injuries, I don't see it happening. But I also know Austin well enough to know he'll never quit trying, and he's building himself up for a huge disappointment."

"If I lost everything, I'd fight just as hard as Austin to get it all back," George said.

"Me too," JC said. "But right now, Austin has tunnel vision and can't see anything except getting back to where he was before the accident. What he did was stupid. He wasn't supposed to be riding a motorcycle. It violated his contract and nearly killed him."

"I bet he feels guilty."

"I'm sure he does, and to be honest, I would, too," JC said softly, admitting it as much to himself as to George.

"He needs to find something else as important as playing basketball," George said.

"To him, there's nothing more important."

The Uber driver pulled to the curb in front of the Williams house on Channing Street, and JC was suddenly a freshman in college again, looking forward to pizza and beer with good friends. He climbed out on one side of the vehicle, George the other.

"You know, we should have walked. I didn't run yesterday or today and probably won't tomorrow either."

George slammed his door. "We would have been late, and you know how Ensley gets."

JC walked behind the vehicle and joined George on the sidewalk. "She cussed me out once when I showed up an hour late with carryout. I didn't know I was supposed to be there at a certain time."

"Sounds like her. She gets something in her mind and won't let it go."

JC followed George up the walk to the white, three-story house. "She should be six feet tall to match her temper."

"Not five foot two and eyes of blue."

"Ouch!" JC cringed. "She hates that song. Besides, in her case, there's a high ratio of mind to mass." He eyeballed the house again as they continued their approach up the walkway with a glance at the upstairs window. The only room on the second floor with a light on was the one she used while she lived there. Suddenly the thought of seeing her again sent a shiver of anticipation coursing through him.

"Mom yelled at me once for criticizing Ensley's temper," George said. "I won't make that mistake again. My parents are overly protective of her."

"Mom's always sending text messages to go see my cousins or call them. I try but fail miserably. Mom still thinks I'm sixteen."

"I bet you text Emily," George said, elbowing JC in the ribs.

"Well, that's a given, but man, she's busier than I am."

"One of these days, something is going to happen between you two, and I plan to be the best man."

"That won't happen. Not with Em. She's like my sister. Sort of like Ensley is to you."

"If you say so, but don't forget I've seen you two together, and there's so much chemistry between you, sparks go off."

"I told you several years ago that nothing is going on between us."

"Shit, man. Yeah, you've told me, but I've never believed it." George punched in the keypad code, then grasped the large bronze knob and pushed.

"I know you haven't." JC followed George into the foyer and closed the door behind them.

"Are your parents still pressuring you to work for your family's businesses?"

"We argue about the business every time we talk. It's gotten so bad that when I see my dad's number pop up on my phone, I cringe and let the call go to voice mail."

George shot JC a hard look. "But you and your dad used to be so close. I can't imagine you being on the outs with him."

JC thought back to the last chewing-out he got for not showing up at a family gathering. "I'm not the only one. All my cousins over eighteen get the same pressure. My aunts and uncles think Dad is a god, but the cousins know he's not. It's an age thing. The younger generation thinks of Uncle David as head of the family, and they don't want Grandpa Elliott making demands on them."

"That's got to be hard on your dad."

"He wants me to be the face of the future, so MacCorp clients will know the business will continue under the same style of management. I can't do that. I see too many things that need to be changed. He has to retire first before I step in. If he's there, clients will continue to call him, not me."

"You don't have time anyway. That firm of yours keeps you busy twenty-four-seven and out of the country more than you're in it. I've met your entire family and attended get-togethers in Virginia, Colorado, California, Italy, and the Scottish Highlands, and I've seen the way your family treats you. Your parents, aunts, uncles, and cousins—"

"See me as a fifteen-year-old. You don't have to say it," JC said.

"I was going to say a college kid. Look, if you don't like the way the company's run, then change it from the inside instead of fighting against it on the outside."

"I don't want to fight at all, inside or out. I don't want to breed Thoroughbreds, and I don't want to grow grapes. I'm focusing on international law and human rights."

"Save the world and make your first billion."

JC laughed. "In that order, although I think I'll make the billion first. Saving the world is complicated."

George flipped on the hall lights and glanced around before yelling, "Ensley, we're here. Let's go to dinner. JC is with me."

JC entered the living room, waiting to hear Ensley yell, "I'm coming." There was no reply, but something was alarming in the room—an earthy smell that belonged in the Scottish Highlands, not inside a house in Cambridge, Massachusetts.

His ears perked up when George called out again, "Ensley!"

The hairs on the back of JC's neck stood on end. He scanned the room as he instinctively reached for the Glock snugged against the small of his back. Then he let his hand drop. The hairs on his neck weren't standing up because of danger to him.

They were standing up because of danger to Ensley.

He walked toward the back of the house and into the kitchen. "She's been here," he yelled to George. "Her computer bag and purse are on the counter, along with an open bottle of Montgomery Winery chardonnay."

George walked in behind him. "What's that weird smell?"

A sense of dread exploded in JC's gut, but his training kicked in. He kept his voice neutral, his face relaxed. "Smells like peat."

"Decayed matter?"

"Have you ever smelled it here before?"

"Never."

The smell of peat and a missing woman meant only one thing. But why this month? There was too much at stake right now for another brooch to show up. "Phone Ensley," JC said.

George made the call, and a phone rang in the kitchen. JC pushed the computer bag aside, and they both stared at the ringing phone like it was a tarantula crawling toward them across the granite countertop.

George disconnected the call. "Where is she?"

"Hell if I know," JC said. And he didn't, but his best guess was another century.

"I'm not surprised she left her purse behind, but she never goes anywhere without her phone. Maybe she's in the bathroom and can't hear us." George walked down the hall toward the staircase and yelled again, "Ensley!"

JC glanced up at the ceiling as if he could see through the dry-wall to the room above. "I don't hear anything up there." The smell of peat and missing women went together like yin and yang, tea and crumpets, salt and pepper, shoes and socks. But there could be other explanations.

Yeah. Right. Like what?

"When was the last time you talked to her?" JC asked.

George scrolled through his messages. "She sent a text ninety minutes ago. She was at the train station waiting for an Uber."

If Ensley disappeared an hour or so ago, would the peat smell still be as strong as it was now? Based on stories he'd heard, the stink dissipated slowly. If she disappeared with a brooch, it happened within the last thirty to forty-five minutes.

"So she disappeared while we were at the Porcellian Club," JC said.

"I don't think she disappeared," George said. "I think she's just missing right now."

If he and George had arrived sooner, they could have stopped Ensley from whirling away in the fog. If Ensley had a brooch, where'd it come from? Her mother's family was from North Dakota, and her dad's family was from Pennsylvania. But Penny Malone-O'Grady's experience proved that the brooches didn't have to come down through a Scottish family.

"Maybe she's downstairs in the exercise room, getting a couple of miles in on the treadmill," JC said.

"I doubt it, but it's possible," George said. "I'll go downstairs and check. You go upstairs."

"Yell if you find her." JC raced up the stairs two at a time. He gained the landing and steadied himself a moment. "Damn." The peat smell was thicker up here, and there was also a thin layer of misty air. He rubbed his fingers along the stair railing, and the dampness glistened on his fingertips. His nose twitched when he sniffed his fingers—peat.

He glanced inside the room George used when he lived in the house years ago. A carry-on suitcase was sitting on the floor right inside the door. If that was George's bag, it was apparent he hadn't gone inside the room since there were no footprints in the vacuum cleaner tracks in the wall-to-wall carpet.

JC chuckled, remembering how Ensley used to leap across her room so she wouldn't leave footprints in the freshly vacuumed carpet. She must have outgrown the habit because the third bedroom carpet had footprints crisscrossing each other. The peat smell was stronger in here. This room was ground zero.

An open suitcase sat on the luggage rack with a pile of balled-up clothes on top. He entered the bathroom and found the air still thick with steam from a hot shower, and a damp towel hung over the shower curtain rod. Toiletry and cosmetic bags were open, with their contents spread out across the vanity.

He returned to the bedroom, slowly scanning the furniture, the floor, and the open suitcase. Nothing seemed out of place.

And then he saw it. "Shit!" His heart pounded for a whole new set of reasons.

Beneath the luggage rack was a brooch identical—except for the stone in the center—to eight others locked away in Uncle Braham's impenetrable safe.

He stooped to pick up the brooch and was surprised that it was still warm. Was it still active? Possibly. He dropped it faster than an argument with his dad, popped to his feet, and stepped away.

If the brooch was here, where was Ensley?

He stared at the brooch on the floor. It must be like the topaz. That stone got so hot no one could hold on to it and threw it away, eliminating any possibility of using it for a return trip. Now, he had to proceed as though the fog sucked Ensley up and spun her through time.

He should call his dad. But that was too dangerous right now. What about calling Uncle David? JC shook that idea right out of his head. That would be the same as calling his dad. Same with Tavis and Remy. No sense involving any of them. He could take care of this quietly.

There was a pattern to brooch disappearances. A woman went missing, members of the MacKlenna Clan rescued her, and she fell in love with one of the rescuers. Well, not always. Twice, the damsel in distress fell in love with someone in the past. Maybe that was Ensley's future, to find someone wherever she went.

He'd read the seven post-action reports. The first one was Aunt

Kit. She traveled back to the Oregon Trail in 1852 with the ruby brooch. The sapphire carried Aunt Charlotte back to the Civil War. A few years later, the emerald whisked Aunt Kenzie back to 1944. Then the diamond carried Aunt Amy back to 1909 New York City. The amber took Aunt Amber back to 1878. The pearl carried Aunt Sophia back to 1789. And most recently, the topaz whisked Aunt Penny back to 1814 New Orleans.

So where had this brooch taken Ensley?

He knew the hardships his aunts experienced and wouldn't want any woman to go through something like that again. But if the past was prologue, Ensley would have a hard time wherever she landed.

"JC, is Ensley up there?" George yelled.

"No! She took a shower and changed clothes, but she's gone now."

"Where the hell is she?" George yelled as he ran up the steps.

"I don't know." JC kicked the brooch under the bed just as George bounded into the room.

"The lights were off in the exercise room." George glanced around. "What was she wearing?"

"Hell, if I know." JC picked up a pair of slacks and a blouse. "She changed, but there's no way to know what she's wearing." He felt like an ass lying to his friend, but he had to get his family's permission before telling George what he believed happened to Ensley. And that wasn't going to happen.

George stood in front of the window and looked out over the front yard, shaking his head. "Wherever she went, she would have taken her phone. Something's wrong. She's missing, and the house stinks." He glanced at her suitcase. "She was meeting friends at a country bar after dinner. They were all wearing boots, jeans, and cowboy hats. I don't see her boots or hat, do you?"

"Maybe she changed her mind."

George sat on the edge of the bed and tapped his fingers on his knees. This situation reminded JC of Uncle Connor when he tried to keep Amber's disappearance a secret from her sister, Olivia, and it almost destroyed Connor's budding romance with Olivia. If JC wasn't careful, keeping this secret could ruin his friendship with George.

"I don't think Ensley changed her mind. She mentioned it in one of her texts while on the train from New York."

"Call your dad," JC said. "Maybe he spoke to her." What had

Connor done to search for Amber when he knew they wouldn't find her? He contacted the sheriff and went through the motions of searching for Amber. That's what he and George should do next.

"Good idea." George placed the call and put his dad on speaker. "Hey, Dad. I'm at the house with JC Fraser, and Ensley's not here. Have you talked to her?"

"Not since last week," Mr. Williams said. "She called to see if she could stay at the house. Why?"

"She knew I was coming to pick her up for dinner, but we're here, and she's not around. Her suitcase, computer bag, purse, and phone are here, but no Ensley."

"That's unlike her," Mr. Williams said. "She told me she was going to meet some college friends. You could call one of them to see if they've heard from her."

"I don't have any names and numbers, and she keeps her phone password protected."

"Then check with Mrs. Taylor next door," Mr. Williams said. "I told Ensley that Mrs. Taylor had been in the hospital. Maybe she went over there to see how the dear lady was feeling."

George let out a deep breath. "That's got to be it. I'll go over there. Thanks, Dad."

"Call me back and let me know. Your mother and I worry about her all the time."

"Mrs. Taylor or Ensley?"

Mr. Williams laughed. "Both of them, son. Enjoy your visit."

George disconnected the call. "Mrs. Taylor was probably so glad to see Ensley that she's talking her head off. I'll go next door. You stay here in case she comes back."

Maybe Ensley was visiting with Mrs. Taylor, but JC doubted it. The smell of peat and the presence of a Celtic brooch pretty much ruled that out.

So what were his next steps? Get the brooch. He couldn't leave the room without it. He snatched it up and shoved it deep into his pocket. Now, what was next?

Figure out where she went. Based on his aunts' experiences, Ensley traveled to a time and place where she had a unique connection. Maybe there was a journal in her bag, or notes, or emails on her computer that would narrow the possibilities. But he already knew she was in Cambridge to meet with the author of a new Teddy Roosevelt book. Was TR's time in North Dakota the unique connection to Ensley?

It made sense to him.

He returned to the den and fixed a drink at the wet bar while waiting for George, sipping it while he looked around. Nothing had changed in the house since they were students. Same furniture. Same books in the bookcases. The same big-screen TV hanging over the mantel. How many of Austin's games had he and George watched on that TV? Hundreds?

JC sipped the whisky, hyper-aware of the brooch in his pocket, warming his leg. The hand on the mantle clock went around once, twice, five times, and his nerves itched like an allergic reaction to spring pollen.

JC paced the room until George returned ten minutes later.

"She's not there, and Mrs. Taylor hasn't seen her tonight. I called Dad, and he said to call the police."

The last thing JC wanted was to involve the police. That meant more lying. But like Uncle Connor's situation, the police had to be involved, at least initially. The New Orleans Police had only done a limited investigation when Aunt Penny went missing, and he doubted the Cambridge police would do any more than the detectives in NOLA.

"They're likely to tell you she's twenty-eight years old, in full possession of her faculties, and there aren't any signs of a crime."

"That's what Dad said, but we still have to file a missing person report."

While George dialed 9-1-1, JC returned to the kitchen and rummaged through Ensley's computer bag. Inside were a laptop, a stack of paper-clipped pages, and a one-page itinerary.

George was penciled in for dinner, followed by a get-together at a country music bar with former classmates. First thing Friday was an eight o'clock breakfast meeting with Professor Whiteside, followed by a work session in his office until noon, then a lunch break, and another work session beginning at two. She had penciled in dinner with McKay and Roanna at eight, whoever they were. Then on Saturday, she had another work session with the professor and a reservation to take the four o'clock train back to the city.

He returned the itinerary to the bag and removed the paper-clipped pages. The top sheet was a query letter from Professor Whiteside, pitching his book covering Teddy Roosevelt's life from 1884—when he had a ranch in North Dakota—until 1895 when he was appointed New York City Police Commissioner by Mayor William Strong. Also attached was a ten-page synopsis, which JC speed-read.

George entered the kitchen. "The police are on their way." He looked over JC's shoulder. "What are you reading?"

"Professor's Whiteside's submission package. His book focuses on Teddy Roosevelt's life from 1884 to 1895. I see why Ensley was interested in the manuscript. TR had a ranch in North Dakota from 1884 until 1886."

"But that doesn't help us find her now," George said.

JC picked up the lowball glass he'd set on the counter, gave the liquid a tentative swirl, then chugged it back.

Oh, yes, it does.

He was now ninety-eight percent sure Ensley had gone back to the Badlands to meet TR. Nothing about that possibility seemed dangerous. It would be rustic for sure, but Ensley was raised there, knew the land, and knew how to hunt for food. And while she would initially be a woman alone, she could handle herself. And according to Whiteside's proposal, there was a woman Ensley could befriend in the town of Medora—the Marquis de Mores's wife—the former Medora von Hoffman of New York City.

The doorbell rang. "That was quick." George headed toward the front door, and JC followed. "Let's hope the police can find out what happened to her."

Two detectives entered the house. Both men were slightly under six feet, with dark hair and dark eyes, but one was in his late forties and carrying a few extra pounds, and the other one was young, probably a rookie. After introductions, JC, George, and the detectives split up.

As JC and the younger cop walked into the living room, the cop asked, "What's with the smell?"

"We noticed it as soon as we entered the house. The odor is thicker in the bedroom, where Ensley showered and changed."

"Have you ever noticed it before?"

JC gave him a sly smile. "Yeah, but it was in the Scottish High-lands."

"It smells like wet grass and dirt. It could be a scented candle?"

"I'm not into candles," JC said. "Most of the scents are too sweet for my taste, but I haven't seen any around here. The hearth is clean, so no one's lit a fire. She wasn't here long enough to cook a meal, and why would she? She was meeting George for dinner."

"I'll include the smell in the missing person report and see if it matches any other disappearances."

If the detective mentioned the smell, the report of Aunt Penny's disappearance might show up in a database of missing persons. But Aunt Penny returned a few days later, unharmed. So if anything, the detectives would find it interesting but not significant.

The detective made a few notes in a pocket notebook, and for the next thirty minutes, JC walked the cop through the house, pointing out everything he'd noticed...except for finding the brooch.

Thank goodness George didn't know anything about the brooch because he would have mentioned it. If the cops entered the brooch *and* the odor into a national database, it would eventually link back to MacCorp—the MacKlenna family corporation—and ultimately to JC.

He and the detective returned to the kitchen. "I went through her computer bag searching for clues, and she has an itinerary if you're interested."

"That'd be helpful," the detective said.

JC pulled out the sheet of paper. "There aren't any phone numbers, and I don't recognize the names of the women Ensley planned to meet tomorrow night. George might know. If not, you could check with Alumni Services. Someone there might be able to track down the women."

The detective squared the paper on the counter and took pictures with his phone. "What else did you find?"

"A proposal from Professor Whiteside. I didn't open her Mac. I assume, like her cell phone, it's password protected."

The older detective and George entered the kitchen. "I've got all I need," the detective said, flipping back through his notebook. "There's no evidence of a crime here. Since Ms. Williams is old enough to walk away and not tell anyone where she was going, there isn't much we can do."

"That's it?" George asked.

"We'll stop by the bar where Ms. Williams intended to meet her friends later tonight," the younger detective said. "And if we can find the women she was meeting tomorrow, we'll talk to them, too."

George ran his fingers through his hair and held his hand there while shaking his head. "You're not giving this the attention it deserves. Ensley wouldn't go off without leaving me a message. I know in my bones something has happened to her."

He shot a distressed look at James Cullen, and JC knew he had to say something. "I agree with George. She didn't leave on her own volition."

Which was the pure, unvarnished truth.

"We'll check with the neighbors to see if anyone has a smart-doorbell camera. One of them might have a video of her coming and going," the younger detective said.

"We'll also call Professor Whiteside. She might have gone off to meet him this evening," the other detective said.

"That doesn't make sense," George said. "She knew I was coming, and if she left with anyone, she'd have taken her phone."

"Do you know how she got here from the train station?"

"Her last text said she was waiting for an Uber."

"We'll check with the car service to see when they dropped her here and if they came back. We'll also notify the NYPD. They can check her apartment and talk to her neighbors."

George shook his head, and his voice was full of frustration when he said, "Look, she didn't disappear from New York. She disappeared from here!"

"She might have said something to a neighbor about meeting a friend she didn't list on her itinerary," the younger detective said.

"I guess anything's possible," George said. "But it's out of character."

The younger detective handed George and JC business cards. "If you think of anything else, give us a call."

George gave the detectives his business card, and the detective glanced at JC, expecting one from him. He grudgingly pulled a card case out of his pocket. He didn't want them to know he was Elliott Fraser's son, but if they googled him, they'd make the connection anyway. And above all, he didn't want his dad or MacCorp connected with another woman's disappearance.

George escorted the detectives to the front door, then returned to the kitchen, his shoulders slumped. "None of this makes sense. I'm going to call Dad back and suggest he hire an investigator. Those detectives will only do a preliminary investigation. We need someone to dig deeper."

"What about Ensley's friends in New York? Do you know any of them?"

"Barb Russell is her best friend in the city. I'll call her." George went to the den to fix a drink. "If Ensley has talked to anyone, it'd be her." He carried his tumbler to the sofa and set it on the coaster on the coffee table while he scrolled through his contacts. "Barb might freak out when I tell her Ensley disappeared."

"Tell her we don't believe—" JC stopped because he didn't know how to finish the sentence.

"What don't we believe?" George asked. "That she was kidnapped? That she walked away on her own? Or maybe she went for a long-distance run to avoid having dinner with me? What?"

"Hell if I know," JC snapped. "Maybe she forgot to bring something and walked to the closest convenience store."

"No matter where she went"—George stabbed JC with a stare that put every ounce of his frustration on full display—"she'd have taken her goddamn phone."

JC wanted to say, "She'll be okay, George. I'll find her." But he couldn't say anything. And being unable to reassure George was pure hell. He had to get back to DC and make plans to rescue Ensley, but he couldn't leave George right now. He was stuck here, doing nothing to help her, and he'd never felt so useless in his life.

George punched the keys on his phone and put the call on speaker. "Here goes."

After two rings, a woman answered, "This is Barb."

"Hey, it's George."

The woman's breath hitched, and a few beats of silence ticked by before she asked in a worried voice, "Are you calling to break our date tomorrow night? I heard you were in Cambridge."

If the woman knew George was here, then she must have talked to Ensley. But what JC found even more impressive was the date part. He gave George a searching look, and George waggled his brows in return.

"I hope I don't have to," George said. "But I have a problem here in Cambridge. Since you already knew I was here, you must have talked to Ensley?"

"Yeah, about an hour ago. I thought she was having dinner with you. Why?"

"I was supposed to pick her up here at the house, but she's gone. Her phone, computer, purse, suitcase are here, but she's not."

JC couldn't sit still. The urge to call his dad was increasing by the minute. It was moments like this when he had flashes of the day he panicked while searching for his dad. Out of fear, he'd run away, gotten lost in the wine cave, and nearly died. He'd been a stupid thirteen-year-old kid at the time. Since then, he'd gone through months of therapy, but occasionally something triggered the memory of being lost and alone, and the anxiety rushed back.

He had better ways of handling it now, though. Thanks to Uncle Jack. Mind over matter. It took thirty seconds of controlled breathing and visualization, and JC was back to normal. He returned his attention to George's conversation.

"That doesn't make any sense," Barb said. "She wouldn't stand you up."

"I called the police. Two detectives came over, but they said she was old enough to leave without telling anyone. They were going to check the bar where she was meeting friends later tonight and then interview the professor she scheduled appointments with tomorrow."

"This is crazy, George. She wouldn't just walk away."

"That's what I told the police. They also said they'd talk to the neighbors to see if anyone had a smart doorbell that would show her coming and going."

"And you said her phone is there," Barb said. "You know Ensley would never go off without it, not after leaving it behind the day her mom had a heart attack and no one could find Ensley."

"Do you have any suggestions?" George asked.

"Maybe she got a call from her client—the author—and went to meet him. But again, she'd have taken her phone."

"We found a book proposal in her computer bag. If she'd gone to meet the professor, she'd have taken that with her."

JC stood in front of the bay window, looking out on the street. The detectives' car remained parked in front of the house. They must be canvassing the neighborhood.

"Look in her wallet," Barb said. "She has an Amex and a Capital One bank card. She wouldn't go anywhere without one of those."

JC signaled that he would get her purse. He returned a moment later and handed it to George. JC had learned early on to never go through a woman's purse. Some women felt it violated their personal space, so he never took the chance. But computer bags were different.

George found the wallet and opened it. Inside were both the Amex and Capital One cards. His face paled. "They're both in her wallet."

"Damn," Barb said. "And there's no sign of a scuffle? Nothing broken? No blood?"

"Nothing. Only a disgusting odor."

"Like what?"

"An earthy smell. There's no explanation for it."

"Smells don't bother her, so it wouldn't have caused her to leave, and she didn't mention it when we talked. I don't know, George." Then there was silence on Barb's side of the conversation. "Would you like me to come to Cambridge? I can help pass out flyers with her picture or something."

That was a great suggestion, and if Barb had been in the room, JC would have kissed her. If she came here to help George, maybe JC could return to Washington and make arrangements to go after Ensley. He nodded to George and mouthed, "Great idea."

George nodded his agreement. "Well, if you're free, that'd be fantastic."

"I'll check the train schedule."

JC googled it, found the schedule, and showed it to George.

George took JC's phone and scrolled through the schedule. "There's a seven-fifty train, a two forty a.m., then six fifty-five, and almost every hour after that."

"If I hurry, I can make the seven-fifty train. If I can't, I'll take the six fifty-five in the morning."

"Gotcha. Let me know."

"The sooner I get there, the sooner I can help you search for her."

"Thanks," George said. "Send a text to let me know what time you arrive, and I'll pick you up. There's an extra room here at the house, so you don't need a hotel, unless, well... You're welcome to stay here."

"Thanks. I'll take you up on the offer."

George smiled as he said goodbye and disconnected the call. "If Barb catches the seven-fifty, she'll be here by midnight." He leaned his head against the back of the sofa, closed his eyes, and pursed his lips. "I don't know what else to do."

"I do. Let's go to the bar and see if we can find the women Ensley planned to meet later. They might know something."

"The cops will be there."

"So... It'd be weird if we don't show up looking for her."

"Maybe the cops will think we're there to change the narrative, put suggestions in their minds that Ensley might stand them up for a man she met."

JC swatted at George's feet propped on the coffee table. "That's the dumbest thing I've ever heard. They don't suspect us of hurting her."

George put his feet on the floor. "How do you know?"

"Didn't you show the detective your last text from her?"

"Yeah. What difference does that make?"

"Everything we've done since she arrived in Cambridge can be verified—the times we arrived and departed the Porcellian Club and arrived here in an Uber. There wasn't enough time for us to kill her, dispose of her body, and wash away the evidence."

"I guess you're right."

"Tell me this," JC said. "Is there any chance she left with a man and didn't want anyone to be able to contact her?"

"Why the hell would she do that?"

JC shrugged. "You tell me."

"There's nothing to tell. Number one"—he held up a finger—"she wouldn't do something like that, and number two"—he held up another finger—"if she was seeing a guy, she would have told me."

"Not necessarily."

George dropped his fingers and rubbed the back of his neck. "Forget it, JC. You know her as well as I do. She wouldn't stand me up. Period."

"Okay. Just asking. So let's go to the bar."

"No, I want to stay here in case she returns."

She's not coming back tonight, George.

"So, who's Barb? Other than a friend of Ensley's and your date for tomorrow night?"

George smiled. "Ensley's tried several times to fix us up. She's an M&A banker at Goldman Sachs. Ens thought we'd have a lot in common, but I was never interested."

"Until you got desperate?"

"Nah, just thought I'd do something nice for Ens. It would make her happy. So I called Barb on Monday and asked her out for dinner tomorrow night. You can meet her later and tell me what you think. But I already know you'll like her. She has *the look*."

"And," JC said, "what exactly is *the look*?"

"You know… Like Ensley, except instead of blonde hair and blue eyes, she has long red hair, green eyes, big dimples, great body—muscular and fit."

"Is she a runner?"

"She's Ensley's best friend. What do you think?"

"Since she's willing to drop everything and come to Cambridge, I like her already." JC lifted his glass. "I need another drink. You want a refill?"

George lifted his empty highball glass. "Yeah, give me two fingers."

JC refilled their glasses, then dropped into the recliner and pulled up the leg rest. Damn, he was tired. He'd been on the go for weeks and only arrived home a couple of days ago. It was time for some R&R.

"I know you've got a heavy schedule," George said, "so if you have to leave tomorrow, I'll understand. I'm going to hang around here for the weekend, and Dad can come up Monday. Somebody should be here in case she comes back…or…"

"There is no…*or*," JC said. "And I'm not leaving you alone with this situation."

"I won't be alone. Barb will be here."

God, he *was* tired if it took him that long to read between the lines. "So, you're saying…what? That you want me out of the way?" JC almost gave George a fist bump, but he corralled his emotions. He didn't want George to know he was anxious to get out of Cambridge and start putting his rescue plan into motion.

"We can handle the weekend, especially if Dad hires an investigator. If we don't have any luck, I might call you to come back."

"Sure. I've got to meet a client out of town for a few days, but when I get back, I'll do whatever I can."

"If she's still missing next week…" George's voice trailed off.

"We'll find her," JC said. "Don't give up hope."

Again, he wanted to tell George the truth, but he couldn't. For the past few years, since the family discovered an evil force was also searching for the brooches, silence and secretiveness were even more imperative. And that was the real reason he was keeping the appearance of this brooch to himself.

6

The Badlands (1885)—Ensley

WHEN ENSLEY CAME out of the fog-induced sleep, she was lying on a vast grassy plain. She rolled over onto her back. The sun was inching above the horizon, filling the sky with a rosy glow, while the dew lay in droplets on the damp blades of grass. If she stayed there much longer, her clothes would get wet, and while it wasn't cold, it wasn't a warm spring day, either.

The vivid green grass brightened the sterile-looking buttes in the distance. She took a deep breath, inhaling the fresh, sweet air scented with the fragrance of silvery purple sagebrush. Either she was dreaming, or she'd taken a magic carpet ride home—back to North Dakota.

She climbed to her feet and looked around, spotting her hat about six feet away. The last thing she remembered was running down the stairs fanning the fog with her hat. And here it was, and here she was. She swiped it up and set it on her head just so.

The Killdeer Mountains were in the distance. The magic carpet had dumped her off only a few miles from the family ranch…

…that she sold just days ago.

From where she was now—probably four or five miles from the ranch near Killdeer on the Spring Creek—it would take ninety minutes to walk across the plains to get there. The new owners wouldn't be there yet, but the caretakers would be, and they'd give her a lift to town.

She checked the time on her Apple watch, but she had no cellular service. That was weird. She always had service out here.

After about thirty minutes walking across the uneven terrain, her hip ached, and her calf muscles cramped. It was time for a water break and a few stretches.

Water? If she wanted a drink, it would have to come from the creek.

Yuck! She'd have to be desperate to risk drinking polluted water. And she wasn't that desperate yet.

She stretched her calves and kept going, following the creek—which probably wasn't a good idea since the rushing water reminded her of how thirsty she was.

When she didn't intersect with the roads she expected to find, she second-guessed her location. She grew up here, rode horses and ATVs, camped out, and hunted. The land was as familiar as the back of her hand.

She ignored her concerns and kept walking. Then, when she reached the cluster of round-top buttes on the north side of her family's ranch, she stopped, and you could have picked her jaw up off the ground.

"What the hell?" There were grasslands and timber and brush-filled coulees, but no utility poles, no roads, no cars, no neighbors. Fear took hold and shook her senseless. "Where's the homeplace?"

She plopped down near the bank of Spring Creek in a belt of cottonwood trees to figure out what happened to her. The peaceful sounds of rushing water didn't help. Neither did the breeze blowing through the trees or the songs of the Western meadowlarks.

Could I be lost? Nope. That's impossible. Well, smarty-pants, there's no other explanation. She could ride through the plains wearing a blindfold, remove it, and know exactly where she was at any time of the year.

This was home or had been until she sold the ranch.

She thought back to the brooch, and the chant engraved on the stone. Did all that swirling propel her into a vortex that carried her to another time? If she hadn't edited a ten-book time travel romance series, the notion would never have occurred to her.

Time travel was possible in fiction, but not real life—not *her* life.

So where should she go now? The nearest town was Killdeer, but if the ranch wasn't here, the town wouldn't be either.

She picked up a stick and drew three equidistant Xs in the dirt. The middle X was the ranch. The X on the left was Grassy Butte. The X on the right was Killdeer. From the first X to the third X was about thirty miles. She could follow Spring Creek to its head at the Killdeer Mountains and then head northwest to the Little Missouri

River, but the journey would take her miles through Dunn County's flat plains and the Badlands areas with little water.

Which was insane.

If she cut across the plains, she could go to Belfield and then on to Medora, which was about twenty miles west of Belfield. Or she could go straight south from her present location toward Dickinson, probably about forty miles.

But would those towns even be there? Weren't Belfield and Dickinson established years after her ancestors built the ranch? If so, that meant she had to go to Medora. Or she could sit right here until someone came by, and she could thumb a ride.

Right. Nobody was coming. She was on her own, without a rifle or even a knife. How would she be able to eat or protect herself?

I'm not helpless. I grew up out here.

Since she needed a knife, she'd have to make one.

She walked over to the creek, hoping for inspiration, and picked up several rocks to skip across the water. She released one with a quick snap of her wrist, spinning it as fast as she could.

Am I really skipping rocks?

Yep, she was. But if she didn't do something, she might just burst into tears.

The stone hit the water parallel to the surface and bounced six times. A perfect throw. She tossed another one, and another, until the only one left was a black stone. She held it with her thumb and middle finger and hooked her index finger along the edge, and was about to release it when her internal voice said,

Stop! Don't throw it. It's obsidian—volcanic glass—sharp as a knife when fractured.

She held up her hand and stared at the stone while accessing an old file from her mental file cabinet—*Improvising in the Wilderness*—and snagged a memory with her father. She'd been, what? Ten, eleven? No, almost ten. It was a birthday camping trip with him. They were setting up camp when he realized he'd forgotten his steel-blade knife. At the time, she'd been afraid they'd have to go home. Instead, her dad used the experience as a lesson in how to survive in the wilderness. And she made a knife out of obsidian.

What happened to that knife? Since she rarely threw anything away, it was probably in a box in her Bismarck storage unit, along with family antiques and heirlooms.

She should have put the brooch in storage, too.

To make a knife, she needed a flat stone to use as a work surface, something hard for a hammer, a sturdy stick for a handle, and something to bind it with. Finding a flat stone was easy, but finding a hammer wasn't.

She picked up several pieces of wood and stacked them aside for later until—"Son of a gun"—she found a piece of petrified wood that might just work.

With the obsidian rock, the flat stone, and the piece of petrified wood, she returned to where she'd been sitting under the tree. If she remembered correctly, her dad cut his finger on the obsidian, but he had a first aid kit with him to clean and wrap the wound. She didn't.

Just be careful.

She put the obsidian on the flat stone and smacked it with the piece of petrified wood. Two good-size slivers broke off.

The stick she'd selected for a handle was already split on one end and would hold the sliver of obsidian. Once she wedged it into the end of the stick, she hunted around for something to tie the split ends together so the obsidian wouldn't fall out.

Her dad used the piece of wire he carried for making rabbit snares. She didn't have anything like that, but she did have a ponytail holder in her jacket pocket, along with a tube of lip balm and a mini tin of breath mints.

What more did a girl need?

She popped a mint into her mouth before carefully wrapping the hair tie around the stick several times, securing the sliver of obsidian into the wedge. Now, if she tied the knife handle to a long stick, she'd have a fishing spear.

She was so pleased she got goose bumps. You'd have thought she solved the problem of world hunger—well, maybe not *world* hunger, but certainly her own.

Since she didn't have another ponytail holder, what could she use as a cord? Roots? Sinew? Plant fiber?

She straightened her legs and crossed her ankles, thinking through her dilemma while watching her feet wave side to side. After a minute or two, she shouted, "Fabric!" If she cut off a quarter-inch of the hem of her jeans, she'd have enough cordage to secure the knife to the longer stick.

Did she want to cut up her clothes? Why the hell not? Clothes wouldn't matter if she starved to death. But they were APO Jeans with diamond-studded platinum buttons—a Christmas gift from

Wyatt. Did she need fancy jeans? Hell no. She was a cowgirl, more comfortable in cheap jeans and boots than sequins and stilettos. And she was in the wilderness, for god's sake, and until she reached civilization, taking care of her necessities—food and water—was her only priority.

That was all the justification she needed.

But wait a minute. Instead of cutting up the jeans, why not use her shirttail? That made more sense. Didn't it?

Sure. Go for it.

She removed her shirt and cut off the half-inch hem, then put it back on. After she tucked in the shirttail, the butchered bottom wasn't even noticeable.

Now, if she cut the half-inch hem in half, she'd have enough to make a spear with some leftover to make tiebacks for her hair until she needed them for another project.

The perfect stick to use for her spear was the hardest to find. But with patience, she eventually found one strong enough not to break, yet easy to handle.

She attached the knife to the end and was about to tie a knot when she thought ahead. It would be hard to untie a wet knot, and she'd have to use the knife to gut the fish. So she tied the end in a bow.

Yeah, it looked silly, but who cared?

She glanced up at the sky to check the sun's location and guessed it might be midafternoon. She was already hungry, and her mouth was too dry to spit. She might as well set up camp now. Once the sun went down, the temperature would drop, and she wasn't wearing the right clothes to sleep outside in thirty-degree temperatures.

The first item on her survival list was to start a campfire. As long as she stayed busy and kept her mind focused on problem-solving, she wouldn't have time to worry about her situation.

Flint, found in chalk and limestone, was readily available along the riverbed, and from where she was sitting, she spotted a piece of limestone that probably had some in it. But what about steel for a striker? Until she went off to college, she always carried a small piece of steel on her keychain. Marcasite would work, but she probably wouldn't find any along the creek bed, although she could find it in the geological formations around the buttes.

That meant if she wanted to make a fire, she'd have to find some marcasite. She picked up a chunk of limestone and threw it down, breaking it into pieces. She searched through them until she found some flint that would work, but she still needed a striker, a piece of steel, something. She stared at the flint in her hand. Maybe her sapphire and titanium ring would work? Titanium would spark. It wouldn't be easy, but it was possible.

Once she created a tinder bundle from roughed-up grass and cedar shavings, she struck the titanium against the flint over and over, watching for sparks. After several attempts and scuffing her fingers, sparks landed on the tinder and started burning.

She patiently fed the flames with kindling and then smaller pieces of wood until she had a good campfire going. After gathering up firewood to last the night, she collected a mixture of green boughs, ferns, and leaves to make a bed. Satisfied she had everything she needed, she grabbed her fishing spear and headed to the creek.

Spearing a fish took patience, and she didn't have much left, but after a half dozen misses, she finally caught a walleye.

While the fish cooked on a stone in the firepit, Ensley harvested dandelions and searched for purslane. Dandelions had more calcium than a glass of milk and were chock full of potassium, folic acid, and magnesium, and because the plant was high in fiber, it would help her stomach feel full. And purslane was like spinach and was high in omega-3 fatty acids. She could also boil dandelion roots and make coffee. It wouldn't taste like Starbucks, but it was the best she could do.

She found dandelions but not any purslane. Maybe tomorrow.

After supper, she nestled into the bough bed that smelled like sweet hay and summertime. The sun dipped below the horizon, and the red and orange sky was simply spectacular. She wasn't afraid of being out here all alone. How could she be? She was back home. But back home *when*?

Sometime during the night, she woke up chilled and piled more logs on the fire, then lay there and listened to the twigs and logs crackling and snapping until she fell asleep again. At dawn, she woke and remained still for a while as yesterday's events played through her mind.

If it was true that she'd traveled to another time, how would she ever get home? Dwelling on that scared the hell out of her. So she didn't. Instead, she fished for breakfast, washed up in the creek, collected her knife, spear handle, and dandelion roots.

Now what?

It was decision time. Which way should she go? Since she had to have access to water, there was only one logical answer. Follow Spring Creek.

The landscape ranged from prairie and prairie dog towns to high plateau plains and narrow, treed coulees. If she'd taken this hike the week before she sold the ranch, she might not have sold it.

In some areas, she had to swing far right of the creek onto a sagebrush terrace and then cut back and forth, slowing her progress. But she couldn't afford to get too far from her water source. Unfortunately, it was a squiggly line, not a straight one, and following it would take twice as long to get wherever she was going. But it was her only sane option.

She was thinking so hard as she navigated one of the switchbacks that she lost her footing, and with nothing to grab hold of, slid down the side of a rocky formation, screaming. Her hat flew off, her full weight landed on her hip, and the impact rattled her teeth.

"Shit!"

Adrenaline stormed through her veins. She froze, not even breathing, barely able to hold her fear in check. It happened so fast there'd been no way to stop her fall. When her breathing started up again, she was panting so hard she was afraid she might hyperventilate.

She had to assess her injuries. Find out what was broken or bleeding.

And she dreaded what she might find.

When the shock wore off, walloping pain rolled over her.

My foot. It's my damn foot.

If a grizzly appeared out of nowhere, she wouldn't be any more terrified than she was right now.

If it's broken, I'll die out here.

Almost paralyzed by sheer terror, she lifted her hip and straightened her right leg. The pain was on the outside of her foot. She could rotate her ankle and wiggle her toes, but the side of her foot hurt like hell. The test would be how painful it was when she stood.

Stand? Hell, no.

She was going to stay right here until help arrived. Then it hit her. *Smack!* Help wasn't coming. Not in an hour. Not in a day. Not ever.

That took a moment to sink in, and when it did, tears rolled down her cheeks. But she couldn't sit here and feel sorry for herself. Well, maybe she could for five more minutes while she tried to breathe normally through the pain. It didn't work. Her foot hurt like hell.

What options did she have? Only two that she could see.

Sit here and die, or get up and try.

She had no choice, and she knew it. It took a few minutes for the tears to dry up, and when they did, she pocketed her fear and confronted reality. "Let's see how awful this is going to be."

She braced against a boulder and pushed up to her left foot, then, slowly, put weight on her right one. Pain shot through her foot and up her leg. "Damn." She immediately shifted her weight off her injured foot.

I've got miles to walk. What am I going to do?

There was no plan in her toolbox for dealing with this. A knife was easy to make, a fire easy to start, but a broken bone in her foot was a death sentence.

The distance across the sagebrush-covered ground from her position to Spring Creek was probably a hundred yards—the length of a football field.

You have to hobble to the river.

"No! I can't do it." She slid back down to the ground, reached for her hat, and plopped it on her head. "I quit."

When have you ever given up, Ensley MacAndrew Williams?

"Never."

Are you going to start now?

"Why not?"

Do you want to die?

"I probably will anyway, so why bother?"

If you do not give up, you will survive.

She glanced around.

Who the hell was she talking to?

She was alone in the wilderness, so it was either a ghost or her thoughts. She often engaged in deep, metaphysical conversations in the middle of the night, with only her thoughts answering back.

But this was different. The voice wasn't hers. It was gravelly yet gentle and caring, and while it reminded Ensley of her dad, it wasn't his voice either.

She continued the conversation asking, "What if I can't make it to the river?"

Stop and rest. Then try again.

"Do you think I can make it?"

He didn't answer. Why? Had she imagined the voice? That was possible, or maybe, if he did answer, he'd have to say, "No."

"You're wrong," she shouted. "I *can* do it"—she snapped her fingers—"just like that." She pushed up to her good foot again. "I'll show you I'm no quitter."

She couldn't put her full weight down, but she could hobble on the ball of her foot. It'd be slow going, but she'd get there—eventually.

She picked up her spear and breathed through the pain shooting up her leg. "I can do this."

Yes, you can.

She jerked, looking left, then right—but he wasn't there. She hadn't expected to see him anyway, but yet she was comforted by his voice.

Ahead of her, the tall grass rippled as if someone was walking through it. Was it *him*? Was it just the breeze? Or her imagination? But the spirit was going in the wrong direction. The shortest route to the river was straight ahead.

"You go on," she shouted. "I'm going this way."

She continued hobbling toward the river and noticed the tall grass stilled. Was he watching her? "I'm not going your way." She kept walking, and a hidden flock of meadowlarks exploded out of the grasses and took flight, startling her. "Jesus!" The birds circled above, then returned to the same spot, which was blocking her path.

Come, Ensley.

"Look here. My goddamn foot hurts like a son of a bitch. The creek is straight ahead."

Come, Ensley.

She jabbed her spear into the ground. "Damn it." As soon as she veered back, the tall grass rippled again.

She hobbled through a grove of cottonwoods and down a slightly-sloping, well-worn path to the creek. She'd never been here before, even though she'd ridden through most of the area.

A few yards from the bank of the creek was a rocky overhang, maybe fifteen feet wide. It was a perfect shelter from bad weather and the heat of the day. Beneath the overhang were remnants of a rock-lined firepit. While there was no evidence anyone had been there recently, it was a popular place. The blackened ceiling above the firepit was proof of that.

She limped to the creek for a drink of water. If it was filled with bacteria, so be it.

Take off the boot.

Just the thought made her cringe. "What? No way."

Take off the boot.

"Who the hell *are* you? I'm not going to do it. You know it'll hurt like hell."

Take off the boot.

"Damn it." She eased to the ground and grabbed the bootheel. But before she could tug on it, she took several deep breaths, and then she yanked hard. "Jesus Christ!" She stopped, tears tracking down her face. "I can't do it."

Take off the boot.

"Go away and leave me alone." Maybe she was losing her mind. On a one-to-ten scale, the pain was a ten, maybe a twelve.

Take off the boot.

"You're a one-trick pony. Go away."

Take off the boot.

She had to try one more time, even if it killed her.

She hissed as if preparing to deadlift a hundred pounds, and she tried again, tugging the boot against the pain. "Shit!"

Take off the boot.

"Shut up!" It was now or never, so she yanked again, screaming, "Shit!" The boot came off, and the pain shot straight up, right off the charts.

She ripped off her sock and sank her foot into the freezing river. The breath-stealing cold swamped the pain. She shivered violently but knew the injury had to be iced. It wouldn't heal a broken bone, but it would numb the pain so she could hobble around and collect kindling for a fire.

How long would she have to sit here, eat fish, and wait for her foot to heal? A few weeks. By then, she'd start getting malnourished from eating only fish. That would trigger a downward spiral until the lack of complex carbs, fats, and vitamins killed her unless she found some purslane.

So what was she going to do? Fall into an abyss of despair without an escape?

Maybe she could chop down a few trees and build a raft. With what? Her little knife? Sure. Why not? At least that thought made her chuckle.

When her foot was completely numb from the icy water, she pulled it out.

It was swelling and turning colors. The injury had to be around the cuboid bone. She'd broken her other foot in the same spot when she fell off a damn bull. Her orthopedist told her how lucky she was not to have a more severe injury and put her in a walking boot for a few weeks. If it was a similar break, she'd recover, but it would take a while. Could she make a walking boot? That would be easier than making a raft, but she'd probably have to shred her shirt down to the buttonholes to have enough cordage.

Before the pain returned, she hobbled around the campsite, collecting tinder to start a fire and logs to keep it going through the night. Then she iced her foot again while she fished for dinner. She was hungry and tired, but she still had to plan for tomorrow.

So what was her plan? Search for purslane while she rested for a day or two and made a walking boot. Then she'd see how far she could go—one step at a time.

7

Washington, D.C.—James Cullen

THE FOLLOWING DAY, as soon as JC finished his meeting with the Manager of Donor Services, he flew back to Reagan National Airport.

He'd made a list of items he needed for his upcoming trip and forwarded assignments to his assistant, Paul Brodie. Paul also managed JC's house and social commitments and, after three years, had become far more than an assistant. He was JC's friend and confidant.

Paul was waiting at the curb, driving JC's factory-fresh Range Rover, head down, probably texting one of his buddies.

JC opened the door to the back seat, tossed in his overnighter, then climbed into the front passenger seat. "Thanks for picking me up. Did you get the package?"

Paul put his phone away and pulled away from the curb. "It's under your seat. I wanted to lock it in the safe but didn't have time to return to the house."

JC pulled a steel lockbox out from under the seat. "Where's the key?"

"In the glove box."

JC unlocked the box, and inside was a leather pouch tied with a drawstring. He untied it and poured the contents into his hand. "Sweet." A handful of gold nuggets glittered in the sun. "What's the value?"

"Hundred grand. Straight from the Black Hills of South Dakota, just as you requested."

JC clapped Paul on the shoulder. "Perfect." He put the nuggets away. "What about the clothes? Did you have any luck?"

Paul lowered his chin, and his eyebrows breached the top rim of his aviators. "Have I ever failed you?"

JC grinned. "Not once."

"And I never will." Paul laughed, flashing straight white teeth against his brown-sugar skin tone. He was twenty-eight, a graduate of Columbia University, the son of New York attorneys Todd and Evelyn Brodie. He was brilliant, handsome, muscular, and could easily be on the cover of *Men's Health* or *GQ*.

Paul merged onto George Washington Memorial Parkway. "I first stopped by two costume shops, but they didn't have what you wanted, so I went to Georgetown's theater department and met with the artistic director. They just finished a production of *Oklahoma!*. Since that musical takes place in the early 1900s, I figured the men's trousers and jackets were close enough to what you wanted."

"I bet the artistic director took one look at you and said you could have whatever you wanted for a small donation."

Paul gave JC another one of those looks over the top of his sunglasses. "I have to up my game if I'm that predictable."

JC gave him a side-eye. "And the artistic director is, what? Under thirty and gorgeous?"

"Closer to thirty-five."

JC shook his head. "So, how much was the donation?"

Paul rumbled out a baritone laugh. "A thousand."

"What? For old clothes?"

"And sponsorship of their next production."

JC had given Paul the authority to spend whatever it took to get the job done, and he never abused it. If anything, his spending generally landed on the conservative side, which meant if Paul thought a thousand would get the job done, JC would have spent fifteen hundred.

"If they have open auditions, I might try out."

Paul sped up and changed lanes. "Sorry. You have to be a student."

"Oh, well, so what'd I get for the donation?"

"Black trousers, white shirts, neckties, vest, and sack coat, which are at your tailor's right now being fitted. They'll deliver them this afternoon."

"What about boots?"

"I compared your boots to pictures of ones worn in 1885, and yours are close enough. I know reenactors are particular, but the

Wellingtons you have will work." Paul clicked through SiriusXM channels, settled on a pop station, and a Selena Gomez song came on. He tapped his long fingers against the steering wheel. "So, what's your plan now? I have a class at two o'clock. Where do you want me to drop you?"

Paul had a degree in computer science from Columbia, and a master's in applied intelligence from Georgetown University, focusing on homeland security and cyber intelligence and espionage. He was now working on a PhD in government. In the time he'd been working for JC, he'd filled in some of the deep holes in JC's knowledge of the dark web.

"Drop me off at the house first. I have some research to do before I go to the office."

"Better get your reports done. Becky's already on the warpath."

JC's office manager had a way of getting what she wanted by needling Paul when she didn't have any luck with JC. "What'd I do now?"

"You didn't call while you were gone."

"Shit. I forgot."

"That's always your excuse. It doesn't work with Becky, so you better come up with something else."

"I brought her a thimble for her collection."

Paul shot JC a quick look and managed a groan. "Good luck with that. She knows you have a memory like an elephant, and you never forget anything."

JC scrolled through his text messages, looking for the most recent one from his office manager. He didn't see one from her, but that didn't mean she didn't send one. He glanced at Paul. "Do you have the same complaint?"

"Me? Nah," Paul said. "If you needed me, you'd call and keep calling until I answered."

"Why don't you explain that to Becky and my parents?"

"It wouldn't work." Paul turned onto 31st Street in Georgetown. "How long are you going to be gone this time?"

"Not sure. A few days or a couple of weeks. It depends on what I find when I get where I'm going."

"And you're not going to tell me where that is."

"Maybe North Dakota. Maybe New York City. I won't know for sure until I get there. That's all I can say."

"Until you get there?" Paul shook his head. "You know that

doesn't make any sense."

"Yeah, I know. But it's the best I can do."

"Okay, man. I'll take care of things while you're gone, as usual."

Paul pulled into the driveway of JC's 10,000-square-foot Second Empire mansion on 31st Street in Georgetown's East Village. His brother would say buying the house built in 1815 for twenty million dollars wasn't a wise investment, but it once belonged to Uncle Braham during the Civil War, and JC wanted the place, so he made the owner an offer he couldn't refuse. Then he hired a decorator to fill the residence with eighteenth- and nineteenth-century antiques. It was a showplace now, and he made it available to a few of his favorite charities as a fundraising venue. It looked more like a museum than a home, but it suited his lifestyle.

JC entered his mahogany study and powered up his desktop. He had access to the MacCorp server and its wealth of information, but he didn't want to leave footprints for Uncle David to find. Even with all the security precautions and firewalls JC and Paul had installed on JC's network, Uncle David could find a back door if he tried hard enough. But so far, Paul assured him, nobody had been snooping around.

For the next two hours, JC did a deep dive into Teddy Roosevelt's life from 1884 until 1895. He printed several summaries and tried to narrow down a specific time in TR's life that might sync with Ensley's.

"I'm leaving now," Paul shouted from the kitchen.

"Okay. I don't have plans for tonight. I'll be here working."

Paul crossed the hardwood floors and stood in the doorway to the office. "You won't leave without saying goodbye, will you?"

"I never do."

"Wherever you're going, I'll go with you. All you have to do is ask."

"I know, man. And thanks, but I don't need you this time. Just take care of things here and do your best to dodge my parents."

"Have you pissed them off enough that they'll show up here unannounced?"

"I haven't yet, but there's always a first time. And if David McBain shows up with Dad, don't let either one of them bully you. David could kill you if he wanted to, but he wouldn't unless ripping you apart was the only way to get the information he wanted."

"About you?"

"About me."

"Got it." Paul turned to walk away, then stopped and turned back. "Hey. You'll be careful, right? I mean, you won't do anything dumb."

JC squared the papers on his desk and fanned one corner of the pages with his thumb. "Do something dumb? I don't think so. I haven't done anything dumb since I was a teenager and ran away and almost got myself killed. Since then, I've never accepted any job before doing risk assessments and minimizing them as best I can."

"I got that," Paul said. "But shit still happens."

God, JC knew that all too well. He narrowly escaped a trap in Asia last week, a trap that could have brought all hell down on the family. "Don't worry."

Paul smacked the door frame. "Okay, see you later."

As soon as Paul left, JC took his TR research and went to the kitchen, fixed a salad for lunch, and read about TR's life in North Dakota while he ate. When he finished, he cleaned up his dishes and left the house.

His first stop was his law office. When he opened the door, he sailed his Sandown Trilby across the room, and it landed on the top hat hanger, spinning. Without looking up, Becky said, "James Cullen, where in the world have you been? I've been calling you for days."

He strode across the room, sat on the corner of Becky's desk, and presented her with a small gift-wrapped box. "I hope this makes up for the distress I've caused you."

She smiled, tugging on the ribbon. Inside the box was a two-inch vintage thimble with six white gold pins. She gasped. "This is gorgeous. Nothing can make up for the distress you cause me, but this comes damn close."

The top of each pin was different. The first one on the left side was a mallet and pearl polo ball, then a pearl and ruby cluster. The third one was a love knot. The fourth had the infinity symbol with a pearl. The fifth was a British crown, and the last one was a Star of David with a pearl cluster. The infinity symbol was JC's favorite pin.

"For your thimble collection, ma'am." He was rather proud of himself for finding it in a London shop, and while it wasn't an actual thimble, he knew she'd love it.

"It's lovely. Thank you." She pinned it to her jacket lapel and patted it gently. "But it doesn't get you out of hot water for not calling. You know the rules."

Yes, he did, and she'd sufficiently chastised him with her tough love.

Becky was a striking woman in her early fifties with thick, shoulder-length black hair, flawless skin, blue eyes, and reminded JC of his mom. She showed up the day he hung the sign with the firm name on the door and told him he needed to hire her. After reading her resume, he hired her on the spot. She was a general with a gentle hand and a big stick, and without her running the place, he'd never be able to do what he did with such success.

"Before you do anything else, you have reports to write, and if you don't..." she tsked.

"I'm heading to my office right now to get them done."

"Good, because I promised them today, and it tarnishes my reputation when I don't come through."

"So you don't care if I'm in the shithouse. You just don't want to be in there with me?"

"You're such a quick learner, James Cullen." She patted his cheek. "Paul said you're going out of town again. Where to?"

JC stepped around to the other side of her desk and thumbed through the documents in her outbox, stalling. There was nothing in the stack for him because Becky always put his correspondence on his chair, which forced him to look at it before he could sit down.

"North Dakota, I think," he said, "but I'll be out of pocket."

"How long?"

"A couple of weeks."

She rolled up the ribbon, put it inside the box, and dropped the box into her oversize handbag. "As long as you write your reports, no one will care."

He held up his hands in surrender. "I promise."

"Can I get the same commitment to call your mother? She doesn't believe I give you her messages."

JC scrolled through his texts, relieved there weren't any unanswered ones from Becky or his mom. "Good. That means she's mad at you, not me."

"Come on, JC. Be nice. She's your mother, and she worries."

"She wants me to find a nice girl, settle down in Kentucky, and start producing grandchildren. It's not going to happen."

"Maybe you should tell her what you're doing."

JC took a step backward as if Becky's words had shoved him. "Are you kidding? You think she worries now..."

"Well, she seems like a lovely woman, and she's always kind to me."

"If she ever gives you any trouble——"

Becky pushed up her sleeves and folded her arms. "Meredith Montgomery doesn't scare me."

"Paul's terrified of her."

"No, he's not. They have a thing." A muscle in the otherwise delicate line of her jaw twitched. She was trying not to laugh at him.

"A thing? What's that supposed to mean?" A pang unfolded in his chest, swift and deep—and completely unexpected. He loved his parents, but he didn't want them to worry.

"They're tight. Paul gives her just enough information to keep her from coming to Washington. And if Elliott Fraser ever storms in here looking for you, I'm running in the opposite direction. I've heard about his temper."

JC's chin dropped. "From whom?"

"Seriously? Just google 'Elliott Fraser's temper' and see what you find."

JC shook his head. "I don't have to google it. I've seen it."

She shooed him away. "Get to work. He's not showing up here today."

"Is that a promise?"

"Not a promise, but it's the best I can do."

His brother would give him a heads-up if his dad headed in this direction. That meant JC had enough time to get out of Washington and find Ensley before his dad started kicking down doors.

He entered his corner office and sat down at his rolltop desk—no glass and chrome for him. Antiques, leather, and centuries-old law books set the tone of the wide-windowed room.

For the next few hours, he wrote detailed After Action Reports, encrypted them, and emailed them to his handler. Then he returned to Becky's desk. "It's all done. You shouldn't get any grief from anyone except Mom. And if she calls, tell her I'll be in Kentucky next week."

Becky glanced up from her computer. "You tried that last time, James Cullen, and then didn't show up. She won't buy that excuse again."

"Well... Tell Mom I have to be in Richmond next week and will meet her at Mallory Plantation."

"You already said you'd be gone at least two weeks, and you

used that excuse the last time you promised to visit Kentucky."

JC scratched the back of his head. "Tell her this time I *will* be at the plantation, and if I don't show up, she can disown me."

Becky cleared her throat. "She's already done that, dear."

He snatched a piece of peppermint candy from the glass dish on Becky's desk. "Then hell, what am I worrying about?" He popped the candy in his mouth and tossed the wrapper. "Just tell her I'll be in Richmond. And don't take any crap off her."

"I never do."

JC laughed. "See ya." He grabbed his hat and left the office to the sound of Becky's chuckles.

As he strolled toward his black Rolls-Royce Wraith parked alone at the back of the lot, he gave his mind permission to wander for a few seconds. Cars, horses, cigars, and fine whisky were his indulgences. He worked hard, played hard, and in between tried to save the world while perpetuating his wealthy playboy persona. Those who knew his dad during his philandering days would see similarities, and that was what JC wanted.

He tossed the hat he never wore into the back seat.

His mind was unsettled, and he had just enough time to clear it before he went after Ensley. A long run would help, but right now, the smartest thing to do would be to find a quiet place to meditate and identify potential complications in his plan. There were a handful of DC locations where he could sit quietly, soak up nature, and listen for his angel. Kristen didn't speak to him often, but before he tackled anything, he opened his heart to hear her if she thought he needed a few words of wisdom.

Since the first time she came to him in a Napa cave more than a decade ago, she'd gotten him out of a half dozen tight situations. Kristen was Uncle Cullen's late sister, who died as a child. Why she picked JC to haunt, he wasn't sure, but he was glad to have her in his head, in his heart.

"So, where should we go today, Kristen?" She didn't speak, but he intuited an answer and plugged Theodore Roosevelt Island into Waze, a GPS navigational software app.

Fifteen minutes later, he turned into the island's almost empty parking lot. On an average day, the island had about four hundred visitors. But today, either they'd come earlier or were coming later, but at least they weren't here now.

Since it was May, pink and white cherry blossom petals now

littered the ground. He crossed the scenic pedestrian bridge that stretched from the Potomac's Virginia side to the island and then plunged into the forest.

Being out here eased concerns about his parents and allowed his mind to sort through the information he'd uncovered during his recent trip. But freeing his mind heightened his concerns about Ensley. With any luck, she would only have been in the past for two or three days by the time he found her.

But there was another concern he'd ignored until now.

All the brooches brought soul mates together, but he wasn't looking for a soul mate. He wasn't sure Ensley was, either. The timing was all wrong—for him, at least.

He pushed forward, climbing over logs and snaking around bushes.

The brooches all had slightly different properties, right? And if the purpose was to enlarge and strengthen the family, that could still happen without locking him in a relationship he didn't want. If he kept his emotional distance—and he was good at that—everything would be fine.

He finally emerged in the clearing where TR's seventeen-foot-tall bronze and granite monument stood with the forest as a backdrop. There was no one else around, so he had TR all to himself.

Saplings grew between granite blocks, proving that groundskeepers didn't overrun the island with hedge trimmers and pruning shears. Compared to other DC monuments, TR's was understated. There were no lawns, no gardens, and nothing cultivated. The forest was allowed to run free, with few man-made touches.

Off to JC's right, a flurry of motion had him reaching for his Glock, but it was only a group of white-tailed deer, flag tails waving, scurrying around the monument. He relaxed his hand, but not his mind or alertness.

"You'd like this, wouldn't you, TR? You'd feel right at home." Although, TR, an avid hunter, would probably shoot the deer.

JC left the monument and hiked the Upland Trail that traversed the island and looped around the old Mason mansion site. He spent an hour walking around the mostly flat, easy trail, thinking about the man the island honored. If JC met him, what would he want to know? Off the top, he'd ask the twenty-sixth president why he found solace on a sweat-soaked wrestling mat while mastering the art of the armbar.

JC returned to the granite-paved oval plaza, which was flanked by two pools with fountains and surrounded by a moat spanned by footbridges. Four twenty-one-foot-high granite tablets inscribed with quotations from TR's writings circled the statue.

The four tablets were titled "Nature," "Manhood," "Youth," and "The State." JC approached the closest tablet and read one of the quotes. "Be practical as well as generous in your ideals. Keep your eyes on the stars, but remember to keep your feet on the ground."

JC sat on one of the benches and listened to the woodpeckers and the croaking frogs. He contemplated life…his life…and the lives of all the MacKlennas. Was he doing the right thing for the right reason? After what he learned in Asia, he was convinced that involving his dad in more brooch business could get them all killed.

One of the white-tailed deer turned and stared at him for a long moment and then walked back into the forest. JC sat still and meditated for several more minutes.

Yes, he was doing the right thing for the right reason. Period.

8

The Badlands (1885)—Ensley

ENSLEY WOKE WITH the morning sun in her eyes. The purple light of dawn rising over the prairie was something straight out of a fairy tale.

And that fairytale included the blanket of leaves covering her. Where'd they come from? Had they fallen on her overnight? Not likely. They seemed to be strategically placed all around her.

So, again, where'd they come from?

Not that she was complaining. The leaves had kept her warm when the temperature dropped during the night. But wait a minute. The fire in the pit was crackling, and she hadn't added any logs. Yet here it was, keeping her toasty warm.

There were only two possibilities: she was a sleepwalker, or she wasn't alone.

The first wave of fear for the day smacked her in the face, and she reached for her little knife. Could she run away and hide? Hell no. She couldn't even walk.

Remembering her foot injury, she wiggled her toes and rotated her ankle. When there were no sharp pains, she tried the other foot, thinking she'd gotten them mixed up, and when that foot didn't hurt, either, she was even more alarmed. It wasn't the kind of injury that would heal overnight. So what the hell happened?

A blanket of leaves, a roaring fire, a healed foot.

None of it made sense.

She lay there, eyes closed, listening to the crisp, dry leaves rustle in the morning breeze, letting her mind wander to wherever it wanted to go.

The image of a giant of a man wearing dark trousers and a red cloak flashed across her mind's eye. The man's right arm was exposed, revealing tattoos from his neck to his fingertips. He must be a member of the Mandan, Hidatsa, or Arikara Nation.

She sat up, scattering the leaves and exposing her sockless feet. Neither one was swollen or bruised. Either she imagined the fall and injury, or her friendly ghost sprinkled magic dust over her foot and healed it.

That's impossible. Ghosts don't have magic dust. Fairies do.

Then how could she explain it? She couldn't. Time travel and ghosts were both unexplainable.

She decided not to dwell on it. There'd be time later to analyze everything that had happened, but not today. She had breakfast to catch and cook and miles to walk.

She reached for her right boot, and as she slipped it on, she noticed scuff marks on the side from the toe box to the heel, exactly where she injured her foot. It did happen, and here was the proof, but how it healed itself overnight had her stymied.

When she reached for the left boot, she spotted a sharp fluted stone sticking up out of the ground. She dug it out and brushed off the dirt. "Cool!" She'd never seen anything like this before.

It's a Clovis Point.

Her head shot up. "Who said that?" The booming voice didn't answer, of course, because she'd only imagined it. But if she'd imagined it, then how'd she know what it was?

Maybe she just assumed it. She'd heard of Clovis Points before, and it made sense that she'd find a prehistoric tool out here in God's country. This one was about four inches long, an inch and a half wide, and fashioned from what? She spat on it and wiped away the dirt in the small waves that resembled ripples in a pond. "I think this is jasper." The stone also had a groove at the base to fit the point onto a shaft.

Finding the 10,000 BC version of a Swiss Army knife was a stroke of luck and the first hopeful sign since this madness began. Well, except for her healed foot. But that was too unexplainable to think about right now.

9

Washington, D.C.—James Cullen

J C RETURNED HOME from Theodore Roosevelt Island, convinced he made the right decision to go after Ensley without telling his family. The goal was to protect them, and not involving them in her rescue was the best way to do that, although they'd never see it that way. Fortunately, by the time they discovered what he'd done, it'd be too late to stop him.

It was easier to beg forgiveness than ask for permission.

He settled into his desk chair and outlined the research he intended to do on TR's time in the Badlands. He started with a YouTube video titled "Theodore Roosevelt and the Western Adventure." While he listened, JC scrolled through book titles on Amazon and downloaded TR's book *Ranch Life and the Hunting Trail.* He also ordered a topography map of North Dakota, paying extra for expedited delivery. If he landed in the wilderness, miles from civilization, he'd have no idea which way to go without a compass and topo map.

For the next several hours, he read and visualized his arrival in the past and the first steps he'd take. Like Roosevelt, JC had traveled around America and hunted moose, elk, caribou, bison, mule deer, and white-tailed deer, so adjusting to life in nineteenth-century North Dakota shouldn't be difficult. And he didn't intend to stay very long or do something idiotic like help Andy Jackson fight the Battle of New Orleans.

Nope. That wasn't for him. He'd find Ensley and get the hell out of there.

"JC," Paul yelled.

"In here," JC yelled back while shoving the pages of research material he'd printed into a folder. Paul wouldn't ask JC what he was doing, but he'd notice and then later slide an "innocent" question into their conversation, like "I thought I'd go deer hunting in North Dakota. Do you know when the hunting season opens?"

As his dad's good friend Louise would say, "What a cheeky bastard."

Paul strolled in and noticed the stack of mail JC had dumped in a side chair. He picked it all up before propping a hip on the corner of the desk. "When are you leaving?"

"Tomorrow."

Paul separated the first class mail from the magazines and junk and tossed the junk mail into the recycle bin. "Do you want me to take you somewhere?"

JC thought a minute. Since he'd decided to take one of his horses, he'd need a ride to the stables. An Uber would work, but what the heck? Paul could take him. "Sure. I'll need a ride to the stables."

Paul gave him a puzzled look as he placed the stack of first-class mail in front of JC. "I'm not even going to ask."

"Good, because I don't have an explanation." JC thumbed through the mail, separated bills from invitations, and returned the bills to Paul. "Pay these. I'll look at the invitations and mark them as usual." Which meant he'd RSVP yes or no, and if no, he'd send donations to the charities.

"I'm going over to the computer lab and won't be back till eight or nine." On his way to the door carrying the fistful of bills, he glanced over his shoulder and said. "Before you leave again, call Ms. Montgomery."

"Have you been talking to Becky?"

Paul turned back toward JC with his lips twitching. "What do you think?"

JC stacked the invitations and put the pile next to his calendar to respond to later. "Since both of you came highly recommended from the same person, I'd say you text each other regularly."

"I don't know what you're talking about, but I do know you should call your mom. I've never met her, but I've heard rumors that she can be a controlling bitch."

JC rolled his eyes. "Who told you that?"

"Your cousins Emily and Isabella. So please call her."

"She wouldn't be ugly to you, and she only acts out when she's stressed. And right now, nothing much is going on in her life, which is why she harasses me weekly."

JC looked at the desk clock. His mother had an appointment with Trainer Ted every afternoon at five for a half-hour yoga class to relieve her accumulated stress. If she stuck to her schedule, she'd be there now and wouldn't answer her phone. He tapped on her number, and the call went straight to voice mail. "Mom, hi. I'll be at the plantation next week, but until then, I'll be out of pocket. Hope to see you at Uncle Braham's." He clicked off. "There, I tried to talk to her. Satisfied?"

"Bullshit. Ms. Montgomery has a yoga class every afternoon at five. You knew she wouldn't answer, so it doesn't count."

"How do you know that?"

"You pay me to know. I'll see you later."

JC cocked his head and watched Paul stroll out of the room. His assistant knew more about JC's life than he would fess up to, but since he trusted both Paul and Becky, he didn't worry about them betraying him.

If he was wrong about either of them, his mistake could be deadly.

10

The Badlands (1885)—Ensley

WHEN THE SUN began to sink toward the horizon in a blaze of red and orange, Ensley decided to stop hiking for the day—her fourth day in the wilderness. Tomorrow she should reach the end of Spring Creek, but she should head southwest first thing in the morning if she was going to Medora.

But if she did that, she wouldn't have water, and right now, her survival depended on it. So, what should she do? Follow Spring Creek until it ended, then go north until she reached the Little Missouri River? If she did that, she'd have to travel several miles without water, and that scared the hell out of her.

She'd sleep on it and decide in the morning.

For now, though, it was time to find a suitable campsite, and the grove of cottonwoods ahead looked like a possibility. After scoping it out and finding a flat area with a few big trees that would provide okay shelter, she gathered wood and started a fire.

At the top of her to-do list was to make a new fishing spear using the Clovis Point. The spear had to be multifunctional. Besides fishing, she required it for protection. She also needed to make containers, and birchbark would work for that.

Following dinner, and after she made preparations for the night, she went looking for a sapling to use for the new spear. But how to chop it down? Her little knife wouldn't work, and if she destroyed her ten-thousand-year-old Swiss Army knife, she'd be pissed. And it would never work as a hatchet anyway. But maybe she could place the blade at an angle against the tree and then hammer it with a piece of wood.

She picked up one of the logs she'd collected for the fire and went looking for a sapling. It had to be a couple of inches taller than she was, which would increase her reach while fishing or protecting herself. If it was shorter and she used it as a walking stick, too, the point could stab her if she tripped.

It took a few minutes, but she found a sapling that was the perfect height and small enough in diameter that she could chop it down.

She pressed the Clovis Point at an angle against the tree trunk and hammered it with the piece of wood, first on one side of the tree trunk and then the other, chipping away at the tree and creating a wedge all the way around until she could break it off.

Snap!

"Ha. That was easy." She examined the Clovis Point and was relieved to find it wasn't damaged. It was now her lucky talisman.

She dragged the sapling back to the campsite to scrape and shape it. When she was a kid, her father taught her how to make a spear. And although she hadn't made one in several years, she hadn't forgotten how to do it.

Looking back on all the things he taught her, she wondered how her father, a kid from the Philadelphia suburbs, had learned so many survival tricks. If anyone could be with her now, she wished it could be her dad. It didn't take much to imagine him sitting next to her, directing each step. "Start at the top of your spear and scrape off about six inches of bark, like you're peeling a carrot."

She sensed his hand on hers as she used the log as a hammer again, banging it against the Clovis Point until she stripped off six inches of bark and shaped the end of the sapling into a sharp point.

Perfect. Now grease the point and roast it over the flames to fire-harden it.

"I don't have any grease."

Then use what you have.

Lip balm! That would work but would require the entire tube to grease the point. Well, hell. What did she want? Smooth lips or a spear? The spear won hands down.

To turn her roughly made spear into a long-term survival weapon was a three-step process. First, she greased up the top six inches of the pointed sapling with the beeswax lip balm. Step two was to fire-harden the edge by toasting it until it darkened. And the third step was to burnish it by rubbing the point with a stone to create a glass-like finish.

She moved through each step methodically, her soul soothed by the simple act of being proactive and creative, and for a while, she forgot about her predicament. And when she finished her project, she held up the spear, grinning. "It's beautiful. A definite keeper."

Now, if she could make a few bark containers, she'd be on a roll.

She wandered through the grove looking for a birch tree and was about to give up and go fishing when something moved, crunching the dead leaves. Her hand shot up, holding the spear at shoulder height.

"Who's there? Show yourself."

Her gaze darted around the shadowed grove until she spotted the leaf-cruncher—a cottontail rabbit, poking its nose around the trunk of the tree. Was she quick enough to spear it? She licked her lips, imagining the taste of roasted rabbit, but no, she wasn't fast enough.

Thoughts of rabbit stew, stuffed rabbit, grilled rabbit, braised rabbit, and—what else? Kentucky Fried Rabbit—lingered long after he hopped away. But the critter had drawn her attention to a birch tree, whose bark had oils that kept it supple and made it easy to fold into shapes.

She banked thoughts of rabbit stew and, using the Clovis Point, tackled the job of stripping squares of bark. When she was satisfied with the results, she returned to her campfire and held a piece over the fire, heating it until it became pliable. Next, she folded it into a square and threaded thin strips of bark in and out of small holes in the corners that she'd punched with the tip of her blade. Pleased with the first container, she made another.

The sun was setting by the time she finished with the second container. She leaned back against a cottonwood tree and admired her handiwork in the dying light—a knife, a spear, and two water-tight bowls. How nice it would be to drink from a cup instead of slurping water out of her hands.

She'd accomplished a lot, but it paled in comparison to what lay ahead.

11

Washington, D.C.—James Cullen

J C STOOD IN his walk-in closet, buttoning the black herringbone vest. But before putting on the sack coat, he used the biometric fingerprint fast-access option to open his tactical weapons safe. The interior had a series of horizontal bars that allowed the attachment of nearly anything with a clip. His holsters, sheaths, and MOLLE-compatible pouches were easily accessible, along with the few antique firearms. He picked up a sleeve gun, à la James West in *The Wild Wild West* TV series, and strapped the slide and derringer to his right arm. Just to be sure it worked correctly, he popped the slide, and the gun appeared in his hand. *Good!* He added a Glock to his hip and another one to an ankle carry holster. A boot knife completed his arsenal.

Three guns and a knife. That should do it.

A black slouch hat completed his costume. He checked his appearance in the wall mirrors and approved of what he saw.

Returning to the bedroom, he folded his extra clothes into the bedroll. He then packed the saddlebags with a Dopp kit, mess kit, rain slicker, canteen, MREs, antibacterial body wipes, water purification tablets, first-aid kit, and energy bars.

Now, what should I do with the gold?

There was always a chance of being robbed, so he didn't want to carry the nuggets in one pouch. He divided them into four piles and wrapped each one in a handkerchief. He shoved one into the side of his boot, another one in his Dopp kit, another in his saddlebag. The last one he hid in the lining of his jacket.

Satisfied with his packing, he slung the saddlebags over his shoulders, tucked the bedroll under his arm, then headed toward the kitchen to get an oven mitt. If the brooch heated the way he expected it would, the glove would protect his hand.

He was tying the saddlebag laces when Paul entered the house and paused in the doorway. "Man, you look like the real thing." He circled JC, checking him out. "The jacket fits. How about the pants?"

"Pretty good. Thanks for finding them."

"Sure. So, are you ready to go?"

JC grabbed his gear and led the way to the garage, and forty-five minutes later, Paul drove into the Meadowbrook Stables in Chevy Chase, Maryland.

"Are you going to ride Mercury to North Dakota or wherever you're going?" Paul asked.

"I've got a ride. A friend's picking us up here in about an hour."

Paul responded with his usual sly eyebrows-above-his-aviators expression. "You've got a brand-new truck and horse trailer. Why aren't you driving?"

"Don't need to." JC climbed out and grabbed his gear. "I'll see you in a couple of weeks. And if Dad shows up, tell him what you know." JC closed the door and headed toward the barn without looking back.

"If you run into trouble, give me a call," Paul yelled.

JC didn't respond. Paul knew he was lying, but damn it, there wasn't anything JC could tell Paul that would ease his mind.

When JC entered the barn, he breathed in deeply. There wasn't anywhere in the world that gave him as much pleasure as a stallion barn. Growing up, he spent more time in the barns than in his playroom. To him, the combination of horseflesh, musty blankets, leather, pine shavings, and hay was as enticing as Aunt Maria's pepperoni bread right out of the oven.

Mercury's stall was at the end, and the horse sensed JC's presence, pawing the floor and neighing before JC appeared at the stall door.

"Hi, there, boy." JC dropped his bedroll and saddlebags outside the stall and opened the door. "Want to go for a run?" Mercury pawed the floor again. JC paid for full-service boarding, and he'd already texted the farm to let them know he was taking Mercury away for a few days.

Mercury stood still, quivering with eagerness, while JC saddled him, using his favorite western saddle with a Cheyenne roll. He removed the oven mitt before tying the saddlebags and bedroll to the back of the saddle, then led the horse from the barn before mounting up.

"Let's go, boy." Mercury carried him across the paddock and into the trees bordering the Rock Creek. "Hold on, buddy," JC told the horse. "You might not like what's about to happen." He put on the oven mitt, opened the brooch, and, holding it tightly, recited the chant...

"Chan ann le tìm no àite a bhios sinn a' tomhais an' gaol ach 's ann le neart anama."

An explosion of sizzling sparks preceded the fog, and an electrical current zapped his hand and ran up his arm to his shoulder. Despite the protection of the thick mitt, he couldn't hold on to the brooch and dropped it just as the fog consumed him and his horse.

12

Chevy Chase, MD—Paul

PAUL'S SPIDEY SENSES had alerted him that something was wrong. He tried to call JC, but it went straight to voice mail, so he returned to the stables to confront JC before he left with Mercury…but arrived just in time to watch him disappear.

Now he emerged from his hiding place in the woods and knelt near the spot where JC vanished in the funny-smelling fog. On the ground was an antique brooch with a hot-to-the-touch orangey stone split in half and held together by a tiny hinge. He picked it up, closed it, and opened it again. If he hadn't known the clasp was there, he never would have seen it.

He walked to the center of the remaining fog. It was thinning, smelled like shit, and the air vibrated around him. The stone glowed and heated. He removed his ball cap, dropped the brooch in it, and held the hat at arm's length while he stepped out of the evaporating fog.

Now he understood why JC threw it away. But what did that mean for JC? If the brooch carried him off, then how would he ever get back?

It wasn't the first time Paul had been alerted to possible danger. He had the same sensation when JC went to Asia, and he'd advised JC to be cautious.

Now JC had vanished. Did it have anything to do with what happened in Asia? And where did this brooch come from? It looked Celtic, not Oriental. Was it a family heirloom?

JC's disappearance put Paul in an awkward position. So what did he do now? He considered the dilemma during the drive back to Georgetown. He had two choices. He could inform Becky or stay quiet and wait a few days. Whatever JC was up to, it was CIA business, and that made it top secret.

By the time Paul reached the house, he'd ruled out informing Becky. He'd catch hell, but JC had an uncanny ability to escape tight situations, almost as if he had a genie on his shoulder who could see twenty steps ahead.

Paul read all of JC's After Action Reviews and knew all about on-the-books jobs. It was the jobs off the books that Paul didn't know anything about. And he couldn't help JC if he didn't know what he was doing.

After locking the brooch in the safe, he went to JC's office to see if he'd left any notes or assignments for Paul to complete while he was gone.

He stood in the doorway to take in the entire room, then zeroed in on the bookshelf. Nothing appeared out of order. JC had a collection of presidential biographies, first editions of several classic novels, all the Greek tragedies, and a fifty-one-volume set of *Harvard Classics*.

Paul ran his finger along the spines, pushing one of the presidential biographies—David McCullough's *Mornings on Horseback: The Story of an Extraordinary Family, a Vanished Way of Life, and the Unique Child Who Became Theodore Roosevelt*—back a fraction to align it with the others. Then he moved to the credenza, noting each of the two dozen framed photographs of family and friends. A picture of JC with his Harvard friend George Williams and George's cousin, Ensley, had been moved from the desk to the credenza. Paul straightened the frame, then crossed the room, and sat down in the desk chair.

Everything on top of the desk seemed in order except for the missing photograph. JC hadn't filled the space with another one, so its absence was more prominent.

Paul glanced through the stack of invitations, but JC hadn't marked any to indicate he planned to attend. Paul checked the dates against JC's calendar and separated the ones that conflicted. Then he opened the center drawer to rummage for a paperclip and pushed aside a newspaper article about North Dakota.

"What the hell?" Under the newspaper was JC's cell phone. He'd turned it off, or else the battery had died. Why did he leave his phone here?

Hell. Why did he disappear in a stinking fog?

None of this made any sense at all.

Paul visually surveyed the room again. Since JC left his phone behind, a whole new level of possibilities opened up. He had hyperthymesia and could recall the majority of things he'd experienced personally in excruciating detail. The syndrome was a blessing and a curse, but right now, as he tried to connect the dots, the blessing part was dominant.

Yesterday the MacKlenna Farm table book was closed, and the antique train on the top shelf of the bookcase was facing the opposite direction. Since he'd entered the office, he'd noticed the Roosevelt book, the photograph of JC's friend George and his cousin, the placement of the MacKlenna Farm table book, the newspaper article about North Dakota, the direction of the train, and the turned-off cell phone. Were they connected?

He didn't know because he didn't know what caused JC to disappear in the fog. Without that piece of information, he couldn't tie it all together, and he didn't dare call either of the people who might have answers.

13

The Badlands (1885)—Ensley

I T WAS ALMOST sunset on the fifth day when Ensley reached the head of Spring Creek. It was time to find a campsite and go fishing. Her hip was bothering her, and she desperately needed ibuprofen. Good luck with that. Was there anything in nature that would work? Yeah. Ginger, but she'd have to be in Hawaii, Central America, or Asia to find that particular plant.

There was still no sign of twenty-first-century life, and she'd given up hope of finding any. As a matter of fact, she hadn't found evidence of any human life at all. If she arrived in the 1870s or later, she'd soon reach the Fort Berthold Reservation on the Little Missouri River's north side. She didn't think they'd harm her, but a woman alone was always in danger. To be on the safe side, she decided to stay out of their way.

The grove of cottonwoods about twenty-five yards ahead looked like a good campsite. It would work fine for a couple of days while she rested and made more containers. The trail ahead wouldn't have water, so she needed to carry as much as possible.

After gathering wood for a fire, she went fishing, caught two largemouth bass, and after gutting and filleting them, placed them on a stone to cook. She'd held it together for five days. Well, mostly together, and now she was tired and hungry for some good old-fashioned carbs like dark chocolate, bread, wine, potatoes, apples, beer, sugar plums.

When visions danced in her head, she got angry because she didn't have any chocolate and didn't know if she'd ever taste dark chocolate again. That scared the crap out of her. And with the fear came tears.

Stop crying. Drink coffee and think about all the things you're thankful for. Yeah, right. Like what?

How about the Clovis Point?

Okay, right. She was thankful for that. And she was grateful she didn't have a broken foot.

But reminding herself of the things she was thankful for didn't stop the tears.

Her dad told her when she was a little girl that it was okay to cry, but that sooner or later, the tears would stop, and whatever caused them in the first place would still be there.

And he was right. When the tears dried up, she still didn't have any chocolate. But she could have a cup of dandelion root coffee.

While she sipped, she considered her situation rationally. She was more than likely stuck here for the rest of her life, and she had to start thinking about what kind of future she could build for herself once she reached civilization.

She was a single woman living in a time when women didn't have the right to vote and were considered a man's property. So, she needed a plan that didn't involve marriage. She was a logical person, and she could figure out something.

But logic, according to Einstein, would only get her from point A to point B. Imagination could take her everywhere else. And she had a fantastic imagination. She'd grown up without siblings, so she had to depend on herself for entertainment.

She'd have to use every bit of her creativity to find a job once she reached the closest town. Towns had newspapers, and all publications needed writers and editors. She could do both thanks to her experience writing for *Flyby*, the flagship blog of *The Harvard Crimson*. Plus, she was a book editor.

All she had to do was convince a publisher to give her a chance.

14

The Badlands (1885)—James Cullen

J C EMERGED FROM the fog in the middle of nowhere.

Surrounding him was a broken landscape full of color, odd-shaped bluffs and serrated ranges of hills, and the occasional lone butte standing sentinel above the surrounding billowy grass country.

His first thought was: *I arrived in the Badlands.* But his second one almost dropped him on his knees: *Oh, shit! I threw away the brooch.*

He groaned loudly enough that Mercury's ears popped up, and he sidestepped. JC patted the horse's neck while replaying what happened in the forest. He didn't throw the brooch away in a bedroom as others had done. Nope. His royal screwup was much worse. He'd thrown it away where none of the family would ever find it.

Dad will have my head unless Uncle David takes it off first.

And JC would deserve it. Why had he done this without consulting his family? Simple. JC wanted to protect everyone. But in fact, his choices would ultimately bring more attention to the clan, which could destroy them all.

What a fucking idiot. This situation was similar to what happened to him as a teenager when he unintentionally locked the wine cave door, and he couldn't get out. It scared the hell out of him and his family.

What would Ensley say when she discovered he'd come to rescue her but had lost their ticket home? Ensley might take his gun and put him out of his misery.

JC dismounted and walked while he considered his options.

What options? He didn't have any, but he had faith in his dad and knew he wouldn't quit searching until he found JC. Paul would find the clues JC left, and Uncle David and Aunt Kenzie would figure out where he went and why.

But it might take them a while.

Right now, though, there was nothing he could do about going home. He had to focus on finding Ensley. Had she been here long enough to reach Elkhorn Ranch? Would Roosevelt even be there? If it was 1885, chances were he was preparing for a cattle drive to round up his herd and ship it off to Chicago. If it was earlier, say 1883 or 1884, TR would be hunting, and it would be harder to track him down.

JC looped the reins around a tree branch and reached inside one of the saddlebags for his topo map and compass. Finding his position in the field was second nature to him, thanks to Uncle Braham and Uncle David, who taught him and his cousins how to find their way in the wilderness. Then the training he went through the past two years had refined all those survival skills.

After he found the declination—the distance between the magnetic north and the true north—he oriented the topo map and rotated the bezel so north lined up with the travel arrow's direction. Then he slid the baseplate until one of the straight edges aligned with the map's right side. Holding the map and compass steady, he rotated his body until the end of the magnetic needle was within the orienting arrow's outline.

With the map oriented correctly, he could identify nearby landmarks, and from that, find exactly where he was on the map and determine the distance to Elkhorn Ranch.

He took his time. He couldn't afford a mistake. A few degrees off, and he could end up in Canada. Well, maybe not that far off, but still way out of the way.

According to his calculations, he was close to Spring Creek and Ensley's ranch. If she landed near here, she would go there first. JC knew her ancestors started the ranch in the late eighteen hundreds, but he didn't know if it was the 1880s or 1890s. If her ancestors were there, Ensley might stay there for a while.

He put the compass away and mounted up again. "Let's go, Mercury."

As Mercury carried him across the plains, the landscape became slightly familiar, but the absence of roads, power lines, and cars and trucks was disorienting. He consulted the map again and confirmed he was on Ensley's property, but nothing was here.

So if the ranch wasn't here, where would she go next? Toward the creek. Finding water was a logical first step.

He turned Mercury toward Spring Creek, and when he reached the water, he dismounted to let his horse drink while he looked for signs of Ensley. He didn't find any footprints or evidence of a campfire.

But how would she start a fire? Maybe she still had the fire starter bracelet he gave her as a joke gift many years ago. He doubted it. So what would she use? There was plenty of flint near the creek, but what about a striker? Marcasite would work, but he doubted she found any here.

He glanced up at the sky. If he had to guess, he'd say it was midafternoon, which left several hours of daylight for him to search. If he followed Spring Creek, he would eventually pick up her trail.

He knew how to survive in this environment, and he could track anything that left a print or a marking on a tree or the ground, or any signs of eating, or other random clues that would enable him to find her.

He consulted his map again. He was ninety-nine percent sure she'd stay close to the water. That meant following Spring Creek to its end and then crossing the Badlands toward Little Missouri State Park, then to the river. It would be a long way around to TR's Elkhorn Ranch—if it existed—but that's where she'd go.

If she had a horse, though, all bets were off.

He mounted up and rode along the bank of the creek, searching for footprints. Within a hundred or so yards, he found some. He dismounted and picked through a rock-lined, shallow firepit, finding fish bones. Next to the pit were shards of obsidian and chunks of crushed rock with pieces of flint.

The footprints were fading but still recognizable: female, size seven boots with one-and-three-quarters ground-to-heel height. Based on the stride, probably five two to five five, weighing about a hundred and five pounds. If these were Ensley's, she was favoring her right hip. His best guess was that she was here about four days ago.

Walking, she'd average about ten to twelve miles a day over the uneven ground. Fewer if her hip continued to hurt. She'd follow the creek but would have to zig-zag when the trees and brush grew up next to the bank. That would eat up the miles and keep her from making much progress.

He mounted up and followed the creek until he had to swing right of the river onto a sagebrush terrace and then cut back and forth, which slowed his progress. As he navigated one of the switchbacks, he followed footprints to the edge of a rock formation.

"Shit." He dismounted to examine the prints. Why the hell did she get this close to the edge? The footprints were overlapping with dig marks made by her heels. "Damn!"

He had to get down there. He visually marked the spot, then led his horse down the switchback until he reached the bottom of the rock formation, where he squatted and examined the ground. This was where she landed. Then she stood on one foot and hobbled.

"Ensley! Ensley!" His voice died on the wind. If she was injured, she couldn't be far away.

He followed her footprints. She was hobbling and had a walking stick for support. Then the prints stopped. He squatted and examined the tall grass, finally finding them again.

Why'd she go this way? She'll get there faster if she goes straight.

He kept losing her prints in the tall grass, but after backing up and searching again, he found them and followed her trail as it angled toward the creek.

And then he found another set of prints. But this set belonged to a man wearing flat-soled shoes, standing about six feet, and weighing close to two hundred pounds.

Ensley's prints were behind his, and he wasn't dragging her.

What the hell's going on. Is he Native American? What tribes are here now?

Sioux for sure. Would they harm her? For the first time, JC was terrified for her.

He followed the footprints to the creek. *She limped here and sat down. Why?* He studied the ground and the trampled grass and then stuck his hand in the water. "Damn. It's like ice." The signs all made sense. She hobbled to the creek, sat down, and iced her foot.

Smart.

He followed her footprints around the campsite. She was still hobbling, but at some point, she walked away on both feet.

What the hell?

How long was she here? He continued his search of the campsite and found the man's prints crisscrossing Ensley's, and then the man walked back through the tall grass and didn't return.

So he left her here?

JC squatted by the firepit and, using a stick, sifted through the ashes, finding a few fish bones. *She wasn't here for more than a day. So how did her foot heal so quickly? Who was the man? And why did he leave her behind?*

A memory pinged in JC's brain.

Erik!

It had to be him or one of the others. The size of the man who left the prints matched the descriptions of the Vikings his dad met at Jarlshof. And according to brooch rules, when a brooch is left behind, the guardian has to stay with it. That meant one of the ancient Council members had to come forward in time to watch over the time traveler.

But wait. Back up a minute. *Why go through all this trouble?*

Guardians had protected the brooches ever since the Keeper dispersed them centuries ago. Since his dad was the Keeper, the guardians were supposed to return the brooches to him. So why send Ensley on a dangerous adventure? She could have pinned the brooch to her jacket, gone to dinner with George as planned, and JC would have seen it. Then he could have bought it from her and saved her from going through all this crap.

He must be missing an essential piece of information. Tavis would know. But JC wasn't exactly in a position to call him. So why hadn't this come up before? Had anybody bothered to ask why the guardians didn't return the brooches?

If I had spent more time at home, I might know the answer.

It must have something to do with activating the brooch.

JC sat back on the ground and took the first deep breath since he arrived in the past while he thought back to Aunt Penny's experience in 1814 New Orleans. Even with a Council member watching out for her, Penny still had a horrible time of it.

What does that mean for Ensley?

He stood and stretched, then walked through the campsite again, noticing even more details, including a birch tree with three squares of bark stripped off. The bark harvest was recent, maybe three or four days ago.

Birchbark was malleable and used throughout the centuries to make dozens of things like containers, canoe coverings, fishing gear. If Ensley stripped bark from this tree, what'd she make? Containers? Probably, but where'd she get a knife? He thought back to the previous campsite he found. There were shards of obsidian.

Slices of obsidian were sharp enough to use for a knife.

She had the means to build a fire, containers, and a knife. But if she was only eating fish and walking a dozen miles a day, she wouldn't last long. He picked up some plant stems and sniffed them. Dandelions. The plant was a good source of protein, and she could boil the roots for coffee, but she still didn't have any complex carbs.

He needed to find her—quickly. She was probably about three days ahead of him by now.

On horseback, he could reach her within a day. He swung his leg up over the saddle. "Come on, Mercury. Let's go find her."

He settled Mercury into a ground-eating lope, determined not to sleep until he had her safely at his side.

15

The Badlands (1885)—Ensley

THE NEXT MORNING, she filled both birchbark bowls with water and covered them with the lids she made last night. She'd be walking a day and a half at least, without access to water other than what she could carry. But if she rationed it, it should last until she reached the Little Missouri River.

She set off on a winding path across the plains with her eyes trained on a row of buttes. Once she reached that landmark, she set another one, which took her through forests and around hills. She had to stop often and reorient herself.

There was no guarantee she was going straight north, but she'd eventually reach the river, even if she went northeast or northwest.

By evening, her water bowls were half empty or half full, depending on how she felt at that moment. And her stomach growled like a lion in the zoo at mealtime.

Half full. She still had hope.

She made camp at the base of the buttes she'd used as a landmark. The lack of carbs in her diet was taking its toll, and her hip was killing her. She was tired, filthy, hungry, and in pain. She'd give all her diamond-stud buttons for a cup of dandelion coffee, but she didn't want to use her water. It had to last another day.

After a fitful night's sleep, she gathered her few belongings and headed northeast again. The ground was rough, hilly, and dry, and it took a further toll on her hip. Black-tailed prairie dogs and a mule deer watched her go by, and a couple of hawks, screaming *kee-eeee-arr* flew overhead. Their presence made her feel not so alone in the vast landscape that extended miles into the horizon.

By midday, both water containers were empty, but she kept

going. And as fatigue set in and her throat got drier, fear rolled over her in waves, and she second-guessed her decision to come this way. If she only knew how much farther she had to go. By late afternoon, she had nothing left in her tank.

She dropped to the ground. "I'm done."

Get up.

She shook her head. "Can't. I'm done."

Get up.

"Go away and leave me alone."

Get up, or you will die.

"I don't care. Go away."

Get up.

He—whoever he was—wasn't going to leave her alone. She reached for her walking stick and held on to it as she struggled to her feet. She managed to stagger several yards before dropping to her knees again. Her mouth was so dry she couldn't work up enough saliva to spit.

If she didn't get up now, she'd die.

Get up.

"No."

Get up.

She shook her head. She just didn't have the strength to go on. In defeat, she closed her eyes and surrendered to the darkness.

16

The Badlands (1885)—Ensley

T HE SOUND OF rushing water brought Ensley to semiconsciousness, and the faint grayish light seeped through her eyelids. It was a blissful, sleep-fogged moment until she remembered…

Thirsty… Can't go on…

And then her blue-tatted rescuer carried her across the Badlands, and she slept deeply for the first time since coming out of the fog.

There was no tossing about, no beasts roaming her uneasy dreams, no sore hip, no tired feet, just rejuvenating sleep, almost like swinging in a hammock on a breezy spring afternoon.

She eased up out of her bough-lined bed and immediately sensed she was alone. A quick shiver slid down her spine. He was gone again, but this time he left a gift. Beside her on the ground was a beautiful, hand-tooled leather costrel with a wooden stopper and rawhide strap. It didn't look like any Native American water bottle she'd ever seen. The symbols appeared much older, possibly from the Greco-Roman world.

Whoever her rescuer was, he must be watching and waiting until she reached a point of desperation before stepping in to help her out and performing a miracle. If he was in the miracle-making business, maybe he could send her home. Was he a shaman or something? If so, he must live on the Fort Berthold Reservation. But if he did, why didn't he just take her there?

She did a full-body stretch and was surprised to discover there wasn't an achy muscle in her body. If she'd taken an hour-long hot yoga class and followed it up with a deep-tissue massage, she wouldn't feel any better than she did right then.

Adding to the feel-good moment was the juicy scent of roasting meat. Man, she was hungry enough to eat a bear. But that wasn't a bear roasting on a spit over the campfire. It was a rabbit, and while she could eat two or three of them, one was enough to take away the hunger pangs.

She climbed to her feet and did a few more deep stretches, still surprised by her pain-free hip. After a quick wash in the river, she sat down next to the fire. A fresh batch of dandelion greens had been chopped up and stored in one of the birchbark bowls, and the roots were simmering in another one.

How thoughtful.

She glanced around, wondering if he was watching her from a distance. But she didn't have a sense of anyone out there. He was gone. And for some reason, she didn't think he'd be back. What did that mean for her? Was she out of danger?

After removing the roots, she sat back and sipped the dandelion coffee while she watched the sunrise. It was incredibly gorgeous this morning and cast its intense, live-coals colors over the glittering cottonwood leaves. They seemed to join her in a quiet sigh.

I almost died yesterday.

She shivered at the thought. It was a wake-up call, and she need-ed to pay attention to it. No matter how competent she thought she was, she couldn't get through this on her own. She had to depend on others to survive.

17

Little Missouri River (1885)—Ensley

AFTER SPENDING TWO nights resting at a sweet oasis next to the Little Missouri River, it was time to follow the meandering river northwest. She couldn't delay any longer. It reminded her of when she boxed up the few belongings she kept at her ex-boyfriend's apartment. She'd put it off until the unfinished business was nearly debilitating. But that kind of delay could be a matter of life and death out here.

It was time. Ensley was refreshed and hopeful and ready for whatever came next.

She didn't know how many miles lay ahead of her, but if she followed the river, she'd eventually reach Medora. And if it was 1885, she'd pass TR's Elkhorn Ranch, and if he wasn't off hunting or rounding up his cattle, he might be there. What would she do then? Go all fan girl on him? Probably.

Since the days blended into each other, she notched a stick every morning so she wouldn't forget how many days she'd been wandering in the wilderness. One day she'd tell her story, and the details would add flavor to her tales, like special sauce or seasoning. That's how she explained it to the authors whose stories she edited.

Damn! She was almost glad the brooch had abandoned her here. At least she didn't have to return to her office to reclaim her stuff. How embarrassing and humiliating.

For now, she'd do what the English did. When anything embarrassing or emotional threatened to come up, she'd discuss the weather. Always a safe topic.

So instead of thinking about her lost job, she studied the sky. No rain today, thank goodness. She didn't have the energy to slog through the mud. The rugged terrain was awful enough, and the constant backtracking—when the heavy-growth forest blocked her path—added miles to the trip. She often ended the day frustrated with her slow progress. Her hip pain returned, and it cut into her mileage. From experience, she knew how many miles she could do in a day, and she was barely getting in eight or nine miles before she had to stop. At that rate, it might be winter before she reached her destination.

After another long day, she found a suitable campsite, started a fire, then went fishing. While dinner cooked, she sipped a cup of dandelion coffee, thinking over what she could add to her diet when the distinct sound of horse hooves clopping through the tall grasses sent her into a panic. The shaman had never appeared on horseback, so it probably wasn't him. Whoever it was, she couldn't sit here and wait for trouble or hope he would ignore the smoke from her campfire and pass her by.

Her mind screamed, *Move! Now!* She grabbed her spear and Clovis Point, and with her adrenaline surging, dashed into the trees for cover.

She peeked through a branch and noticed the horse before the man. That was dumb because the man was the one who could hurt her. But it was rare to see a magnificent black stallion with such fabulous conformation. His head, long neck, and white median star above his eyes were stunning.

Focus on the man.

The rider's posture was perfectly suited to the horse. He sat tall and relaxed in the saddle, shoulders back with both reins in one hand. The other hand rested on his thigh. His black cowboy hat was low on his brow, hiding his face. Any man riding with perfect posture on a beautiful horse couldn't be a threat to her.

Don't be naïve.

The rider approached slowly, the horse snorting.

Could she sneak around and come up behind him? She could try, but the man exuded a shitload of confidence and wouldn't be taken by surprise, especially by a woman half his size.

He was still a good twenty yards from her when he yelled, "Hello, the camp!"

She lowered her voice and gripped the spear at shoulder height. "What do you want?"

"I'm looking for Ensley Williams. Have you seen her?"

Her eyes nearly popped out of her head, and her heart went straight to her throat.

What the hell?

No one knew she was here. "Who's asking?" she croaked out.

"A friend."

"She doesn't have any friends."

The man chuckled. "Yes, she does. Come on out, Ens. It's me, JC Fraser. I've been trailing you for days."

Her legs almost went out from under her. She stabbed the spear into the ground to hold on to it for support while she recovered.

"Ensley, it's safe. Come on out."

Am I hallucinating? If I am, it doesn't matter whether I show myself or not.

She stepped out into the open, barely able to put one foot in front of the other, and asked, "What are you doing here?"

JC laughed as he dismounted. "Looking for you. I almost lost you a few days ago, crossing the Badlands." He looked around. "Is someone with you?"

She rubbed her forehead, her thoughts in tumult. Was someone with her? It was possible, but if she told JC about the shaman, he'd think she'd lost her mind.

"I didn't invite anyone to come along. It's just me."

"It's good to see you." He hugged her, and her soul absorbed the warm wool of his jacket, the muscular strength flexing beneath it, and the sweet scent of wildflowers.

"I'm a bit shell-shocked." She broke away from him. "I need to sit down." She returned to her spot by the fire.

"I'm sure you are." He unsaddled his horse and led him to the river. "I lost your footprints a couple of days ago, and it took half a day to pick them up again." When the stallion finished drinking, JC picketed him with enough slack that he could graze on the native grasses. "The other footprints disappeared for several miles, reappeared briefly, then disappeared again, only to reappear miles later."

"How many times did you see them?"

"I found them at every campsite, but only twice were the footprints near the campfire. The other times they were several yards away."

She stared at him. "At every campsite? Unbelievable." Maybe the shaman was here now. She shot up, hurried into the woods, and walked a full circle around the camp, but she didn't find any footprints or trampled grass.

"I don't think he's here now," JC said.

She returned to the firepit, one hand on her hip. "How can you be so sure?"

"Because I'm here." JC grabbed a currycomb from his saddlebag and took his time, rubbing the horse in circular motions to remove loosened dirt, hair, and other detritus, and then followed it up with a stiff-bristled brush to remove all the material stirred up by the curry.

A defensive stirring in her gut urged her to defend her shaman. "He's not scared of you. He's a noble warrior."

"He is? So you know who he is and where he's from?"

"Of course. He's a shaman from the Fort Berthold Reservation."

JC returned the grooming tools to the saddlebag. "Did he tell you that?"

"No, I figured it out." She sat back down and picked up the warm cup of dandelion coffee. "I've never actually talked to him. I mean, we had one conversation, but it wasn't an actual face-to-face meeting. It was more of a meeting of the minds."

"Did he heal your foot?"

Her head jerked up. "How'd you know I hurt my foot?"

"I found the place where you fell and followed your hobbling footprints to Spring Creek."

"God, that seems so long ago." She stretched out her legs and leaned against the tree. "I heard a man talking to me, telling me to get up, to follow him to the creek. I saw the grass move as if someone was walking through it, but I never actually saw him. He was persistent, so I followed, or rather hobbled behind him until I reached the creek."

"Were you walking in the wrong direction?"

"No. He was leading me to a better camping spot. When I reached the creek, he demanded I take off my boot. I didn't want to because I knew it would hurt like hell. But he wouldn't quit."

"Did you see him then?"

She shook her head. "I don't know where he was, but I heard him. It was weird. I finally got the boot off and soaked my foot in the cold water. Then, I went to sleep, and when I woke up, there wasn't a thing wrong with my foot. I thought I imagined it, but the leather on the side of my boot is scuffed up. So something happened to my foot."

JC squatted and spread his hands to the fire. "I found your footprints. You hobbled in and walked out. So you were injured, no doubt about it. Do you think it was broken or sprained?"

"It was similar to an injury I had several years ago when I broke a bone on the side of my foot. It swelled up and turned black and blue and stayed like that for weeks. My orthopedist put me in a walking boot, but this time the injury healed in less than twenty-four hours." She looked at JC. "Does that make any sense?"

"Yeah, it does. Did you ever hear from him again?"

"A few days ago, before I reached the river, I ran out of drinking water and couldn't go on. The shaman carried me to the river. When I woke up, a roasting rabbit was waiting for me. I thought I was hallucinating, but the rabbit was real, and I didn't trap it."

JC didn't react, taking her story in stride as he sat cross-legged next to her. "You broke your foot, and then it healed. You were dying of thirst, and then you were next to the river. Why do you think he's a shaman?"

"Because he has blue tattoos"—she ran her hand from her shoulder to her wrist—"down his arm. I've never seen that before."

"Was he carrying a weapon?"

She thought a minute and nodded. "A single-handed battle-ax."

"What was he wearing?"

"Dark trousers and a red cloak."

JC tugged at his chin, his head nodding slightly. After a moment, he said, "I think I know who he is. If I'm right, he's a Viking warrior."

Her surprise morphed into *what the hell*. "Not a real Viking. Just some reenactor playing a role. Right?"

JC put his elbows on his knees and tapped his fingertips together. "No. He's an honest-to-God twelfth-century Viking. Dad met him and four other warriors at Jarlshof in the Shetland Islands a few years ago."

"Twelfth century? Really? Wow. I'm still shell-shocked that you're here. Now I'm double shocked that a time-traveling Viking warrior rescued me."

"It's a lot to take in, but Erik and his friends make up the Council and support the Keeper of the Stones."

She cocked her head. "Stones?"

"Stones. Brooches. We use the words interchangeably."

Ensley's jaw dropped, and she slapped her forehead. "Oh, my God, I got all excited about seeing you that I forgot about how you got here. So, you have one of those stones, too, or did you use mine?"

"I used yours."

She jumped to her feet. "Holy shit! Why are we still sitting here?" Her heart fluttered with thoughts of home. "Let's go. You can tell me all about the brooches and the Vikings over a bottle of wine." She looped the costrel strap over her shoulder, grabbed her spear and Clovis Point, and looked around to see if there was anything else she wanted to take with her. "I can't believe I'm going home."

"Ensley, sit down. We have to talk."

"No." She didn't want to hear anything else until she was on the other side of the fog. Then he could talk until he was hoarse. "Look. I want to go home. I need a drink, a long, soaking bath, some real food, and a visit to my hairdresser and manicurist—in that order. You can tell me everything later. Let's get out of here. Do you want me to help you saddle your horse?"

JC reached over and clasped her hand. "Sit down, Ens. I have to explain what's going on here."

"You don't have to. I already know. I came here in a fog after I whispered magic words, and now you're here to take me home. I don't know how or why or anything about the Council. But that's not important right now. Come on. Let's get out of here."

The tension radiating off JC pinged every one of her nerves, but she planned to continue ignoring them. "Should I leave my spear? I've grown accustomed to it, but if you think somebody might need it, I'll leave it behind."

JC shot a stern look at her. "Ensley! Sit. Down."

She jerked her hand out of his grasp. "I don't want to sit. I don't want to listen to you. I just want to go home. I miss my life, and my gut's telling me what I miss doesn't mean shit. I'm not ready to hear that yet. So don't say another word."

She busied herself at the campfire. Doing something construc-tive with her hands gave her brain a chance to play nice with denial. "Do you want a cup of dandelion coffee?"

"No thanks." While she filled the bowl of roots with water from the leather costrel, he said, "I changed my mind. If you have enough, I'll have what you're drinking."

"It's not as good as Starbucks, but it'll do in a pinch." After the water and roots heated, she poured the brew into the other bowl, reserving the roots for another cup. "You have to close your eyes and imagine."

"Are you sure this water is safe?"

The question grated on her last pinged nerve. It was the same one she'd asked herself dozens of times on the first day, not as often on the second, and after the third, she didn't worry about it again.

"I'm not sick yet, and when you're so thirsty you can't work up enough saliva to spit, you drink whatever's available. Drinking a little bit of E. coli in the water is better than dying of thirst."

He sipped the brew. "I doubt this would be a hit with the Starbucks crowd, but it isn't so bad."

She sat down again, holding her bowl of dandelion coffee in her shaking hand, and tried to relax her face, hoping it would lower her stress. "Okay, start at the beginning and ease me into our current reality. Unless this is all a nightmare, and you're only making a cameo appearance."

He didn't smile. If anything, he had a thousand-yard stare. She waved her hand. "Hey, JC. Come back."

He refocused his gaze. "The beginning, huh? That's too far back. Let me start with the most recent events."

"Whatever works for you. I'm in no hurry."

"I met George—"

"My cousin?"

JC smirked. "I thought you weren't in a hurry."

"Sorry. I'll try not to interrupt. Go on."

"I met your cousin at the Porcellian Club the Thursday night you disappeared. He invited me to go to dinner with the two of you. We went to pick you up at the house, and I smelled peat as soon as I entered the house."

"It's a gross smell. What'd you think?"

He smirked again.

"Sorry."

"George yelled for you, and when you didn't answer, I went upstairs to look while he went to the basement. I found your brooch on the floor, and I knew then that the fog had carried you away."

"How'd you know that?"

"I have experience with magic brooches. Just let me tell my story. Okay?"

"But you didn't know where I went. Right?"

"Not then."

"Did you tell George?"

"I couldn't. There are a few brooch rules. And the number one rule is, never discuss the existence of the brooches with anyone outside the family."

"Brooches?" Her jaw dropped again. "There's more than one?"

He groaned before holding up his palm and waiting for silence. "I can answer random questions that you fire at me, or I can take a systematic approach and explain how we got here. Which do you want?"

She ran two fingers along the seam of her lips in a zipping motion.

"I found your itinerary along with Professor Whiteside's proposal. Between your connection to North Dakota and a proposal for a Teddy Roosevelt book, I was able to narrow it down to North Dakota in either 1884 or 1885."

"But that doesn't explain how you knew I went back in time." When he glared at her again, she said, "Sorry. Maybe we better stick with answering random questions."

JC continued without acknowledging her suggestion. "My family has eight brooches like yours, but with different stones. Each one is a time-traveling device with slightly different properties. I made my first trip back to the year 1881 when I was a teenager."

He took a small stick from the kindling pile and sketched the brooch in the dirt. "I was with my parents, aunts, uncles, and cousins. We went back to Napa to save the life of a young girl battling diabetes, which was a fatal disease at that time."

"Did you save her?"

"We brought her home with us, and she's now finishing her internal medicine residency at Johns Hopkins Hospital."

"Are you talking about your cousin Emily?"

He nodded.

"She's from the nineteenth century?"

He nodded again.

"Unbelievable." Ensley's shoulders sagged as overwhelming relief suffused through her system. "That means I have a return trip stamped on my passport."

He used his hand to wipe away the design he'd drawn, then tossed the stick into the fire. "For personal reasons, I decided to use your brooch, go back for you, and return home without involving my family. Since you left your brooch behind, I figured it had the same properties as the topaz brooch. When you activate that one, it gets too hot to hold. So I took precautions and wore an oven mitt." He stopped and looked away, but after a pause, he turned back toward her. "Even with a mitt, it got too hot to hold."

"I know. It got scalding hot for me, too. I couldn't hold it—" And then the realization hit her with the force of a high-speed, rear-end collision and knocked her reality into a concrete wall. "Noooo!"

JC's eyes were on her, but she looked away until she was ready to hear the truth that would shatter her hopes. She counted to ten, to twenty, to a hundred gazillion. He'd thrown her a life preserver, which wasn't attached to a rope to keep her from drifting away. Tears trickled down her cheeks.

Finally, she turned to look daggers at him. "You dropped it, didn't you? And now we have…" She took a deep breath. "We have no way to go home." She forced her features to relax, hoping to erase traces of her growing fear and confusion. Calmly, she dried her tears and waited.

He opened his mouth to say something, but his expression froze as he stared back at her. She set her dandelion coffee aside and pushed to her feet, needing to think, and pacing always helped her uncouple fear from reason. She never once let him get away with anything while they were in college, and she wasn't about to start now.

"Do you want to know my first impression of you?"

"I have a feeling you're going to tell me whether I want to hear it or not."

"You're right," she said, crossing her arms. "I told my girlfriend, 'See that good-looking guy over there? He's a rich, spoiled, intelligent party boy.' And now I can add irresponsible."

"Of all the things I might be, I am *not* irresponsible." His mouth tightened down at the corners, a sure sign that he was getting defensive and refusing to admit what was evident to her. "Why are you giving me such a hard time, anyway?" he asked. "I'm here, aren't I? I came to rescue you."

"Rescue implies freeing someone from confinement, danger, or evil. As far as I can tell, I'm still confined here." Her foot bounced in a pissed-off allegro, her heart squeezed ripcord-tight and, for a moment, forgot to beat.

"I didn't drop the brooch on purpose, Ensley, and if you don't want me here, I'll leave. I'll head toward Elkhorn Ranch. If you change your mind, I'll be there for a few days. After that, I'm going to Kentucky to visit my six- or seven-times-great-grandfather."

"Great-grandfather?" That was a shock to her heart. "How?" She thumped her chest to calm the shock. "How could you possibly have a relative here?"

His reply was a coy smile as if he were secretly holding some mysterious piece of the puzzle and wasn't ready to share. But after a moment, he teased, "It's complicated."

"Say anything, but don't say that. I'm intelligent enough to untangle something complicated."

"Okay, he's the uncle of my mom's several times great-grandmother."

"What's her name?"

"Kit MacKlenna Montgomery."

Ensley rolled her eyes. "That doesn't make any sense. He's not your grandfather. He's your uncle." She plunked down at the bank of the river, her head starting to throb.

He sat down next to her. "It's complicated because my mom's several times great-grandmother is also my dad's goddaughter."

She rubbed her forehead. "You're damn right. It's complicated."

"Let me just say that relationships get screwed up when people time travel. Kit Montgomery should have died by now from a brain tumor, but she came forward in time and is now a healthy woman in her late fifties."

Ensley leaned her head on his shoulder, and he put his arm around her, and she leaned further into him. "We'll have to get jobs. Can you practice law here?"

"Probably, but money isn't a problem," he said. "I've got gold nuggets with me, and if I wanted to practice, we could go to Napa and live at Montgomery Winery, and I could take over my uncle's law practice in San Francisco."

"Your uncle?"

"You've met Uncle Cullen and Uncle Braham. You wouldn't know it, but they were both born in 1824, married women from the future, and came forward to live."

"Seriously? Well, you'd never know it." She sat up and looked across the river as the sun moved below the horizon. "Do you think it works in reverse?"

"What?" he asked.

"That people from the future can fit in as seamlessly in the past?"

"Kit did for thirty years. But look at TR. People out here think he's odd, both in the way he dresses and speaks. We'll sound different, too. But once we find out what year it is, we can consider our options."

She took a deep breath and exhaled with an internal curse. "We don't have any."

"Sure, we do." He capped his statement with a smile, putting a good spin on it, but it didn't work for her. "The good part is, we can travel. Go to Lexington, Kentucky, or Napa, New York City, London, or even Paris. Wherever you want to go."

She liked the sound of that. But going to any of those places in the nineteenth century would require an adjustment she wasn't sure she could make. "If I have a choice, I'd prefer New York City. It would be easier to find employment there, although it would be hard to find a job doing what I want to do."

"I came here to rescue you, Ens, and I failed, but I won't fail to protect you or take care of you financially. If you want to go to New York, that's fine with me. I can practice law or breed horses."

There were dozens of issues to work out while navigating this situation, but it might be manageable if they were honest with each other. "You mentioned brooches. How many are there?"

"Twenty-five. My family has eight."

"Holy shit. Who has the rest?"

His forehead puckered. "We don't know."

"Where'd they come from?"

"Originally? The Vikings and early Celts."

"And your family got them from the Vikings?"

"No, one arrives by indirect routes every two or three years. The first one—the ruby—showed up with my Aunt Kit. She landed on Dad's doorstep when she was a few months old. When she was in her midtwenties, she went back to 1852 and traveled the Oregon Trail, searching for her birth parents."

"How'd she get separated?"

"That's an even longer story. I'll tell you that one later. A few years after Kit went on her adventure, Aunt Charlotte went back to 1864 with the sapphire brooch. Aunt Kenzie worked at Bletchley Park with the codebreakers in England in 1944. Aunt Sophia was Thomas Jefferson's official portraitist in 1789. Aunt Penny went back to 1814 and met Andrew Jackson. Aunt Amber fell in love with a Pinkerton agent in Colorado in 1878, and Aunt Amy went back to—" JC stopped and squeezed Ensley's hand, and she jerked, shocked by the sudden move.

"Oh, sorry. I just thought of something. Aunt Amy traveled back to New York City in 1909, and several members of the family went back for her. If we're in the city then, we can go home with them."

Ensley fell back on the grass and covered her eyes with her arm. *God, this can't be happening to me.*

"What's wrong?"

"A Harvard education, and that's your bright idea?"

"Yeah. What's wrong with it?"

She rolled over onto her side and propped her head in her hand. "Well, for starters, if this is around 1880, then we're talking about thirty years from now. Thirty! I don't want to spend the next three decades hoping someone will—no *might*—rescue me when I'm in my late fifties. Do you?"

She rolled over again and closed her eyes, visualizing herself at that age, and she nearly barfed. "By the time I'm that old, I want to be in love with my soul mate and have a houseful of children and grandchildren. Why would I want to leave at that point? And even if I did, there wouldn't be anything left for me in the future."

When he didn't say anything, she opened her eyes to see what he was doing, half expecting him to be on his phone. But that was dumb. When he glanced at her, there was an intensity in his eyes she'd never seen before. It was almost scary.

"Maybe we won't be gone that long in the future," he finally said.

"What does that mean?"

"Well, after Aunt Kit met Uncle Cullen in 1852, they stayed in California until 1881, and by then, they were both ill. So they came home with us during that trip to rescue Emily. Aunt Kit was in the past for almost thirty years. But when she got home, she'd only been gone half that time."

"How's that possible?"

"It has to do with your age when you're rescued."

Ensley swallowed the knot in her throat as tears stung her eyes, and a rush of confusing emotions surged within her. "I had more hope before you arrived. Now it seems like"—she hung her head—"I don't know…"

JC picked up a twig and snapped it in half, then snapped each half into halves. She watched and knew he was stalling.

"What is it, JC? There's something else. Just spit it out."

"I don't want to give you false hope."

"I don't want it, either. Don't give me castles in the sky, but if it might come true, then tell me."

He turned toward her. "I've been working on a sensitive project for the past several months. And lately, I've been avoiding my parents. My dad has ESP. If I talked to him, he'd know I was hiding something. In our family, lies of omission are as bad as lies of commission. So I haven't been taking his calls."

"What does that have to do with anything?"

"God, you're impatient. I'm getting to it."

She twirled her finger in a speed-up motion.

"I knew Dad would call me, so I turned off my phone and put it in my desk drawer."

"You wouldn't be home to answer it anyway."

JC gave her an exasperated exhale. "When you turn off your phone, the calls go straight to voice mail. Dad won't put up with that for long. He'll go to DC to find out what the hell is going on."

"He won't find you."

"That's the point. If nobody knows where I am, he'll ask Uncle David to find me. And David will be all over it like a beagle following a scent. He'll retrace my steps to Cambridge and will find the missing person report George filed."

"Geez, they'll never find me."

"That's the point. When Uncle David discovers you disappeared, he'll read the report, which probably mentions me and the peat smell in the house. Uncle David will put it together with Professor Whiteside's proposal, and he'll know where we are."

She shot up. "He'll figure all that out? How?"

"Because it fits a familiar pattern. Dad will put a rescue team together, and they'll come after us."

"How soon?"

"Hard to tell. But while the odds are almost a hundred percent that Dad will come, I don't know when. It could be a week, next month, or five years from now."

She shook her head. Years? Did she hear that right? "Why on earth would your dad wait a week, much less a year?"

"He wouldn't. He'll leave almost immediately and will ask his brooch to take him to me. But the vortex might not spit him out this month or even this year. Whatever controls the magic will decide when. I can't explain it any better than that."

She smacked the side of her head. Maybe the tiny crystals in her inner ears had gotten out of alignment, and she didn't hear him correctly. "Vortex? Spit them out? What the hell are you talking about? Are you saying the brooch is alive and makes decisions about where a traveler goes—or even when? Or maybe it's"—she made air quotes—"the man behind the curtain."

"It could be. We won't know until we get four more brooches and can open the door in the cave beneath the castle."

"It's like you're speaking a different language. What cave? What door?"

"You've been to the castle in the Highlands. Well, there's an oak door that dates back several centuries. Around the door frame are twelve slots that match the shape of the brooches. The Vikings told Dad that once he fills up those slots and has possession of the torc, which we already have, the door will open to the other side."

"What's a torc?"

"A necklace that holds a pendant, and the pendant holds a brooch."

This was beginning to sound like a sci-fi movie. "What's on the other side of the door?"

"We don't know, but I have a theory that it'll be like Jodie Foster's experience in the movie *Contact*. We'll go through a wormhole like we do when we travel back in time, then walk out on a beach and meet the man with all the answers."

"Answers to what?"

"Are we alone in the universe? What makes us human? Why do we dream? Are there other universes? How did life begin? What's so weird about prime numbers? Will we ever cure cancer? What's at the bottom of the ocean? Shit like that."

"Seriously?"

"I don't know," he said with a shrug. "It's possible, but I think we'll discover the true purpose of the brooches. Who made them, and why the MacKlenna Clan has responsibility for them. And we might even discover how to solve world hunger."

"That's a lofty goal."

"It is, isn't it?"

JC didn't say anything for several moments, and she had an itchy feeling there was something else he wasn't telling her. "Is there anything more I should know?"

He grabbed his saddlebags and removed a blanket, towel, anti-bacterial wipes, and a Dopp kit. "Yeah, you stink. Why don't you wash up while I catch a rabbit for dinner?"

"I know I'm filthy, but that's not what I meant. Is there anything else I need to know about the brooches?"

"There's a lot we'd all like to know. But that's it for now."

She didn't believe him, but she knew him well enough to know that if he didn't want to tell her, there was no way to get it out of him until he was ready.

He stood, reached down to help her up, and pulled her into his arms. Her head barely reached the center of his chest. "I'm sorry about this, Ens. If George and I had left the Porcellian Club immediately, we would have stopped your disappearance. I'll do whatever I can to make it easier for you. However long we're here, you'll be my top priority."

She sighed a breath, and the breeze scattered it into nothing. Maybe JC wasn't hiding anything after all, and she was just reacting to him and what he knew of the brooches.

"You've already sacrificed your future for me. You've got to think about what's next for you, too."

She took the blanket and Dopp kit and returned to the spot where she'd been spying on him earlier. The wipe had a refreshing, woodsy scent with lemongrass and cedarwood. She started with her face, and the soothing aloe vera and energizing ginseng seeped into her pores. Then she used the dry shampoo and combed it through her tangled hair.

Too bad there was nothing she could do about her filthy clothes. Maybe they could stay here for another day so she could wash her underwear and blouse and spot-clean her jeans.

Just as she finished cleaning up, the tantalizing smell of roasting meat tickled her nose, making her mouth water and her stomach growl. She collected the supplies and returned to the campfire, feeling clean for the first time in days.

JC had skinned, gutted, and skewered a rabbit, then attached each end of the skewer to an upright Y-branch frame to roast.

"How'd you catch that rabbit so quickly?"

He looked up at her, grinning. "When we were kids, my cousins and I competed to see who could catch and skin rabbits the fastest.

I'm good, but my cousin Lincoln is better."

"It smells delicious. My mouth is already watering."

"It's going to take a while to roast. In the meantime, you can eat some of this fish, an energy bar, or an MRE. What sounds good?"

She sat down next to the fire to make another cup of dandelion coffee. "Not the fish. I've eaten enough of that. I'd like an energy bar if you have plenty."

"I do." He dug into a saddlebag and handed her a bar.

"Thanks. Ripping open a package is a nice change from fishing for every meal." She crunched on the sweet and salty peanut butter and honey energy bar. "Do you know where we are? I know where I'm going, but not how much farther I have to walk to get there."

JC flipped the rabbit to cook on the other side, then unfolded his topo map. "I landed here"—he pointed—"and followed you to here"—he tapped the map again. "If we continue to follow the river, it'll take another day or two to reach Medora."

"On this uneven ground, I can only walk about ten miles a day."

"You can ride. I'll walk."

"I'll walk, too."

"You're half my weight. Mercury would rather carry you than me."

"I'm a long-distance runner, JC. I can walk, and I intend to do my part."

"If you insist on walking, we'll walk together."

"Let's play it by ear." She munched on the bar. "Where's Elkhorn Ranch?"

JC pointed to the location on the map. "Here."

"I can't show up there looking like a homeless person. I'll have to stop and clean up—you know, just in case TR's there."

JC folded the map and put it away. "Then we'll check into a hotel tomorrow, and you can have a spa day."

She looked at her broken nails. "Wow. If I could also have a facial and mani-pedi, I'd be a completely new woman."

He hooked her around the neck and pulled her toward him for a hug. "I don't want you to suffer one more day. I intend to pamper you, so hang in there just a little longer."

She pushed away from him. "You don't have to pamper me. No one ever has, and I don't expect you to."

"Maybe not, but I will." He flipped the rabbit again, and the juices sizzled when they hit the flames. "I'm sorry I never called you after your mother died."

"Well, that's a non sequitur if I ever heard one."

His eyebrows hiked up. "You didn't want to hear how I plan to pamper you, so I changed the subject."

She crunched the energy bar and tried to understand what she did want from him. It was just the two of them now, and they had to work together. "I haven't seen this side of you before. We've gone on dozens of camping trips here in the Badlands, and you always treated me just like one of the guys. Why is this different?"

"We had camping gear, rifles, and cell phones in case we ran into trouble. We don't have any of that now."

She glanced at the gear he'd set down near the campfire. There was no rifle or even a scabbard. "You don't have a rifle."

"I didn't have a large-caliber, lever-action Winchester repeater like TR's in my collection, and I didn't have time to search the antique gun dealers to find one."

"You can probably order one in Medora. In the meantime, will you cool the overprotective act? It makes me uncomfortable, and I want to do my share of the work."

"We're in a different era, Ens, and right now, as a woman, you don't have the same rights you do at home. If you're going to get pissed every time I show you deference, you'll be pissed all the time."

He got up and went behind a tree to pee. When he returned, he used an antibacterial wipe to wash his face, neck, and hands before returning to his post near the roasting rabbit.

She leaned back against the tree and crossed her arms. "I don't know if there's anything more calming than the wind whispering through the cottonwood leaves. It makes such a lovely rustle. Don't you think?"

"Talk about a non sequitur."

She smiled. "I don't want to fight with you—at least not at the moment—and I figure the weather is a safe topic."

"Safe enough. Why don't you get the mess kit out of the saddle-bag, and we'll give this rabbit a taste."

"Sure, make the woman set the table."

He whirled around, glaring. "This passive-aggressive shit doesn't suit you."

"Sorry. It's just...I don't know. It's been a hard ten days, and having you here is messing with my mind. This keeps feeling like we're just on an overnight camping trip, and we can go home in the morning. But we can't."

He turned the rabbit again. "There's something else on your mind. What is it? I know you're pissed that I can't get us home right now, but there's something deeper that has nothing to do with here and now. Let's deal with it."

She looked away from him as she shredded the energy bar's foil lined packaging.

"Spit it out, Ens."

She gave him a faint smile while giving herself a motivational talk.

Be a lion, not a mouse.

"Okay, here it is. Why didn't you ever ask me out? For four years, I signaled that I was interested, but you ignored the signals. And then you go and do something stupid like this."

His voice sounded strained when he asked, "Like what?"

"Give up your life to come after me."

"Why wouldn't I? George is my best friend, and you're like his sister. I couldn't date you because of him. If we dated and it didn't work out, he'd hate me, and so would you. It was a lose-lose situation for me."

"Why didn't you tell me?"

"I thought you—" He stared at the ground for a three-count before looking at her again. "I thought you might try to change my mind. And you and George are too important to me to screw it up."

"We're not kids, James Cullen. What I do, the choices I make, aren't George's responsibility."

"He doesn't see it that way, especially now that your parents are gone. Your uncle feels responsible for you, too. And before you claim you don't want them interfering in your life, think about how it would feel if you didn't have them."

Her stomach convulsed, and she punched him in the arm. "Damn it, JC!" She drew in a ragged breath, tears filled her eyes, and her voice quivered. "I don't have them *now!*"

"God, that was thoughtless of me. I'm sorry."

He pulled her into his arms, and although she didn't want to cry because crying was synonymous with losing control, she couldn't hold back the tears. Most of all, though, she was ugly when she cried. She got red in weird places and got snot everywhere. But she couldn't stop the rush of emotions or worry about how she looked, or even what JC thought of ugly-criers.

She buried her face against his chest and broke down, crying in loud, wracking sobs. And he held her. He didn't speak, didn't give her condescending pats on the back, and he didn't try to hush her. He just held her in a secure hold, not too tight, not too loose. Just enough to let her know she was safe and that he didn't care about what she looked like or the snot on his vest.

"I'll get you home, Ens." He cleared his throat. "I promise. I'll get you home."

18

Little Missouri River (1885)—Ensley

ENSLEY WOKE THE next morning to the mouthwatering aroma of fish sizzling on the cooking stone. Was she dreaming? She partially opened one eye to see JC squatting next to the firepit, making a cup of dandelion coffee.

JC's hair was perfectly rumpled, and his jaw was attractively stubbled. The sharp planes of his chin and cheeks gave him a Herculean, chiseled, and battle-weary look that had no resemblance to the immaculately dressed, high-priced DC lawyer who often showed up on the society pages of *The Washington Post* and *New York Times.*

She didn't move or speak. She just watched him. He didn't acknowledge her or even seem aware that she was awake.

He poured the dark liquid into a cup, retaining the roots to simmer for a refill. She expected him to take a sip, but instead, he extended his hand and offered the cup to her. "I know how much you like coffee first thing in the morning. This is the best I can do to satisfy your caffeine addiction."

She yawned. "How'd you know I was awake?"

"Your breathing changed."

"Was I snoring?"

He grinned. "No. Your eyelids fluttered when your optic nerve took in the morning light."

She yawned as she sat up to take the proffered cup. "You had to be staring at me to notice that."

"Nope. Peripheral vision."

"Peripheral vision can't see fluttering eyelashes."

"Have you ever tried?"

"Nope."

He flipped the fish and rotated the rabbit. "This is a protein-rich breakfast, but you should eat one of the MREs for the fat and carbs."

She scrunched up her face. "Yuk. I heard those things are awful."

A frown etched over the already hard line of his jaw, and while the expression probably would've tempted most people to tuck tail and run, it didn't faze her. "You've been living off fish for almost two weeks, and *you're* complaining?"

"I guess it sounds like it, but…instead of an MRE, how about I eat the protein and supplement breakfast with another energy bar?"

"I'm not going to force-feed you."

"Good." She sipped her coffee, and it tasted so much better than hers. "Did you put something in here? It tastes different." She smacked her lips. "I'd say cinnamon, but surely you didn't pack spices."

"I roasted the roots, then added a pinch of cinnamon and fennel seed. And yes, I travel with a mini spice tin. If you add a pinch of this or that, you can eat almost anything."

"I'll remember that for the next time I'm abandoned in the wilderness." She sipped, enjoying the cinnamon taste while watching his efficiency of movement. Even when he ran marathons or competed in equestrian events, he always held his form throughout the course.

"You're staring at me. What's on your mind?"

"I was just wondering what happened last night. The last thing I remember, I was doing an ugly cry on your chest."

"You fell asleep. I figured you were exhausted, so I didn't wake you up for dinner. I ate the rabbit and caught another one for breakfast."

"You ate the whole thing?"

"The whole thing. Getting you through an ugly cry took a lot of energy. I worked up quite an appetite."

Surprisingly, she wasn't embarrassed about crying all over him. She glanced up at the sky and was surprised to see that it was way past sunrise. "It was great to sleep deeply again."

"It's hard to sleep well when you have to stay alert."

"Funny. But I don't remember being afraid at night. I guess my survival instinct didn't sleep." She carefully sipped to avoid swallowing small pieces of the dandelion roots.

JC forked a portion of the fish, placed it on a plate, and handed it to her.

She lifted the plate and sniffed…lemon pepper? "I'm glad you're here, and not because you made coffee and fixed breakfast, but because I don't have to figure this out all by myself now. If I wig out again like I did last night, just pull my circuit breaker."

JC chuckled as he handed her one of the rabbit's crispy back-straps. "It wasn't so bad."

She peeled off the crunchy skin and gnawed on the bone to get every bite of the meat. "I almost got furious with you for coming to rescue me and losing the brooch, but how could I get mad for something I did myself? And besides, nobody can stay mad at you longer than twenty-four hours. Even the women you broke up with always became friends later. You're too much of a charmer."

"I'm Elliott Fraser's son. If there's one thing I've learned in twenty-eight years, it's how to take control by charming my adversary."

"Are you saying you use your charm to manipulate people?"

He tossed a bone into the firepit and pulled off another back-strap. "I use it to benefit my clients and my causes."

"I hope I'm not one of your causes."

He gave her a cheeky, brows-up stare. "Come on, Ensley. You know what I mean."

She forked a bite of fish. "No, I don't."

"Don't be paranoid."

"Don't be a jerk." She shoved the fish into her mouth and chewed.

He made a T with his hands. "Time out. What's really on your mind this morning?"

She sighed. "I just want to go home."

"And I want to get you home, but I can't manage it today. In the meantime, we'd better devise a backstory…like who we are, why we're here, and where we're going. You have any ideas?"

"We can copy TR and be Easterners here to hunt bison. That's believable."

"But what about you and me? Who are we? We can't be travel-ing around the country just as friends. We have to be married or brother and sister."

"There's nothing wrong with being a mature single woman, and

I know they're viewed differently in the nineteenth century. I don't mind being called eccentric, but I don't want to be hit on by a bunch of cowboys who haven't had a bath in months. Of course, I don't smell so good right now, but…"

"Aunt Charlotte and Uncle Jack went back to 1864, traveling as a real brother and sister, which caused her problems as a single woman. She attracted the attention of a stalker, who found a way to frame Jack as a conspirator in the plot to assassinate President Lincoln and then kidnapped her."

"Holy shit. I don't want to deal with a stalker *or* a bunch of persistent cowboys." She blew out a breath. "I guess I'll be your wife, then."

He grumbled. "You guess? Hell! That's not exactly the reaction I thought I'd get from a woman when I popped the question."

"I hope next time you'll get a more enthusiastic response." Ensley reached for another backstrap and gnawed on it. "Charlotte must be one gutsy lady."

JC tossed another bone into the firepit. "She is, and you know what?" He pulled another backstrap off the rabbit. "She's the only woman, other than my mom, who can tell Dad what to do, and he'll do it. My sister-in-law can get up in his face, too, but it's always a battle. Neither one of them wants to give in."

"So what happens?"

"They call a truce and move on."

Ensley shivered. "I've met your dad several times, and he scares me. He also reminds me of the characters in Scottish historicals—fierce and intimidating."

"Yeah, he can be that. And when he comes back for us, I recommend you stay as far away from me as possible so you won't get caught up in the battle of wills."

She stretched her neck to ease the stiffness caused by sleeping without proper head and neck support. "I'll try to remember to do that."

His hand came down on her nape, large and warm from holding the hot dandelion coffee. She groaned at the tender stroking of his fingers.

"So we're James Cullen and Ensley Fraser from New York City. If anyone asks where we live, let's just say the Upper West Side and leave it at that."

"Let's keep it simple. I've edited time travel novels and lies always come back and bite heroines on the ass. I don't want that to happen. A lie could destroy any goodwill we build up."

"When someone lies to me, it's like they spit in the punch bowl. After that, I go find another watering hole."

She couldn't stop the quiver in her cheeks and tug on her lips and finally burst out laughing. It felt good to fall back into their college conversational rhythm.

"I have a question," JC said. "If we're in the Badlands to hunt, where's our gear? Where's my rifle?"

"Oops. That's a problem. Let me think." She took a few sips of coffee, letting her mind wander back through her clients' books, looking for plotlines that would work for them, but came up short.

A morning breeze whispered through the trees, rustling the leaves, and she shivered. She set her plate aside and wrapped the blanket around her shoulders. After a few more moments, she said, "Okay. How about this? We took the Northern Pacific Railroad—"

"What if it's not built yet?"

"It was constructed right after the Civil War, I think. Anyway, we could disembark at Bismarck and change trains to Fort Pembina in northeastern North Dakota."

"What for?"

"Hold your horses. Inspiration doesn't come all at once. I'm getting there."

"We need to stay close to the truth, right?"

"Okay, then let's use my mother's family history. Her several-times-great-grandparents came from Scotland and settled in Selkirk in 1812. The settlement eventually established Fort Daer. My ancestors left there and bought land in central North Dakota to build a ranch."

"But there's no ranch there now."

"Right. So that means my ancestors are still in the Fort Daer area. What if they died and left their property to my parents in New York?"

"Why aren't they here with us?"

"Because…they're too old to travel."

"So we went to settle the estates. And now, instead of returning to New York the way we arrived, we struck out on our own, so I could hunt bison."

"And," she said smartly, "you didn't have any luck."

"And," he said just as smartly, "you complained the entire time.

So we're going to Medora to catch the train back to New York City."

"Then what happened to our other horse and the rest of our gear?"

He glanced up, scratching his jaw. "How about… We left it on the reservation."

"Leaving the gear would make sense, but not the horse."

"So, were we robbed, then?" he asked.

"Why would the robbers leave us with one horse? Because they were dumb, or what?"

"Hey, you're the writer and editor. Keep plotting."

She tapped her fingernails against her chin, thinking about plotlines and what would work. "How about this? Your horse fell and broke a leg several days ago, and you barely avoided a serious injury. Your rifle was damaged, though. That'll explain why you don't have one. We tried to carry the extra saddle and gear but gave up and abandoned everything we didn't need to survive."

"We've got a good start. Let's get moving for now. We have plenty of time to refine our backstory on the way." JC stood and cleaned the plates and cups in the river.

"I'm going to freshen up before we leave, and I'll clean up the campsite when I come back. Can I use the stuff in your Dopp kit?"

He helped her stand, then dug into his saddlebags for the kit and a towel. "Help yourself, sweetheart."

Sweetheart?

That got her attention quicker than a bronc bucking her off its back. She whipped around to face him. "Look. We need ground rules. We can tell people we're married, but we're not sleeping together, and there's no sweet talk or cheek-kissing. Okay?"

His chin snapped up, and so did his hands as he took a step back, pinning her with glittering brown eyes that made her heart pump even faster.

"I don't know about that, Ens," he said. "That goes against everything I know about relationships, both serious and casual."

She grabbed the Dopp kit, towel, and an antibacterial body wipe. "I know it'll be a challenge. But you're a smart guy. You'll figure it out." She marched into the trees, thinking they'd be headed toward a disaster if she still had the hots for him. For now, though, they were just friends, traveling companions, and a faux married couple.

But what if they stayed in the past for months or even years? Would that old spark ignite again?

19

Little Missouri River (1885)—Ensley

FOR THE NEXT two days, they followed the Little Missouri River and skirted the Badlands while they refined their backstories. Since they had JC's canteen and her leather costrel, they could have taken a more direct route to Elkhorn Ranch, but they weren't in a hurry.

They fell into a comfortable rhythm, talking about college and old friends. He shared stories about the lawyers in his firm and his office manager's collection of thimbles, and she shared silly mistakes authors made in manuscripts.

It was easy and fun, and she enjoyed his company, but there was something about his life that didn't ring true. Maybe she'd edited too many romance novels featuring wounded heroes and heroines, and nothing was black and white to her anymore, only multiple shades of gray. And JC had more shades than any hero she'd met in a manuscript. It wasn't just the lack of information or the holes in his stories that concerned her. It was the brokenness that swam in his eyes when he stared off at the horizon.

Book editors sometimes had to play pseudo-psychoanalyst to get to the root of either writer's block or character motivation, and she fell back on that role now.

Of course, she could be completely wrong, but she didn't think so. Something awful happened to JC, and while he tried to forget it, the repression only made it worse. At least that was her (un)professional opinion.

For now, she'd leave it alone. Sometimes—only in the arms of a loving partner—can wounds heal. Since she didn't have any firsthand knowledge, she had to rely on how characters in novels dealt with trauma and eventually recovered.

But JC wasn't a character in a book. He was a living, breathing, sexy-as-hell male. As George Sand said, "Life resembles a novel more often than novels resemble life." Sand believed men didn't want women to accept their faults. They wanted women who pretended they were faultless.

As for her, she would never pretend JC was faultless. But he was a good friend—a cool dude with smooth moves—and he proved his friendship hour after hour, mile after mile.

Late afternoon on the second day, they left the river to go around a forest instead of through it, trudged up steep paths on the red scoria buttes, past magpies perched on a buffalo skull, and finally emerged on the endless stretches of nearly level prairie.

JC stopped and consulted his map. Ensley lowered her hat, protecting her eyes from the sun beating down from a cloudless sky. Objects seem to shimmer and dance in the heat of the sun, and distances were hard to judge.

"According to this map, we're close to the Elkhorn Ranch site."

"How close?"

"A couple of miles."

"Oh, Jesus. I've got to clean up." She glanced around, looking for a private spot where she could strip down and wash and brush her hair. "I can't meet TR looking like this."

"Ens, you're in the frontier. There's no need to clean up." He handed her the canteen, and after she took a long drink, he took one.

She smoothed down the front of her filthy shirt. She'd tried washing it, but it was so stained now, it would never come clean. "I hope I don't go all fangirl over TR."

"If you do, I'll flip your circuit breaker." He folded the map and returned it to the saddlebag. "You want an energy bar?"

"Are there any left?"

"A couple more." He handed one to her. "If I'd known it was your favorite food, I would have packed more than a dozen."

She broke the bar in half and gave the largest piece to him.

"You eat it. You really shouldn't lose any more weight."

She patted her belly while narrowing her eyes at him. She had dropped a few pounds, but how'd he know that? "We haven't seen each other for a while. How do you know I've lost weight?"

He made a show of looking at her ass, grinning. "Your jeans are loose, and, as particular as you are, you'd never wear clothes that don't fit."

He was right about that. When she put on the jeans to go to dinner, they'd been skintight. Now they barely hung on her hips. If she lost any more weight, she'd need suspenders to hold them up. "I think they're just loose because they're stretched out and dirty."

He had the decency not to laugh. "Yeah, right. Look, the MREs are supplementing your fish and rabbit diet. But you're burning up all the calories you're taking in, so you aren't putting on any weight. You need to get to a place where you can rest and gain weight. You've got to stay healthy out here."

"You want me to sit around and eat bonbons all day? Forget it. While I'm here, I plan to work." She finished her half of the energy bar and brushed off her hands.

JC gave her the other half back, and while she eyed it for about two seconds, she took it without objecting.

JC continued, "I agree. You need to work, but that doesn't mean physical labor. You love to write—or did when you were at Harvard. Write the next Great American Novel, *Theodore Roosevelt in the Badlands.*"

"Several authors have already written that book, including my client." Her former client, but she wasn't ready to tell JC about getting laid off.

"Professor Whiteside's book covered a decade. Yours should focus on something specific, like TR's interest in the environment. You can tie his views to those of the twenty-first century, especially his establishment of the National Forests and National Parks, bird reserves, and game preserves, and ensuring the sustainability of natural resources."

"You must have brushed up on him before you came back for me."

JC secured the saddlebags to the D-rings on the saddle and collected the reins he'd tied to a bush. "I did, but mostly I focused on the time he spent here." He clicked his tongue. "Let's go, Mercury."

Ensley sidled up alongside JC, considering a possible angle. "I don't know if I can find a new twist on the body of work that already exists."

"You have a different perspective. You're here with TR…or will be…and I doubt anyone else wrote a contemporary account of his life. And remember, everything TR does here in the Dakotas impacts the rest of his life, and you"—he gazed down at her—"have the benefit of knowing his future."

She munched on the energy bar, her legs swishing through the tall grass, and she thought about the depth of her Teddy Roosevelt knowledge. While it might not be as broad as JC's, it had some substance to it, especially about his time here in the Badlands.

"Here's a question," she said. "Don't you think it's dangerous? What if I suggest something he hasn't thought of yet?"

"It was here in the Dakotas that he conceived many of his ideas about the environment and conservation. I doubt a discussion of those issues will be premature."

"I thought you said the number one rule of brooch management was not to change history."

"That's true. But you won't be changing it. You might be helping TR formulate ideas and beliefs sooner than he would have otherwise, but that's it."

"Shit. That's scary. What if I—"

"You won't screw up, Ens. Just do what feels right."

She followed JC and Mercury down a steep path, leading toward the river. "You know what feels right? A rare T-bone with a loaded baked potato."

"Maybe TR will slaughter one of his cows for dinner."

"Isn't that supposed to be a fatted calf?" she asked.

"Only if you're a prodigal son."

She stopped at the bottom of the path and stared at JC for a moment.

He stared right back. "I know what you're thinking, and you can forget it. Dad won't prepare a feast for me. When this is over, it'll take a while to get back into his good graces."

"He might surprise you."

"Nah. It isn't Dad's anger that I'm worried about."

"God, if he yelled at me, I'd end up in a puddle on the floor like the wicked witch."

"I can handle the cussing-out and throwing stuff. It's his disappointment that will sting. And Mom will get caught in the middle. She'll start crying, and that'll break my heart. Then Dad will blame me for hurting her, and he'll be right, and the fight will continue."

She never had anything like that happen with her parents and could only imagine how awful it would be. JC's grimace showed how hurtful it was for him.

"How do you see it ending?"

"It's only happened once before, and Uncle David intervened."

Ensley grabbed JC's arm as she navigated the last part of the path. "Did your uncle take your side?"

"Hell, no. He just lowered the temperature and sent everyone to separate corners to cool down."

"I guess you didn't consider your dad's feelings when you planned this adventure."

"I did, but I figured this mission would be a quick in-and-out, and he wouldn't know until it was over."

When she reached level ground, she let go of JC's arm. "Aren't you the master chess player who can calculate twenty moves in advance?"

"Twenty-five." He led Mercury toward the river for a drink. "But coming back for you, I couldn't see further than three or four moves."

"You miscalculated."

JC set his chiseled jaw, and it didn't budge.

"Never mind," she said, walking away from the river. "Enough has been said about it. We don't need to keep rehashing it."

Mercury finished drinking, and JC led him away from the river. "Wrong pronoun, sweetheart. I'm not rehashing it at all."

"Don't call me sweetheart."

"Then stop reminding me of my screwup."

They walked side by side in tense silence for several minutes until she decided to get them back on friendlier terms. "I read that TR was probably the most well-read president and perhaps one of the most well-read men in all of history. He usually read a book before breakfast and, depending on his schedule, another two or three in the evening."

"Can you imagine having that distinction on your headstone?"

"I doubt you're very far behind him since you're a speed-reader extraordinaire. How many books do you normally read in a day?"

"It depends on what I'm reading. If it's sad, I follow it with a happy story or some nonfiction book."

"About what?"

He rubbed the back of his neck, grimacing. "I don't know. A couple of nights ago, I read a short story about how threatened animals can bounce back."

"Really? Then you're the one who should write a book about

TR."

"I'm not a writer. You are."

"Okay, then what's your favorite Hallmark holiday movie?"

"I don't have one, but my parents could make a personal holiday movie. They met right before Christmas, and within days fell hopelessly in love. Then they had a huge fight and broke up. After that, they both went through one of those long dark nights of the soul. Then within a few days, they confessed their love and are now living their HEA."

"You've got that whole Hallmark movie plot down pat. So you're a true romantic who doesn't want a relationship. That doesn't make sense."

"I didn't say I never want one. I just don't plan to commit before I'm thirty-six, thirty-seven. Something like that."

"Another decade? Well, good luck with that. When you least expect it, somebody's going to come along and knock you off your feet."

"My parents were older when they met, and I came along eight months after they got married."

She stopped in her tracks. "Really? I never heard that."

"It's not something I talk about. My brother told me Mom wasn't going to tell Dad she was pregnant, but after she was diagnosed with breast cancer, her doctor encouraged her to let the father know, in case she got too sick to care for me."

"I can't imagine that conversation. 'Hi, Elliott. I have breast cancer, and I'm pregnant with your child.'"

"From what I hear, it was pretty bad, but Dad stepped up, quit drinking, and proposed. And as soon as I was born, he became a full-time dad and carried me in a baby carrier around the breeding sheds and the racetrack until I could walk."

She imagined him as a precocious three-year-old dressed in pressed khakis and a green polo shirt with the MacKlenna Farm logo over the left breast pocket, along with a leather belt with a horseshoe buckle. The same pants and shirt she'd seen Elliott and JC's brother, Kevin, wear.

"Would you believe that I could recite breeding statistics before I was three?"

"I can just see you at Keeneland's yearling sales, strutting around the race track with a brochure rolled up in your hand, impressing buyers and sellers with your knowledge of the yearlings by the top commercial sires."

He gave her a puzzled look, and then his eyebrows lifted. "Oh, yeah. You and George went to the sales with me during the spring of our sophomore year. Right?"

"That's when I had the hots for you."

"I knew you did. Now I wish I'd made a move. But at the time"—he shrugged—"I was doing what I thought was best for both of us."

"It was a missed opportunity, but we can't go back now." She was silent for a moment or two while reflecting on that missed opportunity. Then she broke the silence, saying, "It was fascinating watching you bid on a horse. Your moves were so subtle. I don't know how the auctioneer knew what you were bidding."

"He knew his job, and we knew each other. A lift of my finger was the only signal he needed. Then I discovered I was bidding against a family member of the ruler of the Emirate of Dubai. You can't outbid a man with more gold than God. So I bowed out."

"You love the horse business...the auctions, the breeding, the races. So what happened? Why'd you walk away?"

"I had to make the break before the family businesses consumed me. I wanted to make it on my own without using the Fraser and Montgomery names to get there."

"I don't know anything about your financial situation, but you've always had money and cars and planes at your disposal. So how can you complain about family money and then turn around and live off it?"

"I got money from my dad when I turned thirteen, invested it in high-risk, high-reward stocks, and got lucky. Every year my portfolio doubled, and I gave away a percentage of it. Yeah, I have money, but it's money I've made. After that initial gift, all the money they gave me went into an interest-bearing account. When I went off to Harvard, I turned it over to my parents and said, 'Thank you.'"

"You aren't risk-averse at all, are you?"

"No."

"But, if you lost everything you have, you'd still have access to a fortune."

"You're right, and if I had a family, I wouldn't gamble with my assets. I'd be a more conservative investor, but I wouldn't accept family money to start over. I'd use the money I draw out of my law firm. I like what I'm doing in DC. I might eventually end up working for MacCorp, but it'll be on my terms, and Dad's not ready to accept them."

"What does he want?" she asked.

JC paused a moment and glanced away.

"Never mind. You don't have to tell me. I'm sure it's personal."

He looked back at her, and there was tension at the corners of his eyes. "It's not that it's personal. It's just that it sounds selfish to someone who hasn't grown up in the clan."

"Try me out. I'll give you an honest reaction."

"Dad has to retire before I take over. That's my one condition, and it'll never happen. It's not that he thinks his ideas are the best. It's just that all breeders know him and respect him. They know Kevin, too, but he's the money guy. I can get anybody to the table, but if Dad is there, they'll always want to deal with him, not me. So, what's your honest reaction?"

To Ensley, it was as clear as the mud on her jeans, and she couldn't understand why JC didn't see it. "You're very different from your dad. You love the breeding business. That's where your heart is. You just have to figure out why you believe there's not room enough for both of you."

20

Elkhorn Ranch (1885)—Ensley

I T WAS EARLY evening when they rounded a bend in the Little Missouri River, and Ensley stopped abruptly. "Wait!"

She squinted and watched the sun sink behind a cluster of round-topped buttes, glowing chalky white with the sun blazing behind them. "We're close. The landscape looks familiar now."

JC removed his hat and swiped his arm across his forehead. "Good. Our backtracking and river crossings have cost several delays today. It's time to stop and set up camp."

"We probably should have just headed west and crossed the Badlands. But I'm afraid of being too far from the river. Silly, but..." She released a long, slow breath. "I feel like I've wandered in the desert for forty years."

He resettled his hat. "Our wandering is almost over, and soon we'll have a better idea of what year it is. And besides, by staying close to the river, we avoided the possibility of running into a hunting party. I don't think we'd be in danger, but why risk it?"

"We've avoided hunting parties, wolves, rattlers, and grizzlies. It's time to get where we're going before our luck runs out, and preferably before dark."

He reached for the canteen and handed it to her, and after she took a long drink, he did, too. "Let's mount up and cross the river again. At least we'll be on the same side as the ranch."

JC mounted up first, then held out his hand for her. She slung her leg up behind the saddle. "I'm impressed with Mercury. He's yet to balk at crossing the river." She grabbed the Cheyenne roll instead of JC's waist. It was the best way to ride double. If she slid off, she wouldn't take him with her.

"When Mercury was a colt, I had him in the swimming pool first thing every morning. It freshened him up and made him feel good. He'd get frisky as soon as he saw the pool."

"So you trained him?"

"I did some, but a trainer at the farm in Lexington did most of it. After we were named to the Land Rover US Eventing Squad for the World Equestrian Games and competed and came in second, I decided it was time to retire before one of us got injured."

"And you brought him out here? Isn't that risky?"

"Probably, but he's the only horse I had in DC. Mercury's dam is pregnant again, so I might have another horse to train next year."

"Who's the sire?"

"The same stallion who sired Mercury. He belongs to my uncle. The mare I found at an Irish horse show. At the end of the event, I made the owner an offer he couldn't refuse. Then I shipped her to Virginia, and Uncle Braham handled the cover."

"That sounds like a story from a manuscript I read recently. TR saw a horse he liked and wanted, so he pressured the owner to sell and paid him a hundred dollars on the spot."

"Thanks for the warning." JC patted Mercury's neck. "I'll be prepared in case TR makes an offer."

"I read that he can be very persuasive."

JC glanced back at her. "So can I. How do you think I got the mare?"

They crossed the river, and Mercury climbed up the bank on the opposite side. As soon as they were on level ground, they dismounted and walked for about thirty minutes.

When a log ranch house came into view, she stopped a moment to stare and then grinned. "It's TR's ranch. He's here. I just know it. Theodore Roosevelt, the twenty-sixth president of the United States." She held out her arm. "Pinch me, please!"

Instead, he kissed her cheek. "Stay calm?"

"I'll try!" Ensley took off at a jog. "Look at that veranda. It's just like a sketch I've seen. I want to sit in one of those rockers, book in hand, while a cool breeze stirs along the river and drifts across my face, with TR rocking in one of the other chairs." She was about to explode with excitement. "Wait for a second! I need to clean up before I meet him."

JC put his hand on her back to keep her moving forward. "Just be your charming self. I doubt he'll care what you look like."

The one-story ranch house stood near the riverbank with a long veranda shaded by leafy cottonwoods. Directly across the sandbar was a strip of meadowland, and behind that were sheer cliffs and grassy plateaus. Several outbuildings—barn, chicken coop, blacksmith—were nearby. Cattle fed peacefully, pausing to watch as Ensley and JC passed by.

She bounced on her toes, still grinning madly. "This place has been called the Walden Pond of the West. I've been here so many times and imagined the house. Seeing the real deal is sort of mind-blowing. Every time I've been here, I've felt the tranquility and connection to nature. The rangers tell visitors that the land remains unchanged since TR's day. And, now I can see it's true."

When they got within a dozen yards, Ensley yelled out, "Hello, the house."

"Why don't we just knock on the door?" JC asked, heading toward the veranda.

"Stop!" she protested. "That's bad manners. You need to let the people inside peek out to study you and then decide if they want to be neighborly."

"How do you know that?"

"I grew up in North Dakota. Just stand back. If anyone's home, they'll come to the door."

Within two minutes, the door flung open, and a tall thin man bounded out, wearing a fringed deerskin shirt and trousers with boots peeking out the bottom and a neatly tied red scarf around his neck. Cowboys had a thing about having a flash of color in their clothes.

But what distinguished him most was the pair of pince-nez glasses. Oh, and something else. The sterling silver hunting knife rumored to have come from Tiffany's was tucked into a cartridge belt, and a pair of grappling irons inlaid with gold jingled when he walked.

Ensley froze. Although she couldn't move, her heart made up for it, racing heart-attack fast.

It's him. My God, it's him.

For the past two weeks, she'd been trudging through the Badlands, kept moving only by a single goal—meeting TR—but never really believing it was possible.

And here she was. And there he was. And whatever she had to do to spend as much time with him as he would allow, she would do, including riding another bull.

Okay, maybe that was a bit drastic. Still, she had to convince TR that she and JC could be both intellectually stimulating and adventuresome hunting companions to have around for an extended visit.

JC glanced at her, and he must have realized she was tongue-tied, so he said, "Sir, I'm James Cullen Fraser from New York City."

Ensley cringed at the lie, but she had agreed to it, so all she could do now was smile and support his statement with a shy nod.

JC continued, "This is my wife, Ensley. We've been on the trail for a few weeks. And I wonder if you'll permit us to camp here for the night."

"What brings you to the Dakotas?" TR asked.

"It's a long story, sir."

"I just came in from a long day on the trail, and I'm in a mood to hear it. Come inside. We're about to sit down to dinner. It's simple food out here, but you're welcome to share what we have." The man extended his hand. "I'm Theodore Roosevelt."

"Oh, the New York reformer. I've heard of you." JC clasped the hand of the future president. "It's a great pleasure to meet you, sir."

21

Mallory Plantation, VA—Elliott

ELLIOTT FRASER SAT in Braham McCabe's library, reading the *Thoroughbred Daily News* on his iPad while enjoying his second cup of morning coffee. No one knew where he was, and he wanted to keep it that way, at least for an hour. Unless you were alone in a rowboat on the James River, finding a quiet place while visiting Mallory Plantation was almost impossible. But he'd found one and relished his privacy.

Elliott and Meredith flew into Richmond Thursday night with David, Kenzie, their daughters, JL, Kevin, and their bunch. Elliott hadn't taken an official count, but except for the kids away at school, and Austin and James Cullen, most of the family was on the premises.

After having his calls go unanswered for three weeks, Elliott had stopped calling James Cullen until this morning. Now his son had turned his damn phone off, and calls went straight to voice mail. Over the past few years, James Cullen had become more distant, and while his son liked to blame it on family pressures, Elliott knew they weren't the cause.

Sixteen months ago, Elliott became so alarmed that he hired a private military and homeland security agency to investigate his son. What Northbridge Worldwide discovered ripped through Elliott, and he still hadn't recovered.

James Cullen was a Paramilitary Operations Officer for the CIA.

The news was the only thing he'd ever hidden from Meredith, and he still lacked the courage to tell her. Not only had he not told Meredith, but he hadn't told Remy or even Tavis. Why? Because Elliott approved of his son's decision. He didn't like it, but James

Cullen had his dad's seal of approval.

While neither Northbridge nor David had discovered what James Cullen was doing for the CIA, Elliott sensed in his blood and bones that his son's mission, the underpinning of every assignment, was to track down and destroy the Illuminati before the clandestine organization destroyed the MacKlenna Clan.

Whenever James Cullen went AWOL like he was now, Elliott tried to find a project that would keep him distracted until his son returned. This time he'd just identified two yearlings he wanted to buy at the Fasig-Tipton July Sale.

A quick knock on the door preceded its opening, and Penny Malone-O'Grady stuck her head around the partially open door. "Hey. Something's come up. Do you have a minute?"

Elliott turned off the iPad and placed it on the end table as he stood to welcome his daughter-in-law into his sanctuary. "Come in, lass. I always have time for ye." Penny wasn't legally his daughter-in-law, but he had unofficially adopted all the women who joined the family through marriage.

Eight months pregnant with twins, she lumbered across the room and eased down onto the sofa. The babies had to be making her life miserable. Although she never complained, her perpetually pinched face made her discomfort obvious.

"We have a situation," she said, calmly adjusting throw pillows to support her back.

Alarm bells went off in Elliott's head as he reclaimed his seat beside her, wondering if Charlotte had already gone to the hospital for morning rounds. "Is it the babies? Where's Rick?"

"It's not the babies, and Rick took Jean to the golf course."

Relieved, Elliott crossed his legs. "The wee lad's game is better than Tiger Woods's was at that age. At three, Tiger shot a forty-eight over nine holes at the Navy course in California. Jean just shot a forty-seven."

"I realize that's impressive, but Jean isn't a miniature adult. Between the music lessons, horseback riding lessons, and golf, he doesn't have much time to be a kid."

"Ask Kevin what James Cullen was like at three."

"Rick must be talking to Kevin and JL then. Yesterday Rick told him he was going to teach Jean how to wrap his taste buds around the four primary wine descriptors so he could describe the taste of wine to Granny Mere."

"Surely he didn't give the lad alcohol?"

"Hell, no. At least, I don't think he did. He gave Jean glasses of water with different flavors stirred in, so they tasted fruity, earthy, spicy, smoky, and flowery. It cracked me up. Jean insisted on dressing in khakis and a MacCorp shirt and sitting at the bar with a wine glass for his 'instructions.' He'd taste the water, smack his lips, and said 'smoky' after every sip."

"If the lad keeps that up, he'll soon know more than Meredith." Elliott took a sip of coffee, then said, "I don't think ye're here for parenting lessons, so what's on yer mind that ye had to search me out?"

"It wasn't much of a search, boss. I asked Alicyn McBain where you were."

"She didn't see me come in here. How'd she know?"

"To be precise, she said, 'Grandpa Elliott likes to read the TDN with his morning coffee, and since it's the only quiet place around here today—' That's when her twin sister Rebecca butted in and said, 'He's in the cleanroom or the library.' Then Laurie Wallis said, 'Try the library first. He likes the morning sun.' Then she went into a long explanation about why sailors don't like red skies in the morning."

Elliott smiled. "Smart kids. But what'd she say about red skies?"

"That a low-pressure storm system is moving east, so rain is on its way."

"Laurie Wallis has spent a lot of time on the river with Churchill, and whenever he's at the helm of any boat, he's right back in the Royal Navy. Tavis is encouraging him to apply to the Naval Academy."

"Do you think he will?"

"He's worked with private tutors for the past three years, both here and in Italy, so he's not far behind Robbie and Henry. I'm sure everywhere he applies, he'll get accepted. He's a talented artist, a great athlete, speaks three languages, and is sharp as a tack. But ye didn't invade my privacy to talk about Churchill's education."

She hesitated a moment before answering. "I just took a call from a detective with the Cambridge Police Department."

Elliott removed his reading glasses and placed them on top of the iPad. "I assume ye mean Cambridge, Massachusetts, and not Cambridge, England?"

"Yep!" she said.

He couldn't imagine why the police would call Penny, so he didn't waste time trying to guess. "What'd they want?"

Penny rubbed her belly and wiggled to get comfortable. "Have you talked to JC lately?"

He uncrossed his legs and leaned forward. "Let's not dance around a police investigation, lass. What'd they want?"

"The detective was calling Billie Malone."

"Ye haven't been Billie Malone in three years."

"He tracked Billie down through the catering business, and my former partner gave him my mobile number. He's investigating the disappearance of a woman from a house in Cambridge."

Elliott's chest tightened as if a big brown bear had him in a hug, squeezing the last breaths from his body. "Go on," he said, although he knew where this was leading.

"When he entered the details surrounding the woman's disappearance into a national database, my name popped up."

Elliott pushed to his feet and walked over to the window with a view of the James River. "It was the smell of peat. Wasn't it?"

"That's two for two. You're on a roll."

He glared at her. "If ye're afraid to tell me, just spit it out. Ye have my word, I won't yell, and right now ye're the only person in this family that applies to."

"Okay, if you promise."

He shot her with another one of his infamous death rays and raised his arms in surrender.

"Okay. Message received." She adjusted the pillows. "The detective said there was a nasty smell in the hotel room when I disappeared, and the police report described it as the smell of peat. He asked me where it came from. I told him the odor was in a jewelry box I purchased and that it took several months to get rid of the smell. He seemed satisfied, so I asked the woman's name. When he told me, I said I'd met her before, and only then realized I'd probably made a mistake, but I couldn't retract it."

The Hulk-hug tightness around Elliott's chest squeezed even tighter. "Is she a woman you knew at West Point?"

"No, she's JC's friend, Ensley Williams. You've met her. She's George Williams's cousin."

Elliott pounded his fist into his other hand. "Shite. When'd she disappear?"

"Thursday night. But, Elliott, here's the thing. The detective already knew I'm married to the president of Montgomery Winery and that James Cullen Fraser's mother owns it."

"How the hell did James Cullen worm his way into this story?"

"I asked the detective the same question. He said JC and George were both in Cambridge for meetings. They met at the Porcellian Club Thursday night. From there, they went to pick up Ensley and take her to dinner. But she wasn't at the Williams's house. All her stuff was there, including her phone. They got worried, and George called the police. The detectives came and interviewed them, and then George filed a missing person report."

"Does the detective suspect foul play?" Elliott asked.

"He didn't mention it, and I didn't ask."

Someone else knocked on the door, and before Elliott could say come in or go away, David opened it. He looked at Penny on the sofa, then at Elliott pacing. "Looks like I'm too late. Ye heard about Ensley?"

"Aye," Elliott said. "Come in. How'd ye find out?"

David entered and closed the door. "I have alerts set to notify me if a woman goes missing and the investigation mentions the smell of peat. I just got my first one about thirty minutes ago and pulled up a missing person report filed by George Williams." David directed a question to Elliott, "Did JC call ye?"

"No. Penny got a call from a detective in Cambridge."

David glanced at Penny. "I guess he got yer name from a national database?"

She nodded. "I thought you were going to scrub the details of my disappearance so nobody could find me."

"I decided to leave it alone. If my alerts failed, I figured ye'd get a call."

Penny stood and rubbed her back. "You should have warned me. I would have prepared for a conversation with a detective."

"I don't buy it," David said. "Captain Penny Lafitte is always prepared."

"Maybe once, but now I can't even find my feet." She wiggled her eyebrows playfully. "Have you seen them anywhere?"

David gave her a side-body hug. "Ye sound just like Kenzie when she was pregnant. Ye'll be fine." He crossed the room and poured a cup of coffee. "What did the detective say?"

"That my name popped up when he entered 'missing woman' and 'peat smell' into a national database. I told him the smell was in a jewelry box. Then he mentioned that he interviewed James Cullen and that I worked at a winery owned by his mother. He thought that was an interesting coincidence."

David sipped from his mug. "The detective did his research. Did he sound suspicious or sound like he suspected foul play?"

"Elliott asked that, too. The detective didn't say, and I didn't ask. But he did ask if JC knew about the smell in my jewelry box. I told him that as far as I knew, it was so insignificant that there wasn't any reason to mention it."

"Good answer." Elliott was looking out the window at the twin girls kicking a soccer ball around the yard while listening to Penny. "Did the detective ask how long ye were gone?"

"He did, but I had a feeling he already knew the answer. I told him I snuck out to spend time with a married man in Barataria. That pretty much ended the conversation."

"Where's JC now?" David asked.

"He's MIA," Elliott said.

David topped off his mug and carried it to the other window with a view of the yard and the river and watched his daughters play soccer. "Call George. He might know where JC is now."

"Then I'd have to explain how I know about Ensley's disappearance," Elliott said.

"Tell him I got an alert," David said.

"Just tell him the detective called me," Penny said at the same time.

Elliott scrolled through his contact list, found George's number, and punched it in. After two rings, George answered. "This is George."

"George, this is Elliott Fraser."

"Hi, Dr. Fraser. Did JC tell you about my cousin?"

Elliott put the call on speaker. "I haven't spoken to him. What can ye tell me?"

"I've told this story so many times. I wish I'd made a recording. JC and I met Thursday night at the Porcellian Club. Then we took an Uber here to the Cambridge house to pick up Ensley for dinner. She wasn't here, but all her belongings were. We got worried and called the police. They came over to investigate, and I filed a missing person report. We still haven't heard anything. How'd you find out if you haven't talked to JC? Did it make the news in Kentucky?"

"No, David McBain set up alerts when James Cullen went off to school. He's never turned them off. He just now told me about Ensley. Since I couldn't reach James Cullen, I decided to call ye directly. Is there any news?"

"Nothing. A friend of Ensley's and I have been distributing flyers all over town. Nothing's come up yet. I just now called JC and left a message. I didn't expect him to answer but thought if he checked his messages, he'd at least have an update about Ensley."

"Why didn't ye expect him to answer?" Elliott asked.

"He said he was going out of town for a few days and would call when he returned."

"I'm sure he will." Elliott wanted more information but didn't want to press.

"George, this is David McBain. I've been listening to the call. Do ye mind telling us what happened when ye arrived at the house, and what caused ye so much concern that ye called the police?"

"There was a funny odor all over the house. JC said it smelled like peat."

"Did ye search the house immediately?" David asked.

"We did after we found her purse and stuff. I went downstairs to the exercise room, and JC went upstairs. He found wet towels in the bathroom and dirty clothes on top of her suitcase."

"I don't guess ye know what she was wearing," David asked.

"Matter of fact, I do. Unless she changed her mind, she had plans to meet a group of women at a country music bar after dinner. They had all decided to wear jeans, cowboy boots, and hats. We didn't see her boots or hat in the bedroom, so that's likely what she was wearing."

"I assume the detectives interviewed the women Ensley was going to meet later."

"The detectives said they were going to the bar to interview the women, and it turns out one of them was in law school with JC and me. She called me after the interview and volunteered to help hand out flyers. She organized the group, and they spent all day Friday handing out flyers all over Boston."

Elliott glanced at David, then at Penny, and both of them shrugged. "Look, George, I have connections. I'll place a call and get additional help out there for ye."

"Thanks for the offer, sir, but Dad hired a private detective agency that comes highly recommended. If they come up blank, I'll call you back. But if you talk to JC, ask him to call me."

"I'll do that, and if ye think of anything I can help ye with— anything at all—be sure to call me." Elliott disconnected and pocketed his phone. "What are the ladies doing today?"

"We're leaving in about an hour," Penny said. "Charlotte set up hair and nail appointments in Richmond. Why?"

"Meredith and I haven't talked about plans for the day yet, and I'm not ready to tell her about this." He studied Penny's face. "Ye probably should leave the room, lass, so ye'll have deniability."

"I'm already in this, Elliott. I'm not leaving until I hear your plan." She settled in again on the sofa, rearranging the pillows. "So, what are you going to do next?"

"Go to DC, track down my son, and try to figure out where Ensley went."

"I'll go with ye," David said. "But if JC isn't there, I'm not sure what ye can learn."

Elliott gave David a subtle hand signal that Penny couldn't see and wouldn't understand if she did. Through the years, David remained the only person who could read them. Although Meredith knew a few signals, she couldn't follow a conversation. The signal told David not to say anything more.

"JC's assistant, Paul, should be there. He might know JC's whereabouts," Elliott said.

"Paul's a good guy. I'll go talk to him," Penny said.

Elliott sat next to her on the sofa. "I don't know what's going on with James Cullen, but I'm determined to find out, and I don't want to involve ye or alarm Meredith. I'll call a family meeting when we get back tonight, and then we can decide what to do about Ensley."

"So, you're asking me to spend the day with Meredith and the others and not say anything about another brooch showing up? You want me to lie to them."

"Not telling them isn't a lie." A millisecond after he said it, Elliott knew he'd get pushback.

And Penny jumped right on it. "Psssh. A lie of omission is still a lie."

"Wilhelmina, enough! This is how it's going to be. David and I are going to Washington. We'll be back late this afternoon. Ye are going with the other women to the spa. Tonight we will have a family meeting, and ye can tell everyone about yer part in this, or ye can remain silent, and I won't mention yer call from the detective."

"But—"

"There are no buts. Ye're not going to Washington. Period."

"Give me a good reason."

"Ye're pregnant, and we might have to bust some kneecaps. I don't want to send ye into labor. If ye weren't pregnant, I'd let ye have the first go-around with Paul." Elliott stood and collected his mug and iPad. Then to David, he said, "I'm ready to go as soon as ye can reserve a helicopter."

"Do ye want to take Tavis?" Davis asked.

Elliott thought a minute. He wanted to keep this as tight as possible, but Tavis was a former guardian and had a level of insight that neither Elliott nor David had. "Bring him along."

David pulled out his phone and sent Tavis a text. A few seconds later, David's phone dinged with a text message. "He'll be ready in ten minutes." Another message dinged. "Tavis says Remy is rehearsing with a band and wants to know if he's needed."

"Not this time."

David sent another text, and a few seconds later, another message arrived. "Tavis will get a vehicle and be around the front in ten minutes."

"I've got to talk to Meredith. I'll meet ye in the car." Elliott opened the door, glanced back at Penny, and, without saying anything else, nodded to her and left.

He found Meredith in the flower garden picking some nameless—to him—yellow and purple flowers. "Ye going to the spa?"

"In about thirty minutes," she said. "I'm picking flowers for our bedroom. What are you doing? You're wearing that expression that tells me you're up to something, and you don't want me to know about it." She put the cutters in a basket and gathered up the handful of flowers. "Am I right?"

"Aye, my dear. Ye're right. I'll tell ye about it tonight."

"Is it dangerous?"

"Not for me."

"Great. Just great. Take David and Tavis. And don't kill anybody."

He wrapped his arms around her. "I promise not to kill anyone today." He kissed her. "I love ye. Forever and a day."

She smiled. "Same here. And I expect a full report tonight."

He held her close to him for a few more seconds and then let go. "I'll tell ye everything I know."

He got as far as the door to the sunporch before Meredith said, "It's about James Cullen. Isn't it? I've had the strangest feeling all morning. He's in trouble, Elliott. Go find him."

22

Elkhorn Ranch (1885)—Ensley

E NSLEY'S BODY AND mind slowly thawed as she eyeballed the
man on the veranda.

That's Teddy Roosevelt.

And then her new reality hit her with a wallop—not a pinch. She
had time-traveled. JC had already told her so, but now there was no
denying the truth. So, the question was, to what year?

Since both the ranch house and Roosevelt were here in the
Badlands, it had to be the spring of 1885.

Proof positive.

That truth meant she could no longer hang on by bloody fingertips, hoping that the whole time travel bit was an illusion, a dream, a
nightmare.

But there's a trade-off, Ens.

She fastened JC with a hard stare. She'd learned early on to trust
her sixth sense or ESP, and in the last few days, JC had voiced her
deepest fears and loftiest dreams several times, even when they
hadn't previously discussed them.

With as much time as they spent together, it was inevitable that
he'd weasel his way into her thoughts. She'd let him get away with it
this time, but she refused to let him reside rent-free in her head. A
girl had to have some privacy.

Silently, she said, *Yes. There are trade-offs.*

The man on the porch would be the twenty-sixth president of
the United States—the living, breathing man—a man she could talk
to about literature and the Badlands, about the past and the future,
about hunting and conservation.

Roosevelt opened the door and stepped aside. "Come in,

please."

She didn't break stride as she crossed the porch but stopped short of the threshold to use the boot scraper before stepping lightly into the sitting room.

TR closed the door and swept his arm back, welcoming them. "This isn't as spacious as my residence on Madison Avenue in New York City, but it suits me. My partner likes to tell the story that he cut down fifty-three trees for this house, Dow cut down forty-nine, and I beavered down seventeen."

"My wife beavered down a sapling. It wasn't a pretty sight," JC said.

To have found that sapling, JC must have searched every nook and cranny while following her trail. "Well, I did the best I could with limited tools."

She pushed thoughts of JC searching for her aside and studied TR, looking for familiar mannerisms she'd seen in old movie clips, but at twenty-six he had yet to grow into the robust man who appeared in them. There was no barrel chest, or booming voice, or fist propped at his hip. He was pale and thin, and JC could easily span TR's waist with his two thumbs and fingers.

"It's lovely," Ensley said. "And for the Badlands, it's a mansion." Her sense of smell pinged her brain and stomach with an overload of sensory information. "What's that divine aroma? Venison?"

"Yes. I shot it this morning." Roosevelt puffed out his chest. "Field dressed it and brought it back to Mrs. Sewall to slow cook with morel mushrooms and potatoes."

Ensley's mouth watered. She *loved* slow-cooked venison sprinkled with Everglades Cactus Dust seasoning and smothered with mushrooms, onion, garlic, and potatoes. If TR hadn't already invited them to dinner, she'd have offered to wash dishes for the leftovers. She had one foot turned in the direction of the kitchen, but TR seemed to be lingering, studying JC, or as the saying goes, taking his measure.

She'd been to this site hundreds of times, but she'd only been able to imagine the look and feel—not the smell—of TR's ranch house. The National Park Service rangers based their spiel on historical texts. According to them, TR's partners in the cattle business, Bill Sewall and Wilmot Dow, built the house over the winter of 1884. But no one knew for sure what had been inside. Now she did, but she couldn't tell them.

Then write a firsthand account.

Sure. She could do that after dinner. In the meantime, while she waited for TR to finish sizing up JC, she could scribble a few editorial notes. She hoped JC had pencils and paper in his saddlebags. He seemed to have everything else.

A roaring fire of cottonwood logs reddened the hearthstone, bearskins and buffalo robes strewed the chairs, and stuffed heads cast monstrous shadows across the log walls. Rifles stood in the corner, coonskin coats and beaver caps hung from hooks near the door. And the sturdy shelves seemed to groan under the weight of several volumes of Irving, Hawthorne, Cooper, and Lowell. TR was famous for saying, "Books are almost as individual as friends." And she couldn't wait to read some of his favorites.

No photographs of the ranch house survived, but sketches of the floor plan, the exterior of the home, and a layout of the outbuildings were readily available in books and online.

If the floor plan and notes she was familiar with were accurate, the house was thirty by sixty feet, with eight rooms, four on each side of a long hallway. TR's bedroom took up the southeast corner and adjoined the sitting room, which was TR's study during the day and the gathering place in the evenings.

Across the hall was the dining room, and next to it was the kitchen. And that was the source of the mouthwatering aromas of roasting venison, and yes—wait for it—yeast bread.

Oh, my God. I would die for a piece of bread right out of the oven, slathered with rich, creamy butter.

Her stomach growled in anticipation. "Sorry. I've been walking through the Badlands far too long."

"My stomach has been complaining for the last thirty minutes," TR said. "My partners and their wives live here with me, and the women know how to cook wild game."

"You hunt, they cook. Got it! I could write an entire book on the preparation and safe handling of wild game and would be glad to share a few of my go-to recipes."

TR gave her a confused looked that she shrugged off. Okay, starvation had rattled her brain. But now real food, not MREs or energy bars, a hardwood floor beneath her feet, and a fire blazing in the corner reminded her of home and a full belly. She could stay right here, soaking up the warmth and enjoying the rocking chair. TR and JC sat in a pair of leather chairs, perfect for men sporting mustaches and monocles.

Never mind. Forget the rocker. She'd much prefer to curl up with a good book on the brown-bear rug and while away the hours reading nineteenth-century fiction. The bookcase looked interesting. What tomes did TR think worthy enough to ship out here to the Badlands? She'd explore his North Dakota library after dinner.

A child with curly hair—not a toddler, but not school-age either—bounded into the room and skidded to a stop in front of JC, barely reaching his knees. "What's your name?"

JC squatted to be at eye level. "James Cullen. What's yours?"

"Kitty." She bobbed her head, and blond curls bounced around her shoulders. She looked up at Ensley. "What's your name?"

"Ensley MacAndrew Williams...Fraser."

"That's a lot of names. I just have one. Kitty."

"You have more than one. I call you Kitty, but your parents named you Lucretia Sewall," TR said rather matter-of-factly like he renamed children all the time.

"Well, you're a very pretty young lady," Ensley said. "Let me guess how old you are. Hmm." She tapped her chin, thinking back to all the kids from neighboring ranches she used to babysit before she was old enough to tie her shoes. "I bet you are"—she held up three fingers—"Am I right?"

Kitty counted. "One, two, three. I'm three!"

JC gently tugged on a strand of her hair. "For a girl who's only three years old, you sure have long hair. Do you brush it, or does your mama?"

"Mama does." Kitty touched the side of JC's head. "She can brush your hair, too."

He chuckled, a sound that was almost lyrical and in stark contrast to his whiskered-outlaw appearance, which didn't seem to scare Kitty at all. Kids could see a person's heart in the gleam of their eyes. And at that moment, no one could mistake JC's.

"I probably need a haircut, too. Do you have any scissors?" he asked.

She shook her head. "Mama does."

JC's studied, calm, and smiling face reminded Ensley of a Fourth of July celebration she and George attended at Mallory Plantation. The preteen girls were gathered around JC, staring at him with goo-goo eyes. You would have thought he was a movie star or the latest dream pop idol from down under.

To her surprise, he managed to give each of them personal, up-close attention asking about school or sports or boyfriends. He knew enough about every child that Ensley concluded he must be in constant contact with his parents or Emily Duffy, who was like a sister. At the time, Ensley thought what a wonderful father he'd make. And even now, with a child he didn't know, he showed the same unaffected interest.

Ensley glanced up at TR and saw in his public stoicism the grief beneath his facade. He had escaped to the Badlands after his first wife died only hours after delivering their baby. That child, Baby Lee, would be a year old now. It had to be painful to be with Kitty and not his daughter—and not his wife.

Kitty ran from the room, yelling, "Mama, Mr. Roosevelt has company, and he wants a haircut."

JC stood, laughing. "She's a charmer."

"She's in perpetual motion from dawn until after supper. I never knew a child could have so much energy."

"With little ones around, there's never a dull moment," JC said.

"How many children do you have?" TR asked.

"We don't have any." JC smiled at Ensley. "But we have several young cousins."

The sadness deepened in TR's eyes. After losing his wife, he assumed he'd never marry again, and maybe that was on his mind, but Ensley knew he would have another chance at love, and within the next few years, have five half siblings for Baby Lee.

But what about me? I was an only child and planned to have several of my own.

Now she couldn't predict or plan for the future, which didn't sit well with her. At all.

A rail-thin, petite woman with light brown hair entered the sitting room, wiping her hands on her apron. "Should I set another place at the table, Mr. Roosevelt?" Her eyes widened when she took in Ensley's appearance. "Oh. Two more places, then."

"Yes, Mrs. Sewall. Mr. and Mrs. Fraser will be joining us."

"Dinner is almost ready," Mrs. Sewall said.

"A home-cooked meal sounds wonderful," Ensley said. "Trail food gets old after a while. I thought we'd have to wait until we reached Medora."

"How far is the city?" JC asked.

"It's close to thirty-five miles, with multiple river crossings. But right now, the river's too high, too dangerous to cross."

"We followed it for miles, and it was never dangerous."

TR pointed out the window. "See how rough the river is now? It's like that the entire trail to Medora."

Ensley stared out the window. It was a rushing river now, but it hadn't been before. How was that possible?

"We plan to make the trip to Medora tomorrow," JC said.

Ensley made a face. She wanted a long bath, clean clothes, and an entire day to do no walking, no cooking over a campfire, and no washing up in the river. "Thirty-five miles will take us two days."

"Are you in a hurry to return to New York?" Roosevelt asked JC.

"I promised to visit family in Kentucky before I head back east, but Ensley isn't fond of her in-laws, and to be honest…"

When JC hesitated, she added, in her best self-deprecating voice, "They aren't fond of me, either."

They had gone through their backstories several times and quizzed each other, but flat-out lying wasn't in her nature. She wasn't so sure about JC.

"My family wanted me to marry a girl from Lexington, and when I didn't…" He huffed out a soft, half-humorless laugh. "Well, let's just say…families can be difficult and very opinionated."

"Most unfortunate." TR paused, shaking his head, then asked, "What do you do in New York City?"

"I'm a lawyer in private practice," JC said. "And Ensley is starting an editing business."

"You don't say? An editor? Whose manuscript have you worked on?"

She ran through her list of "America's Essential Female Authors" and came up with one that might suit. "I'm working with Kate Chopin on a collection of short stories." Kate wouldn't become known for a few more years, so working with her now would make sense. "She writes about the inner lives of sensitive, daring women. You probably haven't heard of her, but you will. Her stories will be perfect for America's most prestigious magazines— the *Atlantic Monthly* and *Harper's Young People*."

Roosevelt nodded. "I look forward to reading her work." Then he turned his attention to JC. "I studied law at Columbia and marched the fifty-five blocks every day from my home to the law school's location on Great Jones Street in Lower Manhattan. I studied hard, but I was restless and impatient, like a caged lynx. I just wanted to go off with my gun instead of immersing myself in the tedious details of legal cases. Law is a good occupation, but it didn't supplant my naturalist passions. Finally, I decided the law wasn't for me."

"I have that same thought every day," JC said, followed by an unusually hearty laugh. "My clients are likely looking for new representation by now, but hopefully, they can hold off for another couple of weeks."

"How long have you been traveling?"

"About three weeks. I warned them I might be away for a month or more."

"We might be returning to New York at the same time. Mr. Sewall and Mr. Dow are returning to Medora with an extra fifteen hundred cows. Our roundup starts in a few days at Box Elder Creek, so after that, I'll be traveling back east."

"A roundup?" Ensley asked. "I've been working on a short story about a roundup. I'm not quite sure how roundups work here."

"The Cattlemen's Association meets twice a year, divides the area into districts, sets dates for the roundups, and appoints a foreman. The Association sends the information to the newspaper. That way, everyone knows the dates and where to meet. Cattle stray from their owner's range, and it's necessary to throw them back where they belong and identify each owner's calf crop and properly brand them."

"So your district is meeting at the Box Elder Creek?"

"That's correct, but tell me about the story you're editing."

"I'm not editing it. I'm writing it." The lie breezed out of her mouth—just like that. But she'd do anything to go on a roundup, including being rude and inviting herself. "Could I possibly tag along?"

"Whatever for?" TR asked.

"Research. Since you're a writer yourself, you know that firsthand knowledge and experience bring depth and emotion to your writing. I want that for this story. I can compete with women like Annie Oakley and Calamity Jane."

"I'm not familiar with them."

"They're sharpshooters and frontierswomen. Besides, I can take care of myself, and I won't be in anyone's way. I grew up on a ranch and can make biscuits, bacon, and beans just like a cattle-drive cook.

My father wanted a son, but he only had me. So I can also break a horse and rope a calf as well as any man." She slapped the sides of her thighs. *Sell it, Ens.* "Hence the trousers. I'll fill in wherever you're short a man, and most importantly, you don't have to pay me."

Delight blossomed over TR's face. "Well, bully. When I was a senior at Harvard, I wrote my thesis advocating equal rights for women. If you say you can ride and rope, who am I to say you can't?"

JC banded a tense arm around her shoulders, his fingers gripping her upper arm. "Let's talk about this after dinner. We don't have to make a decision right now."

She was about to ask why not, but there was something about JC's touch and in his eyes. Worry? Fear? She wasn't sure, but she understood that it was the wrong question to ask at the moment. So she said, "Okay. I'll go outside and wash up before dinner."

"No. That's not necessary," TR said. "Mrs. Sewall can show you to the guest room. You're welcome to stay as long as you like. It's rare to get company way out here, and I'd enjoy talking about New York. You might even persuade me to discuss law, but absolutely no politics."

"Does that include the election of '84?" JC asked.

Ensley piped in, "You know I've never understood how a Democrat won in the era of Republican political domination."

While TR's reaction to her ranching qualifications was to exclaim "bully," his sharply indrawn breath at her political observation was just the opposite.

I guess women don't discuss politics in your household.

She recalled a Victorian novel she edited last year and drew on the heroine's experience to explain her own. "When I was growing up, the family discussed politics and political activities all the time. My mother and her friends used the kitchen table and drawing room to organize petitions, host committee meetings, and plan campaigns."

"I thought you grew up on a ranch."

"I did, but that didn't stop my parents from enjoying politics. Their views on women's rights are similar to yours."

It's time to bow out of this discussion.

She glanced at Mrs. Sewall. "Which way should I go to wash up? And after that, I'll help you get dinner on the table."

JC stepped in to rescue her. "I believe literature, law, and New

York City are safe topics."

TR clapped him on the back. "Indeed."

Ensley took in a relieved breath as Mrs. Sewall led her down the hallway and entered the room at the opposite end of the house. "I'll bring hot water and towels."

"That's not necessary. You can just show me the way, and I'll manage for myself."

She'd learned growing up on a ranch that everyone pulled their weight, and she intended to do it now. She grabbed the pitcher from the washstand and followed Mrs. Sewall to the kitchen.

"The kettle on the back of the stove has hot water." Mrs. Sewall glanced around the kitchen. "Where'd that child go now? I told her to sit at the table and not move until I came back."

Ensley glanced out the window. "It looks like she's with my"—the next word caught in her throat, but she managed to cough it out—"husband. It looks like he's taking his horse to the barn."

Mrs. Sewall headed toward the back door. "Oh, my. Lucretia will bother him."

"No, she won't," Ensley rushed to say. "He's great with kids." She poured hot water into the pitcher while watching JC give Kitty the currycomb. "I'll be back in a few minutes to help you."

"Let me get you a towel." Mrs. Sewall opened a cupboard and removed a towel just as Kitty ran in through the kitchen door ahead of JC.

"Mama, JC's going to teach me to comb his horse like you comb my hair."

"Oh, is he, now? Don't go bothering Mr. Fraser. He has other things to do."

"No, Mama. He said I'm the most important person right now." She turned and hurried out of the house.

"I'm sorry, Mr. Fraser. When I'm cooking and her father's home, he watches over her."

"I made sure she knows not to go near my horse unless I'm there." JC handed Ensley a saddlebag. "Thought you might need this. As soon as I feed and water Mercury, I'll come in to clean up."

"I'll leave you some hot water." Ensley returned to the bedroom, removed her shirt and jacket, washed her face and hands, then brushed her hair and teeth. Tonight, before she climbed into a real bed, she'd strip down and have a hot sponge bath. Maybe Mrs. Sewall would loan her a skirt tomorrow so she could wash her jeans.

While she dressed, she inventoried the bedroom. She couldn't wait to sleep on the wooden-frame bed, which was a bit wider than a twin but narrower than a double. JC would fill the entire bed, leaving no room for her unless she slept on top of him.

Eck. Not happening.

He'd just have to sleep on the floor.

A buffalo robe blanketed the bed, and she ran her fingers through the thick fur. Sleeping beneath it would be heavenly, and several steps up from cottonwood leaves and boughs. A brown-bear rug covered a portion of the floor, tempting her to remove her boots and socks and scrunch the soft fur between her toes.

JC wouldn't mind sleeping on the rugs. Would he? It didn't matter. She was taking the bed.

Red-checked cotton curtains framed the window. She used the tiebacks to hold the panels in place while she gave the area around the house a good scan through the window. "Wow! A corner room with a view of the river."

She once had a corner room with a view of Waikiki Beach. God, that seemed like ages ago, but it was only a few months. How in the world did she ever believe she was in love with Wyatt? Now she could look through the rearview mirror and see that he was a placeholder. But for whom?

She hefted the saddlebag and placed it on top of a trunk with "TR" engraved on a brass plate. The comb and brush she left on a gorgeous walnut Davenport writing desk. She could imagine sitting in the cane-back chair and working there. And doing what?

Good question.

Maybe she really would write a cattle-drive story—the next GAN (Great American Novel). What better story would capture the spirit of American life? She almost laughed out loud. Wouldn't that be a kick?

Hey, Susan. Since I don't have a job anymore, I wrote a novel. Wanna read it?

The heavy clack of bootheels in the hallway pushed thoughts of writing the GAN to the back of her mind. And she jumped at the rap on the door.

"Ens. Can I come in?" JC asked.

She swung open the door. "It's all yours."

The size of the bedroom suddenly shrank. JC was tall and broad-shouldered, but he was noticeably larger in this confined space than he seemed outside. His footsteps echoed in muted thumps as he moved about the room, stepping over the bear rug.

Guess he figured out he's going to sleep on the floor.

"If you're through, I'd like to wash up, but if you could use more time…"

"I'm done." She opened the window and dumped the dirty water out of the washbowl. "I used your soap."

"Everything I have is yours. You know that." He cocked his head and looked between her and the window. "Aren't you supposed to yell a warning before you dump dirty water out a window?"

"Only if you're on an upper floor and if you're dumping the contents of a chamber pot." She brushed the dust off her jacket before slipping it back on. "I'll see you at the table." She opened the door but then closed it again. "How long do you intend to stay?"

His head jerked, and he pointed a glance at her that held a truck-load of something she couldn't decipher. "Are you trying to get rid of me?" he asked.

"Ah, no, but I want to go on the roundup, and I know you want to go to Lexington. It looks like I could have three weeks with TR. But I don't know how long it takes to get to Kentucky or how long you want to spend time with your family. I'm just trying to figure out how we can both get what we want."

He removed his jacket and hung it over the chair back, then unbuttoned his shirt, slowly and methodically, almost like he was doing a striptease, but he wasn't intentionally provocative. It was just the way he did things.

He hung the shirt on top of the jacket. "You want to sleep out-side on the trail for another three weeks, work your butt off, and irritate the hell out of your hip?"

"Yep. I know it sounds crazy, but that's what I want."

"You'd rather live in the dust and mud than go to MacKlenna Farm and live in the lap of nineteenth-century luxury."

"Even with mud and dust and hard work and hell. Look, I'm not opposed to living in the lap of luxury. I'm just willing to sacrifice comfort for a once-in-a-lifetime experience."

"A once-in-a-lifetime experience isn't always what's it's cracked up to be."

She sat down on the edge of the bed, wrapped her arms around the bedpost, and pressed her cheek against it. "I'm betting this one will be."

"If a roundup was the only option on the bill of fare, I'd go. But eating dust and sleeping on the ground again doesn't sound appealing, and I don't want to put Mercury through that hardship."

"I thought you said Mercury could handle being out here."

"Cowboys ride about a hundred miles a day during a cattle drive, and they go through a string of horses. And from what I've read, some of the horses are at best green-broke. Are you prepared for that?"

"I can break a horse, and I've chased the clouds more times than I can remember."

"I guess that means you've been thrown high off a horse. But think about this, sweetheart—"

"Don't sweetheart me."

"Sorry. But listen, when you rode bulls and broncs before, you had the benefit of a twenty-first-century hospital to put you back together. How many bones have you broken? Huh? That's probably why your hip hurts you all the time."

"I don't complain."

"You don't have to. I can see it on your face. You're hurting now and probably helped yourself to a couple of naproxen to get through the night."

"How many bones have you broken?" she demanded.

"I don't fall."

"Bullshit!"

JC poured water into the washbowl. "If this cattle drive is what you want…"

The muscles rippled in his arms and upper back as he soaped up his hands and slathered his face. He could be a cover model on any of the popular men's magazines: *Esquire, Men's Fitness, Men's Health.* He was fit, sexy, and photogenic.

"If I leave, that will solve the sleeping-together issue," he said.

"Hmm. I wasn't even thinking about that."

He chuckled. "You're a terrible liar. You know that, don't you? You've already planned for me to sleep on the bear rug. Haven't you?"

She ducked her head. "Well, maybe."

"I'll do my best to work it out for you. Let me look at the map and see where we can meet en route to New York. Probably Cleveland."

She looked up at the ceiling, picturing a United States map, and visually traced a path from Medora to New York. "I think you're right, but we'll have to look at the train schedule. How will we communicate, though?"

He splashed water on his face to rinse away the soap, and then he reached for the towel hanging from a hook on the side of the washstand. "Dots and dashes, darling."

She made a face. "Ditto on the word 'darling.'" She stood and stretched. All the talk about her injuries reminded her hip that it was time to give her a painful nudge. "So, by dots and dashes, you mean a telegram?"

He nodded behind the towel covering his face.

"Medora should have a Western Union telegraph office," she said.

After he brushed his teeth, he reached for the hairbrush. "If you go to Medora and send a telegram to MacKlenna Farm—depending on how long it takes to get the message from Midway out to Old Frankfort Pike—I should have it within a couple of hours."

She continued stretching forward, backward, and sideways. "Do you know how obscure that information is? Why would you know that?"

He parted his hair with his finger and brushed the waves away from his face. "Uncle Braham taught me Morse code when I was a teenager. That led to a study of communications techniques from smoke signals and drums to cell phones. I'm sure Medora has a telegraph office at the train station. So if I have any news to share with you, I'll send a telegram and vice versa."

"How will I get it?"

He emptied the washbowl just as she had. "I'll hire someone in Medora to find you and deliver the message." He returned the towel to the hook on the side of the washstand and put away his toothbrush and toothpaste. "Let's go eat before you faint from hunger."

"I'm not that bad."

He pulled her in for a hug and rubbed her back. "If your stomach rumbles any louder, it might bring down the walls."

The embrace gave her warm fuzzies, and for a moment, she lingered there, enjoying the strength of his arms and the solidness of his chest, but it was like hugging a best friend. She stepped back. "Thanks. You give nice hugs."

"Nice?" He grinned. "I'm glad to know you have no romantic

interest in me. It makes things easier."

She smacked his chest. "I know it's a blow to your ego, but you'll get over it."

"Hardy-har-har."

She cocked her head, looking up at him. "You don't have any romantic interest in me, either, and it's no blow to my ego." And it was true, but if they ended up staying in the past indefinitely, that could change. "Now, let's go eat."

He opened the door. "Aye, aye, captain."

They returned to the kitchen to find Kitty carrying a small vase of bright orange wood lily blooms to the dining room. A childhood memory of herself putting similar flowers in a china vase floated around in her head, and she smiled, remembering her parents and missing them like crazy.

"I'll be in the sitting room." JC left the kitchen. Under normal circumstances, he'd stay and help, but tonight he wanted a few minutes alone with TR to firm up their plans.

"What can I do?" Ensley asked Mrs. Sewall.

"The plates and cups are in the cupboard. Would you mind putting them on the table?"

"Not at all." She gathered the items and headed toward the dining room, returning after that task to carry the bread basket and kettle of coffee. "I'll send JC in to carry the venison." She set the bread and pot on the table and called to JC, "James Cullen, will you get the plate of venison off the stove and bring it in here?"

"Yes, ma'am." He hustled through the dining room and returned with the plate and a kitchen knife. "Do you want to carve?" JC asked Roosevelt, who had followed him into the room.

"I'll be happy to."

TR took the seat at the head of the table, picked up the knife, and cut a small portion of venison for Kitty, who sat on his left side. Mrs. Sewall brought a bowl of potatoes and a plate of butter to the table and sat next to Kitty. Ensley sat on Roosevelt's other side, and JC sat at the opposite end.

"What are you reading today, Mr. Roosevelt?" Ensley asked.

"*The Pickwick Papers.* Are you familiar with the book?"

"Certainly. I've read it a couple of times." She held out her plate for a portion of the venison. "You know that book catapulted the twenty-four-year-old author to immediate fame. *Voila,*" she said, flinging her hand.

"Few first novels have created as much excitement," TR said.

JC passed the potatoes, and she helped herself. "I'm captivated by the adventures of the poet Snod—"

"—grass," Roosevelt said, talking over her. "The lover Tupman, the sportsman Winkle, and that quintessentially English Quixote, Mr. Pickwick—"

"—and his cockney Sancho Panza, Sam Weller," she added eagerly, talking over him in turn.

She'd heard a funny story from the rangers about TR's habit of monopolizing conversations. According to them, when TR was president, a world-famous explorer went into his office while reporters hung around outside the door, hearing lots of talking and laughing. After an hour or so, the explorer emerged, and the reporters asked, "What did you say to the president?" The man replied, "I said, 'hello.'"

If Ensley wasn't careful, he'd monopolize all their other conversations as well. While she *was* more interested in what he had to stay than anything she could offer, one-sided discussions weren't discussions. They were monologues.

She patiently waited until everyone filled their plates, then forced herself to eat slowly and let her shrunken stomach dictate how much food she could handle. She bit into the venison and almost sighed, tasting the gamey, lean meat with hints of acorns, sage, and herbs.

As soon as she could speak without food in her mouth, she asked, "What's your opinion of Mr. Dickens?"

"When I read Dickens, Mrs. Fraser, I jump around to get the meaty nuggets of text that inspire me or force me to think critically about something." TR poured a cup of coffee from the kettle.

When he opened his mouth to speak, she jumped in and talked fast. "I've read just about everything he's written. I find it interesting that the women in his stories are pretty and childish, typical of the time, but not at all like the actual women in his life, who were neither domesticated nor compliant."

"The wise thing to do when reading Dickens is to skip the bosh and twaddle and vulgarity and untruth and get the benefit out of the rest."

"Bosh and twaddle?" Ensley asked with a laugh. "I've never heard that expression before." She buttered a piece of sourdough bread, and she did sigh when the sweet butter melted on her tongue.

"You're probably a Jane Austen fan." He set down his fork and wiped his mouth with his napkin.

She chewed slowly, thinking about how best to answer. "I became a 'Janeite'—an unrepentant, lifelong Austen fan—many years ago, but I bet you don't read her."

"It's a slog to read her novels. If I finish anything by Miss Austen, it's because I remind myself that duty performed is a rainbow to the soul." He slowly cut the meat on his plate. "Booklovers who are very close kin to me and whose tastes I know to be better than mine, read Miss Austen all the time—and they are very kind and never pity me in too offensive a manner for not reading her myself."

Ensley tsked. "You're missing out. For me, I appreciate readers whose tastes are different. It's those differences that give us a wide range of books to choose from. I also enjoy finding the little nuances in people's tastes. They remind me of how unique we all are. If we had the same taste in books, that would be boring." She paused a moment to let that idea sink in, then said, "Since we have different impressions of Miss Austen's writing, we can have a more robust discussion."

"If writers write from their own experience," TR said, "how is it that Miss Austen wrote so many masterpieces? She's a shadowy figure who seems to have spent most of her forty-one years being dragged along in the wake of other people's lives."

"But the realistic nature of her narratives was universally praised," Ensley said.

"And her characters had exciting lives," JC interjected. "Miss Austen's father was an orphan who worked his way out of poverty."

She knew JC read widely, but Jane Austen? "Her mother's relative was a duke, yet she was barely able to make ends meet."

"Her aunt Philadelphia's daughter lost her husband to the guillotine during the French Revolution," JC said.

"Her brother George had a disability," Ensley said.

"Her brother Henry bounced from one career to another until he became a clergyman," JC said.

"The brothers, Frank and George, joined the Navy and lived exciting and dangerous lives," Ensley added, laughing.

"You both know quite a bit about her," TR said.

She smiled. "I know my Jane Austen history, sir, but until now, I didn't know the extent of my husband's." JC was such an enigmatic person, and she found it difficult to imagine him relaxing shirtless on the beach with one of Austen's books. Either he was that confident about his masculinity, or he was trying to impress a woman, or he was gay. She immediately ruled out the second and third options. If any man was confident about his masculinity, it was James Cullen Montgomery Fraser.

"I'll bet Mr. Roosevelt enjoys Sir Walter Scott," JC said.

"I certainly do," TR said. "I've read his books over and over again!"

"Did you know Scott was one of Miss Austen's earliest and most prominent supporters?" JC said.

"Are you sure you have the correct Scott?"

Ensley picked up the conversation from there. "There's only one Sir Water Scott, sir, and Mr. Scott thought *Pride and Prejudice* was a finely written novel. He also thought Miss Austen had a talent for describing feelings and characters of ordinary life. And," she said with a sigh, "he thought it a great pity that a gifted writer died so early."

"I wasn't aware that Scott was a fan of Miss Austen's work," TR said. "That's very revealing."

"And even Henry Wadsworth Longfellow agreed that Austen's writings were a 'capital picture of real life,'" she added.

"But he complained that she explained too much," JC said.

Ensley gulped her coffee before asking, "Tell me this, Mr. Roosevelt. Future generations of readers will want to know. Do you dislike female authors, or is it just Miss Austen? I have a cousin who refuses to read female authors. Do you feel the same?"

"Not at all. At the risk of being deemed effeminate, as a child, I enjoyed Louisa May Alcott and the girls' stories—*Pussy Willow* and *A Summer in Leslie Goldthwaite's Life*, just as I worshipped *Little Men* and *Little Women* and *An Old-Fashioned Girl*."

"How about Fanny Fern, the nom de plume of Sara Payson Willis? She's still hugely popular, and her newspaper column was widely syndicated at the time. It was humorous and cutting and smart and accessible, and people gobbled it up." Fern was one of several nineteenth-century female authors whose books Ensley read in a class titled Novels by and about Women in America, 1820-70.

"Not her, but I enjoy Julia Ward Howe and Emily Dickinson. Have you read Milton? I find he's good for one mood and Pope for another, and then there's Whitman and Browning, Lowell and Tennison."

"From Milton to Pope, authors of the scribbling age."

"You are well-read, Mrs. Fraser. I have a little library here at the ranch. You'll find books by Parkman, Irving, Hawthorne, Cooper, Lowell, and a few Southern writers like George Washington Cable and Sherwood Bonner. The books are overflowing into other rooms. I'd enjoy continuing this discussion after dinner."

Ensley buttered another piece of bread. "That sounds delightful. I'll enjoy looking through your collection." She wanted to give herself a high five but didn't. All the pain and suffering she'd gone through to get here vanished into the delights of literature.

"And you, Mr. Fraser. What works of fiction do you enjoy other than Miss Austen?"

"I'm not as well-versed in popular fiction as my bride. I enjoy the Greek classics and Shakespeare, of course, but my power of concentration is so intense that the house can burn down around me when I read, and Ensley gets disturbed when I ignore her." He smiled and patted her hand. "I'm afraid you've opened a can of worms. As long as she's here, she'll want your opinion of every book in your library."

She'd be surprised if JC hadn't already read every book Roosevelt had here. There was rarely a book she read in college that he'd hadn't already read or had it on his TBR list. His goal right now was to direct TR's attention toward her, and she could kiss him for it.

"I can imagine nothing happier in life," Roosevelt said, "than an evening spent in the cozy little sitting room, before a bright fire of soft coal, my books all around me, and playing backgammon. Do you play, Mr. Fraser?"

"I do, although Ensley is a far better player."

"I see." TR sipped his coffee. "Normally, I wouldn't consider your request to join the roundup, Mrs. Fraser. It's a dangerous place for men, but if your husband doesn't object and you agree to follow orders, then I won't deny your request. But I insist on being the first person to read your manuscript."

And just like that, she was allowed to go on a roundup with Teddy Roosevelt.

23

Washington, D.C.—Elliott

D AVID FLEW THE helo into Washington Executive Airpark, and while he took care of filing a flight plan for the return trip, Tavis went to the rental car agency to pick up the car David reserved. After David finished, he took the wheel and drove them to James Cullen's house on 31ˢᵗ Street in Georgetown's East Village.

Elliott had been to James Cullen's housewarming, a half-dozen fundraisers, and a few small dinner parties, but nothing in the past twelve months. When he did see his son, it was usually at Mallory Plantation for a short overnight visit.

David slowly pulled up in front of the house and parked at the curb. "How do ye want to handle this? Except for a barking dog and his owner shushing him, it's quiet around here."

Elliott had given it quite a bit of thought. He didn't want to hurt Paul, but if he sensed Paul wasn't forthcoming, he would give David the nod. "If he resists, let's go in hard and let him know we're not screwing around. I'll knock on the front door. Tavis, ye take the rear and enter through the sunroom, and David, ye go to the guesthouse. There's probably an emergency exit, but I doubt Paul will try to evade us. At least not initially."

"How much force?" Tavis asked.

Elliott looked back over his shoulder at Tavis sitting in the back seat. "Don't maim him."

"He's a nice guy. He won't resist," Tavis said with a shrug.

Before they stormed the house, Elliott needed to bring Tavis into the circle and let him know Paul's and James Cullen's real occupations. Tavis should be fully informed before he walked into a situation that could turn hostile.

"Let's step outside. It hurts my neck to keep looking back at ye."

The three men stood on the sidewalk, facing the house. "Paul might be nice, Tavis, but he's also deadly," David said.

"He must be one hell of an actor, then. He's muscular but not threatening—unless I play chess with him."

"Don't underestimate him. He's a Cyber Operations Officer for the CIA," David said.

Tavis yanked off his MacKlenna Farm ball cap and slapped it against his thigh. "What the fuck! Are you shitting me?" A frown shifted to astonishment. "Hell, I never saw that coming."

Elliott clapped him on the shoulder. "I was just as shocked as ye are."

"Is JC in the Agency, too?"

"Aye. He's a Paramilitary Operations Officer."

Tavis flipped the cap back on top of his head. "I've been trained by the best. I shouldn't have missed that. How'd you figure it out?"

Elliott didn't flinch, even though he knew the answer would piss Tavis off. The lad was a borderline hothead. He'd try to take the news stoically, but he'd still be pissed as hell. "I hired yer old boss."

Tavis's blue eyes turned steely now, and they bored into Elliott's. It was the first time since the night of the museum heist in Gothenburg that Elliott had seen such an intense look.

"Why didn't you give me the assignment?" Tavis asked. "Now Northbridge believes you don't trust me."

"I explained I couldn't handle it in-house and that until I got answers, I didn't want anyone in the family to know what was going on. If it turned out differently, I didn't want it to color yer opinion of James Cullen."

"Goddamn it, Elliott!" He yanked his cap off and smacked it against his thigh again. "You're the Keeper of the Stones, and he's your son. One day either JC or Kevin will demand the Council's allegiance, and I'll give it. I'm here to protect you and the brooches. Don't do that to me again!" He growled the last part between his teeth, an angry flush flooding his face.

Elliott had miscalculated, and that rarely happened. But he couldn't leave Tavis with the impression that Elliott would advise him in the future under similar circumstances. "I won't make ye a promise I can't keep. Ye have to trust me, and if ye can't, then walk away."

"Of course I trust you, but I have a job to do, just like my ances-tors going back centuries. My job is to protect the brooches and the

Keeper. But let me be clear. If it comes to falling on my sword for you or the brooches, I'll choose the brooches every time."

"That's exactly where yer priorities should be," Elliott said.

The flush faded. "Good. That's settled." Tavis refocused, staring at the house. "Do you have a key, or are we breaking in?"

"I don't have a key or code to turn off the alarm," Elliott said. "I assume David does."

"Give me two minutes." David reached back in the car for his laptop, worked his magic, and within his two-minute window, he announced, "It's disarmed. If either James Cullen or Paul is in there, they'll get a signal that the system is disarmed and will be carrying, so be careful. We don't want anyone shot."

They separated, moving quickly in different directions like a fully-trained tactical unit. Elliott's mind churned with a variety of next steps, but each one depended on Paul's reaction.

He approached the front door with the breezy air tingling against his skin. He was coming up on eighty years old, yet he moved with the agility and mental acuity of a man half his age. He attributed his health to his diet and exercise regimen, but he knew it was much more than that. The power of the stones had rejuvenated him.

Meredith often accused him of swimming in the Fountain of Youth. That hadn't happened, but like Brad Pitt in *The Curious Case of Benjamin Button*, he was aging in reverse. Would he live long enough to collect all the stones—even Erik's?

Time would tell.

Elliott stood on the porch, glancing around for the camera he knew was there, but it was well hidden. James Cullen and Paul would be alerted that someone was on the porch, but that didn't matter now. He waited thirty seconds, enough time for someone to welcome him.

When no one came, Elliott opened the heavy oak door, entered the foyer, and walked toward the back of the house. Tavis went through the great room, and a minute later, David and Paul entered through the stainless steel and white kitchen, which looked too sanitized for Elliott's taste.

"Dr. Fraser," Paul said. "I just told David that JC's not here. He was supposed to call you and Ms. Montgomery. I guess he didn't."

"We need to talk. Let's go into his office." Elliott led the way and sat down in the desk chair but didn't pull it up to the desk. He casually straightened the knife-edge crease on his trousers. "Have a seat, please."

Paul showed no fear or alarm. He sat and crossed his legs while David propped a hip on the edge of the desk. Tavis positioned himself between Paul and the door. That didn't seem to bother Paul, either. Elliott sensed Paul had been expecting them, or at the very least, he wasn't surprised they were there.

So what's the game?

"Where's James Cullen?" Elliott asked.

"I don't know. He didn't tell me where he was going."

"If ye don't know where he is, what do ye know about his whereabouts?"

"He went on a reenactment of some sort. He asked me to find clothes from the late nineteenth century. I did, and this morning I dropped him off at the stables in Maryland. He was taking Mercury with him."

"Where was the reenactment?"

"He didn't say, and I didn't ask."

"Was he riding to the reenactment on horseback?" David asked.

"No, he had a friend with a horse trailer picking him up."

"JC has a horse trailer. Why didn't he take his?" Tavis asked.

Paul turned and looked at Tavis. "His trailer carries only one horse."

"We know James Cullen went to Cambridge," Elliott said. "How'd he get there?"

Paul swiveled in his chair, directing his answer to Elliott. "He flew up and back."

"Did he drive to the airport, or did ye take him?" David asked.

This time, Paul didn't take his gaze off Elliott. "I took him and picked him up."

"How many conversations did you have with JC between the time you picked him up from the airport until you dropped him off at the stables?" Tavis asked.

Paul shot his cuffs but didn't look back at Tavis. Instead, he looked at Elliott. "I had three brief conversations with JC after he returned from an overnight in Cambridge. I picked him up from the airport yesterday morning around ten o'clock and brought him here. We had another conversation later in the day before I went to the computer lab at Georgetown. Our last conversation was this morning when I took him to the stables."

"What'd he do when he got home yesterday?" Tavis asked.

Paul continued focusing his attention on Elliott. "He worked in here for a while and then went to the office. You should call Becky to find out if he said anything to her. I know he had several reports to write."

"Reports about what and to whom?" Elliott asked.

"He traveled to Asia for a client, and he had to write a summary of the trip, plus he was behind in writing status reports for other cases."

Elliott looked down and picked at his thumbnail.

So James Cullen went to Asia. Did he learn something about the brooches that scared him? Unlikely, but possible. Or maybe he found a brooch.

If his son had picked up information about the stones or the Illuminati, it made sense that he didn't want to involve the family. Hadn't Elliott just done the same thing?

He looked up, glared at Paul, then tempered it with a slight smile. "Lad, we don't have time to screw around. I have to find James Cullen now. I believe he's in serious trouble, and I believe ye know where he is. I'll give ye sixty seconds to tell us."

"Are you threatening me?" Paul asked.

"We'll do whatever we have to do," David said.

"James Cullen wouldn't like coming home to a blood-splattered office," Paul said in a cocky tone. Then he spread his arms, palms up, and raised his eyebrow in a gesture of openness. "Here's the deal—"

"No deal," David said in a growly voice.

Paul didn't react.

Elliott had never seen anyone seemingly so relaxed around David when he cloaked himself in his Major McBain attitude. If Paul was in the CIA, too, then he knew how to handle himself during interrogations.

Elliott's frustration pulsed through him, sharpening his movements when he shot to his feet and slapped both palms on top of the desk, "Where the hell is my son?"

The fierceness of Elliott's demand didn't seem to rattle Paul. He calmly said, "JC didn't tell me where he was going. If he wanted me to know, he would have. Otherwise, I don't press him for information. That's our arrangement."

At that moment, a memory pinged in Elliott's brain, and he recalled a morning years earlier when James Cullen discovered a Morse code message hidden in Kit's portrait. The painting hung in the Welcome Center at Montgomery Winery in Napa.

Finding that message sent the entire family on a dangerous rescue mission. Ever since then, James Cullen had challenged his family to find hidden messages in the simplest of things. A picture out of place, a clock set to the wrong time, bric-a-brac upside down. The clues had become more subtle and harder to find as he grew up, but he continued to leave at least one every time he came home for a visit.

Wherever he is, he would have left clues to his whereabouts. I'm sure of it.

"Since James Cullen was a teenager, he's left clues for us in the placement of items or bric-a-brac, or by turning an item upside down or sideways. If I'm going to find my son, I have to know what clues he left behind. The clues aren't for ye, Paul. They're for me."

Paul's eyebrow lifted along with one side of his mouth. "I found five. Do you mind if I stand?"

Elliott gestured his permission.

Paul walked over to the bookcase. "When I returned from the stables, I came in here to see if JC left me any instructions to take care of business while he was gone. I noticed four things out of place."

"I thought ye said five," David said.

"I'll get to that." Paul pulled out a book. "This book about Theodore Roosevelt was only slightly out of alignment with the others. All the books in this bookcase, as you can see, are the same distance from the edge. Anytime JC shelves a book, he's very particular about keeping the edges straight. I tease him about his OCD."

"He gets that from his mother," Elliott said. "Although I've never heard either one of them admit it."

David pshawed.

Paul pushed the book back into alignment. "The second thing I noticed was an out-of-place photograph." He stepped over to the credenza. "JC has tons of friends, but his closest buddy is George Williams." Paul picked up a picture of George and Ensley. "Until this morning, this photograph was on JC's desk."

"For how long? A week, a month, a year?" Elliott asked.

"As long as I've been around," Paul said.

"Other than George and Ensley's photograph and a book about Theodore Roosevelt, was there anything else?" Elliott asked.

Paul crossed the room to the coffee table. "The third item is this book about MacKlenna Farm. It's always been here. But it's never been left open before."

"What's on the page?" David asked.

Paul didn't even look at the book. "A chapter on the history of the farm and the long line of Sean MacKlennas." Paul then stepped over to a shorter bookcase on the opposite side of the room. "The fourth item is this train." He pointed to the top shelf. "It's turned in the opposite direction."

"What direction is that?" Elliott asked.

"South," David said.

"Teddy Roosevelt, a photograph of George and Ensley Williams, MacKlenna Farm table book, and a train facing south…" Elliott let his statement trail off, waiting for Paul to volunteer more. When he didn't, Elliott asked. "Ye mentioned five items. What's the last one?"

"Open the top drawer in the middle. There's a copy of a page from *The Washington Post* about the Theodore Roosevelt Presidential Library in the Badlands. Underneath the news article is JC's cell phone."

Elliott opened the drawer, removed the newspaper article, and scanned it before passing it to David. Then he asked Paul, "Why'd ye leave James Cullen before his ride arrived?"

"He told me to leave. And I learned early on not to argue with him. Sometimes I can make a suggestion, and he'll listen, but that's rare. He sets his mind on doing a task a certain way, and there's no changing it."

Paul had James Cullen nailed. "Did ye see James Cullen leave the stables?" Elliott asked.

There was zero hesitation in Paul's voice when he said, "No."

"Did ye find any other clues ye're not telling us about?" David asked.

"No," Paul said.

"Where was the reenactment? And what were they reenacting?" Tavis asked.

"I don't know. I didn't ask, and JC didn't volunteer the information."

"Did James Cullen send ye a text or call ye to do a task before he returned from Cambridge?" David asked.

"He wanted me to get a hundred thousand dollars in gold nuggets and find him some late-nineteenth-century clothing."

"And ye did both?" David asked.

"I did."

Elliott walked over to the bookcase and removed the book Paul had pulled out. It was David McCullough's *Mornings on Horseback: The Story of an Extraordinary Family, a Vanished Way of Life, and the Unique Child Who Became Theodore Roosevelt.* Elliott made a note of the table of contents then returned the book to its place on the shelf, aligning it carefully.

"Did James Cullen ask ye to come back and pick him up in a day or two?"

"No. I assumed he'd call."

"But he left his phone in the drawer."

Paul chuckled. "If JC wants to make a call, he'll find a phone."

"Ye've got that right." Elliott walked over to the coffee table and picked up the MacKlenna Farm table book. On the two facing pages were pictures of Thomas MacKlenna I and II, and Sean MacKlenna I, II, III, IV, and V. Kit had painted the portraits of Thomas MacKlenna II and all the Seans. Elliott closed the book. "We're done here."

"I'm sorry I don't have more information, but I'll call you as soon as I hear from JC."

"I'd appreciate that." Elliott sent a hand signal to David before walking toward the door.

On his way toward the door, David struck like a rattler, grabbing Paul by the throat. "If ye lied to us, I'll find out. Got it?" David released Paul, giving him a shove.

Paul straightened, holding his throat and coughing. "Yeah, I got it."

There was no fear in Paul's expression or body language. Either James Cullen had assured Paul that David wouldn't hurt him, or Paul had ice in his veins. Either way, Elliott found that very disturbing.

Elliott, David, and Tavis left the house and returned to the car. As they drove off, Elliott said, "He didn't tell us everything he knows."

"What's he hiding?" David asked.

Tavis clicked on his seatbelt. "If he lied about leaving JC at the stables and watched him disappear into the fog, he wouldn't mention it to us. He might believe it's classified information."

"If JC went back for Ensley, how'd he travel?"

"He must have found her brooch, assuming hers has the same properties as Penny's," David said.

"Either that or James Cullen went to a reenactment, and he'll be back in a few days."

"I didn't know JC was interested in them," Tavis said.

"He went on a few with Charlotte and Braham, but I didn't know he was still participating. But that should be easy enough to verify." Elliott uncapped his bottle of water and took a big gulp.

"There's another possibility. JC found a brooch while in Asia and is traveling with one of his own."

"Then where's Ensley's?"

"She has it with her."

"Then she'd be in the same position as the others. She'd just have to wait for it to warm up again."

"JC wouldn't have used an untried brooch," David said. "If he found one in Asia, he would have locked it up."

"Where?" Elliott asked.

"A home safe?" David said.

"No. If James Cullen found a brooch, he would have put it with the others at Mallory Plantation. He wouldn't have locked it up in a home safe and left town," Elliott said. "So we have to assume that he either used Ensley's, or he's gone to a reenactment."

"I found a website that lists the top thirty-five battle reenactments this year," Tavis said, "and the Battle of New Market Reenactment is this weekend in New Market, Virginia. Maybe he's doing a weekend thing with a girl."

"Not James Cullen," Elliott said. "His friend Ensley is in trouble. I know in my gut that my son has traveled back in time to rescue her."

"So, what's the plan?" Tavis asked.

David stopped at a stoplight, checked for messages, sent a text, then put his phone away. "Let's return to the plantation, call a meeting, and tell the family what we know. We'll brainstorm the clues, and Kenzie will find the connection."

"I hope it's that easy," Elliott said. "This adventure has the potential of being more dangerous than the last one."

"We can assume all adventures going forward will be more dangerous than the last," David said. "There's more at stake."

"I'd bet my Apple stock that James Cullen stirred up a hornet's nest when he was in Asia." Elliott looked back at Tavis. "Can ye contact Erik?"

"I can go to the Shetland Islands and try, but unless it's a threat to you or the stones, he won't answer."

"Let's see what happens when the family meets." Elliott had screwed up by allowing James Cullen to distance himself from the family. In hindsight, Elliott should have found a way to entice his son back into the fold. But he and Meredith agreed to give James Cullen as much autonomy as he wanted. And now he might be in over his head.

24

Mallory Plantation, VA—Elliott

ELLIOTT SENT A WhatsApp message to all the adults in the family, and everyone responded except for Austin. If the lad didn't snap out of it, accept his bone-crushing disappointment, and find purpose in his life again, he'd end up throwing everything away on drugs and what-might-have-been.

And Elliott understood that. He'd been there, done that, and wallowed hopelessly in emotional and physical pain. If not for Meredith, his alcohol and pain medication abuse would eventually have killed him.

Elliott excused all family members who weren't at Mallory Plantation from virtually attending the meeting, promising a group call later to give them an update. The smaller size would make the get-together more manageable.

At seven o'clock that night, he entered Braham's recently remodeled green conference room. Instead of creating a more contemporary space, Braham and his designer went in the opposite direction. The room now resembled President Lincoln's executive office or "the shop" at the White House, but with twenty-first-century lighting and electronics.

The space was somber and humbling. And Elliott was counting on the room's ambiance to help calm all the participants.

He was the first one there. Before taking his customary seat at the head of the "council table," he poured a cup of coffee, and it wasn't decaffeinated, either. Trainer Ted would jump his ass for drinking caffeine at night, but Elliott could use the kick. The six couples coming to the meeting—JL and Kevin, Pops and Maria, Kenzie and David, Rick and Penny, Kit and Cullen, Charlotte and

Braham—were a tough crowd, and he'd have to play the Keeper card to keep them in line.

The couples, plus Meredith, slowly gathered around the table. He'd already brought Meredith up to speed within minutes of his return from DC. If he ever dared to blindside her at a meeting, he might as well pack his bags and go back to Kentucky—alone.

Just as Elliott was about to close the door, Tavis rushed in, making a beeline for the coffee carafe on the credenza.

"Where's Remy?" Elliott asked.

"He was detained in Richmond and said to go ahead and start. He'll be here in about ten minutes." Tavis carried his coffee to the empty chair next to David and placed his cell phone next to his mug.

Elliott knocked on the table to quiet the side conversations. "Penny, do ye want to tell the others about yer call this morning?"

"Sure, boss," she said. "First, let me start by saying I'm sorry I didn't share this with anyone except Rick earlier, but Elliott asked me to keep it to myself."

"She knows payback is hell." Rick squeezed her neck, and when she turned to face him, he kissed her.

Everything Elliott had hoped for this couple had come true. They worked together, and their joint efforts had resulted in numerous awards for Montgomery Winery: Global Winner: Architecture & Landscapes; Regional Winner: Arts & Culture; Regional Winner: Innovative Wine Tourism Experience; Regional Winner: Sustainable Wine Tourism Practices, and the list went on, including the annual international wine awards.

Besides, Meredith was pleased, and anything that pleased his bride pleased him.

Rick and Penny's three-year-old son, Jean, was probably the best equestrian out of all the children ten and under, and he was a happy, loving child. Instead of calling Elliott "Grandpa" like all the others, Jean called him boss, which always tickled Elliott.

While wee Jean had never met his namesake, Jean Lafitte, he carried himself with a swagger that befitted the famous pirate. It was cute at three, but at ten, he'd probably get his attitude adjusted by one of his O'Grady cousins. Rick was balancing the swagger by encouraging the lad's musical talents—voice, piano, violin, and guitar. The preteen girls in the family already thought Jean was a heartthrob. But they were a fickle bunch.

Penny pushed away from the table and stood. "I can't sit. It's too uncomfortable."

"Take yer time, lass. If it's more comfortable, walk around."

"I'm okay." She pressed her fists into her lower back. "This morning, I received a call from a detective in Cambridge, Massachusetts. He was investigating the disappearance of a young woman. When he entered information about her disappearance into a national database, my name popped up as disappearing under similar circumstances."

"Let me guess," JL said in a sarcastic tone. "The smell of peat?"

Penny nodded. "Yep."

"Did he give you any information about the woman?" Kit asked.

"Yep, her name," Penny said. "She's Ensley Williams. JC's friend."

"Jesus!" JL said. "I met her when she and her cousin came here for the Fourth of July celebration. She was in graduate school at the time, I think. She's beautiful, and, man, can she ride. Did you see her race JC around the training track?"

"I saw it," Cullen said. "Reminded me of Kit racing that cavalry officer at Fort Laramie."

Kit laughed. "You mean the time you almost killed me with the steam coming out of your ears?"

Braham howled. "That was the best race I'd ever seen. I bet the fort commander a five-dollar gold piece based on Cullen's opinion of Stormy. I couldn't figure out what the hell was wrong with Cullen. It turned out he was in love." Braham laughed again. "It was a great race."

"And you were so sweet to me." Kit threw a side-eye at her husband. "But Cullen was in an awful mood."

"In my defense," Cullen said, "that wasn't long after I had to lasso ye in the Kansas River to keep ye from drowning."

"Let's not go there." Kit turned her attention back to the group. "Anyway, Ensley had JC beat at the three-quarter pole, but he overtook her. Then, coming down the stretch"—Kit shot her arm out in front of her—"I thought she'd beat him, but it was a photo finish. After that, I thought for sure something was going on between them. Guess not."

Elliott knocked on the tabletop. "If we can return to Ensley's disappearance, I'll pick up the story. When Penny told me about the phone call, I tried to reach James Cullen, but the call went straight to voice mail. My next call was to George Williams.

"According to George, James Cullen was in Cambridge Thursday night for a Friday morning meeting. They met by accident at the Porcellian Club, and George invited James Cullen to go to dinner with him and Ensley.

"They took an Uber from the club to George's family home where Ensley was staying. When they arrived, she was gone, and a peat smell was stinking up the place. James Cullen searched the upstairs and found evidence that she'd showered and changed clothes. George searched downstairs. When he didn't find her, George called the police to report a missing person, and two detectives came over to interview them. George said James Cullen went back to DC Friday morning, promising to return after a short business trip."

"Have you talked to Paul?" JL asked. "Maybe he heard from JC."

"David, Tavis, and I flew to DC this morning to look for James Cullen. We didn't find him, but we talked to Paul. According to him, he picked James Cullen up at the airport Friday morning after running errands for him."

"Anything particular?" JL asked.

Elliott shot JL an impatient look. "I'm getting there."

"Well, get there faster, will you?" JL said.

"James Cullen asked Paul to find two sets of men's nineteenth-century clothing and purchase a hundred thousand dollars in gold nuggets. Paul also said he drove James Cullen out to the stables in Maryland this morning, where he keeps Mercury."

"I thought JC bought a Morgan for pleasure riding around Maryland's rolling hills and forests," JL said.

Elliott glowered at her, reacting to her tone more than the comment. She rarely used her former NYPD detective voice anymore, but tonight, she was in rare form, and worrying about James Cullen had Elliott on a short fuse.

"The horse wasn't sound," Elliott said.

JL's eyebrows hiked. "Oh. I didn't hear that part."

Braham laughed. "JC was embarrassed because he didn't notice the horse was almost blind in one eye. He believes he knows as much as an equine vet."

And that was Elliott's fault. He'd started out teaching James Cullen everything he knew about horses, and James Cullen had a good feel for the animals, but that wasn't enough. If he wanted the knowledge of an equine vet, he had to go to veterinary school, and James Cullen had turned up his nose at that suggestion.

David sent Elliott a hand signal to get back to the topic of the meeting. "Let's get back to what Paul told us about James Cullen. He told Paul a friend was picking him up to go to a reenactment but didn't mention which one it was. Paul left James Cullen at the stables and returned home, where he found five items that were out of place."

"Like what?" JL asked.

Elliott snapped. "Jenny Lynn O'Grady Fraser, yer impatience is getting on my last, best nerve."

Kevin laughed. "You better watch out, sweetheart. Dad used your full name. That's a good gauge of how much trouble you're in."

She rolled her eyes at her husband. "What's he gonna do? Ground me?" Then she looked at Elliott, grumbling, "Please do. I need a vacation."

Elliott came close to snapping at her again, but Meredith shot him a loaded look. JL was the daughter she never had, and Meredith was overly protective. Then he remembered that Austin had released his surgeon to discuss surgery options on his foot with his mother. The impromptu call must not have been good news.

He and JL were both worried parents. Elliott should cut her some slack. "If ye need a vacation, Meredith and I will watch the kids. Ye and Kevin can go to the condo at the beach."

"Thanks for the offer. I'll take you up on it next week."

Meredith shot him another look that said to drop it. And he did.

"Back to Paul..." Elliott said. "The first item Paul found in James Cullen's office that appeared out of place was a picture of George and Ensley. James Cullen had moved the photograph from his desk to the credenza."

"What's so weird about that?"

Elliott reined in his first reaction, which was to yell at JL, and instead went for an understanding tone. "As long as Paul has worked for James Cullen, the picture's always been on his desk."

"Okay. Got it."

"The second was a book about Teddy Roosevelt, which was out of alignment with the other books in the bookcase. The third was the train engine I gave James Cullen when he was a kid. He keeps it on a shelf in his office. It had been flipped and was facing a different direction. And before ye ask, it was pointing south.

"The fourth was the MacKlenna Farm table book left open to the history of the farm. And the fifth was a *Washington Post* article about the development of the Theodore Roosevelt Presidential Library in Medora, North Dakota."

"Ensley's from North Dakota," JL said.

Kenzie folded her arms and rested them on the table, leaning forward. "I admit I had a few minutes of advance notice of this situation, and I haven't had time to form any impressions, but I do have two questions. Do you believe JC went back for Ensley? And if you do, how'd he do it? Did he break into the cleanroom, steal one of the other brooches from the safe, and vamoose?"

"If he did, he's turned into Houdini," Braham said. "No one can get into the cleanroom without alerts going off. David has tried to override the system, and I've hired others to break in. So far, no one has managed it, but I'm not satisfied with that. I continue to upgrade and test the system. There's too much to lose if anyone gets in. I can assure ye that no one has been in that room since Elliott and I went down there Tuesday afternoon to inventory the brooches. We do it randomly to be sure they haven't been disturbed. There was nothing out of order."

"But you haven't been down there today," Meredith said. "So how can you be sure no one has been in there since the last time you checked?"

Braham picked up a remote, pointed it at the big-screen TV, and clicked. He cycled through several menus until he came to a prompt requesting a password. He entered the required information and cycled through several more screens until the door to the cleanroom slid open. He lifted the remote toward his lips and said, "Show the last person who entered the room."

A video of Braham and Elliott standing in front of the facial recognition scanner popped up. Everyone at the table watched the two men enter the cleanroom. The time stamp indicated it was Tuesday night at nine-fifteen.

"So if our brooches are safe, how'd JC go after Ensley?" Kenzie asked. When no one volunteered an explanation, she continued, "I see three possibilities. JC hasn't gone after her. Or he used Ensley's brooch. Or he found one during his recent trip to Asia."

"For those of ye who haven't heard, JC was on a business trip in Asia last week. Ye know now. If he located a brooch there, he probably didn't have time to bring it to the plantation before he left town again," Elliott said.

"My money," Kenzie said, "is on Ensley's brooch. You mentioned that JC went upstairs to search for her and found evidence that she'd showered and changed clothes. If she had a brooch that reacted the same way as Penny's, then it heated up, and she threw it on the floor."

"If JC found it," JL said, "he would assume, based on Penny's experience, that it got too hot to hold. So he'd plan for that, wear a glove or something."

"If he has Ensley's brooch, then James Cullen can come home," Meredith said. "But how will we know without going back to find him?"

"We?" Elliott said.

"Of course. I'll insist on going," Meredith said. "But maybe the brooch didn't heat up. Perhaps it sparked like the topaz did when Penny reconnected it to the pendant. It could have sent a shock through his hand."

"And he'd have dropped it," David said.

Elliott gave David a sharp look and signaled what he was thinking. If James Cullen dropped it, Elliott knew in his gut that Paul had picked it up. David acknowledged the signal, then picked up his phone and sent a text message to his airport contact.

"If JC went back for Ensley, where did he go, and to what year?" JL asked.

Kenzie opened her laptop, and her fingers flew across the keyboard. "Was the Roosevelt book about his entire life? Or did it cover a particular time, like the adventures of the Rough Riders, or when TR was police commissioner, or governor of New York, or president?"

"It was David McCullough's *Mornings on Horseback*," Tavis said. David and Elliott both turned and glared at him. He shrugged. "I notice things."

"We're looking for something that connects Roosevelt to Ensley, and I think I found it. During the winter of 1884-1885, Roosevelt and his partners built the Elkhorn Ranch on the bank of the Little Missouri River and started a cattle operation there," Kenzie said. "The ranch is about thirty miles from Medora, and, according to this article, he was in the Badlands off and on from 1884 until he sold the ranch two years later."

"Ensley told me she grew up on a ranch in North Dakota and

was a finalist in the Women's Rodeo World Championship. If she went back to the Old West and stayed on a ranch, she'd fit right in," JL said. "I remember thinking at the time that I liked her a lot. She was sweet and loaded with personality, and later, when she was with Lance and Blane, she seemed to take a genuine interest in my kids, and they noticed because they talked about her later."

"What'd they say?" Kenzie asked.

"They were talking about polo, and she knew the top US players—men and women. They thought she was cool."

"I know all the players, too," Penny said. "Lance and Blane don't think I'm so cool!"

Kenzie laughed. "But Robbie, Henry, and Churchill think you are, and they're older and harder to impress." She then turned her attention to Tavis. "What about the guardian of Ensley's brooch? What's his role in this?"

"If Ensley traveled without her brooch, the guardian would have stayed to protect it, and Erik would have watched over her. If JC traveled with it, the guardian would have gone, too."

"Wait a minute. If the guardians have brooches, then that increases the number to more than twenty-five." JL gave Tavis a stern look. "Do you or did you have a brooch of your own?"

Tavis glanced at Elliott, and Elliott heard his unasked question. "Go ahead, lad. Tell them what ye know."

"Erik handles"—Tavis made air quotes—"transportation. He knows when a brooch is activated, and he responds accordingly."

"So Erik goes and gets the guardian of the activated brooch?" JL asked.

"My job was pretty easy."

"Easy?" Kit asked. "My brooch was in the same box with the amber, amethyst, and topaz. You're too young to have gone back with me, but whoever did, didn't help me much. I almost drowned in the Kansas River and was attacked by four men."

"My grandfather almost quit when you jumped into the Kansas River to save that child," Tavis said.

Kit's jaw dropped. "Seriously? What about when those men attacked us? Where was he then?"

"He didn't say, but Kit, we aren't allowed to interfere unless the brooch holder is facing imminent danger or possible death. My grandfather said Cullen had your rescue under control, and you were well equipped to handle the attackers."

"If he had interfered," she said testily, "I might have been able to save Cullen. But never mind, that's water under the bridge."

"Why do ye suppose James Cullen left clues?" Braham asked.

"Insurance," David offered. "He was covering his bases in case he had problems with the brooch. He wanted us to know where he went."

"If JC threw the brooch away, what will he do in the past?" Kenzie asked. "He can't be sure the family will come after him within days or weeks. I mean, look at the Fontenots. They were in the past for almost a decade."

"He'll require plenty of money. Where will he get it?" Cullen asked.

There was silence for a moment, and then Braham laughed out loud. "He'll go after my gold at MacKlenna Farm! That's why the train faced south—toward the farm, which is south of Medora."

"What years are we talking about?" Meredith asked.

"From 1884 until 1886," Kenzie said.

"Sean MacKlenna, Kit's uncle, died Christmas Eve 1885. James Cullen always wanted to go back and meet him," Meredith said.

Braham stepped over to a framed original 1869 US map hanging on the wall. He pointed to the Dakotas then drew a roundabout line from there to Kentucky. "He could take a train from Medora to Bismarck, Fargo, Minneapolis, Milwaukee, Chicago, Cincinnati, Midway. Visit the farm, break into my casket, take a bag of gold, and then he and Ensley could go anywhere in the world."

"It's been two decades since David and I took that train out of Cincinnati en route to Washington to rescue Jack," Charlotte said. "It was hot and dusty."

David gave her a sly grin. "But ye never complained."

"I didn't want you to think I was a sissy."

Kenzie laughed. "You? Never! You broke into a Confederate hospital and whisked Braham to safety to save his life. Plus, I bet you didn't bat an eye when General Sheridan captured you. Nothin' sissy about Dr. Charlotte Mallory."

"Thank you, Kenzie. But you had it a lot worse than I did."

She looked at Tavis. "Yeah, so where was *my* guardian?"

"I don't know who he was, but I guess he saved you from receiving worse treatment when you were locked up in the London Cage, or maybe he was one of the men David recruited to help with the extraction."

David pursed his lips. "I'll be damned. I bet the private investigator I hired, Mr. Teasdel, was yer guardian. That son of a bitch."

A quiet fell over the room, probably because everyone was reliving their moments in hell. And there wasn't a person sitting around the table who hadn't experienced at least one.

Remy entered the room and sat on the sofa across from the conference table, engrossed in something on his phone. Elliott nodded at his bodyguard, and Remy gave him a subtle "Okay" sign.

"We'll use a two-prong approach," David said. "Half the rescue team will go to Medora. The other half will go to MacKlenna Farm."

"I want to go to the farm to visit my uncle before he dies," Kit said.

"Meredith and I will go with ye and Cullen," Elliott said. "If James Cullen goes to MacKlenna Farm, I want to be there."

"I'll go to the Dakotas," Tavis said.

"I'd like to go with Tavis," Remy said.

"If ye're going with Tavis, then I'll call Emily to see if she'd like to go. She can handle medical emergencies and maybe see her parents. They might like to come to Kentucky."

"What a wonderful idea, Elliott," Kit said. "Our son, Thomas, could bring them to the farm. It would be wonderful to see him, and maybe the girls will come from the east coast. We could have a reunion."

"Oh," Charlotte groaned. "Remember what happened last time?"

"Don't remind me," Elliott said.

"Tavis, take Austin with you," Pops said, and every head jerked in his direction, including Elliott's.

Tavis shook his head. "He'll refuse to go, and I'm not sure I'd blame him. It's not the best place for him right now."

"According to this article about Roosevelt, he went on a round-up in the spring of 1885. I agree with Tavis. Austin can't manage that," Kenzie said.

"The hell he can't," Pops said. "I don't care if you have to kidnap him. He has to get out of that gym and face a challenge that has nothing to do with basketball."

"Don't push him, Pops," JL said. "I talked to his surgeon this afternoon. They had hoped to fix his foot drop, but the odds aren't in his favor, and he won't take the risk. He's more bummed now than he was already. An adventure like what David is proposing could break him."

"Bullshit. You've indulged your son for too long. It's time he deals with his shit."

"Pops! We almost lost him in that accident."

"And if you don't take action right now, you might lose him permanently."

JL stared at Rick. "He's your nephew, goddamn it. Tell Pops it's a horrible idea."

"He's getting worse, JL. We've all visited the ranch to talk to him," Rick said, "and he's not listening to any of us. Connor goes out there two or three times a week. A few days ago, Austin told Connor he planned to change the code to the security gate if Connor didn't stop bothering him."

"What'd Connor say?" Elliott asked.

"He laughed and reminded Austin he was VP of Global Security, and if he couldn't get past a locked gate, then he should be fired."

"Great, just great," JL said. "That shows you how messed up he is. He loves you guys. He'd rather spend time with Rick, Connor, Shane, and Jeff than anyone else in the world."

"He's messed up," Pops said. "That's why I want him to go with Tavis."

"But, Pops, if Austin goes cold turkey off pain meds, it could get ugly. No, it *will* get ugly. He'll need to be near a hospital," JL pleaded. "This is a horrible idea. I don't like it, and I vote a big, fat, hell no." She looked from Rick to Pops and back again. "Don't do this. Kidnap him and take him to a treatment facility, but sticking him in 1885 might just kill him."

"Jenny Lynn," Pops said, "you know how much I love Austin and how much your mother loved him, too, but he's on a destructive path, and it's time we did something. I believe this trip is exactly what he needs."

David knocked on the table to get everyone's attention. "If this is what ye want for Austin, it's time for me to share his secret that I swore never to mention, but if he's going on this adventure, there's something ye should know. It could make matters worse."

"I don't see how that's possible," Pops said.

"This might set him off more than being kidnapped."

"Oh, God, David. You've got everybody's attention now. So what's so bad?" JL asked.

"Austin wrote a book about his accident and recovery. I gave him the name of an agent who might shop the manuscript for him. The agent received rejections from a handful of editors. One editor, in particular, wrote the agent back and said the author's situation was unresolved. Until he decided what he wanted to do with his life, the book would never have a purpose."

"I'm sorry it didn't work out for the lad," Elliott said.

"That's not the point," David said.

"Shit!" Kenzie groaned. "Say it ain't so." When David didn't say anything, she said, "The editor was Ensley, and Austin was probably more pissed by what she said than her rejection."

JL said, "If you kidnap him and drop him in the Dakotas to rescue her, all hell will break loose, and he'll never forgive any of us."

"No reason to panic," Tavis said. "We won't tell him. We'll only mention JC."

"Elliott," Meredith said. "You and Pops want to use tough love. I get that. But this isn't the way to go about it." Then to Kevin, she said, "You haven't said anything. He's your stepson. What do you think?"

Kevin took JL's hand and kissed the back of it. "There are enough decision-makers at this table—mother, uncle, grandfather—that I don't need to weigh in unless you want me to make the final decision. In that case, I'll choose what I believe is best for Austin and his mother."

"I don't know what decision ye'd make, but ye and JL had best be on the same page. Austin loves ye, and I'd never want ye to do anything that might destroy the trust ye built up with the lad. And I don't want JL, Rick, or Pops to feel the sting of his anger, either."

Elliott paused and sipped from the mug in front of him. The tension in the room was higher than the cathedral ceiling. He had to make a decision. Now.

"Austin joined this family when his mother married Kevin," Elliott continued. "He was seventeen, and now he's thirty-two. That's almost half his life. Since he considers himself part of the MacKlenna Clan, then I'm ultimately responsible for his welfare."

Elliott sat back in his chair and clasped his hands across his abdomen. "This is the way it's going to be. Tavis and Remy, I want ye two to go to Colorado and invite Austin to go with ye to rescue Ensley and James Cullen. If he refuses, use whatever force is necessary to get him into the fog. If he cusses ye out and wants to kill someone, tell him to take it up with me when he gets back."

Elliott pushed away from the table. "This meeting is adjourned." Then he left the room.

"Well, I'll be damned," Meredith said, hurrying to catch up with him. "Never saw that one coming."

25

Elkhorn Ranch (1885)—Ensley

ENSLEY SAT IN one of the rocking chairs on the veranda of TR's ranch house, gazing sleepily at the fast-moving Little Missouri River while sipping coffee and watching the sunrise bloom over the Badlands. Golden streams of light stretched outward into the vibrant blue sky, and she chuckled at the raspy chatter of a black-billed magpie, sitting on the fence post like he owned the place.

Who are you talking to, little birdie? I can hear you.

It was all so extraordinary.

But this wasn't her first insanely gorgeous Dakota morning. Not by a long shot. And she never failed to appreciate its invitation to enjoy a brand-new day, even when she'd been struggling alone with only her little knife and birchbark bowls.

She rocked while she looked for patterns, shapes, and faces in the weird-looking buttes across the river, their sharp outlines slowly growing more distinct in the multicolored sunrise.

The hairs on the back of her neck suddenly twitched, and her spine snapped to attention. She jerked to find JC gazing at her from the corner of the veranda.

She rubbed her neck to calm her nerves, wondering why she was jumpy now when she had plenty of food to eat, a roof over her head, and a buffalo robe to keep her warm.

"You look beautiful," JC said in a soulful tone. "There's a glow about you this morning that I haven't seen since your freshman year."

"Oh, yeah?"

"Yeah. An unfamiliar world stretched out in front of you, and you were in awe. Is that how you feel now, Ensley MacAndrew

Williams?"

She'd been hoping the caffeine would wake her up, but JC's comment did a fine job all by itself. "You forgot the Fraser part."

"That's just borrowed for convenience. It's not who you are."

Or who I'll ever be.

She stopped rocking and strolled over to the edge of the porch, where she leaned against the railing, sipping the fortifying brew. "As far as the 'beautiful' comment, I'm not sure what to say."

"'Thank you' will do."

The melancholy in his tone was something she'd never heard from him before, and she wasn't sure what caused it.

"Thank you. That was nice. I don't think you've ever commented on my looks before."

He looked away, toward the river. After a thoughtful pause, he looked at her again, squinting in the sunlight. "Are you sure? I remember one Christmas when you, George, and I were invited to a holiday party in Boston. You came down the stairs in a royal blue gown, and I nearly dropped to my knees. Surely I complimented you then."

"Not that I recall. And a girl remembers stuff like that." In fact, at the time, it hurt her feelings. She'd dressed with him in mind, and he didn't even seem to notice. If he'd been about to drop to his knees, he hid it successfully behind a champagne flute.

She took another sip of coffee, letting go of that old rejection. "How late did you and TR stay up after I went to bed?"

"We're still up, I'm afraid."

"You never went to sleep?"

"Nope. And I haven't stayed up all night talking about esoteric shit since I smoked pot in college."

"Oh, wow! I don't think I have, either, but I'm glad I didn't try to hang in there with you guys. As soon as I climbed under that buffalo robe, I was a goner. What'd you talk about other than literature and hunting?"

"He talked. I listened, and occasionally he stopped to take a breath, which gave me a chance to slide in there with a question."

Her ears perked. "And?"

JC chuckled. "I asked for his thoughts about Abraham Lincoln."

She was now fully awake. "Really? What'd he say?"

"He talked about the first time he saw the late president."

"How old was TR?"

"Six. TR was at his grandfather's Union Square mansion, hanging out the window while Lincoln's remains were paraded down the boulevard to the sound of pipes and muffled drums."

"That would make quite an impression on a little boy."

"I think TR was already well aware of Lincoln," JC said. "According to TR, the Lincolns befriended and went to church with TR's father during the Civil War. He said last night that Lincoln was his greatest hero and meant more to him than any other man in public life."

JC glanced around, then leaned closer, lowering his voice. "As president, TR will keep Lincoln's portrait in his office. In times of trouble, he'll look at it and do what he believes Lincoln would have done."

She dumped the dregs in her coffee cup on the ground and set the cup on the railing. "I bet you know tidbits like that about every president."

"I do, except for the likes of Andrew Johnson, James Buchanan, Warren Harding, Franklin Pierce, and a couple of others who failed to safeguard America during a crisis or tainted the office with scandal or incompetence," JC said. "I just finished reading a book on the presidents, so the abuses are fresh in my mind right now, but TR made the protection of human welfare his highest priority."

"Probably thanks to Lincoln's influence."

"I think you're right, but the biggest surprise was that TR isn't a big Shakespeare fan."

"Oh, but he is—or he will be," Ensley said. "When he's in his fifties and travels around Africa, he'll have a collection of Shakespeare with him. He'll write Henry Cabot Lodge and tell him that only a couple of Shakespeare's plays ever appealed to him, but suddenly the sealed book is open, and he's reading all the plays over and over again."

"Was that in the Roosevelt manuscript you read?" JC asked.

"Actually, no. It's from a discussion in a literature class about Bardolatry and famous Bardolators."

JC squinted again. "That's a new one for me. I suppose a Bardolator is someone who idolizes Shakespeare. Hmmm." He paused for a moment. "Wait till I tell Uncle Cullen. He's the one who got me started reading the Bard when I was in high school. I don't think he knows about Bardolatry. But since you do, this is your chance to introduce TR to The Great Bard, and maybe the sealed book will open much sooner."

She gave him a level look. "That's messing with history."

"Is it?" His brows lifted. "Is causing something to occur sooner rather than later altering history?"

"If I alter the past to change the future based on what I believe is best for the rest of the literary world—then, yes, of course. I don't see how you can ask that."

"It's like his passion for conservation that we talked about the other day. You'd just be helping to open his eyes sooner than they would have been. Reading Shakespeare will open him up to so many new literary discussions, in-jokes, and puns. He's losing years of enjoyment."

"Maybe," she said. "I'm still not sold."

"After I discovered the plays were full of universal themes like love and war and fart jokes, I devoured them. Almost all of Shakespeare's comedies explore gender, complex relationships, and cross-dressing women. And *Othello* and *The Merchant of Venice* address privilege and racism. How can you not lead him to a shorter path that will take him directly to a place he'll eventually reach without interference?"

"I'll think about it." She pushed off the railing. "So what started this discussion of Shakespeare?"

He smiled. "I was thinking about Juliet when I saw you standing there."

"Oh, you are such a romantic."

He stepped up on the porch and pulled her into his arms for a hug, holding her tight against him. "I won't see you for three weeks."

She stepped out of his embrace, put her hand flat on his chest, and gazed up at him. "It sounds like you're second-guessing your decision to go to Kentucky."

"I'm second-guessing my decision to leave you here."

"I was alone for two weeks before you found me. I'm from North Dakota and grew up on a ranch. I know all about cattle and horses. My parents let me explore the Badlands by myself or with a girlfriend. If they weren't afraid for me, then you don't have to be, either."

"But you had a phone—"

"Yes, but there were dead spots where only a smoke signal could summon help."

"You're not making this easier for me."

"You said it yourself. Our rescue party could arrive any day and haul our asses out of here. They won't care if you want to see your family or that I want to spend time with TR."

She patted his chest again. "The brooch god dealt us a hand, and we have to play it out. The only way to ensure we both get what we want is to split up. You're a big boy and can take care of yourself, but that doesn't mean I won't worry about you, too. You could get into a gunfight, and I'd never find out what happened to you."

"I promise I won't get suckered into a gunfight."

She reached around his waist to pat the Glock at the back of his hip. "If you believed that, you wouldn't have packed three guns and a knife." He was an expert shot, but that wouldn't matter if he came up against unethical and immoral men with something to prove. "Okay, I admit I'm a little anxious, too, but I'd rather not have you around when I start complaining about being saddle sore or sleeping on the hard, cold ground."

"That did it." A smile teased the corners of his eyes. "I'm not going now. I'd much rather hear you complain about the conditions on the trail, so I can say I told you so."

"You know I don't require watching over, right? And listening to me complain would get old real soon, even if you get to say, 'I told you so.' And you'd get grumpy because you can't see your family. So there. And besides, roundups are inherently dangerous for inexperienced cowpokes."

He squeezed her in a tight hug and rested his chin on the top of her head. "You didn't have to say that. And I'm an experienced rider."

"Maybe, but moving cows isn't easy. So what if you worry but don't obsess?" She squeezed him back, then let go. "I want you to have a great time, and I'll see you in three weeks."

"This is your last chance. If you want me to stay, ask now."

Something came over her, maybe a hint of insecurity, and she wanted to tell him not to go, but she resisted and instead asked, "What time does the train leave Medora?"

"TR said it should arrive late tonight. I should have enough time to buy a ticket and grab dinner."

She looked over his shoulder to see Mercury tied to the hitching rail. "Did TR ask to buy Mercury?"

"Not yet. He hasn't had time to inspect Mercury closely, so I'm getting out of here before he does. He's been so hospitable that I'd hate to be rude and tell him no." JC looked toward the door. "I better leave. Oh, I left a package of body wipes, toothpaste, toothbrush, and lotion for you in the bedroom under the bear rug. I didn't know where else to hide them."

"That was sweet. Thank you."

"I also left a leather pouch of gold nuggets. Buy whatever you need."

"A new shirt would be nice, maybe a skirt. But I don't know when I'll get to a town. Mrs. Sewall said she has a dress I can wear while I wash my clothes. Then I'll feel like a new woman."

"If anything comes up, send a telegram, and if you need me, I'll hurry right back."

"I'll be okay, and if I'm close to a telegraph office, I'll send you a telegram to let you know how I'm doing. I'd text every day if I could."

"I've never been indecisive, but this is driving me nuts with all the second-guessing."

"I'll be with Teddy Roosevelt. I mean, my gosh. I can't be much safer than that."

JC lowered his head and shook it while he scratched the back of his neck. "Just because we know what happens to him doesn't protect you, sweetheart."

"Don't call me sweetheart."

"Okay, darlin'."

She rolled her eyes. JC was trying to pick a fight, and it was time to send him on his way.

The door opened, and TR came out onto the porch. "Are you ready to leave, Mr. Fraser?"

"I am, as long as you haven't changed your mind about Mrs. Fraser joining your roundup."

TR laughed. "I'm looking forward to more literature discussions while I discover if Mrs. Fraser is a backgammon player with an abundance of luck or a player well-versed in strategy."

"I've accepted the fact," she said with a sigh, "that I'm going to lose games, matches, tournaments, and even money, to players who aren't as skilled as I am."

TR threw back his head and laughed even louder. "Now I *am* intrigued, madam."

JC stepped off the porch and tightened the cinch on Mercury's saddle. TR walked around the horse, patting his withers, flank, shoulders, chest, forehead.

"He's a beautiful horse, Mr. Fraser. Weight's good, the coat is slick and shiny, and legs are straight and free of blemishes, eyes are bright and clear, healthy breath sounds, no visible injuries or scars." He stepped back and put his hands on his hips. "I'll offer you a hundred and fifty dollars for him and will write a check this very minute."

JC coughed behind his fist. "Thank you for the offer, sir, but I must turn it down."

"Nonsense. How could you turn down a hundred and fifty dollars?"

"It's easy when you have something irreplaceable. I helped birth Mercury and managed most of his training. I've worked hard to get him this sound and healthy."

"And I'll reward you for your investment. I'll go as high as one hundred seventy-five dollars."

JC shook his head. "Sorry, sir. But Mercury's stud fee is normally a thousand dollars. However, I am willing to waive the thousand dollars, and he can service your broodmare for free. Consider it my thanks for your generous hospitality."

"Hmm," TR said. "I'll have to find a broodmare with the necessary performance, pedigree, soundness, and conformation that will compliment your horse. That might require a trip to London."

"Mercury's dam came from Ireland. You could look there as well."

"We'll have plenty of time to talk further, but in the meantime, I'll send inquiries to associates in New York. There may be a suitable broodmare closer to home."

JC tugged Mercury's reins off the hitching rail and wrapped them around the saddle horn. "Well, I'm going now."

Ensley was determined not to cry, but she did. After their week together, it'd be lonely without JC around, even though she'd have TR for company.

"Be careful." JC used his handkerchief to wipe away the tears streaking down her face. "Don't cry. We'll be okay."

Then, before she realized what he was doing, he kissed her, and it riveted her in place. The kiss wasn't coy or hungry but soft and natural, and he took his time. "Remember your promise."

Ensley was too shell-shocked for a moment to answer. After she took a breath…or two…or three…she said, "I will. And you'll be careful, too, right?"

Most rich kids she'd met were oblivious to their good fortune—born on third base, believing they'd hit a triple—but not JC. He was brilliant, sensitive, and caring and didn't take anything for granted. He was honestly worried about her, and she was concerned about him.

"Always." JC slipped the handkerchief into her hand before mounting up. Then with a flick of his finger to the tip of his hat, he galloped off.

Turn around, JC. Wave. Give me a sign that you'll be all right.

But he didn't. He rode off the ranch without ever looking back.

If I look back and see you standing there, looking forlorn, I'll turn around. Be careful, Ens.

I will. Promise.

26

Washington, D.C.—Elliott

E LLIOTT WAS WAITING in James Cullen's home office, sitting in the desk chair, visualizing him working on the computer, reading, talking on the phone.

Where are ye, son? If anything happens to ye, I won't survive the loss.

So much was at stake right now. It was nine o'clock in the evening, and Elliott and David were in Washington for the second time that day.

Elliott sensed danger in the air and turmoil in the universe. After three years of relative calm, James Cullen had stirred up the evil. What the hell had he done?

Whatever happened to him in Asia wasn't intentional. Elliott knew that. But he had to find his son quickly before a force too large to contain, much too powerful to ignore, and far too extreme to fight in traditional ways, was set loose on the clan, and maybe even humanity.

An exaggeration? Hell, no. It was real, and it was coming—again. They contained it the last time. Could they do it again?

They would sure as hell try.

Elliott licked his lips and tried to calm a sudden upwelling of fear. Paul had information about James Cullen, and whatever it took to get it, short of killing him, Elliott would do. However, the idea of torturing Paul made Elliott physically sick. But he could do it. He had no other choice.

As Keeper and clan chieftain, Elliott was responsible for protecting his family and the brooches. Erik and the other Council members had committed atrocities to protect the secrets and keep the brooches' vast powers hidden from all who would use them for ill. And Elliott could do no less.

The outside door opened, and footsteps echoed through the kitchen and down the hallway. David wasn't trying to mask his passing through the house. He entered the office and stopped, hands on his hips. "The motherfucker's gone. We should have taken him earlier."

Elliott pushed to his feet and slammed his fist on the desk. "Shit! So he packed up and moved out? Son of a bitch. Guess he knew we'd be back."

David paced across the room toward the wet bar. "No. There's a peat smell in the guesthouse. And before ye ask, he didn't throw the brooch. I searched for it. Either he was more prepared than JC for the stone's heat or electrical charge, or the brooch responded differently."

Elliott dropped his head and shook it back and forth as terror raged through him. "So James Cullen told Paul about the brooches. Why?"

David picked up a carafe, uncorked it, and sniffed. "Whisky. Want some?"

"Aye." Elliott's insides curled into the kind of fear that even whisky wouldn't soothe.

David filled two shot glasses, handed one to Elliott, and they raised their drinks. *"Slàinte."* David threw back the contents then poured another, but Elliott waved off a refill.

"Earlier today, Paul told us he took JC to the stables and left him there," David said. "He must have returned, watched JC disappear, and picked up the brooch."

Elliott collapsed in the chair and rolled the crystal glass between his palms. The fear now crawled all over him, freezing the sweat on his back, choking the curses in his throat. *Oh, Jesus. Why now?*

"If Paul returned to the stables, then he went back specifically to spy on James Cullen. The question then becomes, who was he spying for? Himself? Because he wanted to protect James Cullen? The Company? Because spying on my son was part of his job? Or the Illuminati, who possibly planted him here to infiltrate the clan?"

"If the Illuminati planted Paul here," David said, "then they're closer than we thought."

An enormous claw of fear punctured Elliott's stomach and tightened it hard. With a desperate but clear voice, he said, "We're leaving tonight. We have to find James Cullen before Paul does."

"Ye can go tonight with Meredith, Kit, and Cullen, but Emily can't leave until tomorrow. And Tavis and Remy need time to plan and prepare for how they're going to kidnap Austin."

"They should already have that figured out. Clothes, guns, and everything else they need they can find at the plantation. They can fly up tonight, saddle three horses, knock out Austin, and head through the fog before midnight. Call Tavis. Tell him it's go time."

Elliott turned out the lights, David reset the alarm, and they hurried out the door. "If Emily can't leave now, Braham and Charlotte can bring her later," Elliott said.

"If they can't, I'll take her."

Elliott opened the front passenger door and climbed into the rental car. "It's more important for ye to stay and watch over the family. We can't both be gone right now. With ye, Braham, and Daniel Grant protecting the clan, the family will be safe."

David started the car and pulled away from the curb. "Ye better call Charlotte and Braham and explain the situation."

Elliott clicked on Charlotte's phone number, and she answered on the second ring. "Hi, Elliott."

"I'm in DC, but it's become obvious that we have to go back now to find James Cullen. Emily said she couldn't leave until tomorrow, but we can't wait. Will ye bring her later?"

"I just got off the phone with her. She was able to rearrange her schedule, and she's on her way here. What time are you leaving?"

"As soon as we get everyone packed up. David arranged for a pilot to fly us home, so we'll land at the plantation in about forty-five minutes. I'll text Braham to turn on the landing lights, and I'll call Meredith to let her know. She can advise Kit and Cullen. Will ye pack a medical bag for Emily?"

"Already done, and it's waiting in the cleanroom with the rest of the gear."

"Thanks, dear." Elliott disconnected and called Meredith. "Paul wasn't at the house."

"I can't say I'm disappointed," Meredith's tone of voice spoke to her wariness. "I want to know where my son is, but I didn't want you to hurt Paul."

What Elliott had to tell her next wouldn't ease her mind at all. "David smelled peat in the guesthouse."

"So Paul's gone after JC."

"Looks like it. We'll be back at the plantation before midnight, and I want to leave as soon as Emily arrives."

"Have you talked to Kit?"

"No, will ye tell her?"

"Sure. We'll meet you in the cleanroom. Be careful."

Elliott pocketed his phone and leaned back against the headrest. "Ye've met Sean MacKlenna. Will he understand the danger we're facing?"

David drove them across the Potomac by way of the Francis Scott Key Memorial Bridge. "With what Kit told him when she was there in 1852, and what he later learned from Braham, Charlotte, and me, he knows there are more than two brooches, but I doubt he can appreciate the danger involved. Ye'll get on well with him, though. Ye both love the clan, the farm, horses, and Kit."

How well would they get on if Elliott brought a shitload of trouble to Sean's door? About as well as they would if Sean did the same to him.

27

Mallory Plantation, VA—Elliott

ELLIOTT ENTERED THE cleanroom to find Meredith, Kit, and Emily already dressed in period-correct costumes. Trousers, a waistcoat, and a high-button coat similar to what he wore when he went back to Kit's estate in 1881 lay folded on the stainless steel table, along with a shirt, tie, and boots.

Cullen was already wearing a similar suit and was sitting on a stool, drinking coffee from a mug with a Mallory Plantation logo. He looked as natural in nineteenth-century clothing as he did in khakis and a MacCorp polo shirt.

The younger generation, or second-gens, called the khakis and polo shirt a farm uniform. They refused to wear it unless they worked at the barns during the sales or racing season.

Elliott hugged Emily and kissed her cheeks. "Thanks for rearranging yer schedule, lass. I hope ye get to visit with yer family."

"I wouldn't miss this for anything, Grandpa, even if it meant termination from my residency program."

"God forbid! If that were a possibility, I wouldn't have invited ye. Ye've worked too hard to lose it." He then kissed Meredith. "Thanks for getting everyone ready. Did ye pack my journal? I made notes of things I want to talk to Sean about."

"It's there on the table with your clothes. Look under the jacket."

He found it and flipped it open. On the first page was a list of items to check off before he could leave town or leave the century. "Did ye leave our wills and financial arrangements where Kenzie can find them?"

"I took care of everything on your list."

He set the journal aside and spun her around, admiring her feminine silhouette. The dark green and gold silk rustled around her legs. "Ye look amazing. Is this new? I don't think I've seen it before."

"It's one of the dresses Olivia and Amber bought in Denver in 1878. When they heard Kit, Emily, and I were going back to the 1880s, they suggested we check their racks of clothes down here, plus we have the wardrobes from our trip back to 1881 Napa. But I prefer this ensemble." Meredith twirled again. "It makes a better first-impression outfit, don't you think."

"Aye, I do." Elliott picked the coat up off the table and held it against his chest. "So I'm wearing Rick or Connor's Denver clothes, and Cullen is wearing his own?"

"No, you're wearing the same suit you wore back to visit Kit."

"The trip from hell. It's all blurred in my mind."

"I've tried to forget it, too."

"This suit is dated. I should have a first-impression suit." He walked over to the racks of clothes and pushed hangers back and forth, looking for something else to wear that didn't remind him of that godawful trip.

"Elliott," Meredith said, gently guiding him back to the clothes on the table. "Nobody will pay any attention to what you're wearing. Men's clothing didn't change much. So hurry up and dress. We've got to get moving."

Grumbling, Elliott took the clothes into the bathroom. "Mark my words, Sean MacKlenna will notice my lapels are out of style."

Elliott didn't give a flying shit what he wore. He was more concerned about James Cullen than his damn clothes. But complaining about them gave him a chance to vent without addressing the real issue. Meredith was wise to his antics and knew what he was doing, and rushing him was her way of expressing her anxiety. Of course, none of that made any sense, but after living together for almost three decades, it worked for them.

He returned to find the others were arranging trunks in a circle. "Is one of those trunks mine?" he asked.

Meredith pointed. "That's yours over there. Check to see if you want to add anything else."

"Did ye pack it?"

"I packed the clothes. Braham packed the weapons."

"And the gold," Braham added. "Spend it wisely. Kevin is already running a tab on this adventure."

"We haven't spent anything yet," Elliott said.

"Two round-trip helicopter flights from here to DC," Braham said.

"Kevin probably said we should have driven," Elliott said. "He spends more money a year on lotions and potions and hairstylists than I spent on that damn helicopter."

"Everybody knows that, but someone has to count pennies," Braham said. "Ye won't do it, and neither will I. He's including Emily's flight and the corporate jet's cost to fly Tavis, Remy, JL, and Kevin to Colorado. He'll apportion the expenses."

"Why'd JL and Kevin go? Not that I'm complaining. I'd much rather share the expenses with a larger group. But when was that decision made?" Elliott asked.

"Tonight. She wants to make sure the guys don't hurt Austin," Braham said.

"That doesn't bode well for Tavis and Remy. She'll throw her seniority around, and they'll all get into a fight. I'm surprised Pops didn't go." Elliott checked his watch. "Maybe we should wait until they go through the fog, just in case there's a problem."

"If there is, we'll handle it," Braham said. "But knowing Tavis and Remy, once they subdue Austin, they'll get the hell out of there fast."

"As long as JL doesn't forewarn him," Elliott grumbled again. "Her maternal instincts might get in the way of doing what she knows in her heart is necessary."

"Let's hope not," Meredith said, giving Elliott a slight push toward his trunk. "If you need to add anything, do it now so we can be on our way. JL's not the only mother who wants to protect her son, but we have to find James Cullen first."

"Since Braham added the two things I need, I'm ready."

Braham handed Elliott the diamond brooch. "I gave the lads the amethyst since it belonged to Austin's family. It worked fine for Kevin. With Austin in the traveling party, they should take that one."

"Makes sense." Elliott and Braham carried the last trunk over to the circle and placed it between Meredith's and Kit's trunks. Elliott turned to Kit. "Why is it ye have two trunks, lass?"

"Sketching and painting supplies. I promised Sophia I would sketch everything I see."

"Wouldn't it be easier to use yer phone and just take pictures?"

"Not this time," Kit said. "Sophia's giving me painting lessons, and she wants to see which objects I find most compelling in a scene. She wants my eye, not a camera lens, to describe what I see."

"You're already an excellent painter," Meredith said. "What's she teaching you?"

"Right now, some of the techniques she learned from Leonardo."

"Leonardo?" Elliott laughed. "Ye're calling him by his first name, too."

Kit scrunched her face. "So what?" She gave him a one-shoulder shrug. "I tried calling him da Vinci, but it sounded like we were talking about two different people."

"Ye're a good painter. Ye don't need lessons."

"Of course I do. Just because I'm old doesn't mean I can't learn something new. I'll never be on par with Sophia, and my paintings will never sell for hundreds of thousands of dollars, but I'm satisfied with making a few hundred."

Elliott hopped over his trunk and helped Meredith squeeze inside the circle. "I'll give ye a thousand for that Oregon Trail picture hanging in yer bedroom."

Kit's head dropped with a chuckle, and then she glanced up. "You don't stop, do you?"

He gave her a playful raised-eyebrow look. "Stop what?"

"You've always hated that picture. It reminds you of how I snuck off without you and spent months on the Oregon Trail."

"Damn it, Kit," Cullen said. "Are ye trying to pick a fight? Ye know ye never win with him."

The playfulness disappeared, and Elliott set his jaw. "Ye left me at home worrying about ye."

"You were in so much pain you could barely walk. It's time to stop blaming me for something you weren't able to do."

"Ye put me on the no-code list, and off ye went," Elliott answered with a wave of his hand.

Kit opened her mouth to respond, but Cullen jumped in. "I'm looking forward to seeing Sean again. So why don't we go—*now!*"

The pressure doors swished open, and Charlotte rushed in. "Oh, thank goodness I arrived in time." She stopped to take a breath. "I was checking the ancestor book for information on Sean and Lyle Ann MacKlenna. He died of a heart attack on Christmas Eve 1885—at age eighty—and she followed a year later."

"I read that, too," Meredith said.

"But, here's the thing," Charlotte said, getting a cup of water from the faucet at the coffee bar. "If you can convince him to come to the future for a medical exam, we could probably extend his life as we did with Emily, Kit, and Cullen. We won't know until he has a full battery of tests, but we could give him more time than he would have without intervention. You three are the best people to talk to him about treatment. Tell him he can return to his time whenever he wants."

"If Sean talks to these three, he'll believe that once he leaves his time, he'll never go home again," Elliott said.

"We're going home," Cullen said. "One of these days."

Kit glanced at her husband and smiled, and his smile was just as bittersweet. They had a silent conversation, and Elliott wondered if they had made end-of-life decisions about dying at home—at Montgomery Winery—in their own time.

Kit would tell him when it was time for him to know.

"You're traveling with the diamond brooch, right?" Charlotte asked.

Elliott nodded. "And what about Emily and her medication?"

"David engineered a refrigeration system with solar panels and batteries to keep my medicine cold," Emily said. "It's all in the trunk I'm sitting on."

"We'll see that it's set up immediately," Elliott said.

"Travel safely," Charlotte said. "Braham and I will be waiting right here. It'll be lovely to see Sean and Lyle Ann again." Charlotte crossed the room and stood next to her husband, far enough away that they wouldn't get sucked up in the fog. "Good luck!"

Elliott locked arms with Meredith on one side, Kit on the other. Next to her was Cullen, and then Emily completed the circle. Elliott opened the diamond brooch. "Let's focus on James Cullen and MacKlenna Farm. Ready?"

Everyone nodded. Then Elliott recited the chant:

"Chan ann le tìm no àite a bhios sinn a' tomhais an' gaol ach 's ann le neart anama."

Elliott held tightly to the women on each side, preparing for the whirlwind ride through the cosmos, and wondering what he would do when he found his son.

Kick the shit out of him? Or hug him like there was no tomorrow?

28

MacKlenna Ranch, CO—Tavis

TAVIS DROVE THE rental car up to the gate-code box at MacKlenna Ranch and put the car in Park. "I hope the code works." He punched in the numbers, but the gate didn't open. "Shit. Austin changed it." Tavis drummed his fingers on the steering wheel, reviewing his options. "I can ram through it or shoot it open."

"If you tear up the car and gate, repairs not covered by insurance are on you," Kevin said from the back seat. "And you'll have to guard the broken gate until the security company makes the repairs. Plus, you'll have to deal with the insurance company to fix the rental."

"What the hell? That's what your staff does."

"I don't have any staff here," Kevin said. "And I'll be damned if I'm going to stand guard over a busted gate because you didn't come prepared."

"Prepared? Really, Kevin. That's the best you've got? We were wheels up thirty minutes after we got the green light. I barely had time to get the gear together."

JL sat in the front passenger seat, thumbing on her cell phone. "Stop it, both of you. It's late, and we're all tired."

"I would have gotten a couple of hours of sleep if you hadn't spent the entire flight going over every detail of this mission when we already knew what we had to do," Tavis groused.

"Austin's my son. And I don't want him hurt," she snapped.

He's going to get hurt, JL. There's no way around it.

Tavis opened his door. He'd have to jump the gate to get in.

JL grabbed his arm. "Hold your damn horses. I'll get you the code." Her thumbs flew over the tiny keyboard, her gaze fixed on the screen. She stopped, then thumbed again, waited, then continued texting. After a minute or two that seemed more like an hour, she said, "Key in these numbers: 040426030."

"What's wrong with just five numbers? Who the hell can remember a string of unrelated numbers like 0-4-0-4-2-6-0-3-0?"

"You," Remy said, drumming on the back of Tavis's headrest. *Ba-dum-ching!* "Let's get this shit show on the road. I'm playing a gig next weekend to fill in for a drummer who has to be at his sister's wedding."

"*Has* to be?" JL asked.

"Yeah, she's having a baby next month and finally agreed to marry the baby's father."

"What the hell was she holding out for?" JL asked.

"Doan know. Doan care. I'm just happy my sticks are getting some action."

"Drumming is your passion. It has your total focus and energy," Kevin said. "You get lost when you play. Why are you doing this crap when it's not what you want to do?"

"Because I'll never be Art Blakey or Max Roach, but I can fly around the world, stay in five-star hotels, eat the best shrimp étouffée, jambalaya, and gumbo in New Awlins, and date beautiful, sexy women."

"Been there," Kevin said.

"At least Remy has more discriminating taste than you did when you were traveling with Elliott full time," JL said.

"I was just waiting for you to come into my life, sweetheart."

"Yeah, right. You weren't any more ready to settle down when we met than I was." Then JL punched Tavis in the arm. "You just going to sit there and stare at your phone or open the frigging gate?"

"Frigging? What kind of word is that?"

"A nice word. The kids are mimicking me. I'm trying not to cuss."

"That won't last long." Tavis rolled down the window, plugged in the code, and the gate swung open. "Shit! How the hell did you do that? What software program did you use?"

"It's so simple. I'm surprised you don't know."

"Stop giving me shit, JL. Tell me how ya did it."

Kevin grumble-laughed. "Good luck. We've been together for fifteen years, and I still can't get her to give up information."

Tavis put the car in gear. "If it's so fucking simple—"

She held up her phone, showing an open text message from David with the code.

"Son of a bitch." Tavis drove ahead, then looked in the rearview mirror and watched the gate automatically swing shut. "Why the hell didn't McBain tell me he had the code?"

"I guess he wanted me to feel empowered."

"Empowered for what?"

"You're here to kidnap my kid. A locked gate would slow you down and give me a chance to warn Austin."

"But you didn't warn him."

"Not yet. The night's still young."

"Bullshit." Tavis followed the road toward the house. "This family is so fucked up."

Remy drummed the headrest again and laughed. "And you fit right in."

JL's phone dinged with a text message. "Connor's at the barn. He says to stop there first. He's getting the horses ready."

"Hope he picked out a sweet mare for me," Remy said.

Tavis followed the road to the barn. "If he does, you better watch out. If Ferdiad isn't back from the vet clinic, I'm taking Monte Carlo. He's one mean stallion, and I betcha he'll be all over your sweet mare."

"Aw, shit," Remy said. "My mare ain't gonna be your bitch. I'll get me one of those horses who's had his nuts cut."

JL turned up her nose. "Remy, do you have to be so crass?"

Tavis laughed as he pulled up next to a white Ford F150 Super-Crew Cab King Ranch pickup truck and cut the engine. "The *ba-dum-ching* guy doesn't know any other way."

"I can be just as suave and debonair as you, Stuart. So get off my case. Who got the girl the last time we went out?"

"You did, just like always. I called it quits before midnight and Ubered home. You were still buying drinks for a table full of Kappa Kappa Gamma chicks from the University of Kentucky while milking your football stats for all you were worth. I'm not even gonna ask when or how you got home."

"Good, because I doan kiss and tell."

Tavis popped the tailgate and left the key fob in the cup holder. "You're full of shit. Everybody has figured you out. We've got your number."

"Best number ever—eighty," Remy said. "And they retired my

jersey."

Tavis rolled his eyes. "They just told you that. They really threw it in the dumpster."

Remy slammed his door. "Why're you giving me shit tonight? What's pissed you off?"

"Not a damn thing," Tavis said. "But if you slept with that cute blonde with the huge blue eyes, I'm never going out for drinks with you again."

Remy slumped against the vehicle, roaring with laughter. "So…that's"—snort—"what this"—snicker, cough—"is about." He kept laughing. "That blonde left ten minutes after you did. She gave me her number and asked me to give it to you."

Tavis held out his hand, and Remy slapped it. "What? What do you want?"

"The fucking phone number."

"I didn't bring it. It's on my dresser back at the house."

"You're a lying piece of shit."

"Even if I gave it to you, you'd never call her."

JL hopped out of the car, pushed her way between Tavis and Remy, and shoved them apart. "Stop it. We don't have time for this shit. Remy doesn't have the girl's phone number. He's only trying to piss you off because it's so easy to get a rise out of you. Both sets of McBain twins are better behaved than you two. I hope you don't act like this around Teddy Roosevelt."

"Oh, come on, JL. If you can't recognize pre-operation jitters, then you've been out of the businesses way too long." Tavis grabbed Remy around the neck and gave him a loud, smacking kiss on the top of his head. "We're bros. Don't ever doubt it."

Remy flipped his hand over his hair. "Doan expect me to reciprocate."

"Reciprocate? You don't even know what that means. I always buy the beer, and you always say, 'I'll get the tab next time.' In three years, you've never paid once."

"Why should I? You always take care of it," Remy said.

"For the third time, stop it!" JL snapped. "Will you please get your heads out of your asses and focus on what we're doing here?"

JL was right. Goofing off was a great stress reliever, but it was time to get his mind in the game. It was showtime. Tavis checked out the Ford and noticed it had temporary tags. "Is that Connor's new ride?"

"Looks like the picture Olivia sent," JL said. "Connor finally realized driving a Mercedes Coupe when you live on a ranch was pretty dumb."

"Man, he's always been a quick learner," Kevin said. "It only took him—what? Six years? Isn't that how long he's lived in Colorado?"

Connor waved from the barn's end door that opened into the center aisle. "Did you bring the saddles?"

Tavis walked around to the open tailgate. "We brought two. Elliott said there's one here he used last year during the Leadville Boom Days celebration."

"I got it out already. Do you want to saddle the horses now or wait until you bring Austin down?"

"Better do it now and get the gear loaded. Once we knock Austin out, we'll be cutting it close to get back here before he wakes up."

Tavis carried the saddles inside the barn and dropped them on top of a short stack of hay bales. "Remy, get the gear."

JL hugged her brother. "Have you seen Austin tonight?"

"I called to check on him," Connor said. "He told me he's watching a movie and to leave him the hell alone. If I'd been close enough, I would have smacked the crap out of him. If he only knew how many nights I comforted him when he was an infant or a sick toddler or lost a game in elementary school. And now he acts like an asshole."

"You were an awesome big brother to both of us."

Connor gave her an are-you-serious look that must have something to do with Austin's birth parents' identity—JL and an NBA superstar—which made him Connor's nephew, not his brother. Austin discovered the truth several years ago, and it almost destroyed the family.

"By the way, thanks for *not* sending the code," JL snarked.

Connor picked up one of the saddles and grabbed a horse blanket off a shelf. "Austin changes it daily, JL, just for kicks. He likes to taunt us. Something he learned from you. He knows we can get in. He thinks slowing us down will frustrate us enough that we'll leave him alone. He forgets we were cops and spent hours surveilling creeps."

"My son's not a creep."

"I didn't say he was."

"So you figure out the new code every time you come out here?"

"Hell, no. Kenzie's the master codebreaker. She breaks Austin's code every morning with her coffee instead of doing crossword puzzles." Connor looked back at Kevin. "Hey, Kev. Grab that other saddle and a blanket. The horses are back here."

Kevin grabbed both. "I'm right behind you."

"Which brooch are you traveling with?" Connor asked.

"They're taking ours," JL said.

"The amethyst? It's like the diamond and will return us to the moment we leave," Tavis said.

"It better," Remy said. "I gotta be back by the weekend. Damn it." He kicked the hay bale, his pointed-toe boot leaving a dent. "This is my chance to get a regular gig in Lexington. If I doan show up, my name will go on the 'Doan Call' list. That sucks."

"The amethyst will get you back." Connor slung the saddle over the top rung of one of the stalls. "How d'you plan to get Austin down here?"

"I doubt he'll follow us voluntarily. I might have to use a stun gun." She pulled a stun gun out of a holster hidden by her blue jean jacket. "This is on me. I'll do it."

"JL, don't do this," Tavis said. "There's a chance he won't talk to any of us when this is over."

"That's a chance I have to take."

"Are you sure?"

"Stop asking me. I wouldn't do this if it weren't necessary. Pops took a chance on me when he agreed to raise Austin as his son. If Pops believes this will help Austin get his act together, I have to trust my dad. He loves Austin and only wants what's best for him. So"—she took a deep breath and blew it out—"I'll do it."

Tavis rubbed the back of his neck. "I don't like changing plans at this stage of the mission, but if that's the way you want to play it, I'll go along. But, JL"—he shook his head—"if you freeze, Remy and I will take him down."

She lifted her hand holding the taser, then seemed to forget where it was going and dropped it at her side. "I won't freeze."

Tavis was convinced she would. So he mentally prepared for what that meant for him—and Austin.

"That's a little extreme. Don't you think?" Connor asked.

"It's either a stun gun or Tavis will knock him out."

"If you use the stun gun to get the desired effect, you'll have to hold the device against him for more than three seconds. Austin is twice your size. He won't let that happen."

"I know how to use it." The muscle in JL's jaw ticked. "Remy and Tavis will have to hold him down. We'll play it by ear."

"Okay. Say you stun him. Then what? How are you going to get him down here?" Connor asked. "Roll him down the damn hill?"

"Tavis and I both deadlift over three hundred pounds. It'll only take one of us to handle Austin," Remy said.

"You're full of shit," Connor said. "You've seen him on the basketball court. He's a six-five dominator with legs from here to California. You can't deadlift him. He's dropped a few pounds, but he's still close to two-twenty. If you put him in a fireman's hold, his feet will drag the ground."

Remy gave Connor a wry grin. "Then we'll just put him on a dolly and wheel him out."

Connor rolled his eyes. "I'll just bring the horses up there."

"If Austin sees 'em, he'll be suspicious," Tavis said. "That won't work."

"Then take my truck and put him in the back," Connor said. "He knows my truck. It won't surprise him."

"That'll work. Where are the keys?" Tavis asked.

Connor dug into his pocket and handed Tavis the key fob. "Leave it in the cup holder."

"Get the horses ready. We'll be back in under ten minutes." Tavis clapped Remy's shoulder. "Let's roll."

Tavis drove the truck up to the house with JL sitting quietly beside him. Remy rode in the bed, air drumming to a tune no one else could hear.

They entered the house through the basement door. At least Austin hadn't changed the code on that keypad. They moved stealthily through the finished basement, passing the rec room and bar, en suite bedrooms, and a home office on their way to the theater.

They entered the back of a red-walled room with twenty well-upholstered red velvet seats. Four big armchairs with ottomans formed the front row where Austin sat, watching a shoot-em-up with the sound blaring.

JL signaled for them to stand guard at the rear while she went down to the front. That didn't suit Tavis. Instead, he followed her down the right side aisle and signaled Remy to do the same on the left.

As she neared the front row, Austin said, "You don't have to sneak in, JL. I saw you come through the gate." In the seat beside him was a laptop receiving constant video feeds from security cameras placed all over the ranch, including the barn. He pointed over his shoulder. "The stormtroopers don't have to sneak in, either. So, what do you want?"

"We're worried about you, Austin," JL said. "You've cut everybody out of your life. We're here to help you."

"In the middle of the night. Get real, JL. Nobody gives a shit what I do."

Tavis bit back a retort.

"That's not true, Austin, and you know it," JL said.

"Why don't you all take your badassery and get the hell out of here?"

That was all Tavis needed to hear. This was going to go south real quick if he didn't act now. He moved quickly, winding his right arm around Austin's neck and catching him under the chin in the crook of his elbow. With his other hand, he pushed Austin's head forward, knocking him out.

JL rushed to Austin's limp body. "Why the hell did you do that?"

"Get out of the way, JL. We've only got a few minutes." Tavis slipped his hands under Austin's armpits, grabbed hold of Austin's wrists, and pulled them close to his chest. "Remy, cross his feet, grab his jeans at the ankles, and lift on the count of three. JL, clear a path." Then to Remy, he said, "Let's move toward my right." Tavis counted to three, and they lifted Austin and carried him to the aisle. Tavis walked backward toward the entrance.

"Get the door, JL."

When they reached the hallway, Remy took the lead. They exited the house and hurried to the truck parked nearby, where they placed Austin in the bed.

"You drive, JL," Tavis said.

As soon as JL reached the barn, she drove down the center aisle to where Connor and Kevin waited with the horses.

Kevin opened JL's door. "How'd it go?"

"I was going to use the stun gun, but Tavis got antsy and went with the chokehold. We only have another minute or two. Let's get him in the saddle."

"How do you plan to do that?" Kevin asked.

"Lay him over the saddle."

"No, wait," Connor said. "I'll bring the horse next to the truck, and you two can set him in the saddle."

With everyone working together, they got Austin in the saddle, and Connor adjusted the stirrups.

"He's going to fall off," JL said. "Tie him to the saddle, or one of you has to ride with him."

"I'll sit behind Austin and hold him up." Remy climbed on the back of the horse and wrapped his arms around Austin's waist. "Let's go now. If he wakes up, he'll pitch me off the horse."

Connor gave the reins to Tavis.

Tavis wrapped the reins around his saddle horn. "If we get separated, let's meet in Medora."

Kevin tied the third horse's reins to a D-ring on Tavis's saddle. "Don't break the connection between Remy and Tavis, or you'll end up in different locations."

Austin groaned.

"He's coming to," Remy said. "Let's roll."

JL jumped up into the bed of the truck, leaned over, and kissed Austin's cheek. "Take care of him, please. And if you have to wean him off painkillers, don't let him suffer."

Tavis rode around to the rear of the truck and grabbed JL around the waist. He pulled her onto his horse, hugging her tight. He lightly brushed her damp cheek to whisper in her ear. "I'll take care of your boy and will bring him back to you. That's a promise."

JL kissed Tavis's cheek. "Can I take that to the bank?"

"You sure can." As soon as the words left Tavis's mouth, he had a vision of the Council members, but there was an empty chair at the round table.

He didn't have time to analyze what he saw. He'd do that later. He set JL back on the truck bed and dug the amethyst brooch out of his pocket.

"We'll go outside," Tavis said. "I don't want to take anything else with us." He rode outside, leading the other two horses, and recited the chant from memory.

"Chan ann le tìm no àite a bhios sinn a' tomhais an' gaol ach 's ann le neart anama."

The brooch didn't heat. It didn't spark. It glowed a bright purple, and a cloudlike substance swirled around them. There was no smell of peat, no twisting, no turning, just a floating sensation. And while the weightlessness was slightly disorienting, the horses reacted with only a snort or two.

The ride was blissfully smooth, without rough roads and potholes. After a moment or two, in less time than it takes for a high-speed elevator to go from one floor to the next, the weightless sensation ended, and the cloud slowly evaporated until only a thin veil surrounded them.

"What the fuck is that?" Remy asked as he reached out to touch the veil. His hand went straight through the thin barrier, and he wiggled his fingers on the other side.

Tavis had made dozens of trips back in time but never experienced anything like this. The dramatic landscape on the other side proved they had gone somewhere. But were they in the Badlands? He clucked and squeezed his legs to cue the horse forward, and they breached the veil as if walking in and out of a light rain shower.

The rock formations, towering spires, and sprawling grasslands answered his unspoken question. It was Dakota territory, all right. The indigenous people called it "mako sica"—welcome to the Dakota Badlands.

"Where are we?" Remy asked. "And what the hell happened to the roller-coaster ride?"

"I don't know," Tavis said. "I heard once that there was an easy way to get where you wanted to go, but only a few had ever been that way. I thought it was through the door in the castle cave, but it looks like I was wrong."

"It's another brooch mystery we'll never understand," Remy said. "Let's get Austin on the ground before he regains consciousness and throws me off."

"Keep holding him. I'll come around and get him in a fireman's carry," Tavis said. He tied all the reins to a tree branch first. "Okay, tip him toward me, and I'll carry him to that other tree."

Remy tipped Austin sideways until Tavis had a good hold, then Remy slid off the horse and grabbed Austin's legs. It was awkward, but they got him to the tree and propped him against it. Remy straightened Austin's arms, legs, and head and then took his pulse.

"Is he okay?" Tavis asked.

"It's lower than I'd like it to be, but for a professional athlete, a forty-five resting heart rate isn't abnormal."

"You sure all those drugs aren't to blame?"

"He has a trainer and paramedic on duty twenty-four seven and a physician on call. If they were alarmed, they would have admitted him for a workup."

"Well, keep an eye on him. I'm going to get the map and compass and figure out where we are."

"I hope we're close to that town. What's it called?"

"Medora."

"Yeah, that's it. It's close to Roosevelt's place, right?"

"Close enough." Tavis collected the map and compass and spread the map out on the ground. After making a few mathematical calculations, he drew a circle and tapped the marked area with his pencil. "We're about five miles from Elkhorn Ranch unless it's earlier than 1885, and then we're five miles from its future location."

"If JC is there, we can leave right away."

"Only if Ensley is with him," Remy whispered.

Austin opened one eye. "What the hell are you two doing here?" Then he opened the other eye and glanced around, rubbing the back of his neck. "What the hell am *I* doing here?"

Tavis stood in front of Austin, arms folded. "You can blame me for the headache."

"Why'd you knock me out?"

"We didn't think you'd come willingly, and we didn't have time to argue," Tavis said.

"How long have I been out? It was close to midnight when I started the movie I was watching. Now it's"—he glanced up—"late afternoon." He got to his feet, leaning on the tree for balance. "So where the fuck are we, anyway? And where's the car?"

"Ain't no car, man," Remy said. "We're riding horses. How do you feel?"

"Like shit. Let's get the hell out of here. I'm missing a workout."

"Sorry. But we came here to find James Cullen, and we can't leave until we do," Tavis said. "And the sooner we get riding, the sooner that'll happen. So let's go."

"Call McBain. He can track JC's phone and tell you exactly where he is. I should know. The asshole's done it to me. That's why I stopped carrying one."

"JC doan have a phone, and neither do we," Remy said. "And we're in a hurry. You're not the only one who wants to get back."

"If you're in such a goddamn hurry, you shouldn't have brought me."

"Bringing you went with the deal," Remy said.

"What? Did JL hold you at gunpoint? Take my kid, or I'll shoot you?"

"No, it was Pops, you asshole," Remy said, stepping into Austin's personal space. "If you ask me, he misjudged you and the situation. You can't handle this."

Austin's head whacked the lowest branch on the tree, and he swatted it out of the way. "If I can survive the hell I've been through, I can survive anything. Even this. Whatever the fuck *this* is." Austin's eyes and his whole demeanor conveyed a stark, heartbreaking reality. He was only a shell of the man he'd been before the accident.

Tavis regretted not siding with JL at the meeting. Austin didn't need to be here. His heavy scruff and the unkempt hair curling at his collar made him look even more dangerous than he probably was, but at this point, Tavis wouldn't put anything past Austin. He could strike out at any moment, and anyone within reach when it happened would get their ass kicked.

Austin was in pain. That was obvious. But it was more profound than physical pain. He hated life right now and probably hated himself for getting on that motorcycle, and for the past year, it was the painkillers that got him from one moment to the next.

Bringing him here was a shitty idea. Tavis would rather be in Afghanistan right now.

But he wasn't. He was here with a drug addict—or drug-dependent, or, as the scientific community like to call it, someone with substance use disorder. Whatever term he used, it all said the same thing. Austin was abusing painkillers.

Tavis's eyes never stopped moving as he searched the surrounding land for possible danger, but the only real threat within miles was the man standing in front of him.

Austin walked toward the horses. "Which one is mine?"

"The tallest," Tavis said.

Austin grabbed the reins, put his foot in the stirrup, and hissed when he pulled himself up into the saddle.

Fuck this. I'm taking him home.

"What's Pops got to do with this?" Austin asked, reining his horse around so he could glare at Remy.

"Nothin'. Forget it."

"Asshole. Spill it."

Remy was so pissed at Austin he growled at him. "We had a fucking meeting to plan the rescue, and Pops wanted us to bring you along. Nobody thought it was a good idea, but he convinced Elliott, and now we're stuck with you until we find JC. Got it, you shithead? Do you have any idea how worried your family is? No, you doan. You doan give a fuck. Well, from now on, we doan, either."

Remy mounted his horse and moved away from Austin.

"I haven't talked to Pops in weeks. What the hell does he know about what's good for me?"

Tavis mounted up. "I don't care who else you talk shit about, but don't you dare disrespect or criticize Pops O'Grady. They don't come any finer than him. He's fair, honest, and dependable, and for some dumbass reason, he loves you."

"If he loved me, he'd never agree to let you kidnap me."

"If you ever talked to him, you'd know how he felt, and the same goes for your parents and aunts and uncles. So cut the crybaby shit. It's already worn thin. We're the only hope you got of going home again. So shut the fuck up!"

"Where are my painkillers?" Austin demanded as if he hadn't heard what Tavis said.

"We didn't bring them," Remy said.

"What the hell am I supposed to do when I don't have any in my system?"

"They shoot horses, doan they? I guess that's what we'll do to you," Remy said.

For the first time, Tavis sensed they'd pushed Austin too far. He and Remy needed to back off for now and see how Austin handled the trip.

"We're just a few miles from Elkhorn Ranch. If Roosevelt is there, we might find JC. Let's ride."

"I still don't understand why we're on horseback. Isn't it easier to get around in a Jeep?"

"It's 1885, you fucking moron," Remy said. "There ain't no Jeeps."

Austin did a double-take. "What? You kidnapped me and brought me through the time warp without my consent? You can't do that."

"Who says?"

Anger flashed across Austin's face. "What would have happened if we'd gotten separated?"

"You're a smart guy," Remy said. "You'd have figured it out, just like Kit, Charlotte, Kenzie, Amber, Amy, Sophia, and Penny."

But Tavis didn't believe it. Maybe the old Austin would have succeeded, but not this version. He'd have a meltdown, and Erik would have to intervene. Tavis had been on the receiving end of Erik's disappointment and anger, and it was scary as hell to be in the presence of a Viking warrior on a rampage.

Maybe that was just what Austin needed.

29

Elkhorn Ranch (1885)—Ensley

AFTER JC RODE off the property, an overpowering wave of grief rolled through Ensley, and tears streamed down her face. She limped away, praying the peace and tranquility the ranch was known for would soothe the deep-seated loneliness and loss.

A line of poetry by Lang Leav came to mind: *"It should be my right to mourn someone that has yet to leave this world but no longer wants to be part of mine."*

Did she honestly believe that? Or was JC only part of her past wrapped in twine and tossed on the sharp-elbowed, knobby-kneed scrap heap of lost loves and regrets? She mentally shrugged, acknowledging an ongoing tug-of-war with herself and unsure which side would win. The wrong one could unravel it all.

Take a break. Focus on the birdsong and the rhythmic melody of the Little Missouri River.

She turned her face into the sweet breeze blowing through the cottonwoods and pinched the bridge of her nose, distracting her emotional pain long enough to stop the tears.

Slowly her mind panned out, giving her a broader perspective, and it allowed her soul to soak in the surrounding tranquility. It didn't work immediately, but within a few minutes, a smile blossomed, and doubts and grief receded, landing with a thud on top of that scrap heap.

TR cleared his throat and adjusted his pince-nez, pushing them closer to his eyes with the tip of his finger. She had almost forgotten he was standing there.

"You need a horse," he said. "Let's go to the corral and pick one out. Your husband paid me for a horse and saddle."

"He didn't mention that, but, yeah…sure." She wiped her face with JC's handkerchief, and as she unfolded it to blow her nose, she noticed his damn initials and had to choke back a fresh supply of tears. He was the only guy she knew who always had a handkerchief and a monogrammed one to boot.

She pinched the bridge of her nose again, and when that self-inflicted physical pain didn't work, she tried pinching the skin between her thumb and index finger.

"Sorry about my outburst. You can't put off grief, can you? Like, say, ten o'clock next Tuesday morning, I'll grieve until eleven. No, make it eleven-thirty. I had a bad night." It was a rhetorical question, and she didn't expect an answer.

Her breath hitched, and she continued babbling. "Loss hits you out of the blue, and *wham!*" She smacked her hands together. "You're suddenly knee-deep and wallowing in it. If you try to suck it up, it festers like an open wound. Watching JC leave reminded me of losing my parents, and the combined loss of them and JC was like a fresh bucket of hurt dumped over my heart."

TR glanced away, clearing his throat again. "Grief's a burden to bear. I've found it's best not to talk about it. Now, shall we go?"

He might not want to talk about the loss of his wife and mother and missing his daughter, but the pain tightening his face was a tome open for all to read. He walked ahead of her, and she had to jog to keep up with his much longer stride.

When they reached the paddock, she climbed up on the lower rung of the fence and hung her folded arms over the top rail while she studied the horses clustered together on the opposite side.

They suddenly separated, leaving an Arabian stallion with a glistening golden coat and blond mane standing alone. He lit up the paddock like a newly minted 18-karat gold coin.

She had a visceral reaction to him—a giddy, gut-level wave of empowerment. And she had to have him, even if it cost her every nugget of her emergency funds.

She pointed with a shaking finger. "That's…the…one."

TR shook his head. "He won't let anyone on his back." He picked up a lariat and stood beside her. "Pick another one."

There is no other horse on this side of the world, or the other, that speaks to me as he does. He's mine.

"I've ridden horses like him before. Let me try." That was a lie. She'd never ridden such a magnificent horse, and without TR's permission, she'd never get the chance.

The horse turned his head toward her, and her heart thumped like a kettle drum. He was watching, waiting for her—only her—and her fingers itched to thread themselves through his silky golden mane.

"He's too dangerous."

She switched tactics. "Maybe not…for the right person, I mean. Where'd he come from? What's his story?" she asked, but she already knew the answer. The magical horse came here for her.

"I don't know his story, but I bought him off an old man who wandered by here a week or so ago. He wasn't from any of the local tribes, and he said the horse came from the other side of the world."

"Why'd he sell him?"

"He didn't want to, but I kept upping my offer until he finally agreed. He took the money and never looked back. I thought I'd made a great deal until I discovered the horse wouldn't let anyone ride him. We've all tried. So save yourself a few bruises and possibly broken bones and pick another one, Mrs. Fraser."

Impossible. The horse was hers.

"I've got a couple of days to work with the stallion. I'll put him on a longe line to see what he knows. If I can't get him to understand basic commands by the time we're ready to leave, I'll ride another horse and work with him along the way."

"I assured your husband you'd be safe with me. Riding a green horse wasn't part of our understanding."

"Getting along with a horse is all about establishing balance and trust. If the previous owner had a trusting relationship, then it's possible to create another one. Let me give it a try. I promise not to risk injuring myself."

TR gazed at her, one eyebrow slightly raised.

"I promise." She crossed her heart. "If he rears up on me or tries to buck, and I can't get him under control, I'll pick out another one. But if I can ride him, I want to buy him. I know JC gave you money, but it's not enough. I'll double whatever he paid you."

"I'll never try to stop a determined woman. And your husband already paid me twice what I paid for him. Let me cull him from the herd."

She jumped off the bottom fence rung. "Oh, please, let me. It's important to respect the stallion's boundaries. But he needs to understand I'm the dominant party in the relationship, that I can be trusted, and will treat him well."

"Your husband might call me out over this."

"Nah. He's not a violent man." Even as she said it, she wasn't sure it was true. While she'd never seen JC get into a fight, he would never back down from one, either. She was sure of that. But kill a man, especially over something silly like letting her longe a horse? No way. "Can I find a pair of work gloves and a sturdy halter in the barn?"

"I'll get the gloves and halter. Stay right here until I get back." TR headed off toward the barn, muttering under his breath and slapping the rope against his thigh.

"And a longe whip if you have one," she yelled as she opened the gate and entered the corral.

"Let's see how hard you're going to make this." The stallion didn't move. "I'm going to call you Tesoro, which means treasure in Italian." She inched around the edge of the corral, speaking softly and not making any sudden moves. "You're beautiful, Tesoro."

He watched her. His ears were forward, and his dark eyes open and bright.

"You're curious, aren't you? Well, I'm curious about you, too. Why don't you come over here, and we'll get to know each other? You know I won't hurt you. Don't you, Tesoro? You're here for me. Erik brought you to me." As she walked toward the stallion, she pulled out the apple she'd grabbed from the kitchen and used her Clovis Point to cut it into quarters. "I bet you'd like this." He came to her, sniffed her hand, and scarfed up the section she offered.

"You like it, don't you?" She held out another piece on her palm, and with her other hand, stroked his forehead. "You're so beautiful. You're mine, aren't you?"

She fed him the other two pieces and then turned her back and walked away. She glanced over her shoulder. He was following her and nudged her back, gently shoving her forward. She grinned. "I don't have any more apple pieces."

She reached the fence, climbed up, and sat on the top rung. Tesoro stopped in front of her, and she continued stroking his head. "You're not green at all, are you?"

I was born for this moment. A lifetime of training was all for this...

As she stroked Tesoro's refined head and long ears, she realized her mistake. Tesoro wasn't an Arabian. He was an Akhal-Teke. Here. In the Dakotas. A rare breed whose ancestry dated back thousands of years.

"You're pure Akhal-Teke, aren't you, answering to only one master? Even the smell of strangers will make you shy away. Yet you came right to me as if you already know my scent."

The horse nibbled on her shoulder and head, grooming her, and then he breathed on her face, the ultimate sign of trust.

"Will you let me get on your back?"

In response, he rested his head on her thigh.

"I guess that's a yes."

She balanced on the fence and lowered her leg over his back. "Okay, boy. Let's see what you can do." He walked toward the gate without any cues from her. She leaned over and lifted the latch, and they left the corral, pausing so she could close the gate behind her.

Horseback riding was as second nature to her as driving a car. She cued Tesoro into a sitting trot just as TR came out of the barn. He stopped and stood there, as still as his Rough Rider statue at Oyster Bay. If he ordered her to dismount immediately, she'd race off in the opposite direction and pretend she didn't hear him.

When she was comfortable on Tesoro's back, she tightened her lower legs, and he picked up a canter. She forced herself to loosen her legs, and he slowed.

He responded immediately to her slightest movement, and she knew he was waiting for her next command. She liked him moving at a leisurely, rocking canter. A low fence loomed ahead. She cued him into a forward canter with a rhythm of one-two, one-two, then raised and bent her knees so she could grip his back with her inner thighs, and then lifted her weight, and Tesoro sailed over the fence.

"Good boy!"

They trotted toward the barn, exhilarated, and met TR standing in the open doorway, and somewhere during this magical moment, she remembered how much she loved ranch life.

She jumped down and hugged her horse, and then to TR said, "Isn't he fantastic? His trot has a perfect amount of bounce, and his canter is steady and smooth. He's so easy to ride."

"Maybe for you, Mrs. Fraser, but he wouldn't let anyone else come near him." TR's sharp-edged tone cut through Tesoro's rapid breathing and flared nostrils. "I came out of the barn and saw you on his back, and I almost had heart failure." He slapped his chest. "I thought for sure you were going to fall. I couldn't believe what I was seeing. I had to remove my spectacles and clean them. I've never seen a horse take a jump like that."

"What do you mean?" she asked.

"The accepted method of jumping is for the rider to sit back during the bascule phase and pull the horse's head upwards."

"And the first rule of good horsemanship," she said, "is to reduce, simplify, and, if possible, eliminate the rider's intervention. I had no saddle, bridle, or reins. I weaved my fingers through his short mane and let him jump naturally, without my interference."

Then a vague memory hit her. The accepted method of jumping changed in the early 1900s. Had she just shown TR the future of the sport?

"But, madam. You moved with him. You knew what he was going to do."

"And he did it beautifully. Don't you think? Without interference from the rider, a horse can walk, trot, canter, and gallop for extended periods without tiring. When I ride, I give just a few cues and then stay out of the horse's way."

TR reached out to stroke the horse's head, but Tesoro stepped back out of his reach. TR looked confused, his arm hanging there in the air. "You can ride him without a saddle, yet no one else can even touch him." He let his arm fall to his side. "I've seen horses buck off their riders, but this horse won't give a man a chance."

"I don't know why he allowed me," she said. "I've never ridden a horse bareback without riding him under saddle first. But the way he accepted me, I knew it was safe to ride him."

TR shifted the gloves and bridle from one hand to another. "I might as well return these to the tack room." He turned and hurried back to the barn.

Ensley followed him into the shadows, worried that she might have offended him in some way. "Are you angry with me? Did I do something wrong?"

"Angry? That you terrified me?" He hung up the harness and put the gloves on a shelf. He was quiet for a moment as if putting thoughts together before he spoke. "Every man is frightened when he goes into action, but the challenge is to keep a grip on yourself so you can act as if you're not. If you keep it up long enough, it changes from pretense to reality, and you become fearless by practicing fearlessness." He folded one arm across his chest and raised the other hand to fiddle with his mustache.

"When I first came out here, there were all kinds of things I was afraid of—grizzly bears, mean horses, gunfighters—but by acting as if I wasn't afraid, I gradually ceased to be afraid. But watching you on that horse, madam, had me shaking in my boots. So all my practicing was for naught."

"Oh, no, you're wrong," she said. "You weren't afraid for yourself. You were afraid for me, and that had to be worse because you had no control over it."

"No control and total responsibility. How could I possibly explain to your husband that I allowed his wife to kill herself?"

"You didn't allow it. I took advantage of your temporary absence."

"Absence or not, I'm still responsible for your safety. And if you have a habit of disregarding the wishes of others, I might have to put you on the train with a one-way ticket to Kentucky. I would rather send Mr. Fraser a telegram to expect you in person than one to expect you in a casket."

"He wouldn't like either one of those. But here's the thing. I had a similar argument with my parents many years ago. Like you, I had to deal with fear getting in the way, but I wasn't going to let it stop me from doing what I wanted to do. I participated in dangerous activities like breakaway calf roping, tie-down roping, bareback riding, even bull riding. I got over my fear, but my parents were terrified, and there wasn't anything I could say that relieved their worry."

TR gazed out the open door. "You appeared fearless, Mrs. Fraser. And I'll never believe you were scared at all."

"I didn't have to be, sir. You were scared *for* me."

She might have gotten a smile out of him if not for a rider galloping up to the barn, yelling. "Mr. R! Sewall and Dow arrive tonight with the fifteen hundred head Merrifield bought in Minnesota. They need your help to unload the cattle."

"Go change your mount," TR yelled back. "I'll be ready to ride in fifteen minutes."

Ensley put Tesoro in the first empty stall. "I'm going, too."

TR pointed toward a room right inside the barn. "There's an extra saddle in the tack room. Don't make us wait for you." He then whipped around and headed toward the house at a fast clip.

She entered the tack room and collected the saddle, blanket, cinch, and bridle with reins, and saddled Tesoro. He didn't object, even when she tightened the cinch. "I'll be right back, boy."

She grabbed the saddlebags and ran into the house to pack her few personal items. With that done, she borrowed a buffalo robe and rolled it up in the bedroll JC also left behind. Then she hurried from the house, tied down her gear, and was ready when TR said, "Let's ride."

Mrs. Sewall entered the barn with a burlap bag and handed it to Ensley. "I fried chicken for lunch and added some cooked beans and fresh bread. I also packed four apples. You can give one to your horse."

"You didn't have to do that, but thank you, and Tesoro will enjoy another apple." The horse looked back at her, and she could have sworn he smiled. "Later, buddy." She tied the burlap bag to the extra D-ring and rechecked all her gear. "Mrs. Sewall, did you see the man who sold this horse to Mr. Roosevelt?"

"Yes. I was afraid of him at first, but he had kind eyes. And Mr. Roosevelt wasn't concerned."

"This might sound strange, but do you remember what he was wearing?"

"He looked...I don't know...like he didn't belong here. He wore loose trousers, a red cloak, leather ankle boots, and he had tattoos on one arm."

"Interesting." Ensley now had confirmation that Erik brought her the horse. But why now and not while she was walking all by herself? It didn't make sense. It was almost as if he'd wanted her to suffer. But that didn't make sense, either. If he wanted that, he wouldn't have healed her foot. If she ever saw him again, she'd make him stand still and answer her questions.

TR yelled from the yard, "Mrs. Fraser, let's ride."

"Coming." She smiled at Mrs. Sewall. "Thank you for everything. I'll see you in a few days."

He was holding the reins of two unsaddled horses. He gave her the reins to a dun, and he kept the piebald. "You might believe your gold horse can make it thirty miles of hard riding, but I'm guessing he can't. You'll want to change mounts at some point."

"Thank you. It's not worth risking my horse's welfare to prove I'm right." She tied the dun's reins to her saddle and checked one last time to be sure everything was in order. Satisfied, she glanced around. "Where's that man?"

"He changed horses and rode out."

"I'm sorry I made you wait. You could have gone with him."

"He preferred not to wait for me."

"We should get to Medora before James Cullen leaves. He'll be able to help if you want another pair of hands."

"We'll manage. I don't want your husband to miss his train."

She wasn't sure she could bear to say goodbye to JC again. Watching him wave from the train car window might be even more traumatic.

I won't worry about it now.

They rode off the property at an easy trot. "I can keep up with you," she said. "You set the pace."

"The river is too high right here to cross it today. But if we could, how would your horse manage it?"

"Turkmen bred Akhal-Teke horses for the desert, but I doubt he'll have a problem with a river crossing." She wasn't worried yet, but she was concerned for the man who rode hard to get a message to TR. "If your man is riding back toward Medora, that's a seventy-mile ride in one day."

"With all the back and forth and chasing down strays, a hundred miles is a reasonable distance for a cowboy on a roundup to ride in a single day. Then you add in staying up all night on watch and then back at work after gulping down a three a.m. breakfast. You get used to it."

She cringed at the idea of a hundred miles and breakfast at three in the morning. Maybe she oversold herself.

"I've been in the saddle for nearly forty hours before—" TR continued.

I've been on three-day hunting trips. Does that count? Nope. I slept. But I can do it.

"—wearing out five horses and winding up in a stampede. I've roped steers till I flayed my hands—"

I've roped steers, but I wore gloves.

"—wrestled calves in burning clouds of alkali dust—"

Okay, I can do that.

"—and stuck like a burr to bucking ponies with my nose pouring blood, and hat, guns, and spectacles flying in all directions."

And I can do that, too.

"And I bet you thought all that was great fun." She didn't have to ask because his grin said he thought it was just *bully.*

When they reached a safer place to cross, she nudged Tesoro down the bank and into the rushing water, keeping her hands and legs relaxed so he wouldn't pick up any tension from her. Like Mercury, Tesoro took to the river as if he crossed one every day. Since she knew nothing of his past, he might have.

Coming out on the other side of the river, she asked, "If the bulk of the cows are coming up here, where are the rest going?"

"To the Maltese Cross Ranch. It's located about seven miles south of Medora and is the base of my cattle operation."

"Who takes care of it when you're up here?"

"My two partners, Ferris and Merrifield. They manage the place. They're good, honest men and don't know much more than I do about the cattle business. But we're learning. They built a one-and-a-half-story ranch house out of Ponderosa pine, complete with a shingled roof and a root cellar. It's nice by Dakota standards."

"Where are Ferris and Merrifield from?" Like most of her questions, she already knew the answers. She'd been to the Maltese Cross Ranch several times to visit the restored cabin.

"Merrifield came from the East five years ago. He's a keen sportsman. A good-looking fellow, daring, confident, a good rider, and a first-class shot. He's been my *fidus Achates* of the hunting field."

"Everyone should have a companion like Achates. Aeneas was very fortunate to have him, as you are to have Merrifield."

TR laughed. "Bully! I figured Mr. Fraser would be familiar with Virgil, but I wasn't sure if you also enjoyed the Greek classics."

She gave him a side-eye. "So you were testing me?"

He gave her a classic TR grin. "I might have been."

"Well, Mr. Roosevelt," she said, "the ancient classics played an essential part in the development of English literature and are some of Europe's earliest and best works in fiction, history, and philosophy. *The Odyssey* by Homer, *Medea* by Euripides, *Hippolytus* by Euripides, *Antigone* by Sophocles, *Lysistrata* by Aristophanes, *Meno* by Plato, *The Histories* by Herodotus, *The Poetics* by Aristotle, *The Metamorphoses* by Ovid, and *The Satyricon* by Petronius were all required reading in my curriculum."

"Curriculum?" He raised his eyebrows. "Where'd you attend school?"

Harvard.

She couldn't tell him that, so she went with another Massachusetts school. "Smith, but you probably haven't heard of it. It's a small school in Northampton, Massachusetts, with only a few students and faculty."

"I've heard of it."

She needed to change the subject. While she knew a few women who attended Smith, she didn't know much about its history. "And what about Mr. Ferris? Was he a hunting partner, too?"

"He's a tall, fine-looking fellow and the best rider on the ranch, but not a particularly good shot." He glanced at her. "You're a fine horsewoman. What kind of shot are you?"

"I hit what I'm aiming at," she said with a laugh. "I hope we'll get a chance to go hunting."

"Did your husband teach you?"

"To ride or shoot?

"Both."

"I learned to ride and shoot from my parents, but JC is an expert marksman and an incredible equestrian. He could easily qualify to compete in the Olympics."

"But there aren't any equestrian events in the Olympics."

Oops. "Well, if they ever include equestrian events, he could compete, but not me. Give him a course with ten to sixteen obstacles with heights up to five feet and spreads over six feet, and he'll sail over them as if his horse had wings. But he can't rope a calf, so we're even."

"Where is your family ranch?"

The lie she and JC concocted rolled off her tongue. "Pennsylvania. Not far from Philadelphia." She didn't want to talk about her "life story," she preferred to talk about his, but that took a little massaging. "Mrs. Sewall told me you have a daughter in New York City. How old is she?"

TR looked away from her, and she didn't think he was going to answer, but he finally said, "Her name is Alice Lee, and she's fifteen months old. My sister Anna is taking care of her while I'm out here."

"Mrs. Sewall said your wife died within hours of Alice Lee's birth. That's so tragic."

"Mrs. Fraser, I don't know if you've experienced great loss before—"

"I have. I lost both my parents within a short time. I'll never stop missing them."

They rode in silence, and she wasn't sure what he was thinking or even if he would talk about his family.

"Alice was beautiful in face and form and lovelier still in spirit. Like a flower, she grew, and as a fair young flower, she died." The pain in his voice was palpable. "She lived her life in the sunshine and never experienced great sorrow. Everyone loved her and her sunny temper and unselfishness.

"She was loving, tender, and happy as a young wife, and when she became a mother, her life had just begun. Then by a strange and terrible fate, death came for her, and my heart's dearest died, and the light went out of my life forever."

TR was outwardly alive and alert but inwardly shattered. Ensley was too heartbroken for him to say another word, and they rode in silence for the rest of the morning.

After they stopped for lunch, she couldn't hold back her questions for a moment longer, and as they mounted up, she said, "Tell me about the trips you took as a child that made an impression on you."

His eyes lit up. "The family's first grand tour of the continent. We spent six weeks of the trip in Switzerland and stayed at the famous Hotel Baur au Lac, with its flower gardens and meticulously raked gravel walks. I suffered from asthma, and one of my physicians told my parents the bracing air would be the best medicine."

"Is that when your love of nature began?"

"No. That started before I turned ten. My family had to learn to live with my passion. I tied snapping turtles to laundry tubs, brought home a litter of newborn squirrels that I had to feed with a syringe three times daily." He stopped and laughed, clearly reminiscing.

Then he continued, "But when my mother discovered I was storing dead mice in the icebox, she put her foot down and ordered them thrown in the garbage. I was in a state of despair over the loss to science."

Ensley laughed so hard she almost fell off her horse. She'd heard so many stories from the park rangers, but hearing the anecdotes from TR made them come alive. "I'm sorry it was such a significant loss to science." It took a few minutes to get her giggles under control, but when she did, she asked, "So then did you read science books instead of performing experiments?"

"No, but I read a lot, especially the works of John James Audubon and Spencer Fullerton Baird."

"The foremost American naturalist of the day."

"You've read Baird?"

"I haven't read the entire *Catalogue of North American Birds*, but I've reviewed it. Does that count?"

"Sort of," he said.

"What was your first experience in the wilderness?"

"The summer before I turned thirteen. Father initiated an expedition to the Adirondacks. Our destination was Paul Smith's on Lake St. Regis, a favorite summer hostel among well-to-do families. In true Roosevelt fashion, we went in a swarm. My parents, all four children, Uncle Hilborne, Aunt Susy, and Cousin West.

"Uncle Hilborne, Cousin West, and I spent three days roughing it in the bush, and for the first time, I could write in my journal from personal experience of those desolate wilds."

"And I bet for the whole month you were never sick."

"Never. But the next summer, Papa changed my life by giving me a 12-gauge, double-barreled French-made shotgun. It was the ideal gun for an awkward thirteen-year-old."

"I remember my first rifle. I was about the same age. I used to clean that gun every day." When she moved to New York, she packed up all her guns and put them in a safe deposit box. She didn't want them but didn't want to get rid of them, either.

"The year I got that rifle, I also got a large pair of spectacles."

"I bet that made a huge difference in your life."

"Nothing could prepare me for the difference in the world around me. Before then, my range of vision was only about thirty feet. Everything beyond that point was a blur."

"Why didn't you tell your parents?"

"I guess I thought it was normal, so no one knew how handicapped I was, and I had no idea how beautiful the world was."

"What happened once you could see?"

"Birds upstaged everything else in my life, and Audubon became my hero."

A few more hours of in-depth conversation with TR, and she'd have a full notebook, as long as she could remember everything long enough to write it all down.

"You mentioned the first family grand tour. When was the second?"

"The next year, we set out for another extended journey abroad, beginning with winter on the Nile. By mid-December, I was tramping the shores of the great and mysterious river, knocking birds from the sky as rapidly as I could."

"Did you wear a pith helmet like Sir Stanley?"

"Of course." He laughed. "The bird fauna of the Nile is extraordinary. The air is thick with them—larks, doves, herons, kingfishers, and flocks of snow-white cattle egrets, dozens of different varieties of ducks. And, Mrs. Fraser, I could see them all with my new spectacles."

"Would you mind calling me Ensley? Mrs. Fraser is my mother-in-law, and it's way too formal for the Badlands."

His eyebrows pinched together, and he tilted his head. "Mr. Fraser wouldn't appreciate such informality."

"He's not here. And if he were, trust me, he wouldn't mind." It was so strange. Here she was with a man her age whom she just met but knew more about his life and passions and loves than the man she'd recently dated for months.

"I'll call you Ensley unless others are around, and please called me Teddy."

Teddy Roosevelt just told me to call him Teddy. Be still my heart.

"How was your asthma while you were on the Nile?"

"Vanished," he said.

"And you became Natty Bumppo on the Nile. Or maybe Rube Rawlings, Captain Reid's version of Natty."

"I was Humboldt on the Orinoco, seeing new worlds with the eyes of science."

"Sounds like you had a headlong, harum-scarum quality that was more Don Quixote than Humboldt. I can see you with your big spectacles and the great gun slung over one shoulder charging off astride a small donkey, ruthlessly chasing whatever object you had in your sights."

"I was dangerous. The donkey was often out of control, and my gun bounced every which way."

She laughed and suddenly knew what kind of book she wanted to write. She reached for her cell phone to call Susan to pitch her story, only to be shocked back to reality.

There was no Susan, no former employer, no running group, no yoga class, and no job waiting for her return, and she slumped in her saddle.

"Are you tired?" TR asked. "We can stop."

"No, it's just my sore hip. I'll be fine."

Tesoro looked back at her with those huge brown eyes that could see into her soul, and he knew she was lying. He could see the truth, and he wanted to warn her to brace for the crash and steel herself for the fall.

Don't worry about me, Tesoro. It's just one more thing to dump on the stockpile of lost love and regrets.

30

Chicago, IL (1885)—James Cullen

A FTER ENDURING LONG layovers and godawful food from Medora to Minneapolis, JC bought a seat in a Pullman sleeping car with access to a dining room. If Ensley had been with him, he would have leased a Pullman luxury car just for them, but he couldn't justify the expense for one passenger. The older he got, the more his brother's responsible spending mantra had an impact on him.

As the train neared northwest Chicago, he quit reading the collection of Shakespeare's plays—the only book he packed—and spent the rest of the time gazing out the window at the stretches of flat, open prairie. Two-story frame houses stood in open fields with rows of telegraph poles stalking the surrounding areas.

He'd made regular trips to Chicago in the past couple of years. He loved the city and would move here if his business didn't keep him tied to DC. To see the city as it once was made this side trip completely worthwhile. As much as Ensley wanted to be with TR, he knew she'd also love Chicago. As soon as he could, he'd send a telegram to let her know where he was.

He continued gazing out the window as trains rumbled by going in the opposite direction, clacking along the rails. When his train crossed the Chicago River, the brakeman slammed open the door and shouted above the clang, "Chicago! Chicago!"

JC popped to his feet, kicked his legs to straighten his trousers, and reached for his saddlebags in the empty seat. Instead of crowding the door as other passengers were doing, he remained at the rear of the car. He continued to watch the people, taking in details and body language cues for signs that anyone was paying attention to him, just as he'd done during the entire trip. So far, no one seemed overly interested, except a few women whose shy glances he politely ignored.

Call him paranoid, but now that the Illuminati knew about him, they could find him again, regardless of the century or the continent. They wanted information, and under extreme interrogation and torture, JC could reveal enough to destroy the clan. He'd come close and still had bruises and burns to remind him he might not survive another round with its sadistic, indoctrinated members. Without the skills he learned from the monks in the Himalayas, he wouldn't have survived.

"Chicago!" the brakeman called again, drawing out the word. The train moved at a snail's pace now as it pulled into a shadowy train shed teeming with cars and passengers, and he watched with interest at the tide of people pouring out of the depot. They pushed against the horde of new arrivals who hurried in the opposite direction.

JC needed to switch trains here and buy a ticket on the Cincinnati, Indianapolis, St. Louis & Chicago line for the next leg of the trip. But while waiting in line to buy a ticket for a train leaving within the hour, he decided to stay overnight and enjoy an evening in the city.

So he bought a ticket for the train departing tomorrow afternoon at two o'clock and made arrangements for Mercury. While chatting with the agent about the luxury sleeper car, JC asked him for a hotel recommendation.

The agent reached for a piece of paper and handed it to JC. "I recommend the brand-new Hotel Richelieu. It's Chicago's most luxurious hotel. It fronts Lake Michigan and caters to a discerning clientele who demand high-end Parisian cuisine." The agent repeated everything written on the flyer.

JC raised his eyebrow. "French food? What about the rooms?" He waved the flyer. "Should I believe this?"

"I haven't been inside any of the rooms, but I've heard they're elegant."

"And the wine cellar? Should I believe this?" JC read from the flyer, "'The finest assortment of choice wines to be found in any hotel or restaurant in America.' That's a lofty claim."

"I don't have any personal knowledge, but from what I hear—"

"Guess I'll have to find out for myself." JC returned the flyer to the agent. "Sounds like just what I'm looking for." He gave the agent a coin. "Thanks for your help."

He had exchanged one of his smallest gold nuggets for cash at the hotel in Medora. He knew he got ripped off on the exchange, but he needed cash for a ticket, food, and tips.

He turned to leave but paused and asked one last question. "Is there a bank you can recommend?"

Without missing a beat, the agent said, "First National Bank of Chicago. It's on the northwest corner of Dearborn and Monroe."

"Great. Thanks."

"And you need to have your horse loaded an hour before departure tomorrow."

He gave the agent a thumbs-up.

JC now had names for an upscale hotel and a bank. Before he headed in that direction, he picked up Mercury, then stopped at Western Union to send a telegram to Ensley, hoping the Medora agent would do as he promised and get the message to her, wherever she was.

The bank was his first stop after leaving the station. He opened an account and deposited his gold, giving him access to cash and a checking account. He emerged with a full wallet, a checkbook, and a recommendation for a men's clothing shop—the precursor of Hart, Schaffner, and Marx—Hart, Abt, and Marx on State Street.

He purchased a complete wardrobe at the shop, including evening attire, and paid handsomely for a twenty-four-hour turnaround. While the tailors made minor alterations to a suit they had in stock, JC went down the street to the Palmer House Barber Shop for a bath and shave.

Two hours later, after shopping for Ensley, too, he left the men's clothing store looking like the wealthy gentleman he was. And while he appreciated Paul finding him a set of clothes, JC was pleased to wear a fashionable suit when he entered the upscale hotel.

He almost felt guilty for being clean, wearing new clothes, and preparing to dine on French cuisine while Ensley was filthy, chasing cows, and probably eating bacon and beans. But who knows? Maybe she was having as much fun as she expected.

As he mounted Mercury, the hairs on the back of his neck stood on end, and he experienced the same chill of alarm he had in Asia. He didn't turn around, but he knew someone had eyes on him.

His unease rode with him down State Street and didn't let up until he stood in front of the hotel's double doors. He handed Mercury's reins to a boy wearing the hotel's uniform.

JC flipped the boy a coin and then flipped another one. "The second coin is for a proper brushing and fresh oats." Then he flipped the kid one more coin. "And this one is to hire you to take Mercury to the Cincinnati, Indianapolis, St. Louis & Chicago train, leaving for Midway, Kentucky at two o'clock tomorrow afternoon. But he has to be there an hour before the train departs. Can you do that?"

The boy's eyes lit up. "Yes, sir! He'll be on the train in plenty of time."

JC hated waiting for trains and planes. This way, he could take his time getting there and still have a few minutes to check on Mercury before boarding.

Over the hotel entrance stood a six-foot white marble sculpture of the famous Cardinal Armand Jean du Plessis, Duke de Richelieu. Alexandre Dumas depicted Richelieu as the lead villain in the 1844 novel *The Three Musketeers*.

JC wasn't sure why, but he sensed the sculpture had some meaning for him, but at the moment, he had no idea what that could be.

The Three Musketeers?

He shook off the thought and strolled through the lobby, more than ready for an evening of indulgence in fine whisky, a full-bodied cigar, and today's edition of the *Chicago Daily News*.

There was a slight echo as he walked across the almost empty lobby toward the registration desk. Then it stopped, but he kept walking while glancing around. He didn't see anything unusual, but the itch at the back of his neck had returned.

He registered, took the key, and asked about where he could get a drink.

The receptionist nodded toward a corner bar.

"Thanks."

He walked up the sweeping staircase, found his room on the second floor, and dropped his saddlebags without paying much attention to the room's décor. He was just glad he didn't have to sleep on a train tonight.

When he returned to the lobby, he walked down the hall toward the bar, and the back of his neck still itched. He stopped to look at a display case full of grainy photographs taken during the hotel's construction, and he used the reflective glass to scan the hallway behind him. No one was there. But they could have ducked into one of the four rooms that opened into the hall.

He entered the saloon—lit by a gas chandelier and wall sconces—and strode to the end of the bar, where he took the last of several empty stools, passing four men on his way there. The location provided a view of the door and the protection of a wall at his back.

The men glanced at him when he sat down, and he nodded, acknowledging them. All four immediately broke eye contact and returned to what they were doing—drinking and reading the *Chicago Daily News.*

While the bartender conversed with one of his patrons, JC scanned the shelves to find Jim Beam, among other Kentucky whiskys. He smiled when he noticed the labels on the American bottles. The fonts resembled those used on "Wanted Dead or Alive" posters.

Then he spotted a bottle of Old Highland Whisky. That would do. But before he placed his order, he saw a bottle of The Glenlivet and ordered that instead.

He took his time sipping his wee dram while watching customers come and go. After an hour, and with no one paying attention to him, he settled his bar tab and left.

He wasn't two feet from the entrance when someone put a knife against the small of his back and the other hand on JC's shoulder, digging his fingers into JC's deltoid.

"Mr. Fraser. How nice to see you again."

Adrenaline fueled and honed his readiness, making the tips of his fingers pulse. He would never forget that voice, the voice that haunted his nightmares. The man had only one inflection for all situations—callous, gravelly, and evil. Even his monotone questions had a cold-blooded acid wash to them.

"Hello, Sten. I can't say the same about you." JC controlled his voice so it wouldn't reveal his fear. Sten was not a man to mess with or underestimate.

Sten chuckled. "You should have stuck around. You missed the party."

"I got the impression I was to be the guest of honor. I figured the smartest thing to do was skedaddle while I could."

The man tsked. "You ruined my evening, but I'm sure you'll make it up to me. My men are waiting to see you again, with revenge on their minds. Now turn slowly and go through that door on your left."

The door was an exit. Leaving the hotel with Sten was a bad idea. His associates were likely outside, waiting to grab him.

JC's adrenaline surged again, and he used the heightened awareness to his advantage rather than wasting time wondering how Sten found him.

Sten and his people must have information about the brooches the MacKlennas didn't have.

JC needed that information from Sten as much as Sten needed it from him.

"What do you want?" JC had to keep talking while he waited for the moment to strike.

"Don't be naïve, Mr. Fraser. You know what I want. Let's start with the brooch you used to get here."

JC laughed. "If I had it, I wouldn't have stuck around."

"Of course you have it. And before the night is over, you'll tell me where it is. Now open the door. If you make a wrong move, I'll kill you right here."

What an idiot. "That sort of defeats the purpose, doesn't it?"

Sten pressed the knife harder against JC's jacket and shirt, and the sharp point pricked his skin, slicing a hole in his new clothes—and that pissed him off.

"If I don't get the brooch from you, I'll go to the Dakotas to find Ensley Williams. How do you think she'll handle a knife at her throat?"

JC's stomach convulsed. "If you think she'll whimper and tell you everything she knows…which isn't much, by the way…you're wrong." JC was playing with dynamite. Sten was a brutal killer, like Erik and the other Council members. If JC left with Sten, he wouldn't survive, and there'd be no one to protect Ensley from Sten and his assassins.

JC would have more room to fight once they were outside, but if Sten's men were waiting there, it could be disastrous for him. He had to kill Sten—now—and finish what they started in Asia. It was now or never.

JC ran through his options in tenths of a second—that's how it worked for him. When he was in danger, time either slowed down or his mind raced. Hard to say which.

He adjusted his body slightly to the left, and at the same time, backed up into the blade so he'd know exactly where Sten's hand was. The heat of Sten's breath was on JC's neck, along with the stink of tobacco.

JC made his move.

He whipped around in the opposite direction, blocked, then grabbed Sten's knife-wielding arm, twisting it around so the knife pointed into Sten's side. Two seconds max. If he didn't kill Sten now, he'd have to spend the rest of his life looking over his shoulder.

But before he could kill his nemesis, the door behind him opened and one of Sten's assassins wrapped a leather strap around JC's neck.

JC had seconds before the pressure on his carotid arteries knocked him out.

Instead of grabbing for the strap to keep from choking, he turned into the man and used a tiger-claw punch to his face, knocking him down, but it left him open to Sten. JC chambered his knee in a high position and push-kicked Sten, who landed on his back, groaning.

JC swiveled to meet another assassin, who came at him with a haymaker-type cross and then used an eagle claw to neutralize him. But as he defended against the cross, his opponent came in with a ridge hand across JC's neck, then torqued as he stepped in behind JC and, with a hip toss, dropped him to the ground.

The assassin's hand then came in with a straight punch to his nose, and while excruciating pain seared JC's brain, he knew no one would come to his rescue.

And no one would ever know what happened to him.

31

MacKlenna Farm, KY (1885)—Elliott

THE FOG EVAPORATED, and Elliott found himself alone in a lush green pasture. But he knew where he was—the cemetery at MacKlenna Farm was just over the hill, and the mansion, stallion barns, and breeding shed were through the trees a hundred yards or so. He'd ridden over every inch of the farm thousands of times. Every rolling hill was as familiar as the web of veins on the back of his hands.

The absence of utility poles and slowly moving hay wagons pulled by tractors—not horses—on Old Frankfort Pike confirmed he was in a different century.

There wasn't a cloud in the blue expanse stretching above the rolling hills of bluegrass, and the white-blossomed dogwoods and pink azaleas dotted the tree line with bursts of color. The extraordinary countryside never changed, regardless of the season, regardless of the century.

But where was everyone else?

As many times as he'd traveled with Remy, the brooch never separated them—thank God. But the stones had a history of tossing family members around like pick-up sticks every time they whirled through the vortex. If Meredith was alone, she'd go directly to the mansion to wait for him and the others. Until he saw her and held her in his arms, though, he'd worry about her, which he did every minute they were apart. Fortunately, all three women—Meredith, Kit, and Emily—were at home here and wouldn't be alarmed if they were alone.

Elliott was heading through the tree line in the mansion's direction when a horse and rider jumped a rail fence a few yards ahead.

Elliott dodged in time to prevent a thousand-pound Thoroughbred from landing on top of him, but his numb foot caused him to lose his balance, his hat flew off, and he fell back into a blackberry bramble.

"Damnation!"

The only fruit he hated more than kiwi was blackberries. The floral scent made him barf, and the bitter notes were disgusting—even in wine—and then there were the damn thorns. Well, enough said.

But it wasn't the thorns and nettles scratching the exposed skin of his neck and hands that pissed him off. It was his racing heart. It was racing to either get away from the blackberries or leap out of his chest.

And on top of that, he wouldn't be surprised if the pain was a heart attack, and he was going to die while stuck in a goddamn brambleberry thicket.

After the family recovered from the shock, they'd spend the next fifty years talking about how Grandpa Fraser died in a bramble. No one could find out about this. No one. He'd have to bribe the asshole who ran him down.

The man reined his horse and trotted toward him. "Are ye injured?" he asked while dismounting. "Do ye need a doctor?" He reached to help Elliott up. "I could have killed ye."

"I've worked with Thoroughbreds my entire life, and that was the closest one's come to killing me. Kicked, aye! Bitten, aye, but run over... *Never!*" Elliott glared at the man with gray hair and brown eyes. "Are ye Sean MacKlenna?"

"Aye, and who might ye be?" Sean glanced around. "And where's yer horse? Were ye thrown?"

Elliott snarled and narrowed his eyes. "A horse hasn't thrown me since I was a lad!" He extended his arms for Sean to grab hold of.

Sean pulled Elliott to his feet and brushed fruit and stems and thorns off his back. "I'm verra sorry. I jump this fence every day, and this is the first time anyone has ever been on this side of it when I landed."

"Well, someone was here today!" Elliott's tone was sharper than it should have been, but he just had the piss scared out of him. His racing heart slowed but hadn't returned to its regular rhythm. "I've walked, driven, and ridden through this tree line for fifty years, and no one has ever tried to kill me before."

"Fifty years! Ye lost yer mind when ye fell. This is MacKlenna Farm"—Sean thumped his chest with his thumb—"my farm, and I've never seen ye here before."

"Of course ye haven't. I don't live in yer time," Elliott snapped, still irritated at Sean's recklessness. And at eighty, he shouldn't be jumping fences anyway.

Sean's face paled, and his eyes opened wide. "My time! What the hell does that mean?"

"Exactly what ye think it does. I'm Elliott Fraser, Kit MacKlenna's godfather."

"Elliott? Kitherina's Elliott?" Sean grabbed his chest and leaned back against his horse.

Elliott almost laughed until he remembered Charlotte's comment about Sean's heart, and then he was alarmed. "Do *ye* need a doctor?"

"No. I'm just surprised. I never thought I'd meet ye." Tears filled Sean's eyes as he gripped Elliott's hand tighter, then swept him into an exuberant embrace before clapping him on the back. Elliott swallowed the lump in his throat, but he couldn't swallow the tears no matter how fast he blinked them away.

"Ye don't look like Sean VI, but I see a resemblance in yer eyes," Elliott said.

"Kitherina told me ye were like brothers."

"We were, and a day doesn't go by that I don't look for him to share something important that just happened." This time Elliott pulled Sean in for a hug and clap on the back.

The last hug Elliott gave his friend Sean VI was the night before he died. That image flashed before his mind's eye now. Elliott managed to hold it together during the funeral for Kit's sake, but Sean's and Mary's deaths broke off a part of Elliott's heart. And all the love he found since then had never healed that jagged edge. "This is cause for celebration, and I'm embarrassed… I didna bring a flask. What kind of Scotsman leaves his flask a' home?"

Sean bellowed. "A poor one, I reckon!" He picked up Elliott's hat and brushed it off before handing it to him. "I know where there's more than enough to fill a flask and no one to bother us while we celebrate."

"By all means, lead the way."

The two men hit their stride and followed a well-worn path

leading away from the mansion. "I didna think I'd ever say this," Sean said, threading his horse's reins through his fingers, "but thank ye for raising my niece. We were heartbroken when the ship bringing my sister and her babe to America sank during the storm. We believed we'd lost them both, but Jamilyn had the foresight to see to her daughter's future."

"We were gobsmacked when we found her on the doorstep," Elliott said. "Sean pulled some strings, forged a few documents, and Kit became his adopted daughter and legal heir."

"What's so striking," Sean said, "is that Jamilyn's death brought Kitherina to ye, and it was the death of her adoptive father that brought her to me."

"I never thought of it that way, but I guess ye're right."

"And then four years ago, her fall and Cullen's heart attack sent her back to ye."

"And here she is again."

Sean's eyes crinkled at the corners, and he squinted into the distance, as if he could see her already, and asked in a whisper, "Kitherina's here?"

Elliott grinned, and his heart rate finally returned to its natural rhythm. He forgave Sean for almost killing him and was happy for him at the same time. He would soon see his twin sister's daughter after believing for the past few years that he'd never see her again. The moment reminded Elliott of why they were there—to find his son. His displeasure and concerns about James Cullen's actions almost diminished the excitement of Sean and Kit's reunion.

"Did she bring Cullen?" Sean asked, his voice hopeful.

"Aye, she did. And they're looking forward to seein' ye."

"What a blessin'."

"And may blessings follow ye through life."

"Aye, that's two toasts, at least! We're likely to come up with another reason afore we have whisky to drink."

"What about Kit's father? Is he still living?"

"Aye. Donald lives in Washington near Kit and Cullen's daughters."

"Another toast, then."

"I'll send my manservant to the depot in Midway with telegrams for their daughters in Washington and their son in Napa. I'm sure they'll all want to come for a visit."

"Aye, we'll toast to them, too!"

Sean laughed. "I hope ye're keeping count."

"I think we're at four, but we can drink to five just in case we missed one."

They walked into a clearing with a log cabin nestled against a wall of trees and two rocking chairs on a covered porch. Elliott oriented himself and recognized the spot, but it was thick with trees and underbrush in his time. According to the farm's log, there was a fire on the farm in the late eighteen hundreds, and a hunting cabin burned down. Soon after the fire, Sean had his lawyer draft restrictions to protect the site in perpetuity and returned to its natural state. Even if a foundation still existed, underbrush had long ago reclaimed the land.

"Is this a hunting lodge?" Elliott asked.

"No, a hideout. I come here to read, enjoy a wee dram of whisky, or visit with auld friends who are more suited to rustic settings. Lyle Ann knows when no one can find me in the stallion barn or my office that I'm here." Sean pulled out a pocket watch. "It's six thirty. We have an hour before she'll send someone to fetch us."

"I should send word to Meredith that I'm with ye."

"I don't have a communication device similar to what ye have in yer time. But I have a pencil and a piece of paper." Sean removed a pocket notebook and a pencil from his jacket, tore out a piece of paper, and jotted down a note. Then he rolled it up and laced it through the horse's reins that he then wrapped around the saddle horn.

"I believe it'll stay put." Sean swatted the horse's rump, and it trotted off. "One of the grooms will get the message and pass it on to Lyle Ann. That might buy us another thirty minutes. Dinner is at eight thirty, and if we're not back by then, we might as well just stay right here for the night."

"I think ye've hit onto something. I might have to build a log cabin when I go home, or maybe we can come up with a plan to ensure this one survives well into the future."

Elliott followed Sean into a simply furnished room with worn, wide-plank wooden floors and a big stone fireplace. A breeze from the open door disturbed a troupe of dust motes that danced in front of the sunny windows. Elliott sniffed, smelling woodsmoke and age, but not neglect.

"My grandfather built the cabin afore he sailed back to Scotland. I improved on it, adding a shingled roof and glass windows." Sean crossed the room and opened a corner cabinet. "And a supply of The Glenlivet."

"Pour me a double. We have a lot to toast to," Elliott said, studying the collection of books on the bookshelf: *Treasure Island, The Adventures of Huckleberry Finn, The Last of the Mohicans.*

Elliott took the glass and swirled the contents, sniffed, and smiled. "To Kit!"

They drank their first toast.

"To Cullen," Sean said, and they drank their second.

"To Donald," Elliott said, and they drank their third.

"To blessings," Sean said, and they drank their fourth before refilling their glasses. "Here's to yer horses." They drank their fifth toast then Sean asked. "How are yer horses running?"

"I was about to ask the same question."

Sean beamed. "We won the eleventh running of the Kentucky Derby two weeks ago."

Elliott sure liked the sound of that, but he had to dig back into his memory of the farm's history to recall the first Derby winner. "Ah! With Joe Cotton. How could I forget? Congratulations." He held up his glass. "To Joe Cotton."

They drank to the horse's success. "Keokuk tried to steal the race in the early going with a first quarter-mile in 25 ¾ seconds, six furlongs in 1:17 ¼—the fastest clockings in a one-and-a-half-mile Derby."

"The track must have been fast," Elliott said.

"It was wet, but he did a mile in 1:44, the fastest on a wet track in a twelve-furlong Derby. Joe Cotton had moved from seventh in the field of ten to fifth by that point, then unleashed a powerful run—"

"Under jockey Babe Henderson, right?" Elliott asked, following Sean to the front porch.

"Helluva jockey. By that point, even Lyle Ann was excited. Then Joe Cotton gained the lead with a little more than a furlong to run. But Bersan, who had been close to the pace most of the way under Ed West, wasn't finished."

Sean called the race as if it were happening now, and his voice pitched higher as it accelerated. "Bersan narrowed Joe Cotton's lead, and Ten Booker gained ground with every stride. Joe Cotton arrived at the wire in 2:37 ¼—a dandy time on the wet track—a neck ahead of Bersan, with Ten Booker half a length behind."

"Splendid." Elliott lifted his glass in another toast. "*Sláinte!* I've had a few races like that, and every time I say, 'That's it. I'm too old to endure races won at the wire.'"

"It's going to be the death of me, but at least I'll go out smiling," Sean said. "Joe Cotton is racing in the Belmont next week. If it's a race like the Derby, they'll have to carry me home."

"Next week, huh? If it didn't take days to get to New York and back again, I'd go with ye."

"We have a private railroad car. It'll take two days to get there, two to get home. What do ye say?"

"Let me think about it and talk to Meredith. We brought Emily Duffy with us, but she can't stay too long because of her diabetes." Elliott eased into one of the rockers and almost sighed. It seemed like days since he'd paused long enough to breathe easily.

And it was only this morning that Penny brought him news that changed their lives.

They rocked in silence while sipping their drinks. Then Sean asked, "How many brooches do ye have now? When ye went to Napa, Thomas said ye had the ruby, sapphire, emerald, and amethyst. Have ye found others?"

"Four more found us—diamond, amber, pearl, topaz—and a fifth one has surfaced. We're here to find it, as well as my son."

"Yer son traveled with one and didn't tell ye?"

"Aye, and we have reason to believe he's coming here. A friend of his disappeared, but we think the brooch got too hot to hold, and she dropped it. James Cullen found it, and for some reason, decided to rescue her and not involve me. We believe he also dropped the brooch, and a third person picked it up and disappeared. What we don't know is who the third person is working for, or if he's a threat to James Cullen and the brooches."

"Who would want to hurt him?"

"We learned recently that early in the 1600s, the Keeper dispersed the brooches to keep them safe, but we didn't know who or what the threat was. We now believe we know, and it's a threat to all of us, now and in the future."

"But ye can't tell me?" Sean asked.

"That's right."

"Are ye the Keeper in the future?"

"I can't tell ye that, either."

Sean rocked his chair, and it creaked against the oak floorboards.

"When I was about eighteen, I came out here to find my grandfather. He was sittin' on this porch, talkin' to a man in a red cloak. He had markings down his arm to his fingertips. I'd never seen him before or since, but he seemed to know my grandfather well. They laughed and talked in old Gaelic while I hid in the trees. When the sun began to set, they went inside the cabin. I waited for another hour or so, and then my grandfather came out and walked away. I waited a while longer and probably dozed off, but the man never came out. It was getting dark, but I couldn't leave until I found out who he was.

"I knocked on the door. When no one answered, I went in expecting to find the man, but he wasn't there. To this day, I don't know where he went."

There was much more to the story than a disappearing man in a red cloak whom Elliott assumed was Erik, but he didn't know what. "Did ye smell anything unusual inside the cabin?"

"Nothing. And there were no lamps on or a fire in the fireplace. A man went in, stayed for a while, and then vanished."

"And ye never mentioned it to yer grandfather."

"Never. Grandfather would have walloped me if he caught me spying on him."

"Is there a cellar or a tunnel?"

"I've searched several times over the years but never found one."

Just then, Cullen trotted into the clearing. "Lyle Ann got yer message, but she sent me out here to make sure ye both make it to dinner."

"What about Meredith?" Elliott asked.

"The ladies just opened one of the bottles of Montgomery Winery chardonnay Meredith packed in her trunk. She said not to hurry." Cullen dismounted and looped the reins over the hitching rail at the side of the cabin. "It's good to see ye, Sean."

The two men clasped arms, hugged, and thumped each other's backs. "It's good to see ye, too. We need to make another toast. Let me get ye a wee dram."

As soon as Sean went inside the cabin, Elliott said to Cullen, "Sean just told me about a man who was here years ago meeting with his grandfather. Based on the description, it had to be Erik."

"We knew Erik traveled around, but I wonder why he was here," Cullen said.

"I wish I knew."

"Maybe Tavis knows."

"I doubt it, and even if he did, he wouldn't tell me. I've got to get inside this cabin alone and investigate."

Sean returned with Cullen's drink. "Take my chair. I'll get another one."

Cullen took the wee dram and sat on the railing. "Not necessary, Sean. This is fine. Kit told me to come right back. She wants to tour the stallion barn." He held up his glass. "*Sláinte!*"

Sean resettled in the rocking chair. "What's it like living in the future? Are ye happy there? Is Kit?"

"We're both happy, but we miss the children and grandchildren. As for what it's like, it's easy. Kit and I don't have to worry about having food to eat or a place to live, partly because we get a share of the business at the winery since we're legacy owners. We didn't want it, but Meredith insisted, and ye can't argue with her."

"Do ye live here at the farm or the winery?"

"We split our time between MacKlenna Farm and Charlotte and Braham's home in Virginia. Occasionally we go to the winery, but there isn't anything we can do there. At least at the farm, we can work with the Thoroughbreds. Would ye believe travel time between Lexington and Richmond is ninety minutes? Ninety minutes!" Cullen shook his head. "If I want to ask Braham a question, I press a button, and he answers. And not only can I talk to him, but I can see him, too. I could be in Scotland, and he could be in Virginia, and it happens just like that," Cullen said with a snap of his fingers.

"But it's the health care system that keeps us from coming back to this time. We don't have to worry about our health, and at our age, that's important. Maybe in the next few years, we can start visiting the family regularly."

Sean straightened, his eyes darkening as he regarded Cullen, reminding Elliott of how Kit's eyes betrayed her emotions, too. "How can ye do that? I thought each brooch had a particular purpose."

"We're hoping to find a portal that allows us to go back and forth easily."

"How's that possible."

Elliott hissed an annoyed breath. Cullen was talking too much, and it was time for Elliott to cut him off. Sean might be a MacKlenna, but he didn't need to know any more about the brooches than he already did. He might inadvertently say or do something to alert unknown forces that would have ramifications in the future.

"We're hoping for enlightenment," Elliott said.

Sean turned up his glass and finished his drink. "I hope ye don't plan to twist some arms while ye're here to get other family members to travel with ye. I'd hate to lose anyone else to the future."

Elliott finished his drink, too, and stood. "If we don't get a telegram off to the Montgomery children, Kit and Cullen won't be able to see their families. Why don't we go to the house and change for dinner?" He took Sean's empty glass. "I'll put these away. Ye two go on up to the house, and I'll be right behind ye."

He caught Cullen's eye and signaled with a nod that Cullen understood. "We can ride double on my horse and leave Elliott to stroll to the mansion at his leisure. Kit wants to see yer stallions, and she'd prefer to take the tour with ye instead of yer manager."

Sean turned to Elliott. "Ye can ride with Cullen, and I'll walk."

"No, ye go. I want to explore the farm as it is now." What Elliott wanted to do was take pictures of the cabin and the grounds. It could wait until morning, but if he'd learned anything during his travels, it was not to put anything off. The opportunity might not come again.

As soon as Cullen and Sean were out of sight, Elliott walked the perimeter, taking pictures from every angle and on all four sides, paying particular attention to the foundation. If there was anything below the structure, he couldn't find it now, but David could use a metal detector and discover any crevices, caves, or tunnels beneath the cabin.

After taking all the pictures he wanted of the premises, he walked each side, one foot right in front of the other, counting his steps, and came up with a rough measurement of thirty by twenty. Then he opened the cabin door, stood on the threshold, and did a visual inspection of the shadowed cabin. The logs on the back wall appeared to match those on the outside, so it was unlikely there was a false wall. He walked the interior just as he did outside and arrived at nearly the same measurements.

So, where did Erik go?

Elliott lit a lantern and carried it over to the stone fireplace that spanned nearly half the wall's width and rose to the seven-foot ceiling.

I heard a scraping sound…

If a portion of the fireplace swung open into the room, it could lead to a tunnel. But why would Erik have to use a tunnel? He had a brooch that could take him anywhere. And the bigger question…why hadn't Erik mentioned it?

The same reason I didn't explain everything to Sean.

If the fireplace held a secret, it would have to wait till later. He wished David and Kenzie had come along. On the other hand, while Meredith wasn't as good at solving riddles and puzzles, she always had insights into situations that often never occurred to him.

He'd bring her back here tomorrow, tell her what he knew, and let her toss out ideas. Maybe together they could solve the mystery. If not, it would have to wait until they returned home.

32

The Badlands (1885)—Ensley

T HE WEATHER CHANGED drastically during Ensley and TR's hard ride to Medora. By midafternoon she was soaked with sweat, and the chills set in. Before her teeth started chattering, she needed to warm up.

"I have to stop and unpack the buffalo robe I borrowed."

TR reined in his horse. "I didn't know you did."

"Mrs. Sewall said you wouldn't mind. I've gotten chilled, and I don't want to get sick." She pulled up beside him and dismounted.

"You seem to be grimacing a lot. Is it from the cold, or are you in pain?"

"It's my hip." She untied the buffalo robe from the back of the saddle. "I injured it years ago after being thrown by a bull who didn't want me on his back."

"A bull?"

"I know," she said, slipping her arms into the warm robe. "It was dumb."

"You're lucky you didn't break any bones."

She mounted up again. "Oh, I did—hip, arm, wrist, ankle, leg—and now I can forecast the weather. Some believe the change in barometric pressure before it rains changes the pressure inside your joints. But"—she squeezed her legs, urging Tesoro forward—"studies show there's no significant increase in pain. I don't believe it, though. My wrist always hurts before a rainstorm."

"Hippocrates discussed the effects of wind and rain on chronic disease in his book *On Airs, Waters, and Places.*"

"Well, there you go. Who am I to doubt Hippocrates?" She drank from her canteen before splitting the last biscuit with TR.

He gobbled his share up in two bites. "What do you do for the pain?"

"I stretch and try to keep my hip loose, but that's hard to do when I'm riding for several hours. But," she said with a grin, "I can do anything and make it through any day, as long as I know a steamy bath is waiting for me at the end of it."

He grimaced, and it could have been a smile, not of pleasure or amusement, but sympathy. "As soon as we unload the cattle, we'll have to move them out and get them bedded down. You won't have time."

She settled into the soft, thick fur enveloping her. It was almost as welcoming as a bath. "No bath? Then I'll have to rely on my tolerance for pain to get me through."

"You'd have to suffer a lot to develop a pain tolerance."

"I've noticed pain is worse when I'm sad or unfocused. If I stay happy and productive, it's easier to manage."

He studied her for a moment, almost as if he was examining one of the critters he used to keep in specimen jars. "For what purpose would you try to become tolerant of any kind of pain? I understand avoiding it, but why work to tolerate it?"

"If you know it's going to be around for a while, you have a choice. Do your best to tolerate it or be miserable." She adjusted the length of the robe to cover her legs. "Think about the pain you experience when you do physical labor or exercise. If you're like me, you'll push yourself until you can't take any more. Instead of looking at the exertion as painful, I see it as a sign."

"Of what?"

"That I've put in the effort, worked toward a goal, endured the struggle." She let him think about that for a moment before she continued, "The more I'm able to tolerate and deal with pain or painful experiences, the more I can push boundaries and open up to new opportunities. I knew long hours in the saddle would irritate my hip, but I didn't want to miss this chance of a lifetime."

He gave her another one of those looks. "Going on a roundup is a chance of a lifetime?"

She smothered a laugh, and for the first time, she connected with him, not as a historical figure or a future president, but as a man her age who had also suffered a significant loss.

"Of course. Don't you feel the same way? Isn't that why you're here in the Dakotas?"

"I came to hunt, but I don't believe that's why you're here."

He was right about that. "Well, I do love to hunt, but I also enjoy stimulating political discussions, educational pursuits, and reading everything I can find. If I stayed where I was comfortable and never built up my tolerance, I'd have fewer chances to broaden my horizons.

"It's like going on a roundup," she continued. "It's grueling, the weather's horrible, and the food isn't much better. But at the end of it all, there's a real sense of accomplishment. At least I hope there will be. Staying in the saddle for forty hours straight, getting thrown off horses, blistering your hands…you love that, and you're willing to accept the consequences so you can do what you want to do. It's not about living with pain. It's about how you handle it."

He nodded. "And you handle it well, Mrs. Fraser."

She wasn't sure Barb would agree with him. She was the only person Ensley ever complained to, and while it wasn't *that* often, she did occasionally gripe about her hip, her job, her dates, her landlord, whatever pissed her off that day—like bitchy clients. And Barb complained right back to her.

It was part of being yourself with your BFF. Neither of them carried it to extremes, but they were always honest with each other. And right now, she'd have to confess to Barb that her hip hurt worse than it ever had. She'd trade her gold nuggets for a bottle of ibuprofen. Or better yet, a cortisone shot in her hip.

But she and TR didn't talk anymore about pain—emotional or physical—as they continued toward Medora. Ensley spent the time sorting the information she was collecting about TR into mental folders. She originally planned to write a short Great American Novel about TR and the Badlands. But by the time she went home, she'd have enough original material to write a full-length one, and they hadn't even gotten around to the subject of conservation.

A mile outside of Medora, TR pointed ahead. "See that dam? The Marquis de Morès built it to create an ice pond for his refrigerating plant. I'm going to cross there. You can take the footpath between the tracks on the train trestle."

A footpath between the tracks? Seriously? How safe is that?

Ensley studied the ice-cutting crew and how carefully they were moving around the pond. Crossing over the dam wasn't safe, either.

"Teddy, if you fall, you could get severe hypothermia, or drown, or seriously injure your horse."

He studied her gravely and then gave her one of his patented, toothy TR grins. "Once Manitou gets his feet on that dam, he'll keep them there, and we can make it across."

"I won't try to stop you, but you're taking an unnecessary risk. Look at the river…" She pointed toward the water. "It's overtopped the dam, and you can't even see where it meets the bank. If you fall—"

He shot her an irritated glance, then nudged Manitou toward the dam. "I'll be fine, Mrs. Fraser. I'll see you on the other side."

"Give me the reins to the piebald. No point in taking two horses into the icy water."

Just because she couldn't stop his crazy stunt didn't mean she had to stand by and watch passively. She'd been roping steers since she was ten years old. And while she'd never roped a future president to save him from drowning in an ice pond, how different could it be? She quickly tied the reins to the two extra horses over the wheel of a wagonload of ice-cutting equipment parked there, then untied the loop strap holding her rope to the horn.

Her dad's voice played in her head. "Hold the coil, reins, and tail of the rope in your left hand, Ens. The loop in your right."

She smiled, remembering that her hand had barely been big enough to hold all three. But as she grew and her hands got bigger, it became easier to manage, and she kept all of them securely in her hand.

Swinging a rope from the back of a horse was second nature to her, but she was unsure how Tesoro would handle it. Although he hadn't balked yet at anything she asked of him, so he should be okay.

She patted his neck. "Let's be ready, boy. Teddy might need help."

Manitou stepped calmly into the flow, but she held her breath because the tightness around the horse's eyes and muzzle signaled that he wasn't sure of what TR was asking him to do. But not TR. He kept his attention fastened on what was in front of him.

The horse walked only a few paces before he lost his footing. Ensley gasped, and Tesoro stomped his hoof while TR and his mount tumbled into the river, disappearing underwater.

A handful of men rushed to the bank, but she was already there swinging her rope. "Can anybody see him?" she called out.

"He hasn't surfaced yet," one of the men yelled.

"I'll lasso him as soon as I get eyes on him."

Moments later, TR surfaced, swimming toward shore on his horse's downstream side, one hand on the saddle horn and the other pushing ice floes out of the way. He didn't need a rope, but he'd need blankets and dry clothes. She dismounted and hurried to meet him when he climbed out of the ice pond.

She yanked off the buffalo robe and shoved it at him. "That was reckless."

TR laughed, readjusting the glasses that had somehow stayed on his nose. "I suppose it was, but it was lots of fun."

"Well, you'd better get out of those wet clothes, or we'll be going to your funeral." She stomped off, shaking her head and ranting under her breath about stupid stunts that came close to killing people. Austin O'Grady's motorcycle accident came to mind, and she got mad at Austin all over again. "What a waste."

And while she was ranting about TR's and Austin's stupidity, she might as well rant about sports addicts who would rather sit at a bar, drink beer, and watch some stupid basketball game than drink wine and see a new Broadway production.

She yelled over her shoulder. "I'm going to find my husband."

The sun was setting as she walked across the train trestle's narrow footpath, leading three horses into Medora. Nothing about the town's scattered buildings looked familiar except for the Marquis de Morès's chateau, situated on a hill and silhouetted by the setting sun.

She'd toured the historic house museum—a twenty-six room, two-story frame summer home—that belonged to the Marquis and his wife, Medora. Ensley would love to see the house in its original condition and even meet the woman with a town named after her, but she doubted she'd have time.

If not now…when?

Her itinerary had no scheduled leisure time, and she wondered if JC would do any sightseeing, especially in Chicago. He should spend some time there. It might be his only chance to visit the nineteenth-century city.

She stopped near the railroad tracks. Where was she going to start looking? It wasn't like it would take hours. All she had to do was ask the first man she ran into if he'd seen JC.

He'd probably look for a room where he could get a bath and a hot meal. That's what she wanted, too. And he'd also go to the depot to check on the next train heading east. That's where she'd start her search.

Near the railroad track was a rough-board shanty that might be the depot. A single smoky lantern burned inside, illuminating a man with a wiry mustache under a red nose. He looked like he spent more time at the Big-Mouthed Bob's Bug-Juice Dispensary—the town saloon—than he did at the depot.

She tethered the horses, then stood at the window and waited for him to look up from a large ledger book. He must have sensed her eyes on him, and when he looked up, he leered at her. "Can I help ya?"

"I'm looking for my…husband. He's here to catch the next train going east."

The man opened the window. "Only one person boarded that train. Tall feller with a black horse. That your man?"

"He's tall and has a black horse, but there could be other tall men with black horses in town. And his train wasn't due here until late tonight."

The man opened his pocket watch, glanced at the time, then snapped it shut again. "Train came in early. It was going in the right direction, so your man bought a ticket. The rest of the men in town are heading out on the roundup startin' next week."

Her heart sank. She wanted to see JC, but it was better this way. She didn't want to have to tell him goodbye again. Now she'd have to find a room and bath on her own. "What about a hotel? Where can I get a room?"

He pointed across the street. "The Pyramid Park Hotel is right over there. Mr. Paddock and his partner divided the second floor into rooms recently, counting on summer tourists to repay the outlay. Ain't seen any tourists this week. So there might be a vacancy."

"Thanks for your help." She turned to leave but turned back and asked, "Do you know Mr. Roosevelt?"

"Four Eyes? Everybody around here knows who he is."

"Will you tell him I've gone to the hotel to get a room, and then I'm going to get dinner. He's expecting a trainload of cattle tonight. Do you know when the train will come in?"

"About now."

"Now?" She groaned. "Is that a for-sure thing, or just your best guess?"

He held up a piece of paper. "Got a telegram for Mr. Roosevelt from Mr. Sewall. He sent it from Bismarck. Said he'd be in Medora by nine o'clock tonight."

Her empty stomach dropped. As soon as TR and his men unloaded the cows, he'd want to get them out of town. She plopped down into a chair on the small platform to wait for TR, the cows, and a very long night. She leaned her head against the wall and closed her eyes.

"Mrs. Fraser."

Ensley opened one eye. That was all she could manage when she was this tired. "I hate that name. Don't we have an agreement?"

TR glanced around, then looked back at her. "I will as long as no one is around to hear me address you so informally."

"That works for me." She squared herself in the chair. "You put on dry clothes."

He handed her the buffalo robe. "I'm sorry it's so wet."

She folded it inside out to let the underside of the hide dry. "Did you get your telegram?"

"It's from Bill Sewall. They should be here about now. Do you want to get supper?"

She shot up out of her chair. They'd eaten the last of the fried chicken hours ago, and she was hoarding the one remaining apple for an emergency. She'd shared the last biscuit, and, as thin as TR was, she probably should share the apple, too.

"As long as I don't have to cook, I'll eat anything. But do we have time?"

"We'll make time." TR passed a coin to the red-nosed agent. "Send word when the train arrives."

She stepped off the platform, gathered the tethered horses' reins, and led them toward the hotel. "What's your plan after you get the cattle unloaded?"

"Since the river is dangerously high, we can't take the herd across, so we'll have to stay clear of the valley and trek inland."

"No water or rest for the weary. How about I take the horses over to the livery stable and have them brushed and fed, and you go make arrangements for dinner?"

"Tell the owner to put the feed on my bill."

"I can pay for mine."

"I'm sure you can, Ensley. But why would you want to?"

She rolled her eyes. "Because I want to pay my way, Teddy." She emphasized his name as he had done with hers.

"Your husband gave me funds for your care. Save your pin money for new clothes."

If she wasn't so tired, she'd let him know in no uncertain terms that she found his pin money comment offensive. The term pin money had been used in a derogatory way to demean working women's wages since the days of the suffragists. But arguing with him was a waste of energy.

"Okay, then. I'll save my pin money." She snatched Manitou's reins out of his hand. "Save me a seat." Then she tramped through the sagebrush, leading four horses to the livery stable, where she told the owner to put the feed on TR's bill.

"How'd Manitou get so wet?" the owner asked.

"He fell into the ice pond. Will you dry off Mr. Roosevelt's gear, too? And oil the saddle and bridle afterward so the leather won't dry out."

The man laughed. "Did he take Mr. Roosevelt in with him?"

"Sure did. Do the best you can. He's got fifteen hundred head coming in tonight on the train, so he'll have a long night in the saddle."

"Are you Mrs. Roosevelt?"

"No, my husband is a cousin from New York City. We came out to go hunting with Theodore." That was the last lie she and JC concocted before he left the ranch. He thought it would be easier for her if she had a direct connection to TR. And now, even though she hadn't practiced telling that lie, it rolled right off her tongue so quickly she almost believed it herself.

She glanced around, looking for an empty stall or a tack room where she could clean up, but all the stalls were full, and a chuck-wagon blocked the only door that could lead to a tack room. Just as well. She didn't want to keep TR waiting.

She grabbed her saddlebags but didn't want to carry the damp buffalo robe. "Do you mind if I spread this out here? Mr. Roosevelt put it on when he came out of the ice pond, and it's wet."

"Sure." He took the robe and laid it out on top of a stack of hay bales.

"Thanks. I'm going to meet Mr. Roosevelt for dinner at the hotel. We'll be back in an hour."

"This Arabian is a beautiful horse. Never seen one like him. Shines like gold."

"He's an Akhal-Teke, an endurance horse, and gentle as a lamb."

"His hooded eyes are unusual."

"Selective breeding by ancient armies who wanted to intimidate enemies with horses that looked like dragons."

"Dragons, huh?" The owner cocked his head. "Seen a picture of a dragon once. I can't say I agree, but he does look different from other horses."

"Just don't try to ride him. He's loyal and can be ferocious." She rubbed Tesoro's forehead. "I'll be back after I eat. Get some rest, boy. We're going to have a long night." Tesoro nudged her shoulder, and she chuckled.

Before she reached the door, she turned back, and she saw something in Tesoro's marbled brown eyes, a look that said he knew the future and wanted her to know he would always protect her.

I know you will, dear Tesoro.

She tried to shake the feeling as she hurried over to the Pyramid Park Hotel—a crude, nondescript two-story, rectangular building. Still, the feeling lingered like the taste of fine wine, or the emotions evoked by a good romance novel, or the exhilaration of completing a distance race.

Once inside the hotel, she was back to normal.

A corner of the large ground floor served as the manager's office, dominated by a rough desk with a small showcase of brightly labeled cheap cigars. Surely TR wouldn't smoke one of those. She'd gag if he did. Good-smelling cigars reminded her of her grandfather, but stinky ones evoked memories of the drunk driver who killed her dad.

Arranged along the walls were several chairs and benches, all unoccupied right now, and in another corner stood a makeshift sink with tin basins. Dirty towels hung on wall racks. *That's it?* She glanced around.

They sure don't expect women to stay here. Well, to hell with it.

It wasn't like she hadn't just spent a week trekking through the Badlands with JC and little privacy.

She turned her back to the room and used one of the antibacterial wipes to wash up. When she rolled up the used wipe and tucked it into an empty pocket, she discovered a pair of deerskin gloves she'd never seen before.

JC, bless your heart.

After she ran a brush through her hair and tied it back with a strip of rawhide, she then, like a breeze, blew through the lobby toward the dining area, where she found TR sitting at a long table with four other men.

If she acted like it was typical of women in the frontier to wear pants to dinner, maybe the men would take it in stride. Besides, she didn't have the tall, slim-waisted, voluptuous shape of women in the late 1800s, so maybe they'd just ignore her.

When she approached the table, TR stood. The other men, one at a time, smacked the guy next to him on the arm, and they all popped up, one after the other, shuffling their feet and pressing down the fronts of their dirty shirts.

"Welcome, Mrs. Fraser," TR said, pointing to the plate next to him. "This plate is for you."

She smiled, removed her hat, and sniffed. "Smells good."

A man across from TR had the classic western look with a bushy black mustache. Its tips extended to his jawline. "It is, ma'am. Mr. Roosevelt's been telling us you were standing by ready to lasso him when he fell into the ice pond. I'd like to have seen that."

"What?" Ensley asked, giving him a bigger smile. "Mr. Roosevelt pushing away the ice floes or me lassoing him like a steer?"

The men all laughed, and TR right along with them.

"I reckon both," the man said. "Never seen a woman who could lasso a steer, much less a drowning man."

"I wasn't drowning," TR said.

"He wasn't drowning," Ensley said at the same time.

Another man with a full beard passed her a bowl of potatoes. "Here ya go, ma'am. Better eat up. Mr. Roosevelt says you're going on the drive with him. Better eat while ya can."

She took the bowl. "Then I'll shovel in a few of them and take some of the venison, too."

The men passed the rest of the bowls with bacon, beans, biscuits with jam, and fruit, straight out of a can. It wasn't gourmet, but it got the job done. When they finished, she and TR said good-night to the men and left the hotel to pick up their horses.

A long whistle and clacking wheels alerted them the train was coming over the trestle bridge.

"The train's bringing fifteen hundred hungry, thirsty cows. It's not too late to bow out. I can make arrangements with the Marquis for you to stay at his home until the next train heading east comes by."

She put her hands on her hips. "You're not getting rid of me that easily."

He grinned. "I would have been shocked if you'd taken me up on my offer."

The train slowed but didn't stop. "I guess the train isn't stopping in town. How far out is it going?"

"About a mile," TR said.

"I can't believe we're doing this in the dark," Ensley said. "But I guess the cattle can't stay on the cars and hold the train up."

They picked up their horses and rode out to meet the train. The moment they arrived, two men climbed down, carrying lanterns. "Roosevelt, is that you?"

TR rode toward them. "It is. How are the cattle, Bill?"

"They arrived in fair condition," one of the men said. "But since being corralled and branded, they've gone without food while crowded into railroad cars for a punishing three-day ride here."

"Sewall and I moved back and forth among the train's twenty-two cars, checking the animals and keeping them on their feet to save them from being trampled," the other man said. "We got steers mostly, but there are some shorthorn bulls and one polled Angus."

Ensley assumed the two men were Bill Sewall and Wilmot Dow, TR's partners.

"We can't let them get near that river tonight," TR said. "It's a raging torrent, and its bottom is a treacherous mass of quicksand. We'll have to drive the animals down along the divide west of Medora between the Little Missouri and the Beaver."

"They won't like it," Sewall said.

"They can go thirsty or drown," TR said. "I'd prefer they go thirsty."

"Who ya got with ya?" Dow asked.

TR turned toward her. "This is Mrs. Fraser. She's writing a story about a cattle roundup, and she has assured me she won't be a hindrance." TR pointed first to one man and then to the other. "He's Dow. He's Sewall."

"My husband is Mr. Roosevelt's cousin," Ensley offered. "We came out from New York to go hunting, but instead, I'm tagging along." She was over-explaining, and it wasn't necessary. "And I met your wife and daughter at the cabin." Now she was really over-explaining, "Your wife was very gracious, and your daughter is precious." She'd have to explain the lie to TR as soon as they were alone.

Shut up!

"Thank ya, ma'am. I'm sorta partial to them."

Two more men rode up. "Bout time ya got here," one of the men said.

"If they'd let me drive the train, we woulda been here yesterday," Dow said.

One of the men who just rode up said, "We'll cut the first five hundred and head south to the Maltese Cross Ranch. Probably bed down about a half mile from here. How many men do you have with you?"

"Sewall, Dow, Rowe, two others. We'll manage," TR said.

"That's all we need," Sewall said. "Drovers are nothin' but trouble. They work hard, play hard, fight hard. Don't need 'em on this drive."

TR glanced at Ensley. "I mentioned Merrifield and Ferris to you earlier. They manage the Maltese Cross Ranch." Then to Bill Merrifield, he said, "Mrs. Fraser is from New York City. She's writing a story about roundups."

"Welcome, ma'am," Merrifield said. "Don't know why you want to write about this. It's hard work, bad food, and ornery cows."

"Mr. Merrifield, if it was easy, nobody would want to read dime novels about cowboys. How would you like to star in one?" she asked.

Sewall smiled and offered, "*I* would, ma'am. You don't have to write about him. Write about me. Then my sweet Lucretia can read about her papa when she goes to school."

Ensley laughed. "I'll see what I can do."

TR's horse sidestepped. "Let's open the doors and get the cattle off. The night's going to be long enough."

The bawling cattle created a continuous din. And Ensley thought for the second, third, or twentieth time that they should wait for daylight to unload them, but she could tell from their bawling that the cows and steers would probably crash through the walls of the cattle car if they stayed inside any longer.

"You never know what the cows will do. They'll keep us jumping, always on the watch," Dow said.

"They'll need to crop a mouthful of grass before they bed down," Sewall said. "We'll get the herd going north, then turn them into a loose circle until morning."

"Speaking of eating," TR said, "did you get a cook?"

"He should be here with the chuckwagon," Dow said, glancing around. "Don't see him yet."

"I saw a loaded chuckwagon at the livery stable, but I didn't see a driver around," Ensley said.

After the clang and screech of the cattle car doors opening, the bellowing cows and steers leaped out, sounding like the thundering herd they were.

"Take your five hundred from the last seven cars and get 'em out of the way," Sewall yelled.

Before Ensley rode off, she said to TR, "I apologize for the cousin lie. I thought it would be easier to explain my presence."

"I'm not in the habit of encouraging anyone to lie, but it seems harmless enough."

Ensley spurred her horse into a gallop and swung her rope, yelling. "Move out! Move out!" She galloped alongside the emerging herd toward Merrifield, who was riding point, holding his lantern high enough for everyone to see.

The cows were moving in the right direction through buffalo grass, covering almost every inch of the ground. She circled back to get more of the cows and steers and kept doubling back until she reached the end. Merrifield's lantern continued to guide the riders to where they needed to go.

A man whose voice she didn't recognize yelled, "That's all of 'em out of the front cattle cars."

She rode back to tell TR the herd was far enough away that he could let the rest out. The doors squeaked open, and the bellowing increased as the cattle jumped out. Ensley continued riding hard, swinging her rope, yelling directions until she reached the point where Sewall held his lantern aloft as Merrifield had done.

"Get 'em in a circle," Sewall yelled.

All the riders started moving the herd into a circle. Ensley lost track of TR, and without Sewall's lantern, she would have gotten lost herself. Her adrenaline pumped, and her cheeks tingled from the cold night air, but God, she loved this. Once the cattle were all in a circle, they grazed a while before bedding down. She and the men would draw straws to see who would have the night watch.

It was the middle of the night when she followed the circle of torches to the chuckwagon. TR was there, sipping coffee from a tin cup.

"You okay?" she asked, pulling off her gloves to retie her ponytail.

"Bully," he said.

"We sure could use more men."

"I know, but we'll have to make do."

She folded her gloves over her waistband and accepted a cup of coffee from a man she assumed was the cook. "I'm Ensley," she said.

"Norman Lebo."

She sipped the lukewarm brew. It was bitter and full of grounds, but, as tired as she was, she didn't care. "Norman, you make a special blend of coffee from roasted coffee beans strong enough to float a horseshoe, don't you?"

"I try, ma'am." He hung around, holding the coffee pot, acting like he had something on his mind, and was debating whether to say anything or not. Finally, he said, "I heard we had a woman along. Normally it's bad luck, but you being Mr. Roosevelt's cousin and a writer, guess it'll be all right."

"Well, thanks, Norman," she teased. "I guess it'll be all right having a cook along on this drive as well."

He grinned. "You want anything, Mrs. Fraser, just ask."

"I will, but I don't want any special treatment."

"Aw, shucks, ma'am. Kinda hard not to treat you special. Ya better get some sleep. Breakfast is in a couple of hours."

Norman returned the coffee pot to the grate over the firepit, and when he was out of hearing range, TR said, "Only one of the men has any experience. I'm going to make him the trail boss."

"Which one?"

"Barney. The man who showed up at the Elkhorn Ranch with the message."

"Does he have experience as a trail boss or just punching cows?"

"He's never been a trail boss, but he knows cows."

Ensley emptied her cup, hoping the caffeine wouldn't keep her from dozing off for an hour or so. "If he doesn't know what he's doing, everything will get snarled up, and you'll waste time trying to disentangle the situation. I'll watch him, and if I notice anything going off the rails, you'll want to take over immediately. You have too much money in this herd to lose your investment to incompetence."

TR chuckled. "If he can't do the job, then I'll put you in charge."

She laughed out loud. "Not me. I'm no trail boss. I'm just a writer looking for a story."

"You're much more than that, Mrs. Fraser. Get some sleep."

She walked away to unsaddle Tesoro, wondering what TR meant by that. But didn't spend time dwelling on it.

When she put Tesoro in the makeshift corral to graze, she gave his withers a good rub. "You did great today, big guy. I'll give you the morning off."

Tesoro nudged her shoulder. "You don't want to be left out, do you?" She rubbed his head. "Take the morning off. If I don't let you rest, my dad will reach down from heaven and shake me silly. So do me a favor, will you? Just take it easy."

He nudged her shoulder again, letting her know he was there to protect her, and she didn't need to protect him.

"Okay. You win. Get some sleep." She walked away with her bedroll, knowing Tesoro's eyes were on her, and she could almost hear him smile.

33

Chicago, IL (1885)—James Cullen

AWARENESS RETURNED, BUT JC knew if his breathing changed, or if he even twitched, Sten and his thugs would know he was awake, and the beatings would continue. From what little he'd seen from beneath swollen eyelids, he was in a cold, uninhabited meatpacking plant.

Sten had stripped him of everything. He wasn't going to risk JC escaping again.

JC was well-schooled in a Tibetan esoteric meditative discipline. He could control his breathing and block the pain sensations from going to his brain, but he couldn't escape Sten's determination to torture him until he died.

His wrists were bound together by a rope looped over a meat hook hanging from the ceiling, with his bare feet dangling only a few inches above the floor. Before he passed out for the third or fourth time, the two beefy men from the alley used him as a punching bag, laughing as each man landed a heavy blow that swung JC in another direction.

He had a broken nose and broken ribs, and he'd probably be pissing blood for weeks…that is if he survived round three and four and five before they killed him.

The rope had cut into his wrists, and blood was running down his arms, mixing with his sweat. Blood gushed from his nose and ran over his lips, his chin, to his chest.

Sten wanted to know where the Keeper kept the MacKlenna brooches, but JC would take that to his grave—which would probably be in the Chicago River.

He was under no illusion that he would survive whatever Sten had in store for him, but could he die with dignity?

Or would he scream and piss himself? That's what terrified him most.

Jack Mallory had survived weeks with cotton balls shoved in his ears to muffle all sound and his head stuffed in a canvas sack. He could see nothing, hear nothing, smell nothing, except the stink of his own body. Jack would have gone crazy without the ability to escape through meditation.

It was the only chance JC had of dying with honor. He would never give Sten the satisfaction of hearing him scream.

"I know you're awake, Fraser, and I know all about your training at that monastery. But we're not in a hurry. Either you'll tell us what we want to know and die a quick death, or you'll die a slow, painful one. You might be able to control most of the pain, but there is a limit to what even you can control. Tell me where the brooches are hidden, and death will come quickly."

"Don't know…anything," JC said, spitting blood.

"I don't believe you. You know why, don't you?"

When JC didn't answer, the thug who broke his nose hammered him in the gut. JC didn't see that one coming and didn't tighten his abs to take the hit. He groaned.

"Sten asked you a question." The thug pounded JC again. This time a rib snapped. The broken bone could pierce his lung. But since he was going to die anyway, maybe it would help him escape sooner…into death.

"We've searched your clothes, your gear, the room at the hotel. Where's the brooch you traveled with?"

"It got…hot. Threw it…away." JC's muscles bunched, and every part of him fumed. Every inch of him craved vengeance, craved to kill Sten with his bare hands. What had he done wrong? He'd fought three people before and won. What happened this time? Where'd he fail?

The thug came at him again, and JC braced himself. He took a hard right low on the chest, knocking out his breath. His fingers twisted to form a fist and retaliate. But his hands were tied, his arms and shoulders stretched beyond endurance, and while he could probably have pulled a Houdini and freed himself, he couldn't manage it while the men continued to beat him.

The other thug planted his boots wide, squared away at JC, and threw a blow with all the weight of his massive shoulders behind it.

He hit JC full at the jaw hinge, breaking his jaw and knocking out a few teeth. JC's head snapped back, and he didn't have it in him to straighten it again. Blood gushed out of his mouth and splattered on the wood-planked floor.

"Tell me!" Sten demanded.

When JC didn't answer, the goon slammed a punch into JC's kidneys. How much more could he endure?

Whatever it takes.

He would never betray the family.

"Take him down. Chain him to the floor."

When the thugs dropped him, JC crumpled, his stomach doing flips of fear. Before he could try a defensive move to free himself, Sten and the thugs had him spread-eagled and handcuffed to spikes nailed into the floor.

"This is getting tiresome, Mr. Fraser. Tell me what I want to know, and I'll cut your throat and bring an end to your discomfort."

"Don't have...one. Got too...hot. Dropped it...in the woods... Maryland." JC's fingers kept flexing with a primal urge to make fists. But if he tensed up, his body couldn't control the pain as well.

From the sliver of vision he had left, he watched Sten choose a knife from an open black case on a nearby table and then hold it up for JC's inspection.

It was a flaying knife.

JC had seen them in Tibet. On top of the blade was a stylized lion's flayed skin pierced by a Tantric thunderbolt as its handle. Sten held it aloft. "Do you know what this is, Mr. Fraser?"

"It cuts...up...disbelievers and kills...ignorance."

"I have no personal interest in killing you. But I want the brooches and will go to whatever lengths are necessary. I have enjoyed devising many, many deliciously painful ways to question and kill people."

He reached for a pair of gloves and pulled them on, snapping the latex at his wrists. "I'm going to ask you once more for the location of the brooches, and if you do not tell me, I will begin to skin you with astounding skill."

JC didn't doubt Sten would do what he threatened. At that moment, JC sent a spiritual embrace to his parents. He was prepared to die so they would live.

Sten ran the blade through a white cloth, and his lips peeled back in a toothy sneer. "Have you ever watched anyone skin sheep?"

The question was rhetorical, so JC said nothing. He slowed his breathing. It wasn't easy, but in his mind, he escaped to MacKlenna Farm, back to when he was a child and galloped across the rolling hills of the bluegrass.

"You will experience unimaginable pain. You can't escape it in your mind. It takes a long time to die this way, Mr. Fraser. Massive hemorrhaging will eventually kill you, but until then, your screams will wake the dead." Sten held the knife aloft again. In the morning sun, the blade shone with a dull white gleam.

"This blade is sharp as a razor and requires great technical skill. I've learned to take a man's skin off as easily as I peel an apple. I'll do a small area at a time, working slowly. If you ever want to tell me anything, please let me know, and I will stop to hear what you want to say."

Don't be scared, wee laddie. Ye come from a long line of Highland warriors. Don't ye give up. Not today. Not ever. Before ye were born, wee James Cullen, ye were given the gift of sight. Ye're blessed. The ability to see what others cannot. It's time for ye to use yer gift.

A faint breeze washed over him, and his hair fluttered.

Sten began by slitting the skin on JC's chest from his clavicle to his navel, then peeled back the skin—slowly and methodically—first the right side and then the left.

Sten's ecstatic pleasure in torturing JC pulsed like an exposed wire ready to explode.

JC screamed until he passed out, and when he came to again, Sten moved to his shoulder and sliced away the skin on his right arm and then his left. JC's voice became weaker and weaker until he had no voice at all.

Then he slipped into total darkness and floated above his blood-ied body, Sten and his flaying knife, and the other two men.

There was no longer excruciating pain.

Halò, James Cullen.

He glanced around to see who was talking to him and saw a beautiful young girl with black hair and blue eyes. *Who are you?*

I'm Kristen. Don't ye remember me?

You're my guardian, Lady Yoda, a see-through person, or a ghost. Which one?

Whichever makes my presence easier to understand.

He reached for her hand. It was so small in his, but he knew if he laced his fingers with hers, the bond would never break.

You're younger than I thought you would be. I thought you would grow up.
Ye don't age here.
Where is here?
I am where ye are when ye travel through time.
I don't understand.
That's okay. One day ye will.

He smiled and looked around, but it was too dark to see anything other than Kristen. She was a bright golden light in the darkness.

So, I'll never grow old here? Never have gray hair like Dad's?
I don't know, she said. *But I am yer guardian for as long as ye need me.*
I haven't needed you since I was a kid lost in the cave.

She returned his smile. *Most of the time, you haven't been aware of me.*
Why am I aware of you now?
Because ye reached the limit of yer endurance, and I intervened.
Why didn't you intervene sooner?
There are laws from another age that govern my intervention.
But you've always watched over me.
Aye, I have.
Did you help me out in Asia?
I did what I could.
Years ago you told me that I have the gift of sight, but I still don't know what that means.
What did I tell you then?
That I could see what others could not, but the gift would not come all at once.
Aye. That's what I said.
I thought I was hallucinating then.
It's time for ye to develop yer gift, she said.
I'm dead.
Are ye? she asked.
Sten killed me.
Watch. What do ye see?

James Cullen looked below. Sten was standing over him with a bone-chilling expression. "Fuck. The bastard's dead," Sten said.

"He never told you anything," one of his men said, sneering.

Sten's eyes widened, he whirled around, and before anyone could take a breath or put up a defense, Sten whirled with his flaying knife and cut the throats of both men in one move. "Useless bastards." The men dropped to the floor and died in puddles of their own blood.

Sten calmly took a cloth off the table and wiped away the blood on the knife. He glanced down at James Cullen. "Why did you die so quickly? Most men survive a while longer after I finish with the chest and arms. I can usually skin a leg, too. You are such a disappointment."

If others lasted longer, why couldn't I?

It would have been too late.

James Cullen watched Sten while he knelt beside his body and tenderly replaced the skin, smoothing it down, but he felt nothing. No, that wasn't true. He felt his blood pulsing through his veins.

"If not for all the blood, you would never see the damage to your body." Sten stood and gathered his equipment. "If my men don't find the girl, this will have been a wasted trip."

The girl? He's looking for Ensley, isn't he?

When Kristen didn't answer, JC looked around and discovered that, sadly, he was alone in the darkness.

What will happen now? Will someone else come for me?

The steel door to the meatpacking warehouse burst open and slammed against the wall. The clang reverberated through the room and bounced off the plank walls, causing dozens of empty meat hooks to swing eerily back and forth.

Erik charged into the room in full Viking furor, yelling, "Tyr!" and wielding a long-handled battle-ax. "Sten, you have gone too far this time."

Sten threw off a piece of canvas on his worktable, revealing a battle-ax exactly like Erik's. "This is a fight that should have taken place when we were young men."

Erik swung the ax in an arc as he stalked Sten. "The Council saw your black heart. That is why they expelled you. They should have killed you instead."

"They could not kill the Keeper's son."

"But look what you have done here."

Sten glanced down at JC's body. "He wasn't supposed to die so quickly. I expected much more from him."

"You mean you expected him to talk? You should have known better." Erik streaked across the floor, whipped off his cloak, and spread it over James Cullen.

"You cannot save him." A vast, bone-chilling power pervaded Sten's entire being, sending sparks into the air.

Erik faced Sten, rotating the ax handle back and forth. "You are the one who cannot be saved. I will do now what could not be done before."

"It will mean your death," Sten said.

"As long as the future Keeper survives, my life does not matter."

"That cloak and ax should have been mine. Father meant them for me."

"You betrayed him."

"I was framed."

"No one believed you. *I* did not believe you. Nor do I now." Erik raised the battle-ax with his right hand, gripping the bottom and driving the ax with his left. He lunged forward, sweeping the ax down on Sten, but Sten evaded by stepping back. "You cannot defeat the Council or me."

"You are weak. You will never have full control of the garnet."

"As soon as I kill you, I will." Erik attacked with an undercut and caught Sten on the shoulder with the top horn of the ax. The impact sliced off Sten's arm, leaving it dangling by muscle and tendons. Blood sprayed all over Sten and the floor. Erik took advantage of Sten's hesitation, changing his hold on the shaft for his next attack.

But Sten moved too quickly, causing Erik to switch up his attack. Instead of using the head of the ax, he shoved the handle into Sten's chest with such force that his ribs snapped, and he dropped to his knees.

"Mercy," Sten groaned.

"Did you grant the Keeper's son mercy?"

When Sten didn't answer, Erik said, "I do this on behalf of the Keeper. What you have done will take years to undo. Vengeance is his." Erik brought down the ax with such force that it split Sten's skull in half with a resounding crack. Then Erik raised the ax again and severed both halves of Sten's skull from his body.

He looked down at his brother and spat on the remains. "The Council should have ordered your death. The Keeper will remember the Council's failure to do so and one day will demand payment."

Erik turned away from Sten, heartbroken over what had happened to the Keeper's son. "It's time to go home, lad." He gently wrapped the cloak around JC, covering him from his head to his toes, even though he knew that doing so diminished his own power. Then he gingerly picked James Cullen up. "I have failed the Keeper, but I will not fail the son."

34

The Badlands (1885)—Ensley

ENSLEY HAD JUST fallen asleep—or so it seemed—when Norman yelled, "Rise and shine." She opened only one eye to see the gray-bearded cook holding a lantern aloft. "Get up. Breakfast."

She rolled over and covered her head. But all the shuffling, cracking necks and knees, and grumbling, prevented her from going back to sleep. None of the men paid any more attention to her than they did to each other as they wandered around during the blue hour—that particular moment at daybreak when the sun hovered below the horizon and the light's blue wavelengths dominated.

But this morning, there wasn't a thing calming about the hour or the mysterious sky.

With her joints cracking, she dragged to her feet and limped over to a tree where Norman had thrown a tarp over a cottonwood limb to give her a sliver of privacy. She'd grown up camping with men, so even that little bit was a couple of notches above what she was used to having.

As long as men left her alone and didn't get frisky, she'd skate through this time travel adventure without any more trauma. And although she'd taken self-defense classes and knew how to kick a man in the groin or poke a finger in his eye, running like hell was still her best defensive move.

The coffee kettle clanged against tin cups, and forks scraped across tin plates as men shoveled down their breakfast. That alone was motivation to hurry through a wash and brush before they ate all the food.

She did sigh, though, thinking how wonderful it would be to

take a long, hot shower and put on clean clothes. She could almost smell the fresh scent of the Tide Plus Febreze Sport Odor Defense detergent she liked to use at home. But then she sniffed her jacket sleeve and nearly barfed. Thank god she was around men who smelled worse.

How long had she been living in this outfit? A month? At least she washed her underwear as often as she could. She wasn't sure her jeans would ever come clean, and her shirt was beyond repair. It still covered her and didn't have any significant tears, other than a ripped hem, but it quit being a white shirt weeks ago.

She kicked her butt in gear, collected the sighs she just poured out while dreaming of cleanliness, stuffed them in a dirty pocket, and took her clean hands and face to breakfast.

The men had finished eating and gone to saddle their horses when she arrived at the chuckwagon. Norman's territory consisted of the wagon and the sixty-foot radius around it. He was *the* boss, and from what she'd gathered, no one crossed him. He was doctor, gravedigger—if the doctoring part didn't work—equipment repairman, farrier, and could even sew up a cowboy's ripped jeans, or so she'd been told.

Cowboys could manage most situations as long as there was plenty of strong black coffee. And right now, that was all she wanted. Hopefully, the men left more than the dregs at the bottom of the kettle. If not, that would teach her never to be late again.

As soon as she walked up to the wagon, Norman handed her a plate stacked high with bacon, biscuits, and beans. "I put this aside so the men would leave ya somethin' to eat."

She almost laughed at the heap of food she could never finish. "You didn't have to do this, but thank you. I'll get here on time tomorrow."

Norman smiled, showing a mix of yellow teeth and no teeth at all. "I'm pleased to do it, ma'am. If you leave your bedroll, I'll see that it's kept dry for ya."

She flexed her wrist. It didn't ache. "Do you think it's going to rain today?"

He dragged a stool up to the chuck box. "It's not rain that worries me. The temperature's dropping. We might get snow."

"Oh, no. Say it ain't so." She loved the snow, and with her dried buffalo robe, she was better prepared for cold temperatures than hot, but cold temps put the herd in danger.

"'Fraid so, ma'am."

She glanced at the stool tucked under a hinged lid bolted to the rear of the chuckwagon and supported by a stout leg.

She didn't want to invade his workspace. "I can sit by the fire."

"I figured, you bein' a lady and all, that you'd appreciate eatin' at a table, instead of off your lap." He busied himself with cleaning the pots and pans.

"I don't feel much like a lady, but I do appreciate your kindness." Her feel-like-a-lady clothes—suits, silk blouses, and stilettos—were far removed from her life right now. It almost seemed like the stilettos and silk was the fantasy, and the grubby present was the norm.

And maybe it is.

She sat on a ladder-back chair Norman offered, gobbled up the food, and washed it all down with two cups of coffee. She passed on the boiled beans, which she couldn't stomach for breakfast. When she finished, she cleaned her dishes.

Norman handed her something wrapped in a piece of cloth. "Take this. Ya might get hungry later."

She unwrapped the cloth and found an apple and two biscuits. She stood on tiptoe and kissed his cheek. "That's the most thoughtful gift I've received since…I don't know when."

Really, she did know. Erik had healed her foot, fed her, and saved her life. Gifts didn't get much better than those, but Norman's was also impressive.

"Ain't nothin', ma'am, 'cept leftovers."

He'd invited her to sit at his table, and he gave her the leftovers. It was a sure sign that the cook accepted her, and on a cattle drive, except for TR's, no one else's opinion mattered.

She gave Norman her bedroll and headed over to the picket line to saddle Tesoro. She was running a brush over his back when Barney strutted by.

"Ride another mount. You'll break that horse down if you ride him now. Mr. Roosevelt said you rode him from Elkhorn Ranch without giving him a break."

Nothing irritated her more than someone telling her how to care for her horse. Unless they were a veterinarian, and Barney certainly wasn't that. "Thanks for the advice," she said, her voice full of attitude. "Tesoro is an Akhal-Teke. He's an endurance horse. If he needs rest, he'll let me know."

Barney walked away, mumbling loud enough to be heard clearly, "It'll be a shame when he goes lame."

She stroked Tesoro's forehead. "You heard him. Are you up for this?"

The horse nodded, then nudged her shoulder.

She chuckled. "Who am I to disagree with a magical horse?"

Then TR came by, leading his mount. "No one will question you if you stay with the chuckwagon instead of driving the herd."

Damn. Does everyone think my horse and I are weaklings?

"I'm not a slacker, Teddy, and you need me. Where do you want me to go? Pointer? Flank? Swing? Or, god forbid, drag?"

He mounted up, and his saddle squeaked as he settled into it. The squeak was about as annoying as jingle bobs on a pair of spurs. "I told Barney he's in charge. He'll let you know."

Great! I don't have to wonder where I'll end up, then.

Just then, Barney returned. "You can ride drag and pick up stragglers."

She turned away from him before rolling her eyes. She didn't want to give him the satisfaction of knowing it pissed her off. "I'm on it." She overdid the fake enthusiasm just a bit, but so what?

After saddling Tesoro, she dug her square, red-checkered scarf out of the saddlebag and unfolded the face mask part built into the scarf. It was a brilliant design and even included loops for her ears and a nose bridge strip that she could pinch to conform to her nose.

She tied the scarf loosely around her neck and would keep it that way until the herd stirred up the dust and blew it all back on her. She tipped her hat to Norman and rode out with her morning snack tucked away in her pockets.

Rowe came up beside her. "They'll graze for a while so the night riders can eat breakfast before we head out."

Guess they'll get extra beans instead of biscuits. Sorry about that, guys.

"Are you riding drag, too?" she asked.

"Guess so." Rowe adjusted his red bandanna to fit over his nose and mouth, and she noticed for the first time a string from a Bull Durham tobacco pouch hanging from his shirt pocket. That would be a great souvenir to take home.

"Mr. Roosevelt says you know what you're doing. Never been on a drive with a woman 'fore, but since he don't mind, and he's the boss, reckon I don't neither. 'Sides, we gotta have drovers and can't turn away help. Long as you pull your weight, I won't complain."

That's mighty big of you.

She followed him around to the south side of the herd, thinking Rowe and Barney would make great villains in a story. It was hard to guess their ages. They'd spent so much time outdoors that the sun and bad weather had damaged their skin, giving it a leathery texture. If she had to guess, she'd say midthirties, but they could be much younger.

The cattle began to stir at daybreak just as the night riders returned to camp for a quick breakfast and a change of mounts. The cows got to their feet to graze before the day's drive began and drifted some distance away while they ate. When the night riders returned with full bellies and fresh mounts, it was time to turn the cattle onto the trail.

TR was on the right flank, Sewall on the left, and Dow was riding in the swing position. Working together, they began to squeeze the bawling cows into a long, ragged line. Ensley immediately went to work riding back and forth along the edges of the strung-out herd, chasing strays.

The old roan cow and black steer were up front again. Cattle were funny like that. No matter how scrambled the herd was by the time they bedded down for the night, they always sought out their rightful places when the drive began the next morning.

"We got the remuda, too," Rowe yelled. "There aren't enough riders to make one a wrangler. We have to keep the horses in line."

"The unbroken ones will be troublemakers." It was easy now to see how she could travel a hundred miles in a day. Stops and starts and quick turns could wear a horse out in only a few hours. Even Tesoro couldn't keep up that pace. She'd have to switch him out for the bay when they stopped for lunch.

She'd spent all day in the saddle before, but riding drag was probably the worst job she ever had. Worse than mucking stalls. As soon as she drove one straggler back to the herd, another one escaped. It was like herding cats. Not that she'd ever done that, but it was a similarly frustrating exercise from what she heard.

Chasing stragglers wasn't what she had in mind when she asked to tag along. She'd envisioned riding with TR and chatting about his life and books and conservation.

How naïve.

She grew up on a working ranch, and even when she worked side by side with one of the hands, she rarely had time for an in-depth conversation. She didn't even have time to chat with Rowe. If she was going to make him a villain in her story, she needed a few details about him.

By the time the signal came to cut a circle for the lunch break, she was cold, hungry, and tired. Once the herd settled down to graze and rest, she left her position and rode over to talk to TR, who was looking at his pocket watch.

"What's up, boss?" she asked.

"Norman's not here with the chuckwagon." TR waved to Barney, and he galloped over to TR's flank position. "Did you tell Norman where to meet us?"

Barney removed his hat and scratched the back of his head. "Well, I thought he knew."

TR tucked his watch away, then crossed his hands over the cantle, and glared at Barney while his fingers tapped a nervous tattoo. "I appointed you trail boss. That's part of the job. Even I know that."

The other riders joined the huddle but kept their mouths shut and let their expressions speak for them. *Where's the chuckwagon? Where's our lunch?*

Barney looked around the circle of men. "Rowe, go find Norman and tell him where we are."

Ensley watched from outside the circle. If it had been TR's responsibility, he and Norman would have planned a place to meet, and right now, every inch of TR was the embodiment of justifiable, pissed-off masculinity.

He narrowed his eyes at Barney. "It's your mess. You go. We'll camp over there in the trees. Sewall, take the first watch with me."

Barney grumbled as he picked out a horse from the remuda and switched out his saddle. "Norman shouldn't be too far ahead of us."

"Tell him to circle back. He can get here faster than we could get the cattle to him," TR said.

"If he's already cooking lunch, he won't like it," Barney said.

"If that's the case, pack a basket and bring the food to us," TR said.

While the other men remained with TR, watching the confrontation, she left, not wanting to get embroiled in taking sides. She'd already mentally cast Barney as a villain in her story and doubted he'd do anything on this drive to earn a white hat.

She fashioned a rope line and hitched Tesoro there, then set about grooming him. She couldn't wash up until she'd taken care of him, and since she wasn't going to ride him again that day, she concentrated on brushing out the briars and removing the alkali dust. Then she saw to her own needs.

After removing the top layer of dust on her skin, she dropped to the ground and munched on the apple from Norman. She was glad to have a few minutes to close her eyes and rest.

"Mrs. Fraser."

Ensley opened one eye and shaded it with her hand. TR was squatting beside her. "What's on your mind, Teddy?" She sat up straight, yawning.

He sat cross-legged. "I hope you weren't asleep."

"No, just resting my eyes. I've got a layer of dust covering my eyeballs."

He picked a single blade of flat grass and put the blade length-wise between his thumbs, pulling it taut.

She watched with rapt interest. TR's hands seemed preoccupied with the blade of grass, but his mind seemed elsewhere. When he still didn't say anything, she asked, "Are you going to whistle or just think about it?"

He tossed the blade of grass and brushed his hands together. "Did you know a grass whistle isn't technically a whistle? It's a reed instrument."

She chuckled. "I never thought about it, but I suppose you're right. So what's really on your mind? I know it's not reed instruments."

He smiled. "You have an interesting sense of humor."

"Thank you, but I know that's not on your mind, either. Whatever it is, it must be serious because either worry or concern has darkened your blue eyes."

He blinked as if that could wipe away whatever she saw there. "What do you see?"

She cocked her head and studied him. He still didn't look like the Teddy Roosevelt she knew from old photographs, but he was changing before her eyes. Or maybe it was just the trail dust seeping into pores and thin creases on his face and tinting his brown hair prematurely gray.

"Uncertainty, I think," she said.

"I'm putting you on the left flank this afternoon unless you want to stay with the wagon."

She wasn't expecting that and doubted it was the cause of whatever troubled him. "I want to go where I can be the most helpful," she said. "If you want me on the left flank, that's where I'll go." And then she knew what was bothering him. "You're taking back control of the drive, aren't you? And you want to know what I think about the switch-up. Right?"

He straightened out his legs and leaned back on his hands. "I'm taking your advice. One mess-up is one too many. The men are hungry, and their jobs are hard enough without missing meals."

"You should be the trail boss. You have more invested in the herd than anyone else."

"But Barney—"

"But Barney messed up," she said with a shrug. "Everybody's working hard on this drive, and the guys will help with whatever is necessary. You're overthinking this. You have more courage and common sense than all the men here put together. And you'll do great."

"We must *all* dare to be great, Ensley."

"We must?" If she wanted to write the next Great American Novel, then she should take his advice and dare to be great, too.

"Greatness is the fruit of toil, sacrifice, and courage. We must live and risk wearing out rather than rusting out."

"That's profound, Teddy." She made a mental note to use it in the book she was going to write. "Is that a line you've written for a book?"

"No, just a thought I had."

"There's not a chance in Hades you'll ever rust out. You never stop. You live each day as if it could be your last."

He didn't say anything for a moment. "When I was at Harvard, I was told by a doctor that I might die of a heart attack and that I should give up exercise."

"It's obvious you took that doctor's advice," she said straight-faced.

He pursed his lips, thinking about what she said. "If I'd taken his advice, I would have died of boredom."

"And rusted," she added, knowing he struggled to understand her sense of humor. It was fun teasing him. "I think you're much happier than you would have been staying home doing scientific experiments and reading every book you could lay your hands on."

"While that sounds enticing, I would lose my mind if I couldn't go hunting."

"Maybe someday you'll be in a position to encourage all Americans to exercise." *Like when you're president.*

Just then, they heard wagon wheels rumbling over the uneven ground, and they jumped to their feet. "It's about time. Let's eat and get back on the trail," TR said.

An hour later, after a quick lunch, the riders all rotated positions, and she and TR rode the left flank and swing positions for the afternoon. "It'll be a hard ride, Ensley. The cattle are difficult enough to handle without the hardship of crossing the Badlands."

She'd ridden over the Badlands hundreds of times, with all its tangled mass of rugged hills and winding defiles, and even walked a good part of it. But she'd never crossed it with a thousand head of cattle. She had to agree with TR, especially since the temperature was dropping. Norman might well get the snow he forecasted.

When they stopped for the day, Ensley dropped to the ground just as large flakes of snow started drifting down from the sky. If not for the strong winds, she would never have gotten up. But the bad weather forced TR to order the cattle moved to a sheltered valley.

"Ensley, stay here."

She drew the buffalo robe tighter around her. "No can do. I'm not staying behind while everyone else is working in this bad weather. Besides, if I stand still, I'll rust. Then what'll happen to me?"

This time he realized she was joking, and he laughed. "I'll tell Norman to give you some bacon grease to keep you well-oiled."

"Gee, thanks. That'll help a lot."

It was freezing while they herded the cattle into the sheltered valley. Cold didn't bother her as long as she was dressed for it, which she wasn't, but her thin, sweat-wicking socks didn't insulate her feet like wool ones, and her cotton scarf didn't come close to a poly-spandex neck gaiter.

By the time she returned to camp, she couldn't feel her feet or her cheeks.

She slept in fits and starts and finally got settled just as Norman woke her up. No wonder she was shivering. There was frigging snow on the ground.

The snow melted quickly, and within a day, they were sweltering in the heat.

The river remained flooded, so they drove the cattle onto the higher plains, which caused another delay. A cattle drive that was supposed to take three days was turning into much longer, and opportunities to talk with TR grew shorter and more infrequent.

Living in the lap of nineteenth-century luxury at MacKlenna Farm was sounding better every day.

I hope you're enjoying it, JC.

35

MacKlenna Farm, KY (1885)—Elliott

ELLIOTT WAS ENJOYING breakfast alone in the dining room, which except for the wallpaper and drapes, hadn't changed much in two hundred years. Every piece of furniture had been meticulously polished and maintained by a long line of MacKlennas. The food, though, was extraordinary, as was the special blend of coffee beans.

"Excuse me, Dr. Fraser."

Elliott glanced up to see Sean's butler carrying a piece of paper. "Do ye have a telegram for me?"

"Yes, sir. Mr. MacKlenna said if one arrived, I was to give it to you."

Elliott accepted the telegram, nodding as he read the news from Kit and Cullen's son Thomas in California. "There's no return message right now. Thank ye." Elliott refolded it, tapped the edge against his palm, and then tucked the telegram in his jacket pocket.

He took one last sip of coffee, allowing himself a brief moment to appreciate the rich, dark flavor, then set the cup on its saucer and thought back to the family's trip to Montgomery Winery in 1881.

Thomas had blamed Elliott for his mother's fall and even his father's heart attack. The fall was unrelated to the heart attack, but Thomas couldn't separate one from the other. Since he was coming to Kentucky, the visit would be Elliott's opportunity to mend a few fences when he saw the lad again.

Elliott pushed away from the table and walked out onto the rear porch, where Kit was painting MacKlenna Farm's morning colors. He waited until she lifted the brush off the canvas before announcing himself, having learned a long time ago never to surprise an artist. A slip of the paintbrush could ruin a masterpiece.

When she lifted the brush and stepped back, he cleared his throat, and a look of surprise came over her face, changing quickly to a delighted smile.

"You look thrilled, and you're holding what might be a telegram. Is it from Thomas?"

They stared at each other across the walnut porch. The look on her face took him back decades, to when Kit was a teenager and competing in horse shows. He hurried to close the distance between them and pulled her in for a hug.

"Aye, Thomas is coming and bringing Sarah, John, and Frances."

She stepped back out of his arms. "What about Frances's husband?"

"He didn't say, but Clare, Abigail, and Kristen and their husbands are coming from Washington."

Kit's eyes lit up. "And the children? Are they coming, too?"

"The telegram doesn't mention yer grandchildren."

Kit held out her hand. "Let me read it."

Elliott cocked his head. "Was there a please in that command?"

"Please," she said, wiggling her fingers.

"That's better." Elliott handed over the telegram.

She read it slowly before hugging the telegram to her chest as tears slid down her cheeks. "It's really true. They're all coming to see us." She glanced to the side while wiping away tears. Then she let out a deep sigh and grimaced slightly.

"What's wrong? Why the grimace?"

She glanced back at him and managed a smile. "There's so much to do to prepare for all those people. There's not enough room in the house for everyone, and all this company is such an imposition on Sean and Lyle Ann."

"What are ye talking about? Ye're the daughter of Sean's twin sister. Yer family is his family."

"I know, but—"

"But nothing. There's plenty of room here, at the cottage, and at Sean II's house. We'll make do."

"I just wish I knew when they'll arrive."

Elliott looked at the telegram again. "We have to assume they'll be here in four or five days. That's plenty of time to get ready."

"Maybe." She picked up a cloth to wipe her hands. "Have you

told Emily?"

"I came straight to ye."

"She'll be so happy to see her mother and grandparents, but I'm worried about her father since they didn't mention him," Kit said.

"If he'd already passed, Sean would have mentioned it when Emily asked about her parents. He only said that her father's law practice—Duffy and Duffy—was expanding to Chicago. From that, I gathered Christopher is alive and well."

"I hope you're right. Where's Emily now?"

"She went with Lyle Ann to visit sick neighbors. They'll be back by early afternoon."

Kit packed up her paints and carefully lifted the canvas off the easel. "Would you carry the easel, please?"

He picked it up and followed Kit into the house. "Where do ye want to put this?"

"In the library. It'll be out of the way there." They entered the library, and Kit crossed the room to the darkest corner. "Put the easel up here. I want the painting to stay out of the sunlight for now." Elliott straightened the easel, and Kit draped the canvas on it, then set her paint box on the bottom shelf of one of the bookcases.

"Where's Cullen?" Elliott asked.

"The last I saw him, he and Sean were riding off to a neighbor's to look at a filly for sale."

"I thought ye would have gone with them."

"They didn't need me. Cullen and Braham know more about horses than anyone I've ever met, and I've met a lot of horse people."

"Maybe, but ye know how to treat them when they're sick. Cullen can't do that."

Meredith entered the room. "Cullen can't do what?"

"Heal sick horses."

"Oh," Meredith said. "So what have you two been doing? I heard you banging doors."

"Thomas sent a telegram," Kit said, beaming. "He's bringing Emily's mother and grandparents, and the girls are coming from Washington. I'll have my whole family here."

"Did he mention the grandchildren?" Meredith asked. "I know you want to see them, too."

"He didn't say," Kit said. "He didn't mention my father, either. I wish we knew more about his life over the past few years, where he went, what he did."

"None of my genealogists have found any information about him since he sailed away in the fall of 1881. I doubt Thomas has seen him," Meredith said.

"It'd be nice to know what happened to him."

Meredith sat down at the desk and removed a piece of paper out of the top drawer. "We should make lists of how many people we'll have and how many rooms they'll need. We'll probably have to use Sean II's house as well."

"If it makes things easier, Sean and I will sleep in the cabin," Elliott said.

"No, you won't. You'll stay right here," Kit said. "The girls have heard so much about my godfather, and they'll all want to spend time with you. You can't run away from them."

"That's what I'm afraid of," Elliott said.

Meredith made a shooing motion with her hand. "Kit and I have work to do. You should go find Sean or Cullen."

Right then, Elliott knew what he intended to do. "I'm going for a ride and will be back in a couple of hours."

"Where are you going to ride?" Meredith asked.

"I might go to Midway and check out the quaint town. Don't expect me back for lunch."

Kit pulled up a chair next to Meredith. "Have fun."

"Oh, I will." He wasn't going to Midway. Finally, he could go back to the cabin and do some exploring. He'd studied the pictures he took, and there were a few questionable areas he wanted to investigate further.

If Erik disappeared from the cabin, was there a door below ground similar to the one at the castle? Or had Erik traveled with a different brooch, one that didn't stink up the place? If Erik came back, Elliott wouldn't let him leave again until he answered all his questions.

Elliott left the house and walked over to the stallion barn. He got halfway there when he was overcome with emotion, nearly dropping to his knees.

James Cullen, where are ye, lad?

And Elliott knew without a doubt that his son was in serious trouble—and possibly dying. Elliott didn't go to the stallion barn but made a detour and ran toward the cabin.

Where are ye, son? Don't protect me. Save yerself.

36

The Badlands (1885)—Ensley

O N THE FIFTH day, the herd was miles from water and hadn't been anywhere near water since sunrise. As dusk ebbed into darkness, the situation grew dangerous. Thirsty animals might stampede and head for the nearest water source—the river.

Ensley and TR took the first night watch.

Since they were circling the herd in opposite directions, she thought it would be fun to share quotes from favorite books when they passed each other in the darkness.

When she saw him again, she said, "The next time around, recite your favorite Dickens quote."

"Why Dickens?"

"Just a random author selection. You can choose the next one."

When they circled back around, TR whispered so he wouldn't upset the cattle, "'There is nothing in the world so irresistibly contagious—'"

"'—as laughter and good humor,'" she whispered back. "*A Christmas Carol.* That's an easy one."

"Give me a harder one, then."

When they met again, she said, "'Never close your lips to those whom—'"

"'—you have already opened your heart.' Dickens, *Pictures from Italy,*" TR shot back.

Maintaining the same slow speed while singing made-up tunes to the critters made it harder to meet the challenge to come up with profound book lines.

The next time around, he went first. "'There are books of which the backs—'"

"'—and covers are by far the best part.' Dickens, *Oliver Twist*."

"You certainly know Dickens," he said. "I'm going to choose a different author."

"Tell me who so I can start thinking about favorite lines."

He chuckled. "No advance notice. I'm raising the stakes."

Before they could make it back to their rendezvous point on the east side of the herd, the thirst-maddened animals suddenly heaved to their feet and within seconds stampeded, making as much noise as a dozen trains speeding by on parallel tracks.

Ensley jerked her mind away from authors to quote when her survival instincts and training kicked in.

She was on the wrong side, and panic threatened to override good sense. TR would continue riding north and try turning the herd away from the swollen river—in her direction.

If she stayed on the west side, the cattle would trample her to death. TR was riding along the north side. So she'd go south, get behind the herd, and then follow TR up the east side.

She rode like hell to get behind the panicked animals. All they knew was to run as fast and as far as they could from whatever had scared them.

The other riders should be getting their horses saddled by now. There was no way they could sleep through the earth vibrating and the air crackling with the thunder of cloven hooves.

As she started up the east side, Sewall and the rest of the men galloped toward her.

"Where's Roosevelt?" he yelled.

"Up ahead."

"Go back to camp," Rowe said. "It's too dangerous."

"Not any more dangerous for me than it is for you. I'm staying with you to help get this herd under control." She knew there was always a chance the herd would switch on a dime and run over them all. Or they could run for miles straight ahead toward a deep gully. If they hit that, they'd pile up, and TR could lose half the herd.

Barney tossed her a slicker. "Wave that in their faces until they veer away."

She spurred Tesoro, waving the slicker. Never in her life had she ridden so hard in the darkness. All she could see were the shadowy outlines of the herd. She was riding at a dead run across the land full of prairie dog holes, never knowing if the next jump would land her and Tesoro in a shallow grave. She had to get control of this crippling, paralyzing fear.

Focus on what I'm doing and trust my magic horse.

Her stomach did flips of fear as she eased Tesoro up a bit so someone else could take the lead. In the dark, coming from behind was a better position, and she was soon part of a staggered line, following Sewall and Dow, waving her slicker. Right now, her life depended upon Tesoro's sure-footedness.

The herd finally turned, running back to the bedground. But the riders were still in a dangerous position. If the critters turned again, they'd all be goners.

Where is TR?

With the darkness and dust, she could barely see the rider in front of her. But she knew TR had to be up there somewhere.

The herd seemed to know where to go, and the closer they got to the bedground, the more they slowed down until finally, they stopped. If the critters were thirsty before, they'd be dying of it now. At least the run had exhausted them, and they wouldn't race toward the river again.

She spotted TR. His horse was slowing down, too, so she spurred Tesoro, passing the others to catch up to TR. "Are you okay?" she asked.

He removed his hat and wiped his sleeve across his forehead. "Bully. And you?"

"Exhausted."

"I'll get Sewall to ride the rest of the watch with me. Get some sleep. Daybreak is only an hour or two away."

She was about to say that he should rest, too, but he was a big boy and could decide what he needed for himself. "Okay, see you later."

When she reached camp, Norman had already set her bedroll near the side of the wagon.

Tesoro was quivering, and she was almost as bad. The adrenaline shooting through her left a trail of liquid fire that was slowly burning off, and she just wanted to lie down, but Tesoro came first.

She wiped him down, then gave him a proper brushing, talking to him all the while. "Thank you for taking care of me tonight, boy. Any other horse would have failed me, but not you."

She'd kill for a shower, clean clothes, and rest, but only a short rest was available to her. Every muscle in her legs, back, and arms ached, and for the hundredth time, she wondered if she made a mistake by not going to Kentucky.

They'd be back at the ranch tomorrow. Then they'd have a couple of days before they had to leave for the roundup. Sixty-some cowboys would spend five weeks scouring two hundred miles of the Little Missouri Valley—about a hundred miles on either side of the river—combing every ravine, creek, and coulee for all the free-roaming cattle.

After the past few weeks, was that what she wanted? Tonight the answer was no, but who knew what tomorrow would bring?

37

Elkhorn Ranch (1885)—Ensley

E NSLEY WAS RIDING point with TR when they neared Elkhorn Ranch with the herd. It had been a tough week, but despite the hardships, Ensley was jubilant. The experience had stretched her so far past her comfort zone that she knew she would never snap back. She still believed she belonged in New York City working as an editor, but even that had diminished from a hundred percent conviction down to about eighty-five.

Participating in the roundup would either drop that percentage another notch or two or push it back up to a hundred.

And what would happen to her if her conviction slipped to fifty percent? Where would she live then? She no longer had a ranch, but she could buy a smaller one, and it didn't have to be in North Dakota. It could even be upstate New York.

She could go anywhere.

And she didn't have to quit being an editor, either. She could work for authors who self-publish. She'd had conversations with several editors who were considering making the jump from New York to either a small press or working with independents.

What interested her about that possibility was specializing in three or four genres—historicals, time travel romance, fantasy, and sci-fi—instead of slogging through slush piles to find unsolicited books, stories, or poems that merited further consideration.

Quit worrying about that! You're on an adventure—so revel in it!

She scolded herself for planning a life in the future when that possibility was so uncertain. It was times like this—imagining her future—when she missed JC the most. What would he think of the idea? Although first she'd have to confess that her publishing company fired her.

And what was up with the nightmares she'd been having about him for the past two nights? They'd been so unsettling that she hadn't been able to go back to sleep and ended up volunteering for the night watch. Her unease still hadn't gone away. If only she could talk to JC to make sure he was okay, she'd feel better and sleep easier.

The past two days with TR had been so much fun—well, at least, they were after the stampede. But surviving that night and only losing a half dozen cows had given the drovers confidence in their ability to handle the job. And the cowhands' stress vanished with that confidence.

When they reached Elkhorn Ranch, Ensley borrowed a skirt and blouse from Mrs. Sewall to wear after taking a bath in TR's rubber bathtub. Once she was clean, Ensley poured hot water in a tub and used a washboard to scrub her jeans, jacket, underwear, and what was left of her white blouse. She soaped, boiled, rinsed, wrung out, mangled, starched, dried in the sun, and then ironed her clothes. Thank goodness she only had one outfit. But, as soon as her clothes dried, she washed Mrs. Sewall's borrowed skirt and blouse. She'd never take a washing machine for granted ever again.

Somewhere between the rinsing and starching, she found a ragged-edge piece of red linen-type fabric caught in the hem of her jeans and set it aside to study later. It had obviously ripped off something. The only red garment she'd seen was Erik's cloak. Had he wrapped her broken foot in that?

Gold threads in the fabric shimmered in the bright sunlight. According to a nonfiction book on the benefits of wearing gold and silver she'd recently edited, gold supposedly relaxed the body, which in turn improved blood circulation and expedited the healing process.

But a broken bone? Well...why the hell not? Something healed it. Why not Erik's cloak?

She treated the piece of fabric as a talisman and tucked it in her bra to keep it close. If she cut herself, she'd place it on the wound and see what happened.

After finishing her chores, she asked Mrs. Sewall and TR if she could sit on the porch for a while to do some writing. They both encouraged her, saying she should have a day to rest and prepare for the roundup, so that's what she did.

Later in the day, TR joined her on the veranda, carrying a stack of papers, a book, and a pencil.

"Are you working on your manuscript?" she asked.

"Yes, and I intend to write Henry about the cattle drive."

"Henry Cabot Lodge?" Ensley asked.

TR nodded.

"Do you plan to tell him how you risked your life to save the herd during a stampede?"

TR laughed. "I thought I'd tell him I've had a good deal of fun since I came out here. That I've had my hands full working night and day without taking off my clothes but once during the week of the drive."

She looked at him, grinning. "I'm sure after reading your letter, Mr. Lodge will picture you as a ruffian riding hell-for-leather through the wilderness."

TR stared with narrowed eyes and pursed lips, and then after a moment, he gave her a full grin. "That's an apt description, and I could say the same for you, Mrs. Fraser. I should write to your husband and tell him about our adventure."

"He's probably sitting on the veranda at MacKlenna Farm sipping mint juleps and discussing Thoroughbred breeding and racing with his relatives. He'll think we're both nuts for galloping through the Badlands in the middle of the night chasing a stampeding herd."

As soon as she said that, another chill hit her, and she shuddered. She seemed to be having them quite regularly today.

"Are you all right?" TR asked.

"What? Oh, I was just thinking about James Cullen. I miss him." She gave TR a nervous smile. "Now, what were we talking about? Ruffians, right? Well"—she scratched her neck—"no one would believe that of *me*. You maybe," she teased. "But not *moi*."

"Dressed as you are, they might. But if you dressed for an outing in society, no one would believe it."

She knew it was true. People she met in New York City were always shocked when she mentioned growing up on a ranch in North Dakota. She glanced at her right hand, noticing a new blister on her palm from swinging a rope while wearing ill-fitting gloves. It would have been much worse without them, though, so she wasn't complaining. Calluses and blisters used to be normal for her.

"What you just said about society and me reminds me of something I should have mentioned earlier. You probably shouldn't tell your friend Henry or your family about me. People in the East would think my presence here without my husband would be highly inappropriate. And you don't want rumors spreading through New York City that you have a paramour in the Badlands."

His cheeks flushed, and then the tips of his ears turned pink, too. "Henry wouldn't think that. He knows what I've been through."

"Maybe Mr. Lodge wouldn't, but there are other people in society who would. So let's keep what happens in the Dakotas in the Dakotas." If her name appeared in TR's journals, it would perplex future historians. Or if she and JC had to live in this time, society would shun them.

"Your husband wouldn't appreciate rumors spreading, either," TR said.

She felt horrible lying to TR about her relationship with JC. But she didn't know how TR would react to the truth. And if she told TR that she and JC weren't married, then what was their relationship? Brother and sister? That was a lie, too. And what would TR think of her if she told him she and JC were just friends? Wasn't it better to stick with one lie than compound it with several more?

She sighed and pondered her dilemma, falling back again on the plots of her clients' books and not wanting to fall into the kind of idiotic trap so many genre heroines fell into.

So she continued the lie instead of trying to squirrel out of it.

"Knowing my…husband, I'm sure JC must have considered that when he left me in your care. He can't complain about it now, can he?" She went for an innocent tone, but it sounded flat to her ears. "Besides, my nickname *is* Annie Oakley."

"You mentioned her before. You said she's a sharpshooter."

Ensley was almost positive Oakley was in the Wild West Show by 1885. "She's in Buffalo Bill's Wild West Show."

"I thought his sharpshooter was Captain Adam Bogardus."

"He was, but a steamboat carrying the show's performers sank to the bottom of the Mississippi River. The passengers survived, but the captain lost his prized firearms and couldn't adjust to new guns, so Mr. Cody hired Annie Oakley."

"You must spend as much time reading newspapers as you do reading the classics and regular fiction."

"Anything and everything I can get my hands on. But the point of mentioning Annie Oakley is that I fit in here with you better than

I do with JC's wealthy relatives. And on top of that, I'll have enough research to write a great story when I get home."

"I suppose you're right," TR said. "I won't mention you or your husband in my correspondence to Henry and my family."

"And no mention in your diary either. I don't want future historians to scour your notes and journals for your thoughts and feelings and come across my name. What will they think?"

He stiffened, his mouth opened slightly. "No one will want to read my journals."

"Don't historians read everything written by Washington, Adams, Madison, Jefferson, Hamilton, Lincoln?"

"Those men are worth reading about."

"And so are you. You wouldn't be writing books if you didn't believe you had something important to say. And don't you have political aspirations?" Ensley asked, going for an innocent tone again, which didn't sound quite right this time, either. "I can see you running for Congress or even president someday. You're a charismatic person, Teddy, and you'll introduce charisma into the political equation. I bet voters would cast their vote for Roosevelt the man, not Roosevelt the Republican."

"Where'd you get such an idea?" he asked. "I have no such aspirations. I'm a Republican living in a state that Democrats control. I'm not likely to win a general election."

"Based on our conversations the past few days, it's obvious to me that you're a progressive who believes government should serve as an agent of reform for the people."

"I consider myself nothing more than an independent Republican reformer, following in the tradition of national-minded statesmen like George Washington, Alexander Hamilton, Henry Clay, and, of course, Abraham Lincoln."

"Your political career started out following their traditions, but your boundless energy will eventually set you on your path, and I have a feeling if you do that, you'll take the country with you. Not that I'm a visionary or anything."

Careful, Ensley.

She continued to ignore the warnings because JC said it was okay to lay the groundwork. Didn't he?

That was about Shakespeare! No, it wasn't, she argued with herself. *It was about conservation. Oh, whatever. Just slow down.*

She couldn't do that, either. Being with TR was too exciting, too intellectually stimulating, too thought-provoking for her to remain silent. "But I don't think you'll ever be satisfied unless you're making a difference—somehow, somewhere."

"I believe, Mrs. Fraser, that you will make a difference wherever *you* go."

She cocked her head. "Maybe, but not like you. I can't keep up. You run circles around me."

He gazed at her in a contemplative way, then he rocked back in his chair, and their conversation drifted off. Ensley returned to her writing, making notes of their conversation, and TR opened a book and was quickly absorbed in the story.

She was sitting here with Teddy Roosevelt on the veranda at Elkhorn Ranch. Unbelievable.

Even as a Junior Ranger, she'd walk around the cabin's foundation beneath rustling cottonwood leaves, and she sensed the peace and solace TR found here. She'd imagined having conversations with him, and here she was, and here he was. Even though she had a hard time when she arrived, and herding cattle was no picnic, she'd do it all over again in a heartbeat.

It wasn't an hour later that he put his book aside and said, "You're the best-read woman I know."

"Are you still thinking about Annie Oakley?"

"I'm just surprised. Your knowledge seems boundless."

"We're close in age, Teddy. You read one to two books every day. That's *every* day. I doubt there's anyone in history who's read as much as you have. And I'm not anywhere close. I'm more comfortable in a barn than a library."

"I doubt that," he said. "But if you want a book to read while we're on the roundup, take whatever looks interesting from my small library."

"Of the books in your bookcase, what do you recommend?"

He glanced over his shoulder as if he could see the books. "John Burroughs's book titled *Wake-Robin*."

"I'm familiar with Burroughs, but not that book." She had to think back to what she remembered from a high school 4-H project on naturalists. "He once said, 'Leap, and the net will appear.' I love that."

"That's faith."

"I guess it is," she said. "You're the complete opposite of Burroughs."

"How so?"

"You're mercurial, animated, and action-driven. Burroughs is introspective and a poetic observer of nature. But I can imagine you developing a deep admiration for each other."

TR raised an eyebrow. "Mercurial?"

"I think so. When people go through trauma or tragedy, their moods can be unpredictable at times. Grief is like a giant wave you fight against to keep from drowning. It beats you up and exhausts you. But if you stop fighting against it and just float for a while and let the wave wash over you, you'll gain the strength you need to fight again."

TR adjusted his spectacles. "I disagree. You can choose not to talk about it and continue to fight it."

"You've said that before. I have a girlfriend who can always tell when I'm grieving over the loss of my parents. She buys me ice cream in the summer and hot chocolate in the winter. Those are my comfort foods, and it makes me feel better."

"Ice cream?"

Ensley nodded. "Try it." Ensley would give a gold nugget for some homemade fudge or chocolate mint ice cream from Medora Fudge and Ice Cream Depot.

"I have an impressive appetite and a weakness for sweets, especially sand tarts," he said.

Ensley laughed. "Sand tarts? How funny. Mine's fudge."

They both licked their lips and laughed, and she thought how wonderful it would be if she had a car and could drive to Medora, buy ice cream and fudge, and come right back to his time. He would love it.

She went back to writing, smiling to herself, and TR returned to his book.

He was smiling, too.

38

MacKlenna Farm, KY (1885)—Paul

AFTER TUMBLING FOR what seemed an eternity through a black hole and being nearly blinded by intermittent flashing strobe lights, Paul finally emerged from the fog.

He had no idea where he was, other than somewhere in the middle of nowhere with a brilliant blue sky, freshly mowed grass that made him sneeze, and horse manure that saturated the air and made this city boy hold his nose.

Before he met JC, the only horses he'd ever been around were the ones cops rode in Central Park.

Out of habit, he checked his satellite phone. "Damn." No bars. No service. No maps. No GPS. Nothing. Zip. Zero. Zilch. But satellite phones were supposed to work everywhere, even in the most remote areas of the world.

What the hell did it mean that his didn't work here?

After the past three years of working with JC, Paul could count his experiences with international crises like hash marks on the side of a fighter jet, but this one was too damn weird. Did JC emerge from the fog here or somewhere else after his ride through the black hole?

Paul scanned the landscape. To one side was a white plank-fenced pasture and a dirt road to somewhere beyond that. And on the other side was a tree line of mostly elms, maples, and oaks.

He walked between the fence and tree line over rolling hills until he reached the corner of the paddock. Then he headed in what he believed—based on the sun's position—to be a northerly direction.

While he walked, he did a pistol press check and put a round in the chamber. He considered carrying the gun openly, but he wasn't

looking for trouble. While the setting was too idyllic to be dangerous, he'd worked for The Company long enough that he never took
anything for granted. Doing so could get him killed.

After walking about fifty yards to the top of a knoll, he reached a
private cemetery surrounded by a wrought iron fence. A large oak
tree provided a canopy for the two dozen or so gravesites, and at the
center of the cemetery was a monolith.

He chuckled. "Well, I'll be damned. I'm on MacKlenna Farm."
He'd never been here on foot before, or approached the cemetery
from this direction, and he wanted to read the epitaph on the black
stone monolith. The gate squeaked when he pushed it ajar, and he
stepped around the graves until he reached the stone monument.

THOMAS SEAN MACKLENNA II
He saw what others did not.
He lived what others could not.
He dreamed what others dared not.
JANUARY 25, 1770—JANUARY 25, 1853

Paul walked the perimeter of the cemetery and was struck by
how different it was from what he remembered. Then he recognized
what was missing—Sean and Mary MacKlenna's headstones.

No cell reception, no power lines, and missing headstones.

Any minute he expected to hear Rod Serling say, "He will ply his
trade at another kind of corner—a strange intersection called *The
Twilight Zone.*"

Maybe he was here now to narrate the events he would witness
in this convergence of dimensions? Being in another dimension
didn't freak him out, but it was a situation he'd never encountered.

So how was he going to handle it when he met the MacKlennas?
The only way he could. As if he belonged here. After all, the best
intelligence agency in the world had trained him to be a chameleon.

He was the computer guy, the eye in the sky. Being on the
ground wasn't quite what he expected, and he had no one talking in
his ear and warning him about the dangers ahead, the way he did for
the guys in the field.

He closed the gate and headed in the direction of the mansion,
reaching the stone fence he and JC had jumped dozens of times
while horseback riding. Well, to be honest, JC jumped it. Paul rode

around it.

Paul continued walking until he reached a clearing with a *Little House on the Prairie* log cabin. Where the hell did this come from?

No cell reception. No power lines. Missing headstones. And a previously unknown log cabin.

Now he knew he'd arrived in the fifth dimension.

He approached the cabin cautiously, but before he reached the porch, the door flew open. A man wearing clothes straight out of the Middle Ages strode out and stood on the porch. He had muscles like Arnold Schwarzenegger when he filmed *Conan the Barbarian*. His brown, hip-length tunic matched his pants gathered at the knees and tucked into knee-high boots tied at the sides with leather thongs.

"Young Paul!" the man bellowed. "Holster your weapon and come here."

Paul didn't do either. "How do you know my name?"

"I know everything about you. Now put the gun away and come closer. You are not in danger."

How does this warrior know my name?

"I will not kill you."

No, but you might try to beat the shit out of me.

Paul reluctantly holstered his weapon, but he still didn't trust the man in the tunic, especially since he spoke with such proper diction and no discernible accent.

"Who are you, and how do you know about me?"

"I have known about you…" The warrior paused and then said, "I have been watching you since you went to work for James Cullen."

Paul trudged toward the man, knowing he was at a disadvantage and could be walking into a trap. The warrior had a don't-fuck-with-me attitude that convinced Paul he wouldn't hesitate to kill him or anyone else if it suited him. As Paul got closer, he scanned his surroundings to figure out which way to duck and run if the warrior made an aggressive move.

"You still haven't told me who you are."

"I am Erik, and that is all you need to know."

Paul stepped up onto a covered porch that ran the cabin's length, noting the tree line was at least fifteen feet from the edge of the porch. If the warrior came after him, he wouldn't be safe until he reached the other side of the trees. Paul was thirty pounds lighter than the man and probably faster on his feet. Plus, Paul knew the property well enough to get around in the dark. Too bad it was only midafternoon.

"I've never seen or heard of you. Where do you come from?"

"That is not important." Erik lay his hand on Paul's shoulder, and it felt like a boulder weighing him down, making him feel small and inept. "I've brought James Cullen home, and you must go to the mansion at once and bring Dr. Fraser here."

"Home from where?"

"You would not understand."

"I'm tired of your riddles. If you have JC, where is he?" Paul sidestepped Erik and reached for the doorknob, but Erik blocked him.

"He is not well, Young Paul. I must talk to his father immediately."

"Not until I see JC."

Erik had one massive hand at Paul's throat before Paul blinked. "Do as I say and do it now!" Erik released his hold. "I do not have time to bargain with you."

Arguing with Erik was probably a waste of time. "If I hadn't shown up, you would have gone. Right? So—"

"I knew you were coming," Erik said briskly.

"How?" The look in Erik's hooded eyes and the skin bunched around them scared the hell out of Paul.

Erik could have killed him and chose not to, unlike Tavis and David. Paul knew they would try to scare him, but they wouldn't kill him. This Erik guy was different. "All right. I'm going, but what should I tell Elliott?"

"That Erik needs to talk to him. Now. And one more thing. Elliott, Meredith, Kitherina, and Cullen are all visiting the MacKlennas. Bring only Dr. Fraser and Sean MacKlenna, and do not let the others know of my request."

"Sean MacKlenna's dead."

"Sean is very much alive."

"How's that possible? He and his wife died decades ago."

"Young Paul!" Erik barked. "You traveled back in time with the lad's brooch. You should not be here. This is not your time, but I will use your presence for James Cullen's benefit. Bring only Dr. Fraser and Sean MacKlenna." He pointed. "Follow that path over there. The mansion is a kilometer to the south."

Paul's head was spinning. Erik hadn't given him time to analyze the situation, but he didn't want to risk another of those neck squeezes, so he turned and jogged toward the trees.

Before he reached the tree line, Erik yelled, "Wait."

Paul stopped, but he didn't turn around. "You told me to hurry. Now you tell me to wait. What the hell is going on?"

"Bring Emily Duffy as well, but no one else."

"Emily? She's here, too?" Now Paul turned and faced the man. "I should tell you, Elliott might not listen to me. As a matter of fact, he might just shoot me." He realized now that he should have told Elliott the truth about JC's disappearance, but who the hell would have thought they were all involved in this black hole business together.

"You did not tell him James Cullen disappeared into the fog, and you should have done so. It would not have changed the outcome, but Young Paul, do not ever lie to the Keeper again."

"What's a Keeper?"

"You ask too many questions. Now go!"

Paul risked asking one more. "How'd you know I didn't tell Dr. Fraser?"

Erik threw a knife that splintered a tree inches above Paul's head. It happened so fast he didn't have time to duck. "What the shit?" He yanked on the knife but couldn't pull it out, and he was no weakling. "You almost killed me!"

Erik reached into his boot and drew out another knife.

"Okay, I'm going. Don't throw another knife at me, but what year is it?"

"It is 1885, Young Paul."

The whole Young Paul thing was bugging the shit out of him. He might be young compared to the warrior, but why was Erik constantly referring to Paul's age. He didn't call JC, Young JC.

"One more thing," Paul said. "Why do you call me Young Paul?"

Erik flicked the knife back and forth between his hands, and in a voice as unbending as stone, he bellowed, "Go!"

Erik then entered the cabin, and Paul sucked in his first deep breath since landing at this strange intersection of the past and present—a time when ancient warriors roamed the world and spoke in riddles.

He ran like the Devil was chasing him, wondering how in the hell he was going to convince Elliott to come with him?

I'll think of something when I see how Elliott reacts to me being here.

When the mansion came into view, he sucked up the courage to face Dr. Fraser, but by the time he neared the veranda, he slowed to a crawl, having second thoughts about going to the front door. If he went to the back door and asked the kitchen help to get Mr. MacKlenna, he could tell MacKlenna that a man named Erik was at the cabin and wanted to see Dr. Fraser, Emily Duffy, and him. Then Paul could run back to the cabin and find JC.

With a plan in mind, Paul walked around to the back of the mansion.

39

The Badlands (1885)—Ensley

THREE DAYS AFTER returning to Elkhorn Ranch, Ensley packed the Burroughs book and her few things, which now included an extra shirt. TR gave her one of his since he had plenty, and Mrs. Sewall altered it to fit Ensley. She also scrubbed Ensley's white shirt until it was almost clean again. Of course, it wouldn't stay that way for long.

At daybreak, she rode out with TR, Sewall, Dow, and a remuda of about thirty horses, with Norman driving the chuckwagon. They would join dozens of cowboys at Box Elder Creek to participate in the roundup for the Little Missouri District 6. The district, a distance of two hundred miles, ran along the river from the mouth of Beaver Creek to the mouth of the Little Beaver Creek.

While TR, Sewall, and Dow managed the remuda, Ensley rode beside Norman, talking about trail food, the Badlands, and how he came to be a cook.

"I wuz a kid in Texas when the war started," he said. "Everybody I knew was leavin' to fight for the Rebs, so I went, too, an' they put me to work in the mess tent. After the war, I joined a cattle drive. Since I had experience cookin', they put me to work helpin' the cook. Now I drive my chuckwagon from one cattle drive to another."

"Did you ever go back to Texas?"

"Jus' to git another job."

They rode without talking for several long minutes, listening to the chuckwagon jolting and rattling over the uneven ground, along with the jingle of the traces connecting the wagon to the four draft animals…and, of course, the wind. The Badlands was home to

Ensley. No matter how much she loved New York City, this was home.

As the saying goes, you can take the girl out of the Badlands, but you can't take the Badlands out of the girl. But was that an actual place on a map or just a place in her heart?

"What did Roosevelt tell ya about the roundup?" Norman asked, breaking into her thoughts.

"All I know is that at one time ranchers settled disputes over ownership of unbranded cattle with either a neighborly agreement or finding out which rancher had the fastest draw."

"It's not like that now."

"Glad to hear it. I'd hate to witness two otherwise intelligent men try to settle an argument with a six-shooter when they can use their big guns in an arm-wrestling challenge."

Norman gave her a side-eye. "What does that mean?"

She flexed her arm and pointed to her bicep. "Back east, newspaper reporters talk about pitchers having big guns."

"Baseball?" Norman asked.

Ensley made a windup motion and pretended to throw a pitch. "Throw a few of those every day and see how big and strong your arms will get."

Norman laughed as he flexed his arm and pointed to his bicep. "Ya want to hear a story about Roosevelt?"

"Sure. I'm not one to listen to gossip," she said, "but if it's a good story, I might use it in my book and change the names to protect the innocent."

"I jus' thought of it because ya were talking about throwing a baseball."

She'd heard so many stories about TR while growing up near the Theodore Roosevelt National Park, especially during her time as a Junior Ranger, but this might be a new one. "Do tell."

"He was in the Nolan's Hotel and Saloon in a little town west of Medora when a gunslinger pointed his gun at Roosevelt, called him 'four-eyes,' and said he had to buy drinks for the entire house. Roosevelt laughed, then punched the gunslinger twice on the jaw. Knocked him right out."

She hadn't heard that one and would use it for sure. "When confronted by a bully, strike first."

"Which reminds me of something else, Mrs. Fraser."

"Haven't I told you to call me Ensley?"

"No, ma'am, but I'd never do that. It's disrespectful."

"How about Miss Ensley? Is that disrespectful?"

Norman scratched his chin. "I might could do that. But what I wanted ta say is this." He pulled back on the reins. "Whoa." The wagon stopped, and he held the reins loosely for a moment. "When we get to the roundup startin' point, there'll be sixty men or so, most of 'em unmarried. And probably none of 'em seen a woman on a trail drive afore, and not one so purdy."

Norman looked down at his scarred hands, blushing. Then he looked at her again.

"Unless you're with Roosevelt, Dow, or Sewall, stay close to my wagon. None of 'em cowboys will mess wit' me. Nobody with good sense gits on the wrong side of the cook. And if I hear any of 'em disrespect ya, I'll see they git kicked out of the roundup, and that's the biggest disgrace that can attach itself to a cowboy. The shame clings to a man like gumbo mud, and he has to ride far to get another job. But once these men see how hard ya work, they won't cause ya no trouble."

She leaned out of her saddle and gave him a light punch on the arm. "I'll stick to you like flypaper. And thanks."

TR galloped up beside her. "I thought you were going to fall over. What were you doing?"

She lightly punched TR's arm. "Just that. Norman and I have been talking about what I can expect once we get to the roundup, and he's offered me protection at his chuckwagon."

TR nodded to Norman. "I appreciate that. I plan for Mrs. Fraser to ride with me, but occasionally that might not be possible. Knowing you'll look out for her is reassuring."

Her natural reaction was that she didn't need to be looked out for, but in this situation, she wanted what he was offering.

"But what about you, TR?" she asked. "Will the men give you a rough time because you're from the East or because you wear spectacles?"

TR removed his hat, swiped his handkerchief across his brow, then resettled his hat. "If it's like last year, I'll spend the first twenty-four hours living down the fact that I wear them."

"Do they try to taunt you into a fight?"

TR's shoulders slumped. "Occasionally, but I keep quiet unless the men misconstrue my silence. Then it's better to bring matters to a head at once."

"Bullying involves a perceived imbalance of power," she said. "By bullying you, the jerk feels more powerful. Once you show the bully that his perception is wrong, you stop the bullying. So go right ahead and knock his block off. Maybe the next time he sees someone with spectacles, he'll behave."

TR cocked an eyebrow. "Have you worn spectacles? You seem to understand the situation."

"No, but I wore"—she couldn't say braces—"I mean...I wore spectacles as a child, and I was bullied. If someone treated me like that today, I'd challenge the jerk to a bronc riding contest to see who could stay on the horse the longest."

TR pinned her with a stern gaze. "I wouldn't let you do that, and neither would your husband. The cowboys you'll meet at the roundup are lean, sinewy fellows, accustomed to riding half-broken horses at any speed over any country by day or night. You can't compete with them."

She opened her mouth to challenge him, then closed it with a snap. TR was right. She couldn't afford an accident. If she met JC in a few weeks and had a broken leg, he'd be pissed that she took risks when she knew modern health care wasn't available to treat her. And she'd expect him to take the same precautions.

"Okay. I'll challenge them to a horse race, then. Nobody can beat Tesoro."

40

MacKlenna Farm, KY (1885)—Elliott

ELLIOTT ASSISTED SEAN'S farm manager in delivering a foal and afterward hung around to make sure the newborn was standing within an hour and nursing within two hours—the 1-2-3 Rule.

Delivering a foal always reminded him of why he went to vet school all those years ago. It wasn't that it made him feel all-powerful when he brought a new life into the world. Quite the contrary. He found it humbling, and he benefitted from a regular dose of humility to keep himself manageable. At least that's what Meredith said.

He strolled back to the mansion to share the news with her when a tsunami of terrifying sights and sounds slammed into him and forced him to his knees. He was out of control, sliding on black ice toward the edge of a cliff, and unable to stop the vehicle he was driving in his mind.

Death was looming.

He slid down the brick wall at the back of the mansion and collapsed in the garden, waiting. What would kill him? An aneurism? A fatal arrhythmia? A heart attack? A stroke? A massive pulmonary embolism?

Meredith, love, I'm sorry I can't say goodbye.

She would manage without him much easier than he would have managed without her. It was better that he died first.

He closed his eyes and waited for death, unable to move or speak.

A stroke. It must be a stroke.

But even with his eyes closed, he could see color—and not just any color, but bright red. The red turned a dark crimson, and then a man's blood-curling screams assaulted him. He slapped his hands over his ears and fell into a black hole of horror, losing track of time and pleading for death to release him from the abyss.

His entire body broke out in a profuse sweat. The screams grew louder, and then, as suddenly as they started, they stopped—and left his skin burning as if he'd walked through fire.

I've arrived in hell.

"Dr. Fraser! Are you ill?"

No, I'm dead.

Fingers pressed against his neck, but he couldn't talk. His mouth wouldn't work, so he couldn't tell the man he was dead so there was no point in checking for a pulse.

"Dr. Fraser!"

The voice penetrated the bleakness, forcing him to reconsider his condition.

"What's wrong, Dr. Fraser? Is it your heart?"

Not my heart.

"I'm going for help."

Elliott grabbed the long-fingered hand and used it as a lifeline to pull himself back to the world of consciousness. Then he slowly opened his eyes, blinking against the bright sunlight.

"Paul? Is that ye, lad?"

"Yes, sir. Let me get Emily. You're not well."

"She can't help me." Elliott made a move to stand, suddenly aware that he wasn't experiencing his imminent death but his son's. Paul tried to restrain him, but Elliott pushed the constraining arms away.

"Be still," Paul said. "Let me get Emily just to check you out."

Elliott didn't want to waste another minute. He didn't need a doctor. He needed to see his son. Now! "Where's James Cullen?" he growled.

"He's at a cabin not far from here with a big brute of a man with an ax."

"Erik? He's with Erik?" That made no sense. James Cullen was supposed to find Ensley and come here or stay in the Dakotas until Tavis arrived.

But he's here? Why was Paul sent to get me? Why didn't James Cullen come alone to talk to me so we could work out our differences?

"Yes," Paul said. "Erik wants you to come to the cabin immediately."

"What does James Cullen want?"

"I'm not sure. We'll find out when we get there. I'll get a wagon for us."

Elliott grabbed Paul's jacket lapel, remembering the terror he just experienced. "Wait. Is James Cullen alive? Tell me!"

"Erik wouldn't let me see him, but he wouldn't be in such a hurry to see you if JC was…was gone."

Elliott waved his hand toward the barn. "Damn the wagon. Get me a horse."

"Elliott!" A man was running toward them, yelling, "What's wrong?"

Paul recognized him from the family portraits hanging on the mansion's stairwell wall. "You're Mr. MacKlenna."

"Aye." He squatted to be eye level with Elliott. "What happened? Is it yer heart?"

"I found him like this," Paul said.

Sean looked up at Paul. "Who are ye?"

"He's a liar. That's who he is," Elliott's voice was hard and cold as stone. "Get me a horse!"

Sean pressed his hand on Elliott's shoulder to keep him from standing.

Why is everybody trying to restrain me? Don't they understand James Cullen is dying?

"Best ye don't need to ride right now. Let me help ye inside. Emily can examine ye," Sean said.

"No! Enough!" Elliott shook off Sean's hand. "Erik has my son at the cabin."

"Erik? The Viking?"

"Aye," Elliott said. "He wants me there. It's an emergency."

"I don't know about the Viking part," Paul told Sean, "but there's a man at the cabin who insists on seeing you, Dr. Fraser, and Emily Duffy."

"Me? He wants me there? Why?"

"Damn it, Sean." His complacency infuriated Elliott more. "We're not going to learn anything until we get there."

"Only if Emily says it's safe," Sean said. "Ye don't look well, Elliott."

"I'm not ill. My son is. Help me to my feet—or get out of my way, and I'll manage by myself."

Sean and Paul helped him stand, then Elliott sprang forward as though a tether had snapped, and he shoved them away. "I'm going now! Don't try to stop me."

Sean yelled at a groom coming out of the stallion barn. "Jackson, saddle three horses."

"Yes, sir," the groom said, darting back inside.

Elliott strode in the direction of the cabin.

"I'll walk with Dr. Fraser," Paul said. "Will you get Emily? And tell her not to mention this to Meredith."

"Who are ye, again?"

"I'm Paul Brodie. I watched JC disappear in the fog and lied to Dr. Fraser about JC's disappearance. Then I used the brooch to go after him. I just now arrived and was on my way here when I met Erik. He has JC at the cabin, but he wouldn't let me go inside to see him. Please hurry up and get Emily and meet us there."

"Go on, lad. I'll bring Emily and the horses. Stay on the path so I can find ye."

"Don't tell Meredith," Paul reminded him.

"I'll do what I can."

"If ye're coming with me, Paul, don't stand there. Take my arm."

Paul hooked his hand in the bend of Elliott's elbow and forced him to slow down, which irritated Elliott, but right now, he might not get there without Paul's assistance. The horrifying experience had left him weak and unsure of his footing, and if he continued to argue with Paul, the lad might leave him here and return to the cabin by himself.

"Take it easy, will you? Dr. Mallory would be furious with you right now."

"I dinna care." Elliott knew that was a lie as soon as the excuse rolled off his tongue. Charlotte wouldn't even try to understand but would lasso him into submission, just like she did whenever he was sick, even with a goddamn cold.

"Why'd ye lie to me, Paul?"

Paul steadied him as he shuffled down a slight incline. "I believed it was my duty to protect JC's secret. I didn't know the whole family knew about the brooch and disappearing into a fog. I thought it was part of the work he was doing."

"At the CIA?" Elliott asked.

There was something in Paul's expression, in his eyes, that showed how surprised he was that Elliott knew the truth about James Cullen's employment.

"You should have told JC that you know about his job. He hated lying to you," Paul said.

"I knew from the beginning, but it was his choice. I wasn't going to interfere."

"Then you understand why I couldn't betray The Company or JC?"

"No. Not at all."

"I'm sworn to secrecy, Dr. Fraser. That's why I came after JC to find out if he was in trouble. But I don't understand how you arrived here first."

"Ye arrive when ye were meant to arrive. Not sooner. Not later. Now tell me everything from the moment ye came out of the fog."

Paul told him what Erik said and how he threatened him twice. Elliott took it all in, but he wanted to hear it again. So Paul started over and had just finished telling the story the second time when the sound of pounding hooves made them both turn around.

Sean dismounted. "Let me give ye a leg up," he said to Elliott.

"Let me examine him first," Emily said, swinging her leg over the saddle to dismount, but Elliott shot her a look, telegraphing what he thought of her idea, and instead of dismounting, she sat back down in her saddle. "Maybe I'll wait until your ass falls out of the saddle, you pigheaded Scot."

Elliott managed a chuckle. "Ye've spent too much time with Charlotte. I'm quite capable of mounting a goddamn horse."

"Ye're a stubborn old man is what ye are. Now bend yer leg." Sean reached for Elliott's bent leg and gave him a boost.

"Uncle Sean, you shouldn't have helped him. I could see it in his eyes. He knew he didn't have the strength to mount up by himself."

"He didn't fool me, lass," Sean said. "I saw it in his eyes, too. I was only saving his pride. I owed him one."

"If ye two are through talking about me like I'm not here, I'd like to go see my son."

Emily tossed Paul the reins to the horse she was leading, and he mounted up. "Thanks, Emily. Good to see you. It's been a while."

"I'm surprised to see you here," she said. "But I guess I shouldn't be, considering how close you are to JC. What do you know about his injuries?"

Paul settled into his saddle. "Nothing. Erik seems to know everyone in the family, but he wouldn't tell me anything about JC. He just ordered me to bring you to the cabin."

Elliott nudged his horse, and they all galloped off.

Erik was standing outside the cabin door when they arrived. Elliott dismounted, tossed the reins over the hitching post, and stormed the porch, and the others followed.

"Get out of my way, Erik."

Erik shook his head, and his mouth thinned as if he was restraining whatever he wanted to say, which only angered Elliott more. Then Erik put his huge hands on Elliott's chest, and they felt like bricks cementing him in place.

"No. There is much I must tell you before you go in," Erik said.

Elliott jerked his arms up and out, hitting against Erik's to get his hands off Elliott's chest, but he didn't have the strength to do it, which pissed him off even more. All he had was his voice, and he slung words instead. "There's not a goddamn thing I need to know until I see James Cullen. So get the hell out of my way!"

"You can't see him yet," Erik said calmly. "Sit down and listen to me."

Elliott's anger began to burn in his throat like bile as his son's endless screams reverberated through his mind, and his rage, his desperate need to know what happened to his son, seemed to explode through him like a violent storm. He barely held it back.

Elliott glared at Erik. "Is he dying? Tell me that."

Erik released his restraining hands. "He is not, but he needs healing that could require years."

"Years?" The anger seemed to *whoosh* out of Elliott, and he dropped into one of the rockers. "Dear God. What happened?"

"James Cullen is in what you call a coma."

Elliott jumped up. "Then he needs immediate medical attention. Let Emily see him. We'll take him home right away."

"I didn't ask for Emily so she could attend to James Cullen, but to attend to you. You are strong and healthy, but you have unrealistic expectations of what your old body can do. You must calm yourself."

"Can I see James Cullen?" Emily asked.

"Dr. Duffy, even you cannot help him."

She threw Erik an exasperated look. "I'm a medical doctor, and I *can* help him. What are his injuries?"

Paul was standing next to Emily, and Erik grabbed his arm and shook it. "Go inside now and stand by the bed. Make sure no one uncovers James Cullen or touches him. Not you. Not Elliott. Not his mother. Not Charlotte. Not Dr. Duffy. Do you understand?"

"You're putting me between you and Elliott. That's not—"

Erik jerked on Paul's arm again, almost hard enough to dislocate the shoulder joint. "I'm putting you between James Cullen and people who can harm him unintentionally. You must do as I ask, or James Cullen will never fully recover."

"Why?" Elliott demanded. "Why are ye doing this to James Cullen? We've got to get him medical attention!"

Erik whirled around and got in Elliott's face, but Elliott didn't back down.

Erik thumped Elliott's chest with his finger. "You have come to depend more on medicine than on the power you have."

"What kind of power?" Paul asked.

Erik glared at Paul with hard eyes. "Why are you still here?"

Paul looked uncomfortable but not scared. "Uh, I'm going." He opened the door, and hot, wood-scented air flowed out. "It's hot as hell in here."

"Close the door," Erik demanded.

Paul closed the door. "I thought you wanted me inside."

Erik jerked on Paul's arm a third time, and this time Paul grimaced. "Close the door *behind* you!"

Paul shot a glance at Emily, his lip twitching ever so slightly, then entered the cabin and closed the door.

While Elliott watched their exchange, it dawned on him that Paul was too smart to act like an idiot. It had to be a ruse to lower the hostility. If he was willing to risk Erik's temper and abuse, Elliott could force himself to listen quietly. He returned to the rocker and sighed with a heavy heart.

"What happened?"

Erik crossed his arms and said, "Members of the Illuminati captured James Cullen in Chicago, broke nearly every bone in his body, and peeled off the skin on his arms and chest."

Elliott shot up out of the chair, hugged the porch railing, and threw up. Emily handed him a flask from her medical bag. He poured some in his mouth, swished it around, and spit it out. Then he took a long drink.

"How could he survive such horror?" Elliott growled out.

"It wasn't easy," Erik said.

"He never betrayed the family, did he?" Elliott said. "He put himself through all that to protect us. Dear God." Elliott flopped back into the chair. The screams he heard were James Cullen's torture, and Elliott would never forget the sound or the pain. He sat there in mute horror as his mind weighed the implications. A body can heal. A mind cannot.

"James Cullen will come out of the coma when his body is healed, and not before," Erik said. "Any interference from you, and he will die."

"He needs to be in a hospital. Let us take him home," Emily pleaded.

"A hospital cannot heal him. If he is disturbed, the additional shock from the excruciating pain will cause his heart to stop. And even your medicine will not restart it." Eric turned the full brute force of his attention on Elliott. "You must listen to me and trust in the power to save the future Keeper. It will not allow him to die unless you interfere."

"Can we take him home?" Emily asked.

"Not until he wakes up."

"How long do you think that will be?" she asked.

"If he is going to wake up, it will take forty-eight to seventy-two hours," Erik said.

"But he needs—" Emily said.

"He needs nothing!" Erik raised his thundering voice, and the floorboards shook. "If you want him to die, then touch him, uncover him, and give him drugs—because he *will* leave this world again, but he will not return!"

"Again?" Elliott asked.

"When the pain became unbearable, and his heart was failing, his guardian, Kristen Montgomery, interceded on his behalf and took him into her protection until I could reach him and start the healing process. Kristen can only rescue him one more time, and he has a long life to live. Do you want that third rescue to be now because of your impatience?"

A vision of his son standing between his and Meredith's graves slid into Elliott's awareness, blocking out everything else for a moment. James Cullen's hair was gray and thin, his shoulders stooped, but joy illuminated his entire being. What could make him so joyful as he approached the end of his long life?

"Elliott, I must have your word that you will not interfere."

Erik's demand shattered Elliott's vision. In his heart, Elliott knew James Cullen's joy resulted from what Elliott chose at this moment. He clasped Erik's callused hand, feeling the heat of his strength, determination, and truth.

"I trust ye to do what is best for James Cullen and the clan." Elliott squeezed Erik's hand and then released it.

"You have accepted responsibility for your people and the brooches," Erik continued. "You often don't understand, but you dare to live in the cloudy gap in between the two worlds. The lessons you learn never leave you. They pour back in to enable you to make the next more difficult decision—one that benefits the whole and not individual desires."

Elliott found it challenging to argue with Erik's esoteric philosophy. Maybe another time, when so much wasn't on the line.

"Who did this to James Cullen? I want the name of the man."

Erik didn't answer right away, and after a long stretch of silence that raised Elliott's blood pressure, Erik finally said, "My brother, Sten, and his associates."

"Yer brother?" Elliott squeezed his chest, protecting his heart from Erik's pain, understanding that Erik, too, was living in the cloudy gap. "Is this a Cain and Abel story?"

"Similar. Sten and I were alike in many ways until darkness took his soul. Our father disowned and banished him during his youth, but Father could not destroy his knowledge of the stones. Sten took that with him and started a branch of the Illuminati whose sole purpose is to collect the brooches and use them to control the world. I do not know how many stones he has collected or how far his tentacles reach. He was the titular head but did not hold all the power."

"Where is he now?" Elliott demanded to know.

"I killed him," Erik said. "And, as your surrogate, I cut off his head. But his evil has spread too far, and his minions will continue to search for the remaining stones. With Sten gone, the organization has lost its institutional knowledge—but not its purpose."

"I can't worry about that now. James Cullen has to be my focus."

Erik nodded, then opened the door, and Elliott, Sean, and Emily followed him into a sauna. A fire was blazing in the hearth, and Erik poured a few drops of oil from a bottle into a pot of hot water, then drizzled a ladle of water over the sauna rocks until a burst of humidity replenished the warmth and moisture inside the cabin. The cedar walls emitted the forest's subtle scent and mingled with a slight eucalyptus aroma, which must be from the oil droplets.

Elliott put his hands in his jacket pockets as he approached the bed, so his urge to comfort and heal his son wouldn't tempt him to reach out. His heartbeat thudded in his neck and fingertips.

"Is that yer cloak covering his body?" Elliott asked.

"Yes. The heat and steam keep the cloak moist. Don't let the fire go out," Erik said.

Elliott took a step forward. "How do I know it's James Cullen?"

"He has a birthmark on the top of his right foot that resembles an Yggdrasil. Does your son have that mark?" Erik asked.

Elliott dropped his head as tears slid down his cheeks. "His mother told him when he was young that it was a sign he'd been blessed."

"He is blessed, Elliott. You may not believe it, and right now, James Cullen probably would not believe it, either, but in time he will come to accept it."

"Does yer cloak have healing powers? Is that why he's completely covered?"

"Like the brooches, it is made of a substance that came out of the sky. You cannot tear this cloak or cut it."

"But where does the healing power come from?"

Erik went to the stones and ladled more water over them. "It is not for you or me to understand, only to accept what is."

"I'm surprised ye didn't say I'd find out on the other side of the door."

"It is possible you will never know. The cloak is thousands of years old and is the only one of its kind. Each generation has passed it down to the next. Now it belongs to the Keeper's son. He cannot give it away until he is dying, or it will lose its power."

The realization of what Erik said weakened Elliott's legs, and he reached for the chair at the foot of the bed for support. "How can ye give it away, then?"

Erik's face was gray and lined with a lurking sorrow, and it added to Elliott's overall sense of gravity. "It has served my purpose, and I do not need it now. It belongs with the Keeper."

"But James Cullen isn't the Keeper yet," Elliott said, wondering if he, like Erik, had served his purpose, and it was time for the next generation to take the lead.

"He will be the Keeper in due time. When his healing is complete, James Cullen will awake. But his mind will not be the same.

The cloak cannot heal the terror and pain he experienced. He has to find peace in his way and at his own pace."

"How?" Elliott asked.

"I do not know, but I suggest Young Paul take James Cullen to the mountains, to the monks, to live there until his mind has settled. But darkness will remain deep in his soul until he finds his true purpose."

Elliott covered his face with his hands. "Why?"

Erik gripped Elliott's shoulder. "You walked in darkness for decades to gain the wisdom you have. Now it is your son's time to walk in the shadow. He will have wisdom beyond his years and will lead the clan into the next century. Be not afraid for him. Have patience. This battle is won, but the war is not yet over. When James Cullen wakes, you can take him home, but he must leave immediately for the mountains."

"I'll go with him," Paul said.

"One more important matter. James Cullen must wear the cloak for the rest of his life. It folds up into a small square that he can wear in a packet around his neck. But while he is at the monastery, he should wear it as a cloak."

Erik clasped arms with Sean. "You were brave to wait outside this cabin all those years ago. I regret not having time to spend with you. When Elliott takes his family home, you must burn this cabin down, and the land around it must return to its natural state. It cannot be sold or developed. It is now sacred ground. Treat it as such. No evidence of the cabin's existence should remain."

"Why?" Elliott asked.

"You will know in time." Erik then clasped Elliott's arm. "I will not see you again until you reach the other side."

"Of the door?" Elliott asked.

"No," Erik said. "When you take your final breath, I will welcome you to the beyond."

Elliott shuddered. "I hope that's not any time soon."

"There is one more thing I must tell you. Walk with me." Erik picked up his battle-ax and escorted Elliott out to the porch, then closed the door. "The Council, which included my father, failed to destroy my brother. Since Sten almost killed the future Keeper, the Council owes you a favor. Only one, though. Whatever you ask, the members cannot deny your request. Use it wisely."

Elliott looked back toward the door. "What could I ever want from them? Every question I've asked, the answer has been to wait until we reach the other side of the door."

"The day may come when I'm not there to intervene on your behalf."

"Why wouldn't the rest of the Council be receptive to my request?"

"I am not saying they would refuse it. I only want you to be aware of the possibility. If you come back and I am not there, prepare for a battle."

Erik ran the ax handle through his leather belt to hold it in place. "Be well, my friend. Do not lose faith in James Cullen. You saw the vision I sent you. He will find joy."

Elliott blinked, unsure he heard Erik correctly. "I had a vision of James Cullen as an old man standing over my grave, and he radiated a kind of joy I've never witnessed before."

"I sent it so you would have hope."

Elliott's eyes watered, and he struggled to see clearly through his tears, trying to understand what Erik was saying. "Ye can see the future?"

"Not everyone's. But I can see James Cullen's and my own." Erik glanced off toward the trees, and a few beats passed before he said, "I have a request that I hope you will honor."

"Anything," Elliott said.

Any pretense of presenting a calm front vanished when Erik said, "Treat Ensley, Tavis, and Mark as if they were children of your blood. I will not be here to watch over them. And I trust you to see to their welfare."

"That's an odd request. Why them?"

"They are my children. They are Viking warriors by blood."

Elliott tried to hide the shock he knew was creeping across his face, but if Erik could send him visions, he could probably read his mind, too. "Do they know?"

"No, and there is no reason they should."

"Did ye rape their mothers?"

"No. I loved both of them, and I believe the women loved me as well. They were unable to have children with their husbands. As I was your proxy when I beheaded Sten, you will be mine in acting on my children's behalf."

Elliott held up his hands in surrender. "I refuse to behead anyone. But I will treat them as I treat my two sons."

Erik nodded. "I trust you to do whatever is required, and that is all I can ask. I must go now. My work is not finished."

"Where are ye going?"

"To watch over my children for as long as I can."

"James Cullen went back to find Ensley."

"He found her and left her with Mr. Roosevelt in the Badlands. They intended to meet later and travel to New York City."

"Thank God she wasn't with him."

"If she had been, James Cullen would have revealed every secret he knew to save her life. And they both would still have been tortured and killed."

Nausea crawled the walls of Elliott's stomach again, but he clenched his teeth and strove for control. "That would have started a goddamn war."

"Indeed." Elliott could hear Erik's effort to convey a level of reassurance, but his sadness and regrets were clearly audible.

"I've delayed too long."

"I'll never be able to thank ye."

"Take care of my children, and that will be all the thanks I would ever want. Goodbye, my friend."

Erik stepped off the porch and walked toward the grove of trees behind the cabin. Elliott squeezed his eyes to wipe away the messy tear film, and when he opened them, Erik was gone. There was no fog, no smell of peat, just an emptiness where the Viking once stood.

Goodbye, my friend.

41

The Badlands (1885)—Tavis

TAVIS RODE TO the top of a butte overlooking the Little Missouri River and reined in his horse. They'd been riding about two hours, and he was pretty sure Roosevelt's Elkhorn Ranch was right around the bend in the river. He dismounted, took the binoculars out of his saddlebag, and studied the landscape out over the river.

A trail of chimney smoke wafted up behind a smaller butte.

Right location. Must be the ranch.

He lowered the binoculars and considered the best way to approach the ranch. If JC was here, it would be simple enough to ride in without setting off alarm bells. If he wasn't, the presence of three armed men might frighten the occupants. And if Ensley was there, she wouldn't recognize them.

Was there a way to signal her?

It would have to be a signal only a time traveler would understand. Like what? She wouldn't know the Army, Navy, or Marine signals. How about the V sign? Its first use was in 1941. Or he could flash his Superman T-shirt and sing a line from "Wish I Could Fly Like Superman."

He rubbed his chest. The shirt was a gift from his two-year-old nephew. Well, it was actually from Tavis's brother, who put his son's name on the birthday gift. Tavis liked wearing it. Not that he thought of himself as Superman, but the shirt reminded him—as did the silver medallion with Odin's spear, Gungnir, in the center, which dangled from a stainless steel chain around his neck—that he had loved ones, besides the MacKlenna Clan.

He stood at the edge of the butte. If he were Superman, he

could spread his arms and fly off this hill with its steep, vertical sides and find JC. *Where are you, bro?*

The wind lifted his hat, and he grabbed it before it could sail over the edge and across the plain.

A knot locked down his throat. *What the hell?* When the knot tightened, he knew something was desperately wrong, but he had no idea what or where.

He glanced down and noticed a purple flower growing out of a crevice. He snapped it off the stem, and after a quick sniff, tucked it into his shirt pocket. The sweet scent smelled better than he did.

Remy rode up behind him and dismounted. "Do you see it?"

"No. But there's a smoke trail over that closest butte that looks like it's coming from a chimney. I'll know for sure after I check the map." He glanced around. "Where's Austin?"

Remy pointed with his chin. "Taking a leak."

Tavis stared in the direction Remy indicated. "I'm worried about him. Keep your eye out for trouble, will you? If anything happens to him, JL will lay into me worse than any commander I ever reported to."

"I doan have to keep an eye on him. He's not letting me out of *his* sight. I have drugs, and if he wants painkillers, I'm the only game in town." Remy stood in his stirrups. "I can see him. He's coming up now."

"Don't give him any."

"Doan plan to."

Tavis unpacked the topography map and compass and took a few minutes to orient himself and do the calculations. "The smoke should be coming from Elkhorn Ranch. At least we know someone's there."

Remy opened his canteen and took a long drink. "So, what's your plan? Are we just going to ride in and ask about JC?"

Tavis shook his head. "No, I'll go in alone while you stay here with Austin. If JC isn't there, I don't want to alarm President Roosevelt. Look at us. We could easily pass for outlaws. I don't want to make anyone trigger-happy. There isn't much law out here, and some dumbass might just shoot us first and ask questions later."

"By the way, Roosevelt's not president yet."

"I know, but he still deserves our respect, and his vision is terrible. He might not see our good hearts and intentions."

Austin rode up, dismounted, lay down in the shade, and plopped his hat over his face. He was larger than a bear, meaner than a mad dog, and usually spewing cuss words like a sailor on stormy seas.

Austin was the incarnation of his sports nickname—the Dragon. His height, broad shoulders, muscular arms, and hands the size of a small state would scare sensible people shitless. But men with something to prove would give him what he wanted—trouble, big trouble. Before the accident, Austin had been a marshmallow off the court, but now his attitude screamed, "Try me."

"Look at him," Tavis said.

"Yeah. His attitude sucks. We're in the Wild West. Somebody might just push him hard enough, and he'll get himself killed." Remy scratched his chin, and his nose twitched as if nerve endings were collecting sensory information like cat's whiskers. "We could all be pushed further than we want to be, overreact, make a mistake, and end up dead." Remy was quiet for a minute. "If I get shot, can you go back in time before that happened and stop it?"

"I asked that question once. I didn't get a straight answer. But I believe if something happens while we're out of our time we can't undo it. It is what it is. If you get shot—"

"That's not true. Kenzie changed her grandfather's history."

"That's different." Tavis thought back through the clan's history to find an example. "Here's what I mean. If Kenzie had died on Omaha Beach, David couldn't have rewound the clock and gone back for her at a different time. Dead is dead."

"Fuck." Remy thought a minute. "Nope. That isn't right. Remember what happened to Jack? He died, and Charlotte and David went back to a time before the Union could hang him and kept it from happening."

"I guess dead isn't dead," Tavis said. "But Jack might be the exception. So let's don't test the theory, okay. We're trained soldiers, sailors, and Marines. We know what we're doing."

Remy pointed his thumb over this shoulder. "He doan know what he's doing, and if ya ask me, bringing him was a shitty idea. He's been doing nothing but complaining. He might push me to do something I'll regret."

"What? Cut out his tongue?"

"Doan tempt me."

"You know he's doing it on purpose. If he makes us miserable enough, we might give in and take him home. Just ignore him."

"I wish I could."

Austin lifted his hat. "You two just going to stand there and whisper about me, or are you going to figure out where the hell we are? I'm done with this. Take me home. I've got work to do."

"We're not going home, you son of a bitch. Stop complaining," Remy snapped. "We'll go home after we find JC."

Austin dropped his hat over his face and crossed his arms and ankles.

Tavis had been having prickling sensations ever since he arrived, and he wasn't sure what they meant. There was a disturbance in the unfolding of time. He felt it every time he traveled, but this was different.

He also sensed Erik was here. If so, that meant he was watching over Ensley and JC. They'd still have trouble, but nothing they couldn't handle. If their lives were in danger, Erik would step in, but sometimes the Viking waited too long. At least in terms of Tavis's definition of "lives in danger."

"I'm going down alone," Tavis said. "If the three of us ride up unexpectedly, unannounced and uninvited, there'll be trouble. I'll signal if JC's there. If not, I'll come back to get you, and we'll reevaluate."

"Does that mean we can go home?" Austin asked, this time not even raising his hat.

"Hell, no. We're here to find JC, and we woan leave till we do." Then Remy said to Tavis, "I'll give you fifteen minutes. If you doan signal for us to come down, we're coming after ya."

"Okay. Fifteen. But don't start counting until I cross the river." Tavis put the map and compass away and remounted his horse. "Don't beat the shit out of Austin while I'm gone."

"I'll try not to," Remy said.

Tavis rode down off the butte, crossed the river, and trotted toward the ranch. He checked the time. It was almost noon. There was a chance they'd be back at the Colorado ranch by supper. But if that was the way it was supposed to work out, why bother to kidnap Austin?

Because this isn't going to be easy, and we won't be going right back. The shit's going to hit the fan. I feel it in my bones.

Tavis followed the smoke and arrived at a ranch house built about thirty yards from the cottonwood-lined riverbank. The cabin looked substantial enough, with two chairs on the porch, gently rocking in the breeze. He rode slowly into the yard and stopped a few feet from the porch.

"Hello. Anybody here? I'm not looking for trouble. I'm searching for James Cullen Fraser. Have you seen him?"

Nothing happened for a minute, then another, and another. Tavis was about to ride around to the back of the cabin when the door creaked open, and a woman came out, holding a rifle like she knew how to use it.

"Why you lookin' for him?"

"He's my cousin. I heard he might ride out here to do some hunting with Teddy Roosevelt. Is he around?"

She shook her head. "Rode off a week ago."

"Do you know where he was going?"

"Kentucky."

"Lexington, I guess," Tavis said. "Was he traveling by himself?"

The woman shook her head again. "Had his wife with him."

Tavis's gut reacted before his mind did. But then it made sense. JC must have found Ensley and used a fake marriage to protect her.

Tavis took off his hat and slapped his leg, grinning. "Hot dang. Guess he finally convinced Miss Ensley to marry him."

Tavis's informality relaxed the woman, and she lowered the rifle. "Miss Ensley didn't go with him."

That didn't sound like JC. Something else was at work here. Tavis worked up a laugh he didn't feel, so the woman would keep feeding him information. "Aw shucks, ma'am. Are ya telling me they broke up already?"

"Oh, no." The woman smiled. "You could tell they're mighty fond of each other. Miss Ensley wanted to go on the roundup with Mr. Roosevelt to research a book she's writing, but Mr. Fraser wanted to go to Kentucky to visit his family. Mr. Roosevelt agreed to watch over her until they could meet up in Cleveland and return to New York City together."

"New York City, huh? So JC and Miss Ensley plan to live in New York City instead of Kentucky."

The woman gave him a suspicious look. "That's where they've been living. You didn't know that?"

"Hmm," Tavis said. "My mama's family news is a bit behind. I'll be sure to catch her up. Now, you mentioned a roundup? When did they leave?"

"This morning," the woman said.

"Then I could catch up with them. Where were they going?"

"They were meeting the other cowboys at the mouth of Box Elder Creek on the Little Missouri River to take part in the District 6 roundup. It's about thirty miles north of here."

"Thank you, ma'am. You've been most kind." Tavis tipped his hat. "Oh, one more thing. Was it just Miss Ensley and Mr. Roosevelt? Cause they could ride pretty fast. But if they had a wagon and extra horses, it could slow 'em down."

"Four men, a chuckwagon, a remuda of thirty horses, and Miss Ensley."

"Then I can catch 'em. I bet they could use another set of hands, too. Thanks again."

He waved and rode away from Elkhorn Ranch, returning to Austin and Remy with a minute to spare.

"Where's JC?" Austin demanded.

"He went on a roundup with Roosevelt. They left about four hours ago. If we ride hard, we'll catch them within a couple of hours."

"We can't catch two riders with a four-hour head start in just two hours," Remy said.

"He's traveling with three men, plus a cook driving a chuckwagon, and a remuda of thirty horses." Tavis wasn't going to mention that JC wasn't with Roosevelt, nor was he going to mention Ensley.

If Tavis did, Austin would just start bitching louder. And Tavis wasn't in the mood to listen to him. This was a need-to-know mission. "Give me five minutes to look at the map and chart a course."

It took him ten.

Ninety minutes later, Tavis spotted a dust cloud. It had to be Roosevelt's party.

How was he going to handle this now? He hadn't had a chance to pull Remy aside and tell him JC went to Kentucky. So both Remy and Austin would react to the news in front of Roosevelt. Tavis could count on Remy playing along with him. But Austin was a wild card. And if he recognized Ensley's name, then all hell could break loose.

This reminded him of Elliott asking him to stand down while Rick and Remy broke into the Gothenburg Museum. He knew what they were doing and why but he couldn't tell Elliott how he knew. Elliott took the deception in stride, but Tavis couldn't count on Austin doing the same. His behavior was too erratic right now.

Tavis mentally sifted through possibilities. The logical next step was to collect Ensley, ride to the nearest telegraph office, and send a telegram to MacKlenna Farm. Once Tavis confirmed that JC was with Elliott, Tavis's team could take Ensley home.

But what concerned Tavis was their delay in getting here. Why had they arrived now instead of shortly after JC's arrival? Maybe Elliott and the others weren't even at the farm yet.

The Council knew more about the brooches than the travelers did. But there were still details the Council didn't understand.

And as a guardian, Tavis knew even less.

He closed his eyes and steadied his breathing—and for a fleeting moment, he heard a man's blood-curdling screams, and Tavis's skin burned hot as fire.

42

MacKlenna Farm, KY (1885)—Elliott

AFTER ERIK'S DEPARTURE, Elliott returned to the cabin and its dueling aromas of cedar and eucalyptus to find Emily scooping water onto the stones and Sean filling glasses with whisky. He handed one to Elliott, but Elliott couldn't bring himself to drink it while he stood by James Cullen's bed, silently praying for his son's recovery.

"We can't keep this from the women," Sean said before taking a hefty swallow. "If they find out from someone else, Lyle Ann will never forgive me, and I doubt ye'll fare any better with Meredith."

Elliott stared down at the glass of whisky in his hand, needing a drink more than he'd realized until now, but also knowing that if he started drinking today, he might slide down the slippery slope to alcohol dependence again.

He set the drink aside and wiped the sweat off his forehead with his handkerchief. It had to be over a hundred and fifty degrees in here.

"I'll tell Meredith as soon as I return to the house." Elliott looked at the drink he'd set on the table—wiping his upper lip—and reconsidered but arrived at the same conclusion. He couldn't escape this reality in an alcoholic stupor.

"Kitherina and Cullen's children should be here by the time we get back," Sean said. "Thomas Montgomery sent a telegram saying he'll be here with Emily's parents before dinner."

Emily hung the ladle on a hook by the hearth before tossing a log on top of the flames. Her face was dripping sweat, too. "I hope they recognize me. I've changed a lot since I left Napa. They'll be astonished that I graduated from college and medical school."

"It might be sixteen years for ye, but it's only been four years for them. They'll recognize ye. And besides, ye look just like yer mother."

"I hope you're right, but it'll be a short visit," she said. "We'll have to leave as soon as JC wakes up."

"We'll make the best of the days we have." Elliott checked the time on his Rolex. "I have to head back and talk to Meredith."

"What do you think she'll say?" Emily asked.

"She won't believe an ancient cloth can heal James Cullen. I'm not completely convinced myself, but I have to be committed before I talk to her. If I waver, she'll balk and demand we take James Cullen to the hospital."

Never taking his eyes off James Cullen, Paul rolled his shoulder repeatedly and stretched his neck from side to side. "Look at it this way. Since we're here in 1885, it's obvious traveling through time is possible. If that sci-fi fantasy is true, then it's not a stretch to believe a twelfth-century Viking has a magic healing cloak?"

"I hope that argument works with Meredith." Elliott watched Paul rub his shoulder, and it reminded him that he hadn't asked about a possible injury. "Yer shoulder's bothering ye. Let Emily look at it."

Paul waved away Elliott's concern. "Erik knows his strength and how to use it. He could have ripped off my arm. It's a little sore, but it's still attached. JC is more important right now. Don't worry about it."

Emily put her hand on Paul's shoulder. "I'm sorry, I should have looked at it immediately, but I got distracted."

He removed Emily's hand and kissed it. "Thanks, but don't worry about it. The heat and humidity here will increase blood flow to the muscles and keep them loose. I'll be fine." He released Emily's hand.

"Okay, but if you change your mind—"

"I'll let you know," Paul said in an irritated tone as he rotated his shoulder. "But I have another problem." He held up his satellite phone. "This doesn't work here, so once you guys leave, I won't be able to communicate with you. I could try smoke signals I guess, or a string and a tin can."

Elliott drummed his fingers on his hips as he stared out the window at the four horses hitched to the rail. "Sean, if ye have a loose horse on the farm, will it return to the barn?"

"Usually. Why?"

"It could solve Paul's problem. If I unsaddle his horse, he could send it back to the barn as a signal. As soon as the horse shows up, I'll ride out here."

"Or I could send a farmhand here to sit on the porch and wait for a message," Sean said.

"That would start rumors," Elliott said. "Best to keep this quiet for now."

"There could be more men out there looking for James Cullen or even Ensley," Paul said.

"Shit!" Elliott punctuated the expletive with a flat-palmed blow to the wall. "God*damn* it. We can't let our guard down. I'll talk to Meredith and come back with weapons and ammunition." He glanced at Paul. "Ye're armed, aren't ye?"

"Yeah, but I only have one extra magazine. I didn't come here planning to defend the OK Corral."

"Is that the gunfight in Arizona between the Earps and Doc Holliday and the cowboys? I'm surprised ye know about it," Sean said.

"It's one of the most infamous stories of the Wild West."

"Hmm. The strangest things are important in yer time," Sean said, walking toward the door. "I'll unsaddle yer horse, Paul. But if ye release him before Elliott returns, be sure to tie up the reins so he won't get tangled in the briars or bushes."

"Okay," Paul mumbled, glancing away and massaging his shoulder.

Elliott shot a glance at Paul, knowing the lad was sensitive because he wasn't a skilled equestrian, but after watching Paul with Erik, Elliott realized Paul wasn't at all who he appeared to be.

"If you change your mind and want me to look at your shoulder—"

"Not now, Emily!" Paul snapped and gave her a look that could have held back a weather front. But Emily just gave him a Charlotte smile—a Southern bless-your-heart look to soften the condemnation that followed. Elliott had learned to brace himself every time he saw one coming.

"Erik could have torn your rotator cuff. That arm won't do you much good. I hope you're left-handed." She gave him that smile again. "I'll be outside with Sean."

When the door closed behind Emily, Elliott crossed the room to stand at the foot of the bed. "Is there anything I can bring back for ye?"

"Paper and pencils or pen and ink," Paul said.

"There's plenty in the cabinet over there. Sean comes here to sketch, so he keeps it well stocked. There's also coffee and whisky. Nothing to eat, though. I'll have meals prepared and sent down from the house."

"Appreciate it," Paul said.

Elliott closed his eyes, trying to free his mind for a few moments before he left to talk to Meredith. An image of James Cullen's broken and bloodied body fixed itself in front of Elliott's mind's eye. While most of his son's skin was black and blue, the rippled skin on his chest and arms was the color of rot. If not for the cedar and eucalyptus aromas inside the cabin, the stink of decay would have sickened him.

The horror of it all knocked Elliott off balance, and he swayed.

Paul rushed to his side. "Take it easy." He hooked his foot under a nearby chair's spindle and dragged it close to the bed. "Sit here. I'll get Emily."

"No need, Paul." Elliott held on to the top rail of the chair. "Sometimes I see things."

Paul's questioning stare went from Elliott to the bed and back to Elliott. "Can you see beneath the cloth?"

Elliott's eyes watered, his spirit nearly crushed, but he had to tell someone the truth. It would be a burden for Paul, but someone needed to know. He dropped into the chair and fingered the thick fabric of his trousers, trying to straighten the stiff crease, but the trousers didn't have one. He stilled his hands.

"Except for the birthmark, James Cullen is un…recognizable. They broke his nose and jaw, knocked out his teeth, and broke his legs, hips, and fingers. The skin on his arms and chest is black and shriveled up, but his organs are functioning as if he's only asleep. He's alive on the inside but rotting on the outside."

Elliott clasped Paul's arm. "Meredith must never see him this way. Ye must do whatever it takes to keep her from pulling back the cloth. She'll get pissed, but getting over that would be easier than being haunted for the rest of her life by the sight of her son's mutilated body."

"Ms. Montgomery has a steel backbone. As long as you're up-front with her, she can handle anything. But Dr. Fraser, I could never use force to restrain her."

"Ye'll do what ye have to do." Elliott held on to Paul's arm as he stood. "I have to go, but I'll be back in an hour or so and will bring food." He shuffled toward the door. "Lock it behind me, and don't let anyone else come in."

"Take your time. We've got a long wait. The Viking said it could be seventy-two hours before JC wakes up."

"Ye'll need to sleep."

"I don't require much sleep. I'll start to doze after seventy-two hours, but I'm fine until then."

Elliott dropped his head and rolled it back and forth. "This is my worst nightmare."

"If I had told you the truth, none of this would have happened."

"This is not yer fault, Paul." Elliott raised his head and looked Paul in the eye. If James Cullen didn't survive, Elliott didn't want Paul to feel responsible for his death. "James Cullen knew what he was doing, but I have to accept a share of the responsibility. This business is bigger than all of us, and no one is capable of handling it alone. James Cullen had an exaggerated sense of his capabilities, and I never discouraged it. That's my fault. Even if ye told us what happened, this would have played out the same way."

"You're trying to ease my guilt."

"Ye're a man of character, Paul. Now guard James Cullen well. If the Illuminati show up to steal the cloak, kill them. Yer automatic is loaded, isn't it?"

"Yes, sir."

"I'm glad to have ye on our side." Elliott shuffled toward the door and opened it. "Bolt the lock and shutter the windows." He peered out the door, looking both ways. "Sean's stacked more wood on the porch and unsaddled the horse. It's hobbled nearby to graze."

As soon as Elliott stepped down off the porch, he heard the bolt slide into place and flinched, remembering Charlotte's description of walking past Braham's jail cell and hearing the bolt slam into place. The horror of Braham's imprisonment in Richmond in 1865 was almost as shocking as what was happening here.

Elliott snapped his mount's reins off the hitching post and swung up into the saddle. "Let's go." He rode back to the mansion with Sean and Emily in silence. When they reached the stallion barn, four men dressed in livery were unloading baggage from two carriages.

"Company's arrived. Let's keep James Cullen's presence quiet as long as possible," Elliott said.

"I'll go talk to my farm manager about Paul's horse," Sean said.

Elliott dismounted, handed the reins to a groom, and then helped Emily dismount. "We'll go on up to the house."

"Tell Lyle Ann I'll be right there," Sean called after them.

Elliott agonized over the next few minutes. The house would be a beehive of activity, and Kit, Meredith, and Lyle Ann would be competing for the queen bee's role. He'd put his money on Kit.

He walked toward the front door with Emily. "I have to pull Meredith aside, tell her what's happened, then return to the cabin. With all this company, it's not going to be easy."

"I'll do what I can. But, Elliott, JC's condition is stressful. I noticed you didn't drink the whisky Sean poured for you. That was smart, but if a sedative would help you or Meredith deal with the very understandable anxiety, I can give you something."

"Meredith's never relied on medication, and I doubt she'll start now, but ye never know. Having a mild tranquilizer on hand might be a good idea." As for himself, he wasn't drinking, and he wasn't about to drink plus take a sedative.

Emily opened her medical bag and put two pills in a small Ziplock pill bag. "Here are two diazepams, but don't mix them with alcohol."

Elliott put the bag in the pocket of his waistcoat. "If Meredith doesn't want them, I'll give them back." He patted his pocket. If he had to sedate his wife, he'd put them in a cup of tea. She had never been an overprotective mother, but James Cullen was her only child, and he couldn't be sure how she'd react. His calm and always-in-control bride might not be able to handle this. But she surprised him sometimes.

He steeled himself for what was to come and entered the mansion, where chaos ruled. Three petite blondes in their thirties buzzed around Kit, squealing, which Elliott somehow found amusing. If these three women were Kit's daughters, they hadn't inherited their mother's personality. Kit never squealed over anything. He didn't have time or the inclination to visit with them right now, but he couldn't be rude.

Emily dashed off as soon as she saw her parents.

Traitor.

"Momma, Pappa." Emily embraced her parents, and Elliott's

eyes watered again, forcing him to look away. The sight of Frances and Christopher Duffy embracing Emily was too emotional to watch. They had their child back…while he might never hold his son again.

"Elliott," Meredith called. "Come in here when you have a minute."

He was thankful for the reprieve, but only momentarily. Meredith would know as soon as she looked into his eyes that something was wrong. He mustered as much courage as he could and stepped into the parlor.

43

The Badlands (1885)—Ensley

ENSLEY RODE TESORO through the Badlands alongside Norman's chuckwagon. They were about a half mile behind the dust thrown up by TR and the others who were moving the remuda north. Her horse's smooth gait and the warm sun on her face lulled her to sleep.

"Miss Ensley! Riders comin'," Norman shouted.

She jerked her head up, her eyes wide open. "What? Where?"

"Behind us. Three of 'em. Keep your rifle close."

She looked over her shoulder and saw three men heading toward them, riding hard. Maybe fifty to seventy-five yards out. A heavy dose of adrenaline pumped through her. It wasn't the first time she'd worried about her safety, but now she had a good reason. It was time to put her plan into place.

What plan?

"Pshaw." Right. She had no plan, except this… She pulled TR's Model 1876 Winchester repeater out of its scabbard and held it pointing toward the sky with the stock against her thigh.

"Yer holdin' that rifle like ya know how to use it."

The tip of her finger slid back and forth along the rifle's brass plate above the trigger. "I'm a damn good shot, Norman." She looked over her shoulder again to see how close the riders were now—about twenty-five yards. "Do you have eyes in the back of your head?"

"No, ma'am. But I got a mirror. I keep my eyes on what's in front and what's behind me. If a stampedin' herd's headin' my way, I wanna get out of the path. Sometimes ya can see a dust cloud before ya hear the poundin' hooves."

She didn't doubt Norman would try to protect her, but she sure wished TR was here. "Do you have any idea who they are?"

"Likely drovers on their way to the roundup. Don' know why they'd be ridin' so fast, though. Got plenty of time to get to the meetin' place. Sometimes drovers are troublemakers. If they're in the mood for trouble, we're on our own. Roosevelt and the others are too far ahead to hear gunshots."

Great.

"But most cowboys ain't good shots."

That made her smile. "Thanks, Norman."

Right then, she remembered what had been bugging her about him. He reminded her of Randy, her dad's ranch manager. He'd ridden so many bulls and broncs in the rodeo that he had a permanent limp, and he was always watching out for her and offering comments like the one Norman just made.

When she competed all those years ago, he stood on the chute's left side and hooked her bull rope. He was the last person she saw before the gate swung open.

Randy had invested every penny he made, and when she sold the ranch, he retired to a place in Colorado with a healthy retirement fund and a bonus from her. It was almost as if Norman was the reincarnation of Randy. No, wait. Randy had to be the reincarnation of Norman. But whatever. They didn't look alike, but their minds seemed to run on the same track, and they had a similar sense of humor.

"Let's stop and face them. If the men want trouble, I'd rather they'd be in front of us."

"If you say so, but you can outrun 'em and reach Roosevelt afore them men get a hold of you. And if they chase you, I kin always shoot 'em."

"Maybe they want you, not me," she teased. Why the hell was she taking this lightly? She wasn't. The joke was step one to relieve tension. Step two—she blew out a breath. Step three—she steadied her nerves.

"It's tempting to run, but I'd rather confront trouble I can manage than run from it." What in the hell made her think she could handle three troublemaking cowboys? Overconfidence? Or stupidity? Or Mr. Winchester?

Norman stopped the wagon, tied off the reins, and stood up in the box, the barrel of his rifle resting in the crook of his arm. He wasn't much taller than she was, but he was lean and tough and had enough experience to turn his hair gray.

She studied the three men as they rode up while her heart pounded and a knot the size of a bowling ball stuck in her throat. She'd never pointed a gun at a person before, but if these men threatened her in any way, she'd do whatever was necessary.

"They don't look friendly," she said.

"You're right, ma'am. Never seen a man as big as 'at one in the middle."

"Looks like an NBA player," she mumbled.

"What's that?" Norman asked.

"Oh, just a dumb jock without the brains to do anything except kick, throw, or bat a stupid ball. All brawn, no brains." But she couldn't deny that he rode like a knight who'd come into the world atop his black destrier. The stallion had to stand eighteen hands, with a colossal head that likely weighed more than she did.

But she wasn't intimidated. Tesoro might be smaller, but he had power and endurance and could outlast Monster Black.

The men pulled up in front of her. Monster Black didn't even need a tug on the reins to know what his rider wanted from him. He stopped when he was almost nose to ears with Tesoro.

She glanced up and gave each man a practiced looked that said she might be small, but she wasn't about to be pushed around.

There was something odd about them. Their haircuts, clothes, saddles, and the caliber of horses screamed they had money and lots of it. They smelled like sandalwood and musk and outdoorsy, not at all like the men she'd been around lately.

The guys on both sides of the tall cowboy had that testosterone-overload look common to men in the military and law enforcement. While they were all handsome, the one in the middle—the knight— had the broadest shoulders she'd ever seen. His wingspan had to be seven feet, and his face belonged on a statue representing a Timeless Handsome Man like her mom's all-time favorite—Cary Grant. It was incongruent to be a knight and an old Hollywood hero, but it somehow worked for him.

Wowza!

But when she gazed into his leaf-green eyes and saw emotional pain lurking there, her heart did an ultra-fast *thump-thump*, and then *thump-thump* again, and then again. She dropped her gaze, unable to maintain eye contact. TR lived with grief and sorrow, but it never stopped him from living each day to the fullest. She wasn't so sure about the green-eyed guy.

The scruffy-faced, Spanish-looking guy on the left, riding a bay stallion, flashed the V sign. "Peace," he said, with a deep Cajun voice and dark, sparkling eyes.

She managed to match his peace sign with one of her own. "Peace, bro."

Okay, this is too weird, but it does lower my stress.

"So, you guys on your way to the roundup?" she asked.

"No way in hell," the knight said. "We're looking for James Cullen Fraser. Have you seen him?"

The question was like a punch in the gut.

Damn. They're here.

She knew…or hoped…that sooner or later, someone would show up to take her back to the future, but not today. She wasn't ready. But why were they here? If they stopped by Elkhorn Ranch, Mrs. Sewall would have told them JC went to Kentucky.

"It depends on who's asking," she said.

"JC's my cousin," the knight said. "My mother married his half brother Kevin."

Ensley cocked her head and looked into those damn green eyes again, and she shivered at the intensity of his glare. "The way I understand family trees, that makes him your uncle, not your cousin."

The knight gave her a blank look. "He's younger and shorter. I refuse to call him uncle."

What an asshat.

JC had dozens of cousins, so she wasn't surprised she hadn't met this one, and with his attitude, she was glad she hadn't.

She needed to talk to them and didn't want Norman hanging on her every word while his finger twitched near the trigger. She turned her horse around and said in a low voice to him, "I'm safe with them. The tall guy is my husband's cousin. I've never met him, but I have to explain why James Cullen went to Kentucky without me. You can go on. I'll only be a few minutes."

Norman glowered at the three men. "I don't know, Miss Ensley. They don't look so reputable."

She turned to look back at the men. "They don't, do they? Well, I'll just shoot them if they misbehave. How's that?"

Norman plunked down on the bench seat, stored his rifle, then picked up the reins. "If I hear gunfire, I'll come back and help ya bury 'em." He snapped the reins. "Git-up." And the wagon rolled away. "I'm goin' slow," he called over his shoulder. "And I'm not lettin' ya outta my sight."

"I'll be right behind you." She hoped she hadn't made a mistake trusting these guys. Just in case, she didn't lower her rifle. "Let's walk the horses so Norman won't worry." She maneuvered Tesoro in line with the others. "So the big guy is James Cullen's cousin. Who are you two?"

"I'm Tavis Stuart, a distant cousin of the Frasers and VP of Global Security for MacCorp."

"Are you a Marine? You look like one."

"Navy SEAL."

"Is that once a SEAL always a SEAL?"

He gave her a heart-melting smile. "Something like that, ma'am."

She leaned forward and looked at the guy on the other end, riding the bay. "Who are you? You sound like you're from New Orleans."

"Originally, yeah, and I'm not a cousin. Name's Remy Benoit. I'm Elliott Fraser's personal EMT and bodyguard."

Ensley looked behind her. "Where is he?"

"Who?" Remy asked.

"Dr. Fraser. If you're his bodyguard, shouldn't you be guarding him?"

Remy smiled, and she honestly couldn't decide who was sexier—Remy or Tavis. They both had killer smiles. But if the knight could manage one, his just might be sexier than the other two.

"Elliott and his wife traveled back to MacKlenna Farm. We had no idea where you would end up—here or there. So we drew the long straw."

"This was the long straw? Good God." She returned her rifle to its scabbard, confident now that the men wouldn't harm her. "You know you could be sipping mint juleps at the farm. Instead, you'll end up participating in a roundup."

"The hell we are." The knight then said to Tavis, "If Elliott wanted me to go on an adventure, why in the hell didn't he take me with him?"

"Why would he want to? You're an asshole," Remy said.

Ensley covered her mouth to stifle the laugh gurgling up. "What's your name, JC's cousin?"

"Austin O'Grady," he grumbled.

Her eyes nearly bugged out of her head. Surely not.

This can't be the same man who sent me a manuscript. The same man I told to resubmit when he got his life figured out. The same man I didn't google.

"The basketball player?" she asked.

"Yeah, so what?"

Of all people. Did his agent mention my name?

"Ah, no reason." She snuck a quick look at Tavis, and he winked. Why? Was it a sign or signal, or was he flirting with her?

"You know who I am," Austin said. "So, who the hell are you?"

"Your attitude sucks. But you know that already, right?" There'd been an inkling of regret that she might have rejected his manuscript too quickly. But if she'd known about his attitude, she would have put the rejection in a special delivery envelope marked extra-special delivery. The thought of working with him repulsed her. Why the hell did they even bring him along?

"I don't care what you think about my attitude. I just asked who the hell you are."

"Chill," Tavis said.

She guided her horse over a little bit to get out of the fight zone before the Navy SEAL challenged the knight to a fight to the death. When the challenge didn't come, she said, "I'm a friend of JC's. We went to Harvard together, and my cousin is one of his best friends."

"What's his name?"

"George Williams."

"I think I've met him before. He came to a game with JC when we played at Madison Square Garden a few years ago. Is he a Wall Street guy?"

"Yep. He works at Morgan Stanley."

Austin dropped back, then rode up next to Ensley, sandwiching her between him and Tavis. Her horse was almost as tall as Tavis's, but the two men still dwarfed her, and she almost felt like their prisoner.

Norman was maybe twenty-five yards ahead of them and would hear her if she screamed, but she'd feel better if he was closer. She nudged Tesoro with her knees, and he moved into a trot. The men did the same.

"So you traveled with JC?" Austin asked.

"No. He came after me."

"Why'd he do that? I mean, how'd he know you'd traveled back here? When women go missing the way you did, Elliott calls a family meeting and tells us what's going on. He didn't do that for you." Austin then glared at Tavis and Remy. "Or maybe he did but didn't invite me."

"JC didn't tell anybody," she said.

"That must have pissed Elliott off," Austin said.

"He was avoiding his father because he didn't want to have to lie to him."

"About what?" Tavis asked.

After she cut the distance between her and Norman down to only a few yards, she slowed Tesoro to a walk. "JC told me he'd been working on a project and couldn't tell anyone about it, not even his dad. So JC was avoiding him. He believed his dad would sense something was wrong, and JC would have to lie, and he didn't want to do that."

Tavis looked over at Remy. "JC could have had a run-in with our competition."

"Or heard something," Remy said.

"Who's the competition?" Ensley asked.

"An evil force that's trying to get our brooches," Austin said.

"I hope it's not here in the Dakotas," she said.

"God, that would be shitty," Austin said.

"If they knew about JC, they could have followed him here. There's no way to know," Tavis said.

"This is so fucked up," Austin said. "There are significant missing parts to this cock-and-bull story. How'd JC know to come here for the damsel in distress?"

That thought made her dizzy, as if her horse tilted eastward, tumbling her into the early weeks of her adventure. She couldn't deny that she'd been in distress or how close she'd come to dying. And that pissed her off because she'd always been independent and able to take care of herself.

"Here it is. Now pay attention. If that's possible," she said in a snarky tone.

Austin's brows creased in a slight frown. "Talk about *my* attitude."

"Austin, read my lips," she said, pointing to her mouth. "If people around you develop an attitude, it's because they have to defend against yours."

Remy burst out laughing, which spooked his horse and caused it to jump sideways, but Remy quickly got both himself and the bay under control. "Damn, that was good. I wish I'd thought of it."

She snapped her fingers in Austin's face. "Are you paying attention? I don't want you to miss this."

Austin gave her a crooked smile that surprised the hell out of her. "Coaches have always commented on my attention span. When you get back, read the press reports about my focus under pressure."

She didn't have to read his press reports. His manuscript had a chapter about how he'd developed his phenomenal ability to focus, tune out all distractions, and get into what he called "the zone," which was why his free throw stats were record-shattering. She wouldn't know one player's stats from another's. But Austin's ability to swish free throws in tight games was indicative of his ability to shut everything else out. Everything but the nail on the free-throw line, and then the basket, and to hold his follow-through.

According to another chapter, he tried to use those same skills during rehab but failed. And that led to his dependence on pain medication.

She didn't care about what he did to try to play again. She wanted to know how he handled the tragedy, made worse because he had no one to blame but himself, and how he moved on with his life. The manuscript ended without that answer.

Was he still dependent on opioids?

"As soon as I get home, I'll google you. How's that?"

He shrugged like it didn't matter, but his eyes said the opposite. Everything mattered to him. She read that between the lines of his manuscript, and she saw it now in his leaf-green eyes as they flickered from one emotion to another.

"Great. You do that," Austin said. "Now tell us how JC knew you traveled here."

"I had dinner plans with my cousin, George, and JC came with him. But when they got to the house, the fog had already carried me away. JC found my brooch on the floor and used it to come back for me. I was by myself for several days before he arrived and probably would have died if not for a mysterious man who healed my broken foot."

"Tell me about the mysterious man," Tavis said. "What'd he look like?"

"He was an Indigenous Person, but when JC heard my description, he said he sounded like a Viking warrior named Erik."

"When was the last time you saw him?"

"The days have all run together, but two, maybe three weeks ago."

"Fuck! How long have you been here?" Austin asked.

Damn. She tried biting her cheek, then her tongue, and then she rolled in her lower lip. His tone, language, attitude, and whining were exhausting. She stood up in her stirrups so they'd be face to face, and she poked him in the chest with her finger. "In the last fifteen minutes, you've used fuck as a verb, adjective, subject, object, noun, gerund, predicate, and even an appositive! I half expect to hear you using it as a comma next! So if you wouldn't mind, stop cussing and shut the fuck up!"

Remy and Tavis both howled, laughing so hard they almost fell out of their saddles.

Austin huffed. "Fuck isn't a cuss word. It's a sentence enhancer. And what the hell are you anyway? Some fucking editor?"

Ensley bit her tongue again. Tavis signaled Remy, who dropped back and pulled up next to Austin.

"Ride with me," Tavis said to Ensley. He moved his horse into a trot, and she followed while Remy caught Austin's horse's bridle.

"What the hell are you doing?" Austin demanded.

"Stop!" Remy said. "You're acting like a complete jerk."

She and Tavis quickly moved from a trot to a gallop, and they rode some distance away from Austin and Remy and past Norman.

"Sorry about that." Tavis slowed his horse again. "This is the first time he's been out in months, and he's forgotten how to behave. If his father was here, he'd disown him."

"Who is his father?" As soon as she asked, she remembered he was an NBA player who got his girlfriend pregnant when they were both in high school, and no one ever told Austin until he was a teenager.

"Chris Dalton. He was a six-time NBA Finals Most Valuable Player, ten scoring titles, five MVP Awards—"

"Okay, I don't follow sports, but even I get that his father was a special player. He must have taken Austin's accident especially hard."

"Chris was there for Austin. As soon as the doctors released him to practice, Chris was on the court with him every day. But it only reminded Austin of what he lost, so he locked his father out, too."

"I can see everyone giving Austin a break, but his behavior

would get old fast. I've only been around him a few minutes, and he's already worn out his welcome with me."

"Yeah, I know. I'll do what I can to keep him away from you."

"I'd appreciate it. I'd like to enjoy the rest of the time I have here with TR."

"How long have you been here? And why'd you and JC split up?"

"JC said his family would rescue us, but he didn't know when. And he was worried about having enough money. He had gold nuggets but thought we'd be better off with more. So he wanted to go to MacKlenna Farm and borrow some from Braham McCabe's secret stash."

Tavis chuckled. "It's a good idea. But why didn't you go?"

"I grew up here just a few miles from the Theodore Roosevelt National Park. As a kid, I was a Junior Ranger. I'd walk around the park and have imaginary conversations with Teddy. And right now, I can have conversations in person. I didn't want to leave. Roosevelt said he was going back to New York City in a couple of weeks, so the three of us made plans to travel together. JC's meeting us in Cleveland, and we'll all take the train to New York."

"He didn't count on his parents coming after him. They'll insist he go home with them."

"He won't go. We talked about it, and he promised me time with TR. I'm going to hold him to it." She glanced behind her to see where Austin and Remy were. "You winked at me. Was that a 'we're in cahoots together' wink?"

"I know you rejected Austin's manuscript, and I didn't want you to say anything. He was pretty ticked about it, and probably still is. I wouldn't bring it up."

"I won't, but you make it sound like I broke his heart. He's got a big enough ego to survive a rejection letter."

"Maybe at one time, but not now."

They had slowed down while they chatted, and now Remy and Austin caught up with them.

"So, what are we going to do?" Austin asked. "Go home now that we have her?"

"Erggg."

"We can't leave until we hear from JC," Tavis said.

"I agree," she said.

"We need to send a telegram to the farm to make sure he's there and let Elliott know we're with you. Where's the closest Western Union?"

"Probably Medora," Ensley said. "It's about thirty-five miles south of Elkhorn Ranch. You all can do that while I go on the roundup with TR."

"No, baby doll. We're all going," Austin said.

"What'd you call me?"

"Baby doll. You're five-two, blue eyes, blond hair. Yep, a baby doll."

Her cheeks heated, and she had to be careful not to strangle Tesoro with the reins. "You. Are. A. Total. Asshat. I've got to go. TR will wonder what happened to me."

"Wait a minute," Tavis said. "We've got to send a telegram. So who's going?"

"We shouldn't split up," Remy said. "Look what's happened here. JC left Ensley. Now we're here, and we don't know for sure where he is."

"I'll go, then," Tavis said. "I need to update Elliott anyway. I'll take Austin with me, and we'll be back tomorrow evening."

"I'm *not* going! You want to go, go! I'm staying put," Austin said.

Remy looked at Austin, and his upper lip curled. "You're an asshole." Then to Tavis, he asked, "If you leave, how will you find us?"

"I'll probably hear Austin bitching from a mile away."

"JC said he would send a telegram when he got there. He planned to hire someone in Medora to deliver it to me, but I haven't received one. Chances are the person took JC's money, and the telegram is still waiting there for me. Will you ask?"

"Of course," Tavis said.

Ensley looked at his lathered black stallion. He couldn't possibly ride to Medora on his Thoroughbred. "Take Tesoro. He's built for endurance, and I haven't ridden him hard today."

"None better than an Akhal-Teke. Where'd you get him?"

"I think Erik sold him to TR, but nobody could ride him but me, so I don't know if he'll let you."

"He will," Tavis said. "I normally wouldn't borrow someone else's horse, but in this situation, yours looks fresher than mine." He hesitated a moment. "I'll take you up on the offer."

She dismounted and unsaddled Tesoro. Then she kissed his forehead. "I'll see you soon."

Tavis put his saddle on Tesoro, then saddled his horse with Ensley's tack. "Remy, leave me some signs. And I'll see you guys tomorrow."

Ensley folded her arms, watching Tavis as he mounted Tesoro, and waited for him to buck. But he didn't. Tesoro remained as still for Tavis as he did for her.

Tavis settled into the saddle and patted the horse's neck. "Arthfael, run like the wind." The horse flicked his ears then reared in a perfect hi-yo Silver. That made her think of her mom again. She loved old TV shows, and she loved them most of all when Ensley watched them with her.

Ensley yelled, "What does Arthfael mean?"

Tesoro galloped off, and Tavis yelled back, "'Bear strength.' See you in twenty-four hours."

The sun glinted off her golden horse as he grew smaller and smaller until he was just a dot on the horizon. "Why'd he call my horse by a different name?"

Remy shrugged. "Tavis is as mysterious as Erik. Come on. Let's go find your hero."

She was surprised by the grief that overwhelmed her. She was unsettled, and it wasn't just the loss of her horse. "I don't even know his horse's name."

"It's Ferdiad," Austin said. "It means ancient hero."

"How do you know?" Remy asked.

"I helped train him."

"You what?" Remy said.

"His owner sold him to Elliott, and Elliott brought him to the ranch for retraining."

"From what?" Ensley asked.

"He was a racehorse, and his career was over. The owner didn't want the upkeep, so he was getting rid of him."

"Why'd Elliott want a used-up racehorse?"

"He started the Colorado ranch a few years ago and turned it into a haven for former racehorses to keep them from being neglected. We have twenty-five right now."

"I didn't know former racehorses were neglected."

"Yeah. It's a problem. The 1986 Derby winner Ferdinand's life ended in a Japanese slaughterhouse, and they used his carcass to make pet food."

"A Derby winner. Are you serious?" Her stomach roiled. "That's disgusting."

"Elliott didn't want that to ever happen to another racehorse."

"Ferdiad doesn't look old or broken down."

"He came to the ranch with mild lameness and a gastric ulcer. Elliott treated him, and I took a liking to him. We were both broken, I guess. I started working with him, and when Tavis met him, it was a match made in horse heaven."

"Why didn't you keep him?" she asked.

"I have several horses, and Ferdiad needed an owner who would ride him a lot. Marengo doesn't care if I ever get on his back. Do you, boy?" Austin said, patting the horse's neck.

"I thought you were only interested in horsepower. *Varoom.*" Remy played his fingers like drumsticks, tapping the horse's head as if it were a crash cymbal.

"That's not me. That's you," Austin said. "How many cars you got? Four?"

"Not as many as you," Remy said.

Ensley watched the two men bickering back and forth and honestly couldn't tell if they even liked each other. "Do you two hate each other, or what?" she asked.

Remy glowered down his nose at Austin, then turned toward Ensley. "After his accident, I was his private nurse for six months, wiping his ass. But when he could do it for himself, he kicked me out and wouldn't even take my calls."

Austin shrugged. "Because you bugged the hell out of me."

Ensley lifted her hat with both hands and slammed it back on top of her head. "You're *both* bugging the hell out of me. So just shut up!" She closed her eyes for an instant, breathing slowly.

"What'd I do?" Remy asked. "I thought I was funny."

When she was calm again, she opened her eyes and put her hands on her hips. "If you want me to think you're funny, don't tell me you're funny. Tell me a frigging joke." Several moments passed as the two just stared at each other, then Remy burst out laughing.

"Tell you a fucking joke? That's what you want? Okay, here's one." He drummed his fingers again. "Two career swabbies were sitting at a bar. One of them says, 'Look at those two dunks across the bar. That could be us in ten years.' The other guy says, 'You asshole, that's a mirror.'"

She rolled her eyes. "That's not funny." She mounted Ferdiad, keeping her head down so he wouldn't see that she was about to laugh, too. "There's someone for everyone, and the perfect person for both of you is a psychiatrist."

"A joke. She told a joke." Remy burst out laughing again. "A psychiatrist. Now that's funny."

"I hope you find one soon." And with that, Ensley took off at a gallop, riding Tavis's black stallion across the Badlands.

44

The Badlands (1885)—Ensley

ENSLEY RODE ALONGSIDE the wagon, talking to Norman while Remy and Austin trailed behind them. Then they disappeared and returned an hour or so later with four rabbits and a white-tailed deer slung over the back of Austin's horse—already field dressed.

Damn. That's impressive. How'd they do that so quickly?

"Looks like we're havin' rabbit stew and deer steaks fer dinner," Norman said. "The rest of the deer, I'll smoke it into dry meat fer the men to carry in their saddlebags fer snacks."

"And me," she said.

"I was hoping ya'd stay in camp."

She gave him an arch look. "Come on, Norman. I can't get much research done if I stay put."

He slapped the reins and ignored her for a moment and then said, "It'd be safer."

"I know you think so, but—"

"Miss Ensley," he interrupted. "Ya don't need to be out there wit' them cowboys. Ya need to be with yer husband and startin' yer family."

Norman sounded so concerned it made her lies feel like lead weights around her conscience. She couldn't be candid with him, so she had to tell him another lie. "Here's the thing, Norman. I can't have children. I fell off too many broncs years ago, and it messed me up. So you see, my work is a substitute for a family."

He snapped the reins again. "Don't matter none. Ya still should be wit' yer husband."

And that ended their conversation.

She uncapped her canteen and took a long drink, then capped it again. When she did, she bumped the blister on her palm. Hard.

Damn, that hurts.

She yanked off her gloves and cringed when she saw the quarter-size blister that needed cleaning and an antibiotic ointment. She almost asked Norman if he had a remedy in his medical box, but she wasn't sure she could trust his treatments.

Maybe Remy had something.

And then she remembered the piece of red linen she found in the hem of her jeans. She slipped her fingers inside her bra and pulled it out. If he wrapped her foot in his cloak and it healed, maybe it would do the same for a blister.

As soon as the piece of linen touched the open wound, her hand warmed and tingled. She put her glove back on and didn't give it another thought.

They reached the meetup point at sundown, and Norman drove the wagon into a grove of cottonwoods near the river and set up camp while Ensley went looking for TR. She found him with a group of men gathered around a fire, telling stories and smoking. When he spotted her, he left the group and sauntered over to her.

He fixed her with a stern gaze. "Did two men ride in with you?" He didn't say hello or even ask about the trip but went straight to Austin and Remy's identities.

"News travels fast around here."

"A rancher knew Norman was working for me and asked about the three cowboys coming in with the chuckwagon."

"Three? There were only two."

"He said one was huge, and another was so small a cow would be chasing him instead of the other way around. He didn't realize you were a woman."

"The big man is JC's cousin, and the other is a family friend. They heard JC was here to hunt, so they came out to join him."

That was one of the lies she, Remy, and Austin had dreamed up shortly before they arrived at the meetup place.

I'm stacking up lies like firewood, and I hate it!

"Where are they now?" TR asked.

As if on cue, Austin came out of the early evening shadows and campfire smoke like a wraith walking the desolate landscape one final time before descending into hell. Loud gasps circled the camp like a stadium wave at an athletic event.

"That's Austin, his cousin," she said.

"Man, you're tall," a cowboy said.

The crowd laughed.

"How's the weather up there?" another one asked.

A third cowboy strutted up to him. "Hey, can you see tomorrow? What's gonna happen? Tell me so I can sleep all day."

The crowd continued laughing, with many of them forming a semicircle around Austin. If Ensley had been wearing a gun, she would have pointed toward the sky and fired a couple of rounds. Even though Austin pissed her off most of the time, she hated the jerks for taunting him.

Another one said, "Let's set him up on a hill so he can spot all the roamin' cattle. Then we'll know where to go get 'em."

They treated Austin like he was a freak, and all she could do was stand there helplessly.

What could she do?

Something. Anything.

She adjusted her stance and prepared for action, legs apart with one foot back, shoulders back, arms free. She didn't know what she'd do if given a chance, but she readied herself anyway and watched. Austin didn't toss out threats or instigate a fight.

"You know… It doesn't seem to bother him," she said.

"I agree," TR said. "He doesn't seem daunted by their jeering."

Show those assholes the superstar still exists.

Austin went over to the line of bedrolls nearby and snatched up a pillow from one of them.

"What's he doing?" TR asked.

Austin squashed the pillow into a ball, and even the cowboys around him looked confused.

"Hey, that's my pillow. Leave it alone," one of the cowboys yelled.

Austin took three steps, and she knew what was coming.

"Oh, my God," she said.

Austin levitated into the stratosphere in an impressive display of power and skill and stuffed the pillow into a tree crotch about ten feet off the ground.

"Whoa!" She expected an updraft to catch him in midglide and carry him up and over the top of the cottonwood, like an eagle soaring into the night sky. Then, as if a parachute had opened, his feet descended slowly to touch the ground. If she hadn't been looking at his face, she would have missed his tense jaw. The landing must have hurt like hell.

It was one of the most graceful exhibitions of athleticism she'd ever seen outside of a performance by the New York City Ballet. The leap was an art form that showcased his power and made mincemeat of the human body's perceived limits.

There was a chapter in Austin's book about how he spent hours as a teenager perfecting his dunk, playing in the driveway long after the sun went down and the stars came out. While reading the manuscript, she thought it was such a waste of time. He could have been studying or reading a book that would have given life meaning.

Damn. I'm such a snob.

Is this what Harvard and New York City had done to the rodeo queen from North Dakota? A deep sadness welled up inside her. It was partly because of what she'd given up, another part because of what she'd run from, and the rest for what she could never replace.

The man whose pillow Austin had stuffed into the pocket at the connecting point of two limbs yelled, "Hey. You can't leave my pillow up there."

The rest of the cowboys laughed until they were rolling on the ground. A couple of them tried to imitate Austin's move but fell way, way short, literally falling on their asses, and the men all laughed harder.

And Austin O'Grady, the jerk she'd met hours earlier, became an instant hero.

"I've never seen anyone do that. I've got to find out how he did it," TR said.

"Years of practice, but I think he'd prefer to throw a ball into a basket than stuff a pillow into a tree crotch."

Austin jogged through a gauntlet of cheering, back-slapping cowboys, and he headed toward her with a slight limp that she noticed because she was looking for it. With the problems she had with her hip, she knew his landing after the pillow dunk must have sent a razor-sharp pain up his entire left side.

He reached TR first and extended his hand. "Sir, I'm Austin O'Grady. And it's an honor to meet Theodore Roosevelt."

"That was an amazing stunt, Mr. O'Grady. Can you teach me?" TR asked.

"Throwing down a one-handed dunk takes a great deal of skill, sir. I started practicing as a kid, and it took a lot of time. I can teach you the dynamics, but the execution requires strength, coordination, and a thirty-five-inch vertical jump, for starters. The rest is finesse."

"How high can you jump?"

"Two years ago, forty-four inches on a good night. Now it's about thirty-eight."

TR gave Austin a head-to-toe appraisal. "Abraham Lincoln was tall like you."

"He was six four, sir. So am I. But he wore that stovetop hat, which made him about seven feet tall. I've played against seven-footers—"

Ensley's first reaction to his comment was to slap her hand over his mouth, but she doubted she could reach it, so she stepped on his giant foot. "Oh, I'm sorry. I didn't see your foot."

"That's almost impossible, Ensley, but you can walk on top of it all you want."

"In what sport?" TR asked, picking up on Austin's comment.

"Sport?"

"Yes, that you played against seven-footers."

Austin glanced up and rolled in his bottom lip.

"Polo, I believe. Wasn't it, Austin?" she asked.

"No," he tweaked his chin. "It was hockey. Like polo, it's one of the five oldest sports in the world."

"What are the other three?" She was embarrassed that her sports knowledge was so limited, and she hated not knowing something Austin knew.

"I believe, Mrs. Fraser, that would be running, wrestling, and—"

"Javelin throwing," Austin said. "And with the length of my arms"—he demonstrated throwing a spear—" I'd win a gold medal, don't you think?"

"I think you're right," TR said. "Do you wrestle?"

"I did when I was young, but once my arms and legs sprouted like weeds, no one would wrestle with me anymore."

Ensley's eyes bounced from Austin to TR and back again. It was like an entirely different person showed up once the sun went down. What happened to the bad-tempered jerk she met earlier? She tried looking into his eyes but couldn't see into them in the dark. He must have taken pain medication. His personality couldn't flip like that in such a short time.

Remy joined them. "What's all the cheering about?"

TR pointed. "Mr. O'Grady stuffed a pillow up in that tree."

Remy turned to watch a man climb on another man's shoulder

to reach the pillow. "You're off your game, Austin. That's only about eight, maybe nine feet."

Austin shrugged. "I knew I couldn't make twelve, so I settled."

Ensley's jaw dropped. "How did you judge the distance to the first crotch and then to the second? There wasn't enough time."

"The accident didn't hurt my eyesight, Ensley, only my leg. You put me on a ninety-four by a fifty-foot rectangle, and I can tell you the distance from any point inside that area."

Austin stared at some invisible point, and Remy took advantage of the silence. "I'm Remy Benoit, Mr. Roosevelt. A friend of James Cullen's. It's a pleasure to meet you, sir."

"Where are you from?" TR asked. "I don't recognize the accent."

"New Awlins, sir. But I call Kentucky home now."

"That's where Mr. Fraser went."

"I heard that. I hope he has a pleasant visit. Now"—Remy gestured with his index fingers, air-playing them like drumsticks—"Norman said to round you guys up for dinner."

"Have you been cooking?" Austin asked.

Ensley couldn't tell if the question was wry or delighted.

"I made Cajun rabbit stew," Remy said.

"To be official Cajun rabbit stew, doesn't it require a squirrel? I didn't see one in the carcasses you brought into camp," Ensley said.

"No squirrel. Just salt, garlic powder, paprika, chili pepper, cayenne pepper, a little dry rub with black pepper, powdered tomatoes with chicken broth, cherry-berry homemade wine, a little peanut oil to brown the rabbit, and then whatever else Norman had to add to the pot."

"I'm not familiar with Cajun cooking, and I don't have much use for exotic food," TR said.

"This isn't exotic. It's just spicy with a bite," Remy said.

What's with MacKlenna men carrying spices in their saddlebags?

They returned to their campsite, and Ensley excused herself to go wash up for dinner. She removed her gloves and fingered the red fabric she'd put on her palm earlier. She blinked. "Damn." The blister had healed, and the skin was as smooth as a baby's butt.

"Mrs. Fraser, dinner's ready," TR called out. "The rabbit stew smells like it came from Delmonico's kitchen."

"Coming!" She packed up her toiletries, tucked the two-inch square swatch back into her bra, and returned to the wagon.

Along with Sewall and Dow, Austin and Remy carried two boards they placed over a tree stump, forming a tabletop.

"Bring your saddles to sit on," Austin said.

"Get your chair, Norman."

"Don't need to eat yet," he said.

Ensley grabbed his ladder-back chair and placed it at the end of the makeshift table. "Of course you do. You're part of the team."

The stew was spicy with a kick and a real crowd-pleaser. Several of the other cooks followed the Cajun scent and came by to see what they were eating, but Norman stayed mum. "I don't never tell cookin' secrets," he whispered to Ensley. "So I'll always have a job."

They were all too hungry to do much talking. When Ensley's stomach was full, she dumped her dirty dishes into Norman's wrecking pan. She'd learned early on that it was the ultimate no-no to leave dirty dishes behind.

She picked up a dishrag to dry the dishes, but Norman shooed her away. "Ya better get to sleep soon, so go be with Roosevelt and your husband's cousin. Tomorrow you'll be too busy to talk."

"Are you sure?" she asked. "I'm glad to help. I didn't do any of the cooking."

"Not your job. Do ya think I'll feel bad for not findin' any strays tomorrow?"

She folded the dishrag and handed it to him. "Okay, I'll do as I'm told."

Norman laughed and shook his head.

TR produced a backgammon board. "Do you play, Mr. O'Grady?"

Wait a minute! I'm supposed to be your partner.

"I do, but it's not my best game," Austin said.

"What is your best game?" Ensley asked. "Old Maid?" As soon as she'd thrown out the insult, she wished she could rake it back in. Austin was acting decent, and she shouldn't pick on him.

He gave her a half grin. "Pops taught me to play chess as a kid and made me play thirty minutes every night."

She returned to her saddle, put her elbows on the table, and laced her fingers. "It must have taken a while to finish a game."

"Sometimes, it took a week. But it wasn't until I got older that I realized Pops used that time to pass along words of wisdom. And the game taught me how to eliminate distractions, learn strategy, and see my next move. It also taught me how to flip a switch in my brain and get back into the game immediately, psyched up and ready to play, even after twenty-four hours." Austin went quiet and swiped at his nose. It took a few moments before he continued. "Pops raised a family that loves to play games. It gets rowdy at the O'Gradys'."

"How large is your family? Do you have many brothers and sisters?" TR asked.

Austin's eyebrows knitted together. "I grew up believing I had one sister and four brothers, but when I got older, I discovered that my brothers were my uncles, my sister was my mother, and my father was my grandfather."

In the torchlight, she saw shock register in TR's eyes. "That surely caused a scandal."

"Nah. The secret stayed in the family." Austin took his white checkers and arranged them on the backgammon board. "I was mad at them because they lied to me, but I eventually got over it. They're still the same people, and it didn't change how much I love them."

TR placed the black checkers on the board, and then they both rolled one die. TR had the highest roll, so he went first. The game moved quickly, and they were soon down to the same number of checkers on their home board. TR lost by one checker and asked for a second game. He won the second game and requested a third, but Austin stood and stretched.

"I'd like to walk a bit before I turn in, sir. But I'd like to play another night." He reached for Ensley's hand. "Will you walk with me, cousin?"

Austin caught her off guard. She didn't want to be rude in front of TR, so she said, "Sure," and accepted his offer to help her up. "I know you want to catch up on what James Cullen has been doing, and we haven't had a chance to talk."

Her hand looked like a miniature in his foot-size palm, and when she stood, her head barely reached the middle of his chest. The difference in their sizes was stark. He was a giant redwood, she was a sapling, and he could easily block out all the light. She wasn't sure if that thought had a deeper meaning or revealed something lurking in her subconscious. But she decided not to waste time thinking about it.

They strolled through the adjoining campsites, and even though his stride equaled three of hers, she managed to keep up with him. They detoured and walked through all the other camps. The men at each one gave Austin an appreciative nod. After making the rounds, he directed her back toward the river. It wasn't until they reached the water that she realized what he had done.

"You made a name for yourself today."

"I didn't intend to bring attention to myself, but when I saw what those assholes did to Mr. Roosevelt, I couldn't help it."

"What'd they do?"

"They made fun of his glasses, and a guy from Texas called him Storm Windows."

"What'd Teddy say?"

"He told him to put up or shut up, fight or be friends."

"And…"

"The guy let it go. It took guts. So after watching the way Roosevelt handled it, I took his advice, more or less, and did it the only way I knew how."

"And you did it brilliantly. But I think this walk through the campsites was about something else."

"Like what?"

"You were telling those men that I'm under your protection and not to mess with me."

"I saw the way they look at you, Ensley, and I wanted to knock the lustful smirks off their faces. I won't tolerate their disrespect. Tonight, though, not one of them glared at you. They all nodded and then looked away."

"Was that a signal?"

"Yep. They received my message. But I can't promise the men will behave, but if anyone steps out of line, the rest will deal with him."

"How do you know? This *is* a different time."

"Maybe, but men aren't any different. They still act like jerks."

"Coming from you, that's a real ha-ha."

He dropped his chin and gave her a half shrug. "Look, I'm not a complete jerk. Pops made sure I always minded my manners and respected women. So I know I acted like an ass this afternoon. I wasn't mad at you, but you were a handy target."

She couldn't hide her flash of surprise that he'd intentionally taken it out on her. "If I'd been a man, would you have been so obnoxious?"

"It wouldn't have mattered, even if you were a kid. Well, I take that back. I wouldn't have done it to someone who couldn't fight back."

"And you thought I could? At five foot two?"

"I have a couple of aunts who aren't any taller than you, and what they have in spirit and drive more than makes up for their short stature. And I knew it would piss off Remy and Tavis. But it's not them I'm pissed at. It's Pops and Elliott. They shouldn't have done this to me. I can deal with almost anything except when people lie."

That yucky rush of adrenaline a person got when they did something wrong and knew they were going to get busted surged through her once again, and she turned slightly so the moon wouldn't illuminate her guilty face.

"I don't think they lied to you," she managed to say.

"Sure they did. If you know something and don't tell the person it affects, then it's a lie of omission."

"Sounds like you haven't gotten over the first big lie your family told you, so all lies since then are just dumped on top and compound the pain." She picked up a handful of rocks to try to skip them by moonlight and threw one. It bounced once and sank.

"Are you a shrink, too?" His afternoon tone of voice was rising to the surface.

"No." She wasn't even an amateur psychologist. But she had edited a book by a real one. The author explained that self-improvement, when done correctly, was the key to getting everything you wanted. Self-improvement would either light a fire under your ass or present the information in a way that compels you to act. And it wasn't long after that book was released that she sold the ranch.

"You have a dark side, Austin. If you can harness it, you'll go from good to unstoppable."

"You *are* a damn shrink."

"No, but I do read a lot," she said quickly and then moved on to another topic. "So tell me this, if Remy and Tavis had asked you to go with them, what would you have done?"

"Told them to go to hell."

This was her chance to tell Austin the truth and confess that she was the editor who rejected his manuscript. She opened her mouth, but closed it again. She couldn't do it. If she told him the truth, it would destroy the delicate balance between them. He'd go back to being ugly and cussing at her. And she liked this version of him—a lot.

He took one of the stones from her and threw it. The damn thing skipped four times before it sank. Was there anything he couldn't do?

Yeah, play basketball.

He took another stone from her. "It's beautiful here. I can see why you love it."

"It's a serene prairie paradise full of natural wonders."

"That sounds like a marketing tagline."

"It does, doesn't it? But it's true. It has all four seasons, and it's a leader in the agriculture industry and aerial drone development."

He laughed. "Really? Aerial drones?"

"Yep, and look at the sky. Even in the twenty-first century, light pollution is almost nonexistent in this area. You have unfettered views of the stars, just like tonight."

He glanced up. "It's a beautiful sky." And then he looked at her, and what she saw in his eyes took her breath away. It was an unbridled need, and she stepped back, almost gulping for air.

"Here," she managed to say and held her palm open so he could take the remaining three stones. Her rock-skipping was off tonight. And she wanted to keep him talking so he wouldn't look at her like that again. "Where's home for you now?"

"I left New York City to attend a special high school in Napa. Then the University of Kentucky recruited me, and I moved to Lexington. And then I was drafted by Golden State and moved to San Francisco. Then I was traded to the Cavs. Since the accident, I've been rehabbing at the family ranch near Denver."

He took the last stone, rubbing his thumb across her healed palm, and the brief touch tingled across her skin.

She cleared her throat. "Is the accident a touchy subject, or can I ask about it?"

"I had a motorcycle accident," he said as if he still couldn't believe it.

"Yikes."

"I lost control of the bike. My mind flew through the options. I could jump off and probably break something or stay on and take my chances on a minor injury. I was wrong. I could have broken a leg and been out for a season instead of having a possibly career-ending injury."

She reached up and put her hand on his arm, which was almost the diameter of her waist. "I'm sorry. When you have to make a split-second decision, you've got a fifty-fifty chance of getting it wrong."

"Maybe, but I don't see you having to make a split-second decision that could tear your body, and your life, to shreds."

"Not anymore, but I participated in more rodeos than I care to remember and have constant pain in my hip."

He looked like she'd sucker-punched him. "Rodeos? Like bucking broncs and roping bulls? Nah. Don't believe it."

She nodded. "Yep. Dumb, huh?"

He gave her one of his sexy half grins. "Yeah, pretty dumb, especially for someone as smart as you."

"What makes you think I'm so smart?"

"Because you told me I'd used fuck as a verb, adjective, subject, object, noun, gerund, predicate, and even an appositive! I don't know many people who are familiar with all those parts of speech."

She chuckled. "How in the world did you remember that?"

"I have a pretty good recall and," he said with a grin, "I also have two degrees—one in accounting and one in creative writing."

No wonder he was such a good writer. The logical thing to ask at this point in the conversation was, "Have you written anything for publication?" But she wasn't about to bring it up.

"Earning two degrees while playing college sports, that's impressive."

TR came through the trees, making enough noise to wake all the nocturnal animals that weren't already awake. "It's late, Mrs. Fraser. We'll be up early."

"Hi, Teddy. You're right. The evening got away from me." She looped her arm with his. "Good night, Austin."

"'Night, cousin."

She and TR walked along the river on their way back to their campsite. "Mr. O'Grady seems like a nice fellow. He's certainly a good backgammon player," TR said.

"I haven't spent much time around him, but I think you're right. He's recently gone through a rough patch. This roundup might be good for him."

"Norman said there was a third man who took your horse. What happened?"

"Tavis was worried about JC, so he rode back to Medora to send a telegram to his family's farm. Since he'd already ridden so hard, I offered to switch horses. He didn't want to at first, but then realized it made sense."

TR scratched the side of his face, squinting. "He rode Tesoro? That's a surprise."

"Yeah, I know. But Tavis mounted him and rode off as if he'd been doing it for years. He plans to meet up with us tomorrow night."

"Do they want you to leave?" TR asked.

She glanced back to where they left Austin. "They do, but I'm not ready to go."

TR turned to face her. "I don't want to sound improper, but I do enjoy your company, and I'm looking forward to the time we have here. I hope you'll stay."

The shadow of a tree in the moonlight hid his face, and he stepped farther back into it, as if he was suddenly shy, or feeling guilty, or even embarrassed by what he just confessed. It was a gesture both respectfully sweet and utterly charming.

She didn't deserve sweet and charming.

If life imitated art, she knew what would happen here, just like all the lying heroines in stories she'd edited. They all got busted, and the heroes ended up hating them.

Just thinking about Austin and TR hating her for lying made her sick, but she couldn't be honest with either of them…at least not right now.

45

The Badlands (1885)—Ensley

THE AIR WAS thick with the smell of unwashed men, cattle, horses, early morning dew, and topped off with the tempting aromas of sizzling bacon and black coffee. The moos and bellows competed with the grumbles and cracking joints from dozens of cowboys.

And Ensley felt right at home.

She was sitting in Norman's chair, drinking her third cup of coffee and hoping it would wake her up when Austin and Remy arrived at the campfire. She hadn't seen either of them since she said good-night to Austin after his pillow-dunking exhibition and their stroll along the river.

As tired as she'd been, thoughts of him interfered with the deep breathing and relaxation techniques she used to calm her body and mind so she could fall asleep. Then when she finally drifted off, erotic dreams starring Austin woke her. Damn. Why *him*? Why not JC, or Remy, or even TR? It made no sense.

Remy and Austin couldn't see her sitting in the shadow of the wagon, but she could see them easily in the firelight. Austin's height and broad shoulders made him recognizable anywhere. Man, he was big. Her mind replayed a reel of one of her dreams—the hottest one, and her face flamed.

"This sucks," Austin grumbled. "I'm not here to play cowboy and chase down rogue cows. Let's grab Ensley and go home."

His grumbling threw cold water on her fantasies, and her face cooled.

"Shut the fuck up." Remy grabbed a tin cup off the pot rack in the firepit and poured in the thick, black brew. "If you want to sit your ass right here, do it. But if you want to prove to all those cowboys that you deserve last night's accolades, then get some coffee and saddle your goddamn horse."

"I will, but I want pain meds."

"Not happening. If you act like a human, I'll give you something tonight to take the edge off."

"You're an asshole," Austin said. "Do you have any idea how much pain I'm in?"

"Not as much as you think you are. You're so used to taking something when you get an ache that now even a pinch makes you yelp. And, by the way, you're an asshole too."

Ensley had heard enough and wanted to get far away from Austin and his foul mouth. She dumped the coffee dregs on the ground and left the tin cup in the wrecking pan. But before walking away, she shoved her bedroll into the front of the wagon and collected the snack Norman left for her—biscuits wrapped in a piece of cloth.

"How long is this going to take?" Austin demanded.

Take for what?

She'd already lost the thread of Austin and Remy's argument. It was time to get to work. She grabbed her tack and rushed off to meet TR at the remuda, finding him in a huddle with Sewall and Dow. He was passing out assignments from the captain of the roundup.

"Morning. Are you men ready to catch some cows?" she asked.

"Yes, ma'am," Dow said. "We got our orders and are heading out. Are you riding that big black horse you rode in on yesterday?"

She dropped the saddle, and in the blue light of dawn, did a visual sweep of the thirty horses TR had in his remuda. They were all tied to one of four picket lines. "Ferdiad's not trained to be a cow pony. I'll ride one of your cutting horses."

"They're barely saddle broke, ma'am," Sewall said.

"I can handle 'barely,' but a green horse would be a challenge this morning." She pressed a hand to her hip in anticipation of how much worse it would feel later. Maybe Remy would give her one of Austin's pain pills.

Don't even go there. Stick to stretching.

"But I'll ride whatever you give me." If the horse threw her, she couldn't walk away, or she'd lose respect. Maybe not with TR and his crew, but with the others in camp. And the news would spread quickly. She'd have to get up, brush off her ass, and do it again...and again…and again.

The roundup was one big competition, and as the only woman there, she had to prove herself. Austin and TR's protection would only carry her so far. The rest she had to earn on her own.

"My favorite cutting horse is Muley," TR said. "You can ride him."

"I don't want to take your horse." She spotted a chestnut quarter horse at the end of one of the picket lines that reminded her of one she'd seen at a rodeo many years ago who had lots of cow sense and athleticism. Maybe this horse would, too. She pointed to the chestnut. "I'll take him. What's his name?"

"Lucky, and he's too green, Miss Ensley. Pick another one," Sewall said.

She'd argued with TR about riding Tesoro and ended up with a remarkable horse. This morning she was willing to trust her judgment again. "Nope. He's the one I want."

"I agree with Bill, Mrs. Fraser. Pick another one," TR said.

"Today is my lucky day. Might as well ride a horse named Lucky."

Sewall threaded the brim of his hat through long, slender fingers. "If you insist on riding him, then let me help you saddle up."

"I won't object to that." She followed him over to the horse, lugging her saddle. "Has he ever been saddled before?"

"A few times. He'll calm down once he figures out you're in charge."

She knew how to ride a bucking horse. As long as she didn't panic, she'd be okay. "Switch out the halter for the bridle, and I'll see how Lucky handles the saddle." She walked around the horse, patting his withers, flank, shoulders, chest, forehead, just as TR had done with JC's horse the morning he left for Kentucky—which reminded her that if JC sent her a telegram, Tavis would bring it back to her. Having news from JC would be a great way to end the day.

Sewall switched out the halter and held on to the reins. "I'll hold him until you tell me to let go."

She stroked Lucky's head and shoulders again. "Okay, big boy, let's make this easy on both of us."

A few more men paused to watch. It wouldn't surprise her if one of them was taking bets. When she competed years ago, the competition often bet against her. Sometimes they lost, and sometimes she ended up on her ass. Her goal was to stay on the horse, establish a rhythm, and go forward until he quit bucking.

If only she had an apple for Lucky.

I don't have an apple, but I have something just as good.

She unwrapped Norman's biscuits, took one, and put the others away. It was a biscuit in name only. Where she grew up, it was called a molasses cookie, and horses love sugar. She broke off a piece and held her hand out flat, fingers down so Lucky wouldn't bite one of them off.

"Hey, boy. Want some? Yum." The horse nipped the cookie out of her hand.

"You like that?" She rubbed his nose. "If you let me saddle you, I'll give you another piece." She swung the blanket over his back, and when he didn't object, she gave him another piece. She followed with the saddle, and when he didn't object to that, either, she gave him the rest of the cookie before tightening the cinch. "He doesn't mind the saddle. Let's see what he thinks of a rider."

"Good luck, Miss Ensley. Tell me when to let go."

"Thanks, Bill."

Austin walked up to the picket line. "Hey, don't do this. Remy can set broken bones, but he won't be happy about it."

She was psyching herself up for the mount, visualizing putting her foot in the stirrup and swinging her right leg gently over Lucky's back. "Good to know. Now leave me alone."

"I'm serious," Austin said with more urgency. "That horse isn't ready for prime time."

"It's not prime time. Go away." Austin was getting in her head and messing with her concentration. "I'm an experienced rider. Leave me alone."

"You should listen to me. I know what I'm talking about."

Sewall handed her the reins but continued to hold on to the bridle. "Tell me when to let go."

"If you're gonna do this," Austin said, "keep his head up. Keep your center of gravity as close to the horse's center of gravity as possible."

"Stop bugging me," she snapped. "I know what I'm doing."

"I doubt it. So listen to me. Keep your shoulders back over your hips."

"Shut up," she yelled. "You're making me nervous." She put her foot in the stirrup, sprung up, and settled into the saddle. Lucky immediately pushed off the ground. He bucked through the air, and his body lifted her legs.

"Scoot back in the saddle," Austin yelled.

She did. Not because he yelled instructions, but because she already knew what to do. She kept her knees bent, and the bucking sucked her back into the saddle. Her heart was in her throat. Everything was a blur in the hazy morning.

"Keep your heels down and forward," Austin yelled. "When he descends, he'll leave you hanging in midair. Bring your legs back and up."

"Shut *up!*"

Austin stayed close but kept a safe distance. "Keep your right arm straight. When he comes down, pull his head up. Don't pull back on the reins. Pull your arm up. Bring his head up over his shoulders. Leverage the bit."

She had to tune Austin out. He was interfering with her focus. She knew what to do with the reins, with her arm, *and* with the freakin' horse.

"Establish a rhythm."

What the hell!

"Shut up!" she yelled.

"He's bucking like a jackrabbit. Pump your legs faster. Lower your center of gravity. Shoulders back."

Not since her father yelled instructions at her when she was a preteen had anyone else tried to do it. Austin sounded like her dad, and it bugged her. She didn't want Austin in her head.

Go away!

She quickly moved into the horse's rhythm and tugged Lucky's head up, which automatically raised his shoulders and made his back hollow out. After several more bucks, each one less effective, Lucky stopped bucking and just stood there, breathing heavily.

Woohoo!

She felt like the rodeo queen she'd always wanted to be, but every single year lost out in the finals.

Sewall was jumping up and down, waving his hat and shouting, "Yee-haw!"

TR yelled, "Bully, Mrs. Fraser. Bully!"

She trotted the horse around in large circles, and he bunny-hopped, but it was ineffective. It was a damn good ride, and she was tickled and so thankful that her ass wasn't on the ground. Her hip thanked her, too.

She rode over to where Austin was standing, slapping his hat on his leg instead of clapping. "Damn good ride, *ragazza tosta*."

"What the hell does that mean?"

"Tough girl."

"Oh, well… How'd you know what to do?"

Austin held Lucky's bridle while he stroked his forehead. "I've been to a few rodeos."

"Admit it. You've been to those bars with mechanical bulls."

He grinned. "Maybe a couple. But remember, I spend a lot of time in Colorado. The state has a slew of rodeos that have been going on for a hundred years. And Denver has a massive—"

"National Western Stock Show. I know. There was a time when I went every year."

TR rode over. "Mrs. Fraser, you have surprised me once again." Then he looked at Austin. "You knew what she should do. So I want you to teach me."

"Ensley already knew, sir. I was just keeping her focused."

"Well, I'd appreciate it if you'd keep me focused this afternoon when I come back to change ponies."

"I'll do what I can, sir," Austin said.

A cowboy walked up to Austin. "I'd like to see the teacher ride next time."

Austin shook his head. "I can't ride like that now. I had an accident that makes it impossible for me to ride broncs."

"But you can jump," the cowboy said.

Austin glanced down at his feet. "I'm wearing special boots that help me do that, but I've got nothing to protect me from falling on my ass."

The cowboy slapped Austin on the shoulder and walked away, laughing. "Keep jumping."

Now she felt guilty for yelling at him when he knew what he was talking about, but she was still annoyed that he didn't trust her to know what *she* was doing.

Lighten up! He doesn't know me. He doesn't know what I can do.

"Are you coming, Mrs. Fraser?" TR trotted ahead of her with such exuberance she almost laughed. She was enjoying the hell out of this roundup, too. They both must be nuts.

Her horse managed a few more bunny hops—his last feeble attempts to toss her off his back—as she trotted off after TR. She had Lucky under control now, and he was coming to realize it as well.

"This is the best part of cowboy life," he called out to her. "We have decent food. We sleep soundly, and the work is exciting..."

I wouldn't go that far.

"It's a competitive group," he continued. "Cowpunchers are alone so much of the time that the roundup is like a long Fourth of July celebration. A man's reputation is won or lost by the way he handles himself, and if you fail to respond to a challenge or insult, you'll lose face."

She glanced over her shoulder and was surprised to see Austin leaning against a tree, arms and ankles crossed, watching her, and when he grinned, a slight dimple popped out above his right cheek.

"Are you talking about anyone in particular?" she asked.

"Mr. O'Grady is an odd sort."

"Because he's so tall?"

"Out here, they say you can always spot an Easterner. But Mr. O'Grady's differences, aside from his height, are more than geographical. He doesn't act as if he belongs anywhere."

"Why do you say that?"

"He grumbles about being here and wants to go home, but he doesn't leave. He's an accomplished and educated fellow, but his anger gets in his way."

TR was right about Austin, and she found it prophetic. If TR had heard Austin grumbling, she needed to remind Austin to watch what he said because people listened to him. They would quickly become suspicious if he talked about home and the conveniences he missed.

They rode out toward their assigned section of the Badlands to search the high plateau plains and narrow, treed coulees for roaming cattle, and she couldn't stop thinking about Austin and her dreams about him.

"Austin had an accident that ended the career he spent his life training for." Explaining Austin's situation reminded her that she lost her dream job, and she hadn't had time to deal with the disappointment.

My career isn't over, though. Only delayed until I find another job. But Austin can't play for another team.

"I believe Austin is trying to figure out where he fits in now," she said.

"What'd Mr. O'Grady train for?"

"To play sports."

"Which one? Baseball? Golf? Rowing? Rugby football?"

She knew James Naismith invented basketball in the late eighteen hundreds but didn't know when exactly. There was a framed newspaper about Naismith hanging on the women's restroom wall in Wyatt's favorite sports bar. She'd waited in line dozens of times, and reading notices on the wall was the only distraction from listening to women gush over sexy athletes.

"Basketball," she said, more as a question than a statement.

"I haven't heard of that. How's it played?"

"Two teams of five players run up and down a court and try to throw a ball into a basket. At the end of the game, the team with the most baskets wins."

"Like Mr. O'Grady stuffed the pillow into the tree."

"Yes," she said, "but I don't know all the rules. You'll have to ask him."

"I will," TR said. "He's a complicated man."

"You can say that again."

She and TR rode out on their day's assignment, and she set thoughts of Austin aside…for now.

46

The Badlands (1885)—Ensley

ENSLEY WAITED UP, hoping Tavis would return. He was late, and she was worried, but Remy told her not to be, which of course didn't help.

She'd only spent a short time with Tavis before they traded horses, and he rode off in the opposite direction, but she sensed he was much more than a Navy SEAL. He seemed like an old soul—older and wiser than other men his age—and fearless. She'd watched his face when he mounted Tesoro, and she saw nothing except absolute confidence.

Who was Tavis Stuart? The real Tavis. Not the one he allowed the world to see. He knew who he was, but she doubted any woman would ever get close enough to find out, and, Ensley chuckled, she pitied the woman who tried.

When she dozed off in her chair while watching Austin and TR play backgammon, Austin shook her shoulder to wake her up. "Why don't you turn in?"

She rubbed her eyes, then set her elbow on the plank table and rested her chin in her palm. She didn't have the strength to hold her head up without support. "I want to stay awake until Tavis gets back."

"But you're barely awake. And besides, Tavis might not make it here tonight. Go to bed. If you're rested, you can handle whatever news he brings back."

She sat straight up, fear spiking through her, and she shuddered. "That sounds ominous. Do you think something happened to JC?"

"Nothin's happened," Remy said, playing the plank as a drum with two sticks he'd lifted from the kindling pile. *Ba-ba-boom!*

"No, but JC might want us to come to Kentucky," Austin said.

TR rolled the dice and moved his checkers. "Where's your home? You never said."

"Originally, New York," Austin said, shaking the dice in his hands. "Now I just move around."

Ensley tapped on one of the points in his home quadrant on the gameboard, but Austin brushed her hand away, then moved where she suggested. "JC and I had an agreement," she said. "My time with Teddy isn't up yet."

TR picked up the dice. "If Mr. Fraser requests that Mr. O'Grady escort you to Kentucky, I will insist you go."

She gave TR a side-eye. "Traitor."

He clamped his teeth over his lower lip, and while he didn't laugh, his eyes twinkled. "I must respect your husband's wishes, even if they aren't mine."

She had nothing in her arsenal to use if she wanted to bargain with Tavis. If he had a telegram from JC that said he wanted them to come to Kentucky, she'd have to go. She had a notebook full of TR's stories and thoughts about everything from hunting in the Badlands to life in New York City. More than enough material to fill up a book.

But still, she wasn't ready to leave him. "That wouldn't be my wish, either," she managed to say without releasing the tears burning her eyelids. "Sometimes we don't have choices." She gave him a sweet smile. "I'm going to bed. If Tavis returns, tell him I want to talk to him first thing in the morning."

"Good night, Ensley," Austin said.

She turned in time to catch his wink, and it tickled her because it was so innocent. It wasn't flirting. It was more of a we're-in-this-together look.

"Good night, Mrs. Fraser," TR said.

Remy played the table again and broke one of his substitute drumsticks. "Damn. It took me hours to turn that into a perfect drumstick."

"I'm sure you'll find another one," Ensley said, yawning. "But Norman is protective of his kindling. I wouldn't take too many of them."

"Doan worry. I'll leave him the broken ones." *Ba-da-da-boom.*

She dragged herself to bed and fell asleep, but she woke up sev-eral times with the same haunting dreams of Austin that she had the night before. But once she was awake, all she could think about was Tavis. And wondering if he'd made it back yet with news of JC.

She had three men in her head—JC, Austin, and TR—and there was no elbow room. Once Tavis returned with news of JC, she could push at least two of them aside.

Why not all three?

There wasn't an answer floating around in her heart, so she ignored the question and managed to fall back to sleep until right before dawn. Her first thought was that it was exactly like yesterday—the same smells, the same complaints, the same creaking joints, the same weather. But today, the reek of manure from the cow pasture and the smoke from the branding fires was more potent.

She crawled out of her bedroll and washed up before going to the chuckwagon for breakfast. When she arrived, Norman was holding a welcoming cup of coffee for her.

"That Tavis fella dragged himself in about midnight. Crashed down by the river. Never seen a man so worn out and a horse so fresh. Tesoro coulda run right back to Medora without breakin' a sweat."

"I'm glad Tavis's back, and I'm glad he's exhausted and not my horse." She sipped the coffee. "That sounds mean, doesn't it?"

"Not a mean bone in yer body, Miss Ensley. Ya let him borra your horse and expected him to return Tesoro in good shape."

"Tesoro is only on loan to me."

"I heard ya bought a wild horse from Mr. Roosevelt. He won't take him back."

"He's on loan to TR, too. Tesoro needs to return to where he came from."

"Where's that?"

She looked off into the distance as if she could see Turkmenistan's Karakum desert where the Akhal-Teke originated. "Far away," she said with a sigh. As much as she wanted to take Tesoro with her, she couldn't take him to the future. He didn't belong there. And she was certain Erik would reclaim him. If that was true, then he was around somewhere, watching. She didn't know why she thought that or why Erik would take Tesoro home with him. It was just one of those gut feelings.

She sat down at the chuckwagon's tailgate and spread a large spoonful of jam on a biscuit. "Did Tavis say anything about a telegram from JC?"

"Didn't say nothin' to me, and everybody else had turned in afore he got here."

"Where's TR?"

"Mr. Roosevelt finished breakfast and rushed off to get his horse."

"Damn. How long ago?"

"A bit afore ya got up."

She let out an exasperated huff. "And you let me sit here, jabbering away when TR was getting ready to leave. He probably left without me." She bit into the biscuit and washed it down with a gulp of coffee. "Where's Austin?"

"They left at the same time."

"Damn, Norman. Why didn't you tell me that first?"

"Because ya need a good breakfast before ya spend the day roundin' up strays." He refilled her coffee cup and flipped another piece of bacon on her plate. "Finish eatin'."

"I can't believe I slept so late."

"Ya didn't. They started early."

"I don't get it. Why didn't they wake me up?" Pouting wasn't doing her any good.

Eat and go find them.

She ate the bacon and only a few spoonfuls of beans. "Maybe I can catch them before they ride off." She dumped her dirty dishes in the wrecking pan. "Gotta go. Thanks, Norman."

She grabbed her tack and raced off to the picket lines where Bill Sewall was saddling a horse. "Bill, where's TR?"

"Rode off with two of the fellas ya brought with you."

Her pulse drummed with a mixture of anger and disappointment. "Austin and Remy?"

"No," Bill said. "The one what rode in last night, and the one he calls 'Cajun.'"

Tavis left without talking to her? Damn him. Now she was sorry she loaned him her horse. Forget the disappointment. She was pissed now. "That's Remy. What about Austin?"

Bill raised his hand over his head. "The tall one?"

To Ensley, everyone was tall. "Yeah, him."

"A cowboy from another outfit rode in to say he spotted a grizzly a mile or so north of camp. Your tall friend went hunting. Mr. Roosevelt said you should stay in camp today."

"Because of the bear?"

"Guess so."

"That's crazy. The bear sighting was north, and TR's rounding up cattle southeast of here. I'd be perfectly safe. He must have forgotten he gave me a rifle." TR knew she could shoot. So why leave her behind?

She could ride after them. Yeah, right. That sounded like one of those heroines who was "too stupid to live."

"Why didn't you ride out with them?" she asked.

"I'll be dragging the steers to the branding irons today. Not my favorite job, but I'm one of the few who knows all the brands."

Since the thick-headed men didn't want her with them, she had the day to herself, but that was a waste. She wanted to be part of the action, not sitting around Norman's wagon, rewriting the notes from her interview with him about the Civil War and the role he played. At first, he'd been reluctant to talk about his experiences, but he slowly opened up, and as he did, an idea for another book started to bloom.

"How about I hang around with you? I can rope 'em and drag 'em to the branding fire just as well as anyone else."

Bill jumped, raising his arms in self-defense. "No! Those cowboys won't let a gal anywhere near those fires. And besides," he puffed up his chest, "you don't know the brands."

"That's ridiculous. They know I can ride, and I know all three of TR's brands. I can cut his calves and steers from the herd."

"Roosevelt said no. And if you get hurt, he'll for sure blame me."

"No, he won't. He'll blame me! He didn't want me to go with him today and left me to fend for myself. So that's what I'm going to do."

"What are you goin' to do?"

"Saddle Lucky." And that's what she did. Then she rode over to the branding fires and hung out for a couple of hours, watching the action until she knew the procedure and had all the brands memorized.

When she was confident she knew the process, she rode over to the hot branding fires. The smoke burned her eyes. The smell was so familiar to her, and it brought back memories of the ranch and her father. She took a few deep breaths along the way, as she would when preparing for any job interview.

"Hey, guys. I've been watching, and your horses need a rest."

I can do this job if you'll give me a chance.

She squared her shoulders and continued. "Lucky's fresh and ready to work. Let me cut out some steers for you."

"It's dangerous work, ma'am," one of the cowboys, whose leathery skin made him look the oldest, said. "And it ain't suited for a gal."

I'm not letting you bully me.

She relaxed her shoulders and crossed her hands over the saddle horn. "Ever heard of Annie Oakley?"

"Ain't she that gal in Buffalo Bill's Wild West Show?"

"She sure is. So if she can shoot well enough to be in Buffalo Bill's show, surely I can drag some steers to the branding fire. C'mon, give me a chance. If I mess up, I'll walk away. Promise."

The corner of the old cowboy's mouth twitched, but she couldn't count it as a real smile. The beginning of one, maybe. Or it was the beginning of a smirk, expecting her to fail.

I won't fail.

"Start with the calves, Miss Ensley. Leave the steers for the men. But if you tell us the wrong brand to use, you'll have to deal with the rancher."

"Sounds reasonable." She mounted Lucky and headed into the herd, confident of Lucky's skill as a cutting horse. She spotted a cow with her calf, confirmed the Maltese Cross brand on the mother, and cut the calf away from her. Lucky was almost on his knees, dancing back and forth to keep the mooing calf from returning to its mother.

Ensley swung her rope, lassoing the calf, catching his two hind legs. Then she dragged him over to the branding fire. "Use the Maltese brand on this one." Branding wasn't an easy job, and you had to be fast and careful because no one wanted to hurt the animals. She'd learned how to do it without watching because the smoke rose into your face, blinding you. And the air stank, making it hard to breathe without throwing up.

She lost count of the number of calves she dragged to the branding fire, but the men hadn't lost count and kept a record of which brand each calf received.

"The calves are done, Miss Ensley. If you want to rope the cows, go ahead," the old cowboy told her. "Just be careful out there."

"Sure." Feeling like the cool kids had invited her to sit at their lunch table, she and Lucky galloped off to find her first one.

The first one she cut wasn't having any of what Ensley had planned. She forgot to lasso its legs and instead got her around the neck. Lucky backed up until he was almost on his haunches, digging in his hooves. When the rope was taut, she jumped off, rushed over to the animal, tied three of her legs together with a piggin' string she'd been carrying in her teeth. When the tie was complete, she threw her hands in the air to stop the clock.

"What are you doing?" the old cowboy hollered. "Drag her over here."

Oh, God. This isn't the rodeo.

She mounted up and dragged the cow to the branding fire. "Sorry about that. I thought you were timing me."

"What for?"

"I thought we were competing for the best time. Playing a game, you know."

Good try, Ensley.

"A game? I'll play," one of the other cowboys said.

"Bring another one down, and we'll time you. Who's got a pocket watch?" the old cowboy asked.

"I got one," another cowboy said, opening up his pocket watch. "This belonged to my pa. It works good."

She collected her rope and piggin' string. "Start the count as soon as I cut a cow." She rode off to find another one to rope. Her best time was ten seconds. Let's see how she could do now.

She cut out a cow, chased after her, lassoed, then dismounted. Seconds were ticking in her head as she tied off three of the legs then threw her hands in the air. "How'd I do?" she yelled.

"Eleven seconds," the cowboy with the watch yelled.

"I'm next," another cowboy said. He roped one in ten seconds.

She knew she could do ten, but could she do nine? She mounted up and cut another one, and when she finished, the cowboy with the watch yelled, "Ten seconds."

After five attempts, neither of them could break ten seconds, and Ensley called it quits. "I'm done." Her hip was killing her, and there wasn't a patch on her that wasn't coated with mud or cows' blood. And the stink of burning hide stung her nose.

"C'mon over, Miss Ensley, and have some roasted testicles."

Cowboys had bullied her into eating her first roasted testicle when she was a teenager, and she had to eat it or lose face. The funny thing was, they weren't awful. Roasted, they looked like slices of ham, crisp and brown on the outside, and on the inside, they had a meaty flavor. Bull balls were slightly sweeter than ram balls.

She removed her gloves and tossed one from hand to hand while it cooled. Then she popped it into her mouth and chewed. "Not bad," she said, smiling. "Now I've had enough fun for one day. I'm going to clean up and work on my book for a while until Mr. Roosevelt comes back." She waved. "Thanks, guys."

She returned Lucky to the picket line and unsaddled and brushed him, then left him to graze while she went to Tesoro. "Come on, boy. You deserve a good brushing and a bath."

She gathered hers and the horse's grooming supplies and led Tesoro through a grove of cottonwood trees down to the river away from the camp. She wanted privacy to take a sponge bath. This was probably the filthiest she'd been during her entire time in the past. Her clothes would never come clean, but at least she could wash underneath them. She would never get used to putting on dirty clothes after a bath, but she loved being here. That could all change at any minute, but for now, she was a happy camper.

While she was brushing Tesoro, he started acting jittery, jumping to the side, swishing his tail, and neighing louder than usual. "What's wrong, boy?" He wasn't a sensitive horse, so when he acted like this, she was alarmed but remained calm. If she didn't, he'd never settle down.

When he curled his upper lip, she knew he sensed danger.

She glanced toward the grove, and the hairs on the back of her neck twitched. "Okay, I believe you. Let's get out of here." She gathered the supplies and untied the rope, becoming more alarmed by the absolute silence surrounding them. Even the river, turbid brown from eroding the banks, grew still. And the stone-gray sky seemed to meld with the earth, blurring the line between them.

What the hell's going on?

The wind picked up and tugged at her hat. They must be downwind of something unsettling because Tesoro broke loose, neighing louder than any horse she'd ever heard. The glands around his shoulders and neck emitted a reddish liquid that made his fur look darker, giving the appearance of bleeding, stark in the grayness of the late afternoon.

Then he reared, and his legs climbed the air, fighting some unseen foe. His feet touched the ground, and he reared again.

Now she was seriously alarmed. No, she was downright terrified.

She reached for her rifle, but it wasn't there. It was with her tack at the remuda. Her heart beat faster, diverting the blood from her gut to her limbs.

Run! Now!

But before she could move, a black bear appeared at the edge of the grove.

"Holy shit." Fear skewered her heart. Her gut tightened, and stomach acid driven by that fear heaved up into her throat.

Tesoro's feet touched the ground, and he reared again, screaming.

The bear dropped and ran toward her, but Tesoro stood between them. She expected Tesoro to run, but he didn't. He reared again, and his scream was even louder. That's when she realized it wasn't a black bear. With a shoulder hump and those short, rounded ears, she knew it was a grizzly, and his four-inch claws could rip her horse apart.

The bear could rip her apart, too. It could outrun, outswim, outdistance her on its worst day.

The bear lurched at Tesoro, batting at him with one of his giant paws, scraping his claws down Tesoro's golden underbelly, shredding the skin, and Tesoro's screams grew louder.

"Run, Tesoro!" she shrieked. "Run! Before he kills you." She waved her arms to distract the bear. "Run, Tesoro."

Tesoro screamed again, rearing and biting the bear. Why didn't anyone hear the shrieks? They were loud enough to wake a village.

Tesoro was sacrificing himself for her.

Run—now!

But she couldn't abandon her horse.

What the hell can I do?

She ripped the tie-back off her hair and attached the Clovis Point to a long stick. She'd done it so many times it only took a couple of seconds. Now she had a weapon.

"Tesoro!" she screamed as terror punched her heart. Why didn't anyone hear the commotion?

The bear wrapped both arms around the horse and threw him on the ground. Then he fell on top of him, biting his neck with jaws that could crush a bowling ball. She threw her spear, but it didn't penetrate the bear's tough hide. Instead, it hung there, caught in its fur. The bear ripped off more of Tesoro's skin with its deadly claws.

Oh, no! Please, get up, Tesoro. Get up. Run.

But as still as he was, she knew he'd never run again.

So she ran, and when she reached the grove, she glanced back. The bear climbed over Tesoro's body, growling. Then it dropped down on all fours and lumbered toward her. His giant paws left bloody footprints in his wake, and the shaggy hair on its neck and shoulders bristled as he moved. His fangs were red with Tesoro's blood. The bear's glittering, evil eyes glared at her.

If she ran, he would chase her. If she climbed the tree, he would climb it too. If she ran into the river, he would swim after her.

Run. Weave. Scream.

Indecision would get her killed.

Out of the grove came a sound more terrifying than the bear's, and Erik appeared, yelling, "Tyr," and wielding his ax. The bear jerked and lunged for Erik. He slashed the bear again and again. Undeterred, the bear grabbed him in a hug, shaking him until Erik dropped the ax. But that didn't leave him defenseless. He had a single-edged knife that he used to jab the bear in the side—again and again.

When they moved away from the ax, she picked it up. She wasn't a weakling, but even with two hands, she couldn't swing the steel blade with enough force to cause much damage. She swung it against the bear's legs, but she only nicked him, and the bear scarcely reacted.

That pissed her off. She was holding a deadly weapon that could kill the monster if only she was strong enough. If she was the son her father always wanted, she'd be able to kill the goddamn bear.

Erik was a large man, slightly broader than Tavis, and each arm probably weighed as much as the ax. But compared to the bear, the difference was as stark as her standing next to Austin.

Erik continued jabbing the knife into the bear's side, and the bear growled, becoming more aggressive, and finally swatted away the blade just as he had the ax.

Approaching a full-blown panic, she searched the ground for a weapon, for inspiration, for something—anything—she could use to stop the bear before it killed Erik too.

Erik was buried deep in the bear's thick fur. He reached up and latched his arms around the bear's neck, squeezing with huge hands, but to little effect.

I have to do something. I can't let the bear kill him too.

She grunted, adrenaline surging, and she raised the ax again. Her hip screamed, and her leg buckled, but she straightened quickly against the sharp pain, and with all her might, she swung it against the bear's back. The bear stumbled, but the strike didn't stop it from clawing Erik's flesh, rending it with deep, bloody gouges. Her muscles shook from strain, but she *had* to strike again.

The bear tried to shake Erik loose, swinging him back and forth, but Erik held on. Grunting, she raised the ax, her muscles quivering, and she wielded it again, slashing the bear near the first strike. The squealing bear lost its balance and fell, trapping Erik beneath his several hundred-pound mass of claws, teeth, and muscle.

Hit him again.

The coppery smell of blood, the human screams, and animal growls, the earthy stink of the churned, moldy dirt at the bank created chaos and roiled her stomach.

Don't get sick now. Fight!

She lifted the ax, her muscles screaming, barely able to hold on. She was demanding more than her body could give, and she wasn't sure her hip would hold up if she strained it again, but she couldn't stop trying. She must do everything she could for Erik, no matter what it cost her.

This time she had to strike down instead of swinging to the side, and she barely got the ax lifted with shaking arms when a horse galloped into the clearing.

"Run, Ensley!" Austin roared as he grabbed his rifle and leaped off his horse without a hitch, pause, or wasted movement. "Run!"

His shouting penetrated her tunnel vision, and she ran, not toward safety but to Austin's warhorse.

Austin balanced, squared his shoulders with the target, braced the rifle buttstock close to this right shoulder, pressed his cheek firmly against the stock, and fired. There was a pop and then a loud crack.

Ensley used her remaining strength to pull herself up into the saddle. She would spur Austin's horse and charge the bear if she had to.

Austin quickly got off another round, hitting the bear in the heart and lung area. He cocked the rifle a third time, moved slightly to adjust to the bear's jerking, and got off two more rounds.

The thrashing and bellowing quieted as the bear fell and rolled over onto its back—dead.

The grizzly had mauled and bitten chunks out of Erik's shoulders and neck, leaving him bloodied and shredded beyond recognition. If not for his blue tattoos, she wouldn't have known him. She dismounted and dropped to the ground at his side, ignoring the blood, shredded skin, and exposed muscle and bone.

She found a faint pulse in his wrist and yelled to Austin, "He's still alive. Find Remy."

Austin fired one more shot between the bear's eyes, then mounted his warhorse and rode off, leaving her with the dying Viking and her beloved horse.

"You can't die," she pleaded. "Fight for your life the way you fought the bear." Then she remembered his red cloak. It had healing powers. "Where's your cloak? It'll heal you."

He opened his eyes, and the irises were the most beautiful shade of Artic blue she'd ever seen. "It's too late, Ensley. Tell Tavis to take me home. I must go back."

Ravens cawed overhead, and the wind sighed through the pines and cottonwoods. And she had to wonder if the wind was trying to get her attention or had something important to tell her.

"Will you heal there?"

"My time is done. It's time for my heir to take the empty seat at the table."

She didn't know what he was talking about. "You're not going to die. We'll take you home. The doctors can save you. Hold on just a little bit longer."

He coughed, and blood spilled out of his mouth. "I must go home, and the horse must go with me."

"Tesoro is dead."

"He will live again."

Her sobbing seesawed between hyperventilating gasps. "No! Don't go. Please."

"You have been brave...and resourceful," he said, his entire body trembling. "I'm proud of you. I...didn't know if...you had it"—he patted his chest—"in here. You do... Don't ever doubt yourself. The Keeper...will need your skills...for the coming...battle. Train hard...until you can wield...the ax. It is yours now. Carry it proudly. You have the handprints of your ancestors on your heart."

She swiped at her tears. "I heard that once before, on my last bull ride."

"I was there. I did not want you to give up." With a bloody

finger, he drew a mark on her forehead. Then he closed his beautiful eyes, and his entire body sighed.

"No!" she screamed. "Don't take Erik, too." The walls she'd constructed around her heart crumbled in a tsunami of tears, exposing the grief from losing her father, mother, ranch, job, horse, and now Erik.

I can't take any more.

All her sorrows knotted together in one humongous heartbreak and shattered into millions of pieces, and she doubted she'd ever recover from this furnace of pain and loss.

47

The Badlands (1885)—Tavis

AUSTIN RODE INTO camp, yelling, "Need help!" Then he jerked his horse around and galloped back the way he'd come.

Tavis simultaneously dumped his coffee, yanked the reins off the wheel of Norman's wagon, and galloped after Austin while swinging his leg over the saddle. Remy was only a beat behind him as they raced through the cottonwood grove.

Tavis didn't know what happened, but either pain or fear had to be responsible for the pale, haggard, desperate look on Austin's face. Acute pain wasn't an unusual look for him, but fear? This was different. Austin went to great lengths to hide his fear from everyone, including himself.

"Is it Ensley?" Tavis yelled.

"Hurry!" Austin yelled again, but with much more urgency.

If Ensley was in danger, Erik would have intervened and protected her, but she still could have been injured. Tavis's gut knew that's what happened, but his mind lagged a bit behind accepting it. This business had no fucking guarantees. And that gave him heartburn.

His training in both the future and the past prepared him for what lay beyond the cottonwood grove. But the coppery stench in the air sent his stomach acid straight to the back of his throat.

He roared, "Tyr!" The war cry gave him a boost of adrenaline—strength from within, empowering him to handle what lay ahead. His warrior spirit was fully engaged and dispassionate. He scanned the killing field for the dead and injured. Dead—one horse, one bear…one Viking. Tavis's gut roiled.

Alive—one sobbing woman covered with blood.

Within seconds, his mind developed a scenario: a bear appeared. Erik's golden horse attacked it and fought to the death. The bear went after Ensley. Erik arrived in time to save her but ultimately lost the fight.

But who killed the bear?

Ensley? Not likely. If she had a gun, the bear wouldn't have been able to kill Erik or his horse. Tavis glanced at Austin. His face hadn't changed, confirming for Tavis that pain wasn't contorting Austin's chiseled features. It was terror, and he hadn't cycled out of it yet.

Austin's mind was replaying what he saw when he pulled the trigger. And there was no doubt in Tavis's mind now that Austin had killed the bear. He was an expert shot, and it would have been an easy kill for him. But the slaughter and knowing how close Ensley had come to suffering the same fate as Erik was a harsh reminder of the fragility of life and how easily it could change in mere seconds.

Tavis jumped off his horse midstride and ran to Ensley, dropping to his knees. He pulled her into a sitting position. "Where are you hurt?" She had blood all over her clothes, her hair, her face. He did a quick assessment to see if any of it was hers. "Where do you hurt? Are you cut? Bitten? Answer me!"

Tears streaked the mud and blood down her face and neck, her eyes were glassy, and she was unresponsive.

"Remy, bring your kit and check her out. She's in shock. See if any of this blood is hers, and give her a shot of morphine," Tavis said.

Remy dropped to his knees and set his kit on the ground beside him. "Ensley, I'm going to take off your jacket. I have to see where you're injured."

Tavis helped Remy peel off the worn, bloody denim jacket. The blouse beneath it was so threadbare Tavis was surprised it still held together.

Remy ran his hands over her chest, arms, and back, and then down her belly and legs. "I doan see any open wounds or indication of broken bones. Nothing's swelling. Plenty of bruises and scratches, but most doan look recent." He removed a tin box from his saddlebag and, using an autoinjector, gave Ensley a dose of morphine.

She didn't react to that either.

Tavis looked down at Erik and just as quickly looked away. He couldn't allow himself to look at his body yet or react to his death.

Erik had been a father to Tavis, and he would grieve later when he carried the Viking king home for burial.

"Austin, take Ensley down to the river and wash her up. It looks like her gear is still there. Dig through it until you find what you need."

"Are you crazy? Dig through a woman's gear? That's a sure-fire way to get myself killed."

"You're safe this time. She's in shock and won't remember."

Austin's expression was no longer strained, and his cheeks had pinked. "Come on, baby doll. Let's get you cleaned up." When Ensley didn't stir, Austin picked her up as if she weighed no more than a kitten.

A vision appeared in Tavis's mind's eye of Austin carrying Ensley through the snow to the Colorado ranch house, her skis dangling. They were both laughing, as young lovers do, over silly shit. Then the vision vanished as quickly as it appeared.

Tavis's visions were always insights into a future event, but he never knew why he had them or how far in the future they'd happen, so he never told anyone about them. Not even Erik.

"Let me help you wash up," Austin said, looking down at her. "Tavis, what's this mark on her forehead?"

"It's an Yggdrasil, a Viking symbol. Don't wipe it off."

"Why not?"

"I want a picture of it."

Austin patted his shirt and pants pockets. "I have my phone somewhere. I'll take one, but did Erik put it there?"

"I reckon so," Tavis said.

Ensley turned her glassy eyes toward Tavis. "Erik said to take him and Tesoro home."

Her voice held no emotion or inflection. And Tavis was pretty sure she had no idea where she was or what just happened to her.

He lightly traced the Yggdrasil. The blood had dried, but it was hot to the touch. Tavis brushed her nose, cheek, and chin with the back of his hand—all cold next to his skin.

"What'd he tell you about this mark?"

She put her hand to her forehead. "I'm chosen."

Tavis knew there was more because Erik said the same thing when he drew the mark on Tavis's forehead a dozen years ago. He didn't know how many others were marked, and Erik never answered when Tavis asked.

"Find his cloak," Ensley said, slurring her words.

Tavis pushed Ensley's hair back from her face. "How do you know about his cloak?"

"I found a piece of it"—she ran her fingers across her palm—"and it healed my blister."

Tavis knew what Ensley said was true. Something similar happened to him. But his injury wasn't a blister. It was a cut on his head, and it wouldn't stop bleeding until he used a scrap from Erik's cloak.

Where was the cloak now? With JC? If that was true, Erik already knew his death was imminent, and he couldn't risk the cloak falling into enemy hands.

He signaled to Austin to take Ensley away. Then he knelt beside Arthfael, the horse Ensley named Tesoro, and examined the horse's mortal wounds. Tavis stroked his long neck, remembering his birth. Erik had been so proud, and he knew the stallion's destiny would be remarkable. He'd been Ensley's first line of defense, giving Erik time to get here.

"Did you get a telegram from Elliott?" Remy asked.

Tavis went to Erik's body to help Remy prepare it for the trip home. Tavis looked into Erik's blue eyes—the same color as his own—and then solemnly closed them.

"There was a telegram waiting for Ensley," Tavis said to Remy. "JC sent it from Chicago. He also shipped clothes to her. The boxes are waiting at the depot in Medora."

Tavis crossed Erik's calloused hands over the gaping chest wounds. It would take Remy hours to sew them up. Hours Tavis didn't have. The Council members were probably already sensing their chief's death. He had to leave soon.

"So JC's okay?"

"I don't know. I got a strange telegram from Elliott. He said he, Meredith, and Emily were taking JC home and that we're to go to Kentucky to bring Kit and Cullen home with us."

"Why didn't they go with Elliott, and why would they take JC home?" Remy's eyes narrowed, and then he said, "Unless…"

Tavis heard what Remy didn't say. It confirmed what Tavis thought might have happened, and it was like a spike to his heart.

"I spent the trip back here thinking about that. And I tried to read between the lines of Elliott's telegram."

"What'd you read?" Remy interrupted again.

Tavis hesitated a moment, unsure if he should tell Remy, and then decided that was stupid. Remy expected and deserved complete honesty from him, and vice versa.

"You're not going to like this."

"Shit, bro. Spill it."

Tavis rolled in his bottom lip then released it. "Based on my experience, I believe the Illuminati found JC and tortured him."

"Fuck. No!" The muscles directly under Remy's eyes quivered. It was Remy's tell when he was tense, concerned, and maybe scared. "What kind of experience you got, man? I got experience, too, but I couldn't come up with something like that. What kind of proof have you got? And if you doan have any, you damn well shouldn't be telling anybody that. It's pure fiction, and it'll give me the willies. So stop it!"

"Sorry. But you asked. I don't know if Elliott was taking JC's body home, or they were taking a broken man home. If it's his mind, JC might never recover."

Remy stopped midstitch to still his shaking hands. "Fuck! I doan like the direction this conversation's going. And how the hell could the Illuminati find him here?"

Tavis brushed the dried clumps of blood and debris off Erik's trousers. Then he straightened the Viking king's legs. While doing that, he looked for Erik's brooch and found it pinned to the inside of his trousers.

"Do you see his other leather ankle boot?" Tavis asked Remy.

Remy looked up from what he was doing and glanced around. "It could be anywhere. Look under those leaves."

Tavis walked around the clearing and found it under a pile of leaves and branches. The strap had broken. Tavis reknotted the leather thong and slipped the ankle boot on Erik's foot. He remained there, sitting on his haunches, looking up at the Viking king, recalling his early impressions of Erik's broad, muscular shoulders. Tavis didn't believe at the time that he would ever be as large as Erik. He shook his head at how dumb he'd been. By the time he entered the Naval Academy, he was bigger and broader than Erik and most of his classmates.

"JC was in the Far East recently," Tavis said. "I don't know what he was doing there. It's possible he had a run-in with the Illuminati and left enough breadcrumbs behind for them to follow him home and then here."

Remy cut the thread and put the needle aside. "Are we in danger?"

Tavis couldn't help but crack a crooked smile. "You mean more than usual?"

"Hell, yeah. Braham's fixation with security at Mallory Plantation is enough to make us all paranoid."

"I believe the Illuminati's tentacles may have already reached Ensley. Her father's car crash was suspicious, and so was her mother's heart attack. The woman was healthy and in great physical shape when she died."

"You're promoting a fucking conspiracy theory?"

"I might be, but on its face, it is suspicious. I believe the Illuminati wanted Ensley's ranch and somehow manipulated her into selling it."

"How'd they do that?"

"I don't know yet."

"Asshole. Doan be so cryptic. If you know something, tell me."

"Come on, Remy. You know the deal. Not until I have more to go on than just a hunch. But when you get back, get the lawyers working on it. Find a way to repurchase Williams Ranch, plus all the ranches adjoining it. Tell Kenzie and Kevin to go through a shell corporation. There can't be any connection to MacCorp."

"Spend millions of dollars on your hunch?"

"If I'm right, it'll be worth it. If I'm wrong, we'll put whatever we buy back on the market. Or Kevin can pay for it out of my share of the Lafitte treasure, and I'll own ranches in North Dakota."

"What if the owners won't sell?"

"Then we'll use drone technology and keep eyes in the sky to watch what they're up to."

Remy packed away his supplies, shaking his head. "I doan know what this is about, but I'll talk to Elliott and David as soon as I can. But you didn't say why Kit and Cullen stayed behind."

"Probably to extend the visit with their family. You should probably leave for Kentucky in the morning or as soon as Ensley feels like traveling. Tell Roosevelt that JC wants his wife to join him there. He won't object. But here's the thing. Once you leave here, Austin and Ensley need to travel as a married couple. I don't want them separated, not ever. It's too dangerous."

"Why Austin?"

"He's the most accurate shooter in the family. I already knew he was good. I've been hunting with him enough times, but until I saw that bear, I didn't know *how* good."

"I didn't notice."

"Two shots into the heart-lung area. Two shots in the head."

"You haven't been anywhere near that bear. How do you know?"

"There are four shells on the ground within fifteen feet of the bear. If I had to get off four shots guaranteed to kill a grizzly, that's where I'd aim."

"Yeah, but I'm a good shot, too. So it makes me wonder if you're playing matchmaker, and if you are, stop it. All hell's going to break loose when Austin figures out Ensley was the editor who rejected his manuscript and then lied to him."

"She didn't lie to him. She just didn't tell him who she was."

"Can't believe you're one of those jerks who believe a lie of omission isn't a lie. You asshole. You know it is."

"I'm not a jerk. Just be sure you're close by when Austin puts it together. Ensley won't be in any condition to set him straight. Tell Austin he's got an assignment, and there'll be plenty of time to hate her later."

"She'll want to go back to New York when we get home."

"Elliott might be too worried about JC for a while, so lean on David and Kenzie. They'll make sure Ensley understands her life is in danger. She has got to learn fighting skills, and Braham has the best setup for that."

Tavis glanced across the clearing and watched Austin gently cleaning Ensley's arms and hands. He remembered the vision of Ensley in Austin's arms, and he reconsidered the best place for her to go.

"If Austin is still speaking to her after this is over, she could go to Colorado to live. David can hire special ops guys to teach her everything she needs to know. And as soon as Penny delivers, she might like to spend time at the ranch training with Ensley."

"You and I could teach her."

"I might not be back for a while, and she should start immediately. Plus, Elliott will need you. If the situation with JC is as bad as I'm afraid it is, Elliott might start living out of a whisky bottle again."

"Meredith won't let him."

"Meredith might be in that bottle with him. JC is her only child. Talk to Kevin. He was with Elliott years ago when he was drinking and living on painkillers."

"From what I hear, Kevin was an enabler. Gave Elliott whatever he wanted."

"Then find out what he did and do the opposite."

Remy shrugged. "That makes sense." He sat back and packed up his gear. "I've done the best I can do for him with what I have. How do you want to handle this transfer?"

Tavis looked around the clearing again. "Let's move Erik next to Arthfael. Then I can hold on to both of them."

"What's going to happen when you get to Jarlshof? You're returning with their dead chief. They might decide to kill the messenger or, in this case, the delivery boy."

"They'll know these are animal wounds. I'll be okay, but the funeral might be a problem. The traditional funeral for a chief is violent and goes against everything I believe. I'll refuse to participate, and that won't sit well with the rest of the Council."

"They woan hurt you, will they?"

Tavis looked off at the rich orange colors of the setting sun, recalling the ancient stories of funerals for Viking chiefs, and he shivered. "I don't think so."

"Doan go, then. We'll bury Erik here, then return in the future and give him the burial he deserves."

"I don't have a choice, Remy. And I'd never disrespect Erik."

"You should take someone with you."

"Who? Elliott depends on you." He glanced back over at Austin and Ensley. "And looking at those two, Ensley might be just what Austin needs—and vice versa. Keep 'em safe. Okay?"

"Austin can be the biggest asshole I've ever been around. If he acts up, I'll shoot him."

Tavis looked back at Remy, wishing he could see this mission through before going back to Jarlshof. But the funeral of a Viking chief was his priority—before any other obligation.

"One more thing," Tavis said. "If you go through Chicago, don't even step off the train. Send your porter to the local Pinkerton office and hire half a dozen agents to travel with you."

"Should I mention Daniel Grant recommended hiring them?"

"Play it by ear, but if you find someone who knew him, you'll have to make up a cover story. It might not be worth it." Tavis pulled the amethyst brooch and the telegrams out of his pockets and gave them to Remy. "Leave as soon as possible, and never let down your guard."

"Got it."

Tavis glanced across the killing field. "Help me carry Erik over to his horse."

They laid Erik next to Arthfael just as the sun peeked out from behind the clouds, and the blood-streaked hair on the golden stallion shimmered in the setting sun.

Tavis unpinned the Mandarin Spessartite Garnet brooch from the inside of Erik's trousers.

"Is that the brooch Erik promised to give Elliott once he had twelve brooches to open the door?"

Tavis nodded. "Rare and extremely beautiful. I don't know where it came from, and we won't know its secrets until we can go to the other side."

"Who will wear it now?"

"I don't know." Tavis glanced at Ferdiad, grazing on the tall prairie grass. "Tell Austin to take my horse back to Colorado and make sure he's ridden daily."

"I'll tell him. Anything else?"

"Nope, that's it." Tavis gave Remy a back-thumping man hug.

"Aren't you going to tell Austin and Ensley goodbye?"

Tavis glanced over at Austin and Ensley. "They'll ask too many questions, which will only delay my departure. It's hard enough to leave, knowing it could be a while before I return. And remember, do not get off the train."

"Doan stay away too long." Remy stepped away from Tavis, squeezed his eyes shut for a moment, and then looked at Tavis again. "I'll miss ya, bro."

Time for Tavis to disappear before the tears stinging his eyelids spilled over. He stretched out over Erik and Arthfael, opened the brooch, recited the chant, and disappeared into the fog. When it evaporated, he was once again in Erik's smoky longhouse, listening to the chatter of the women who lived there.

Then silence, followed by shrieks, and a young woman whose voice he knew intimately shouted, "Tavis has come home!"

His heart warmed at the sound of Astrid's voice—his beautiful, beloved wife.

48

The Badlands (1885)—Ensley

ENSLEY WOKE UP in the dark, feeling as if she'd swallowed an entire pharmacy while fighting Leif Erikson for control of the Americas. Her head was about to explode, she was queasy, and tremors shuddered through her body and down her arms. The muscles were so sore she could barely lift her hands.

Luckily, she managed to roll over before she vomited—again and again—until she completely emptied her stomach. At the same time, vivid images of the Viking mauled by the grizzly scrolled through her mind like ghastly hallucinations.

She crawled to a sitting position, holding her head and groaning, "What the hell happened to me?"

Long, muscular arms covered in wool flannel wrapped her in a warm embrace, and a man crooned an Irish lullaby in the smoothest tenor she ever heard—*Austin.*

"Too-ra-loo-ra-loo-ral / Too-ra-loo-ra-li / Too-ra-loo-ra-loo-ral / Hush now, don't you cry…"

She leaned back against him, quieted by his soothing voice, and took the canteen he offered. She swished the water in her mouth, then spit it out, and repeated the swish-spit, again and again.

"This water tastes funny. You sure it's safe?"

"It's a Remy Benoit special blend of filtered water mixed with electrolyte powder guaranteed to rehydrate you."

She took several long drinks and capped the canteen while he pulled her bedroll away from the vomit. "You killed the bear." Her voice sounded gruff and flat as if she'd strained her vocal cords. Maybe she screamed during the attack. She couldn't remember much after he shot the grizzly.

"I got lucky," he said.

Austin eased her down onto the bedroll, and she didn't resist. Sitting up made her dizzy. She lay flat and stared at the night sky, trying to judge the hour by the stars, a skill she learned as a kid. By finding the Big Dipper and the North Star, she could create a mental twenty-four-hour clock. But her head hurt too much to think it through right now. And hell, it didn't matter anyway. It could be midnight or four in the morning. The time wouldn't change what happened to Erik and Tesoro.

Their loss folded into all the other losses in her life and quadrupled her emotional pain. Losing someone she loved or cared for deeply sucked the energy out of her, numbed her, and wreaked havoc with her desires and purpose, forcing her to reevaluate everything that once mattered.

What did she believe? What did she want? What did she need?

She thought she'd answered those questions when she sold the ranch. But she'd only postponed them, and now nothing was the same, and she was right back where she started. No, forget that. She was in minus territory.

She rolled onto her side and, in the moonlight, studied Austin's chiseled profile. "How'd you end up here in just the nick of time?"

"Got lucky on that one, too."

"It wasn't luck. It was something else, but I don't know what to call it."

He chuckled softly. "If you don't know the proper word, just use fuck. As someone told me recently, it's a very versatile word."

She wanted to elbow him in the side, but her arm wouldn't cooperate. "Don't tease me. My head hurts too much."

"Remy has drugs for that. I'll go get you something to relieve the pain."

He put his hat on and made a move to stand, but she held him back. "It can wait. And besides, the way I feel, it's obvious he's already drugged me. So what's the deal? How'd you get to the right place at the right time?"

"Are you complaining?"

"Hell, no. It's just such a coincidence, that's all."

"Not really. I'd been following that bear all day and lost him earlier. Shot an elk, then picked his tracks up again late in the afternoon. I'd been trailing him just about an hour when I got to the clearing."

"I think someone summoned you."

"Like who?"

"Whom?" She couldn't see his eyes, but she imagined him rolling them when she inadvertently corrected his grammar.

He tensed against her and cleared his throat. "By whom was I summoned, the grammar police?"

"I'm not *that* bad." She knew she was, but hey, she was an editor—a fired one, but still an editor.

"Yes, you are, and Aunt Sophia is just as picky. It's annoying as hell."

"She's the artist, right?"

"She's married to Pete Parrino, my uncles' best friend, and JL's former partner at the NYPD."

"I've met them both. JC took me to an art exhibit featuring paintings of the Battle of New Orleans. The paintings of the battle scenes, Andrew Jackson, and Jean Lafitte were so realistic you could imagine the artist painting while watching the battle."

"She was, along with her husband, and my uncle Rick and his wife, Penny. It was hell on all of them, and Rick and Penny still have PTSD, but it's manageable."

"That sucks. Did the accident give you PTSD?"

"No, I already suffered from it. I was kidnapped by a Mexican cartel when I was seventeen."

She gasped. "Damn. Were you hurt?"

"No, just scared the piss out of me. The whole family got involved. It was a mess. I'll tell you about it another time."

"The MacKlenna Clan could produce a TV series or movies based on all the family adventures and become a best-selling franchise."

"Except that Elliott has locked up the brooches and all the secrets in a vault that has more security than the gold at the Fed Building in New York City. The family is flying under the radar, not on top of it."

"Yeah, well, I guess you're right. A movie would blow the clan's cover. But a book or movie script could explain some details that are hard to understand."

"Like what?"

"I don't know. Maybe the brooch gods. That's who I believe summoned you to the clearing just in time to kill the bear."

"Oh, them." Sarcasm saturated his comment. "I'm not sure they exist, and if they do, they have no sense of humor. My family might agree with you, though. They wouldn't agree with me and haven't for a while."

"Is that what you want, for people to always agree with you?"

"No, not always. Just when it comes to my health. I can make my own decisions, but they treat me like I'm still a kid."

"You should discuss it with your family instead of ignoring them. When you talk to people who have opposite viewpoints, it forces you to grow and define your own."

"That sounds like a line in a self-help book."

"No, I paraphrased a quote from a famous liberal jurist who was best friends with a conservative one."

"I don't need to grow or define my views. I've been making my own decisions since I went to California to finish high school. And I don't appreciate my family jumping in now and trying to run my life. It's not going to work, and it'll only widen the breach between us."

"They're your family, Austin, and you're lucky to have them. But look at it this way. Playing basketball has given you a skill, like a plumber, nurse, teacher, coach. But to be a true professional, you have to do something outside yourself, something that makes life better for people less fortunate."

He mumbled, "I do."

"What?"

"I don't publicize it, and if this gets out, I'll know who blabbed."

"A secret?" She cheered up at that, remembering how her dad always told her what he planned to give her mother on their wedding anniversary. "I love secrets, and I never blab. What is it?"

He didn't say anything for a frustrating minute or two or five, and she resisted the urge to nudge him as a reminder that she was still there. Besides, he was stroking her arms, so he knew she hadn't gone anywhere. And as good as his hands felt, she wasn't likely to get up and run away.

Finally, his hands stilled, and he broke the silence. "Do you remember when I was talking about Tavis's horse, and I mentioned that Elliott buys former racehorses and transitions them into second careers? Well, when I find one that's gentle enough for my foundation, I purchase the horse. Then with the help of Special Olympics and therapeutic riding centers, I match the horse with a challenged young adult and teach him or her to ride at an indoor arena I bought in Denver. You wouldn't believe what it does for their self-esteem.

"I've also retrained twice as many Thoroughbreds since I got hurt. I couldn't have gotten through this past year without these remarkable young men and women. They see me struggling just like them, and they believe if I can do it, they can, too. I guess you could say we inspire each other."

"Wow! I didn't expect that." Her opinion of him did an instant three-sixty, or rather a one-eighty. He'd already made it halfway by killing the bear. "You should tell your family."

"Not a chance. They'd butt in. Elliott would want to give me his professional opinion of the horses I buy, and Kevin would want to give me financial advice. I don't want any of it. I'm keeping it completely separate from the family's businesses."

"You should tell your family, so they won't worry so much."

He started stroking her arms again. "How do you know they do?"

"Remy told me."

"He has a big mouth. But here's the thing. If I told the family, the press would find out and make a big deal of it. The young riders don't need the press interfering in their lives. It's hard enough for them without reporters asking them about me."

"Maybe they'd leave you alone. The press, I mean."

"Not likely. Sports announcers and commentators are always talking about my comeback. I want to punch them all out. I might never be the caliber of player I was, even if I have more surgeries. It just might not be in the cards. This trip has forced me to come face-to-face with that realization.

"The guys here at the roundup don't know I was a superstar and wouldn't care if they did. They just know I'm different, but I can do the work just like them. I lost count of the number of cowboys I worked with over the past couple of days, just giving them pointers about riding broncs, especially Mr. Roosevelt. I'm not just a one-trick pony to them."

"I figured that out when you were yelling at me."

"When was I yelling at you?"

"When I was riding that green horse."

"I had to yell, or you wouldn't have heard me."

"You were distracting me, but later I was impressed that you knew so much."

If she'd known he wasn't a one-trick pony when she read his manuscript, would it have made a difference? It might have.

Damn him. He should have included his business venture in the manuscript, and because he hadn't, it said a lot about him. Bottom line: she'd been the wrong person to read his work since she had little respect for men in his profession. She owed him an apology, but now wasn't the right time to confess.

"You know, if you get bored and are looking around for another side venture, you can sign up to rescue damsels in distress. Without you, I'd be dead. Just a few seconds, and it wouldn't have mattered."

He took her hand and kissed the back of it, then snugged it between his large hands.

The intimate touch made her muscles tighten in exquisite anticipation. "That's a smooth move, O'Grady."

He chuckled. "My uncles are all badass warriors, but when it comes to their women, they're marshmallows, very romantic, and love to sing and dance. At one time or another, I've seen all of them make that move, even Elliott. I've never done it before. It just seemed like the natural thing to do. And just for your information, it would have mattered to me if I'd arrived five minutes later. I'm just sorry I wasn't there in time for Erik and Tesoro."

"Yeah, me too." The pounding in her head had subsided, but now, thinking of how different the outcome would have been if Austin had arrived earlier caused a louder timpani roll to move wavelike from the front of her skull to the back. But she didn't want any more drugs in her system that would mask the gut-wrenching hurt.

"I guess you buried them last night. I'd like to go to the graves as soon as its daylight."

Austin released her hand and went back to stroking her arms. He was so reliable, so safe, that she relaxed till even her bones seemed to turn to putty. He tilted his face down to hers, and while the hat brim cast a deep shadow in the moonlight, she could still see his expression. Warm and waiting.

It was one of those rare moments when she knew in her heart, in her brain, in every part of her being that if she kissed him, it could have life-altering consequences. She lowered her head, unwilling to take the risk. It was easier to be a coward than a trailblazer.

No, that's not it. I'm not a coward. I'm a liar. I can't kiss him until he knows who I am and what I did to his soul-searching manuscript.

"There aren't any graves," Austin said.

Her head jerked up. "Why not?"

"Tavis took them back to Jarlshof. Erik is like a king or chief of his village and head of the Council. He deserved a proper Viking funeral."

"I wish I'd known. I would have gone."

"To the twelfth century? Not a good idea. You might have been in danger, especially without Erik there to protect you. I can't imagine what all those Vikings would do if they saw such a beautiful woman."

Her cheeks flamed, and she was glad Austin couldn't see her blush in the darkness. He'd gone from calling her a baby doll to a beautiful woman. That was quite an upgrade.

"Doesn't a traditional Viking funeral involve putting the king on his ship and setting it afire?"

"Eventually, but there are some disgusting things that happen before then. And don't ask me what, because I'll never repeat it. My stomach curdled when Remy told me."

She sat up, and her alarm antenna went *bong!* "Tavis could be in grave danger, then. He shouldn't have gone by himself. If he doesn't come back right away, we should go after him. How long has he been gone?"

Austin tapped the light on his wristwatch, shielding it so no one could see what he was doing. "It's four thirty. Almost twelve hours. He gave the amethyst brooch to Remy and said someone on the Council would bring him back, but he didn't want us to wait here for him."

She almost smacked her forehead when she remembered the purpose of his trip to Medora. "I completely forgot. Did he bring back a telegram from JC?"

"There was one waiting for you at the depot. JC sent it from Chicago and said he ordered clothes for you and had everything shipped to Medora."

"Wow! That's sweet." Thinking of those clean clothes reminded her of how filthy she was. She groped in her duffle bag for a cleaning cloth and used it to wash her face, then tried to bush her tangled hair. "What's in my hair?"

Austin picked through the tangles. "Dried blood. I tried to wash it off your face and hands, but I couldn't get it out of your hair. You kept swatting my hand away."

If she could leave the mats alone, she would. But wearing Erik and Tesoro's blood seemed a rather ghoulish way to remember a man and a horse, both too extraordinary ever to forget.

"Here, let me try again. You've got a lot of tangled pieces." He worked through the matted hair using his fingers.

He was much gentler than her mom used to be when trying to get the mud out of Ensley's hair. "What are you doing?"

"Just following the knots with my fingers and unraveling them. It's just like a horse's mane, except prettier."

"Well, thanks…I guess." She pulled a section of hair over her shoulder and worked through several tangles while Austin poked at a thick tuft on the back of her head.

"Are we still meeting JC in Cleveland?"

"Tavis sent a telegram to Elliott at MacKlenna Farm, and Elliott sent one back. He said he and Meredith are taking JC home, and he ordered us to go directly to the farm."

She stilled her hand, recalling JC's concerns about how pissed his parents were going to be. But he wouldn't have returned with them willingly, not without sending her another telegram.

"This sounds fishy. JC wouldn't have left with his dad. Not willingly, anyway. So what happened, and why do we have to go to the farm?"

"Kit and Cullen stayed behind, and we're to bring them home."

"I don't like the way this sounds. JC mentioned that something happened to him in Asia recently, and he couldn't tell his dad and didn't want to lie to him."

"So maybe when JC got to the farm, he told Elliott, and they decided they better go home and take care of business."

"Maybe, but he would have told me."

"Not necessarily. Elliott could have told JC he would send the telegram."

"I don't know. I don't like it. Something's wrong. I can feel it in my bones."

"How about we recover from yesterday's trauma before we waste time imagining another one? We'll find out as soon as we get to the farm."

"Okay, I'll try. But do we have to leave right away? I'd like a couple more days with TR if that's possible."

"We gotta go, Ens. Tavis said not to wait."

"Did he say why?"

"If he did, Remy didn't mention it."

"I'll ask him later." She snuggled into Austin's embrace, not wanting to move but knowing she had to. Norman would be preparing breakfast, all the cowboys would be waking up, and she didn't want anyone to find her in a compromising position. TR would be very disappointed in her. Reluctantly, she cranked herself up to her feet and shivered in the early morning chill.

Austin popped up and stood behind her, wrapping her in his embrace again. "You're shivering."

"My body chemistry is all messed up."

She'd always thought that women who dated big, tall guys must have some kind of complex, but standing in Austin's embrace was like having outside heaters blowing hot air all around her. In the summer heat, it might not be as welcoming, but hell, it sure was right now.

She rested her head back on his chest. "I have to buy another horse from TR."

"Tavis left his for you."

"Didn't he need one where he was going?"

"Guess not. I was busy with you, and Remy hasn't told me everything Tavis said."

"Thank you for taking care of me. I was so out of it. If we're going to leave today, I'd better tell TR goodbye before he rides out this morning." She sighed and relaxed, letting Austin support her. "It sucks, but I can't complain. I've had weeks with him, hours of conversations, and heard stories I've never read about before."

She stepped away from Austin, but as soon as she did, her head started swimming, and she swayed. Austin caught her before she fell, sweeping her up into his arms.

She put her hand to her forehead. "What'd Remy give me? I feel like I've spent a week stoned out of my mind."

"I'm surprised you know what that feels like."

She tilted her head up. "Why are you surprised?"

"Because you're JC's friend, and he's Mr. Goody Two-Shoes. He's never done anything he wasn't supposed to do, except for the time he ran away and got lost in a cave."

"I heard about that. The experience traumatized JC, and I don't think he's ever recovered from it. And I don't know if I'll recover from what happened here. I may never recover my usual *joie de vivre*."

"There's nothing simplistic and relaxing about you."

Damn. He surprised her again. She expected him to ask what *joie de vivre* meant. But no, not Austin. He spoke French. "Is French the only foreign language you speak?"

"I know a little bit of Italian and Spanish, too. I spent a summer playing basketball in France and picked up a few words. And Remy speaks Spanish and Sophia speaks Italian and French. And I have an aunt and uncle who are polyglots. So it's common to hear foreign languages spoken at the dinner table. I think I know cuss words in a dozen different languages."

"So if I hear you speaking a foreign language, I can assume you're cussing."

"Maybe." He grinned. "But back to you and your lack of *joie de vivre*. You're used to speeding through life at ninety miles an hour, regardless of what you're doing. That's why you feel thick-headed right now. You don't know what it's like to slow down. And," he said in a lowered voice, "Remy gave you morphine."

"What? Why the hell did he do that? I wasn't in physical pain."

"There was blood everywhere, and Remy didn't know what kind of injuries you had. He'd read a study that giving a person morphine after a trauma, even when they don't have a serious injury, would decrease post-traumatic stress."

"Well, I've never wanted to be a test case, but—"

Sticks and leaves crunched nearby, and Ensley jerked around to look in that direction. Her heart thudded hard and fast while fear clogged her throat.

A bear!

"Mrs. Fraser. Is that you?"

No. Not a bear. It was TR. She took a deep breath, but it took a few moments longer before the wild rhythm of her heart steadied once again.

"You better put me down."

"Are you sure?"

"Yeah. TR won't like it."

Austin set her down close to a tree so she could use it for support.

"Yes, Teddy. Austin's with me." TR appeared in the moonlight. "He's been telling me what happened after he killed the bear. I don't remember much."

"Bully! Mr. O'Grady is not only the best horseman but the best hunter I've ever met. He skinned that grizzly as if he did it every day and even gifted me the head."

The thought of the bear's head roiled her stomach, and she

leaned against the tree. Austin made a move toward her but stopped himself and didn't try to pick her up again.

"The head? How nice." TR's opinion mattered to her, and she was relieved and satisfied that he not only thought so highly of Austin, but his opinion also affirmed what she'd been thinking.

"Mr. Benoit said you weren't injured but that you were in shock from the attack. I'm sorry about your horse and the warrior who fought the bear. Horrible. Just horrible."

"Their deaths are a great loss." She didn't want to talk about it again, so she changed the subject. "Did Remy tell you about the telegram from James Cullen?"

"He said your husband requested you leave immediately for the farm in Kentucky. As your protector, I encourage you to do that."

"We have so many more books left to discuss. I'm not ready," she said.

"Ensley, you have been a charming guest, but you must go. If you give me your New York City address, I will send you and your husband a dinner invitation."

Oh, God. How was she getting out of this?

"They might not be back for some time," Austin said.

Thanks, Austin.

"I'll write to you as soon as we get back, and we can plan an evening."

"Bully. I'll look forward to it. And I hope you'll let me read your manuscript when it's finished."

Austin chuckled. "She couldn't handle a critical critique. You'll have to go easy on her."

"That's not true at all," Ensley said, ignoring Austin. "I'll take all critiques seriously." She didn't dare look at him for fear that he'd finally linked his manuscript's rejection with her. If he wanted to talk about it, she would later, but damn, she wasn't about to bring it up in front of TR.

"Besides," she said, "you might not like my writing style. Remember, you don't read Jane Austen."

"Even if you write like Miss Austen, I will force myself to read it."

"For you, that's saying a lot. But you're safe. Our styles are completely different."

TR laughed and offered his arm. "Come along. We'll eat breakfast, and then I'll see you off with a promise to dine together as soon as you return."

An hour later, they'd saddled their horses and strapped on their bedrolls while TR rushed off to find Sewall and Dow to say their goodbyes. Ensley found Norman packing biscuits and cans of fruit into a burlap bag.

"For you. O'Grady hunts, so now ya'll will have plenty to eat."

"That's so thoughtful." She handed him her pouch of gold nuggets. "I want you to have this. I won't need it where I'm going."

Norman bounced the pouch in his palm, and the nuggets rattled against each other. He untied the thong and emptied the contents on his palm. He whistled. "Miss Ensley, it's too much. I hardly did anythin'."

"It's a small stake, so you can go back to Texas, buy a tavern, find a good woman, and have lots of babies."

"I dunno," he said, grinning. "A tavern *and* a family…that's a lotta work."

"If anyone can make a success of it, you can. Now tell me where you'll go, and I might look you up someday." Unless she followed TR to San Antonio, where his Rough Riders trained before going to San Juan, she'd never see Norman again.

He returned the nuggets to the pouch and tucked the pouch into his vest pocket. "Mebbe back home to San Antonio."

Damn. Did she just read Norman's mind, or was this another coincidence? She kissed his whiskered cheek. "Be safe, Norman. And thank you for everything, especially all the coffee."

"Thank you," he said, patting his pocket where he'd stashed the pouch. "I'd do anythin' for ya, Miss Ensley. Be careful, now."

TR returned with Sewall and Dow. "We've come to say goodbye, Miss Ensley. Sure has been nice knowing ya."

"Thanks, Bill, and you too, Wilmot. I appreciate you putting up with me."

"It was nothin' Miss Ensley," Dow said. "Hope you come back next year."

"If I can, I will, and please tell your wife and daughter, Bill, that it was a pleasure to meet them."

Sewall and Dow tipped their hats and left, and TR said to Ensley, "Will you walk with me?"

He took her arm and threaded it through his, and they set out in a direction leading away from the clearing where the battle took place. Instead, they approached the river by way of a path farther north.

"I will miss our book discussions," he said, "and I will also miss your company. I have to admit I didn't fully believe you when you said you could handle yourself on a cattle drive. But you more than proved me wrong. It's been a pleasure having you here. I'm sorry we won't be traveling home together."

"I am, too." They walked for several minutes without speaking. Then she broke the silence. "Teddy, I think you should resume your social life when you return. You're a young man, and you'll find love again."

"I do not agree, Ensley."

"Well," she teased. "With an attitude like that, maybe you won't. But look, you have a long life ahead of you, and you're going to do amazing things."

He stopped and faced her, and she dropped her arm. "You said something similar before. Can you foretell the future?"

She wanted to hug him out of both amusement and affection. "Are you just now figuring that out?"

He chuckled. "Then tell me. Will I marry again?"

"Hmm." She closed her eyes for just a moment. "Since I don't have my crystal ball, the future isn't as clear, but I see you with a woman who is an excellent judge of character."

He belted out a laugh. "Then why would she marry me?"

"Because"—she tapped her forehead as if waiting for more ideas to materialize—"she has loved you for years and will be a reliable partner in all your affairs."

"Loved me for years. I can't imagine—" He quieted and gazed out over the cottonwoods toward the river. "There is one woman, but…"

"No buts. When I see you again, I want to meet her." She retook his arm and turned back the way they'd come. "Austin and Remy are probably getting restless, and we have a long way to ride today. I should go."

"I don't want to lose contact with you. What is the name of your husband's family in Kentucky?"

"MacKlenna, and the farm is in Lexington."

"If I do not hear from you by the end of the year, I will write to Mr. MacKlenna."

She rubbed a finger beneath her nose and tried to think of a response that would make sense if he did write to her and she didn't write back. "If we decide to travel before we return to New York, I'll ask Mr. MacKlenna to reply to your correspondence." She'd have to tell JC's relatives that if TR contacted them, they should tell TR that she and JC went to Europe or California for an extended visit.

They arrived back at the campsite to find Remy and Austin hanging out at the chuckwagon, drinking coffee with Norman.

Austin looked her way. "Are you ready?"

"I guess so." But damn, she hated this. She would never see TR again, and there was still so much she wanted to know.

She and TR stood there awkwardly until she just threw her arms around his neck and hugged him. It took him a moment to hug her back, and they just kind of sighed into each other.

"I don't think this is at all proper," he said.

"I don't care. Do you?"

He separated from her. "No, but your husband would."

"No, he wouldn't. Where we come from, friends give friends hugs when they meet, when they depart, and sometimes just for the heck of it."

"You are too thin, Mrs. Fraser. Be sure your husband's relatives feed you plates of fried chicken, dumplings, cornbread, biscuits, and gravy."

"Cornbread *and* biscuits? Do you want me to get fat?"

"No one would notice a few pounds," TR said.

"I'll keep that in mind." She gathered up Ferdiad's reins.

Austin stepped over to her side. "I'll give you a leg up." He reached for her bent leg and gave her a boost, then adjusted the stirrups. "They hit right at your ankle. How do they feel?"

"Good. Thanks."

TR smiled up at her. "Be careful. And write when you can."

She leaned out of the saddle and kissed his cheek. "I'll never forget you, Teddy. Thanks for giving me a chance. We'll dine in New York City soon. Until then, work on your manuscript, socialize with friends, travel, and enjoy your daughter."

He removed his glasses and cleaned them with his handkerchief. "I will."

She nudged Ferdiad forward but wanted to leave TR with a lasting impression. Using her legs and hands, she signaled the horse to rear. As the stallion pawed the air, she waved her hat. "Every beginning comes from another beginning's end. Farewell, my friends."

Ferdiad's front feet hit the ground, and he took off at a gallop. Ensley let him run full out while tears streamed down her face. Finally, he slowed to a trot, and Remy and Austin caught up with her.

"The lady knows how to make a fuckin' exit. Impressive," Remy said. "I'd be playin' a drum roll if I had my sticks."

"That was straight out of the movies," Austin said, grinning.

She wiped the back of her hand across her face. "I just wanted it to be memorable. I don't want TR to forget me. I thought that image would stick in his mind for a while. I know it's selfish, but being with him has been the highlight of my life."

Austin pulled up his horse, and so did she. He used his thumb and rubbed it across her cheekbones rhythmically as he wiped away the remainder of her tears. "Then, Ensley Williams, it's time for you to have more memorable experiences and create another highlight of your life."

"Do you think that's possible?"

"I do. So hang on for the ride."

There was a wistfulness in his voice, a hint that maybe he was afraid he'd changed something in their relationship—if that's what they had—with his unexpected declaration.

They nudged their horses and joined Remy to ride off toward Medora and the train to take them home.

And in the back of Ensley's mind, she knew the ride would be on a bronc, not on a gentle mare.

She still had a confession to make.

49

The Train (1885)—Austin

BY THE TIME they reached Medora late the next afternoon, Ensley was nodding off in the saddle. If Austin didn't find a place for her to sleep in the next few minutes, she'd fall off her horse and land on the muddy ground. Even if he had to buy a house in Medora to use just for the night, he would find her an un-infested bed and a clean bathtub.

Watching her head bob when she jerked awake, he marveled at the small bundle of flesh and bones and muscles that made her a warrior woman. She was strong in all the right places. Soft in all the important places. And hotter than hell in all the desirable places. And he hadn't been this hot for a woman since...well...he couldn't remember when.

Ensley was different, and his interest in her surprised the hell out of him. She wasn't his type. He went for model-gorgeous women with big boobs and full lips, and Ensley was more like some of his aunts—small and slight but muscular, intelligent, beautiful, coura-geous, and funny. The type of woman you married. Not the kind you screwed for a few weeks and then moved on.

Remy caught him staring at her yesterday and gave him a look that said, "Watch your ass, man." And he knew what Remy meant. She was a five-foot-two ballbuster who could ride a bronc and wouldn't put up with any of his shit.

When she was in his arms the morning after the fight with the bear, he'd been afraid she'd notice his hard-on and move away from him, but she never did. He didn't know what that meant and damned if he'd ask Remy. Maybe she didn't notice, but he wasn't a small guy. How could she not?

Hell, she'd almost been killed by a bear, and then Remy drugged her, so his wood was probably the last thing she would have noticed.

He tried to redirect his man-brain to focus on protecting her, not on screwing her. But watching her ass move in the saddle just fed his fantasies further. His uncles often said he learned his raunchy, free-wheeling attitudes about women and sex from Uncle Rick, and maybe he did, or at least the way Rick was before he settled down with Penny. Austin never thought Rick would ever be satisfied with just one woman, but man, he was head over heels in love and about to have two more kids.

"Hey, asshole!" Remy shouted, pointing at his own eyes with two fingers, telling Austin to look at him, not at her ass. "We should go to the depot first and check the train schedule."

Austin studied the three hundred feet of the trestle that crossed the river into town. "Is that the only way across?"

"Yeah, it's safe enough…as long as a train doesn't come along," Ensley said.

Remy pulled up his horse and shaded his eyes with his hand. "It could get tight up there if one comes barreling along, but it's easy to see a quarter-mile in both directions, so we'd have enough time to get the hell out of there."

"And let's remember to ask about your packages from JC when we get to the depot," Austin said.

"Good idea. I want a bath, a hot meal not cooked over a camp-fire, and a clean bed," Ensley replied. "Clean clothes would be a cherry on top."

Austin winked. "If I can make it happen, baby doll, I will."

She rolled her eyes. "What have I told you about calling me that?"

He led the way onto the bridge, and they trooped across in single file. "That it offends you."

"Then why do it?"

"Because you're so cute when you get pissed."

"So, if I make ugly faces and growl at you, you'll stop?"

He looked over his shoulder, grinning. "Probably not, but you could try."

"What happened to the grouch I met a few days ago? You weren't just mean. You were a bastard. Now you're just irritating."

Remy chuckled. "Watch out, Ensley. He's trying to impress you."

"Well," she grumbled, "it's not working."

They reached the other side of the bridge and rode into town. Ensley yawned, pointing to a rough-board shanty next to the railroad track. "That's the depot. The first time I saw the agent, I thought his red nose made him look like he spent more time at Big-Mouthed Bob's Bug-Juice Dispensary than working here."

Remy laughed. "Bob's Bug-Juice?"

"Big-Mouthed Bob…the town saloon. And the hotel is over there. Food's decent, but I can't say much for the cleanliness."

"What? That would bother you after washing up in the river every day?"

"Not days, weeks. I know what to expect on the trail, but a railroad town is different. I expect an upgrade from sleeping outside on the ground."

Austin pulled up in front of the depot, dismounted, and stepped up on the platform.

A man with a mustache and a red nose opened a dirty window. "Can I help ya?"

"When's the next train coming through heading east?" Austin asked.

"Should arrive 'bout nine, but could be later." He shrugged. "Ya never know. All three of ya want tickets?"

"Yeah," Austin said.

Ensley dismounted and stepped up on the platform. "Are you holding packages for Ensley Wi…Fraser? If so, I'll take them off your hands."

The agent scratched his head. "I put 'em on the private car like I was told."

Austin tensed, and for the first time, the possibility of danger smacked him in the face. How could anyone know they were coming? He was steps away from his gun, not close enough. He glanced over his shoulder at Remy, and Remy immediately reached for his rifle.

"Private car? I think you're mistaken," Austin said.

"That Stuart fella chartered the private car and said to put the packages on it when the car arrived. That's what I did."

Austin shook off the tension and gave the agent a lopsided grin. "You're a good man. So where's this car?"

He pointed toward the siding yard. "Right there."

"Tavis leased a private car?" Ensley asked. "How thoughtful."

"He didn't do it for Austin or me," Remy said. "If you weren't with us, we'd be lucky to have a stall in a cattle car."

She swung around. "Did you know?"

Remy shook his head. "Fuck, no. It wasn't like he had time to give me an itinerary."

"What about our horses?" she asked.

"The train from Billings is bringin' the stock car. The carriage came in from Chicago this morning," the agent said. "The cook and steward are at the hotel. I'll go tell 'em you arrived."

"A cook?" Ensley asked. "Seriously?"

"Yes, ma'am. See? This here advertisement said the leased car 'comes with iceboxes containing comestibles for the most exacting palate for a full week.' Not sure exactly what it means, but sure sounds fancy."

"Shit! Tavis must have the hots for you, Ensley." Remy shot an eyebrow up at Austin.

Austin wanted to knock Remy off his horse. Besides, he doubted it was true. Tavis left shortly after meeting her and only returned in time to take the Viking home. He hadn't spent any time with Ensley, and Austin had never seen Tavis hit on a woman before. He spent time with Emily, but they seemed more like friends than lovers.

Remy dismounted and joined them on the platform. "Do we have the carriage all the way to Kentucky or do we get off in Chicago?"

"I believe it goes through to Kentucky, but lemme check. I wasn't the agent who leased the car." He went inside, and after a few minutes returned with an open journal. "Says here, Mr. Stuart leased the car to your final destination. No return trip. Just one-way."

Ensley grinned. "Sounds like a great way to travel. So can I get on the carriage now to get some clean clothes?"

The agent shrugged. "Don't matter to me when ya board. Suit yourself. I'll go tell your staff."

"What about a key?" Austin asked.

"Ain't locked. Jes' open the door. But I tell ya, it's pretty fancy. Ya might wanna wash off the trail dust afore ya go inside."

Austin glanced down at his boots.

"The livery stable is down the street," Ensley said. "Let's board the horses until the stock car gets here, and we can wash off the worst of the dirt while we're there."

"Which way?" Austin asked.

"Down the street on the right. Miz Fraser's been here afore wit' that big gold horse. She knows whar it's at."

Austin glanced at Ensley, and it nearly broke his heart to see tears gathering on her lashes. When he returned home, he would scour the planet until he found her another Akhal-Teke.

He took her elbow and gently turned her away from the agent. "Let's go. The sooner we get to the train, the sooner we can get cleaned up and relax. If it's got an icebox full of food, there should also be a well-stocked liquor cabinet."

"Pour me a double and keep the whisky coming," she said.

"You can get blootered for all I care."

Remy burst out laughing. "Hey, you're Irish. 'Blootered' is Scottish."

"How the hell do you know?"

"I've heard the old men at the pub in Inverness talking about getting blootered. Where'd you hear it?"

"I've been part of the clan since I was seventeen, and except for the O'Gradys, everyone's a Scot, and they all love whisky." Austin followed Ensley and Remy down the town's main street toward the livery stable.

"I'm not a Scot," Remy said. "Ensley's not."

"Yes, I am," she said. "My mom's family came over from Scotland and settled in Selkirk in the northeastern part of the state."

"My bad," Remy said. "That makes sense since all the lost heroines have had Scottish ties."

"So that's what I was? A lost heroine? At least you didn't call me a helpless one."

"There's nothing about you, Warrioress Williams, that screams 'helpless.' Do you remember how many times you hacked at that bear? A dozen at least."

She grimaced, and Austin wanted to punch Remy for mentioning the attack. He watched her closely, unsure how she'd react, and he readied himself to pick her up instantly and carry her straight to the carriage if she started crying, screaming, or throwing something. Thankfully, she wasn't holding anything she could throw. He'd seen women do all three during times of emotional distress. And to be honest, he'd done all that and more himself.

Her shoulders slumped, and she knotted her hands but otherwise held her shit together. She might not have PTSD, but nothing could hide grief and loss. He should know.

She grabbed Remy's arm, forcing him to stop. "I just remembered the ax. Where is it? Erik wanted me to keep it."

"I have it," Remy said. "It's rolled up in my bedroll. I didn't think you'd want to see it right now."

She let go of Remy and continued walking. "I don't, but one day I will. Thanks for holding on to it."

As Austin walked down the muddy street, listening to constant hammering, thinking back to Rick and Connor's adventure to Leadville and Denver in 1878. He compared what he heard about those towns to this one, and there wasn't much to compare. To him, Medora was a lonely place surrounded by barren hills.

Not at all like Colorado. Of all the places he'd lived, Colorado was his favorite. He loved the ranch and wanted to buy it but doubted Elliott would sell it to him. And the way Austin had behaved over the past year, he couldn't blame him.

"This is a one-street town, for sure. Not much here," Remy said.

"It doesn't look like much," Ensley said, "but right now, it's one of the most prosperous and rapidly growing towns along the Northern Pacific line, full of grand dreams and sordid gunfights. TR said Medora was a place where pleasure and vice were synonymous. New buildings are going up as fast as carpenters can do the work, and there's hope it might be the state capitol."

"The capitol's Bismarck, right?" Austin asked.

"Right. Although early on, Medora thought they'd get it. It didn't work out. But just look around. It's the jewel of the Badlands and has all the important businesses," she said, pointing from one to the other. "A hotel, saloon, blacksmith, slaughterhouse, a twenty-six-room chateau on a hill, and a newspaper office—the *Bad Lands Cow Boy*. When I thought I was going to be stuck here, before JC showed up, I planned to apply for a job at the newspaper."

"No church?" Austin asked.

"Nineteenth-century cowboys are highly irreligious and irreverent. They believe Sunday stops at the Missouri River and look at religion as an institution for old women and weaklings. But civilization is coming, and everything will change. The new community won't get along with the half-tamed open-range cowboys. The sad thing is that the town will collapse by 1887. In our time, most of the people who live here work for the Theodore Roosevelt National Park."

"I'm glad we're only staying a few hours," Remy said, leading the way inside the stable.

While Remy made arrangements for the horses, Austin and Ensley carried their gear out back, washed the mud off their boots, and brushed trail dust off each other.

"I'm throwing these clothes away. Never in my life did I even imagine I'd wear the same outfit for several weeks straight."

"I'm not sure even the homeless would accept your clothes."

"Ah!" She slapped her chest. "I'm hurt. I can't believe you said that."

When he laughed, she swiped her hand through the trough water and splashed him, which he didn't mind at all. He considered spraying her back, but the temperature was dropping, and from what he could feel of her the other morning, she had very little body fat to keep her warm. But on the other hand, if she got chilled, he could be a hero and warm her up.

"I'll get even. Just wait." He used his sleeve to wipe drops of water off his face. "I grew up in a house full of guys, and we were constantly fighting. Drove Pops crazy. No one would get away with what you just did. If it was warmer, I'd toss you in the trough, but I don't want you to freeze. You get a break this time, but I wouldn't try it again."

He watched her eyes and could see the mischief there. She wanted to splash him again and was weighing the odds of getting dunked.

"If it was summer, I'd splash you again."

"Listen, when we get out of here, why don't we go to the beach, and you can splash me all you want?"

"Sounds like fun. But I've got some stuff to work on when I get home. It might take a while."

Remy came out. "Horses will be delivered to the train when it arrives. Let's go. I want to see this hotel on wheels."

"You couldn't care less," Austin said. "You just want the whisky."

"Well, that too."

"Connor leased a private car in Denver in 1878. It was a double-decker with two bedrooms up top."

"A double-decker wouldn't have as much headroom, would it?"

"Not enough. I'd still be walking hunched over."

"That's a problem I never have to worry about," she said.

Austin led them over to the carriage and up the steps to the canopied open platform. "This is perfect for a whistle-stop. Anyone interested in campaigning?"

"Hell, no. I just want the whisky," Remy said.

Austin stepped aside for Ensley and followed her inside, humming "Beautiful Dreamer."

If I can't get lucky with a sexy woman in a place like this, then I've lost my touch.

The carriage resembled a nineteenth-century drawing room, complete with mahogany-paneled walls and ceiling, deep-cushioned chairs and matching settee, blue shaded lamps, and crystal chandeliers—pretty much the way Connor described the carriage he leased in Denver. But this one had oriental rugs and a liquor cabinet.

Remy beelined it to the mahogany cabinet, opened it, and pulled out a bottle of The Glenlivet. "Fuck, yeah! I'm going to wash up, then sit down in that comfy chair and drink until I pass out. Unless anyone has any objections."

"None from me." Ensley crossed the room toward a hallway. "Let's see what else this hotel has."

Austin followed her for the tour. Next to the drawing room was a stateroom with an attached bathroom complete with a bathtub and an Italian marble sink.

Ensley shrieked. "Look! I can't believe it. Does it have hot water?"

Austin turned on the faucet and put his hand under the stream. It was hot. He cupped a small amount of water and flung it on her.

She shrieked again. "It's hot!"

"Now we're even." He didn't think he'd ever seen something as simple as hot water please a woman as much as it pleased her.

"I've washed with cold water for weeks. I may never get out of a tub full of hot water."

There also were boxes of different shapes and sizes stacked up on the floor. "Looks like you've got some work to do unwrapping all those. You want some help?"

She glanced at them. "It's like Christmas. I think JC went overboard."

"After what you've been through, he probably wanted to spoil you. I would have done the same."

She gave him a suspicious look. "Why?"

"Because...you deserve this. You've had a rough time, and you should be going home, but you can't yet. So why not spoil you?"

"I haven't done anything to deserve it, but come on. Let's check out the rest of this rolling hotel."

He didn't want to leave this room. He wanted to strip Ensley naked and wash her hair while she soaked in the tub. And whatever happened after that was up to her. And right now, she was impossible to read.

Next to her stateroom was another one but without a bathtub. "You'll have to take a bath in my room."

He waggled his eyebrows. "We could save time and water and take one together."

She put her hands on his back and pushed him down the hallway. "As big as you are, there wouldn't be any room for me."

"Oh, baby—"

She stopped, put her hands on her hips. "Don't you dare say it."

He pressed his lips together and pantomimed zipping them. "You'll never hear me say, 'baby doll' again."

"Is that a promise?"

"Probably not."

She gave his arm a knuckle punch. "I knew it."

He rubbed the spot on his arm and groaned. "You're killing me."

"You know I don't take you seriously, don't you?"

He clapped his hand over his heart. "Say it ain't so, babe."

"There you go again."

"You're so easy to tease. Come on, let's go find the refrigerator."

"I think it's called an icebox."

"Whatever. As long as it keeps shit cold."

Next to the second stateroom was a small bathroom and storage closet, and the apartment-size kitchen was on the other side. There was room for a sink, range, fridge, heater, and a small work table. And next to the kitchen was a dining room with an extension table and sideboard.

"I wonder where the staff sleeps."

"Probably in here." He crossed to one side of the dining room and ran his hand along the polished satinwood that formed the bottom of a sleeping berth. "This is a folding sleeping berth, and there's one on the other side."

"I can't believe Tavis did this. I never expected anything so grand. Although I've been to Mallory Plantation, MacKlenna Farm, and the Upper West Side house in New York City, so I should have expected it. Wherever Elliott goes, it's first-class all the way, but this is way too much."

She walked back down the corridor. "I'm going to open the boxes, find something comfortable to wear, then take a bath. You might not see me for a couple of hours. What are you going to do?"

"Clean up and pour a double. Do you want a drink to sip while you're in the bath?"

Her eyes brightened. "Hmmm. That sounds wonderful. Sure. Bring me one."

She went into her stateroom and closed the door. He waited, curious to see if she would lock the door. She didn't, and he smiled. But he wasn't dumb enough to take the unlocked door as an invitation, so he returned to the drawing room. Remy had kicked back and was reclining on the sofa, sipping from a crystal glass.

"You look out of place without a remote in your hand."

Remy twirled one of his drumsticks. "Glad I brought a book to read. No TV, no laptop. And you and Ensley are almost eye-fucking, so I'm on my own."

"Don't be crude."

Remy almost sprayed out the whisky he was drinking. "Me? You're the crude one, and it's hard to believe, but your language is worse than Rick's."

"Penny's made him clean it up. It's not so bad now, and mine's getting better."

Remy shrugged. "Whatever. So what's your game plan?"

"Wine and dine her and see where it goes."

Remy sat up and put his feet on the floor. "I finally figured you out, O'Grady. You've been fucking with the whole family. You're not on painkillers, and you're not an asshole. You were, right after the accident, but not now. You haven't bugged me for painkillers in twenty-four hours, and I think you were palming them anyway. So what's the deal?"

Austin ignored him while he poured a drink. "I know you tell Elliott everything. All I'm asking is that you don't mention the painkillers for a few days. Give me time to talk to JL and Kevin first. I owe them that much."

"What about your Dad?"

"I'll invite him out to the ranch and talk to him after I talk to Elliott."

"I hate to tell you, but if JL knows anything, Jack knows. If Jack knows, Charlotte knows. If Charlotte knows, Elliott knows. So how the hell are you planning to keep it from Elliott for more than two hours after you tell JL?"

Austin ran his fingers over his scruff, making a scratching noise. "I don't know. Ask her to keep it to herself for once."

"Impossible, but I have a question. Why'd you want everyone to think the worst of you?"

"I was mad, frustrated, and sick of all the interference. I was busting my ass to make a comeback and going cold turkey, and the pressure from the family was messing with my focus. So I cut everyone off. It was easier. In hindsight, it probably made it worse, but..." He smiled, thinking about Ensley. "If I hadn't been an ass, Pops wouldn't have insisted I come on this trip, and I would have missed getting to know Ensley."

Remy upended his glass over his mouth to catch any remaining drops before heading back to the liquor cabinet for a refill. "You're not stepping on JC's turf, are you?"

"I don't think so. They've known each other for a decade and never pursued a relationship. If Ensley has feelings for JC, she'll let me know. Short of that, I'm going for it. I might crash and burn, but I gotta do it."

Remy refilled his glass and clinked it against Austin's. "If you want me to get out of the way, just send me a signal."

"Once the train leaves the station, we have orders not to leave it. So if it works out, cover your ears."

Remy clinked his glass against Austin's again. "I doan expect a detailed report, but if there's anything you feel like sharing, I'm all ears."

"I'll either have a smile on my face, or I'll be begging for pain-killers to help me survive the rejection."

Remy slapped him on the shoulder. "Forget it. I know the truth now. You're on your own."

"Shit. I knew I shouldn't have trusted you."

"Austin," Ensley yelled. "Where's my drink?"

Austin made a fake jump shot. "Three for O'Grady." Then he poured Ensley's drink and whistled his way out of the drawing room.

Remy drummed his stick on the top of the liquor cabinet. *Ba-dum-CHING.*

50

The Train (1885)—Ensley

ENSLEY STRIPPED OUT of the clothes she'd worn for weeks and kicked them into a corner. "Ugh. Gross." She should throw them away but knew if she did, she'd just dig through the trash and salvage them. They were so dirty they could stand up on their own, but she had an emotional attachment to the clothes that she couldn't break—yet.

If she soaked them in the tub overnight, maybe the filth would wash out.

She rolled up the jeans, blouse, and underwear, tucked them inside the jacket, then tied the sleeves together, making a tight bundle of stinky clothes.

From the window, she caught a glimpse of the shining black hulk of a locomotive. It was slowly backing up to their car. She braced for the coupling, and the force pitched her onto the bed. "Well, damn." She gripped the headboard, waiting for the train to jerk forward, which wasn't nearly as bad. The conductor blew his whistle, and the train picked up speed. They were finally on their way to Kentucky.

Now she needed something to wear while she unwrapped packages.

At the foot of the bed was a lightweight blanket. She shook it out and wrapped it around her like a Turkish towel. Then she relaxed in a tall-back occasional lounge chair. It seemed like the first time she'd been able to sit down and take a deep breath in days…or weeks. Her life had been in survival mode since the day she arrived here. And except for those evenings with TR talking about books and history, this was the first time she felt completely safe.

In front of her was a lifetime's worth of Christmas presents. She'd never seen so many packages in one place at one time. There were hatboxes, shoeboxes, and a dozen or more coat-size boxes. She didn't have the energy to go through all of them, but she had to find something to wear after her bath.

The first few she opened had silk and cotton dresses in earth tones, with ruffles and high collars that would create body-hugging silhouettes with narrow shoulders and tight sleeves. Gorgeous clothes, and if she wasn't so tired, she'd try all of them on—after her bath—even the corsets, petticoats, and bustles.

She glanced at the dresses draped over the furniture and spotted a two-piece chestnut brown silk outfit with a long peplum bodice trimmed in brown and blue-striped floral brocade, pipe stand collar and cuffs, and brass buttons. If she could figure out how to put on a bustle, she'd wear that one to dinner. But what she really wanted and hadn't found so far was a pair of lounging pajamas. Did they even exist in 1885? If they did, JC, knowing her preference for wearing comfortable clothes at home, would have included them.

In the very last box, she found a gorgeous semi-sheer white peignoir set with ruffled sleeves, pink ribbons, beige floral embroidery, and a matching pair of cotton and silk slippers. It was so delicate she was afraid to wear it, but after what she'd worn the past few weeks, the luxurious fabric would feel fantastic against her skin, so how could she resist?

She hung the gown on a hook in the bathroom and was about to start the water when she remembered the promised drink.

Before opening the door, she readjusted the blanket tightly around her. Then she called down the hall, "Austin, where's my drink?"

"Just a minute." Within moments, he was walking back down the corridor toward her room, humming "Beautiful Dreamer."

"You must like that song a lot. I've heard you hum it before. Or, are you just dreaming?"

"Both. It was one of Maggie O'Grady's favorites." He held out the glass, singing…

"Beautiful Dreamer, beam on my heart / E'en as the morn on the stream let and sea; Then will all clouds of sorrow depart / Beautiful dreamer, awake unto me / Beautiful dreamer, awake unto me!"

She accepted the drink. "You have an amazing voice."

"Thank you. Now, do you need help? Can I carry away the

trash?"

"Maybe later. I'm still admiring all the beautiful things JC picked out."

Austin leaned against the doorjamb, trying to block anyone else's view into the suite. "I doubt he picked out anything. He probably walked into the most expensive women's dress store in Chicago, gave a clerk your measurements, and hired her to select a wardrobe for you."

Ensley took a small sip and shivered as the burning sensation traveled from her mouth and down the delicate lining of her throat. She coughed. "JC doesn't know my measurements."

"Hell, Ensley. *I* know your measurements."

She didn't grasp but wanted to. Austin's certainty about something so personal freaked her out. "Did you measure me in my sleep?"

He crossed his arms. "You're five foot two and normally weigh"—he wiggled a hand—"about a hundred and two pounds, give or take a few ounces. Your BMI should be around eighteen, but you've lost weight since you've been here. Your measurements are thirty-two, twenty-two, thirty-two. You wear a size seven shoe and zero in clothes. Am I right?"

Her mouth gaped open, and her pointy-toe red slipper bounced in a pissed-off tempo. "You're sick, is what you are. How could you know any of that?"

He fidgeted with his shirt collar and looked down at his feet before returning his gaze to her. "It was sort of a game I played at the gym with my trainer, guessing a woman's measurements. Sounds dumb now, but am I right or wrong?"

"It's none of your goddamn business. I don't want to be a collection of numbers, and I never go to the gym."

"I know that. During the week, you go to yoga classes and do short runs. Then on weekends, you run ten to fifteen miles. You've run marathons but prefer halves. They're challenging enough and not as hard on your body."

He was dead on, but she'd never admit it. "You spend too much time in the gym." She took another sip, and this time it didn't burn as much. The next swallow shouldn't burn at all.

"Nah. Working out at the gym was part of the job."

He reached up and gripped the top of the door frame. Sometimes, when she stood next to him, she felt like David next to his

Goliath-size body. And for the hundredth time, she fantasized about going to bed with him. It was scary and sexy at the same time. And she scratched her head, unable to figure out how Peg A could fit into Slot B.

"If you get in the tub and want a refill or want help washing your back or even your hair, I'll do…whatever. And I'll even close my eyes."

"If you expect me to believe that, you're crazier than I thought. Now run along." She pushed on the door, but his big feet were in the way. "Goodbye, O'Grady."

He still didn't move. "You sure you don't need any help?"

"I'll let you know if I do."

He inched his feet out of the way so she could close the door.

"Goodbye." She clicked the latch bolt into place and leaned against the door for a minute, imagining him on the other side, his green eyes darkening. She took another sip and wondered if it was the desire in his eyes or the whisky shooting steamy heat through her that made her want to jump into his arms.

Definitely his eyes!

As the train clattered over an uneven section of the tracks, she tossed the blanket aside and entered the bathroom, still fantasizing about Peg A and Slot B.

An hour later, she was squeaky clean and warm inside and out. The nightgown was like silk against her skin, fresh and soft, and reminded her of home. Not New York. The ranch. And she wasn't sure what that meant. She untied the towel she'd wrapped turban-style around her head and shook out her wet hair, making a frustrated face at herself in the mirror. Without a hairdryer, it would take hours to dry.

A knock sounded on the door. She glanced that way and smiled as if she could see through the solid mahogany. It was Austin. Don't ask her how she knew. She just did.

"Ens, can I get you anything? Another drink? A snack? A fresh towel?"

"You can come in," she said.

The knob twisted, but he didn't push it open, and he sounded puzzled when he asked, "Are you sure?"

"If I didn't want you in here, I would have said so."

He pushed open the door and stood there looking at her. He cleared his throat before asking, "Do you need…a refill?"

She choked back a laugh. "I tell you to go away, and you stay. I invite you in, and you hesitate. What's up with you?"

"Remy will kick my ass if I piss you off."

"I doubt that." She handed over her glass. "One more drink, and I'll fall asleep, which probably isn't such a bad idea."

"Whatever makes you happy." He took the glass and headed out the door. "I'll be right back."

She dug through her gear for a comb and had it in hand by the time Austin returned with her drink.

"I'll trade you this drink for the comb."

"You don't have one?"

He ran his fingers through his hair, making tracks through his thick auburn waves, and damn if his cheeks didn't turn pink, which made her wonder what he was thinking.

"I don't need one for me, but I thought…I'd volunteer to comb…yours."

Remembering how good it felt when he untangled her knots, she gave him the comb and angled sideways into the high back chair. "What's Remy doing?"

"Drinking. It's weird to see Cajun lying on a sofa with a drink and no remote in his hand. He's a maniac when it comes to sports."

"And you're not?"

"Sure, when it comes to basketball, but Remy will watch anything, even curling." Austin glided the comb through her hair in long, even strokes.

"How'd you learn to comb a woman's hair? You seem to know what you're doing."

"My cousin Betsy has long brown hair."

"Who does she belong to?"

"Uncle Connor and Aunt Olivia. And Betsy thinks it's funny and giggles when I brush it. She's watched me on the basketball court from the time she was a year old. I don't get it, but she's in awe when she puts her little comb in my hand."

"I understand the feeling. Your hands are huge. They could span my waist. So how old is Betsy now?"

"Almost ten, going on fifteen."

"You must be her favorite cousin."

"Not anymore. The younger guys have taken my place." He combed Ensley's hair, then rolled sections around his finger. "Do you want me to break down the boxes and dump them in the trash?"

"They probably recycle, don't you think?"

He dropped each curl, letting it drape over her shoulders to dry. "I doubt they call it recycling, but I'm sure they reuse anything and everything they can. In which case, they'd probably prefer we leave the boxes intact."

Remy came to the partially open door. "The cook and steward arrived with dinner from the hotel."

"I wonder who paid for it?" she asked. "Not that I'm nosy or complaining, but it seems weird that they'd buy precooked food when there's so much here to fix."

"They thought we'd be hungry after traveling all day." Remy entered the room and closed the door behind him. "I guess they have an expense account so they can buy supplies. But... I only got a quick introduction to the steward, and all I can say is, I'd rather have Norman here."

Austin dropped the last curl over her shoulder. "Are you being paranoid?"

"Maybe." Remy turned around and left—but came right back. "Look. Tavis was worried. Maybe he was just upset about the Viking, but it made an impression on me. After you meet the steward, if you feel the same way, we'll dismiss them, and they can get off at the next stop."

"Then we'll have to cook for ourselves," Austin said.

"I doan mind cooking," Remy said.

"I don't, either," she said.

Austin scratched his whiskers. "If someone sent them after us, if we kick them off the train, others will come to replace them."

"Why would somebody want to hurt us?"

"Because of your brooch," Austin said.

"I don't have one. JC and I both tried to hold on to the sun-stone, but it got too hot. It's still in the twenty-first century."

"I doan want to scare you, Ensley," Remy said, "but the enemy doesn't know that and woan believe you. They'd likely torture and eventually kill you while trying to extract what you doan know."

Sh...

She tried to say shit, but no sound passed through her constricted throat, and not much air came out of fear-frozen lungs. This was her worst nightmare. When her throat relaxed, she said, "But...those two men could really be a cook and a steward. Right?"

Remy rubbed the back of his neck without saying anything, but she wanted an answer.

"Tell me the truth."

"If you want me to agree with you, I can't."

She stood and paced the room. Where was her Clovis Point? She needed protection. And then she remembered. The last time she saw her little knife, the point was dangling from the bear's fur.

"Let me get dressed, then let's have dinner. We can decide what to do after we check the guys out. I'd prefer it if we could at least start by believing they are who they say they are."

Austin looked around the room. "Did you find anything comfortable to wear in all those boxes?"

"Other than two peignoir sets, the dresses all require a bustle except the black wool riding outfit. That's probably the least complicated one in the collection."

Austin winked. "Yell if you want help with zippers or back buttons."

"I don't think zippers are a thing yet, but if I need help buttoning, I'll be sure to reach out."

It took about thirty minutes to get the skirt and peplum jacket buttoned up and presentable without the corset. And besides, she wasn't in the mood to be that trussed up. She picked through the box of elastic garters and knit silk hose in yellow, pink, white, and black, all with white lace trimming. Her feet almost sighed at the warm luxury. It was better than a pedicure.

Then she remembered the small piece of red fabric. She unwrapped her dirty jacket and found the fabric stuck to her bra. Now where to put it. The skirt should have a hidden pocket sewn in for a handkerchief. It took a minute of searching the folds to find it. Perfect. She just hoped she didn't forget it when she changed clothes.

Inside a shoebox with a pair of riding boots, she discovered two small boxes. One held an ivory handle comb and brush set and hairpins, and the other had an exquisite pearl necklace and earbobs. The jewelry didn't exactly go with the riding habit, but what the hell. She wore them anyway.

The last thing she did was pin up the slightly damp waves, letting them cascade down to her shoulders. Now, presentable for the first time in weeks, despite the pain in her hip, she had a bit of a bounce in her riding boots when she opened the door and stepped out, savoring the aroma of roasting venison.

She immediately grabbed the hall railing to stabilize herself on the swaying train as she made her way to the drawing room.

When she entered, she found Austin and Remy huddled near the liquor cabinet whispering and figured they were talking about the steward and the cook.

She cleared her throat to announce her arrival. Both men looked up, whistled, and stared a moment too long with an intensity that was so delicious she had to freeze in place like a model in a window display so she could soak it all in. After knowing she looked like a homeless person for weeks, their appreciation made her feel desirable. And maybe pretty, as well.

"You clean up *good*." Remy studied every inch of her from face to feet, grinning.

She curtsied. "Thank you. Soap and clean clothes work magic on a girl's psyche."

Austin noticed Remy's attention and stepped in front of him, blocking his view. "You look beautiful. It wasn't hard to see the beauty beneath the grunge, but without the grunge, you're a knockout, baby—"

She growled, "Don't you dare say it!"

"If I can't say baby doll, can I say…babycakes? Sweetcheeks? Turtlecakes?"

"Turtlecakes? Seriously?"

"Well, hell, I was just going with the Mutant Ninja Turtles theme."

"What are you? Five?"

He peered down at her as if he wore glasses. "I hang out with the second-gens. I know all about Ninja Turtles."

"Oh, good grief." And then she smiled. She adored it when he talked about the kids. It made him so normal, even lovable.

He grinned, and that dimple popped out above his right cheek again. She didn't always notice it because every time she gazed up at him, she got lost in his green eyes. The color was every hue of a forest and reminded her of a New England summer.

"You're a knockout." He held an elegant elbow out toward her. "May I escort you to dinner?"

She tucked her hand into the crook of his proffered arm. When he looked at her the way he did now, she simply couldn't resist him. If he had asked for a kiss, she would have given him that and more.

As soon as they entered the corridor, she dropped his arm and grabbed the railing again. The hallway was too narrow to walk side by side, and the swaying too dangerous not to hold on to something.

She entered the dining room first and paused to appreciate the ambiance. The candlelight reflected off the china and silver, and the room beckoned with its romantic glow and the scent of warm bread. Plus, a silver bucket held an open bottle of chilled champagne, ready to fill the three stem wineglasses next to it.

All that was missing was soft jazz playing in the background.

Remy played his drumsticks at a super-low volume against the table. *Ba dum-bum ishhh.*

"If I had a piano," Austin said, "I'd play some sweet jazz with warm tones and clear melodies."

"You play the piano?"

"My uncles play piano and guitar, and when I was a kid, I wanted to be like them, so I took lessons. Pops told me that as long as I practiced guitar or piano at least thirty minutes a day, I could play sports the other twenty-three and a half hours."

"And chess?" she asked.

"Thirty minutes of piano or guitar and thirty minutes of chess. Pops was determined to make me well-rounded."

"What about studying, eating, and sleeping?"

"He left that up to me, but he told me if my grades ever dropped, he'd put his foot down. But Rick's the one who helped me the most. He taught me how to balance my time."

"Are you any good?" she asked.

"Not as talented as Rick on piano or Connor on guitar, but I can keep up with Remy."

"You get Austin or Rick on the keys, McBain on sax, Connor on jazz guitar, JL or Amber on vocals, and my sticks," Remy said, "and we've got a band that can bring the house down."

She gave Austin a caressing smile. "I'll look forward to hearing you play." And for the briefest of moments, all the horrors of the last few weeks vanished. *Poof!*

A man who looked to be in his thirties or early forties with a dark brown comb-over and dressed in a neatly pressed three-piece suit with a standup collar and cravat entered the room carrying a serving tray with slices of venison. He bowed slightly. "I'm Mr. Bailey, your steward. Whatever you need, please ask."

"I detect an English accent," Ensley said. "What brings you to America?"

He set the serving tray on the sideboard. "Employment, ma'am. If you'll excuse me, I'll bring out the rest of the food." Once he moved away from the sideboard, he smelled like the cowboys who hadn't had a bath in weeks.

After he left the room, Ensley looked over at Austin to let him know she didn't notice anything suspicious. But his eyes were flashing with anger vying with fear, and Remy was reaching for his pistol.

"What's wrong?" she whispered.

Austin put his finger to his lips, and Remy gave his head a quick shake.

"Shit," she mouthed.

Fear was a funny thing. It enabled her to do tricky things like hacking away on a bear or riding a bronc, but it could also paralyze her—as it did now—crippling her mind and making it hard to control her breathing.

This paralyzing fear had only happened once before, on the night the drunk driver killed her father. But watching Remy and Austin react to the steward boomeranged all that emotion, and she shook so hard her slightly damp curls bounced against the sides of her neck.

Austin pulled her into an embrace and whispered, "Shh... I'll explain everything later, but this could get nasty. Stay alert. Remy and I won't let anything happen to you. But right now, you're shaking like a two-year-old throwing a tantrum, so cup your hands over your mouth and breathe slowly."

She *was* almost hyperventilating. When she didn't cover her mouth, Austin did it for her. "Breathe." Then to Remy, he murmured, "Pour the champagne or get the whisky."

"Don't leave," she whispered into her cupped hands. "Who is that man? I need to know." She could hear the panic in her voice, and that scared her even more. "Use the brooch. Let's get out of here. Now!"

"Shh..." Austin held her tighter, and she was comforted by the rhythm of his heart. If he was calm, she could be just as controlled. So she allowed herself to relax in his arms and let her panic attack subside.

"Mr. Bailey is wearing a ring identical to one worn by a man who terrorized Aunt Penny. It's associated with the Illuminati."

"It could be a coincidence," she said, infusing a bit of hope into her voice.

"When you see Elliott, ask him what he thinks of coincidences," Remy said.

She crossed her arms and wondered why she should care what Elliott thought of coincidences. "So give me the Cliffs Notes version, and if I remember to ask him, I will."

"He believes that if fate or mystery or God—or even brooches—can cause coincidences, then the cause is known, and there are no coincidences."

She tapped her fingers against her crossed arms, thinking through what Remy said, hoping it would make sense if she thought about it long enough. "So if God causes a coincidence and you believe it was God, it wasn't a coincidence because you know the cause. Is that it?"

"Something like that," Remy said.

She was still trying to figure it out when Mr. Bailey returned, carrying a tray with several serving dishes.

"Would you like me to serve?" Mr. Bailey asked.

Austin laughed and stepped away from Ensley but kept his hand on her shoulder. "If my fiancée can keep her hands off me, I'll serve us. Thank you, Mr. Bailey."

She patted his hand that wrapped her shoulder. "Me, darling? It's obvious it's the other way around. What do you think, Mr. Bailey?"

His eyes flashed, and then he answered, "I never offer an opinion in matters of the heart. If you ask me if it's going to rain tomorrow, I'll tell you what I think." He nodded, but before leaving the room, he pulled on a cord. "There's one of these in every room. Pull it, and it rings in the kitchen. I'll come immediately."

As soon as he was gone, she whispered, "Mr. Bailey is wearing a ring with a crossed-keys insignia. Is that what you associate with the Illuminati?"

Remy put his finger to his lips as he crossed the room, looked out into the hallway, then closed the door. "Let's fix our plates and act like nothing's wrong. We have to assume they're spying on us."

"Why don't we just leave?" she asked.

"We can't leave yet, and we don't know if both men are involved. Plus, our orders are to go to the farm and collect Kit and Cullen." Remy picked up a plate and loaded it with venison and potatoes. "Excuse me while I eat. I think better on a full stomach."

"Do you want me to fix you a plate?" Austin asked.

She sidled over to the table and poured a glass of champagne, hoping more alcohol would calm her. At least she had stopped hyperventilating. "No, I want you to be honest with me."

Remy sat and poured a glass for himself before taking a big bite of a buttered biscuit. "These could be the same men who caused trouble for JC when he was in Asia. Or at least from the same organization."

"How do you know?" she asked.

"I doan. I'm just guessing. But Elliott took JC home under mysterious circumstances. It could have something to do with the Illuminati. If they found JC, then they must know about you and your whereabouts."

Dumbfounded, she asked, "How would they know that?"

"I doan know. But the Illuminati knows a lot of shit we haven't figured out yet. The MacKlenna Clan is a small organization. The Illuminati is worldwide. We doan know how many people they have, the number of brooches, or how much they know about the stones' history and purpose. Based on what happened to Penny, I'd guess the Illuminati have been a step ahead of us all along."

"But the agent at the depot said they came in on the train today. So they haven't been hanging out waiting for me to get here."

"He said the cook and steward came in on the train from Billings. He didn't identify them. Maybe the men who are here now aren't the same men who came in on the train."

"Damn, Remy."

Tension flexed in the tendons in his neck. "I'm worried about ya, and I wanna be sure you're aware of the danger. Stay alert. We'll have your back. But it's you they want. Not me. Not Austin. We're in their way, and they'd just as soon shoot us now."

The worry she saw in Remy's eyes sent a shiver across her skin, and it zip-lined down her spine. She turned toward the food in an attempt to hide how scared she was but doubted she fooled anyone.

"This looks like the food I ate at the hotel. Which was not 'comestibles for the most exacting palate.'"

"If I add some seasoning, it woan be too bad." Remy's voice was as bland as the food, and that sent the shiver zip-lining in the other direction.

She sat down next to him but had little appetite for what was on her plate. She pushed it away. "I can't eat this." She sipped more champagne, which made her head swim from anxiety and fear. How long had it been since she'd injured her foot? Weeks? She'd been scared to death that she'd die because of the injury, and now here she was facing another terror. But this time, thank God, she knew from the outset that she wasn't alone.

As she waited for them to finish eating, she refilled everyone's champagne glass, then placed the empty bottle upside down in the bucket. Austin straightened his legs out under the table and accidentally nudged her calf.

"Ouch," she said.

"Sorry. I misjudged how much room I had."

"I thought you were always aware of how much space you had to do your *thing*!"

"I do." He winked. "So why aren't you eating?"

"My stomach's upset. When I get worried or stressed, that's where it hits me."

"JL's like that. I can always tell when something's on her mind. She glares at food as if it's the enemy."

Austin went back to eating, scraping his fork across the china, and she swayed with the rocking train clattering down the tracks, hurtling through the night with two possible assailants onboard.

Remy wiped his face and hands and dropped the napkin next to his plate. "Let's go back to the drawing room and come up with a plan."

She wrapped her hand around her glass tight enough to break it. "What's to stop them from attacking us now?"

"They want us alive—or at least you—and will wait until they believe they have an advantage," Remy said.

"I know self-defense. I'll fight," she said. "But if you have to shoot me, you know, like in the arm or leg, to get to them and save us all, do it."

"That's the dumbest thing I've ever heard." Silence ticked the moments away before Austin added, "Remy and I would rather die than hurt you."

"I don't mean, kill me. I mean—"

"Give it up, Ensley. Neither one of us will shoot you or at you, unless..." Austin dropped his voice, "it's to save you from something horrific, something worse than death."

She shivered. "Like when Heyward in *The Last of the Mohicans* is being burned alive, and Hawkeye shoots him so he won't suffer more?"

"Yeah, something like that."

Remy knocked on the table. "Can I have your attention?"

She and Austin looked at Remy, who arched an eyebrow at them, while out of the corner of her eye, she saw him do something weird with his fingers like a baseball coach giving the runner signals. But she dismissed it, thinking he was playing a miniature drum set.

"We should return to the drawing room now and set up our defenses there. Both of you need to focus on how this is going down. I'll lead, and Austin will bring up the rear. Stay close to him, Ensley, and stay loose. If I do anything strange, just follow along and wing it."

"Like what?" she demanded, feeling a little testy.

Remy gave her a *what the hell* look. "I doan know."

Well, hell, she didn't know, either, and the unknown was killing her. She jumped up, knocking her chair to the floor, and shook her finger at him. "Don't get short with me, Army guy. You know lots of things I don't know. I'm just a book editor from New York—" She dropped her finger, cringing. She'd avoided telling Austin what she did for a living or what she used to do, and now she just screwed up and blurted it out.

"A book editor from New York City?" Austin asked. "Who do you work for?"

"I don't work for a publishing company...now."

"Who did you work for? Harper Collinsworth?"

She looked at him, and their eyes met. It was like a thunderbolt, and it hurt like hell, and she felt like a horrible person, and she knew he was feeling the same way about her.

"Ensley Williams, editor, Harper Collinsworth. Oh, yeah, I recognized you from your picture on the website."

"Why didn't you say something?"

"Because I wanted to see your face when you discovered I knew all along you're the editor who rejected my manuscript."

Her frantic, chaotic mind waffled between being pissed as hell and guilty as hell. She framed her face, making a little box with her fingers and thumb, and gave him a fake smile. "I hope my reaction meets your expectations?"

Remy pushed to his feet. "Can you two shut the fuck up?" He opened the door, looked out, closed it again. "They're not hanging out in the corridor, so they're probably in the kitchen. If you two can put a hold on your argument until we're safe, I'd appreciate the cooperation."

The muscles in Austin's jaw ticked. "Sure. Let's roll."

She lined up a foot behind Remy and glanced over her shoulder at Austin, who was standing two big feet away. "I don't know why you're pissed now if you've known the truth for days. Can you explain that?"

"It reminds me of how shocked I was when you rejected my manuscript. It's a damn good book, and it would have put me on the best seller lists."

She made a T with her hands. "Time out."

"Damn, woman." Austin took her hands. "A time out T is made by putting your fingertips to your flat hand. Not the flat of your hand. You don't know anything about sports, do you?"

Her lip curled while anger and disappointment warred for the privilege of taking a swing at him. "I don't know much, but that's not what we're fighting about."

"We're not fighting."

"We aren't? Good. Then let's shelve this for later when I have time to explain my decision."

"Your decision was obvious. You thought my writing sucked."

"If that's what you think, then you didn't read my letter."

He leaned away from her. "Whoa. Never saw a letter. I just heard you thought it wasn't worth your time."

She stared at him, hands on her hips. If she could annihilate him with a death ray, she would. "Damn, Austin. There's a lot more to it. Didn't your agent send you a copy of my letter?"

"I told him I didn't want it. The bottom line was all I needed to know."

"Well, hell. Since you haven't read it, I'll write another one and address it to you. And I'll soften my response. But why are we talking about this right now?"

"Why not? We could be dead in five minutes."

"Good. Then I'm glad you brought it up. I'd hate to die without telling you I was the wrong person to read your manuscript. Someone who didn't have a prejudice against professional athletes should have read it."

He crossed his arms, and every damn muscle in his supersized body figured out how to display itself, even those hidden by a flannel shirt. "Prejudice. I missed out on an offer from a New York publishing company because the editor was too prejudiced to give me an honest evaluation."

"She's pissed enough now, man. Let's go," Remy said.

She blinked. "What the hell? Pissed enough? Was this all a set-up?"

"Sort of," Austin said.

"God, that pisses me off."

"Good. We wanted you pissed," Austin said. "It'll give you an edge."

"Wait a minute." She punched Remy's arm. "You sent Austin a hand signal. Didn't you?"

"I doan know what you're talking about." Remy returned to the table and picked up the bucket with the empty champagne bottle. "Let's try this again." He reached for the doorknob. "If I notice anything, I may veer from the script."

"What script?"

"The one that says ad-lib all your lines," Remy said.

Terror seized her, bringing memories of the growling bear and smell of blood and Erik yelling, "Tyr!" as he attacked the grizzly.

"Relax," Austin whispered in her ear. "I've got your back."

The terror lasted only a second and then vanished like a vapor, allowing her anger to return. She marched into the dark corridor, knowing Austin had her caged in between him and Remy.

Remy stopped at the open kitchen door and held out the bucket. "Excellent choice of champagne. Do you have another chilled bottle?"

"Yes, sir," the cook said. "We have several."

"I'll bring a bottle to the drawing room," Mr. Bailey said. "And if you require anything else, pull the bell cord, day or night."

"Why doan I take a bottle with me and save you the trip?" Remy said.

"Certainly." The cook opened the refrigerator and handed a bottle to Mr. Bailey, who then wrapped it in a cloth napkin and exchanged the full bottle with the empty one.

"Would you prefer I carry it?" Mr. Bailey asked.

"Nope. I can manage." Remy smiled, but it wasn't his natural smile. Ensley knew then that this was all for show. He was checking out the cook. So was she. The cook and Bailey wore identical rings with a crossed-keys symbol.

She caught a whiff of the terror that had only just evaporated, but this time it was a chill that blew through her like a winter storm.

Austin must have sensed something in her body language because he locked his arms around her, and the two men standing in the kitchen couldn't help but notice Austin's protective stance.

Remy accepted the bucket and carried it under his arm. "Let's go. We have some celebrating to do."

"Oh, wait. We need glasses," Ensley said.

Mr. Bailey removed three from the cupboard, and Ensley took them from him. "I'll carry them, thanks."

When they reached the drawing room, Remy closed the door, set the bucket aside, and did a pistol press check to make sure he had a round in the chamber. "As I see it, we have two choices. We can kill them both, dump them off the train, and continue our trip to the farm. Or two, return home now and go back later for Kit and Cullen."

"Even if they're a threat, I can't condone killing them," she said.

"If we do kill them, won't the people they're working for come after us?" Austin asked.

Remy holstered his gun. "Yeah, they'll come after us or try to. But hell, they'd probably come after us anyway, or if they doan, someone else will."

"I bet David would want to interrogate them, but taking two members of the Illuminati to the plantation would breach Braham's security," Austin said. "I'm not sure that's a good idea."

Remy did a press check of the pistol in his boot. "We can blindfold them, and they woan know where they are."

Austin did a press check of the automatic in his boot. "How do you plan to disarm them?"

"They're probably thinking the same thing about us," Ensley said. "Whatever we're going to do, we'd better do it now."

Remy dug into his duffel bag and pulled out a weird-looking gun. "This is a Taser X26P, ready and set to use."

Austin returned the gun to his boot. "Taser or drug them. I don't care, but let's do something before they come in here with guns blazing."

"They doan want to kill us—yet—but they will once we're no longer useful." Remy opened the bottle of champagne and filled the three glasses Ensley was carrying. "How do you think we should play this?"

"Carefully," Ensley said. "Is there any way we can take this carriage home with us?"

"We could try, but we might end up with the whole damn train," Austin said. "Kit traveled back with a covered wagon, a cat, a dog, and a Thoroughbred. But I don't want to risk taking all the passengers. That would be a disaster."

"How about I go back to my room, stack up the boxes, and ask Mr. Bailey to carry them away? One of you can come in behind him and taser him."

"I won't risk you being in your stateroom alone with him," Austin said. "He could take you hostage. We've got to stick together."

She gave an exasperated huff, set down the glasses, and sat on the sofa before the swaying train knocked her over. "Then do you have a better plan?"

"I agree that whatever we do, we need to do it now," Remy said. "They could be planning to overpower us tonight and take us off the train at the next stop."

"Is there a chance we're overreacting?" she asked.

Austin sat beside her and rested his arm along the back of the sofa. "They both are wearing crossed-keys rings. It's possible, but I don't think so."

"If we leave now, with or without prisoners, what about Kit and Cullen?" she asked.

"After we turn these creeps over to David, we can return for them," Remy said.

"Elliott might not let us come back, although I don't know who's in the mood to travel right now," Austin said.

"Sophia. She's always ready," Remy said. "But with the Illuminati searching for you, Ensley, Elliott might not let you go."

"Let's worry about that when we get home," Austin said. "For now, let's figure out how we're going to get those two disarmed."

"Okay, listen," Remy said. "Austin can hide in your bathroom, Ensley, while you ring for Mr. Bailey to come and do something. Clean your room, remove the trash, bring a glass of water. Whatever. When he gets there, I'll come in from behind and taser him. As soon as he's down, I'll go after the cook. You two tie up Bailey. As soon as the cook is disabled, I'll drag him to your stateroom, and we'll get the hell out of here. But if this goes south, be prepared to take him down any way you can. Got it?"

"Got it," Austin said.

"I'll hide in the second stateroom," Remy said. "As soon as Bailey goes by, I'll come in behind him."

"I want a gun," Ensley said. "I've never shot a person, but if it's him or me, I'll do what I have to."

Remy gave her the Glock he carried in his boot. "There's a full magazine with a bullet in the chamber."

She took the gun and looked it over. "Cocked and ready."

"You act like you know how to use it. Any questions?" Remy asked.

"Nope." She stood and slipped it into the back of her waistband. "Let's get the show on the road."

He looked her in the eye, and she did her best to tamp down a hundred emotions flapping around in her system—dread and terror being the two headliners—yet still, she was ready for the show. And when Remy signaled and opened the gate, she'd barrel through without hesitation.

"I'll go first. Give me a count of twenty to get into position," Remy said, then closed the door behind him.

Austin took Ensley's hand and started counting. When he reached twenty, he opened the door and led her toward her stateroom. The train swayed and rattled, and she held tightly to the railing.

He led her into the bedroom, leaving the door slightly ajar, and kissed the top of her head. "I'll have eyes on you the entire time."

As soon as Austin was out of sight, she pulled the bell cord and expected any minute to see Mr. Bailey at her door.

Earlier she had tossed boxes everywhere and strewn clothes on the furniture and the floor. She made quick work of the trash, stacking the boxes at the foot of the bed. She picked up one of the dresses and was in the process of folding it when Mr. Bailey knocked on the partially open door.

"Ma'am. Did you need something?"

"Yes, Mr. Bailey. Would you mind removing these boxes? I've unwrapped everything."

He came into the room, and his gaze crawled across her before he pushed the door shut. "You have several beautiful dresses. I look forward to seeing you wear them."

As soon as he took a menacing step toward her, any remaining hope that they were wrong about Mr. Bailey evaporated. A seven-inch fixed blade knife appeared like magic in his hand.

"If you scream, my associate has orders to kill your bodyguards immediately."

She'd never seen an evil gleam in anyone's eyes like the one she saw in his. Evil had ripped out his heart, chopped it up, and littered tiny pieces along the trail for vultures to eat.

"Associate?" That meant just one. "You mean the cook?"

Mr. Bailey chuckled. "The hotel food is gourmet compared to any food he can prepare."

She swallowed hard. "Where's the cook hired by the railroad?"

"He took another job."

She didn't believe that for a minute.

Mr. Bailey's eyes bored into her, making her downright terrified.

"So I guess this means you're not going to dispose of the boxes."

Don't get smart. He's more dangerous than the bear.

Mr. Bailey's features became taut with malevolence. "The only thing I intend to dispose of is…well… There's no need to talk about it right now. Where's the brooch?"

"I don't have one," she said.

"Don't be coy, Miss Williams."

"How do you know my name?"

He took a step closer, tsking. "I know all about you, your sunstone brooch, and your friend Mr. Fraser."

"I haven't seen James Cullen in weeks."

"When you split up, we had to make adjustments, but it worked out." Mr. Bailey held out his hand. "Mr. Fraser didn't have the brooch, which means you do. Give it to me and save yourself a great deal of pain."

Austin, why the hell are you waiting?

"I don't have it. It got too hot to hold and was left behind. The same thing happened to JC when he used it."

Mr. Bailey laughed, and the sound scraped across her skin, chilling her to the bone, but somehow she remained calm, using every bit of the control she learned at the rodeo.

"That's impossible. No brooch acts like that."

Now she laughed—or made her best attempt at one—but it sounded more sarcastic than humorous. "You'll have to take that up with the brooch gods because mine did. And JC dropped it at the stables in Maryland. By now, someone has probably found it."

Mr. Bailey's knife hand shot out and sliced down the front of her jacket, cutting off the buttons. He was as emotionless—soulless—as anyone she'd ever encountered, and it was terrifying. She had no doubt he would do everything he threatened to do—and more if the mood struck him.

Whatever self-defense she knew would be ineffective against a man with a knife used by Special Forces.

Special Forces.

Nothing stupid about her. She connected the dots and knew then that Mr. Bailey was a traveler, which made him even more dangerous. Plus, now he reeked of liver and onions.

"That wasn't nice," she managed to say as she pinched the ends of the jacket together. "I don't have a needle and thread. How am I going to sew them back on?"

She flashed back to being in the chute, ready to ride a bronc, waiting for the gate to open. *Get ready. Breathe.* During the next few seconds, she could live or die.

His brown teeth showed in a sadistic grin that nearly made her throw up.

Where's Austin? Where's Remy?

She couldn't make a move until one of them burst into the room.

"No corset?" Mr. Bailey asked. "Hmmm." Using the knife, he swatted her hand away and sliced down the front of the chemise, nicking her skin and exposing the curve of her breasts. Then he used the blade's tip and flipped the sides farther apart, exposing more of her.

He pressed against her, and before she could anticipate his next move, he grabbed the back of her head and held it still while he kissed her with stiff, unmoving lips. It wasn't a kiss at all. It was strictly intimidation.

"Before I kill you, I'll enjoy taking what you'd never offer."

The hell you will. Enough of this bullshit.

When he kissed her again, she reached behind her back, eased out the gun, and slammed it into his gut. His head whipped back, and she only saw the bear. His eyes widened with surprise as he realized what she was doing. Before he reacted, she fired.

There was a pop and then the jingle of the brass bullet casing hitting the floor.

The look on Mr. Bailey's face said, "You bitch. You shot me." He clutched the hole in his gut and fell backward. "What have you done?" he groaned, dropping the knife at his side.

She kicked the knife out of his reach as she pressed the gun to his forehead. "I shot you, you goddamn bastard, and I'll do it again. Where are my friends?"

"They're dead," he said, blood trailed from the corner of his mouth down his chin. "Just like James Cullen."

"You lying piece of shit." She was now a cold-blooded murderer, and she didn't care. She racked the slide, putting another bullet in the chamber. "Where are they?"

"Shoot…me." His tone was as flat as his eyes.

Instead of shooting him, she grabbed the knife and the sheath tucked into his trousers. "You goddamn bastard." She searched his pockets and took everything she could find, including his tobacco pouch, and shuddered when she saw a picture of herself and JC at Sophia's art exhibit in New York City. Before she could ask where he got it, he breathed out a raspy breath and died.

"Enjoy hell." She stood and kicked him in the ribs.

A chill swept through her at how close she came to being raped and killed. She was a warrior now, and she couldn't fall apart until she found Austin and Remy.

You were always a warrior.

She jerked around. *Who said that?* She kicked open the bathroom door, and it slammed back against the wall. She had an uninterrupted view of the room, and Austin wasn't there.

"Shit! Where the hell are you?" There had to be a secret door, which meant there were two ways to enter her room. She hurried back to the entry door and scooted a chair in front of it. Then lodged the back under the doorknob so no one could open it from the other side.

She returned to the bathroom to search for a secret panel in the wall that opened and connected the two rooms, hoping working on the puzzle would keep her from freaking out.

Since her dad gave her a gun, he'd stressed safety to keep her from shooting anyone. And now, damn it, she had.

Don't think about it.

She ran her hands down one wall and then another, and when she glanced in the mirror and saw herself, her knees buckled. Her jacket was open, her chemise was ripped in half, and a bloody red line went from the sternum notch to the bottom of her rib cage. She pulled hairpins out of her hair and pinned the chemise together, then went back to searching for a lever to open the door.

But when did Austin disappear? Was she so distracted that she didn't hear a fight in the bathroom?

Is he dead?

No, she refused to think that. The Illuminati didn't want any of them dead—yet. They planned to torture them until they gave up whatever information they had. The cook would wait until Bailey finished with her. But didn't anyone hear the gunshot?

The bathtub was under the window on the left. The sink was directly in front of her, and the toilet was on the right. That meant the only portion of the wall that could slide open was next to the sink. But how did it work?

She tucked the sheathed knife in her waistband. Then she ran her hands up and down the wall again but couldn't find a lever. There had to be one here somewhere. She removed the framed picture of a train engine and *voilà*.

A knob!

Clever.

But what would she find on the other side? It didn't matter. She had to look. If the cook was in there holding a gun on Austin, she'd kill the cook, too.

She raised the Glock, steadied her hand, and with her left hand turned the knob.

The wall wisped open into the adjoining stateroom, flickering the candle flames in the brass wall lamps. The sight of Austin hogtied on the floor nearly ripped her heart out.

Oh, my God.

Words died in her throat. She couldn't speak, couldn't even whisper to him to let him know she was there.

His arms and legs were up in the air behind his back, tied together. She hurried to him and felt for a pulse. Thank God he was alive.

Moving quickly, she used Bailey's knife to cut him loose and spotted a knot the size of a goose egg at the base of his skull. No telling how long he'd be unconscious. She couldn't do anything to help him, but damn, he was going to have one hell of a headache.

In the meantime, if they didn't find a way out of this mess, they'd all be dead, and it wouldn't much matter.

What was she going to do now? And how long did she have? Bailey probably told the cook to tie up Remy and Austin and wait until he finished torturing her before deciding what to do with them. She could look for the cook, but what if he captured her? There wouldn't be any backup. She had to find Remy. But did she dare leave this room? And where the hell was the cook?

Where would she want to be?

The drawing room. It was more comfortable and had a supply of liquor. That meant the cook would have tied Remy up in the dining room. But what if she was wrong?

Channel your inner Viking warrior woman.

Before she cracked open the door, she removed her shoes, tucked the knife in her waistband, and checked the gun. Another round had automatically entered the chamber after she fired once.

I'm ready. Let's get this done.

She opened the door and listened. No voices. But as loud as the rumbling train was, she wasn't surprised she couldn't hear people talking at either end of the carriage.

Right or left? Do or die. What the hell? Go for it. Warrior woman.

She reached the kitchen and listened before revealing herself. Then she tried to still her racing heart as she turned, holding her firearm in a high ready position, which reduced her profile. The room was empty. She turned toward the dining room, maintaining her grip, her finger on the trigger.

No voices were coming from the dining room, either. She'd give her last dollar for a mirror with a direct view of the room's interior. Her field of vision around the corner and into the room was zero.

She had no business trying to clear the room by herself, but she had no choice. Should she go at top speed or a slow creep? Before she could decide, she had to know if Remy was in immediate danger. Bulldozing her way into a room could get them both killed.

She hugged the wall, and when she was ready, she took one step and got a look at a slice of the room. Nothing there.

She took another step and saw another slice of the room. Nothing there, either.

She took a third step and spotted Remy hogtied on the floor— but was anyone else in the room? If she took a baby step, she'd have a complete view.

Do it.

She took the last step and let out a breath of relief. No one else was in the room.

She hurried to Remy and felt his pulse. He was still alive but had a similar knot on his head. She quickly cut the ropes binding his arms and legs, wondering how long he'd be out. It was impossible to know.

So what was she going to do now? Sit here and wait? No. She had to go after the cook. None of them would be safe as long as he was alive.

Don't stop. Don't think about it. Just do it.

She patted him down to see if he had another weapon. She was checking his boot when he grabbed her arm.

"Shhh," Remy whispered.

"Well, scare the shit out of me, why don't you," she whispered. "I thought you were unconscious."

He rubbed the back of his head. "I'm not now. Where's Austin?"

"Knocked out in the other stateroom."

"Where's Bailey?"

"Dead."

"Good. And the cook?"

"I don't know. Let's get Austin and go home."

"Can't leave the cook behind. If you haven't seen him, he's probably in the drawing room. Give me your gun." He put his hand on the top of the barrel and lowered it. "Release your grip, Ens."

Her fingers were frozen to the weapon.

"Relax your hand, baby doll. Let me have it."

Baby doll?

She glared at him, but his eyes were soft and smiling, and she understood that he called her that for shock value, and her hold relaxed.

"Did Bailey have a weapon?"

She nodded and handed over the knife.

"Keep that. Do you know how to throw it?"

She nodded again.

He kissed her. "You'll do great, baby doll. Stay behind me, and if shooting starts, hit the floor."

"Hit the floor? Okay, but don't do the honorable thing. Kill him as soon as you see him."

"Can't do, baby doll. We need the information he has."

Remy led the way down the corridor and reached the drawing room, signaling to her to stay back while he stepped out and searched wedges of the room exactly as she had done.

"Shit." He grabbed Ensley's hand, hurried back down the hall to the stateroom, and shoved her inside, and shut the door.

"Get down and stay close to Austin." He dug into the front of his pants and pulled out a brooch similar to her grandmother's, but Remy's had an amethyst stone. "We've got to go now. Focus on Mallory Plantation and Charlotte."

Ensley didn't ask why.

Remy laid down over her and Austin and recited the chant: *"Chan ann le tìm no àite a bhios sinn a' tomhais an' gaol ach 's ann le neart anama."*

They were disappearing into the fog just as the cook burst into the room, firing an automatic, and Remy returned fire.

51

MacKlenna Farm, KY (1885)—Meredith

M EREDITH WATCHED ELLIOTT enter the mansion and knew
something was wrong. It wasn't how he looked that concerned her, but the way he moved—slowly as if he had lead weights
in his shoes. He always carried the heavyweight burden of the family
on his shoulders, but never like this. In their almost three decades
together, she'd never seen him look so demoralized.

No, that was wrong. Years ago, she went to Elliott's house and
told him she was pregnant and had breast cancer. That was a shock.
But when she told him if she didn't survive, she hoped he would
raise the child, that was an even bigger shock, and he had the same
weary look that he had now.

What could have caused it?

He'd been at the foaling barn most of the morning. Maybe he
lost the mare or the foal. No, that would upset him but not devastate
him. It surprised her that he even came back to the house so soon.
He needed time to regroup before tackling a houseful of people he
didn't know.

It was at moments like this that she worried about his health. He
looked on the verge of another stroke. She had to get him out of
here now.

She stood when he approached the sofa where she'd been sitting
with Kit and her father, Donald McCabe, the one person she and
Elliott never thought they'd meet. She kissed Elliott's cheek. "You're
just in time to meet our wonderful surprise. Kit's father came from
Washington with his granddaughters."

Elliott smiled, but it was one of his I-don't-have-time-for-you
smiles, and he expected her to bail him out. Although he was

gracious enough to extend his arm. "Captain McCabe. I would know ye without an introduction. Ye look exactly like Kit's paintings of ye. I never thought we'd meet, though."

The captain offered his bruised, purple-veined hand. "I didn't, either, Dr. Fraser."

Meredith could see Elliott meant what he said, but it didn't ease the tension in his jaw and around his eyes.

A line of concern drew Kit's brows together as she searched Elliott's face. "What's wrong, Elliott?"

He reached for Meredith's hand and squeezed it, an urgent request to help him out. How could she orchestrate a polite see-you-later?

But Elliott beat her to it. "An issue's come up. I'll tell ye later. But yer father looks tired. Why don't ye take him to his room to rest before dinner?" Then to Captain McCabe, he said, "I have dozens of stories to tell ye over a glass or two of whisky and a cigar. Why don't ye get some rest first?"

The captain smiled at Kit. "Dr. Fraser's a wise man. I would like to lie down for a bit."

Elliott managed to chuckle. "I believe that's the first time anyone's called me a wise man. People usually say I'm a goddamn son of a bitch."

Captain McCabe laughed, but it quickly turned into a coughing fit. He put his handkerchief to his mouth, and when he pulled it away, there was blood. Meredith's heart leaped to her throat. When Captain McCabe arrived an hour ago, his frail appearance shocked her, but she chalked it up to exhaustion from a long trip. Now she knew why he was so tired. He was dying.

Meredith glanced up toward the bedroom where James MacKlenna died over thirty years ago, surrounded by his family singing him into Heaven. She'd heard different versions of the story from Kit, Cullen, and Braham, and now Kit would bury her birth father in the same cemetery where her adoptive father would eventually rest.

Kit stood. "Come on, Dad. I'll show you the way."

Elliott helped the captain stand, and then Kit held on to his arm. "When you wake up, you can have a whisky with Elliott. Would you like that?"

Captain McCabe looked back over her shoulder. "I don't know, lass. From what ye told me about yer Elliott, there might not be any left." The captain laughed and coughed as he shuffled out of the room.

"Come on," Meredith said to Elliott. "Let's leave through the side door."

They crossed the brick drive that fronted the stallion paddock and walked down to the lake, delaying their conversation until they reached the wrought iron bench sitting in the shadow of a large oak tree.

Meredith didn't want to sit. She had too much pent-up energy, but she sensed Elliott needed to get off his feet, so she sat close beside him, gazed out over the water, and enjoyed the lovely scent of nearby azaleas. Elliott rested his arm across the back of the bench and toyed with the lace around her collar.

After a couple of minutes, she asked, "Did you lose the mare or the foal?"

"Neither one. They're both fine." That was all he said, and they sat in silence, letting the gentle breeze waft over them. The quiet stretched longer than she wanted, and it fed her anxiety. But it was his issue to share, and when he was ready, he'd tell her. She closed her eyes and let the sun warm her face.

She was almost dozing off when he said, "Paul arrived."

Her eyes flew open. There was more in what Elliott didn't say than in what he did. "Where's James Cullen?"

"They're both at the cabin."

"Then why are we still sitting here? Let's go see them." She popped to her feet and headed off toward the cabin. She planned to have a few words with her son and Paul, too, but that might have to wait until later.

"Where are ye going?" Elliott asked.

She stopped and turned to face him. "Where do you think? To see James Cullen, of course. Although I don't know why he didn't come straight to the mansion."

Elliott patted the bench. "Come sit down, Mere. There's a lot to tell ye first."

Tell me…first?

She didn't like the sound of that at all, and Elliott's dire expression only made it worse. She dragged her feet, returning to the bench. "Tell me quickly, then let's go."

He cleared his throat, his face nearly bone-white now. "Erik brought James Cullen here."

Her head jerked as if the words were bullets, and her forehead the target. "Erik? The Viking? How in the world did James Cullen hook up with him?"

"I'm not sure."

Erik was a violent, uncivilized man from the twelfth century who was capable of unimaginable atrocities. What he and the other Council members did to Colonel Bowes, Penny's professor at West Point, still made her stomach churn, and the thought of her son being anywhere near the Viking made her heart thump in her ears, behind her eyes, in her throat. Her body was suddenly on fire, like a night's worth of hot flashes hit all at once.

Her mind took off in fifth gear and tried to speed ahead of what Elliott intended to tell her about the Viking and James Cullen. But her mind suddenly detoured and ran smack into the memory of Montgomery Winery's security, informing her that her first husband had a massive stroke. She shivered before crawling back out of that memory, furious that it invaded her mind right now. It took all of her reserves to steel herself. She knew intuitively that her world was about to crash into the abyss—again.

She took a shaky breath. "Spit it out."

Elliott took a shaky breath, too, which wasn't at all comforting. She was rarely, if ever, out of control, but right now, she was borderline. She fisted her hands, hoping to keep that control from slipping through her fingers.

"James Cullen found Ensley in the Badlands and left her with Teddy Roosevelt—"

"Why on earth would he do that?" she interrupted.

Elliott held his hand up to quiet her down. "Paul was at the mercy of the brooch and only just arrived. Erik said a man named Sten, along with his associates, captured James Cullen while he was in Chicago."

"And Erik helped him escape?"

"Eventually."

She read volumes in her husband's choice of words and knew James Cullen's capture had involved much more than simply being detained.

Erik brought him here.

There was a tome in those words, too. Reading between the lines—James Cullen was unable to travel on his own.

"Dear God," she moaned. "Just tell me, is he dead?"

"No," Elliott said.

She lifted her eyes to gaze into Elliott's, rimmed with tears. "Is he dying?"

Elliott slowly shook his head. "His injuries are severe, but Erik assured me James Cullen would survive."

"Erik is a twelfth-century Viking, not a doctor! A broken bone might heal on its own over time, but that doesn't mean the person can walk normally again. James Cullen needs to be in a hospital."

Elliott stood and paced in front of her. "Erik arrived in time to save the lad, but not before the men broke almost every bone in his body."

"Dear God," she moaned. "How could anyone recover from that kind of trauma? He should be in a medical facility with access to specialists. I saw Emily walk in with you. That means James Cullen isn't getting any medical attention at all. We have access to the best medical care in the world, Elliott. Why are we sitting here?"

She shot to her feet. Elliott might have his priorities screwed up, but she didn't. She intended to take James Cullen home. But how? She didn't have a brooch, and she'd bet the winery Elliott wouldn't give her the brooch he carried. But if Paul just came through the fog, he'd have one.

"I'm taking my son home," she said, poking him in the chest with her finger. "And don't try to stop me. If you do, and James Cullen dies, it'll be your fault."

Elliott jerked back as if she'd slapped him, and that was just what she wanted to do.

"As long as we follow Erik's instructions, James Cullen won't die."

She blinked at the absurdity of his statement. "All those trips through time have short-circuited the wires in your brain. Neither one of us would be here right now if it weren't for the medical attention we received. James Cullen is seriously injured, and you're taking the word of a goddamn Viking."

She threw up her hands. "Go to hell." God, this couldn't be happening. She and Elliott were always on the same page. But this time, they weren't even reading from the same script. This was disastrous for their marriage, but more importantly, for James Cullen's survival.

She wasn't going to stand around and wait another minute. Elliott's delaying tactics had failed, and he couldn't stop her from seeing James Cullen.

The path to the cabin was on the other side of the lake. She bolted in that direction, with Elliott storming after her. It seemed like a ten-mile hike through the desert to get there. For the first time since that Hogmanay celebration all those years ago, when he blamed her for his horse's death, she felt the same emotional disconnect, and she hated it. But right now, she hated him more.

He caught up with her. "I have to tell ye the rest of the story, and this is going to be hard to believe."

She walked faster. "Not any harder than what you've already told me."

He took her hand, and her skin tingled where they touched. His energy was an electrical current supercharging hers, and she yanked her hand away. She might be the yin to his yang, but not today. She refused to get sucked into his absurd theory.

He opened his mouth to say something but must have thought better of it, and that suited her just fine.

It wasn't until they reached the clearing in front of the cabin that he said, "Meredith, stop. Ye have to listen to me, or ye can't go inside. There are rules."

"Screw the rules," she said as she marched toward the door.

He grabbed her arm. "Sit down and listen to me. Ye can bang on the door all ye want, but Paul won't let ye in. Ye're acting like—"

"A mother? You're damn right, I am." She sat down on the tree stump used for splitting wood and relaxed her neck and shoulders—or tried to. "You've got two minutes." Then she would use everything she could think of to get inside. Elliott was not going to keep her from her son.

"Erik killed the men who attacked James Cullen. Then he wrapped the lad from head to toe in his red cloak."

"Why?" she nearly shouted.

He shushed her. "It's a special fabric with healing powers."

"Like what?"

He shushed her again.

She folded her arms. "You have ninety seconds."

"The ancient people—those who lived long before the Vikings—made the cloak using the same materials used in the brooches."

"But the brooches are stones. How can a fabric last that long?"

He shushed her a third time, which infuriated her. "You have sixty seconds. And stop wasting your time shushing me."

He bit his lip, took a breath. "I don't know, but it's as ancient as the brooches. I don't have all the answers, Meredith. But I know this… If we believe in the power of the stones, then how can we not believe in the healing power of the cloak?"

"I don't have the same faith you have."

He squatted to be at eye level, and she wanted to shove him over, but she didn't.

"Ye have the same faith I do. It dims, then brightens, then dims again just like mine. But it's always there. Sometimes yers dims when mine brightens and vice versa, but it never goes completely dark."

"James Cullen still needs to be in a hospital. I won't change my mind about that."

Elliott stood and ran his hands over his thick gray hair. "Damn it, Meredith. If ye move him, he'll die. And I won't let ye do that. There's only one way we can play this. Erik said James Cullen should sleep for forty-eight to seventy-two hours, and when he wakes up—"

"If," she said, spitting out the word.

"No! Meredith! He *will* wake up. The cloak is his only chance. I've seen him, and God bless his soul. The only recognizable part of him is the birthmark on his foot. He had the shit beaten out of him, and the goddamn bastards took a knife to him and tried to skin him alive. If not for Erik, he would have died, and we would never have known what happened to him."

She screamed, "You goddamn bastard. I'll never be able to unsee that." She pushed away from him, lifted her skirts, and ran until she dropped to her knees in the freshly cut grass, doubling over in the most unbearable pain she'd ever experienced. She felt like she, too, was being skinned alive. She sucked in oxygen and screamed out in pain. "Not my beautiful boy! Tell me it's not true! I want my son back!"

Elliott knelt beside her and held her while she cried.

"He can't survive this, Elliott! He won't want to live with being disfigured and disabled."

"He won't be disfigured or debilitated."

"Good God. Are you that gullible? You believe everything that horrible Viking told you. Well, it's not true."

"People think time travel is impossible, but we know the truth, and James Cullen's body will completely heal."

Something about that didn't sound right to her. What was Elliott not saying?

His body will heal.

If she couldn't unsee James Cullen's tortured body after Elliott's description, James Cullen couldn't unsee it, either.

His mind.

"Oh, God!" she screamed again, ripping up handfuls of grass and shredding them until she exhausted herself. "He'll suffer emotionally from this, won't he?"

Elliott didn't say anything.

"You still remember crying in the barn when your mother left all those years ago. You have nightmares and call her name. James Cullen will scream out just like that. You never forget trauma. What happened to James Cullen will replay in his mind, torturing him for the rest of his life."

"We don't know what he'll remember."

She pulled up to a sitting position and wiped her eyes with her sleeve. "Even if James Cullen doesn't remember, the memory will still be there and will haunt him. But he won't understand why his heart races or why he runs away in fear. That's almost worse."

"Erik suggested he go to the monastery. And I agree. That's the only place his mind will have a chance to heal."

She swiped at her nose. "For how long?"

"As long as it takes."

"Months?"

"Maybe years."

Those words were like knives piercing her heart, each one plunging deeper than the last. "The monastery doesn't allow women, visitors, or phones. We won't know how he's doing."

"Paul is going with him."

"This is all Paul's fault anyway."

"No, it's not! If the brooches had taken him to James Cullen in Chicago, Sten and his henchmen would have tortured and killed them both. James Cullen will recover."

"I don't know how you can be so sure."

"Because I had a vision of James Cullen standing over our graves. He had gray hair, hunched shoulders, and a joyful smile. It'll work out for him. We just have to give him time, and we need to be patient."

"Paul can leave the monastery and call us, right?"

"Probably."

She glanced toward the cabin, where smoke poured from the

chimney. It had to be hot as hell in there. Paul should open the windows and allow in some fresh air and the scent of spring flowers.

"Let's go to the cabin. I want to see him."

"He's in a coma and completely covered with Erik's cloak. Ye can't touch him or look beneath the fabric."

"But you did," she said.

"No, I had a vision."

She gave a frustrated sigh. "When will he come out of the coma?"

"Two or three days. Just try to have faith in the process."

"In a magic cloak." She shook her head. "Why don't we go back a few days and prevent this from happening? We can stop Sten from finding James Cullen in Chicago and torturing him."

Elliott gave her a pitying smile like she was a child asking a ridiculous question, which pissed her off—again!

"Well, why not? I'm surprised Erik didn't try it. He seems to be able to come and go anytime he wants."

"The only time we tried to change history, we ended up with the same result," Elliott said.

"You're thinking of Kenzie's grandfather?"

"He still died, but he died a hero instead of a traitor. If we go back and try to stop it, we might be collateral damage. Not that I wouldn't give my life for my son, but it might make it worse for him. When we get home, let's talk to David and see what his thoughts are."

"Ask Erik."

"I don't think I'll ever see him again."

"Why not?"

Elliott gave her an exasperated look. She was frustrating him, but she didn't care.

"I don't know, Meredith!" Elliott took a deep breath and blew it out. "There are things I sense and other things I know for sure. The answer to your question lies somewhere in between."

"I intend to stay here with him until he wakes up," she said.

"I know it's what ye feel compelled to do, and I want to stay as well, but we have to keep this quiet. We can't tell anyone."

All these damn rules were too much to handle. She was close to screaming again but forced herself to moderate her voice. "Why the hell not?"

"Think about it. Sten knew where James Cullen was, which

means he must have come from the future and brought men with him. There might be others looking for him. We're all in danger here."

"Oh, no," she groaned. "That means Ensley and the guys are, too." Her panic and fear, after a momentary reprieve, spiked again. She reached for her phone, which of course, she didn't have. "We have to get word to them."

Elliott seemed to puzzle through that suggestion while pinching his fingers against his thumb and rolling them as if he held a cigar. And then he stilled his hand. "I can send a telegram to Ensley in care of Mr. Roosevelt, letting her know Tavis is on his way, and she's to leave with him immediately."

"Maybe Tavis, Remy, and Austin aren't even there yet. I mean, Paul left before we did, and he just arrived. Or did he just arrive here?"

"He just came through the fog."

"The brooches have even less control than we thought. Three different brooches carried travelers to different locations within hours of each other, but they arrived days apart. I wonder if we'll ever understand them."

"Since the ruby carried Kit off that ship and brought her to the farm, I've spent decades trying to work out their riddle. I've made notes of successes and failures. I struggle with how to be fair, how to hurt others less, and how to love ye more. I want to find meaning in all this, Meredith, but it seems the more I know, the less I know."

"Maybe your riddle is unsolvable." She moved to get up, but Elliott stood first and helped her to her feet, which wasn't easy considering the corset and layers of cotton and silk. It was comforting to feel the strength in his hand, his arms, and she thought she'd kiss him, but there was still too much tumult rampaging through her.

Plus, she had yet to find her balance with him. That would come. It always did, but in the meantime, she considered his dilemma for a moment and then said, "Until we have possession of twelve brooches and can unlock the door and its secrets, we won't be able to solve your riddle. I don't think anyone has ever mentioned whether Kit's father knew about the brooch."

"He knew it was a wedding gift, but not about the magic," Elliott said. "But speaking of the captain, he's not well."

"I think he's dying. As soon as Kit saw him, she turned white. I'm afraid he might not survive this visit."

A veil seemed to cover Elliott's eyes for a moment and then cleared. "From the look of Captain McCabe, he probably didn't think he'd survive the trip. His health might cause a problem for Kit and Cullen."

"Other than losing a beloved family member?"

"Aye. As soon as James Cullen wakes up, we need to return home, but Kit won't want to leave her father."

"Kit has said several times that she and Cullen might return to Napa, but the longer they stayed in the future, the less likely it seemed. Cullen won't decide to stay here without weeks of deliberation and consultation with Braham."

Meredith stepped up on the cabin's porch, steeling herself for what was to come, but wanted to settle Kit in her mind first. Once Meredith walked through that door, she wouldn't be able to focus on anyone or anything but her son.

"This riddle is easier to solve," she said. "Send the telegram and tell Ensley that Tavis is to bring her to Kentucky. That will give Kit and Cullen extra time to make a decision, and they should know more after Emily examines the captain. If modern medicine can help him, Kit will want to take him to the future. If his illness has progressed too far and he can't recover, then she'll want to stay until he passes."

"Then we'll wait for Emily's prognosis before I send the telegram."

The shutter on the window that opened onto the porch cracked open, and Paul peeked out. When Elliott waved, Paul slid back the bolt and opened the door. Hot air scented with cedar and eucalyptus blasted Meredith in the face.

Paul stared hard at her. "You understand what's happening here?"

She nodded. "I do." Then she brushed past him and swam through the thick, hot air toward the bed. "It's like a sauna in here."

"Erik said the heat and humidity keep the cloak moist, which helps the healing."

"How do you know it's James Cullen?" she asked.

"Erik described the birthmark on his foot," Elliott said.

She sat in the chair next to the bed. "Has he moved? Groaned? Made any sound at all?"

"Nothing," Paul said.

"What about his kidneys? Shouldn't he have a catheter?"

"I think he should have that and much more, but the Viking said he didn't need anything except the heat, humidity, and the red cloak."

"Do you want to take a break? I can sit with him," she said.

Paul shook his head. "I can easily stay awake for several days. After that, if JC isn't awake, I'll need to rest. But until then, I have plenty to do."

She noticed paper scattered across the table. "What are you working on?"

"I'm writing pseudo code on paper. I'll convert it later to programming language syntax."

"It looks like Greek," Meredith said.

"I read Greek, and it's quite different."

She reached out to touch James Cullen, but Paul snatched her hand back. "If you can't abide by the rules, you'll have to leave."

Meredith hissed at him. "This is your goddamn fault. If you hadn't screwed up in Asia, this never would have happened."

"JC left town without telling anyone where he was going, including me," Paul said. "By the time I arrived in Thailand, he'd covered his tracks, and I couldn't find him. I paid a dozen operatives to search for him. When I got word he'd escaped, I returned to the States."

"You should have told me."

Elliott flashed a stern look at Meredith and then another one at Paul. "Ye two barely know each other. What the hell is going on here?"

Meredith replayed the conversation. Had she outed herself? She cringed. Yep, she had. "It's not what it seems."

"It's exactly what it seems. Ye two"—Elliott wagged his finger from Meredith to Paul and back again—"have something going on. And I want to know what it is." When neither Meredith nor Paul said anything, Elliott yelled, "Now!"

Paul stepped away from the bed. "I'll be outside."

Elliott grabbed Paul by the lapels. "Sit yer ass down. Ye're not going anywhere."

"Stop it, Elliott," Meredith said. "Let's focus on James Cullen, and I'll explain everything when we get home."

Elliott released Paul with a slight shove, and his eyes flashed like daggers at her and Paul. "Ye're not going anywhere until ye tell me what ye're hiding."

She never wanted Elliott to find out what she'd done, and now really wasn't the time to explain it. "It's complicated."

"Bullshit!" Elliott walked over to the table where he'd left his drink earlier and tossed it back. "I don't know what the hell ye two have been doing, but if ye don't tell me the truth right now, ye won't like what comes next."

Elliott wasn't a man to throw down threats and not act on them. If he wanted to keep her away from James Cullen's bedside, he could do it.

"A few years ago, my researchers came across Paul's family. His mother is a McBain, and she is distantly related to David's father."

"Does David know?"

"I've never told him."

"Don't you think ye should have?"

"Probably. But David will understand why I didn't."

"I doubt it, but go on."

"I had background checks done, and when James Cullen went to work at the CIA, I opened some doors for Paul and put him in a position to work for James Cullen while Paul finished at Georgetown."

"Did Paul know what ye were doing?"

"Not at first. But after about a year, James Cullen was driving me crazy because he rarely took my calls and wouldn't answer my text messages. I talked to Paul and asked him if he would text me two to three times a week to let me know James Cullen was okay, and maybe once a week encourage James Cullen to call me. He agreed to do it if I stopped bugging James Cullen."

Elliott pointed his angry eyes at Paul. "Did ye tell James Cullen what ye were doing?"

"No," Paul said. "The point was to make life less stressful for him."

"It was an easy and uncomplicated way to tell me James Cullen was okay," Meredith said.

"So ye both knew James Cullen went back in time?"

"I told you I left JC at the stables. What I didn't tell you was that I watched him disappear, but I thought it was part of the work he was doing at the CIA," Paul said.

"I didn't know anything until you came back from Washington," Meredith said. "I tried to call Paul, but he didn't answer."

Elliott poured another drink. "Ye lied to me."

"It wasn't a lie."

He shot her a look exactly like the one he'd given her that night all those years ago that sent her running back to California. "How many times have we gone through this, Meredith? Failing to tell someone the truth is a lie of omission. Yer actions were both a lie and a sign of disloyalty. After all our years together, how could ye do that?"

"If I had suggested we arrange for someone to work for James Cullen to report back to us about his health and well-being, what would you have said?"

"It's out of the question."

"Well, it wasn't out of the question for me. I hired a family member to work for James Cullen as an insurance policy."

Elliott took his drink and dropped into the chair by the table. "How much did she pay ye?"

Paul looked at Meredith, and she nodded. "Nothing directly. She made large annual contributions to a charity of my choice—the Boys and Girls Clubs of America."

"How much are you getting from James Cullen?"

"Fifty thousand, plus room and board."

"How much were ye making at the CIA?"

"Elliott, stop it!" she snapped. "What's your point?"

"There hasn't been a day that I haven't worried about James Cullen. But unlike ye, when he told me to stay out of his life, I respected his request."

"But you knew he worked for the CIA, so you didn't stay completely out of his life."

"Unlike ye, I didn't act on what I knew."

"You might respect his boundaries, but I never could," she said. "He's my only child. I carried him for nine months, knowing cancer might kill me, but his life was and is more important than mine." She stopped and stared at her son lying motionless on the bed, completely covered by the red fabric. "I don't regret anything I've done."

"I'm sorry ye see it that way." To Paul, he said, "Give me yer pistol."

Paul handed it over, and Elliott did a pistol press check. "Now give me yer brooch."

Paul handed that over, too.

"Now take her to the house and send Cullen down here."

"I'm not going anywhere," she said.

"Fine."

Fine?

Elliott never gave up that easy.

He went to the cabinet, poured her a glass of whisky, handed it to her, and then picked up his glass. *"Slàinte mhath."*

Meredith raised hers, finding his actions highly suspicious, but she tossed back the drink and set the glass aside. If he could act normal, so could she.

Fifteen to twenty minutes later, the quiet, the warmth in the room, the eucalyptus-scented air, and the whisky all combined to make her so sleepy she could barely hold her eyes open.

"Ye look tired, Meredith. Go back to the house and rest."

She couldn't argue with him. If she didn't lie down, she'd fall over. Everything in the room was going out of focus, and it was then that she realized he'd drugged her.

"You…sssson…of…a…bitch," she said, slurring her words.

And that was the last she knew.

52

MacKlenna Farm, KY (1885)—Elliott

A LIGHT RAP on the door awakened Elliott from a sound sleep. He'd dozed off while browsing through the collection of Shakespeare from Sean's library. He immediately looked at James Cullen on the bed, still hidden by the red cloak, and let out a deep sigh.

No change.

Elliott closed the heavy leather volume and stretched.

Another knock, and then a woman's whispered announcement. "It's Kit."

Of all the possibilities to show up on the doorstep, he preferred Kit above anyone else. If she gave him grief, he didn't have to worry about pushing back and hurting her feelings. She gave as good as she got.

He shuffled across the plank floor and peered out between the slats. She was standing on the porch alone, with the handle of a straw basket slung over her arm. He slid back the bolt, opened the door wide enough for her to enter, then closed it and slid the bolt back into place.

Kit lifted the veil attached to her black riding hat. "You're acting like a jerk, but you know that already. Right?" She peeled off her gloves, finger by finger, and clutched the kid leather in a stranglehold.

"Aye. I'm an asshole. I won't disagree. But are ye complaining about anything in particular?"

She stepped over to the bed and looked down at James Cullen's motionless body hidden beneath the cloak. "Let's see. For starters, how about keeping a mother from her child?"

"Leave it alone, Kit. Ye know the rules."

He tossed an extra log on the fire, then poured a few drops of oil into a pot of hot water before drizzling the scented water over the sauna rocks, increasing the humidity and eucalyptus aroma.

Kit's gaze slowly moved from James Cullen's feet to his head and back again. "Has he moved at all?"

"I thought so, but I decided it was my imagination." He lifted the basket off her arm and carried it over to the table. After three days, his nose was so full of the stink of eucalyptus that he could barely smell the fried chicken and yeast rolls.

She removed her hat, tossed the gloves into the upside-down crown, and placed the felt hat on the table. "You'll regret what you're doing. You better fix it soon."

He walked back to the door and reached for the bolt. "If ye're going down that road again, ye can leave and not come back, which is what I told ye yesterday. So where's Cullen?"

"You've run off everybody else. I'm sticking around and taking your abuse because you're acting just like the jerk I remember from my childhood. I ignored you then, and I'm not paying attention to you now. And Cullen's not coming back. He's pissed at the way you're treating Meredith. He said if he came back, he'd knock you out."

"I'd like to see him try."

She rolled her eyes. "You're so full of yourself. No one's going to take your side on this. If we were home, the family would ostracize you until you make up for drugging and excluding Meredith, and as mad as everyone is, a simple, 'I'm sorry,' won't do the trick. You've got to go big if you ever expect to get out of the doghouse."

Kit didn't have to tell him what he already knew. He blamed Meredith, but truth be told, it was his fault. He should have gone with his gut and kept tabs on James Cullen—and communicated with her about what he was doing. Meredith had wanted to be discreet, which was fine, but she didn't have enough control over her plan. And that was her mistake.

Kit dug into her skirt pocket and pulled out a piece of paper. "Here's a telegram from Tavis. They found Ensley and will bring her to MacKlenna Farm to return home with Cullen and me."

"Good. When do they arrive?"

She thrust out her hand. "Read it yourself, and you'll know everything I know."

He took the telegram and read it. "I'm relieved. That frees ye and Cullen to stay as long as ye want."

He reached for a plate in the cabinet and put two pieces of chicken on it. "If ye're going to stick around and annoy me, tell me about yer father."

"It's not my goal to annoy you, but there was a time when you didn't want me to leave you."

That certainly gave him pause. It nearly destroyed him when Kit returned to the past to marry Cullen, but it ultimately led Elliott to Meredith. He sent Meredith away before and restored the relationship. If he played it right, he could do it again.

Aye. I'm an asshole.

Kit sat in a chair at the table and unwrapped the biscuits. "Emily examined Dad. He has symptoms common in both TB and lung cancer."

"Jesus Christ!" Elliott said midbite. "TB? Get him out of the house now before he infects everyone else."

"Without a skin test, Emily can't be sure. But Dad's coughing up blood, has a non-specific fever, dramatic weight loss, hoarseness, and deep breathing aggravates his chest pain. The symptoms point more toward cancer than TB."

"Emily still needs to be careful."

"She's put protocols in place. There're only a few people who can go in his room, and those who do must keep their distance, wear masks, and wash their hands."

"Have ye suggested he go to the future for treatment?"

"He won't go. He said he's been like this for months, and he's not going to last much longer. He'd rather die here than in a future world."

"But maybe modern medicine can extend his life. Can't ye talk him into it?"

Kit shook her head. "God knows I've tried." She picked up her suede gloves and straightened the seams. "I'm not here to talk about *my* Dad's life"—she pointed to JC—"but his."

Elliott picked up a biscuit. "Don't go there, missy."

She smacked her gloves on the tabletop. "Damn it, Elliott. You have to allow Meredith to come in here. You can't tell me to take care of my father and ignore her request to sit with her son. It's not fair."

Elliott looked at James Cullen's lifeless body. "I don't give a flying fuck what's fair. Those assholes didn't think about what was fair when they tortured and tried to kill him. And as for Meredith, she was hoist with her own petard."

"She what?"

Elliott ate the last bite of biscuit, then bit into a chicken leg. The tasty, juicy meat exploded in his mouth. "It means to be caught in a trap of yer own making."

"I know what it means." She flipped open the book on the table. "What are you reading, Shakespeare? Must be *Hamlet*." She closed the book and tapped her fingers on top of it. "Look, Elliott. If I had been around during that first Hogmanay when you scared Meredith off, I would have told you to go after her, and that's my advice now. You can't blame her for what happened to James Cullen. That's just as illogical as blaming her for the death of your horse."

He put the chicken bone down and pushed back from the table. "It's time for ye to leave." He stepped over to the door and opened it. "Thank ye for the food."

Kit snatched up her hat and stomped toward him. "You're making a mistake, and don't come crying to me when Meredith won't take you back."

"Ye don't have to worry about that."

"What? That you'll come crying to me, or that Meredith won't want you back?"

"Goodbye, Kit."

"Not going to answer? Suit yourself. But if you continue to be such an ass, you'll lose even me."

As soon as Kit strode out, he slammed the door and bolted it. His vision blurred. If there was ever a time he needed Meredith, it was now. But she betrayed him. And he couldn't get past his anger. He watched through the shutter slats as Kit mounted her horse and rode off.

"Dad. What are you doing here?"

Elliott jerked around to find James Cullen sitting up in bed. The red cloak had dropped to his waist. The glistening skin on his arms and chest was void of hair, and other than sweat beading on him, there wasn't a scratch or bruise, not even on his face.

It was a miracle. Tears streaked down Elliott's cheeks, and he crossed himself. "Do ye know where ye are?"

James Cullen glanced around the cabin. "I've never been here before. Where are we?"

"In a cabin on MacKlenna Farm. It's 1885."

"Oh, right. I left Ensley with Teddy Roosevelt and came here to rob Uncle Braham's casket of a few gold bars." Then James Cullen's face drained of color, and he started shaking so hard the bed rocked.

Elliott had to get James Cullen home ASAP. Charlotte could sedate him or something until he could get his son to the monks.

"We need to go home." He walked toward the bed, but the closer he got, the more agitated James Cullen became. "I'm not going to hurt ye, son."

James Cullen snarled like a rabid dog. "Stay away from me!" He held his hands out as he scooted backward and pulled the cloak up to his chin. "Don't come any closer."

"I have to. We must hold on to each other to go through the vortex."

"Don't. Touch. Me."

Elliott paused. Maybe he couldn't do this alone after all. But he had run everybody off, and now he was stuck. He had no one to help him restrain James Cullen. Elliott sat in the chair next to the bed and maintained his distance.

"It's time to go home, or do ye want to stay here?"

"In 1885? No."

"Then let me take ye home."

"As long as you don't touch me."

Treat him like a skittish colt and take advantage of the first opportunity.

Elliott fumbled with the diamond brooch in his pocket and finally popped it open. All he had to do was recite the chant he knew by heart, and they'd be off. "I won't, lad, but can ye hold on to me? We have to stay connected."

"I can't leave without Ensley."

"Tavis, Remy, and Austin are with her now."

"How do you know?"

"I sent them a telegram, and Tavis sent one in return."

"So you have two recovery teams here?"

"Aye. One here and one in North Dakota."

James Cullen glanced around the cabin. "Did Mom come with you?"

"Aye, but it was my turn to sit with ye. Kit just left. She brought a food basket. Are ye hungry?"

"No. I must have had a big dinner. I'm not hungry at all. We can wait until Mom comes back."

"She might not be here until tomorrow. Tavis is bringing Ensley here because Kit and Cullen aren't ready to return. Mom can come with them."

James Cullen closed his eyes and relaxed a bit. The cloak dropped to his waist again, giving Elliott an even better look at his son's skin. It was as smooth as a baby's butt. Not a blemish of any kind. But what struck Elliott the most was the development of James Cullen's body. He looked like Captain America in the *Avengers* movies the grandkids watched all the time.

His chest was broader, fuller, more three-dimensional, and his neck and arm muscles bulged. He looked strong enough to pick Elliott up with one hand, lift him over his head, and toss him out the door.

"I can't think about it right now," James Cullen said. "You decide."

"Then we should leave now. I'll write a note, so yer mom will know we've returned home."

"Which brooch does Tavis have?"

"Since Austin was going, they took the amethyst."

"I'm surprised Austin agreed to go on an adventure."

"He didn't have a choice. Thanks to Pops. But I'll tell ye about it later."

Maybe Elliott could get James Cullen home and on his way to the mountains before the rest of the group arrived. That would save him from having another battle with Meredith.

"I don't know, Dad. Mom will be pissed if we go off without her."

"Well, here's the deal, son. Ye don't have any clothes, and I can't leave ye alone to go up to the house to get her."

"Why not?"

"If I left ye alone, yer mother would kick my ass back to the twenty-first century."

James Cullen fiddled with the red cloak. Then before Elliott could take a deep breath, James Cullen's expression changed into a potent, churning cocktail of rage and fear that must have permeated his brain chemistry.

His dark brown eyes hardened like black granite with bits of history locked inside, and they transformed into a frightening coldness that made Elliott afraid of his son.

His gut tightened, and stomach acid heaved up into his throat. The thumping of his pounding heart dulled the sound of the popping and crackling fire.

He couldn't rid himself of images of his son's torture. And based on James Cullen's terrified expression and rigid body language, he couldn't rid himself of them, either.

Elliott started reciting the chant, and as the fog swept up around his feet, Elliott tackled his tortured son.

53

Mallory Plantation—Ensley

THE RIDE THROUGH the vortex seemed to take only seconds, but the swirling made her so dizzy Ensley couldn't piece together what happened on the train in those last moments before their escape.

Once the swirling stopped, two muscular bodies held her sandwiched between them.

Gunshots. Remy. Austin.

Remy's warm breath brushed her neck, and Austin's fluttered across her cheek. They were alive. And so was she.

With anxious anticipation, she did what she'd done dozens of times during her short bull riding career—breathed deeply and cleared her mind. That was the only way to prepare for what was about to happen—the unknown. Although she mentally choreographed the possibilities, shit happened. She fumbled for her knife.

The fog cleared slowly, but her heart beat faster. All she could see through the thinning, misty veil was a concrete floor, stainless steel cabinets, and bright lights that made her blink.

It looks like a prison. Where am I?

JC's aunt and uncle, Charlotte Mallory and Braham McCabe, rushed toward her.

"Remy's bleeding," Charlotte said.

"They fired several shots," Ensley said, peering between Remy's arms still folded over her head. "Austin was knocked unconscious before the shooting started."

Remy rolled off her, groaning. "Fuck! Those bastards shot me in the ass."

"Where are you hurt, Ensley?" Charlotte asked, kneeling beside her.

"I'm not."

"You have blood on you, your buttons are gone, your chemise is torn, and you have what looks like a knife cut down your sternum. You don't need stitches, but I need to clean the wound."

Ensley tugged the pieces of her jacket together. "It can wait."

"Why doan you ask me where *I'm* hurt?" Remy whined.

"I see two wounds. How many times were you hit?" Charlotte asked.

"Twice. Give me the auto-injector in my bag."

"You're ten feet from my exam room," Charlotte said. "Let me look at the wounds."

"Look all you want, but get me the fucking auto-injector, or I'll get up and do it myself."

Charlotte checked Austin's pulse, and he opened his eyes as soon as she touched his wrist. "What happened to you?" she asked.

"Son of a bitch caught me off guard and bashed me on the back of the head. I've got a hell of a headache," Austin grumbled. "What's wrong with Remy?"

"We were trying to get away when the cook and another guy burst into the bedroom and started shooting," Ensley said. "He got hit twice in the ass."

Austin chuckled. "That's what you get for riding on top, cowboy."

"Where the hell do you expect me to ride, asshole?"

Austin chuckled again. "On the bottom."

"You fuck. Stop trying to make me laugh."

"Clean up your language," Charlotte snapped.

"Sorry, but when you get shot, off-color language is permissible."

Charlotte looked up at her husband. "Austin has a knot on the back of his head with a possible concussion. Ensley has a minor six-inch laceration on her sternum that doesn't require stitches, and Remy has two gunshot wounds in his buttocks. As soon as I get his clothes off, I'll know how serious they are. Call David and Kenzie. We need help down here."

Braham moved away and made the phone call.

Charlotte dug through Remy's bag. "Ensley, take these scissors and cut off his trousers. Start at his waist and cut straight down until I can see the entire upper outer quadrant, then continue until his entire right buttock is visible."

Ensley took the scissors and started cutting through Remy's wool trousers and black briefs. As soon as she uncovered the two wounds, Charlotte cleansed the skin with alcohol wipes, removed the red safety plug from the injector, placed the yellow end of the injector against Remy's skin, and depressed the black firing plunger.

"They're on their way," Braham said. "What else can I do?"

"Write down the time of the injection and get me more compression pads." She unwrapped the few pads she found in Remy's bag and pressed them against the two wounds.

Austin rolled over, and his green eyes widened when he saw her, and they were naked with feeling. He was genuinely worried about her. "Goddamn it. What'd he do to you?"

"When you didn't show up, I knew something was wrong. He threatened me, and I knew I was on my own." Her lip quivered, remembering the pop of the bullet, the shell casing pinging on the floor, and the warm blood splatter. "I shot him."

"Shit!" Austin said. "Dead?"

"Dead."

"Jesus," Charlotte said.

"Goddamn," Braham said.

"Ensley's got fucking balls," Remy mumbled. "She was calm as Hang Drum music when she found me tied up. She's a fucking warrior."

Austin kissed her forehead. "She sure as hell is. You should see her on a bronc. Got nerves of steel." He pulled her into his arms and hugged her. "Talk to Charlotte later. She's our resident shrink, too. What you went through might prey on your mind for a while."

"We'll do that today," Charlotte said. "When I tell you it's time to talk, don't put me off. It's important to work through what happened as soon as possible."

It wasn't Ensley's first trauma, but she'd never talked to anyone before. This time was different. It was trauma upon trauma. What other counselor would even believe she was abandoned in 1885, broke her foot, almost died of thirst, nearly killed by a bear, watched the bear maul and kill her horse and Erik, was assaulted, shot at, and forced to kill a man?

It was all too much, but Charlotte would understand. "I won't put you off, believe me."

Braham returned with a handful of gauze pads. "What now?"

"Wheel the gurney over here, and let's get Remy on it."

"I can walk," Remy said.

"You can walk out tomorrow. Right now, I'm trying to control the bleeding. So be still."

"Can ye take care of it?" Braham asked, "or should we take him to the hospital?"

"I can do it. Both are flesh wounds. He got lucky."

Braham lowered the gurney, and Remy used his forearms to pull himself on it. "Yeah, real lucky."

"Let me take the brooch and lock it in the safe before it gets lost."

"Sure," Remy said, slapping it down on Braham's palm.

"What can I do to help?" Ensley asked.

"There's a chart on the wall of the exam room with concussion symptoms. Run through the checklist with Austin."

"He ain't got a…con…cussion," Remy said, slurring his words. "Bastard's head's too hard."

"You're probably right," Charlotte said, smiling at Ensley, "but just in case he has a soft spot we haven't seen before, Ensley should check him out."

"I don't need a chart. I learned all the symptoms during my bull-riding days and never forgot them."

"Bull riding?" Braham asked, giving her an appreciative nod. "That does take balls."

"I haven't been on a bull in over a decade," she said. "My last ride didn't have the best outcome."

"But you just rode a bronc," Austin said.

"I shouldn't have, but I couldn't resist the temptation." Ensley went through her mental concussion checklist and asked Austin, "Do you know where you are?"

"The cleanroom."

"Where's that?"

"On the plantation near Richmond."

"Okay, now follow my finger." She held up a finger and slowly moved it side to side. "How many fingers do you see?"

"One."

"Are you sick to your stomach?"

"Not sick. Not dizzy. Just a headache." He grabbed hold of one of the steel table's legs and pulled himself up.

"Are you dizzy now?" she asked.

"Nope." He reached down for her. "Are you?"

"No. I'm good. We're both good, Charlotte. What else can I do?"

"The shower is over there," she said, pointing to a door beneath a sign that said Locker Room. "Go get cleaned up. You'll find everything you need, from scrubs to shampoo. Help yourself."

Double doors swished open, and David and Kenzie strode in, stopped short, and David's brown eyes lasered in on Ensley, Austin, and then Remy. "Welcome back, but where the hell is JC?" He then looked at Braham. "And Elliott and his crew?"

"Forget them. I'm shot...in the ass." Remy flung out his hand. "Hold my hand, Ensley."

"Leave my girl alone, man," Austin said, grinning at her.

"Your girl? Fuck... Since when?"

Yeah! Since when?

Kenzie made a beeline to Ensley and hugged her. "I hope it wasn't too horrible. It seems every new adventure is worse than the last."

Ensley accepted the warm hug and tried to smile, but her face failed to cooperate. "I made it back, and that's all that matters right now."

"How long were ye in the past?" David asked.

"Weeks," Ensley said.

"Three days," Austin added.

Kenzie threw shade at Austin. "Three days, and you're already calling Ensley, 'my girl.' Damn, you O'Grady men move fast. You've even got Rick beat. Can't wait to hear this one."

Ensley tipped her head back so she could look up at Austin. "He's exaggerating. He calls his horse 'my girl,' too."

"My horse is a stallion, and I'm as straight as that ruler over there." Then Austin slapped his chest and crooked up a corner of his mouth in a too-knowing smirk. "I thought you had feelings for me. Did I misread your signals?"

Before she could respond with something not too off-color about a holiday romance, fog rose out of the concrete floor next to her. Startled, she forgot about Austin and jumped out of the way before the fog snatched her up and carried her off again. No mulligans for her. No double-whammies. No repeat performances. Her feet were staying safely in the twenty-first century.

A man's voice yelled from inside the fog, "I'll kill you if you don't get off me."

That's not just any man's voice. It's JC!

David darted over to a storage cabinet and threw open the doors. Kenzie and Braham joined him, and they all grabbed a weapon and extra mags. When Austin and Ensley saw what they were doing, they both reached for guns and mags. Then, taking their cues from the others, they chambered a round. The five of them formed a circle around the fog and took up shooting stances.

When the fog cleared, Elliott was sitting on top of JC, pinning his muscular arms to the floor. *Shit!* JC had expected the reunion with his father would be testy, but it looked far worse than that.

Ensley lowered her weapon, as did the others.

JC wasn't wearing a stitch of clothing, but a swath of red fabric was tangled around his abdomen and thighs. *Where'd he get those pecs?* He looked like one of the bodybuilders who worked out at her gym, complete with bulging veins. But wait a minute… When he stripped off his shirt to wash up that first night at Elkhorn Ranch, he didn't look like he did now. And that was only a couple of weeks ago.

"Settle down, son, before one of us gets hurt."

JC pulled up his legs and twisted his upper body, unbalancing Elliott. Then using the power in his legs, he rolled over, reversing their positions.

David shoved his gun into his waistband, came up behind JC, and grabbed him in a chokehold. "JC, calm down before ye hurt yer father or I hurt ye."

"Let go of me, David. I don't want to hurt you."

"Stop fighting yer da. Now!"

When David didn't release his hold, JC flipped him, and David landed on his back.

JC jumped to his feet. "Leave me the hell alone. That means all of you."

The red cloak clung to him, rippling over his muscles and genitals, and she couldn't stop staring. When she finally took her eyes off him, she realized the red cloak was identical to the one Erik wore in her dreams. Was it Erik's? And if so, that must be why he wasn't wearing it when he fought the bear. But why give it to JC?

"JC," Ensley said, as calmly as she could manage. "Did you see Erik after you left me? Is that how you got his cloak?"

JC glanced down at the fabric clinging to him as if static held it there. "I don't know… I don't remember…" And then his eyes glazed over, he convulsed, and his tortured screams echoed off the walls.

Ensley cringed. Never in her life had she heard anything so harrowing, so gut-wrenching. She'd been in the arena when cowboys were being trampled and gored by bulls, but they never sounded like JC's agonized, enraged screams.

Elliott climbed to his feet, and David shot up off the floor. They both remained where they stood, watching JC, searching for an opening. When JC stopped screaming, he reached for Kenzie, catching her off guard. He yanked the gun out of her hand, pulled her close, and wrapped his arm around her neck.

"JC, drop the gun. Now!" Braham barked, pointing his weapon at JC.

"Yer fight's with me, James Cullen. Let Kenzie go," Elliott said.

JC looked over his shoulder, retaining his hold on Kenzie, did a quick sweep of the room with his gun arm outstretched. "My fight is with every fucking one of you." His gravelly voice made him sound possessed.

Out of the corner of Ensley's eye, she watched Charlotte, armed with a hypodermic syringe, tiptoe out of the room where she'd taken Remy. JC continued waving the gun. She snuck up behind him and jabbed the needle into his ass, pressed the plunger, and pulled it out—two seconds max.

Braham used his gun to signal to his wife to move out of the way. She backed up, but before she could get out of range, JC hooked his other arm around her neck while still gripping the gun.

"What the hell did you give me?" he snarled at her.

"A sedative," Charlotte said in a smooth, calming, almost hypnotic voice. "You'll start to feel sleepy very soon. Why don't you give me the gun?"

"Hell, no! I need it to get out of here."

"Where are you going?" Charlotte asked as if talking to a frightened child.

JC swayed and loosened his grip on her, but she didn't move.

"I've...got...to find...Kristen," he said.

"Did you see her recently?"

He nodded. "She...saved me."

"She saved you before, didn't she? When you were lost in the cave," Charlotte said.

JC blinked. And blinked again, obviously struggling to keep his eyes open.

Ensley watched the tableau play out, and Kenzie impressed her as much as Charlotte. There was no fear in Kenzie's eyes, only alertness and confidence. Kenzie knew she could take JC down but was waiting to see what he would do next. When he swayed again, she did just that, and JC sprawled on the concrete floor. If Ensley had blinked, she would have missed it.

David yanked the gun out of JC's hand and shoved it in his waistband with the other Glock. "Good work. Ye okay?"

"Nobody's gotten the drop on me before—ever," Kenzie said, looking down at JC. "But I'm fine. I hope I didn't hurt him."

"He wouldn't know if ye did."

The sedative finally took effect, and JC's eyes rolled back in his head while his ferocious smile faded. And the resemblance to his father was never more pronounced. He'd aged. Not by much, but he did look older. The changes were so subtle that if she hadn't just spent days looking at him, she might not have noticed. And his hair was lightly salted at the temples.

Braham shoved his gun into his waistband before pulling Charlotte into a ferocious hug. "Don't ever do anything like that again."

She hugged him back. "I've known JC most of his life. He wouldn't hurt me."

"The James Cullen ye've known wouldn't hurt ye, but this one isn't himself."

"I'm sorry I scared you. I won't do it again."

He kissed her. "Ye haven't changed since the day I first laid eyes on ye in Chimborazo Hospital. Ye risked yer life then, and ye risked yer life today. And I doubt ye'll do anything different tomorrow."

"You know me well, don't you, major?"

He patted her ass. "Damn right, I do, Cap'n Mallory."

"I haven't played the role of Cap'n Mallory since I rescued you from that Confederate hospital. One of the smartest things I've ever done."

He kissed her again. "And not a day's gone by that I don't appreciate it."

She tugged on her earlobe, drawing attention to the diamond stud earring. "And I like the way you show your appreciation."

"Anything for my bride."

"Then, will you put JC in the bed next to my exam room?" she asked. "As soon as I finish with Remy, I'll examine him and do some blood work. But for now, restrain him. I don't want him getting up and threatening anyone else." She shot an intense look at Elliott. "What in God's name happened to him?"

Completely out of character, Elliott looked ready to cry. But he straightened, took a breath, and released it slowly. "Members of the Illuminati captured him in Chicago and tortured him. Erik barely arrived in time to save his life."

"He doesn't have a mark on him," David said. "Was it psychological torture?"

"They broke every bone in his body and skinned his arms…and…and…chest…" Elliott's voice trailed off, and he looked pale and forlorn beneath the scruff, which was also out of character for the man who always appeared tanned, trim, and perfectly coiffed.

It was one of those brief moments when Ensley's brain couldn't wrap itself around what Elliott just said. She didn't want to think about how horrible everything was now, and she wished, for just a brief second, that it was all a bad dream.

And then reality returned with a *wham*. And she nearly dropped to her knees. Austin must have sensed she was close to freaking out because he was immediately at her side.

"I've got you."

She leaned against him, appreciating the simple courtesy and concern. Austin took her gun, ejected the mag, racked the slide, removed the chambered round, and then did the same to his before placing both Glocks on the stainless steel table.

Charlotte sucked in a deep breath. "Dear God. No wonder his mind is so distressed and agitated. But if they did all that to him, I'm as confused as David. How's it possible JC doesn't have a scratch?"

"If ye can figure out how that happened, clue me in. I doubt even James Cullen knows." The color slowly returned to Elliott's face. "Let's carry him over to the bed." He bent to pick up his son's legs, but David stepped in front of him, and, with Braham's help, they carried JC and placed him in the bed. Elliott straightened the red fabric, so it covered JC from neck to toes. "James Cullen needs some of those heated blankets from the warmer."

"I'll get them." Kenzie pulled two out of the warmer, and she and Elliott, who was on the other side of the bed, quickly cocooned JC in the warm blankets.

Ensley stood there, helpless, still breathing uneasily in the aftermath of JC's violence. Austin tightened his hold, and she tried to relax against him, and just as the heat from the warming blankets soaked into JC, Austin's heat seemed to flow into her as well.

Elliott tilted Kenzie's chin and studied the red marks on her neck. "I'm sorry the lad did that to ye. Erik didn't mention James Cullen could be violent."

"No one knows what's going on inside another person's head. Erik is a Viking. What's violent to us might not be violent to him," she said.

Braham returned to the bed with two pairs of handcuffs. "JC will be furious when he wakes up and discovers he's restrained, but Charlotte's right. We can't take the risk. Sorry, Elliott."

"Do what ye have to do."

"How long was he with Erik?" Kenzie asked.

Elliott shrugged.

"JC left me over two weeks ago to go to MacKlenna Farm," Ensley said.

"Why'd he leave ye, lass?" Braham asked.

"He said there was gold in your casket there. He was going to borrow a few gold bars, and then we were supposed to meet in Cleveland and travel to New York City with Mr. Roosevelt."

"He shouldn't have left you. That's the number one cardinal rule of time traveling," Kenzie said.

David coughed. "Did ye really say that, Kenz? Don't ye remember running away from me and nearly getting yerself killed?"

"The situation was different."

"The only difference I see is that this time it was JC and not ye."

"Okay, you're right. Almost getting killed is the reason it's the cardinal rule. And I'm guilty of breaking it, but if you'd been honest with me, I wouldn't have run away."

"I accept my share of the blame," David said.

She chuckled. "I love it when you show vulnerability. It makes you even sexier."

He winked at her.

Kenzie returned the wink, and in that quick opening and closing of her eye, she telegraphed an "I love you" to her husband, and it gave Ensley goosebumps to witness the love flowing between them.

Then Kenzie turned her attention to the red fabric she was caressing. "What kind of material is this?"

"It's like linen." Ensley reached inside her pocket and pulled out the piece she'd found in the hem of her jeans. "Shortly after I arrived in the past, I fell and broke my foot, and it scared me to death. I went to sleep, and when I woke up, my foot was no longer broken. It wasn't till later that I found this little scrap. It came off Erik's cloak."

"I didn't notice a tear in the fabric," Elliott said.

"I didn't, either," Kenzie added.

Ensley held her piece against the cloak. "The fabric's the same. Maybe Erik had another cloak, but if he did, he would have worn it when he fought the bear."

"What bear?"

"The bear that killed him," Ensley said sadly.

"Erik's dead?" Elliott asked.

Ensley nodded. "Can I tell you about it later? There's too much going on right now."

"Sure," Elliott said. "But I doubt Erik has…had…another one. He seemed oddly resigned when we talked, but he was firm about James Cullen having the cloak now. And he said James Cullen was never to be without it."

"For how long?" Kenzie asked.

A worried frown creased Elliott's brow. "The rest of his life."

"Did he say why?" David asked.

The creases in Elliott's brow deepened as he considered David's question. "No. Just that he must always have it with him."

"Like Superman's suit underneath his clothes?" Ensley asked. "Erik should have explained. Why would JC ever believe that?"

"He seems attached to it already," Kenzie said, "or rather, his body seems attached to it. Did you notice the way it clung to him?"

Did I notice? How could I not?

"It has static," Ensley said.

"Maybe it's a shield that will protect him in the future. If I believed that, I'd never go anywhere without it." Kenzie then crossed her arms and leaned against the stainless steel table. "Elliott, where are Meredith and the others? Did you drop them off somewhere, or did you intentionally leave them behind?"

Elliott ignored the question and walked over to the drink station, where he put a pod in the coffee machine. "Anyone want coffee?"

"No!" Kenzie snapped. "Where is Meredith?"

"And Kit and Cullen?" Braham added.

Charlotte popped her head out of her exam room. "And Emily?

I could use her help right now."

"They're still at MacKlenna Farm," Elliott said, stirring a dollop of cream into his cup of coffee, which Ensley thought was odd. He drank his coffee black, just like JC. Was he even aware of what he was doing?

Kenzie gasped with such force it almost sucked all the oxygen out of the room. "You left Meredith—"

"And my best friend—" Braham said.

"And Emily!" Charlotte added.

"And Kit," Elliott confessed. "When Erik brought James Cullen to the farm, he was in a healing coma. Erik said no one should touch him or lift the cloth to check his injuries until he emerged from the coma in forty-eight to seventy-two hours."

"If he was that injured," Braham said, "ye should have come home."

"Erik said if we touched him, he would die."

"And you believed him?" Kenzie demanded.

Elliott slammed his fist on the countertop. Ensley jumped, Austin jerked, David glared, Braham clenched his fists, and Kenzie shot Elliott full of eye darts.

"Dammit, Kenzie. I had to do what I thought was best for my son, and ultimately the family. I couldn't risk any interference."

Kenzie tapped her fingers on her crossed arms. "You believed a twelfth-century Viking over Charlotte's medical knowledge. Is that what you're saying?"

When Elliott showed more interest in his cup of coffee than in answering her question, Kenzie looked from David to Braham, to Austin, to Ensley, and back to Elliott.

"I've known you and Meredith for almost twenty years. You are two of the strongest, most bull-headed people I've ever met. If you believed in Erik and Meredith believed in Charlotte, then what we have here is the unstoppable force paradox."

"An unstoppable force cannot be unstoppable in the same universe where an immovable object exists, as it would no longer be unstoppable. And Meredith and I do live in the same universe."

"I hate your esoteric arguments. You pull them out every time you need a distraction. Well, it's not going to work this time."

"Ye started it, lass."

Kenzie pushed away from the table and approached him. "When was the last time you saw her?"

"Not that long ago."

Kenzie punched him in the chest with the heel of her hand. "You asshole. You shut Meredith out, didn't you? She disagreed with you, so you took JC and hid him away from her. And then you abandoned her." Kenzie held out her hand. "Give me the damn brooch."

"No. I'm the—"

"Don't throw that Keeper shit at me. You abandoned your wife in another century. That's unforgivable. I'm going back for her, and if she never wants to see you again, if she wants a divorce, I won't blame her. She forgave you once, but I don't see it happening again. Now give me the goddamn brooch."

Ensley had never heard anyone talk to another person like Kenzie spoke to Elliott, and if she could talk to him that way, why was JC afraid to confront his father?

"Kenzie, get off yer goddamn high horse. Ye've overstepped the boundaries we've set. After I take James Cullen to the monastery, I'll go back for her."

"Bullshit," Ensley said under her breath.

"Like hell!" David's brown eyes turned almost black. "If ye leave right now, ye could spend six weeks making things right with Meredith and come back, and ye'll only be gone a few minutes. JC won't even be awake from the drug Charlotte gave him. Ye have no excuse."

"I just want to know one thing, Elliott." Kenzie tunneled the fingers of both hands through her hair and held it back for a second or two before letting it go. The strands resettled like a fine curtain framing her face. "What was so damn important that you had to hurry back here?"

Elliott sipped his coffee. When she was very young, Ensley had once watched her mother do the same thing Elliott was doing now—stalling, thinking of a way to explain the unexplainable.

She still had no idea what her mother had wanted to tell her father, but it was life-altering. Her mother first ushered her from the room, and by the time Ensley was allowed to come in again, the tension in the air was still there and never went away. Ever. How odd that she remembered it now, after all those years. There was probably even more that she'd blocked out.

And then another memory of that day flashed by. When she was in her bedroom, she looked out the window and saw a man wearing a red cloak watching the house.

Ensley took a deep breath. Now was not the time to strip down those memories.

She glanced at Austin to see how he was handling the confrontation. He looked like a scared kid ready to bolt. If what was happening was a reminder of her parents, what event in his past was Austin remembering?

Elliott carried his coffee over to the stainless steel table and pulled up a stool. When the ceramic mug clinked against the stainless steel, the sound punctured the silence and reminded her of the shell casings pinging on the hardwood floor of the luxury railroad car Tavis had reserved for them. She shivered. The simplest things rolled back to painful memories—a bit of PTSD that probably stemmed from that horrific bull ride.

"I didn't want Meredith to see her son like this," Elliott said. "If she heard his screams, if she saw the agony in his eyes, on his face, she'd have nightmares for the rest of her life. We have unleashed monsters that will commit atrocities. I am responsible, and so is my son—the last MacKlenna."

The only sound in the room was the quiet hum of the generator. And except for Elliott, everyone stared at their feet while the stink of peat mingled with the steam from Elliott's coffee, the coppery taste of blood, and the sting of antiseptics in the exam room.

No one said anything until Ensley cleared her throat and said, "It's not your fault. If I had gone with JC, it might not have happened."

Then she shuddered as another memory, more vivid than the last, surfaced.

If I hadn't gone to town with Momma that day, we wouldn't have seen the man in the red cloak who thought I was beautiful. Who said I was born to be a warrior. Who caused the fight between my parents.

"Thank God ye didn't go, lass. They would have done horrible things to ye, and ye would have begged to die."

Bile rushed to the back of Ensley's throat, and she hugged herself and wanted to curl up in a corner. "Dear God. The pain…"

Austin wrapped his arms around her, and his warmth and secure hold kept her feet on the ground.

"He survived it, Ens," Austin kissed the top of her head. "But we need to give him time to heal."

"If I hadn't opened that damn brooch, I wouldn't have disappeared, and JC wouldn't have come after me."

"The brooches have minds of their own. We can't pick and choose what we do or don't do," Kenzie said. "Each one has a plan, and we're merely players."

"Speaking of players, did Paul show up?" David asked.

"He arrived right after Erik brought James Cullen to the farm. When Erik suggested James Cullen go to the monastery to finish his healing, Paul agreed to take him there."

Kenzie glared at Elliott. "So you left Paul behind, too? That's five people."

Elliott growled. "I had a choice to believe Erik or not. I made my decision based on what he told me. Then he said he had to leave to finish his work." He looked at Ensley. "He went to protect ye, lass."

"He came to my rescue several times before JC found me. The last time I saw him was a couple of days ago when he fought the grizzly bear. Austin arrived in time to kill it, but it was too late for Erik. His sacrifice was—"

"Personal," Elliott said.

"Yes, that's exactly how I feel."

"I'm sorry Erik died," Kenzie said. "But right now, I'm more worried about Meredith and the others. We've never left anyone behind before, and it could be hours or years before we see them again, just like Philippe and Rhona Baird. So I don't give a damn what you thought you had to do, Elliott. You screwed up, and you have to go back right now."

"Then Austin and I should leave right now, too," Ensley said. "We left Tavis."

David's eyes flashed. "Ye what?"

"Calm down, Uncle David. We didn't exactly leave him," Austin said. "It's more like he left us. He had to take Erik's body back to his time. He said if he didn't come right back, then we should go get him."

"Retrieving Tavis might not be so easy," David said. "If he's gone back to the early 1100s with the body of a Council member, the rest of the Council might take it out on Tavis. We might have to fight for him."

Elliott scratched his forehead. "There might be another way. As soon as James Cullen has settled in at the monastery, we'll go back for Tavis."

"We can't make any plans until you go back and bring the others home," Kenzie said.

"What about the Illuminati?" Ensley asked. "If they knew about JC and me, do they know about MacKlenna Farm? Are Meredith and the others in danger?"

"Jesus Christ," Kenzie said. "Yes, they're in danger. If they found JC, we have to believe they're a step or two ahead of us and could well be on their way to the farm."

"I'll go with you," Ensley said.

"If you're going, I'm going," Austin said.

"Ensley, after what you've been through, you should take time to decompress and write a post-action report," Kenzie said.

"The lass can come if she wants to," Elliott said.

That's a surprise. Why do I feel that he knows something he's not telling?

"Kit's father is there," Elliott said.

"Uncle Donald?" Braham asked.

"Aye. He just arrived, and he's very ill. Kit wants to stay until… Well…she wants to be there at the end."

"Then I must go," Braham said.

"I think you should," Charlotte said. "If I didn't have two pa-tients, I'd go with you. I'll pack extra vials of insulin for Emily."

"When do you want to leave?" Ensley asked.

"I'm going to go up to the house, get something to eat, and clean up. Say, an hour?" Elliott asked.

"I have to find something else to wear. I shouldn't show up with blood all over my dress."

"I'll pick something out for you from our wardrobe depart-ment," Kenzie said. "What size do you wear? Your bone structure suggests a size zero, but with all the layers you have on, it's hard to tell."

"She's a zero," Austin said. "I've seen her in jeans. She's not any bigger than JL."

"Good. I've got dresses down here for Kit and JL. I'll find something."

"I'd rather wear pants."

Kenzie shook her head. "Nah. Not to MacKlenna Farm in the eighteen hundreds. You'd cause a stir. JL's clothes from our trip back to 1881 should fit you. I'll find something while you take a shower."

Ensley entered the locker room, where she found four bathrooms along one side, each with a shower, toilet, and sink. The other side had cabinets holding towels, scrubs, underwear, and toiletries. The scrubs were organized by size, as were the men's and women's underwear. Whoever they gave the job of keeping this place organized was a neat freak.

After gathering toiletries, clothes, and towels, she entered one of the bathrooms, where she stayed in the shower until she almost shriveled up. She towel-dried her hair, slipped on a pair of scrubs and disposable flip-flops, and dumped her bloody outfit into a dirty-clothes bag.

"Ens," Austin said, knocking on her door. "Want me to do your hair again?"

She got a hot flash just remembering the sensual feel of his fingers in her hair. Do her hair again? Hell, yeah! She opened the door and almost fainted at the sight of him wearing only a pair of gym shorts. There had to be ten miles of him. Without clothes, his long, lean body and muscular limbs went on forever and a day.

She held up the hairdryer. "You have competition."

Austin leaned against the doorjamb. "My hair might be short, but I know how to use one of those."

David barged in. "Good, ye're out of the shower, Austin. Pops is on the house phone."

"Shit. How'd he know I was back?"

"I sent him a text. He wants to speak to ye before ye take off again."

Without taking his eyes off Ensley, Austin said, "Will you tell Pops we're good and that he did the right thing, insisting I go after Ensley? I'll call him later."

David frowned. "I doubt that'll satisfy him."

"Then tell him I'm standing here with my girl"—he winked at her—"and we're both partially undressed, and I'm not worried about his feelings right now."

David shrugged. "Hell, that might work."

After David closed the locker room door, she smiled up at Austin. "That's the second time you've called me your girl. Are you just giving the rest of them a hard time?"

"No, ma'am. I just figure if you hear me say it often enough, you might believe it."

If her head had been swimming before, it was now swirling in a whirlpool. "Are you always this pushy?"

"I was one of the best offensive players in the league before I got hurt. So yeah, I push for what I want."

She gulped. "And you want me? Do I get a say in this?" She was back to fantasizing about his Goliath-size body.

"I know we've only just met, but it's like I've been waiting for you all my life. If you want to return to New York City, that's where I'll go. If you want to come to Colorado, you can live in one of the guesthouses for now, until, you know… Until you're ready to take it to the next level. I don't want to pressure you."

"Then why am I getting the full-court press?" she teased, actually thrilled that he was ramping up the pressure.

The door opened again, and this time Kenzie came in rolling a garment rack with several long dresses. "Move out, Austin. Elliott will be back in about twenty minutes, and if you guys aren't ready to go, he might leave without you."

"I don't suppose you have anything in that wardrobe closet that will fit me."

"David's looking right now. He ordered generic clothes for you when he upgraded our wardrobe closet a while back, so there should be a jacket and trousers that will work for 1885."

"I don't care if the jacket and pants aren't in style. I just don't want to wear a coat with sleeves stopping at my elbows and pants barely covering my knees."

Kenzie tsked. "Picky, picky."

He glanced down at Ensley. "You'll have to dry your hair, but I'm calling dibs on the next time you wash it." He left, whistling another unfamiliar tune.

Kenzie licked her finger then touched the back of her hand. "Hiss. Damn, girl. He was sizzling. No telling what would have happened if I hadn't walked in here."

Ensley looked at the door as if she could see Austin standing on the other side. "He's just playing games with me."

"I've seen him play games, and that wasn't what he was doing. But I do have a question. Is he high right now? He's happy, and we haven't seen him in a good mood for two years."

"The whole drug thing was a ruse. He used it to keep people away so he could do his thing without interference."

"Nothing illegal, I hope."

"Not at all. Austin's a good guy with a good heart."

"He sure had us all fooled, and Pops will be thrilled." Kenzie wagged her finger back and forth. "So, are you two a thing?"

"I wouldn't call it a thing. I mean, we haven't even kissed, but we're getting to know each other. With all that's happened, we should take it slow. Life and death situations draw people together because they have to depend on each other. I want to make sure I'm not attracted to him as a reaction to danger."

"From watching the two of you, I'd say it's much more than a reaction to danger." Kenzie held up a shapeless white gown. "This is a chemise. I also have a pair of open-crotch drawers and a corset. Let's get you dressed."

Ensley pulled the scrubs top over her head, and just as her pants hit the floor, Austin returned. "Jesus Christ, Ensley!" He wiped his hand across his forehead. "You're goddamn gorgeous."

Ensley didn't get all bashful and try to cover herself with her arms and hands. Instead, she calmly reached for the chemise and slipped it on. "Go get ready, cowboy." She gave Austin a coy smile, and he left muttering something about "hot as hell."

Kenzie held her laugh until Austin was gone, and then it burst out. "My God. You're cool as a cucumber. How'd you do that?"

Ensley shrugged. "I spent a few years riding bulls, and guys were always walking in on me. I learned not to overreact, and they left me alone. I was just one of the guys."

"Trust me, Ensley. You are not one of the guys now. You're beautiful, and you have a gorgeous body except for that scar on your hip. It almost matches mine."

"Did you have a hip replacement, too?"

"No. While deployed, I was several feet away when an IED hit. I got hurt, but it killed my best friend."

"How awful. I can't imagine the horror of being injured and losing a friend in a war."

"Well, I can't imagine staying on the back of a bull for eight seconds."

"How'd you know the ride was eight seconds?"

Kenzie laughed. "When I was at West Point, a few friends and I went to a bar that had a mechanical bull. We all had to ride it. No way in hell could I ever get on a real one."

"Yeah, but I did something dumb. You did something brave."

They chatted and laughed while Ensley put on several layers of clothes. When she was fully dressed and her hair pinned up, she said, "Can I ask you something that's sort of, I don't know, personal?"

"You can ask me anything except what it's like to make love to David McBain. I only share that when I'm drinking with the girls and they're talking about their men, too."

"Well, it's not about making love to David, but…doing it with Austin. How do you think two people as different as we are can align our bodies to hit all the right spots?"

Kenzie burst out laughing and kept laughing until she doubled over. Finally, she got herself under control, wiping tears off her cheeks. "Girlfriend, you have to figure that one out on your own, and when you do, please share it with the rest of us because we all tried to figure it out."

"You've talked about Austin's sex life?"

All Kenzie could do was nod and then burst out laughing again. "I'm sorry. Really. But over the past decade, the girls have had several conversations about it, but I can't offer you any practical tips, except this one. I've met a couple of his dates who didn't play for the WNBA, and they were all small like you."

Now Ensley laughed. "Good. That means he knows what to do with little women."

A knock on the door quieted both of them. "Kenz," David said. "It is safe to come in?"

"Sure, hon."

He came in and stood still for a moment, arms crossed. "The only time I hear ye girls laughing so hard is when ye're talking about us men. From the guilty look on Ensley's face, ye've been talking about"—he stroked his chin—"Austin's…height?"

Kenzie's jaw dropped. "McBain, sometimes you're entirely too perceptive."

"No, just observant. I don't know what Austin saw a few minutes ago, but he walked out and went straight to the liquor cabinet."

Ensley and Kenzie looked at each other, and Ensley put her finger to her lips. "Shhh."

Kenzie drew a cross over her breast. "The secret is safe with me."

David leaned close to his wife and whispered, loud enough for Ensley to hear, "Ye'll tell me later, right?"

Kenzie patted his cheek. "No, hon. You'll have to find out from Austin."

David gave her a big, whopping kiss, complete with bodies leaning into each other, and Ensley was in awe of their relationship. They'd been married for years, and the passion was still there.

"Talking privately to Austin will have to wait. Elliott's back and ready to go." David swatted Kenzie on the ass before opening the door. "Ensley, do me a favor. Keep yer eye on him."

"Austin? He's fine."

"No, Elliott. There's much more going on than what he told us. We all worry about his health. Don't let him blow a gasket—and do what ye can to get him and Meredith in a room alone. They're our foundation, and if they can't work this out, it'll destroy the clan."

"I'll do what I can, but I doubt either one of them will listen to me."

"Don't be so sure. I sense Elliott will. I see it in his eyes when he looks at ye. I believe he has a message for ye. I don't know what or from whom, but when the time's right, he'll tell ye what he knows."

Kenzie cocked her head, then looked at David. "That's perceptive, McBain."

"Aye, but ye would have noticed if ye hadn't been so busy busting Elliott's balls."

Kenzie elbowed David in the ribs. "Next time, tell me to shut up and listen with my eyes."

"Nah. Elliott deserved it. Ye were much easier on him than I'd have been."

They walked out of the locker room to find Austin, Braham, and Elliott standing at the refreshment center scrolling through mobile devices.

"There's the lass. We can go now," Elliott said, pocketing his phone.

Austin smiled at her. "You look beautiful, but you looked more beautiful before."

"Good try, Austin. I'm sure I'm not the first naked woman you've seen, and you probably told all of them they were beautiful."

David laughed and slapped Austin on the back. "Watch out, ol' soul. Ensley will give as good as she gets."

Austin winked. "I figured that out when I first heard her name mentioned."

Ensley immediately knew what he was talking about, but she didn't respond. They still had a few unresolved issues concerning his manuscript, and beyond that, she wanted him to rewrite the ending and resubmit to a publisher. But they'd deal with that later.

"Do you have an extra laptop I could borrow? I'd love to get the notes from my time with Teddy Roosevelt typed out."

"There's no electricity where we're going," Austin said.

"Duh. You're right." She smiled. "I teased JC that he was going to stay in the lap of luxury at MacKlenna Farm and drink mint juleps on the veranda while I slept on the ground and ate dust on a cattle drive." She squeezed her eyes shut to keep the tears at bay. "And look what happened to him. Damn. It sucks."

Austin stood there, barely breathing, taking in every word. He reached out for her, and the look on his face said he needed her more than she needed him. But she didn't think that was possible. A large, adoring family loved and supported him. How could he ever resent their interference? The only family she ever had consisted of her mom, dad, and grandmother, and now they were gone, and so was her ranch. No, he didn't need her more than she needed him.

"Now *you* can go drink mint juleps on the veranda," Kenzie said.

Charlotte stuck her head out of her exam room. "And if that doesn't work out, you can drink mint juleps on our veranda any time you want to visit."

"I can't think of anything I'd enjoy more as soon as this is all over."

Kenzie's eyes lit up. "I can. You and Austin can stay in the cabin. It's secluded and backs up to the river. You'll love it. And you'll have plenty of uninterrupted time to work out all your concerns while you're there."

"That's where Penny and Rick stayed when they came back from the Battle of New Orleans," Austin said, grinning like the Cheshire cat. "You'll like it."

Sensing there was a big story there, she said, "I'm not going to ask."

"That's smart," David said. "Now, to answer yer question about a laptop, I have one ye can use along with a portable solar power bank." He opened another cabinet full of devices and picked out a laptop and a small orange pack that resembled a charger. "This should be all ye need."

Ensley hugged her gifts. "That's impressive. Is there anything you don't have in here?"

David looked around the room. "I don't think so."

Kenzie gave her a black and gold tapestry bag. "I put clean drawers and chemises in here. If you end up needing another dress,

Kit can share what she has."

"Perfect." Ensley stored the laptop and charger in the bag. "I guess I'm ready."

Austin took the bag. "I'll carry it. You'll need to hold on to me when we go through the vortex."

"Let's get in position," Elliott said.

"Oh, Ensley," Kenzie interrupted. "Wait a minute. I forgot to tell you something. Come here."

Ensley walked over to Kenzie, who lowered her voice. "I have one piece of advice. If you have sex, use a condom. Several of us have gotten pregnant with twins while traveling."

"Ooh. Twins! Don't worry. I don't intend to have sex," Ensley whispered.

"The way that man is looking at you, he's already got it all mapped out. I put condoms in your bag just in case."

Ensley glanced at Austin, and the sparkle in his eyes confirmed what Kenzie just said. *Holy moly.*

Ensley returned to the men and squeezed in between Austin and Braham. "If we get separated," Austin said, "make your way to the mansion, and I'll meet you there."

"I'm sure the farm doesn't look the same, but it is recognizable?" she asked.

"The house looks the same," Braham said. "At least it did when I was there in 1865. The grounds aren't as manicured. But ye'll recognize it. Follow the white fences."

"Do you think we'll get separated?"

"If we do, we'll find ye," Elliott said.

"Good to know." She linked her arms with Austin and Braham. "I'm ready."

Elliott opened a diamond brooch. "Concentrate on Meredith." Then he recited the chant, *"Chan ann le tìm no àite a bhios sinn a' tomhais an' gaol ach 's ann le neart anama."*

As the fog engulfed them, Ensley had a sudden thought that she was slipping into a cloudy gap between two worlds.

54

MacKlenna Farm, KY (1885)—Elliott

ELLIOTT EMERGED FROM the fog—alone.

That didn't bother him, and it wouldn't bother Braham, either, since he was here during the Civil War when it likely didn't look much different. Austin would easily find his way around. During his years playing basketball at the University of Kentucky, he brought his teammates and their girlfriends to the farm for cook-outs, swimming in the Olympic-size pool, and horseback riding. He knew pretty much every inch of the property.

Ensley, though, wasn't as familiar with the layout. JC had invited her to visit the farm several times when they were in college, but she rarely saw more than the mansion and stallion barns. But she was her father's daughter. She'd find her way.

And then he remembered. Ensley was *his* daughter now, and Tavis was his son. He would have to tell them sooner or later, but first, he needed to tell Meredith and then Kevin.

Elliott paused and studied the landscape. He was close to where he landed last time. If he wanted to be a coward, he could stop at the cabin for a bit. Give the others time to reach the mansion and let Meredith know he was back. That would give her time to prepare for a confrontation.

No, not her. She wouldn't need or want prep time. She'd already know what she wanted to say, and she'd throw words at him with the finesse of a dartboard champion.

Was their marriage strong enough to survive this?

He honestly didn't know. They'd argued about everything from soup to nuts during their marriage. But they had always been on the same page when it came to JC—until now.

He would fight for her and ask for forgiveness, but if he had to do it all again—he'd make the same decisions. It was part of living in the cloudy gap where nothing was black or white. Protecting the brooches from evil was his foremost responsibility, and that obligation extended to protecting the future Keeper. Period.

But—and this was a big one—without stability and the clan's cohesiveness, Elliott's job was almost hopeless. Without Meredith at his side, her absence almost guaranteed both would be impossible. So what did that mean for his relationship with her?

Simple. He had to take a knee, beg for forgiveness, and recommit to being partners in life and love. She was everything to him, and if he had to grovel, he would. But it was also vital that he protect his family from evil forces determined to destroy it, steal all the brooches, and try to control the world.

With his eye on the path forward and steel in his spine, he set out to find his wife. But when he saw smoke coming from the cabin's chimney, he decided to stop and see if there were any clues to give him an idea of how long he'd been gone.

The temperature was the same, the spring leaf-out was the same, and the sweet smell of flowers hadn't changed. So maybe he'd only been gone a few days.

As he approached the cabin, he noticed the eucalyptus-scented air was also the same. "Shit." The brooch had returned him close to the moment of his departure. But after he thought about it, he decided that was the best possible outcome. He could rip up the letter he left for Meredith and explain in person what he'd done. And why.

He opened the door and stopped in his tracks.

Goddamn it.

Meredith sat at the table, reading his letter with her lips as white as her fingers gripping the page. When she looked up, her eyes were shiny with tears—the furious kind, not the sorrowful kind. And he braced himself for what he knew was coming.

"You're a goddamn bastard, and I hate you." She balled up the letter and threw it in the fire. Then she stomped over to the hook by the door and snatched up her bonnet. Slapping it on her head, she shouldered past him and out through the door he held open.

"I hated you that night at the farm all those years ago when you accused me of killing your horse." She paused at the hitching rail and gripped it tightly. "The rage and hurt I felt then fades to insignificance compared to what I think of you now."

She walked away but stopped again. "Kit's father is dying and might not last the night. We'll leave right after the funeral. Until then, don't you dare come near me."

His stomach heaved, and he had to swallow quickly to keep from vomiting. "Please, Meredith. Give me five minutes to explain."

She glared. "Not five, not four, not even one." Her claws came out, and she said even more viciously, "I'll never trust you again, and I will never forgive you."

She turned her back and strode away, and his heart splintered into tiny shards that stabbed and drew blood and even laughed at him for being such a shithead.

Before she left the clearing for the path to the mansion, she turned back once more, and he steeled himself against another verbal assault. Why didn't she just slap him or punch him in the gut? It couldn't hurt him any worse.

"It would have taken me a while to forgive you for drugging me, but locking me out and taking my son away are unforgivable."

He hovered beneath the porch's eaves, desperate for something to say, actions to take, and it occurred to him that he'd have to shatter all her illusions to get her attention.

"His body is perfect."

"Why, Elliott? We've shared everything in our marriage. Why'd you do it?"

He held up his phone to show her a video and turned it up as loud as the iPhone would play.

"I'll kill you if you don't get off me."

"Settle down, son, before one of us gets hurt."

"JC, calm down before ye hurt yer father or I hurt ye."

"Let go of me, David. I don't want to hurt you."

"Stop fighting yer da. Now!"

"Leave me the fuck alone. That means all of you."

"JC, did you see Erik after you left me? Is that how you got his cloak?"

"I don't know... I don't remember... Aaah!"

"Drop the gun. Now!"

Meredith sat down on the tree stump, and she bent forward at the waist, looking like she might throw up. She didn't, but her silence attested to the lockdown of her emotions, and it was much worse than vomiting or yelling at him would have been.

He was a bastard for blindsiding her like that, but he had to use everything in his toolbox to get her attention.

"Charlotte was able to sedate him before he hurt himself or anyone else."

"How'd you get him home?"

"He woke up and asked about ye."

"What lie did you tell him?"

Ouch.

"That we were taking turns watching over him. When he screamed, I activated the brooch, and as the fog appeared, I tackled him."

"That's why he was yelling to get off him?"

"Aye."

"What does Charlotte suggest?"

"We didn't talk about it. Kenzie was furious that I left ye behind. She insisted I return immediately, so I was only there for less than an hour."

"I can't believe you videotaped James Cullen in that condition."

"I didn't. Braham activated the audiovisual equipment as soon as the fog appeared."

"This doesn't change anything, Elliott. I understand how fragile James Cullen is right now, and he's where he needs to be, but it doesn't excuse your behavior. You know how unreliable the brooches are. It could have been years before they allowed you to return."

"Kenzie pointed that out."

If Elliott asked Meredith about hiring Paul right now, their delicate dance might turn into a martial arts exhibition, and they'd try to kill each other. Besides, this particular fight was about his behavior, not hers.

Meredith stood and walked toward the tree line. "I'm going to the mansion, and I'll ask Sean to send someone down here with food later today, but I suggest you sit your ass in that damn rocking chair until we're ready to go home."

"Why are ye so hateful?"

"Me? Hateful? You're the one who drugged me and kept me from my son. Then you left me, risking all of us, especially Emily, who would die without insulin. What were you thinking? Or maybe you weren't thinking at all."

"I didn't have time to think. I reacted. I just wanted to get James Cullen home, and I didn't want ye to hear him scream. Ye'd have never forgotten it."

"But you played the video so I *could* hear him, and you're damn right. I'll never forget it. But I think the brooches have given you too much power, and if you don't get control over them, they will control you. I thought I had a partner. But it appears I'm married to an autocrat."

"I'm not an autocrat."

"Really? Well, just think about how you handled this situation— even the issue with Paul. We would have talked about it before. But over the last couple of years, it's become your way or the highway."

"That's not true."

"Why don't you ask Kenzie what she thinks?"

"She's not here, but Braham, Austin, and Ensley came back with me. Braham wanted to see Donald before he passed."

"Were they in the room when you and James Cullen returned?"

"Aye, they were."

Meredith didn't say anything for a few moments, and Elliott hoped she'd give him a break, maybe even accept his apology. He walked toward her—hoping—but she held up her hand, palm out.

"Stop!"

He eyed her with uncertainty, afraid of what she'd say next.

"As soon as we return from settling James Cullen at the monastery, I'm moving back to Napa. I don't want the winery's daily management. Rick is doing a great job as president. But I'd like to help him develop a new label."

"This isn't about the winery or a new label, is it?"

She didn't meet his gaze. Instead, she stared off into the void for a long time, saying nothing. Then she answered him. "I just don't want to be around you for a while."

For a while? She was leaving the door open for him. "Ye've thought this all out. What do ye want from me? I said I was sorry."

Her tense blue eyes didn't soften at all, and she seemed to lapse into an old memory, and he knew then his apology meant nothing.

"I told you once before that you're as close to Jekyll and Hyde as any man I've met. I went back to you once, but I don't think I can do it again."

Then she was gone, taking everything that mattered with her. No, that wasn't true. His son mattered. The clan mattered. Protecting the brooches mattered.

But, ye dumbass, Meredith matters most of all.

55

MacKlenna Farm, KY—Ensley

E NSLEY WANDERED AROUND the farm, trying to figure out which direction to go, when she spotted Meredith stomping through the pasture, her sunbonnet brim flopping with every fierce stride. Ensley stood on tiptoe and waved frantically and then stopped and laughed at herself. Would a few extra inches make her more visible behind the rolling hills? Hell, no!

"Ms. Montgomery! Wait up!"

Meredith shielded her eyes with her hand and waited for Ensley to reach her. "Please call me Meredith. Ms. Montgomery makes me sound ancient."

Ensley's cheeks heated. "I'll try, but my mom would shoot me for being so informal with you."

A flash of sadness crossed Meredith's features. "I'm sorry about your parents. Losing one is hard enough to cope with, but losing both so close together prolongs that raw and intense grief."

"It's been hard, and selling the ranch recently just brought it all back again. But I'm getting by."

"What always gets me with a surprise *wham* is the way grief seems to relish catching me in a snare. Emotions shouldn't have so much power."

Ensley connected with Meredith's grief, so heavy in her voice, but Ensley didn't remember JC ever mentioning his parents had experienced a tragedy.

"I agree with that. Grief pops up and sinks me in a puddle of despair without a moment's notice, and God forbid if I try to fight it. Resisting gives it more power."

"Exactly," Meredith said, tugging on the brim of her sunbonnet.

"Let's go over to those trees, where there's shade. The sun's too bright out here, and I don't have sunglasses." They quickly fell into a comfortable pace over the uneven ground. "I'm sure being abandoned in the past didn't help with the grieving process. I hope the adventure wasn't too awful."

"Spending time with Teddy Roosevelt was incredible, but being alone in the Badlands without a knife, gun, or even a fishing pole, created a whole set of problems I've never faced before. Then I broke my foot, got caught in a cattle stampede, was attacked by a bear, and then threatened by members of the Illuminati."

Meredith pressed her hand on Ensley's forearm, and the weight of it wasn't at all reassuring. It was shaking slightly, and from a woman of steel like Meredith Montgomery, Ensley found it disturbing.

"They found you, too? Oh, Jesus. But you got away? They didn't hurt you?" Meredith lifted her skirts high above her boot tops and picked up speed.

Ensley easily kept pace but was unsure why they were hurrying. Did Meredith think the Illuminati would find them here?

God, that's a terrifying thought.

She glanced around and realized they were in a vulnerable position. If riders came after them, there was nowhere to hide. Ensley didn't voice her fear, and neither did Meredith, but when they hurried toward the trees, it was apparent they had scared themselves. They paused in the shadow of the elm and oak trees and searched the pasture in both directions.

"Tell me what happened when the Illuminati found you and how you got away."

"It happened the first night we were on the train coming here. Remy and Austin noticed our steward had a ring with a symbol used by the Illuminati. We escaped with guns blazing. Austin and I are fine, but Remy got two flesh wounds in his butt. Fortunately, he should be up and about later today."

"Knowing Remy, nothing will keep him down as long as he has his sticks. But what about Tavis?"

"About three days ago"—Ensley rubbed her forehead—"I've lost track of time, but I think it was three days. Anyway, I went down to the river to clean up and was attacked by a grizzly. I bought an Akhal-Teke stallion from TR a couple of weeks earlier and named him Tesoro. When Tesoro saw the bear, he didn't run away but instead got between the bear and me and fought it until the animal mauled him to death."

Meredith gasped. "Oh, my God! But you had a rifle…"

"Yeah, but I left it with my tack at the remuda."

"I can't imagine how horrifying that was."

"It was, and just when I thought I was going to die, Erik ran into the clearing yelling, 'Tyr!' He was mortally wounded fighting the bear. Then Austin galloped into the bloody clearing, jumped off his horse while reaching for his rifle, and got off four kill shots as if he'd choreographed the scene in advance."

"I've watched him perform under pressure," Meredith said. "He knows how to do it. But what happened to Tavis?"

"Before Erik died, he told me Tavis had to take him home. Tavis arrived right after that and returned to Jarlshof with Erik's body."

"And he's still there?" Meredith's terrified expression only heightened Ensley's fears.

"He told Remy that if he didn't come back, we should go get him."

"There's no doubt in my mind that the brooches might eventually kill us all." Meredith grabbed Ensley's hand. "Come on. Let's get out of here."

They ran from one tree line to another and paused when they could hide in the shadows. "What can we do to protect ourselves from the Illuminati?" Ensley asked.

"Short of returning all the brooches to the Council, there isn't much we can do."

"Wouldn't that be worse? Remy and Austin told me about the Council and Erik's home in Jarlshof. It seems to me that it would be easy for the Illuminati to invade Jarlshof, kill the Council members, and take all the brooches."

"You're right. That would be worse." Meredith glanced behind her and sucked in a breath. And it was hard for Ensley to tell if Meredith was disappointed by what she saw or relieved. "I saw Elliott at the cabin. He told me what happened."

There was something bleak in Meredith's voice, and it told Ensley the meeting with Elliott didn't go well at all. Ensley touched Meredith on the back, finding her muscles so rigid that it was like patting cement. Meredith tensed even more for a moment, and then her shoulders drooped a little as she released some of the tension.

"I'm new to this whole time-traveling business, but Kenzie was afraid it could be years before we came back for you. How long was Dr. Fraser gone?"

"Call him Elliott. No one calls him Dr. Fraser." Meredith checked the time on an antique diamond and platinum watch pendant pinned to her lapel. "Maybe an hour. Kit had taken food to the cabin, and when she returned to the mansion and told me what he said, I decided it was time to talk to him. The fire was blazing when I arrived, and I was only there a short time before Elliott walked in. We talked for a few minutes, and then I left."

"An hour to return to the future and come back. Is that unusual?"

"Each brooch has different properties, and I don't know which one Elliott used."

"The diamond, I think."

That was all the small talk Ensley could manage. And as tense as Meredith was, she wouldn't be interested in anything else, either. Ensley's conversations with JC's mom had always been about literature or the latest New York City restaurants, never anything about personal stuff. And right now, everything was personal.

Where was Austin? Ensley sure could use a rescue right now. She glanced around but couldn't see over the next hill.

"Austin and Braham should be at the mansion by now. Donald McCabe will be pleased to see Braham."

"Elliott said he's very ill."

"Emily wasn't sure at first if he has lung cancer or TB. She's leaning toward lung cancer and doing everything she can to keep him comfortable. He doesn't have much time left."

Ensley saw a long-legged man coming over the knoll in a blaze of sunlight, and her heart rate skyrocketed. "There's Austin." She darted out from under the trees and waved, yelling. "Austin!"

His face lit as he spotted her, and his stride lengthened. When he reached her, he picked her up and kissed her. "I was so worried. Are you okay?"

"Yes! Yes! Put me down!"

What will Meredith think?

He set her gently on her feet. "I can't believe how scared I was when I came out of the fog and you weren't there."

Meredith stepped out into the sun and walked a few steps closer, brows puckered. "Have you seen Braham?"

"Oh, hi, Meredith. No, have you seen Elliott?"

Meredith glanced over her shoulder. "He's at the cabin. Let's go find Braham." She took off, leading the way. "Ensley told me about you shooting the bear."

"Lucky shot," Austin said.

"Four shots," Ensley said. "And luck wasn't involved."

"Sounds like Pops made the right decision when he insisted you go rescue Ensley."

"It was a good idea, but Ensley didn't need rescuing."

"I didn't? What about the bear?"

"Tavis was only a few minutes behind me."

Ensley punched him in the ribs, and Austin faked a reaction, grabbing his gut and bending over. "Damn, that hurt."

"Yeah, right. My elbow bounced off you. But seriously, that bear would have mauled me to death by the time Tavis got there."

The wind sighed across the pasture, bringing the scent of horses and springtime. And it wafted the folds of Ensley's skirts about her legs, an odd sensation for her. She took in a deep breath of the breezy air, letting go of some of the fear and anxiety. No, it wasn't the breeze. It was Austin's presence. He was with her now, comforting her, willing to help carry the heavy load of her worries.

"I want to hear all about it," Meredith said, sounding only half interested. "But a story like that deserves a good bottle of wine. So how long were you gone?"

"A month for me," Ensley said.

"Three days for us," Austin said.

"In three days, you've grown very…close. I'm surprised." Meredith looked up at Austin. "What happened to the surly man who didn't want anything to do with his family?"

Austin scratched his scruffy chin but didn't say anything.

Ensley put her hand at the side of her mouth like she was telling Meredith a secret. "It was a ruse to keep people out of his business."

"A ruse? Austin! Is that true?" Meredith tsked. "You were officially my first grandchild, and you lied to me?"

"I never lied, and besides, I was sixteen when I went to work for you at the winery. I will never call you Granny Mere."

"Good, because I'm not sure I'd answer. But after worrying about you for months, JL will be extremely pissed."

"I sent a text to Pops with a big thank-you for insisting I go on the trip. He'll give JL a heads-up."

Ensley marched along, keeping up but remaining silent.

"I hope you plan to do more than a heads-up," Meredith said.

He stared at her briefly. Then he cleared his throat. "Let it go, Meredith. I'll take care of it."

Tension seeped back into Meredith's face, so Ensley stepped between them. "Do you want to hear what I enjoyed most about the time I spent with Teddy Roosevelt?"

Oh, God. How lame.

Meredith gave her a forced smile, obviously not at all interested, but being polite, she asked, "What? Politics?"

"No, he said upfront that talking about politics was strictly off-limits, although JC did get in a few questions about the election of 1884."

As they walked, Ensley rattled on about the cattle drive and book discussions, and Austin mentioned playing chess with TR.

"Who won?" Meredith asked.

"I was very competitive, but TR won two out of every three games."

"I didn't know you were that good," Meredith said. "If you can keep up with Teddy Roosevelt, you've got to be the best chess player in the family."

"Jack gives me a good game," Austin said.

As they neared the mansion, they spotted Braham crossing the drive.

Austin yelled, "Braham!"

Braham acknowledged them with a quick wave, then waited there for them to catch up. He gave Austin a hug and slap on the back, and Meredith and Ensley each a kiss on the cheek.

"How's Uncle Donald?" he asked.

"He's declining by the hour," Meredith said. "Only his determination to see Kit kept him alive long enough to get here from Washington. He has mentioned you several times, so I know he'll be happy to see you."

"I'll go to his room right away. Has anybody seen Elliott?" Braham asked, searching each of their faces, his brow etched with worry.

Meredith didn't answer right away, and Ensley wasn't going to speak up. It wasn't her news to share.

"Meredith saw him at the cabin," Austin offered.

Meredith glared at Austin as if to nail him in place to deal with later. Ensley had a similar reaction, but she'd put him in a jar with holes in the lid. Where was his tact?

"We talked…briefly," Meredith said in a tone both deliberate and cold.

Braham's brow smoothed out, and his concern visibly fell away. "Good."

Good? What's wrong with you men? Can't you see there's a problem here?

"I'm glad he arrived safely," Braham continued. "I assume he told ye about JC?"

Meredith winced, and the muscles in her jaw flexed. "Elliott played the video. It was horrible."

There was sympathy in Braham's eyes, a quiet understanding. "I downloaded it for him but didn't watch it. The real scene was horrific."

"It just breaks my heart, but thank God he's alive and not physically handicapped or disfigured. That's a start," Meredith said. "But I'm not convinced he should go away right now. We can hire the best therapists to treat him."

It would be easy to shy away from that line of thought like a spooked horse, but it was a problem Ensley had to face as well. "JC can't tell anyone what happened to him, and I have the same problem. With all I went through, I could use counseling. But I can't tell a therapist that I traveled back in time and hung out with Teddy Roosevelt, or got caught up in a cattle stampede, or was threatened by men from an evil organization, or rescued by a Viking from the Middle Ages."

"No, of course not," Meredith said. "That's always been a problem for the family. We have to consider other options, but I prefer he didn't go to the other side of the world for months, possibly years, to find the healing he needs."

"Do you think Jack would go with him?" Austin asked.

"It depends on where he is with his latest manuscript," Braham said. "Jack hates to write longhand, and the monks don't allow computers. If he's on deadline, he won't be able to go, but otherwise, maybe."

There seemed to be an easing in Meredith's tension, and by the time they reached the mansion, she almost cracked a smile at Austin's exaggerated story of how he taught Ensley to ride a bronc.

Kit was walking down the sweeping staircase when they entered the residence. She halted, her mouth agape. "Braham? How'd you get here?"

"Same way the rest of ye did. I clicked my heels. Do ye remember when I showed up with Donald all those years ago?"

She smiled. "Of course I remember. Dad and I have relived that moment over and over again." She kissed her cousin and looked up at Austin. "I wasn't expecting you for a few more days." Then to Ensley, she said, "We met briefly a few years ago."

"I remember," Ensley said.

Kit put her hands on her hips and looked from Braham to Austin to Ensley and finally to Meredith. "This doesn't add up. Let's go to the dining room. Cullen's eating a late lunch. Are you hungry?"

Austin rubbed his belly. "Have you ever known me to turn down a meal?"

"Never."

Meredith removed her sunbonnet and placed it on the hall tree. "My head hurts. I'm going to rest for a while."

"I'll ask Emily to check on you," Kit said. "I'm sure she has Tylenol."

"I have some," Meredith said. "I'll be down in about an hour."

"We'll leave you alone, then." Kit laced her arm with Braham's. "We weren't expecting you. Why didn't Charlotte come?"

"She has patients who need her, and I wanted to get here quickly to make sure I can see Uncle Donald before…"

"Your visit will make him very happy. There's a nurse with him now, so just go on up."

"Should I wear a mask?"

"Emily is pretty sure he has lung cancer, but we're still taking necessary precautions. The nurse will help you mask up. Dad is using my old bedroom."

"I'll go on up."

"Wait. Come say hello to Cullen first, and you can tell both of us at the same time why you're here with Ensley, and Tavis and Remy aren't."

Ensley walked through the front room. It was quiet, save for the fire's murmur and the gentle creak of settling timber. She wasn't familiar with all the eighteenth- and nineteenth-century furniture styles, but everything looked similar to the room in the future, except for the draperies and upholstery. And the same painting of the destroyed Eilean Donan castle was hanging over the fireplace.

She followed the others into the dining room, where Cullen sat at the head of a table for twelve reading a newspaper. He glanced up, stared, and then shot to his feet. "Braham! What are ye doing here?"

Braham gave Cullen a fist bump before going to the server to pour a cup of coffee. "I wanted to see Uncle Donald."

Cullen then hugged Austin. "Good to see ye, lad." Then he removed his glasses and looked closely at Ensley. "What's going on here? We didn't expect ye and Austin for a few more days, and we didn't expect Braham at all, which means ye returned to the future and made another trip to the past."

"I'll tell you everything I know if I can eat a few pieces of fried chicken first," Austin said.

Cullen slapped Austin on the back. "Fix yer plate, and we'll talk."

"I'm going up to see Uncle Donald," Braham said. "I'll catch up with ye later."

"What about ye, Ensley? Are ye hungry?" Cullen asked.

"Not really," Ensley said.

"Good," Kit said. "Let's take a walk. I want to hear about your trip." Then she glanced at Cullen. "Unless you want to hear it, too."

"I sense yer interest in Ensley's journey has a different focus than mine." He signaled, fine, go ahead, and Kit pulled her out of the room.

"Get all the scoop so that you can share it with me later," Austin said.

"What kind of scoop?" Ensley sensed he wanted to kiss her, but the public display of their affection had already surprised Meredith, and Ensley didn't want anyone gossiping about them.

"The farm, the horses, the crops. Whatever is going on out there."

"Oh, okay. I'll take notes." Ensley followed Kit through the house, into the office, and out the French doors to a patio lined with sweet-scented spring flowers in reds and golds.

"Let's walk down toward the lake, and you can start your tale from the beginning."

"Which beginning?"

Kit's head tilted curiously. "I guess the beginning of the beginning. From the moment you first disappeared in the fog, how you found JC, how you separated, and how you got here."

"Can I give you the Cliffs Notes version?"

Kit looked over the edge of her glasses. "You're teasing me, right?"

Ensley laughed. "I was talking about my adventure with Meredith, but she wasn't interested, and I realized I was giving her way too many details for right now. Her mind is somewhere else."

"Yes, I imagine it is."

By the time they reached a wrought iron bench next to the lake, Ensley had summed up her trip, her separation from JC, and what happened on the train.

"So Tavis is back in the twelfth century, Remy got shot in the ass, and you and Austin are…?"

"…exploring a relationship."

"That surprises me. I thought you and James Cullen were—"

"—and still are, friends," Ensley said. "We missed that window and moved on. And now, after everything that's happened, it'll be quite a while before he's ready for a relationship."

"So you know what happened to JC?"

"A few minutes after Austin, Remy, and I landed in the clean-room at Mallory Plantation, Elliott and JC came out of the fog. It was horrible. JC and his dad were physically fighting. David tried to subdue JC, but JC flipped him, and then he attacked Kenzie, took her gun, and threatened everyone. And suddenly, he screamed the most horrific scream I've ever heard. Charlotte was treating Remy's wounds, but she sneaked up on JC and jabbed a needle into his ass to sedate him."

"Oh, my God! But what I don't understand is why Elliott took JC home. He put all of us at risk by doing that."

"JC woke up in the cabin and started screaming like they were torturing him all over again. Elliott activated the brooch, tackled JC, and they returned."

"Meredith will be furious when she discovers Elliott left her."

"Kenzie told him he had to return immediately."

"So where is he now?"

"When I came through the fog, Meredith was the first person I saw. She told me she'd just seen Elliott at the cabin, so she knows he took JC home."

"That's not good."

"I overheard Elliott tell Charlotte that he and Meredith were taking turns watching over JC."

"That's a damn lie."

"I know that now, but he said he was afraid JC would hurt his mother, so he brought him home."

"I just took Elliott some food a little over an hour ago, and he still refused to let Meredith come inside the cabin."

"Why?"

"Meredith disagreed with Elliott's decision to follow Erik's instructions. She wanted to take JC home to the hospital."

"JC looks perfect, except his muscles are more developed, and he doesn't have a scratch or bruise on him, but his mind can't forget the torture."

"Meredith will be livid."

"She was preoccupied but not angry. There was a sadness about her, but she wasn't furious."

"That's not good," Kit said. "That means…well, I don't know what it means, but it's not good. Did JC ever mention to you about how his parents met?"

"In Scotland over Christmas, and Meredith got pregnant at the same time she was diagnosed with breast cancer. It was a very traumatic time for his parents. JC said Kevin told him the whole story."

"Meredith doesn't handle medical situations very well. Her first husband had a stroke, and after a few days, she had to take him off life support. Before that, her father had a heart attack, and her mother died when she was young. I think her father was very demanding, and Meredith could never live up to his expectations. When Elliott locked her out of the cabin, it brought back a lot of past trauma."

"I can't believe Elliott locked her out because of a difference of opinion. JC always said his parents had the strongest marriage of anyone he knew."

"Elliott also discovered Meredith hired Paul to report to her about what JC was doing."

Ensley gasped. "To spy on him? JC would be furious over that. But I still don't understand why that caused so much anger."

"Elliott was furious over what she'd done, and he didn't trust her to follow Erik's instructions about not touching JC. So he drugged her, and Paul carried her back to the mansion."

"Jesus!" Ensley said. "If somebody did that to me, it'd be all over."

"Well, that's what Meredith is saying, but we can't let that happen."

"Have you talked to Elliott?"

"Cullen and I are so incredibly pissed at him, and I told Elliott how we feel. He told me not to come back to the cabin if I was going to criticize him."

"JC wouldn't want his parents' marriage to fall apart because of him."

"That's for sure."

The sound of galloping horses had them both turning around. Cullen was riding toward them, leading two other horses.

"Oh, dear," Kit said. "It must be Dad."

When Cullen reached them, he jumped down. "Emily said to hurry. Donald doesn't have much longer. Braham's with him now."

"Give me a leg up," Kit said, and Cullen tossed her up into the saddle.

"Let me help ye, lass," he said to Ensley.

"I've never ridden with all these clothes before."

"Pull up your skirts and go," Kit said.

And that's what Ensley did.

When they reached the mansion, Paul was pacing on the veranda.

"Ride over to the cabin and tell Elliott that Donald's time has come." Cullen swung down and handed his reins to Paul. "Take one of these horses with ye and don't accept no from him."

"Yes, sir," Paul said, mounting Cullen's horse.

When Kit, Cullen, and Ensley reached the foyer, Austin was there. "Kit, your uncle Sean says your dad wants you to sing."

A man carrying a violin entered the foyer from the back hallway. "Donald asked if ye would sing 'Simple Gifts.'"

"Of course," Kit said. "I haven't sung it in years, but I'll do my best." Then she pointed to Ensley. "Uncle Sean, this is Ensley, another traveler."

"I've heard all about ye, lass. I'm looking forward to hearing yer opinion of Mr. Roosevelt."

"Yes, sir. He's a remarkable man," Ensley said.

"I met him briefly at the 1884 Republican National Convention in Chicago."

"I wonder why he didn't mention meeting you when JC told TR he was coming here?"

"Mr. Roosevelt wouldn't remember me. I was with a group of local Republicans, and there was only a general introduction. But I did hear his speech supporting John Lynch. His decision to back James Blaine against the wishes of other Independent Republicans did great damage to his immediate career."

"I think he'll manage just fine." Then she whispered, "If you want me to tell you what happens, let me know."

Sean grinned. "I think I can manage to know his future. We'll talk later."

"My favorite quote of his is, 'Believe you can, and you're halfway there.'"

"I haven't heard that sentiment before."

Ensley clapped her hand over her mouth. "Oh! Maybe TR hasn't said it yet."

Sean laughed. "That must be a constant problem for ye time travelers."

"I'm new at this, but I can see how it would be."

He hooked his hand in the bend of her elbow and escorted her toward the stairs. "I look forward to a longer conversation."

When they entered Donald's sunny bedroom, Ensley was surprised to see a stoic Meredith with glistening eyes sitting near the open window.

A light breeze softened the scene with the heady fragrance of lilacs. But the farther Ensley moved into the room, the distinctive acetone odor of a dying person overpowered the sweet-scented flowers. The smell triggered memories, but she set them aside for now. This moment wasn't about her grief, and the intrusion of her memories seemed disrespectful. Her focus—in fact, everyone's—should be on the dying man and the people who loved him.

Several pillows propped Mr. McCabe into a semi-reclining position while Emily leaned over him, pressing the drum of a stethoscope on his chest. His desperate gasps for breath signaled the end was near.

"Daddy, I'm here now." The mattress dipped when Kit sat on the edge of the bed and threaded her fingers with his.

"My precious Kitherina. Sing for your da." Her father managed to smile between gasps.

Kit nodded to Uncle Sean. He lifted his violin, tucked it under his chin, and, after tilting the bow's angle, began to play. Kit blinked away tears and started singing in a beautiful contralto voice.

"Tis the gift to be simple, 'tis the gift to be free, / 'Tis the gift to come down where we ought to be, / And when we find ourselves in the place just right, / 'Twill be in the valley of love and delight. / When true simplicity is gain'd, / To bow and to bend we shan't be asham'd, / To turn, turn will be our

delight, / Till by turning, turning we come round right."

When she finished, she kissed her father's cheek, then smiled up at her husband, and Cullen mouthed, "I love ye."

Ensley couldn't imagine singing to her parents as they died, but she wished she'd had the chance. Everything in the room seemed to unfold in slow motion, and she couldn't stop what was about to happen. No one could.

Tears streaked down Kit's face, and Cullen handed her his handkerchief. It reminded Ensley of the times JC gave her one with his initials—JCF—embroidered in one corner.

Sean lowered the violin. "Donald has requested the men sing 'Auld Lang Syne.' Please gather close so he can see ye."

The clouds drifted in front of the sun, leaving the room draped in shadows.

Sean, Cullen, Braham, and Austin stood at the end of the bed.

"Austin, why don't ye play the guitar? There's one by the bed. Kit's been playing it for her father," Cullen said.

"Sure." Austin picked up the instrument and strummed a few chords, then nodded to Sean.

Sean lifted the violin again but was interrupted when three couples entered the room with Elliott trailing behind them. Kit signaled to the women, all younger versions of her, to join her at the bedside. The men gathered with the others.

Elliott's gaze went directly to the corner where Meredith sat, but instead of going to her, he went to stand next to Sean. Her eyes glinted at him, but other than that, Meredith didn't acknowledge his presence.

Even now, two people who were deeply involved in Kit's life couldn't manage to put their differences aside for her emotional well-being, and their behavior damaged Ensley's opinion of them.

The men lifted their voices…

"For auld lang syne, my jo, for auld lang syne, / We'll take a cup o' kindness yet, for auld lang syne. / And surely ye'll be your pint-stowp! / And surely I'll be mine! / And we'll take a cup o' kindness yet, / For auld lang syne."

The voices blended beautifully with the two instruments, and Ensley couldn't take her eyes off Austin. He played the guitar with the same intense focus he had when he dunked the pillow, played chess, and shot the bear, and he stirred her heart.

In the midst of death, love is born.

No. It was born somewhere in the pages of Austin's manuscript.

She had identified with him when he recounted lying in the hospital bed. Every time he closed his eyes, his motorcycle hit the pole, over and over again, each time more brutally than the last.

It had been the same with her. But instead of smashing into a pole, a damn bull bucked her off its back. And the bull did it again and again, every time harder than the last.

Somewhere deep in his soul, Austin knew her, and she knew him. They had fought their demons and, despite them, they survived.

Her eyes slowly drifted from Austin to Donald McCabe. His last breath was a gentle rush of air, and his life drifted away like the last wisps of smoke from dying embers.

56

MacKlenna Farm, KY (1885)—Austin

T HE MACKLENNAS COVERED the furniture and paintings with black shrouds and held Donald McCabe's wake that evening. When neighbors, friends, and associates heard the husband of Sean MacKlenna's twin sister had died, they came in droves from Midway, Frankfort, and Lexington.

Almost every guest was curious about Austin's height and good looks. He tried explaining the distant relationship between his family and the MacKlennas, but that only drew more questions than he could answer. Emily finally took pity on him and came to his rescue, explaining that the two families' link came through an illegitimate child.

That shut them up.

Austin caught up with Ensley going through the buffet line. "I thought you ate already."

"That was appetizers. What you see on my plate is the full course." She licked her lips. "It seems like months since I've had decent food."

"I thought you liked what Norman cooked."

"It was okay, but this"—she licked her lips again—"is gourmet food in comparison."

"Wait till you sample Amber Grant's food. Now, that's gourmet. There are lots of good cooks in the family, but Amber has them all beat." He looked around for a place to sit. "Let's go outside. It's too crowded in here."

They found two wicker chairs on the veranda, and he carried them out into the yard to get away from the crowd.

Ensley followed him into the evening shade beneath the oaks.

"Are you hiding from someone?"

"The women inside couldn't stop staring, and the men treated me like a freak in a carnival show. They were worse than the press corps and twice as annoying as my family."

Ensley covered her mouth to stifle a laugh, but he tugged her hand away. "Stop laughing."

"I'm sorry, but it seems weird that these Southerners sipping mint juleps on the veranda think you belong in a cabinet of curiosities, and the cowboys treated you with the utmost respect."

"Hey, you're right. They treated me like a regular cowboy and thought *you* belonged in a cabinet of curiosities."

"They did not."

He laughed. "You're right. It wasn't curiosity. It was fear."

"Afraid of me?" she asked, pressing her hand to her chest. "That's impossible. What'd I do to invoke fear in them?"

"Oh, let me count the ways. You cussed like a damn sailor. You rode a gold horse like a goddess. You broke a bronc no one would ride. And you had Norman eating out of your hand."

"I did not. Norman ruled the roost."

"With an iron hand and an iron skillet, but he doted on you. They were all terrified of him. So they figured if they were scared of someone who doted on you, then you must be a terror."

"Oh, that's bullshit."

He leaned over to kiss her, but she popped a deviled egg into her mouth just as he made his move. Instead, he kissed the tip of her button nose. "You're too cute for anyone to be scared of."

"Cute?" She gave him a side-eye. "I'm twenty-eight. I don't want to be cute."

"Would you rather be sexy and gorgeous?"

"Sure. Wouldn't all women?"

"Yep, but not all women can be cute, sexy, and gorgeous."

"You can't be cute and gorgeous."

"You can't? Hmm. Well, right now, you're cute with that bit of egg on the side of your lip." He took her napkin and wiped it off. "When you're horseback riding in jeans, you're sexy as hell, and when you come out of the bath with wet hair and glistening skin, you're gorgeous."

"I bet that's the one you like the best. The wet hair and glistening skin."

"Nah. I like watching you on horseback."

She blushed, and he laughed. He knew where her mind was drifting off to, and he wanted to push it further. But he didn't want anyone to think badly of her or to offend Sean and Lyle Ann.

No, he'd wait until he had Ensley alone with time to explore—possibilities. And while his ultimate goal was to get her in his big bed at the ranch, he'd take whatever she offered, wherever she offered it. Taking the next step had to be on her terms, though.

"You look damn good on your horse, too," she said. "The first time I saw you, I thought you looked like a knight riding his black destrier."

And then she stared at him in open-mouthed horror, and on the heels of her shock, he had a punch to his solar plexus. He knew, without doubt, what she was thinking, and he didn't like it any better than she did.

Black destrier? Mercury. Ferdiad.

"They're gone, Ensley."

"No!" she gasped. "I lost Tesoro to a bear, and I *promised* Tavis I'd take care of his horse."

Austin squeezed her arm affectionately. "There may still be hope. The horses were booked on the train from Medora to the Midway Depot. Maybe they're in Midway waiting for us to pick them up."

"But that's dangerous. I mean, the Illuminati know we escaped. Maybe they'll be in Midway thinking we'll come back for the horses. We might end up leading them here to Elliott and his brooch. That would be a disaster. I bet that's why Elliott didn't want anyone to know JC was here."

"Shit! You're right. As much as it pains me to leave them behind, we can't do anything to draw attention. I'll let Sean know the horses might show up."

"Won't that put Sean and his family in danger?"

"I don't think so," Austin said. "The Illuminati want the brooches, and if we're not here, the brooches won't be here, either."

"But they still know we have them. So what are we going to do? Spend the rest of our lives looking over our shoulders? I can't live that way. We have to end it now."

"No one in the family will object to that, but we're not ready for a showdown—yet. At least not here. Once we get home, we can have a family meeting, discuss it, and come up with a plan."

Ensley rotated her head like she was spinning thoughts in her mind, coming up with a plan to fight the Illuminati. "Okay. I get it. We can't take action on our own. And I'm not physically fit enough yet to wield Erik's ax. I'd better start training as soon as I get home."

"Which brings me to a topic I've wanted to discuss with you."

"It sounds serious."

"Anything that involves you, as far as I'm concerned, *is* serious. I'm used to being around you now, and I don't want us to go our separate ways when we return to the future. And now that we know about the danger, we should stay close to each other."

A maid came by, took her plate, and refilled her glass of sweet tea. "I've got to go back to New York City, clean out my office, and find a way to explain to my best friend and my cousin where I've been all this time."

"I can help with that. You can't tell them you've been through the vortex and back again, so I suggest you tell them you've been with me."

She burst out laughing. "They would believe I traveled through time before they believed I shacked up with you for several days or weeks, or however long I've been gone."

He rested his head against the high back of the wicker chair and closed his eyes. "Damn. That hurts my feelings."

"Oh, it does not. Your ego is as big as you are."

"Maybe it was once, but I'm more grounded now." He picked up his chair and placed it in front of her so they'd be knee to knee...or would be if his legs weren't so long. It was time to fess up and share one of his biggest secrets. "I've had a reputation for going through women faster than basketball shoes. But it's not like that at all. The women are girlfriends. Friends *without* benefits, by the way, and most are basketball players in the WNBA. I don't sleep around. I never have."

"But you let others believe you do."

He shrugged. "The press wouldn't believe the truth, so I don't bother to correct them. But here's the thing. I learned growing up to treat women with honesty, respect, and appreciation. I've been in four long-term relationships in my life, and they've been the only women I've invited to my house."

"I'm surprised. I thought professional athletes were philanderers."

"And I thought all book editors were stuffy former librarians."

"Touché. And I don't think I'm stuffy. I've been in a couple of relationships, too. The last one ended several months ago."

"Why'd it end?"

"Because all he wanted to do was go to sporting events or watch games on TV at his favorite sports bar."

"Instead of what?"

She glanced away as if the truth was embarrassing. "Instead of anything."

"Like what?" he pressed.

"Like going to the opera or a Broadway musical or The Met."

"You won't have trouble getting me to a show. Mom was a professional singer and dancer who performed on Broadway for years. That's why music is such a big deal in my family."

"Broadway? That's cool. Does she still sing?"

"She died when I was a baby."

"I'm sorry."

"Yeah, me too."

"My BFF will never believe I'm interested in a professional basketball player. And believe it or not, our last conversation was about you."

"Me? How's that possible? You didn't even know me, except through the manuscript I submitted."

She had the grace to look embarrassed.

"So you told your BFF that you were interested in me?" he asked in a teasing tone as he met her gaze.

"No. No. Not at all. But we were talking about you…you know, in general."

He grinned like a high school kid pressing his best friend for the goods on the cutest girl in their class. "You've piqued my interest now. You have to tell me what you said."

The maid returned to refill her glass, but Ensley didn't care for more, so she took it away. "If you want to know, you'll have to ask Barb. She'll be happy to repeat every word of the conversation."

"So when do I get to meet her?" he asked with that same high school eagerness.

"When you have an opening in your schedule, why don't you come to New York? We can all go to dinner, and she can tell you the story."

This was his big chance, but he didn't want to blow it by being too pushy. After all, they hadn't even shared a passionate kiss yet. How lame was that? He clicked his tongue, acting like he was mentally reviewing his calendar. "I don't have anything coming up right away. We can take the company jet to New York, and I'll stay at the Riverside Drive house for a while."

She cocked her head. "Really? But don't you have to practice basketball or something?"

"Practice? Yeah, and you might not know this, but New York City has hundreds of gyms. My staff will be glad to relocate for a while."

"Your staff?"

"I have a full-time trainer, physical therapist, massage therapist, nutritionist, chef, and assistant. I know it sounds like a lot, but I'm still recovering, and it takes several people to keep me healthy. Plus, I manage my portfolio, but I need help with my Thoroughbred business and scheduling community and charity events. It takes a village."

"Sounds like it. Do you have a valet, too?"

He laughed. "No. I wash my clothes or take them to the cleaners."

"Good to know." She glanced around. "Let's go for a walk and find some privacy so you can kiss me."

He gave her a slow smile. "On top of your head like I've done a dozen times, or did you have something else in mind?"

She grinned right back at him. "Let's find the place first, and then we can negotiate."

The way she looked at him made him wonder how he was looking at her. He wanted to do a lot more than kiss her, and that had to show on his face. Not that he was desperate for her, but it was pretty damn close.

He stood and reached for her hand. "I know just the place. It's a bit of a walk. Is that okay?"

"Lead the way. After shoveling down all that food, I'd better get some exercise."

He knew how she could burn off a few calories without taking a step, but he kept that to himself. His size was intimidating enough. He didn't want to bombard her with sexual innuendoes.

"I was going to offer a shovel, but I didn't want to embarrass you."

She elbowed him in the side.

"Ouch," he said. "Why do you keep trying to beat me up?" Her elbow punches lacked power, but it was fun to tease her. He rubbed his side. "You should see the bruises on my ribs from all the times you've punched me."

"Your body's like granite. You don't have a soft spot anywhere. And if we checked each other out, you'd see I'm the one with the bruises. Not you."

He didn't miss a beat replying, "I'm game."

She was smiling, but something changed in her eyes. They got warmer, more inviting—not uninviting, as he might have expected. And her gaze slipped briefly down to his mouth. Damn. He tried not to think about easing her down on his dick, but he couldn't help himself, and several times he had to realign his body so she wouldn't see the size of his boner.

"Let's go this way," he said, pointing. "There's a cave about a quarter-mile from here. JC and I found it by accident years ago, and we swore each other to secrecy. We both had a cave trauma, so we used it a few times to challenge each other to confront our fears. It became our sacred ground. That's why we never told anybody about it."

"Did it help to be in there?"

"I don't know. We always snuck a bottle of whisky out of the house and passed the bottle back and forth until we reached the cave. By then, we were laughing like goofballs."

They walked for about ten minutes until they reached a grove of trees. "Come on. It's this way." He took her hand and tugged her along. The hem of her skirt kept snagging on briars and brambles, and he had to stop and untangle her, but each time he did, he snuck a quick kiss, starting on her head, then the tip of her nose, and both cheeks, and was disappointed when he didn't make it to her lips. But he would get there eventually.

"In our time, this area is still in its natural state, but not this overgrown. And it's rumored to be haunted."

"So only the ghosts come here? Is that what you're saying?"

"Years ago, Kit and Meredith both saw Cullen's ghost on the farm."

"That's weird. I guess that was before he came here to live."

"Traveling back and forth between centuries messes everything up." Austin stopped and looked around for a minute, getting his bearings. "It's this way." They kept walking until they reached a creek.

"Does this feed the lake?"

"No. An underground stream feeds it."

They reached a wall of trees in front of a grassy knoll with a huge boulder, surrounded by thickets. "It's a prickly squeeze, but we can make it. Come on."

"Wait a minute. We need a light."

Austin dug into his jacket pocket and pulled out a penlight. "I was never a Boy Scout, but I'm always prepared."

A corner of her mouth curled up. "Always?"

He knew what she was thinking, and he patted his breast pocket. "Always." He was lying. He didn't have a condom. But there was no chance in hell they would ever reach the point of needing one without a serious conversation about what they were looking for in a relationship, which for him also meant kids. He wanted four or five. None of the women he'd dated before fit in the category of his "forever girl." Ensley was different. Not only did she fit in the category, but she defined it.

He squeezed in behind the boulder and clicked on the penlight.

"So why'd you bring a flashlight? I'm just curious."

"Swiss Army knife and flashlight. I never leave home without them."

"Seriously."

"Of course. I'd think a woman like you would also carry both, along with a pistol. Am I right?"

"I used to, but not now."

"Well, while you were checking out the laptop and battery, I picked up the light and knife." He retook her hand. "We have to duck. The opening is only about three feet high."

"You mean crawl?"

"You can duck. I'll crawl."

Once they got through the opening, Austin used the light to show her the cave's dimensions, which were about the size of a triple-bay garage with a height of about ten feet.

Ensley ran her hand along the sidewall. "I think this is gypsum. There are a couple of sites in North Dakota with deposits of gypsum."

"What's it used for?"

"Fertilizer, plaster, chalk, and sheetrock—"

"Ah! Gypsum board."

"Oh, and look at these!"

"They look like balloons," he said. "We wondered what they

were. If JC researched them, he never said."

"They start with dripping water. The magnesium in the water becomes concentrated. If there's enough evaporation, the magnesium forms this pasty white substance which can inflate and cause these pearly balloons."

"That sounds very technical."

"I think it's word-for-word how my 4-H instructor explained it."

They stepped farther into the cave, and Austin's beam of light traveled along the walls, ceiling, and floor.

"Stop! Stop!" she squealed. "Look."

"At what?"

"Those markings on the wall." She took the flashlight from him and let the beam of light spotlight what she wanted him to see. "The markings extend from the top of the wall to the floor. Do they look familiar?"

"We noticed it years ago, and JC thought it resembled his birthmark."

"Crap. It does. But you know what? It's gone now. Did you notice his foot?"

"No, I was watching JC's eyes. Not his feet."

"Kenzie mentioned his skin was as smooth as a baby's butt. I guess he got new skin all over." She shivered, and Austin rubbed her arms.

"It's cool in here. Let's go."

She looked at the drawing again. "Erik drew that design on my forehead."

"I know. I saw it. He drew it in blood."

"Oh, right. Well, he also drew it on my forehead when I fell off the bull and almost died. I saw it then."

"Did you have an out-of-body experience?"

"I guess so. I saw my body on the ground, but I couldn't feel a thing. Then I woke up in the hospital. I think Erik was with me."

"It sounds like he's always been around to protect you. When we get back, we can show this to David. He has equipment that can map it out, and if there are clues, he and Kenzie will find them."

"Clues to what?"

"Who knows? But there's a connection between you, this cave, and JC. I want to know what it is and what it means for the family."

They left the cave, and Austin decided to take the longer route back to the mansion. The sun was going down, and it was an easier path. He led her around the side of the mound, through the tree line, and stopped.

"I'll be damned. Never seen this before. It must be the cabin where Elliott kept JC."

"Is it on the farm in the future?"

"Someone obliterated the cabin and its foundation. Come on. Let's get out of here. It's giving me a creepy feeling."

Ensley grabbed Austin's arm to hold him back. "Wait." She let the light shine on the ground. "See these footprints?" She squatted and studied them closely. "I've seen these before. They're Erik's."

"They're going in both directions."

Ensley glanced behind her. "I wonder if he came from the cave and went back again the same way?"

Austin helped her up. "Why would he need a cave?"

"We won't know until we study the drawing. But what if there's a secret passage in there that allowed Erik to move laterally? We know he was here and in Chicago and North Dakota. How'd he move around so easily?"

"With his brooch."

"But so far, none of the brooches have been dependable that way. That's why Kenzie got so mad at Elliott. She was afraid the brooch wouldn't take him right back to get Meredith."

"I still don't see why Erik would need another way to move around."

"Because he can't fly."

"Another mystery will drive the family nuts. Come on. Let's get out of here. If the Illuminati know about the cave or caves, we could be in even more danger. Let's keep this quiet for now. We can tell David and Kenzie as soon as we get back."

She looked up at him. "Do you have your phone?"

"Is there someone you want to call?"

"No, I want pictures of the footprints."

"I don't have it. Tavis and Remy knocked me out and abducted me. I must have dropped my phone in the movie theater."

"They abducted you from a movie theater?"

"It's not what you think. There's a small theater in the ranch house."

"Of course there is. I know it's not a typical ranch house like the one I grew up in, but a movie theater?"

"Elliott wanted it to be a winter resort for the family. It has everything. And I love it there."

"Why?" Her expression was a curious mixture of wistfulness, loss, and something harder to identify.

"The mountains, winter sports, and hunting and fishing."

"North Dakota has all that."

"Do you want to go back there?"

She shook her head. "No, I sold the ranch. It was time to move on."

"I'll take you to Colorado for Christmas. Unless you decide that you're ready to leave the city for the mountains now."

"Let's get through this adventure first. Okay?"

He took her hand and led her across the clearing, looking for the perfect spot to kiss her. It had to be a place they could easily find later if they wanted to reenact their first kiss. When he saw a tree stump, he made a beeline in that direction.

"Hey, slow down. Your legs are twice as long as mine. I look like a hobbit next to you, mister gargantuan hardcourt hero."

"I'm no longer a hardcourt hero, and you don't look like a hobbit." He sat down on the tree stump, pulled her onto his lap, and didn't give her a chance to back out. He cupped her jaw with one hand and the back of her head with the other. Then he tilted her face up and melded her mouth with his.

His tongue slid past her lips, and she stroked his tongue in an irresistibly erotic rhythm. They shifted the angle of their heads several times but didn't break the kiss until he pulled away and pressed his lips against her neck just beneath her ear. She probably knew he was aching to enfold her tiny body in his arms and hold her so close against him that he could feel her heartbeat.

He didn't want to stop, but somehow—only God knew how—he kept his hands on her hips instead of exploring the hollows and mounds he'd visually charted when he barged in on her in the locker room.

He ended the kiss long before he wanted to, knowing he had to table his dirty thoughts and raging hard-on while he was still able. He looked deeply into her eyes, then released her. "You better hop up, or I'm going to toss up your skirt and petticoats and do it right here."

He willed her to comprehend the intensity of his feelings, but he must have gone too far because she stood up abruptly.

"We should go."

"I'm sorry—"

"No, don't be, and I'm not at all sorry. The kiss was perfect, and I didn't want it to end, but I don't want our first time to be on the ground at sunset, although that does sound romantic. But if we return to the mansion all disheveled, Sean will frown at us. And I don't want to offend our hosts."

"You're right. But help me understand something. If it wasn't important for us to look presentable when we returned, you might consider doing it here?"

She shook her head. "No. I'm holding out for a big bed, so you can show me how to make love with a man twice my size."

He rolled back his head and laughed. "Oh, darlin'. It might seem impossible, but it's not. We'll fit just fine. All you have to do is trust me not to hurt you."

She met his gaze with her usual immutable calm. "Everything about you invites trust, from your commanding stature to your sharp eyes and ready smile. Plus, you saved my life. How could I not trust you?"

A faint carnal tremor raced through him. Faint? Bullshit. It was a tsunami. And he wanted her more than he ever wanted a championship ring. And that was saying a hell of a lot.

The stroll back to the mansion was tense, but only because they were going in the wrong direction—away from privacy and possibility while watching the sun dip lower in the sky. And when they reached the house, Austin was relieved the company had left, leaving everyone exhausted except Braham.

"Austin, let's play chess."

"Good, you do that," Emily said. "I've been trying to get a few minutes alone with Ensley. You two go play while we find a quiet place to talk for a while."

Ensley gave him a mellow smile that tilted the corners of her mouth upward just slightly, and his heart snagged on the soft, erotic way she looked at him. "Maybe I'll see you later?" he asked.

Emily grabbed Ensley's arm. "We can drink an entire bottle of wine before those two play best two out of three."

"Ye better not be drinking a bottle of wine," Braham said. "Charlotte would shoot me."

"You know me, Uncle Braham. I'm careful." Then to Ensley, she said. "They are the slowest chess players I've ever seen."

"Not tonight, Emily," Austin said. "If I have to blow a game to finish sooner, I will."

Braham laughed. "Ye'd never do that. Ye're too competitive. Sean has the chessboard set up in the library, and I have something ye can't refuse." He dipped his hand into his inside jacket pocket and pulled out two cigars.

Austin glanced back at Ensley. "Uncle Braham, you know I don't smoke cigars."

Braham laughed. "If Ensley doesn't know you like them as much as Michael Jordan, Charles Barkley, Shaquille O'Neal, Karl Malone, and Steph Curry, then she'll find out now."

"Steph Curry?" Ensley asked.

"Only when he celebrates," Austin said.

"The first time I saw JC with a cigar," she said, "I had a fit and told him to get the nasty thing out of the house. But since then, I've discovered that puffing on a good cigar just slows everything down and allows smokers to relax. And you, my dear, deserve that tonight. So enjoy it."

"I'm curious. Where'd you learn that about cigars?" Austin asked.

"I edited the *Unequaled Cigar Book* and even smoked a few myself."

Braham clapped Austin on the shoulder. "Looks like ye've found the perfect girl. Don't let her get away." He handed Austin a cigar, and he held it to his nose for a moment, taking in the sweet aroma.

Braham was damn right. He winked at Ensley. No way in hell was he letting her get away from him.

57

MacKlenna Farm, KY (1885)—Austin

REVEREND BRECKINRIDGE FROM the Presbyterian Church in Lexington officiated at the funeral the following day, with Braham delivering his uncle's eulogy.

Austin was worried that the minister, who was as old as Christmas, might not make it through the service. But he did, then finished it off with a glass of whisky—or maybe two—before one of his parishioners carted him home.

It wasn't only Donald McCabe's death that hung over the family like black shrouds. It was worry over JC, concern for Elliott and Meredith, and fear that the Illuminati would strike again.

After everyone departed late in the day, Braham asked Austin and Cullen to meet him in Sean's office.

Austin was the last one to arrive and closed the door behind him. Braham was staring out the window that overlooked the paddock and turned when Austin entered. Cullen sat in one of the wingback chairs fronting the fireplace, thumbing through *The Naval War of 1812* by Theodore Roosevelt.

"Are you interested in the War of 1812 or the author?" Austin asked.

Cullen closed the book and set it aside. "After Rick and Penny's and Pete and Sophia's involvement in the war, I've read several books, but I missed Roosevelt's contribution. Sean said it's the definitive book on the subject."

"Let's hope no one in the family has to fight that one again. So what's going on? I told Ensley I didn't know what you have in mind but that it was important."

"What are the women doing?" Braham asked.

"Sitting on the veranda watching Kit sketch pictures of her daughters. It makes a man self-conscious when a group of women can't stop spitting iced tea because they're laughing so hard."

"The girls are exactly like their mother," Cullen said wistfully. "We've missed them and the grandchildren terribly."

"Enough to return permanently?" Braham asked.

Cullen stretched out his legs and crossed his ankles. "I wish I knew the answer to that. Kit and I have tabled the decision for now. It's easier to leave it hanging than to commit. The girls are happy, involved in their causes, and don't need us to take care of the children. But still…" Cullen finished his thought with a slow shake of his head.

Braham came around the desk and propped his butt cheek on one corner. "One day, we'll be able to travel back and forth freely, without worrying we might get stuck somewhere, but for now, without ye around, I'd be lost."

Austin grinned. "You can't leave, Uncle Cullen. If you did, I'd end up stuck playing chess and beating his ass every time we play. He needs someone who will let him win once in a while."

"Next time I offer ye a cigar, it won't be from my premium selection," Braham scolded.

"Damn. I know when to reel back an insult. You'll always be a better player than I am. And that's something I never admit."

Braham laughed. "And don't ye forget it." Then he dug into his inside jacket pocket and pulled out three cigars. "A man thinks better when he has one of these."

Austin accepted one and toyed with it for a moment, rolling it between his fingers, and for some reason, he thought of Ensley, about the kiss they shared and about how much more he wanted to share with her. But he wasn't entirely sure about her. Did she feel the same?

Braham handed one to Cullen before clipping a cigar and lighting one for himself. Then he walked back around the desk and sat in the swivel chair, exhaling. A blue cloud of smoke soon hazed the air throughout the room.

Austin sniffed the cigar before striking a match against his thigh and waving it in front of the tip. He took a long, satisfying draw, leaned his head back, and blew smoke at the ceiling. "Ensley asked where I was going, and I told her you wanted to meet. She's curious and might barge in here to find out what's so important."

"She's welcome to join the discussion." Cullen took a deep draw. "This has to be from Cuba. It's as smooth as the inside of a woman's thigh."

Austin choked on the smoke and coughed, replaying what his uncle just said.

Braham balanced his cigar between two fingers. "Correct all around. And I expect a review, and that goes for ye, too, Austin."

"Sure. I know that's always part of the deal." Austin's eyes were still watering from choking on the smoke. Cullen's comment shouldn't surprise him. He'd heard plenty of sexual innuendos from all the men in the family. And there was never a shortage of PDAs at family gatherings.

"This won't take long," Braham said, "Ye can bring Ensley up to speed as soon as we make a decision."

"About what?"

"It's time to go home, and trying to talk to Elliott is useless. I've never seen him like this. He reminds me of ye, Austin," Cullen said, waving his cigar, leaving a trail of smoke in the air. "But from what Kit tells me, ye weren't on drugs all this time. Ye just wanted more independence from the family."

"Something like that." Austin brushed off Cullen's comment. He didn't want to discuss his life with his uncles right now. He wanted to go home. Figuring out how to do that was his number one priority. "I don't understand why Elliott doesn't want to leave so he can take care of JC."

Cullen rolled his cigar ash into a crystal ashtray. "He did, but now he's given up. He just sits in his room, drinks whisky, and won't talk to anyone."

"Can't Meredith talk to him?" Austin asked.

"She won't, and Kit tried," Cullen said, "but he locked her out. He realized it doesn't matter how long he stays here because he'll only be gone a few minutes in our time. So he can sit his ass here for a year or longer. And by staying, he doesn't have to confront what's waiting for him at home."

"That doesn't sound like Elliott. He never lets any grass grow under his feet."

Braham puffed on his cigar, blowing rings, which seemed to entertain him. "He's afraid he's lost his son *and* his wife."

Cullen took a short draw, then removed the cigar from his mouth and studied it. "I'm afraid Meredith isn't much better off."

"Yeah, I know. She looks like she's lost her best friend. And I guess she has," Austin said.

"Then we have to find a way to get them in the same room. Alone. And soon." Braham looked down at his cigar and used the stub of the match to trim the ash evenly. Then his attention lifted. "I wonder if Ensley can reach him."

"Elliott hardly knows her." Austin glanced at his cigar, using how much he had smoked of it as a measure of time, knowing Ensley would be getting impatient if she was kept in the dark much longer. "But she does or did know Erik. This might sound crazy, but Elliott had a connection with Erik, and Ensley did, too. She can try to draw Elliott out by telling him what Erik told her before he died. It's worth a try, isn't it?"

Cullen flicked his cigar's gray ash. "It won't hurt. Maybe we should try that before we lock Elliott and Meredith in the attic."

There was a quick rap on the door before Sean partially opened it and stuck his head into the room. "The conspirators have been missed. Ye should come on out."

Braham chomped down on his cigar. "Come in. After all, it is yer office."

Sean walked in and closed the door. "Did ye come up with an idea?"

Cullen frowned behind a cloud of smoke. "We're implementing a plan to use Ensley first. If she can't intercede and break the stalemate, then we'll lock Elliott and Meredith in the attic until they resolve their issues."

"If using Ensley or putting the contrarians in the attic don't work, I know a brambleberry thicket Elliott can't get out of by himself."

Braham took one last puff on his cigar before extinguishing it in a silver-hinged ashtray sitting on a desk. "I'd hate to leave him in a thicket, but that might be the best outcome we can hope for."

58

MacKlenna Farm, KY (1885)—Ensley

TWO HOURS AFTER Braham, Cullen, and Austin met to plan an intervention that hopefully would get them all home, Ensley, the designated sacrificial lamb, carried a dinner tray to the wounded lion's den.

Every step she took, she wondered how she got nominated to take one for the team. If this was a newbie's initiation into the family's rites and rituals, then she couldn't wait for the next newbie to come along. Not so Ensley could help terrorize her, but to stand in solidarity against such awful treatment.

She was acting overly dramatic. After all, the men gave her an option. The choice was to do nothing or do something. So, after consulting with Austin, she decided to do something because her home was calling. It was time to end this adventure and get back to her life, in whatever form and fashion it would take. A new job? A new relationship? A new adventure?

She was game!

But back to Elliott and the task ahead. She hardly knew the guy. Their conversations over the years had been superficial and usually involved horses. This conversation wouldn't be either one. It would be a gut-level, personal one.

And this would be a good time for the voice she'd carried in her head for most of her life to offer advice. She never realized how vital the mind-to-mind communication was until the brooch abandoned her in the Badlands. Since her dad's death, she'd assumed the voice was her dad's, but could it have been Erik? If so, she had to ask why. Why had he chosen her to haunt?

But he was gone now, and she'd never know the answer.

Since she had no head voice to advise her, she decided to channel her best Kenzie McBain impersonation. Man, that woman was one badass vet—totally fearless.

I want to be her when I grow up.

Ensley trudged down the hallway, composing a variety of mantras. She'd need plenty of oomph to confront the—indomitable, unconquerable, invincible—Dr. Elliott Blane Fraser.

How about I'm a badass warrior? And I have a battle-ax to prove it.

She tried it out to hear how it sounded. "I'm a badass warrior."

"You sure are, ma'am."

She whipped around, rattling the tray full of dishes, to see Austin behind her. He put his finger to his lips. "Shhh. I'll be outside the door in case you need help."

She gave him an evil-eye look. "You just agreed I'm a badass warrior, and you muck it up by telling me you're here to help. Talk about siphoning off some of my confidence."

"I didn't mean it that way. Don't be so sensitive."

"Go away."

His eyes widened. "Sorry."

She tilted her head back. "Kiss me, *then* go away. I have to focus and get into my zone before I go in there. I know you understand *that*."

His eyes lingered on her lips a moment, then he bent down and swiftly kissed the tip of her nose. "I understand completely." Then he turned and walked away.

"Well, I'll be damned," she whispered.

A soft chuckle floated in his wake as he strutted toward the landing. When he hit the top step, he looked back and winked. Then he was gone. But Ensley knew he was only out of sight. Austin Klenna O'Grady was a keeper-man.

He'd lifted her spirits, and there was a spring in her step as she continued the long walk to Elliott's bedroom. Although it seemed shorter now that she didn't dread her assignment as much as she did before. She chuckled. Yeah, before the kiss on her nose.

Only Austin would do something so silly but so significant to help her ease into her zone. He *got* her. And she *got* him.

When Ensley reached Elliott's bedroom, she'd shelved most of her anxiety, leaving only a slight unease that she could handle. It gave her an edge, which was a good thing. She set the tray down on a hall table before knocking on the door.

"Elliott, it's Ensley. I have a dinner tray."

"Leave me alone."

"You need to eat."

"Got all the nutrients I need right here."

"In a bottle of whisky? That's all sugar. Open the door, okay? If you don't eat some protein and complex carbs right now, you'll get sick."

"The only thing I'm opening is another bottle of whisky. Now. Go. Away," he said, slurring his words.

"I brought a bottle with me. You want it?"

"Leave it and go."

"Well, that's the thing. I can't go away, so I'll just sit here and wait. Sooner or later, you'll have to open the door."

"No reason to open it."

"You'll run out of whisky eventually, and then you'll remember there's a bottle out here." She wasn't going to give up, so she leaned against the door and slid down it until she was sitting on the floor in a pile of petticoats and silk. "I want to talk to you about Erik and my childhood memories of him. Memories I don't understand, but I hope maybe you will."

"What makes ye think I'll understand?"

"You know Erik, and you've had long conversations with him. You know things about him that I want to know."

"I can't help ye."

"I think you can."

"Ye're wrong, lass."

There was one thing that might pique his interest enough to open the door. She didn't have permission to share Austin and JC's secret, but the guys told her to use her vast repertoire of skills to get inside the room.

"Hey, Elliott. Did you know there's a cave behind the cabin?"

"No."

"JC and Austin found it when they were teenagers."

She paused to listen for a response or movement in the room. There was nothing. Now she had to go big or go home.

"There's an Yggdrasil on the wall. It's identical to JC's birthmark and the sign Erik drew in blood on my forehead before he died."

Nothing.

"Austin and I found footprints identical to the ones I followed in the Badlands. They were Erik's. Some were going to the cabin, and some were going to the cave."

There was still no movement on the other side of the door. She had to keep going. Some part of the story might entice him. She summoned her best storytelling voice and continued.

"Austin and I believe there's an opening in the fabric of time inside the cave. We think it lets a person travel from one place to another along the same time continuum. That's how Erik could travel from the Badlands to Chicago to here and back to the Badlands as quickly as he did."

"He had a brooch, lass. He could go anywhere."

Bingo! She had him engaged.

"Could he?" she asked. "Go anywhere? You know the brooches aren't dependable. That's why Kenzie insisted you return immediately. She was afraid it could take years to get back here for Meredith and the others. Erik couldn't take that risk. He needed a reliable method to reach JC before it was too late and then get to the Badlands before the bear killed me."

She paused again to wait for a response. He didn't say anything, but after a minute or two, the lock clicked, and Elliott opened the door. *Woohoo.* She high-fived her persistence.

"Where's the whisky?"

She forced a smile. "Well, I sort of lied."

"Don't ever do that again."

Elliott headed toward a chaise lounge near the window. Plates full of partially eaten food, overflowing ashtrays, and empty whisky bottles littered the floor around the chair. The smell of decay, an unwashed body, and stale cigar smoke stank up the room. Before she did anything else, she had to let in some fresh air.

She threw back the heavy floor-to-ceiling velvet drapes.

"Leave those alone. I want it dark in here."

"I don't care what you want. I'm opening the windows, too. It stinks in here, and you need a bath."

"I didn't ask ye to come in."

"Yes, you did. It was a silent invitation when you unlocked the door."

"If ye want to talk about Erik, talk. Then get the hell out of here."

She picked up the plates of half-eaten food and set the china on a serving tray. "I heard you were an asshole, but I didn't believe it until now."

"Do ye think I care?"

"You don't care about anything or anyone." She tossed three empty whisky bottles into the trash basket. "But for some strange reason, people care about you, and that's why I'm here."

"If they cared about me, they would have sent ye with a bottle of whisky."

"Goddamn it, Elliott. Your pity party is disgusting. And you don't deserve the kindness of others."

"Then leave!" he growled.

"You're a goddamn bastard, and I don't know why anyone depends on you." She went over to the bed and threw back the quilt to straighten the sheets. "I'll leave when I'm ready and not a minute before." After making the bed, she picked up two pairs of trousers, folded them neatly, then placed them in the chifforobe. Boxer briefs went into a clothes basket along with dirty shirts and socks.

"When I was sixteen, a bull bucked me off, kicked me, and broke my hip."

"When ye get on a goddamn bull, what the hell else would ye expect?"

She almost threw a pillow at him. "A wild, eight-second ride, the biggest adrenaline rush imaginable. There's nothing like it."

"If ye want a wild ride and a rush of adrenaline, try having sex with the love of yer life. It won't kill ye."

She emptied the ashtrays full of ash and cigar stubs, then cleaned her hands on one of the cloth napkins on the dinner tray. "I've had wild sex, and it was an adrenaline rush. But man, it didn't compare to riding a bull."

"If ye ever have the good fortune to be with the one God meant for ye, ye'll find out it's an order of magnitude better than riding a goddamn bull."

She held the chamber pot at arm's length and set it out in the hall. Her willingness to clean up Elliott's shit only went so far.

"I died that day, you know. Left my broken body behind and hovered above the arena, watching the medics tend to me." She sat in the chair across from him, and for the first time, saw a disheveled older man without an ounce of resemblance to the great Elliott Fraser.

What a damn pity.

She doubted he would ever regain the respect of those who loved him. And in the state he was in, he would never regain his wife's love and trust, either. The situation tempted her to pack up and leave, but she hadn't finished her story. And when a cowboy had a captive audience—as she did—there was no quitting.

"After that bull kicked me and I went flying across the arena floor, I heard a man's voice. He said, 'Be strong and fight to survive. You are the chosen one, and the Keeper will depend on you for the coming war.'"

Elliott shifted slightly in his chair, his eyes closed, but she knew he was listening.

Help him to find himself. No one else can lead the clan through the approaching darkness except Elliott. He is the Keeper.

She shivered. *You're back.*

I never left you, my child. But you have to guide the Keeper and his woman. The clan is weak without them together. They cannot win if they're divided. It's up to you now.

Why me?

You are the chosen one.

Chosen for what?

When it is time, you will know.

"Did Erik tell ye what war?"

She jerked. Elliott's question brought her back to the nasty room that reeked of stale food and whisky. "I asked him, but he said, 'You will discover that in time. But always remember you have the handprints of your ancestors on your heart.'"

"Do ye think that was Erik?"

"I'm sure it was. But it wasn't the first time he played a role in my life. When I was a child, my parents were arguing one day, and my mom sent me to my room. I saw Erik out in the yard. But I had met him earlier that day when my mom and I went to town."

"What were yer parents arguing about? Do ye remember?"

"No, but I remember the tension in the air. Why?"

Elliott didn't say anything for countless seconds, and she was starting to believe he had quit talking, but then he said, "There's no easy way to say this, lass, but to just come out with it. Erik was in love with yer mother, and ye're his child."

Ensley turned stone cold, and the bear's growl grew louder and louder in her mind. And she heard Erik's voice again, *Run, child run!* Another time he had said, *Be still, and I will heal you.* But when was that? When the bull bucked her off or when she broke her foot? Both? And there was another time, too. When she almost died of thirst.

She wanted to go somewhere quiet and think about this and decide if she believed it or not.

But why would Elliott lie to her?

Because he's binge drinking and doesn't know what he's saying.

That was believable. Erik being her father…well, that wasn't.

"I find it hard to believe—no, impossible to believe—that my mother cheated on my father. But after what Erik did for me, it's not a stretch for me to believe you. But why didn't he tell me? Or here's the bigger question. Why'd he tell you?"

"He said he acted as my proxy when he beheaded the man who tortured James Cullen. And he asked me to be his proxy and always protect ye in return."

"And you agreed to that?"

"He gave me back my son. I wanted to repay him. That was his price."

"On behalf of Erik the Viking, I release you from your obligation. I don't require the protection of a self-pitying drunkard." She pushed to her feet. "Thanks anyway."

She walked toward the door but stopped. She had one last thing to say. "Death leaves its mark in grooves and patterns. You have those grooves all over you, and I bet this drunken stupor is a pattern in your life when you feel sorry for yourself. People have probably bailed you out of it in the past. Well, guess what? Nobody's doing it this time." She opened the door. "And you want to know why?"

"Sure."

She held up her hand. "I've got this, and you can go to hell."

He wobbled, but with effort, he made it to his feet. "Where'd ye find that?"

"In the pocket of your trousers."

"Ye don't want that brooch, Ensley. It comes with too much responsibility, and it's taken too much from me."

"From you?" She stomped over to him and got as close as she dared. "Is that what you think this is all about? You? The brooches and the evil in this world have taken Erik, and they've taken JC's mental health, and God knows what's happened to Tavis.

"If Erik had wanted me to know he was my father, he would have told me before he died. He chose not to do that. But you couldn't resist, and you're a bastard for revealing it."

"Damn it, Ensley. Ye can call me all the goddamn names ye

want, but ye're the daughter of a Viking warrior, and ye got what it takes to win this war. I can't do it any longer. It's up to ye now."

"Hell no, it's not, and it's past time for you to get your goddamn life in order."

"It's as orderly as it's going to get."

She stomped back to the door and threw it open. "You can wallow on your ass right here, but we're going home, and Meredith's going with us. You see, I talked to her first. And she was willing to give you a chance, but not now. I won't let her."

Ensley saw the dinner tray she left on the hall table. She couldn't leave it there, so she picked it up and carried it across the room. "You still should eat."

"Take it away. I don't want it."

She returned to the door and decided to channel Clark Gable this time. "Frankly, Elliott, I don't give a damn."

She slammed the door and ran down the hall—smack into Meredith.

59

MacKlenna Farm, KY (1885)—Ensley

"**W**HOA!" MEREDITH GRABBED Ensley's upper arms to keep from losing her balance. "Where's the fire?"

Ensley couldn't speak, nor could she stop shaking. You would have thought she'd escaped a lion's den. Hey, wait a minute. That's just what she did. She took deep breaths to help her calm down a bit, but it didn't happen right away.

"He's…a g-goddamn bastard."

Meredith managed a snort that passed for a laugh. "I assume you're talking about Elliott. Forget about him." She waved her hand as if flicking him off. "Come with me. I have a bottle of Manzanilla Pastrana, a single-vineyard sherry. A glass of this is the perfect aperitif before dinner, and it will calm you down enough to tell me what he did to make you cry. Although I can probably guess." Meredith glanced toward Elliott's room, scowling.

Ensley wasn't sure, but she thought Meredith muttered, "Bastard." At least they agreed on that!

But of all the people to run into, why'd it have to be Meredith? Ensley needed to find Austin and tell him about her ordeal. But he more than likely used his mind-to-mind communication skill—a common trait in the MacKlenna Clan—and already knew what happened. Then she spotted him in her peripheral vision, sitting on the bottom step with his legs stretched out from here to Tennessee!

But since Meredith had hold of her hand, short of yanking it out of her grasp, Ensley had to go wherever JC's mom led her. Ensley could drag her feet, but she still had to go. From what she knew of Meredith Montgomery, "no" was an unacceptable response.

Ensley did drag her feet as she followed Meredith into her bedroom and intentionally left the door ajar. But Meredith reached back and pushed it shut. *Slam!*

Ensley noticed three things right away.

The setup in this bedroom was similar to Elliott's. But it was clean and smelled like lilacs instead of shit.

Oh, and one more thing. It reminded Ensley of the Victorian bedroom described in a novel she edited recently, right down to a small table with a tassel-fringed green velvet cover between two needlepoint-upholstered armchairs.

Meredith sat at the cute little table and gestured for Ensley to sit, too.

God, I need to get out more often and stop living in fictitious worlds.

Then she almost laughed out loud. She'd been hanging out with Teddy Roosevelt and a Viking warrior. Plus, falling in love and fighting evil. Her experiences were wilder than any book she'd ever edited.

Meredith poured sherry from a crystal decanter with a surprisingly steady hand. "This is a carefully blended sherry I brought from home. You'll notice the apple, citrus blossom, and roasted nut flavors. I hope you like it." She handed a glass to Ensley and lifted the other. "To what should we toast? Wounded lions and lambs?"

When Meredith asked the question, her eyes, her whole demeanor, conveyed a stark, heartbreaking reality. She was also a wounded lion and, in many ways, the wounded lamb as well.

"How'd you know?"

"I was in Lyle Ann's sitting room across from Elliott's room."

"So you heard us yelling."

"Most of it." Meredith sat with her back ramrod straight, her chin lifted ever so slightly, and the force of her iron will on full display. Angry waves still rippled off her, but at least they weren't white-capped now.

Ensley raised her glass. "Let's toast to wounded lions and *sacrificial* lambs." She pinged her glass against Meredith's, hoping she didn't look as stark and heartbroken as Meredith.

"So, Braham and Cullen sent you in there to talk Elliott out of his pity party?"

Ensley shrugged. "Something like that. How'd you know?"

"I know them. This situation is very stressful, and it's their natural inclination to try to fix it, but they can't."

"Who can?"

"Only Elliott. He messed up this time, and it's going to take more than an apology to make it right again. But what I don't understand is why they thought you could."

Ensley gnawed on that question for a moment. It had to be more than her connection to Erik. But for the life of her, she didn't know. Probably that telepathy thing again.

"Maybe they thought I was spunky enough to give him hell and fast enough to take cover before the cyclone hit."

Meredith smiled. "You, Kit, Kenzie, and JL have a lot in common. I'm sure Braham, Cullen, and Austin saw the similarities. But there *is* a connection between you and Erik, and Elliott thought it was his job to tell you."

"How'd you know?"

Meredith sipped from her glass, then held the crystal between her palms and slowly rolled it back and forth as if she wasn't even aware she was doing it. She didn't answer immediately, and Ensley wondered if she was going to ignore the question.

Then Meredith took another sip. "I've studied genealogy for decades, and when I met you and your cousin, I did a background search. I wanted to know your family's country of origin. Your mother's family came from the Scottish Highlands and settled in North Dakota, so you're from a branch descending from Thomas MacKlenna's brother Edward."

Ensley's jaw dropped. "Are you serious? Am I related to JC? And you never said anything?"

"Very distantly related, and I didn't want to interfere. I liked you instantly and hoped one day you might be our daughter-in-law. If a relationship developed between you and James Cullen, I would have told you, but I didn't want it to influence you either way."

"Does Elliott know about the connection to the MacKlennas?"

"Elliott has never been very interested in genealogy. The hows and whys don't concern him. He just wants to know the bottom line. I never told him about your connection to the family."

"So you're in the habit of keeping secrets?"

"Secrets and acts of omission. They seem to be a family curse. But I heard Elliott tell you about your other parent."

"Erik. Did you know?"

"I suspected. Sophia painted a portrait of Erik based on Penny's description. When Elliott told me about your disappearance, your photograph triggered something in my brain, and I went back to

Erik's portrait. You have his eyes—glacial blue—and his high cheekbones. You look too much alike not to be related."

Ensley popped up out of her chair as her heart slammed urgently in her chest. "I can't believe my mother was unfaithful. She just wouldn't have cheated. That's not who she was."

"Your father was injured in Iraq and couldn't have children. Erik was a sperm donor."

A second slid off the mantel clock, then another, both of them drenched in tension. "How could you possibly know that? It's private information and violates all sorts of HIPAA regulations."

"You're right on both counts. And I'm not proud of everything I've done through my network of detectives and genealogists. They often tread lightly into the gray zone."

"But Elliott said Erik loved my mother."

"I'm sure he did. But that doesn't mean your mother was in love with him."

"Are you just saying that to make me feel better?"

"I don't think words can make you feel better right now, Ensley. You have to look at what people do, not what they say. That's where you find honesty."

"Elliott opened the door and let me in. What does that mean?"

"What did he tell you?"

"That Erik stood in as Elliott's proxy when he beheaded the man who tortured JC. And he asked Elliott to be his proxy and watch over me as if I was his child."

"And he will when he comes to his senses again." Meredith sipped her sherry. "That makes you a Viking warrior. How do you feel about that?"

Ensley lifted her chin. "Proud. But it doesn't take anything away from how much I still love my dad."

"And it shouldn't."

"But this story isn't about my Viking father. It's about the clan, which right now is rudderless. It can't survive without you and Elliott. Everyone would splinter off. It's the cohesiveness that strengthens the family and protects the brooches."

"You're very insightful."

"Not any more than the others. So what do you want from Elliott? What will it take to get your issues resolved? I can tell you're putting up a good front, but you're crying on the inside. What do you need? If words don't matter, what do you want to see?"

Meredith stood, set her empty glass aside, and walked over to the window, hugging herself. She didn't speak, didn't move, didn't even seem to breathe. Finally, she said, "I want to see James Cullen."

Ensley walked over to Meredith and held out her hand. The diamond brooch glinted on her palm. "Nothing and no one should ever come between a mother and her child. Take it and go see your son."

60

MacKlenna Farm, KY (1885)—Ensley

MEREDITH SNATCHED THE brooch from Ensley and held it against her heart like it was a secret talisman that would solve all her problems. In Ensley's limited experience, brooches caused more problems than they solved, and giving one to Meredith wouldn't fix any of the bad shit between her and Elliott.

Ensley eyed the door and planned her escape. As far as she was concerned, she couldn't get away from Elliott and Meredith fast enough.

"You're coming with me!"

Ensley glared at Meredith in a way that should have frozen her feet to the floor. "You're *not* serious."

Meredith crossed the room, locked the door, and pocketed the key. "I most certainly am. You're coming with me. I can't do this alone."

Then take your husband, damn it.

"You can't lock me in here. I'll scream. Austin's sitting on the steps and will barge in here to rescue me." Ensley glanced out the window overlooking the paddock. Her best guess was that the second-story room looked out over the patio and flower garden outside Sean's office. She could drop from the windowsill smack into the lilacs and daylilies and come out smelling sweet and maybe a little bruised. So what if the fall hurt her hip more than it already did? At least she wouldn't get shanghaied.

Meredith put her hands on her hips. "If Austin comes in, he'll have to come, too. But why involve anyone else? You have to come. If we're kicked around the vortex and tossed out somewhere else, I want a Viking princess with me."

That term was annoying as hell, or in cowboy lexicon, as prickly as a burr in her saddle. "I'm *not* a princess." She thumped her chest. "I'm a warrior."

Meredith hurried over to her traveling trunk. "That's even better. But we should take some money, jewels, or gold with us, just in case. Do you have anything on you? Ring? Necklace? Earrings?"

"A sapphire and titanium ring."

"Austin needs to give you some jewelry for your birthday next month."

"How do you know…? Never mind." Meredith was a font of information about her. And Ensley didn't like it at all. It put her at a disadvantage, and that was never a good thing. Meredith probably even knew how much she had in her stock portfolio. "I don't even have any money."

"I know that's not true, but you probably mean you don't have any with you."

Yep. Meredith even knew Ensley's net worth. "That's what I meant," Ensley grumbled.

"If my son intentionally abandoned you, he should have left you with some money."

"He did. But I gave that to a man who was very kind to me."

"That's valiant and goes with the whole"—Meredith waved her hand around her head—"warrior persona."

Meredith grabbed a leather case from her trunk. "I have diamonds, rubies, and pearls. That should be enough." She glanced around the room again. "Clothes. We need capes. It might be cool in the evenings." She grabbed two from the chifforobe and tossed one to Ensley. "What did you wish you had when you landed by yourself?"

Ensley swung the cape over her shoulders. "A gun or knife, food, water, a container, something warm. Lots of things."

"Grab the bottle of sherry and two glasses and put them in that basket on the floor by the bed. Our only option for a weapon is a letter opener unless you see something else that will work."

"That's better than nothing, but let me get Austin. We won't need a weapon with him along."

"No! We're doing this by ourselves. We're taking action. No words. Got it?"

It looked like Ensley was stuck. *What a story this will make.* "A blanket. I would have killed for a blanket."

"Good idea. Grab the quilt off the bed."

Ensley folded the quilt and packed it neatly in the basket with the sherry and glasses. The letter opener fit perfectly between her corseted breasts. If something went wrong, she wanted quick access to the only thing they had for protection.

"Meredith, I want to go on the record as saying this is a horrible idea, and if Elliott discovers we left—"

"I'll leave him a letter just like the one he left me. That'll make us even."

"Getting even won't help the situation."

"You're right, of course. But I'll feel better, and it will shock Elliott senseless."

"I still don't like the idea of zipping off into the stratosphere."

Meredith stared up at the ceiling as she tapped her chin with a manicured fingernail. Then, after a minute, she returned her gaze to Ensley. "I've heard your objection, considered it, and passed on it. But you shouldn't worry."

"Yeah, right. You might as well tell me to stop breathing."

"Okay. Here's the deal. Charlotte, Kenzie, Amber, Amy, Sophia, Penny, and you were all abandoned by your brooches. But we're traveling with the diamond, and it's the most reliable one we have."

"But which one of those women was abandoned by the diamond brooch?"

Meredith let out an exasperated sigh. "Amy, but after it refused to work for her temporarily, it's been very reliable since. We'll be okay."

It wasn't that Ensley was anxious about traveling again. It was about traveling alone with Meredith. She had no idea how JC's mother would react in a crisis. If they landed in a Scottish castle in the 1700s, would she be any help at all?

There was only one way to find out.

Ensley looped the basket handle over her arm. "Letter opener, sherry, glasses, and a quilt. But we still need food…"

Meredith snapped her fingers. "I've got just the thing." She returned to her trunk and pulled out a Ziploc bag full of energy bars. "These will get us through a couple of days, I think."

They would have gotten Ensley through a week in the Badlands.

"We've got everything now, so let's go." Meredith tried to return the brooch to Ensley. "Here, you do it."

"Me?" Ensley shoved her hands behind her back, refusing to

retake possession. But it was a surprise twist. And come to think of it, her only chance to bail.

Take it and run!

Ensley glanced at the door, then back at Meredith, and felt defeated. JC's mother had coerced her into doing something against her better judgment.

"You keep it. I don't have the right mindset."

"Please take it. I'm afraid I'll drop it," Meredith said.

Ensley widened her eyes for emphasis. "Then I *definitely* shouldn't hold it." She moderated her tone of voice to convey the seriousness of her excuse. "Remember, I dropped mine and started this whole mess."

Meredith made an exasperated sound. "Don't worry. You won't drop this one."

Ensley made the same exasperated sound. "If we get stranded, I'll remind you of your misplaced confidence." She somehow, even with shaking hands, managed to open the brooch. "Let's concentrate on JC."

Meredith laced her arm with Ensley's. "Okay."

"Here we come, JC." Then Ensley recited the chant, hoping this wasn't a huge mistake.

61

Mallory Plantation, VA—Ensley

THE RIDE THROUGH the vortex tossed Ensley here and there, and when it finally ended, she was tangled head to foot in the cape Meredith had given her. As the fog started lifting, she pocketed the brooch before placing the basket on the floor and untangling herself. Then she dug into her bodice for her lame excuse for a weapon.

When enough of the fog lifted that she could see her surroundings, she shook the tension out of her shoulders and relaxed her grip on the silver-gilt letter opener.

Kenzie spotted her and blinked. "That was quick!" Then alarm replaced her surprise. "Where's everyone else?"

Ensley looked around the room, and her shoulders knotted again. "Oh, God! I lost Meredith."

"What about the others?" David asked.

"Others?" Ensley asked.

"Where's Braham?" Charlotte asked.

Ensley was too worried about Meredith to think about the others right now. "It's just the two of us, and Meredith was afraid we'd get separated. We have to find her. She's so distressed she might panic."

"Meredith doesn't panic," Kenzie said. "Calm down. Don't worry. The brooches have never spit anyone out along the way."

"There's always a first time."

"She's on the property," David said, "and she knows her way around. I'll notify security so they can pick her up."

Just then, the door swished open. Meredith marched in and scanned the room. When she saw Ensley, she said, "Oh, good! You made it."

Meredith didn't seem particularly surprised or concerned, but Ensley was so relieved she plowed into Meredith and hugged her with such force they almost tipped over. "You scared me to death. Are you okay? You must have been so afraid when you landed alone."

Meredith patted Ensley's back. "There, there. I knew where I was, so I wasn't scared." She released Ensley. "Where's James Cullen?"

"Over there," Kenzie said, pointing in the direction of Charlotte's exam room.

Meredith headed in that direction, but David blocked her path. "Not until ye tell us why it's just the two of ye. Where the hell's Elliott?"

"Where's Braham?" Charlotte demanded.

"Braham is one of the instigators. He, Cullen, and Austin cooked up a plan for me to confront Elliott. I did, and here we are."

A frown rippled over Meredith's face, like a stone thrown into black water. "Elliott's drunk and locked in his room. Now get out of my way, David. I'm not in the mood to put up with anybody's shit right now, and that means you, too. I'm going to see my son, and Ensley can fill you in on what's happened. Move!"

Kenzie joined David, so they stood side by side, arms crossed, wearing identical frowns. Talk about a power couple. Man. Double the power. Double the trouble. Surely Meredith would back down now.

"We didn't let Elliott get away with brushing us off, and we're not going to let you do it, either," Kenzie said.

David snapped his hands to his hips, determination prickling like barbed wire on top of a chain-link fence. Nothing was going to get past him. "What's the deal?" he demanded.

Meredith looked at Ensley, almost pleadingly. All she wanted was to see JC, and Ensley didn't think Kenzie and David should interfere.

Ensley picked up the basket and pulled out the bottle of sherry, like a rabbit out of a hat. She'd much rather have a shot of whisky, but this would do for now. "Let Meredith see JC. I have here a bottle of her best sherry, so let's each have a glass, and I'll tell you what happened and how I channeled my best Kenzie McBain."

A smile winked at the corner of Kenzie's mouth. "I hope it got you what you wanted."

"I wasn't sure what I wanted, but I certainly got more than I expected." It was weird how her voice sounded confident while her insides were churning.

David muttered, "A glass of sherry in exchange for information. No Scot in his right mind would ever agree to that."

"Well, I'm offended. I'm mostly a Scot, and I don't think it's such a bad deal."

"If it's Meredith's Manzanilla Pastrana, I'll drink with you." Kenzie went to the drink bar and collected two beer glasses. "Sorry about the glasses, but it's either whisky, beer, or coffee down here."

"I brought the glasses. You can't drink this sherry out of a mug."

While this was going on, Meredith tried to step around David, but he blocked her again, and Ensley was relieved she had the letter opener and not Meredith. The daggers flying out of Meredith's eyes were dangerous enough.

Charlotte joined them while snapping off her latex gloves. "Meredith, JC's sedated. He's over here. Did Elliott tell you what happened before you left my husband behind?" Charlotte's Southern accent was a hundred percent stronger than before.

David gave Meredith a small grunt of disapproval but otherwise moved out of the way. Meredith swung off her cape and dropped it on the stainless steel table.

"Elliott played the video of James Cullen's violent outburst for me," Meredith said, following Charlotte to an alcove with a single bed. "I can't get the sound of his screams out of my mind. It was terrifying."

"It was for us as well. But how did you get here without the others?" Charlotte persisted in a more pronounced Tidewater accent than usual.

Meredith walked over to the bed to gaze down at her son. "I have to give Ensley credit for that."

Ensley ignored the glares from everyone while she uncorked the sherry and poured the pale, light wine into the glasses she'd packed in the basket. "As I said, the three guys thought I was the perfect person to interrupt Elliott's pity party. I accepted the challenge, but he wasn't having any part of it. So I sat outside his door and bugged him until he opened it."

"I sat outside Braham's room once. He'd locked himself in there with a bottle and his guilt because he wasn't able to save President

Lincoln's life. I imagine Elliott was in the same rare form. If Elliott let you come in, you must have been very persuasive."

Ensley handed Kenzie a glass. "I lied about having an unopened bottle of whisky."

"Ooh. I doubt that went over well," Kenzie said.

"You know, he didn't seem to care. He just told me not to lie to him again. But man, his room was disgusting. I made his bed and picked up his dirty clothes while he drank, and I talked. When I found the brooch in his pocket, I palmed it, and then Meredith shanghaied me."

Meredith looked up from the careful study of her beloved son and gave Ensley a lopsided grin. "You didn't steal it. Elliott knew you took it, but you only took the diamond. He has your brooch, too."

"But I didn't take it so we could sneak back here. I took it so Elliott couldn't hold us captive."

"He was manipulating you, sweetie. He would never leave a brooch unguarded. He knew you, Kit, Emily, or I would eventually come into his room, pick up his clothes, and yell at him. And while we were there, take one of the brooches, feeling justified in doing it."

"He's not that controlling, is he?" That was a stupid question. After butting heads with both of them, Ensley had already learned how controlling both of JC's parents were.

"Doesn't matter. We're here, and we'll get back before anyone knows we're gone." Meredith stroked JC's head. "He looks so peaceful." She leaned over and kissed his forehead. "How long will the sedative last?"

"Two to four hours."

"How long has he been out?"

"An hour."

Meredith slowly drew back the blankets. "He's still covered with the red cloak. Why?"

"Elliott was told JC should always wear it."

"But he's healed. Right? I mean, I can lift it and see for myself."

Charlotte nodded, and her eyes softened.

Meredith slowly drew back the cloak to JC's lower abdomen, and her breath rushed out in a hiss. "He's perfect. He's more than perfect. He could be the model for Adonis." She glanced down his covered lower body. "Is the rest of him like this? Perfect, I mean."

"We saw pretty much all of him, and there's not a bruise or cut anywhere," Charlotte said.

Ensley almost mentioned the absence of JC's birthmark but decided that would only stir things up, so she kept quiet and hoped no one else would bring it up.

Meredith replaced the cloak and blankets. "His muscles are more defined. He's been working out more, and he's like his dad. He's turning prematurely gray. He's aged since I saw him last. What do you think, Ensley? You've seen him more recently than I have."

If Ensley told Meredith that JC looked older and more muscular than he did a few weeks ago, it would alarm her, so she punted. "He didn't have gray hair the last time I saw him, but you know JC. He's always so manscaped, he could have been coloring his hair for a while, and no one knew it."

"That's possible." Meredith then turned to Charlotte. "James Cullen needs extensive therapy, but we can't take him to a psychiatrist or therapist. No one would believe he was beaten almost to death and then..." She closed her eyes and cringed. "I can't bear the thought of what happened to him."

"That's why it's a good idea to take him to the monks," Charlotte said. "Jack went after he returned from his horrible experience during the trial of the conspirators. I don't think he would have fully recovered if he hadn't gone there."

Meredith clenched her fingers around the bed's side rails. "I'm not so sure."

"You and Elliott will need to discuss it in depth. And I'll be glad to talk to both of you, but right now, I need to finish up with Remy."

"How is he?" Ensley asked.

"He fell asleep. I've cleaned and stitched both wounds, but I still have to apply the dressings. I won't be much longer." Charlotte returned to her exam room, and Kenzie tugged on Ensley's arm.

"Let's go to the locker room. You probably want a shower or something," Kenzie said with a wink.

Ensley nodded. What did Kenzie have in mind? News of Austin? Probably. "Great idea."

Kenzie took Ensley's hand and dragged her toward the locker room. "You owe me a story."

"Story? Hmm. What kind of story?"

"Don't play dumb with me." Kenzie's forehead creased, a delicate little V forming right between her eyebrows. "How long have you been gone?"

"Three days?"

"That's more than enough time. That man is an O'Grady. They don't let the grass grow."

Ensley followed Kenzie into the locker room, and when she saw the shower, she wanted to strip down and stand under the water until she emptied the hot water tank. But it would have to wait.

Kenzie sat on the built-in bench and patted the spot beside her. "Sit. Start from the beginning, and don't leave anything out."

Thirty minutes later, David walked in, catching Ensley in the middle of the chess story.

"Have ye gotten to the good stuff yet?" he asked.

"Good stuff? Are you asking about my argument with Elliott?"

"Matter of fact, I am. Knowing Elliott, he was either yelling or not talking."

"He didn't want me there, but he did want information, so I told him about the cave Austin and JC found when they were teenagers."

"Where is it?" David crossed his arms and stood with his feet slightly spread, his muscles bulging in his green MacCorp polo shirt. His dark brown eyes studied her intently, and for a split second, she wondered how Kenzie tamed a man like him.

"About a ten-minute walk from the mansion."

A look of surprise came over his face, changing quickly to a delighted smile. "I have a feeling this is a significant find. Go on."

"They never told anyone."

"That was a mistake."

"In hindsight, Austin would agree with you. He took me there, and we explored a little bit, but we only had a penlight and couldn't see much. But I found an Yggdrasil painted on the wall similar to JC's birthmark and the sign Erik drew on my forehead. But what makes this find so significant is that we found Erik's footprints coming and going from the cave to the cabin."

"What cabin?" Kenzie asked.

"It's several yards from the cave. All but the immediate area in front of the cabin is undeveloped and overgrown. Erik took JC to the cabin, and that's where Elliott stayed with him. Austin said the cabin doesn't exist in the twenty-first century."

"I know the place," David said. "The history of MacKlenna Farm mentions a fire burning down a cabin. Following the fire, the land surrounding it was allowed to return to its natural state, and every four or five years now, workers thin out the overgrowth. There's a rumor that it's haunted. Nobody wants the job, so the farm manager always gives it to the newest employees."

"Haunted? Well, that's one way to keep people away. If you give me flashlights and a camera, we'll go back and take pictures."

"I'll do ye one better. I'll go with ye," David said. "This is too important not to go see it myself."

"But you can see it without going back in time. I mean, JC and Austin found it about fifteen years ago. Surely it hasn't changed much."

"That's probably true, but if Erik has been inside the cave, I want to see what he saw. We have all the equipment here that we'll need to do a cave survey."

"I missed all the fun when you guys found the cave with the Confederate treasure, so make room for me. I'm going, too," Kenzie said.

"You think this cave has a treasure?" Ensley asked.

"We won't know until we get in there and have a look around," David said.

"Do you have a theory?" Ensley asked.

"Not yet. Do ye?"

"Well, since you asked… Austin and I think Erik used it to travel from the Badlands to Chicago to MacKlenna Farm and back to the Badlands."

"But he had a brooch," Kenzie said.

"We talked about that, too, but we decided they aren't dependable enough. You can't rely on a brooch to take you to an exact time. You could get within a few days or weeks, but when it's imperative to move from one place to another in an hour or so and don't have an airplane, you need another method."

"Interesting theory, but I'm more inclined to believe Erik's brooch has different properties that allow him to go anywhere at any time. But until we survey the cave, we won't know if it has any significance," David said.

Ensley looked at the clock on the wall, anxious to tell Austin what all had happened. "We should head back. The sooner we get started, the sooner we can put this adventure to bed."

"I'll pack up the equipment," David said, heading toward the door. "Will ye find me something to wear?"

"Sure, babe," Kenzie said.

When the door closed behind him, Kenzie said, "Quick. Tell me about you and Austin."

"We just kissed and talked about going back to New York City when this is over. He said he could train in the city as easily as he can in Colorado."

"I guess I'll have to visit New York City for updates," Kenzie said. "Come on. I've got to find something to wear."

"I'll check on Meredith and JC while you do that."

Ensley returned to JC's bedside to find Meredith holding his hand, tears streaming down her face. "He hasn't moved. Not even an eyelash flutter." Meredith snatched a tissue from the box and wiped her eyes.

Then as if summoned, JC slowly opened his eyes. "Hi, Mom. Hi, Ens. Where are we?"

"In the cleanroom at Mallory Plantation. How do you feel?" Meredith asked.

"Groggy. Where's Dad?"

Meredith shot a glance at Ensley. "He just…stepped out. He'll be back in a few minutes."

"I hope he's not too pissed."

"Why would he be mad?" Meredith asked.

"Because I went back for Ensley without telling him."

"Darling, don't give it another thought."

He yawned. "I won't." And then he fell asleep again.

Meredith sat there a minute or two with tears continuing to stream down her cheeks. "He doesn't even remember fighting with Elliott."

"That might be a good thing."

Meredith threw the tissue in the trash and reached for another one. "Now that I've seen him, I can't leave. Do you mind going back for the others?"

Ensley gasped. "Are you serious? You'd bail out on me and force me to face everyone else alone and confess what we did? No way. That's not going to happen. And besides, we'll only be gone for a few minutes. JC will still be asleep when we get back. And as Charlotte said, you need to have a conversation with Elliott before you can decide what to do about JC."

Meredith lightly combed JC's hair with her fingers. "You're right, but we don't have to go. Elliott has the other brooch."

"I don't care if he has a dozen. I don't want the others to think we abandoned them. It might not matter to you, but it does to me. And David and Kenzie are coming with us."

"He doesn't trust us to travel alone."

"*I* didn't trust us traveling alone," Ensley said, "but David and Kenzie want to visit the cave Austin and JC found when they were teenagers. Austin showed it to me, and when I described it to David and told him we found Erik's footprints going in and coming out, he said he wanted to do a cave survey."

"Can't he just fly back to Lexington to do that?"

"He could and probably will, but he wants to see how it looked in 1885."

"If they show up with us, everyone will know we went off without them," Meredith said. "And they'll be furious."

Ensley almost huffed at Meredith. Instead, she said, "Really? You think? Just like Elliott pissed everyone off for taking JC home?"

"That was different," Meredith snapped.

Ensley was gobsmacked but refrained from smacking her forehead by holding her hands together prayerfully. "Was it, now?"

"I hear the sarcasm in your voice."

"Good. Because I intended it to be there."

"What's up with ye two?" David asked. "If I didn't know better, I could have sworn JL was in here bickering with Meredith."

Kenzie swished up to David in all her silk and petticoats. "Not JL. Just her future daughter-in-law."

"Whoa, Austin and I have barely shared a kiss, and you're marrying us off. Stop it! Now I see why the family drove him away. Please don't put pressure on him like that."

"We'll back off, Ensley," Kenzie said. "You're just the new kid on the block."

"Well, the initiation period is over. This will be my third trip back in time, so I'm no longer a newbie."

"You're right. So, let's go. Are you ready, Meredith?" Ensley asked.

Meredith made no effort to move, just sitting there staring at JC, ignoring the question.

Ensley took Meredith's hand. "You have to go back and get things settled with Elliott. The two of you can't debate what to do next while he's freaking out. That won't be good for anybody."

"Ensley's right, Meredith," David said. "Ye can't put it off. There's too much at stake."

"I'm not sure I agree with you," Meredith said.

"I don't give a shit if ye do or not. Ye don't have a choice, and ye don't want me to throw ye over my shoulder."

"You wouldn't dare."

Ensley tugged Meredith out of the chair. "I have a feeling he would, and while it would be a funny story to tell, it's undignified. So cut it out, and let's go."

Meredith's eyes flicked at Ensley, and for a moment, Ensley was afraid she'd pushed too far, but damn it, the woman needed to get her shit together. Being a wimp wasn't doing JC any good. The time had come for Meredith to man up—well, woman up—and straighten things out with Elliott.

"If I hadn't heard the video, I never would have believed James Cullen was violent. He looks so peaceful."

Ensley tugged a little bit harder to get Meredith moving. "And he'll look just as peaceful when we return."

Charlotte came out of her exam room again. "I'm going to do an updated test on his telomeres and compare the results with his previous report. It might give us some indication of how long he was in the past. I also want to do some blood tests to be sure he's well enough to go to the monastery."

"Do you think something's wrong with him?" Meredith asked.

"I have no reason to believe he's sick, but I want to be sure. In any case, he's been severely traumatized," Charlotte said, "and it might be a rough trip up the mountain."

"May is the end of the spring travel season," Meredith said. "Maybe it won't be so crowded. As soon as we get back, we should notify the flight crew. They'll need to file a flight plan for Paro International Airport."

"Jack's favorite hotel is the Zhiwa Ling Hotel, and you'll need horses for the trek up the mountain," Charlotte said. "Tiger's Nest in Bhutan is so much easier to reach than the monastery in Tibet. I'm glad JC prefers that one."

"We'll figure it all out when we come back." Meredith glanced at JC again. "I can't get over how peaceful he looks."

"And he'll be at peace again one day." Ensley gave the diamond brooch to David. "You can do the honors."

Ensley, Meredith, Kenzie, and David gathered around the two trunks full of equipment. "See ye soon, Charlotte."

"Don't come back without my husband."

David opened the brooch and recited the chant while Ensley's mind teemed with images of Austin riding his warhorse, dunking the pillow, kissing her…

And then they all disappeared in the fog.

62

MacKlenna Farm, KY (1885)—Meredith

WHEN THE FOG lifted, Meredith was back in her room at MacKlenna Farm and very much alone, which was as much an emotional state as a physical one. She glanced out the window and was relieved to see David and Kenzie talking to Sean.

That makes three of us.

If Ensley was with Austin, then they all arrived safely. Meredith opened the door to see Ensley at the bottom of the staircase with Austin.

Good. Everyone's here.

She didn't know how long it would take David and Kenzie to survey the cave, but she figured she had a few hours to straighten things out with Elliott. They couldn't return home without reaching an agreement about James Cullen's immediate future. And that agreement might lead to their reconciliation.

They couldn't continue to live like this. It wasn't healthy, it forced the family to take sides, and that realignment could tear the family apart, which would be a disaster for all of them.

As for Meredith, she was starting with a handicap. James Cullen's near-death experience set off every one of her death and dying triggers. And God knew she had a dozen of them. The fact that she could function right now was nothing short of a miracle. Unless she and Elliott could be calm and rational, they'd never move beyond the current impasse.

She emerged from her room to trek down the hallway, but there was no rush to get there. So she limped along emotionally, visualizing their conversation. But when she got there with her heart in her throat, his door stood open, and the room was clean and empty, except for Elliott's signature scent of leather and cloves and balsam.

She walked around the room, searching for evidence—clothes, Dopp kit, attaché case—that he'd even been there.

She had an old memory of him leaving Edinburgh without telling her. It had almost broken her heart. So why remember that now? Because just like then, he left unexpectedly. But where would he go now? Anywhere he wanted. He had a brooch.

And that fact skewered her heart with terror. She dropped into a wingback chair and fought the tears that swamped her as fiercely as she had wept for James Cullen. Elliott was gone, and there was only one place he'd go. Back in time a week or two to prevent what happened to James Cullen.

If she'd been standing in front of a speeding freight train, she wouldn't have been any more terrified than she was at the thought of Elliott confronting that evil Viking.

She buried her face in her hands and tried to process, which wasn't easy with her heart traveling at ninety miles a second. He didn't leave from here. There was no smell of peat. So maybe he hadn't left yet. He could be activating the brooch from somewhere else on the farm.

But where?

The cabin? The cave? Ensley said she told Elliott about the cave. He had traveled without telling anyone before—several times—but he always had Remy with him. Remy wasn't here, but Paul was. And Paul felt guilty enough right now that he'd do whatever Elliott asked of him.

Oh, God!

She raced out of the room and down the stairs.

"Meredith, what's wrong?" Austin asked.

"Have you seen Elliott?"

"No," Austin said. "Is he not in his room?"

"He's gone."

"I've been here for most of the past hour, and he hasn't come down these stairs. If he went out, he must have taken the back staircase."

Meredith headed toward the door. Her determination had changed from saving her marriage to saving her husband's life. "I have to find him. Now!" She flung open the door and raced across the veranda.

"Meredith, where are you going?" Kenzie asked.

"I have to find Elliott. He might be at the cabin or the cave."

"We're heading in that direction as soon as the wagon gets here to carry the equipment."

"I can't wait!" Meredith hurried past them toward the path that would take her to the cabin. The freight train was barreling down on her, and Elliott's life hung in the balance.

"I'm coming with you," Kenzie said as she reached Meredith's side with long strides.

Ensley caught up with them. "So am I."

"I'll get horses and meet you there," Austin said. "Unless you want me to go with you."

"I'll get the horses and the wagon and meet ye at the cabin," Sean said.

"Get the gear loaded on the wagon," David said. "Austin and I will saddle the horses."

Meredith started jogging. "Come on. We have to hurry."

"Why?" Ensley asked.

"Because Elliott has your brooch, and I believe he intends to go back and try to stop James Cullen's torture."

"Shit! That's a horrible idea," Kenzie said. "He'll just make a bigger mess of things."

"Maybe we should take Austin or David in case we have to restrain Elliott," Ensley said.

Meredith stopped and looked back to where the guys had been standing, and Ensley and Kenzie stopped as well. "Maybe we should."

"Oh, ye of little faith. I can take Elliott down," Kenzie said.

"I know you took JC down, but you caught him off guard. If Elliott sees us coming, you'll lose that advantage." Meredith started running again, hoping they wouldn't have to use force. But if it came to that, she'd help Kenzie do whatever was necessary. "Just do it before he opens the brooch."

"If he opens the brooch, I'm running in the opposite direction," Kenzie said.

Meredith had run hundreds of miles with Kenzie, and although Kenzie could run at a faster pace, she never did. Now running in layers of cotton and silk and laced-up ankle boots, she wished Kenzie would run faster, but Meredith knew she wouldn't. Kenzie was pacing them to get there quickly yet still fired up and ready to respond to the situation.

"If we don't stop him," Meredith said, "he'll go confront Sten, and the Viking will use James Cullen to extract information from Elliott. If Erik has to choose which one to save, he'll choose the Keeper, and James Cullen will die."

"Don't you think Elliott knows that?" Kenzie asked.

"I'm not sure what he knows, or even if he's thinking straight. He sees a problem and has to fix it, regardless of the cost."

They stopped talking and concentrated on running over the uneven ground, lifting their skirts like cancan dancers.

They reached the clearing in front of the cabin before David and Austin caught up with them.

"Wait here. Let me go in first. I don't want to put either of you in danger."

Kenzie stood in front of Meredith. "You're not going in there alone."

Meredith didn't have time to argue with them. "I have to find out what he's doing. Sit on the porch. If I need help, I'll yell, and you can storm the cabin."

"I don't like that idea at all," Kenzie said.

"I know you don't, but that's *my* husband in there, and I get first dibs on dealing with him."

She got a snort out of Kenzie and a reluctant grin from Ensley. Occasionally Meredith was pretty good at defusing tense situations—if only her luck would carry her through the next few minutes.

Kenzie stepped aside. "You can have first dibs, but if he continues to act like an asshole, I'm going in there, and it won't be pretty."

Meredith jogged up on the porch and didn't bother to knock. She barged right in to find Elliott sitting on the bed, clean-shaven and dressed immaculately. But when he looked up at her, his eyes told a different story.

"Elliott!" She shuddered with relief so deep and absolute that tears burned her eyelids and spilled over and down her cheeks.

"You're here!" A vise gripped her heart, squeezing so hard she couldn't breathe, couldn't think, as her blood pumped hotter and faster, and the tightness in her chest blocked out everything but the fact that she hadn't lost him.

"Where'd ye think I'd be?"

She nodded to Ensley and Kenzie before closing the door. "Gone." She waited, but she wasn't good at this—the patience part—and it had never been Elliott's forte, either.

"In another couple of minutes, ye wouldn't have found me." He opened his fist, and a brooch the color of sunstone gleamed in his hand.

"What were you waiting for?"

He looked down, the long lashes hiding his eyes, and he hesitated for a moment before confessing, "A voice told me to wait."

"Did you recognize it? The voice, I mean?"

His mouth quirked up at one corner. "An ornery cuss with a deep, booming voice."

Meredith sat beside him, her hands in her lap and clasped so tightly together her knuckles turned white. There was an aura about him. She couldn't see it or touch it, but she sensed its presence, and it stood as a barrier between them.

"Your father?" she asked, not at all doubting that he'd heard a voice.

The suggestion seemed to catch him off guard. "No, not him or my grandfather. I believe it was Erik."

"Really?"

"Aye. I didn't know he was going to haunt me."

"Maybe he thought you were about to make a mistake, and he decided to intervene."

"Protecting James Cullen would never be a mistake."

"I tried to protect him, and it was—" She stopped midsentence and closed her mouth firmly, her time-tested method for not escalating an argument.

"Ye weren't trying to protect him, Meredith. Ye wanted to maintain some control over him. Paul understood that."

She let silence stretch between them for several beats while his statement replayed in her mind. "Good God! He's my only child. What'd you expect me to do?"

"Ye smothered him, and he had to get away."

"Did James Cullen tell you that?"

Elliott clenched his jaw, then said in a low voice, hardly above a whisper. "He didn't have to. And that's why I let him go."

This argument was escalating anyway. To hell with it. "Are you saying this is all *my fault?*"

"Of course not."

"That's the way it sounds."

"Look, we both put too much pressure on him."

"I don't think I did." She put steel in the velvet of her voice. "But if James Cullen believes I did, then it doesn't matter what I think or what my intentions were."

Elliott crossed his legs and straightened the crease in his wool trousers, an annoying habit that showed how calm he was, but this time the comfort move was a fake. She could see it in his darkening eyes and the jerky movement of his hand.

"From the very beginning, we wanted him to be perfect. He's brilliant and handsome—"

"—with an inflated opinion of himself," she added.

"He believes he's invincible, and because of that, he took on our archenemy, overestimating his abilities and underestimating their depravity."

"We assumed they were evil, but they surpassed even that." She stood and paced in front of the unlit fireplace that still smelled like eucalyptus, and it reminded her of the day she was here to see James Cullen.

"When I came here with you to see him, I was reminded of my late husband and how I sat at his bedside for days following his stroke. The doctors finally told me his condition was hopeless, and they recommended discontinuing life support. I thought that was what I'd have to do for James Cullen—to let him die—and I couldn't bear to do that to my son. And I resented you."

"Why?"

"Because you refused to see what was ahead of us and the decisions we'd have to make. And then you exiled me."

"I'm sorry."

She stopped walking and stood in front of him. "I've seen James Cullen, and I believe one day he'll be free of his demons. But navigating the path to freedom will be difficult."

"It doesn't have to be. I can undo it all."

"No, Elliott! You can't. Sten would use James Cullen to get information from you, and then he'd kill you both. Erik would only be able to save one of you, and he would save you—the Keeper."

"I would insist Erik save James Cullen."

"You might not be in any condition to insist on anything." She spotted the whisky bottle and poured herself a drink, hoping Elliott hadn't doctored the entire bottle.

"Ye're still angry that I drugged ye. I'm sorry I did that."

She gave a brief, shocked laugh. "I didn't expect you to apologize. Thank you. Emily already apologized for the part she played, but what I don't understand is why. What'd you hope to gain?"

He swallowed, appearing puzzled by the question. "To protect the two people I love most in the world."

"That doesn't make sense."

"Ye didn't trust me, Mere, and I couldn't risk losing our son because of that. If ye had touched him or uncovered him, he would have died, and ye would have realized too late that Erik spoke the truth. Then ye would have spent the rest of yer life knowing ye killed him, and I would have lost both of ye."

With their honesty, the aura that had separated them slowly began to fade. And for the first time in several days, there wasn't as much tension between them. If they released the tail of their anger, it would fade completely.

"Elliott, I'm sorry for what I said, for how I acted, for not trusting you, and for letting my fear co-opt my love and respect."

He seemed to think about it for a minute, and she wasn't sure if he would accept her apology. He cleared his throat, his eyes suddenly glistening. "I have loved ye since the day I met ye, Mere. Ye're the love of my life. Without ye, the sun doesn't shine, and the days are dark. But with ye, every day is a new beginning."

Her legs wobbled, and she sat down again. All she was expecting or hoping for was a blanket you-are-forgiven. Instead, Elliott recommitted to her using vows similar to his proposal all those years ago.

And then he surprised her with a kiss, and the scent of leather and cloves and balsam tickled her nose, and she tasted coffee on his tongue, not whisky. He hadn't isolated himself to get drunk but to clear his head and find a way to save their son and a path back to her.

Whatever fears she had, her all-consuming need for her husband quieted them, and her body ached more insistently with each kiss and stroke of his fingers along the side of her neck. And his breath flowed warmly over her face. Slowly, slowly, his mouth traced the line of her jaw with touches that lingered, tantalizing and spicy.

She wrapped her arms around him, anchoring herself once again to the man she loved. The only man she'd ever loved.

63

MacKlenna Farm, KY (1885)—David

D AVID AND AUSTIN galloped into the clearing, each leading an extra horse. Kenzie and Ensley were on the porch in the rocking chairs, chatting and rocking back and forth as if there wasn't an emergency. The sight lowered David's stress level since it meant Meredith must be in the cabin with Elliott. And since Kenzie didn't seem alarmed, Elliott must not have activated his brooch for a quick getaway.

David dismounted and tied the reins to the hitching rail. This entire adventure was only three-quarters done, and he'd be glad when they finally wrapped up the loose ends, wrote After Action Reports, and locked the brooches away in the safe. His bones were getting too old to continue playing dodgeball with the universe.

Why in the hell was he complaining? Elliott was much older and hadn't missed a step, and he planned to leave here and climb a goddamn mountain. Even now, locked in a cabin with his bride, he was probably having makeup sex. His stamina was that of a forty-year-old.

Whatever McBain did during this trip, sex with his bride was out of the question. Every time they traveled with a brooch and stayed longer than a few hours—surprise, surprise. She got pregnant.

Five wee McBains were plenty. Although Robbie and Henry were at Cambridge, raising hell in the UK instead of the States, they still found a way to create disruption, which required a monthly parental trek across the pond to settle disputes. They were good lads, but their pranks on each other often went too far.

David hopped up on the porch, his bootheels clicking against the slats, which for some damn reason, reminded him of being in

Leadville, Colorado. But it wasn't the kids or even previous trips that were on his mind. It was the vision he had three years ago that led the family on a quest to find the torc.

He didn't understand the significance of recalling it now, and when he didn't understand the whys and wherefores, it frustrated him and interfered with clear thinking. He hadn't mentioned it to Kenzie yet, or anyone else for that matter. They would just ask the same question he was asking—"Why now?"

"That was quick," Kenzie said. "Tell me you didn't saddle three horses and ride over here in under fifteen minutes. If you did, remind me to check the tack before I mount up."

He gave her a light kiss on the lips. "Ye know me better than that."

Austin laughed. "McBain can do the impossible with one hand tied behind his back, but it takes him fifteen minutes to saddle *one* horse."

Kenzie quirked her eyebrow. "So you lazy butts didn't saddle any of them while the women ran a six-minute mile in layers of silk and lace."

"And a corset," Ensley added. "It felt like I was running with only one functioning lung."

Austin winked at Ensley. "I know how that feels. But you and Kenzie are Amazon women, and Uncle David and I were saving ourselves for the heavy lifting." He leaned over the railing and reached for Ensley's hand, which she eagerly gave him. "Truth is, Sean just snapped his fingers, gave the order, and here we are."

"Without the gear," Kenzie said.

"We could have waited for Sean and the wagon but thought we should be here." Austin glanced at the cabin door. "You know, in case we needed to…whatever."

A frown knitted Kenzie's brow. "So you two didn't think we could handle this situation. Is that what you're saying?"

David leaned over for another kiss. "Ye always handle situations better than me, Kenz."

"Then what?" she shot back while they were still kissing.

It was such a deliberate tease, it sent a spike of lust through his gut, and he had to remind himself—no sex…no sex…no sex. "If the fog sucked ye in, I wanted to be with ye."

"Ah…" Ensley said. "He's a softy at heart, isn't he?"

David winked. "Ye best disabuse yerself of that thought."

"Sorry. Too late. I've always thought of you as William Wallace in *Braveheart*. But now I know you're more like Shrek. Sweet and mean, charming, and charmless."

Kenzie rolled her head back and burst out laughing. "Mean and charmless."

David snarled up and narrowed his eyes. "Yeah, but she also said I was sweet and charming."

"Oh, McBain. You're that for sure." Kenzie finally stopped laughing and wiped her eyes. "So, where's Sean now?"

"He told the men to saddle the horses first, so he'll be along shortly." Austin nodded toward the cabin door. "What's going on in there?"

David glanced at the door. "It's quiet. Ye sure they haven't vanished?"

"I assume they're still in there since we haven't smelled stinky peat," Kenzie said.

"Elliott's a true Scot. He has priorities."

"What's that supposed to mean?"

He pulled Kenzie up out of the chair and into his arms for a twirl, dip, and kiss. "If I hadn't been with ye for days, we'd be having makeup sex."

"If you're so sure about that, then we don't need to hang around here. Let's go to the cave and leave Elliott and Meredith alone."

"We can't yet. We have to wait for the gear. I want one of the cameras to take pictures of the footprints before everyone tromps all over them," David said. "I've met Erik. I know how big he is. By measuring the footprints, I can determine the size and weight of the person who made them. Then I can rule Erik in or out."

"We know Erik was here, so we should find his prints," Ensley said.

David twirled Kenzie one last time before releasing her. "But if we find prints in the cave, I want to be able to rule him in or out."

When he heard the rattle of an approaching wagon, David said, "Austin, why don't ye show me where the footprints are, and we can figure out how close to the cave Sean can drive the wagon."

Austin kissed the back of Ensley's hand, fixing his eyes on her with such devotion that David looked away before they caught him staring. Austin had returned to the personable college student version of himself, and David couldn't be happier. Pops knew what he was doing when he insisted his grandson participate in Ensley's rescue.

"Sean can't go any farther than the side of the porch," Austin said. "A few yards beyond that, you'll reach the trees with heavy undergrowth, but there's a deer path through the thicket. That's where we found the footprints. It's not wide enough for a wagon or even two people walking side by side."

"Got it. Then Sean knows where to put the wagon. I'll walk on ahead."

"I'll go with you." Kenzie jumped off the porch. "How far is the cave beyond the prints?"

"Probably ten to fifteen yards. See if you can find the entrance," Austin said.

Kenzie's eyes snapped into focus as if she'd been only half awake before. "Is this a challenge?"

David smiled. That was all Kenzie needed to hear. Whenever she had a chance to match her wits against a clock or an opponent, she jumped on it. And her complicated, brilliant mind was possibly the reason he loved her most.

"Kenzie," Austin smiled. "I've never beaten you at anything except our only game of horse."

She pantomimed the act of shooting a basketball. "Who in the hell has ever made a backward over-the-head basket from eighty feet?"

He tilted his head to one side, narrowing his eyes. "If I remember right, it was Thunder Law of the Harlem Globetrotters on November 2, 2014. It was eighty-two feet, two inches."

Ensley rolled her eyes. "That begs the question, what was yours?"

"About eighty. But that's not the bet I want to make."

"Okay, so what's the bet?"

Austin grinned. "That you can't find the entrance to the cave in under fifteen minutes."

Kenzie glanced at the tree line. "You're on. If two teenagers can stumble over a cave entrance, two former special forces officers can find it."

Austin checked his watch. "Ready? Go!"

David took Kenzie's hand, and they dashed toward the deer path. A spring storm was rolling into the area, making the air heavy and thick with the forest's green scents.

They didn't have long before the rain would wash away the

evidence they hoped to collect.

"How long do ye think it will take us?"

"You want to make a bet within the bet?" Kenzie rubbed her hands together gleefully. "Hmm. I love betting with you, McBain, since I usually win. So I'll bet that we'll find the cave in under ten minutes."

He gave her a once-over. "Since ye're dressed like that, I'll go with over ten."

She fluttered her eyelashes. "What does the winner get?"

"Whatever they want."

"Ah, you're living dangerously, McBain. You're on." Kenzie pulled the back of her skirt between her legs and tucked the end into her waistband.

"Hey, that's not fair. Yer long skirt was part of my calculations."

"I figured that. But it's too late now."

As they stepped onto the deer path, David spotted the first footprint and realized he'd already screwed up. This was a mission, and they had to treat it as such, or their hurry could destroy evidence they'd regret losing later.

And since Sean was pulling the wagon into the clearing, David would have access to the tools and equipment he'd need to do this right.

"Hold up and turn off the clock," he yelled.

"You giving up already?" Kenzie asked.

"No, we need a plan. Hey, Ensley," David yelled. "As soon as Sean parks the wagon, get the Canon and Nikon cameras out of the smallest trunk and take pictures of these footprints. Ye'll also need a tape measure. Get the length and depth of each one, plus the distance between them. Austin, grab the evidence flags and mark each footprint. That'll keep us from walking over them. Once we get inside the cave, one of ye shoot stills and the other shoot videos."

"Got it, boss." Then to Sean, Austin called, "Pull the wagon up as far as you can."

As soon as the wagon stopped, Paul jumped out. "What do you want me to do?"

"Get the trunk with the lights and generator, then wait here until we find the entrance."

"Doesn't Austin know where it is?"

"Aye. But he's challenged us to find it in under fifteen minutes."

Paul walked around to the wagon bed and unloaded a trunk.

"Knowing what I do about this family, I can safely predict that not one of you can pass up a challenge."

"We should decide how we're going to work once we're inside the cave, so we don't destroy any evidence," Kenzie said.

David wanted to punch himself for not thinking this through. What the hell was going on with him?

There's a cave involved, dumbass.

He shook away the thought for now. "Let's work in two-person teams. One to survey and the other to take notes. Since Kenzie and I are the only ones here who know how to use the surveying equipment, Paul, ye work with Kenz. Sean, ye work with me to take notes. Austin, ye and Ensley go ahead with what we just discussed."

"If you see anything you want us to focus on, give us a shout, and we'll get pictures and videos of it," Ensley said.

"Everybody clear on yer assignments?"

"Aye," Sean said. "Do ye have paper and pencils, or should I get some from the cabin?"

"Elliott and Meredith are still in there. But ye'll find notebooks and pencils in the small trunk."

Sean looked over at the door. "Guess they're talking about what happened."

"Maybe. Now, let's get to work before the storm hits." David did a visual search. Among the scattered elms and birch trees was a giant oak, and near it was a mini rocky defile that had thrust up from the forest floor like the edge of a serrated knife. It was a unique and out-of-place land feature. Trees would die, but that defile would last through the centuries—a perfect X to mark the spot.

He squatted at the last footprint, and Kenzie did the same. "What do ye notice first?"

"Whoever made these prints wore flat-soled shoes," she said.

"Aye. How tall? Can ye tell?"

"You love testing me, don't you?" She used her forearm to measure the distance between footprints. "Based on the distance between them, I'd say six feet."

"And weight?"

She stuck her finger into the heel of one of the prints. "Based on the depth, I'd say one-seventy-five to two hundred pounds. I never met Erik, but that fits his description, don't you think?"

"Close enough."

"That's large for a Viking, isn't it?"

"He's an unusual man."

"Was," Kenzie corrected.

"Aye. Which reminds me, if Tavis isn't home when we return, we should get moving on his rescue."

Her eyes were suddenly as wide as a deer's facing headlights. "To Jarlshof? In 1100 AD? No, you can't go. What if your vision comes true?"

The question caught him unprepared, and he tried to gather up his thoughts by focusing harder on the dark mass of trees.

When he didn't answer, she said, "McBain. What if it comes true?"

Although he tried to hide his fear from her naked gaze, it was fruitless. "I don't want to talk about it, Kenz."

The vision had haunted him every day since it first invaded his mind, and now that he knew he'd probably have to go back for Tavis, it was even more terrifying.

He didn't want it invading his mind right now, or ever, but there it was…

Dozens of warriors with tattoos of mythological creatures from the tips of their fingers to their necks filled the vision. Each warrior carried a broadsword with ridged blades and wore a cloak covering half his body. They were spread out on a slanting, rocky field, yelling, frightening the red grouse that flew low over a peat bog, squealing.

Warriors stood guard over a man lying on the ground—a man believed to be James MacKlenna. One of the warriors removed a torc from around his neck. He poured water from a drinking horn to wash off the blood and then placed it around David's neck.

A woman standing nearby aimed a tall longbow made of yew at a target he couldn't see. Her arm muscles were lean, flexed, and still.

Now, three years later, David knew the woman's identity. But, goddamn it, that only increased his fear of the vision.

"Don't snap at me," Kenzie said. "Your vision has been on my mind since I heard Erik was dead. If you're planning a trip to Jarlshof, it could come true."

"Not now, Kenz."

"I understand why you don't want to talk about it, but just so you know, if you go there—to Jarlshof—I'm going, too."

"That sure as hell won't happen." When he saw the shock in her eyes, he knew he had to backtrack. He'd never had any success telling his bride what she could or could not do. "Let's talk about it later."

"You bet we will. Now, start the clock. I'm going to win the bet."

David stood and turned in a slow circle, studying the landscape from the ground up, finding bootheel prints, broken twigs, and smashed ground cover. The bootheel prints matched Austin's.

He checked the time. "It's three ten."

"You're on, McBain."

Kenzie took off, following leads of her own, while he followed broken twigs and crushed leaves until he reached a huge boulder impossible for one person to carry. Kenzie arrived simultaneously, coming from a different direction.

"Let's call it a tie and figure this out together," David said. "It'll save time."

"If you want to do that, ask Austin and Ensley where it is. Otherwise, get to work. The defile is one marker, and this boulder is another. It's somewhere in between. Austin said the entrance was behind a boulder. But I don't see a way in." Kenzie removed her shoes and started climbing the rocks next to the boulder.

"Be careful. Lichen and water stains cover this gray monolith, which means the rocks will be slick. If we take another patient home to Charlotte, she might close up shop on us."

"But we have Emily here with us, and we have time to get patched up before we go home."

David stepped back and watched her climb, prepared to catch her if she slipped. The distance gave him a different perspective of the boulder. It was too large to fit into a camera frame unless you stood back several yards. But if you stood back that far, trees would block the view. Clever.

The fifteen-foot-tall boulder was half-buried in the side of a grassy knoll that Kenzie had now scaled. But at the top, gnarly trees and underbrush made it all but impossible to stand at the edge and look down on the boulder without first clearing a path.

If there was an entrance behind the monolith, the knoll and trees had it so well camouflaged that he wasn't surprised it had gone undiscovered, except for Austin and JC.

The bramble bush on one side had several broken shoots, and blackberries were rotting on the ground. He pushed the thorny, arching stems aside and smiled. "Beat ye, Kenz."

"Where is it?"

"Ye're standing right above it. The top of the boulder is buried in the side of the knoll, so ye can't see the opening. Come on down. I'll help ye."

"Wait a minute. Do you have your phone? I didn't bring mine. There's a petroglyph up here."

"Of what?"

She squatted and brushed away debris. "Call me crazy, but it looks like a Viking longship. Long and wide with a shallow-draft hull."

David climbed up halfway and passed her his phone. "How big is it?"

"About three inches wide, and with a square-rigged sail makes it one and a half inches tall. What do you suppose it's doing here?"

"It's another marker. Take yer pictures and come on down." He waited for her and then climbed down first so he could catch her if she slipped. When they reached the ground, she sat to put her shoes back on while he scrolled through the pictures. "It's another X marks the spot."

He pocketed his phone and picked up two long, thick sticks, staked them in the soft ground, crisscrossed them, and then wove a piece of twine around the stakes to hold back the bramble bush. The string didn't come in handy every day, but it had often enough that he never finished dressing without a piece in his pocket, along with his Swiss army knife.

"It's a tight squeeze. The trunks won't fit. We'll have to unload them here. I'm going in to look around."

"Good," Kenzie agreed. "And while you're there, why don't you scare away the rats and make sure there aren't any booby traps."

"Like the search for the Holy Grail in *Indiana Jones and the Last Crusade*. I doubt we'll find either a treasure or booby traps, Kenz. Kentuckians didn't see Vikings very often."

"Ha! Ha! Try again. Erik was here a few days ago."

The opening behind the boulder was about three feet by three feet and looked almost as dark and foreboding as any hole he'd ever seen. Only adventuresome young men and undeterred lasses like Ensley would have dared crawl in there with just a penlight.

"How in the world did those two teenagers find this?" she muttered.

"I was wondering about that, too. Pass the lights and generator through as soon as they bring the trunks. I'm going to get a few initial pictures."

"Mr. Boy Scout, did you bring a flashlight?"

David dug into his pocket. "Damn. Where is it?"

"I saw you put it down on the stainless steel table before you put on your jacket. Did you forget to pick it up?"

He'd been watching Meredith cry over JC and barely got his jacket on.

"Use your phone," Kenzie said.

"I don't want to use up my battery. Paul!"

"Coming!"

"Bring me a flashlight." While David waited, he struggled to manage his overactive sweat glands and a racing heart. Was he sure he wanted to do this? Hell, no. Kenzie complained about rats but wasn't afraid of them. She'd go inside without giving it a second thought, but he'd rather battle his demons than send her into an unknown situation by herself.

Although it wasn't unknown, Ensley and Austin had been inside the cave recently, and he could send them back in. But they might overlook details that could be significant. Paul could go in and set up the lights, and if there were clues or signs, he'd spot them.

But to send Paul in there, I'd have to admit my irrational fear.

The trunk's metal handles clunked against the leather sides when Paul set the gear down in the crunchy underbrush. "Where's David?"

David stuck out his arm. "Right here. Give me a flashlight."

Paul opened the trunk and handed one to him. "I can't believe there's a cave in there. How'd you find this, Austin?"

David wiped his sweaty face and waited to hear Austin's explanation so he could give his racing heart another moment or two to slow down. Unlikely, but he could hope.

"It was dumb luck!" Austin and Ensley joined the others at the bramble bush, carrying another trunk. "JC and I were looking for a place to drink a stolen bottle of whisky and confront our cave fears. He ran ahead of me and hid. I was mad as hell that he was hiding because he had the bottle. I almost pissed my pants when he jumped out from behind that bramble bush. He was laughing his ass off, lost his balance, and fell backward.

"I watched him try to get out of the bush. It was too dense for a gnat to wiggle through, much less JC. I'd give anything for a video of it now. But while he was struggling with the damn thing, he found the entrance and didn't tell me. He just climbed in and disappeared. When I stopped laughing and realized he was gone, I got pissed again. Anyway, a few minutes later, he yelled at me to get over there. I was excited about the cave, but he'd dropped the damn bottle when he fell, and all the whisky was watering the damn bramble bush."

David chuckled. He didn't have any trouble picturing that fiasco. He'd sneaked his own purloined bottle of whisky out to the barn when he was a kid. The joke was on him when he realized he'd stolen a bottle full of tea. Auld Fraser had an odd sense of humor.

"Where'd everybody go?" Sean yelled.

"We're over here," Kenzie hollered back.

A moment later, the weight of another trunk crunched in the underbrush. "Where's the entrance?" Sean asked.

David stuck his arm out again and waved. "Here. The bushes and shadows keep it well hidden. Unpack the lights and generator and slide them to me. As soon as I get the lights set up, I'll do a short video of the cave. I want to be sure we don't destroy any evidence once everybody gets in there."

"Ensley and I probably messed shit up the other day," Austin said.

"I'll recognize yer footprints," David said. "If I don't see anything else on the cave floor, the rest of ye can come in. Give me the Canon and a few minutes to set up."

"Hey, McBain..." Kenzie knelt to be eye level with him, speaking softly. "This isn't the best time to mention this, but...you're claustrophobic and hate caves. Are you sure you want to do this? Austin and Ensley have already been in there. Let them set up the lights."

"Aw, geez, Kenz. I almost forgot. Thanks for the reminder," he said in a voice laced with sarcasm. There was no way out now. He had to go in or lose face. And what kind of warrior allowed that to happen?

"Ensley and I can go in first," Austin said. "Places like that don't bother me, except when I can't stand up straight."

No way in hell were the youngsters going to show him up.

David steeled himself for the inevitable and came up with an excuse. "Ye've been in here too many times. I'll see things ye might think aren't important. But keep talking and send in the equipment."

"I'll sit here at the opening and pass things through to you,"

Kenzie said.

He kissed her. "Thanks, babe." Having her close would keep him grounded when the walls started closing in on him. But as he crawled through the entrance, the memory of lumbering through the cave below Fraser Castle when he traveled back to 1944 to rescue Kenzie hit him hard, and his heart rate accelerated into super-fast gear.

"You okay, McBain?"

"Don't ask me again, Kenz. Every time ye do, it reminds me of how much I hate closed-in spaces. If ye're going to sit there, be helpful."

"How about pretending we're having phone sex? You know, don't you, that you can't have two emotions at the same time. So if you're sexually excited, you can't be scared."

"I'm *not* scared. And getting me turned on will only get my ass out of here before I can get anything done."

"Gotcha. No sex talk. Well, how about politics?"

He growled. "That'll only get me pissed off."

"Okay then, you're on your own."

He crawled inside, then pushed to his feet, shook off his nerves, and swept the flashlight beam around the interior. He did a three hundred sixty-degree sweep to determine if any dangerous obstacles would impede progress once they started the survey. He ballparked the dimensions, guessing the ceiling to be twelve feet, the width approximately thirty feet, and the depth about the same, give or take a few feet in depth and width.

There were no stalactites and stalagmites. The walls were limestone with deposits of gypsum, and the floor was hard dirt. There were several partial footprints and three complete sets—Austin's, Ensley's, and Erik's.

Kenzie slid the generator and lights through the opening. "You doing okay in there?"

"Haven't seen any rats so far."

"That's encouraging."

David quickly set up the lights in the middle and along the walls, and when he found the Yggdrasil, he couldn't stop staring. The resemblance to JC's birthmark was uncanny.

As he moved farther into the guts of the place, he stopped short. "Goddamn. What the hell?"

The rear wall was an art exhibit, with dozens of pictographs and petroglyphs similar to the Yggdrasil and the Viking ship marker outside. It would take years to decipher them without expert help to identify patterns in these signs, and he knew hiring cave art researchers was out of the question.

"David, can we come in now?" Kenzie yelled. "There are five impatient people out here."

"Yeah, come on in," he said, unable to take his eyes off the paintings.

"You don't sound so sure."

He didn't answer.

He'd just spotted the petroglyph of a brooch, similar to the ones surrounding the cave door at Fraser Castle on the far right side of the wall. The pictographs were of an island, Viking ships, North America's coastline, objects falling from the sky, ax-wielding warriors, and several figures and shapes he couldn't identify.

Kenzie came in first, brushing dirt off her hands. "What are those pearly balloon thingies on the wall?"

"Deposits of gypsum. Forget about them and come here. Ye won't believe this."

Kenzie stood beside him, staring. "Holy shit! What does it all mean?"

"It'll take years to figure it all out, but once we do, we'll be able to verify what we know about the brooches."

"Seriously?"

David laughed. "Aye. But it'd be nice if we could hire cave art researchers to explain it all."

Ensley entered, and behind her Austin, and they joined Kenzie and David at the wall.

"What the hell?" Austin said. "JC and I were in here dozens of times, but we never saw this. How'd it get here?"

"When was the last time ye were here before the other day?"

"If I remember right, it was the night before JC graduated from high school. You have to remember we were teenagers. But if we'd seen this wall, we would have told Elliott."

"We didn't have the best light the other day," Ensley said. "Austin showed me the Yggdrasil, but we never noticed this. Although, honestly, we weren't interested in spelunking right then. So I can't say for sure whether these paintings were here or not."

Sean walked up and stood beside David. "I thought I knew every inch of the farm. I can't believe this is here and I didn't know about it. But it does make me wonder if my grandfather knew. And if he did, why didn't he tell my father or me?"

"I've been coming to MacKlenna Farm since I was a teenager," David said, "and like ye, I thought I knew every inch of the farm. I might expect something like this in Scotland, but not here in Kentucky."

David watched Paul walk a grid that only Paul could see in his mind. When he reached the back wall, he slowly walked side to side and back again.

"What are you doing, Paul?" Kenzie asked.

"I have hyperthymesia and can recall most of what I experience in excruciating detail. In the future, whether it's twelve hours or twelve years, you could ask me about the day I first visited the cave. I could tell you the date, time, and everything about this place."

"Does your mind take pictures that you can recall later?"

"The occipital lobe, located in the back of our brains, is responsible for processing visual information. Mine takes distinct pictures of my experiences, and I can recall in minute detail what happened and when. It's a curse and a blessing."

Kenzie smiled at David. "I wish I had Paul's...hmm...unique ability. Then I could remember everything about the first time I saw you. All I remember now is that you acted like an ass."

"Wasn't Jack there? He has a pretty good memory," Austin said.

David growled at Austin. "Don't ask Jack. He'll agree with Kenz."

"Can we talk about these drawings?" Ensley asked. "There are historians and specialists who could date and explain what's going on here. I edited a manuscript about the antiquities trade, and I could contact the author. I'm sure he could give me the names of experts."

"That'd be too dangerous for the family," David said. "I believe these petroglyphs and pictographs tell the story of who created the brooches and the source of the magic. Some of it we already know, but there's more here that we don't. If we brought in experts, the Illuminati might find out what we're up to."

"That's a terrifying thought," Ensley whispered.

"Why do you suppose the artist put a brooch at the far end of the wall?" Kenzie asked. "It looks like all the slots around the door in the cave. But why just one?"

"Why don't we insert a brooch and see what happens?" Austin

suggested.

"Elliott took Ensley's away from me, or you could use that one, which seems appropriate since it started all of this," Paul said.

"I have the diamond," David said. "But that might be premature. One of these pictographs might explain its purpose. Suppose Ensley's theory about a door that allows travelers to move from one place to another on the same day without going through the vortex is correct. Then we might all end up on a fast train to Chicago or the Badlands and a run-in with the Illuminati."

"Nobody wants that," Kenzie said.

"Aaaaa-MEN," Austin said.

"This might be an anteroom like the pyramids with rooms behind walls or even below ground," Paul said. "I wouldn't be surprised if there's at least one more room here. Electrical resistivity tomography measures the shapes and distances under the ground. That's how they discovered tunnels in pyramids. If we had that technology, we could find out."

"Then we'll get the equipment when we go home," David said.

"How do you know about all that?" Ensley asked.

"I read an article in National Geographic about the Teotihuacán Pyramid of the Moon. They discovered a tunnel using electrical resistivity tomography, but the purpose of the tunnel was unclear. There's evidence the inhabitants of Teotihuacán used the pyramid for rituals, including human sacrifices."

Ensley grimaced. "That's just gruesome."

"Since it looks like we'll have to wait until we get home to find out more, what are our next steps here?" Kenzie asked. "Hon, do you want to put your brooch into the petroglyph?"

"Let's do the survey and then decide if we want to try that." David just wanted to get the hell out of there, but knowing Kenzie, she wouldn't leave until she satisfied her curiosity.

"Kenzie, why don't ye and Paul take the right side. Sean and I will survey the left."

It took two hours to get all the measurements, photographs, and videos, and if they were going to put the brooch into the petroglyph, it had to be now.

"If you want any help writing a program to analyze the data, I'm your man," Paul said.

"I'd appreciate the help," David said. "I've heard about yer expertise, but I think Elliott and Meredith want to leave for Bhutan as soon as we get back, and if ye're going with them, ye won't have time."

"I'll have time during the flight to write some code. Send the data in an email, and I'll do what I can."

Sean slapped David on the shoulder. "I'm sorry I'll never know the results of yer study or understand what all this means."

"Come home with us," Kenzie said. "We'd love to have you and Lyle Ann come to the future for as long as you want to stay."

"That's a tempting offer," Sean said. "I'll mention it to Lyle Ann."

David returned to the back wall to take a last look at the pictographs. His rising panic was clouding his mind, and he had to get out of there.

Kenzie joined him at the wall. "Are you okay?"

"Sure. Let's just get this done."

"Then tell me… What's the story here?"

"There is a map of Jarlshof and Scotland. To the right are the Scandinavian countries. Several Viking ships are sailing from there to Jarlshof, and other ships are sailing from Scotland during the Middle Ages. Those pictographs represent the Celts, and we know they were devoted to magical practices." He somehow rattled off most of the descriptions in a single breath.

She gave him a critical look. "If you want to leave the cave, I'll go with you."

"I just want some fresh air. Ye stay here while I go stand by the entrance for a minute." He left Kenzie, Austin, Ensley, and Sean at the wall and Paul walking another grid.

Paul stopped as he walked by. "You okay, David?"

"Why does everybody keep asking me that?" David growled. "I'm fine! I want to stand back from the wall and get a different perspective."

"I don't like closed spaces, either, so I imagine the walls are blacked-out windows that I can crash through and get out of here in an instant."

"Does it work?"

Paul shrugged. "No. But I try."

David fisted his hands, trying to contain the energy building in his gut to an explosive level. "Next time ye offer advice, offer some that'll work."

Paul stepped back, arms raised. "Man, I'm not messing with you.

Just trying to be helpful."

David brushed past him and crouched at the entrance while he took gulps of fresh air, but that only made his need to get the hell out of there stronger. He forced himself to watch and listen and stay engaged.

"Does anybody have an opinion about why these drawings are in a cave on MacKlenna Farm?" Austin asked.

Nobody offered one.

"If my grandfather knew about this," Sean said, "then it explains why he wanted the land and convinced Virginia's governor to give him the grant."

"So the cave was here, and Erik finagled a way for the MacKlennas to own the land? Is that what you're saying?"

"Since both my grandfather and father are dead, we'll never know."

"It makes sense to me," Austin said. "Only a time traveler would know about the MacKlennas' and Frasers' involvement with the brooches. If it was Erik, he was planning for the future."

"David, I think you should put your brooch in the slot and see what happens," Kenzie said. "If the drawings are gone in the future, we'll never know if it was significant."

I don't give a shit. I just want to get the hell out of here.

Kenzie walked toward him. "David, let's try it. Then we can pack up and go."

If that will get me out of here faster, I might as well do it.

David returned to the wall and removed the diamond brooch from his pocket. He was responsible for protecting the brooches and the clan. Was he putting the stones or their lives in danger? Should they vote, or was the decision his to make?

He turned to Ensley, hoping she could guide him one way or the other. "Ye're Erik's daughter. What do ye think?"

"Erik brought JC here to the farm, then hurried back to the Badlands to rescue me. We don't know how he did that, but this wall might explain it. I want to know. Don't you?"

"So do I," Austin said. "I agree with Kenzie. These drawings may not be here in the future. I mean, I've never seen them before."

"Okay then. Everybody move back, and if we get even a whiff of peat, run like hell!" David's gut was in his throat. He took Kenzie's hand. "Stay behind me."

"No, McBain. I'll stand beside you. If you get sucked into the void, I'm coming, too."

He wiped the sweat off his brow. Kenzie's declaration should have worried him, but he found it comforting. "Then let's do this together." He put the diamond brooch in her hand and placed his over hers. Then he guided their hands to the petroglyph, and together they pushed it into the carving. For several seconds, nothing happened.

And then the wall began to open to the cranking sound of a grinding chain. David shoved Kenzie behind him. "Back up, everybody. We don't want to get sucked in."

Austin wrapped his arms around Ensley. "Please don't rush in there."

She looked up at him. "Don't worry. I want us to make it home in one piece. We have a lot to do."

Austin kissed her, and the couple melded into each other. David had seen Austin with dozens of women, but he'd never seen the former basketball star so enamored, and Ensley was equally enamored with him. No, they weren't enamored. They were definitely in love.

When the gears ground to a halt, the door stood open about ten feet. "Everybody grab a lamp." They all grabbed one and turned them to shine into the darkness, illuminating a room twice the size of the anteroom.

"Goddamn," David said.

"I second that," Kenzie said. "Is this what the Confederate treasure looked like when you saw it for the first time?"

David was momentarily speechless, and all he could do was shake his head. Finally, he found his voice. "It was nothing like this. That was a small cave with chests of gold and valuable artifacts. What ye're looking at here is a hundred times the size of that treasure."

Then to Ensley, he said, "Do ye still have room on the camera's memory card?"

"I think so," she said. "I'll shoot as much as I can."

"I'll get videos," Austin offered.

David led the group into the cool room, shivering at the stark temperature difference. The room looked like the inside of a junkyard, with random shit piled floor to ceiling. But it wasn't piles of junk. It was a treasure of inestimable value.

There were dozens of Roman statues, scrolls, chests of gold, silver, and bronze coins, large silver serving vessels, silver spoons, marble furniture, a reclining couch, and even a chariot with four bronze horses. David was mistaken about the size of the room. It wasn't twice the anteroom's size, but more like four times, and it must have taken years, maybe centuries, to accumulate it all.

"David, if the Illuminati knows about this, they might want it more than the brooches," Kenzie said. "We should move all this to our secure storage. But, how'd it all get here?"

"Through the vortex, I guess," David said, "But once I go through the data, photographs, and videos, I might find a clue."

She walked away. "I'm going to look behind some of the larger items. I might find evidence of another entrance."

"Be careful," David said.

Austin sidled up next to David, opened his hand, and whispered, "I just found this gold ring. I don't know what the stone is, but can I have it and give it to Ensley someday? I mean, if this all came from Erik, it already belongs to her."

David didn't like the idea of taking anything out of here until there was a complete inventory. Still, since the ring was for Erik's daughter, he decided to keep his opinion to himself.

"Sure," he said. "It'll be beautiful when it's polished. But"— David glanced around to see if he could signal Kenzie to help Austin with his ring selection, but she was crawling around on the floor— "if ye're thinking of an engagement ring, it'll need a matching wedding ring, and possibly one for ye, too. I mean, this could all be gone by the time we get home."

"I'll look," Austin said, pocketing the ring.

Ensley joined them, beaming. "Is this the treasure of the Knights Templar?"

"No, they came after the Romans. The Romans left England in the early 400s AD, and the Vikings settled in Jarlshof about four hundred years after that. I don't know for sure, but I bet it came from the Roman occupation of England. Maybe the Caledonians collected part of it, and the Vikings stole it from them."

"David," Kenzie yelled from across the room. "Look over there." She pointed. "Sunlight. There's an exit to the outside."

David dashed toward the light. "No! Stay back! That's not sunlight."

"What is it?" she asked, hurrying to his side.

He wrapped his arm around her. "It's the bright light we see when we go through the fog."

Ensley walked toward the light too, but David wrapped his other arm around her shoulders. "Stop, lass. We can't go any farther. Erik went in and out of here, but he knew how to use this chamber. We don't, and until we have more information, we're not going close to that light. We all need to back out and close the door before we trigger something. Maybe when we understand all the drawings on the wall, we might know more, but until then, we can't afford to open the door for the Illuminati to come in."

"Good point. But tell me this. How did Erik accumulate a hoard this size?" Ensley asked.

"If Erik traveled around the world throughout history, he could have amassed a fortune, and he needed secure places to hide it. We got the Roman hoard. No telling how many other hoards he left behind. He could have caves like this all over the world."

"But why hide it on MacKlenna Farm in Lexington, Kentucky?"

No one said anything for several seconds, and then David said, "Because the farm has a connection to the Keeper."

"But why?"

"To support the war against the Illuminati."

"But we can't sell this stuff to raise money. Who would buy any of it? We can't provide documented evidence of provenance," Kenzie said.

"We could sell it to anyone willing to buy antiquities on the black market," Ensley said.

"Well, we aren't selling anything today. So let's go home," David said.

"But what if the hoard isn't here in the future?" Ensley said, "I mean, not that we can do anything with it, but it'll be a shame if we can't do a full inventory to find out what's here."

"We'll worry about that later."

They gathered up the lights they'd brought into the treasure room, and David was the last one to leave.

"Hey, McBain. Did you lock the doors and turn out all the lights?"

"Aye, and I tried to leave it the way we found it." He looked one last time before he removed the brooch. "Look, the light's faded."

"Maybe we triggered something when we walked in there that activated a motion sensor security light, and when we left, it turned it off."

"That's possible, but we can't stick around here any longer. Let's go home," David said.

Kenzie linked her arm with his. "I wish closing the door would wrap up this adventure, but there's still too much to do."

"Maybe Tavis will be home when we get there," David said.

"We can only hope."

The door closed with a clang. "Before ye ask, I have no idea who built this door. But if Erik traveled as much as we think he did, he easily could have found an engineer to build whatever he wanted."

"Or he twitched his nose," Kenzie said.

They carried the gear out of the cave and packed up the trunks, and as they carried them to the wagon, Sean said, "Elliott asked me to burn the cabin to the ground and remove all evidence of its existence. Is that still the plan?"

"Aye," David said, taking his first deep breath since the moment he crawled into the cave. "And find a way to keep people away from here."

"Do ye have any suggestions?" Sean asked.

David set his trunk in the bed of the wagon, thinking of places he'd seen in his life that encouraged people to stay away, and then he laughed. "Aye. Post signs that say the area is haunted. We know ghosts have been sighted on the farm before. Just ask Kit and Meredith."

64

MacKlenna Farm, KY (1885)—Ensley

ELLIOTT AND MEREDITH rode off on the extra horses David and Austin brought with them, so, instead of riding double, Ensley and Kenzie rode on the wagon's damp tailgate with their legs dangling while they chatted and laughed their way back to the mansion.

As they rode up to the barn, the horses in the paddock caught Ensley's eye, and she did a double take. "What the hell! They're here!"

"Who's here?" Kenzie asked.

Ensley pointed. "The horses! Mercury and Marengo and Ferdiad, and Remy's horse, too, but I don't know his name." She jumped down, yelling, "Austin, look! The horses. They made it."

Kenzie jumped off the tailgate and joined Ensley at the fence. "Mercury's JC's favorite horse. How'd he get here?"

"JC was riding him when he left Elkhorn Ranch, so he must have had Mercury in Chicago." Ensley climbed up on the lowest rung and rested her folded arms atop the rail, eyes fixed on the stallion. "I know JC went shopping and bought clothes for me. He probably left Mercury at the train station while he did that."

"Marengo and Ferdiad are here, too," Austin said, kissing her. The contact was startling but warm and compelling. He sipped at her lips gently, drew away for a breath, and came back for a firmer, more possessive kiss. His stubble rasped her chin, and she couldn't have cared less.

Kenzie cleared her throat.

But Ensley ignored Kenzie's warning to curb their display of affection. She was so overcome with relief that she kissed him back in front of God and Kentucky and the entire SEC, whatever the hell that was.

"They all made it here. I thought we'd never see them again," he whispered against her mouth. "Wait till you see them running on the ranch with the mountains in the background. It's a magnificent sight."

"I can't wait."

Ferdiad saw her but kept looking around. "Look at Ferdiad. He's looking for Tavis."

"He'll come to me," Austin said. And then he called, "Come here, boy. Come here, Ferdiad." The Thoroughbred clopped over and nuzzled Austin's shoulder. "We miss him, too." Austin scratched the horse's forehead. "We're going to bring your master home."

Ferdiad nodded his head as if he understood and then nuzzled Ensley's shoulder. "You'll see him soon," she said, stroking his muzzle.

Austin whistled, and Marengo trotted over to him and rested his head on Austin's arm, whinnying. "I never thought I'd see you again." The expression on Austin's face was one of pure joy. She'd known he was attached to his horses, but the way he looked now told her the depth of that attachment. They were his kids, his team, and he needed them as much as they needed him.

Mercury stood alone in the paddock, watching as if he knew JC should be there, and he was going to stand back until he appeared. Elliott jogged over to the fence, and when Mercury saw him, he pawed the ground and shook his head. Then he trotted over to Elliott and nudged his chest until Meredith walked up, and he left Elliott to lay his head on Meredith's shoulder.

She hugged him back, crying. "You miss him as much as we do." She petted and stroked him. "James Cullen will be so happy to see you again."

It was a miracle that Mercury was here, and Ensley saw it as a good sign that JC would again sit tall and relaxed in the saddle, shoulders back, hat tipped low on his forehead. She would keep that image front and center in her heart and pray for his full recovery.

Meredith smiled at Elliott. "It's a good sign. Don't you think?"

"Aye. A good sign." Then he turned around and addressed the gathering of family members. "Let's pack up. It's time to go home."

Sean came out of the barn, carrying a saddle. "The owner of the

Midway Livery said they arrived two days ago. They didn't know who they belonged to until one of the hands discovered a MacKlenna Farm logo on the back of the saddle. He brought them here to see if they were mine. I wish I could claim them."

"All but Mercury are retrained former racehorses."

"What about the bay stallion?"

"Remy Benoit, who works for me, calls him Gumbo, but he calls all horses that."

"Aye. Emily mentioned he got shot during the escape from the train."

"Not seriously, thank God. He'll recover just fine, but he's not attached to Gumbo. Ye can have him. He was a fantastic performer, but he never produced offspring of comparable quality. At least not by twenty-first-century standards."

You can't give away one of Austin's horses.

As soon as Ensley had that thought, she almost smacked herself. Sean and Lyle Ann had been wonderful hosts, and the gift of a Thoroughbred was a perfect thank-you.

"Thank ye for the offer," Sean said, "but I remember Kitherina's story about her Thoroughbred Stormy and why she decided to leave him in the future. She was afraid the horses he sired couldn't establish legitimate pedigrees, and that eliminated a racing career."

"Good point. Well, if ye won't take the horse, then come to the future with us."

Sean kicked at several clods while he thought about the invitation. "I don't know, Elliott. It's tempting. Lyle Ann and I have a good life here, and as much as Cullen and Braham enjoy their lives in the future…" Sean shook his head. "It's not for us right now."

"Does that mean it might be later?"

Sean laughed. "I don't think so."

"Well, I tried." Elliott pulled Sean in for a hug and slap on the back. "I'm glad we finally got to meet. If ye change yer mind, leave a message in the cave. Bury it beneath the Yggdrasil, and we'll come back for ye."

"I'll do that."

Elliott faced the family again. "We'll leave in an hour."

Austin took Ensley's hand. "Let's walk. It won't take us long to pack."

They walked over to the veranda and sat in the wicker chairs. Austin looked around for a minute before clearing his throat.

"We've talked briefly about our options once we get home, but we didn't talk about JC's trip to the monastery or Tavis's rescue. You mentioned you wanted to go with Elliott and Meredith. If you still want to go, I'd like to go with you."

"Sure, that'd be great," she said.

"As soon as we get back from Bhutan, Elliott will want to plan for Tavis's rescue."

"I'm going, and I don't care what Elliott says."

"He'll probably consider it too dangerous."

"After what I've been through, I'm ready for it. Bring it on." As soon as the words spilled out, she realized how cocky it sounded, and she tried to reel it all back. "That didn't come out the way I intended. It's just that, besides rescuing Tavis, I want to see Erik's home and meet his family, and this will be my only shot. Elliott can't leave me behind."

"I'll leave it up to you to persuade him. But Ensley, you'll be going back to medieval times when life was hard and dangerous, and since we're on a rescue mission, it might not be peaceful, either."

"I know that."

"Then we have to be prepared. Erik wanted you to use his ax. If you commit to six weeks of training, you'll be able to swing it as easily as a broom."

"You think?"

"It won't be easy, but I think you can do it, and I have the perfect trainer and training facility."

"Austin, we've talked about this. I have to go back to New York to settle things and talk to my cousin and Barb."

"We should be able to accomplish that in a couple of days. Don't you think?"

She had the urge to stomp her feet. He was trying to manage her, and she didn't like it at all. She'd been gone for weeks and wanted to go home for a while to soak in her tub, wear her comfy clothes, nap on her sofa, cook her favorite foods, and read her mail. She was homesick. She might get un-sick in a couple of days, but she wanted a chance to find out.

"You're pressuring me to make a decision right now, and I can't do that. Give me a chance to go home and wrap up my business. It'll take as long as it takes. If you have to get back to the ranch, go on, and I'll come later."

Austin smiled, almost sadly. "I don't mean to pressure you, and I did agree to go to New York and stay as long as needed, but I have to admit I am anxious to get back to the ranch."

"Then go," she said without really considering what that would mean if he did.

He dropped his head and gave it a little shake. "I don't want to go home for my convenience. I want to go for us. Once you see the ranch, I bet you'll fall in love with it, just like this city boy did. As much as you enjoy sunsets, you'll go nuts when you see Colorado's."

"That's the way I felt growing up in North Dakota."

"So the plan is to FaceTime with George and your friend Barb to let them know you're safe. Then we'll go with JC. When we get back, we'll go to New York City."

They hadn't made plans for Tavis's rescue, so the discussion wasn't over. But she was okay with banking the rest of the decisions until they got back from Bhutan.

"Let's pack up and go home." She took his hand and tugged him out of the chair. If he hadn't wanted to stand up, one little tug in the opposite direction would have toppled her into his lap, and she was proud of him for resisting the urge to do just that.

"How come I think the ranch and sunsets aren't all you want to show me?" she teased.

He winked. "Wait till you see the theater, my dear."

65

Jarlshof (1125)—Tavis

ASTRID THREW HER arms around Tavis's neck, and he hugged her to him, digging his fingers deep into her thick, blond, waist-length hair, fragrant with the fresh, briny scent of the sea. The hot, unfettered sensations from contact with her after so long stunned him.

Astrid parted her lips, and he kissed her senseless, right there in the middle of the longhouse, momentarily ignoring the other women standing nearby, who were now weeping over Erik's body.

Astrid broke the kiss. "Father said you would come soon but didn't say why." Her chin quivered when she looked across the room at the bodies of Erik and his horse, and she blinked back tears. She looked back up at Tavis. "Are you hurt?" She ran her hands down his chest and arms then clasped the sides of his face. "I don't see any blood. Tell me you're not hurt."

"I'm not hurt." God, he was so glad to see her, to hold her in his arms again, to feel her luscious body beneath the long green dress and white apron. Her breasts felt heavier, and her hips broader. But he didn't care if she put on a few pounds.

"I arrived after the attack was over. There wasn't anything I could do. He was already dead. Erik fought the bear until Elliott's grandson arrived and killed it."

"The Keeper's grandson?" She glanced to the ceiling, at the skylights cut into the thatched roof for light and ventilation. "That would be"—she tapped her chin—"Blane or Lance."

Tavis kissed her again. "Ah, but there is one more grandchild." He had drawn a family tree with all the MacKlenna Clan members, and she painted it on the wall so others would know the Keeper's family and where she and Tavis fit in.

She raised her hands and pushed them into the air as if shooting a basketball. "Aus...tin. But he is injured."

"Just his leg. He's an excellent hunter and shot the bear four times."

"Shot? Oh, with what you call a...gun."

Erik's widowed sister and her two unmarried daughters began gathering bowls of water, soap, and cleaning cloths. "You must tell the Council," Erik's sister said, her voice cracking.

"My husband will tell them," Astrid said. "Come, I'll walk with you."

Tavis helped her with her cloak, and they left Erik's longhouse. The house and all Erik's belongings now belonged to Tavis. He held his wife close, sheltered under his arm, as they walked across the windy hill toward the longhouse that had been her home until her father and Erik signed the marriage agreement.

"After you meet with the Council, you will meet your son."

The word *son* hit Tavis with the force of a two-by-four, and his knees nearly buckled. He'd never given much thought to having a family because he didn't think he'd ever get married. That all changed when Erik insisted he select a wife. And now, here in a Viking settlement in the twelfth century, he had a son.

"But how's that possible?" When he left the last time, Astrid wasn't pregnant. Or was she? When was that?

She gasped. "Possible!" She pushed away and gave him a killer look that did make his knees buckle. And if that wasn't enough to make her point, she reached for the dagger at her waist.

He jumped back a couple of steps.

You asshole. You all but accused her of infidelity.

He put his hand over hers so she wouldn't pull the dagger on him. "I'm sorry, I didn't mean to offend you."

"Offend?" The killer look flared again. "I don't know that word."

"Make you mad. Hurt your feelings."

She shoved his hand away. "I am your wife. As long as you live, I belong to you. No one else."

He pulled her to him again, stroking her hair with soft caresses. "I'm your husband, Astrid. As long as you live, I belong to you. No one else."

"But you are gone for months at a time. Other men take women wherever they go."

"I'm not like other men, and if you ever doubted that, Erik would have told you not to worry." A hint of self-doubt colored his tone when he remembered how close he and Emily came to having drunk sex. Fortunately, they sobered up before it could happen, and their make-out session hadn't affected their friendship.

"Erik told me. But it was hard not knowing when you'd return."

"He would have told you that, too."

"He said when he had news, he would tell me."

Erik had brought him to Jarlshof to meet the rest of the Council members a few years ago, and Arne introduced his daughter. She was fourteen, old enough to marry in their culture. Unbeknownst to Tavis, Erik and Arne arranged for their marriage. When Erik told Tavis he was to wed her, he was furious and explained that in his time, fourteen-year-old girls were too young to marry, and he refused to consummate the marriage until she turned eighteen. That didn't sit well with the Council, but Tavis refused to bed her. He would support her, but he wouldn't be a true husband to her yet.

Astrid had grown from a timid young girl into a beautiful and desirable woman—a Valkyrie—who possessed all the intelligence, skills, and passion he wanted in a wife. Her English was almost perfect, and she read every book he gave her. He had told her about the lands and centuries beyond Jarlshof. The information excited her, but she didn't want to travel. He intended to pressure her again while he was here.

He nuzzled her neck. "Where's my son now?"

"My slave has him. They went to the storeroom for vegetables."

The girl had served Astrid in her father's house and was given to her when she married Tavis and moved to Erik's longhouse. She was only about twelve, but Astrid depended on her to do most house-hold cleaning tasks.

"What's his name?" When Tavis thought about children, usually during MacKlenna Clan get-togethers, he wanted to honor his grandfather and name his child Joseph.

Astrid looked surprised. "He has no name other than Son of Tavis. We have been waiting for you to give him a proper one."

Now he felt like a real cad. "How old is he?"

She held up two fingers. "Two months."

Now he knew he was a real asshole. His last trip here was to celebrate Astrid's eighteenth birthday and consummate their marriage, and she had conceived during the three months he stayed here. Why hadn't he asked before he returned to his century?

"You should have told me."

"I didn't want to be a burden and hold you here when you had work to do in your time."

"I would have stayed. Nothing is more important than you."

He grimaced, knowing how dangerous childbirth was in the twelfth century, and the infant mortality rate was so high. What if he'd returned and learned that she and their son had died in childbirth? With that thought, terror rolled over him. And now that Erik, his mentor, was gone, and Tavis didn't have a brooch of his own, what would he use to travel back and forth?

Astrid rested her hand on Tavis's chest and fiddled with the chain and silver medallion he wore against his skin. The jewelry had been a wedding gift from her, and he never took it off.

"From the first time I saw you, I imagined having a son with your eyes and hair, and I finally got my heart's wish."

He smiled, appreciating the wish of a maiden, and he realized only now how much she'd given up when she agreed to wait four years for him. He'd forced her to sacrifice her childbearing years to accommodate the standards of the future and his sensibilities.

He kissed her. "I'm sure he's a beautiful baby, but I'd rather he looked like you, not me."

She stood on tiptoe and kissed him back, and he looked down and slowly raked his eyes over her. He knew the feel of every curve, every bone, every muscle in her body. But her body had changed. The changes made her even more desirable, and he hardened in anticipation of making love to her.

She teased him with a provocative smile. "A son should resemble his father, not his mother."

He didn't have an answer for that. But he had the answer to a question he'd asked dozens of times: *Will you go to the future with me?* He had a child now, and it was important to him to do what was best for his family. He would talk to Astrid's father first. Without buy-in from him, she would never leave her home by choice, and he'd never take her away against her will.

"I will leave you now," she said. "Come to me as soon as you finish with the Council."

Since he didn't know how long it would be before they had time alone, he thought about his upcoming conversation with the

Council, which immediately killed the boner.

She sauntered away but looked back at him, smiling. "Hurry."

Damn right, he'd hurry. And after just that saucy smile, his hard-on was resurrected.

He waved and then walked toward the cliff, where he gazed out over the sea. The chilly breeze blowing off the water tensed the muscles in his neck and shoulders. He rolled his neck, but it didn't help, and nothing would right now, other than a few hours alone with his wife. And that wasn't likely to happen until after the funeral.

How many times had he stood here with Erik, talking about the future and the Celtic brooches? Dozens? No. Hundreds. And each time Tavis asked about the stones, Erik always gave him the same answer, "When the time comes, you will know all there is to know."

But Erik often made random comments about the stones and their power, and when he did, Tavis didn't spend much time putting them into context. He wrongly assumed he would have many more years with Erik. Now, when it was too late, he had questions.

Tavis thoughtfully scraped his thumb across his stubbled chin and considered his relationship with the remaining Council members. He didn't trust them the way he trusted Erik. They weren't untrustworthy. It was just that he didn't have a connection with them, but that was about to change. As Erik's heir, he inherited a seat on the Council, or maybe they would hold it open for Tavis's son. The Council could vote to do either one.

He glanced across the remnants of the ancient civilizations dating back to 800 BC. It always fascinated him to walk the grassy hills, knowing which buildings had crumbled and which ones the community would construct in the future.

He would never walk these ruins with Erik again. He would never hear Erik's stories or watch him laugh at a simple tale told by another Council member. How often would Tavis be able to get back here to tell those same stories to his son?

That's why Astrid had to leave with him this time.

"Tavis!"

He turned to see Astrid's father striding toward him. "I heard you were here. Where is Erik?"

Tavis squeezed Arne's shoulder. "A grizzly was about to attack Ensley, but Arthfael tried to fight the bear. The stallion succumbed to his wounds. Erik arrived in time to save Ensley, but...he..."

Arne clasped his hand over Tavis's, and then they both dropped their arms. "He didn't survive?" Arne glanced off toward the sea, and his face turned ashen as he closed his eyes.

After a moment, he opened them again, and they were glistening. "Before he left, he said it was time for him to go to the other side to be with the elders, and he might take the Keeper with him." Arne looked at Tavis. "Did he?"

Tavis gave his head a hard shake, trying to jostle Arne's statement around in his brain until it made sense. "I'm pretty sure he didn't, but he might have taken James Cullen. The Illuminati might have tortured and possibly killed him."

"And Ensley? What of her? Was she injured?"

"Elliott's grandson shot and killed the bear before it could reach her. But Erik didn't have his cloak when he fought the bear."

"Where is it now?"

"There was no sign of it anywhere near his body. If I had to guess, I'd say he wrapped it around Elliott's son."

Arne fingered the ends of his long mustache. "I doubt the Keeper understands the full power it holds. He'll either lock it up with the brooches or bury it with his son. Either way, it will be safe. Where is Erik's garnet brooch?"

Tavis wanted to keep it and hoped it was part of his inheritance. "I have it."

Arne held out his hand. "The brooch belongs to the Council, not Erik. He has carried it for many years, but it is mine now."

Tavis didn't know if that was true or not, but until the Council met and told him what to do, he wasn't letting it go. He might be making an enemy of Arne, but it was better to piss off one member than all of them.

"I'll bring it to the Council meeting. If it's yours, they will give it to you."

Arne's brown eyes flared, but he didn't challenge Tavis. Instead, he said, "Come. I will send word to the others. We must meet immediately to plan Erik's funeral and settle the matter of his brooch."

Tavis crossed his arms. "Before I sit down with the full Council, you should know that I won't participate in raping a slave girl. I haven't been with my wife in months, and I won't dishonor her by doing something I find repulsive."

"Every man in the village will participate."

"I don't live here or live by your customs. Erik understood my values, and it would dishonor him to participate in the rape and murder of a child. It's a tradition that should end right now." Tavis's pulse flared, along with his anger, but he moderated his voice to keep Arne from knowing how angry this made him. "Tell the men it's Erik's wish."

"You can argue your position to the Council, and we will vote. Then you will accept the Council's decision. You are my daughter's husband, but I will not spare you if the Council decrees you are to accompany Erik to Valhalla."

Arne's statement struck swift and deep, and Tavis's anger flared into a full burn, beckoned from the place in his gut where he'd kept his emotions well-checked until now.

Arne was threatening him, but Tavis didn't understand why.

They reached Arne's longhouse, and he lifted the latch and pushed open the door. "Have you seen your son?"

"Astrid just told me. I'll see the baby after I meet with the Council."

Tavis followed Arne inside the dark and smoky longhouse, coughing. The stone hearth was located in the center of the longhouse and provided heat, light, and fire for cooking, and was the household's center of activity. It always took Tavis a couple of days to adjust to the smoky darkness. He nodded to Frida, Arne's wife, and their two youngest daughters, who were not yet old enough to marry. Frida had two sons between Astrid and her sisters, but neither one survived infancy, which made Tavis's son Arne's male heir.

Tavis's spidey senses were on high alert. It was time to gather his family and get the hell out of here.

The women sat on the compacted dirt floor next to the stone hearth, weaving a multi-colored cloth on weighted looms. The clicking of the stone weights sounded almost like a metronome— *click, click, click.* The women glanced up when he entered, smiling, and Tavis mustered a faint grin.

Their smiles dropped, and Frida stood and poured ale in carved horn mugs and offered them to Tavis and Arne. "It is good to see you, Tavis. Have you seen your son?"

"Not yet. I just arrived." Tavis took a long drink then swiped the back of his wrist across his mouth. The ale smelled earthy, not sweet, and was bitter, with a dry taste. After two gulps, warmth from the alcohol flowed down his throat.

"Send our daughters to collect Bjørn, Birger, and Forde," Arne told his wife. "We have urgent business to discuss."

Frida asked no questions but alerted her daughters, who grabbed their cloaks and rushed outside.

"Come, sit, and I will prepare some fish."

"Not yet." Arne led Tavis over to a bench built into the far wall, the only piece of furniture in the stone-framed longhouse. "You may speak to the others, but then you will leave while we discuss what we need to do next."

Tavis's anger flared. If they left him out of the discussion, they would never understand his position. "I insist on presenting my case."

Arne sat on the bench away from the hearth, leaning against the wattle and daub wall, pulling his cloak around him. Tavis wasn't the least bit chilled. If anything, he was scalding. He sat cross-legged on the dirt floor in a circle of foggy firelight.

"The Council is already aware of your…case…as you call it. The funeral of a Viking chief will proceed according to our traditions. The head of Erik's household will select a sacrificial female slave. She will drink large amounts of alcohol before every man in the village rapes her. She will then be strangled with a rope, stabbed by a village matriarch, placed in the boat with Erik, and set ablaze."

Tavis almost threw up at the viciousness of their tradition. If they forced him to participate, they'd have to kill him first. He took another swig and used all his reserves to hold it together. There was still an issue he had to discuss with his father-in-law.

"After the funeral, I want to take my family to the future. Life here is harsher than in my time. I want to give my family opportunities they'll never have if they stay here. And Astrid won't go unless you give her permission."

Arne's face remained stoic, and Tavis couldn't read anything in his dark eyes. "The Council will discuss it."

If Tavis had to bet, he'd say his odds weren't good at all. He'd have to convince Astrid first and ask her to put pressure on her father.

Yeah, right. Good luck with that.

A few minutes later, the other three Council members entered the longhouse. Tavis stood to greet them, then returned to where he'd been sitting on the ground while the four men sat on the bench, leaving the center seat empty.

Erik's absence suddenly became very real, not that Tavis wasn't already grieving. But the empty seat forced him to face the stark reality that Erik's moderating influence, so crucial to the Council's objective view of the future and the brooches, no longer existed.

And he no longer had an advocate.

Which one of these men would become the moderating influence? None of them. Unlike Erik, they didn't have negotiating skills, insight, or forethought. The Council would be rudderless without their chief.

And he was unsure of what that meant for his future and his family's. Although he did have the Keeper's protection, he had no way to contact him, but he was confident Elliott would show up eventually. Remy would see to it.

"Erik didn't mention bringing you back with him this time," Bjørn said.

Tavis opened his mouth to explain his presence, but Arne spoke first. "Erik was killed fighting a bear while protecting Ensley Williams. Tavis returned with his body."

The other three Council members jumped to their feet, and Bjørn shouted, "Impossible. Erik could fight a bear and live to tell the story."

"There had to be two to kill him," Birger said.

"Only one," Tavis said. "It was a grizzly bear, taller, bigger, meaner."

"His cloak should have protected him," Birger said.

"He didn't have it with him. I believe, but I won't know until I go back to my time that Erik gave it to the Keeper's son."

"What makes you think that?" Forde asked.

"Erik saved Ensley's life at least twice, and both times she remembers the red cloak. He didn't have it on when he fought the bear. Elliott sent two teams back to rescue Ensley and James Cullen. The team that included Elliott and his wife went to MacKlenna Farm. The other team, which I led, went to the Badlands in the Dakotas. Elliott sent a telegram saying he was taking his son home. There are only two reasons he would do that. Either JC was seriously injured or dead. If he was injured, maybe Erik gave James Cullen his cloak."

"The Keeper will protect the cloak," Arne said.

"What about his brooch?" Forde asked.

"I have it," Tavis said.

"Your inheritance does not include the brooch," Bjørn said. "The Council will keep it in the box."

"We must plan Erik's funeral and Tavis's formal induction," Forde said.

"Induction to what?" Tavis asked.

"A seat on the Council. However, you will not be entitled to the knowledge until you have earned it," Arne said.

"Erik never mentioned a formal induction. Give the seat to someone else."

"You are Erik's heir," Forde said. "The seat is yours. Now we must talk about the funeral. Erik told us you would object to the tradition, and we should weigh your objections when we make arrangements."

Bjørn looked directly at Tavis. "Leave us. We will give you our decision shortly."

Tavis returned to the cliff to await their decision. It didn't take long, but by the time Birger came for him, he was shivering from both cold and, to be honest, fear.

He retook his position on the floor and remained stone-faced.

"We will respect Erik's request and excuse you from participating in the tradition. You will, however, sit on the dais," Arne said.

"And watch the debauchery?" Tavis swallowed the bile rushing up to the back of his throat. He would have to shut down his mind to get through it. "It goes against everything I believe in."

"But you are here, and this is our tradition," Arne said. "As for your other request, we deny it. You will remain here and take Erik's place on the Council."

"Or," Bjørn said, "one of us will escort you and Astrid to the future, but your son must remain here. He has Erik's blood, and he will not be allowed to leave."

Tavis jumped to his feet. "That's outrageous! How could you possibly think I'd go without my son? When I leave, he will go with me. And he doesn't have Erik's blood any more than I do."

"You are Erik's son, which makes your son his as well," Arne said.

Tavis shook his head. "No, I am his heir, but not connected by blood. I grew up with both my parents. I didn't see them very often, but I know I'm theirs."

"Why do you think I agreed to let my daughter marry an outsider?" Arne asked. "I agreed because of who you are."

"I don't believe you." Tavis's mind did a quick data search. Were there any clues in his life that he wasn't his father's biological child? No. Not that he recalled. And he and his brother even resembled each other. Arne was lying. But why?

Arne crossed the room and collected an ebony container the size of a shoebox. He returned to his seat and opened it. From where Tavis stood, he couldn't see the contents.

Arne held out the box. "Please put the brooch in here."

Tavis removed the brooch from his pants pocket and set it in the box on top of a photograph. He turned his head to look at it right side up. "That's my mother with Erik. How the hell is that possible?"

Arne removed the photograph and held it up. "You are correct. It is a picture of your mother and Erik. This is evidence that what I said is true."

The hairs on the back of Tavis's neck stood on end. "Where the hell did you get this?"

"Your mother had it taken when they were in Rome. That was about two weeks before you were born."

"I don't believe you, and besides, my brother and I are too much alike not to be full brothers."

"Erik is also his father. Your grandfather knows the truth. His son had an illness in his childhood, which made him unable to father a child. Your grandfather made all the arrangements. And Erik gave me this picture to explain this truth to you."

"I don't believe it. Erik would have told me something this important. And why did he pick me and not my brother?"

"Erik and your grandfather had to decide which one of you would be a guardian. You were chosen."

Tavis dropped to the floor as his emotions spun around in circles. He didn't know if he was pissed, hurt, betrayed, or mad enough to kill. "Why didn't Erik tell me? He had plenty of time."

"He intended to when your son was born, but he was away on Council business and unable to bring you here. He was waiting for the naming ceremony."

If Tavis had thought he lived in two worlds before, now there was no doubt. "This doesn't change anything. I still intend to take my family to the future.'

"You and Astrid are free to leave, but your son will be raised here and take your place on the Council when he comes of age. He will not travel until he's an adult, so the riches available in the future won't influence him."

Tavis was aghast. "What?" he shouted. "You expect me to leave my child behind? That's not happening. He's leaving with Astrid and me."

"He cannot leave," Bjørn said.

"You can't do that," Tavis said. "Erik would let me go and take my family."

"Erik is no longer here," Arne said. "But there is another option for you. Ensley Williams is also Erik's child."

Tavis clutched his head. In all his years in the Navy, fighting in Afghanistan, or dealing with Elliott, he'd never gotten this pissed. "How many more children did Erik have?"

"We only know of you, your brother, and Ensley. He chose the mothers because of their lineage."

"What's so special about that?"

"Both your mother and Ensley's have direct lines to us."

"Not to Erik, I hope."

"No, to the first Keeper," Arne said. "You have a choice, Tavis. Your family or Ensley."

"That is no choice at all. I won't leave my son, and I won't exchange my life for Ensley's, for my half sister."

The Council members stood. "We are finished here. It is now time to prepare for Erik's funeral."

They all walked off without speaking, and Tavis returned to his place on the cliff and sat on a boulder. He'd been sitting there alone, trying to figure out a way to resolve the situation, when Arne joined him.

"Whether you believe this or not, I did argue your case. But Astrid would never be happy in your time."

"Without our child, neither one of us could ever be happy. But what I want to know is why did Erik go to the future to impregnate women? Surely there was one here who would have accepted him."

"He lost three wives in childbirth. After that, no one would agree to marry him, and he didn't want a slave girl. He thought medicine in your time would save his child. He searched for years until he found your mother and Ensley's mother, hoping one of them could give him what no other woman could."

"Shit, Arne! You've manipulated me for years, first locking me into marriage and now blackmailing me. You knew I'd refuse to leave without my child or sell out Ensley Williams. You now have what you wanted. I'll live here with my family, but when the Keeper comes for me, and he will, my family and I are leaving. All of us. Together."

Tavis marched off. Hell, he was pissed. How long would he have to wait for Elliott to come for him? Elliott could come immediately, but it could be years for Tavis. That's the way the damn brooches worked.

But Elliott would come, just not soon enough.

66

Mallory Plantation, VA—Ensley

W HEN THE TRAVELERS came through the fog, Ensley found herself in the cleanroom for the third time in under twenty-four hours. And man, not only was she exhausted, but her hip burned like a branding iron had stamped her initials on it.

Time for some ibuprofen with a whisky chaser.

Once she dulled the pain, she could easily sleep for an uninterrupted twenty-four hours. But before she put her head on a pillow, she wanted a long, hot bubble bath and a bowl of chocolate mint ice cream. She'd fantasized about both for weeks.

The cleanroom soon became a beehive of activity, with four horses neighing and stomping their feet and eleven travelers shaking off the temporary disorientation from speeding through the vortex.

"Let's get the horses out of here," Braham said.

"Kit and I will take them to the barn," Cullen said. "We're ready for dinner and baths and quiet time after all the excitement of the last several days."

"I'll help you get them out of the house," Paul offered.

Kit and Cullen's goodbyes with their children had been heart-wrenching to watch. But Elliott's promise to take Kit to Washington, DC someday so she could visit with her daughters again had lightened the moment. From what Austin told her, Elliott was the only family member to ever take a trip back in time for personal reasons.

Maybe they could go when TR was president between 1901 and 1909. If they did, Ensley would insist on going along, too.

Charlotte was standing right where they left her, relief flashing over her face as she hurried across the room to hug Braham.

"You're never going without me again."

"I won't." Braham kissed her. "But I'm glad I could say goodbye to Uncle Donald, and I needed to keep an eye on Kit and Cullen to make sure they didn't stay behind."

"Did they consider it?"

"Aye, but since Cullen's heart attack, he doesn't like being away from twenty-first-century medical care for longer than a few days."

Elliott and Meredith hurried to JC's bedside. Ensley wanted to go but thought JC's parents should be alone with him for a few minutes.

"How long were we gone?" David asked Charlotte.

Charlotte glanced at the bank of wall clocks. "Seconds, I think. Braham distracted me, but the fog that took you away merged with the fog that brought you back."

David picked up a trunk and placed it on the stainless steel table. "Hmm. That's a record."

"How long were you in the past?" she asked.

He opened the trunk and started unloading equipment, taking his time to answer her. "Well… Long enough to find a priceless Roman treasure."

Charlotte's blue eyes opened wide. "Where?"

Braham released her to pick up one of the trunks, placing it on the table next to David's. "In a cave on MacKlenna Farm—and it puts the Confederate treasure to shame."

"Larger objects? Or the size of the hoard is larger?" she asked.

Braham unloaded the cameras. "Ten times larger? Although I didn't see it firsthand, I did scroll through a few dozen pictures while I was waiting to leave."

"I can't believe you didn't go see it."

"Cullen and I were busy looking at horses on adjoining farms, but if ye ever need a photographer, ask Ensley. She has a good eye, and it's all captured in her photographs and Austin's videos. The cave has a stunning collection of artifacts, life-size bronze statues, and frescoes that might even prove the Romans traveled to North America."

"It might be true," Ensley piped in. "Several caches of Roman coins have been found buried in North America, dating back to the sixteenth century. Some think collectors deliberately placed coins as hoaxes. But I don't believe the hoard in the cave was put there by collectors to prove a point. I believe Erik put the collection together over time to finance the war against the Illuminati."

"I'm with ye on that, Ensley," David said. "But once we analyze the data and study the videos and photographs, we should have more answers."

"I'll get it all uploaded, and we can get to work." Braham took the cameras and walked into a glass-walled office with large monitors and multiple computers.

"I'll add Ensley to WhatsApp and give her an email address," David said. "When ye have the pictures and videos uploaded, I'll send out a link."

"Is the system secure enough that I can send emails about the trip?" Ensley asked.

"We have an encrypted system as secure as the Pentagon's," David said, "but let's keep this quiet for now. I want to go to the cave tomorrow and make sure the treasure is still there before we bring in everyone else."

"I'll go with you," Braham said.

"If the Illuminati picks up on this, nothing will stop them from engaging in the battle from hell to steal it all," Kenzie said.

"We have to be mindful of that possibility, especially when we're inside the cave. There's something strange about the place, and it'll take a while to discover its secrets," David said. "And we need to map the cave as it is today and compare the data to see if there's any change."

"But we didn't map the treasure room," Kenzie said.

"I realized that too late, but I'm pretty sure I can reconstruct the dimensions based on the photographs and Paul's recollections," David said.

The crease between Kenzie's auburn brows marked her doubt, which matched Ensley's. Although David probably didn't make mistakes like that very often.

Ensley tried not to limp to the drink bar to get a bottle of water out of the mini-fridge but failed.

Austin spoke from right behind her. "You're in pain."

She sucked in her breath with a sudden hiss. "Do you know where I can find ibuprofen?"

Austin opened the cabinet over the sink. "Right there. Pick your poison—aspirin, ibuprofen, acetaminophen."

"Ibuprofen." She grabbed a bottle of water, popped two pain relievers into her mouth, and swallowed them with a long drink.

"If Anne's available, she can give you a massage. Do you want me to call her?"

"We don't have time right now. It can wait." She walked toward JC's bed with a wave at Remy, who was still lying on his stomach and looking bored and restless, and she arrived just in time to hear Elliott say he planned to leave for Bhutan within the hour.

"What's the plan for keeping him calm during the flight?" Meredith asked.

"I'll go with you," Charlotte said. "If JC needs to be sedated again during the flight, I'll take care of it. I want to keep him comfortable."

Emily entered the wardrobe room, stood behind a privacy screen, and tossed clothes over the top of it as she stripped out of her nineteenth-century day dress, "Charlotte, I can go and take care of JC."

"And I can go, too," Remy hollered from the exam room.

"You're not going anywhere, Remy," Charlotte said, "and Emily, you have to be at the hospital. You can't take six days off."

Emily emerged wearing blue scrubs, and Ensley almost drooled to do the same. But when she stripped out of this dress, she wanted to be heading for the tub. She could wait a few more minutes.

"I can call and ask," Emily said, pulling pins out of her updo. "I have vacation days that I haven't taken."

Charlotte plucked out a few pins Emily missed, then handed her a hair tieback she found in the pocket of her white lab coat. "If this was an emergency, I wouldn't stop you, but it's not necessary."

Remy shuffled out of the exam room. "I'm fine, and I want to go."

"Charlotte just removed two bullets from yer ass. Ye're not going anywhere," Elliott said. "Ye can't even walk without pain. How do ye think ye can climb a mountain?"

"If you and Emily both leave, then I have to come with you. Who'll take care of me if I relapse?" Remy said to Charlotte.

Charlotte looked at him over the rim of her glasses. "Good try, Remy, but I won't agree to let you go. JC might be a handful on the flight, and I don't want you moving around and ripping out your stitches."

"You're not the boss of me."

"While you're under my care, I am."

"Charlotte's right, lad," Elliott said. "I need ye healed up and healthy to go back for Tavis."

"What the fuck am I supposed to do while I'm left here by my-self?"

"You can start with cleaning up your vocabulary," Charlotte said.

"I thought you had a gig you wanted to play this weekend," Austin said. "If you go, you'll miss it."

Remy shuffled back to bed. "Fuck it!"

"It's a sixteen-hour flight, plus fueling in Luton, England, and Istanbul, Turkey, and ye can't sit down," Elliott said. "So relax, enjoy the time off, and rehearse."

"It takes several hours to hike up the mountain, and even under normal conditions, it's difficult. The humidity will make it much worse," Charlotte said. "With that kind of physical exertion, your stitches *will* come out."

Austin chuckled. "Ensley and I plan to go so we can help with JC."

Elliott studied Ensley briefly. Then he cleared his throat. "I appreciate ye wanting to help James Cullen, but ye've had a rough few weeks, lass."

Ensley stared back in a panic, her heart galloping. Elliott was going to tell her she couldn't go, and that was unacceptable. "He came to my rescue at great cost to himself. I'm not going to bail out on him now."

"I'm not sure ye're up for it," he said.

She licked her lips before taking a deep breath. "Of course, I'm up for it. And if you leave me out, I'll find another way to get there. I know! I'll go through the cave."

"Good try, lass. But ye can't open the wall without a brooch. And neither Braham nor I will give ye one—and this time there isn't one to steal."

"But the sunstone brooch is mine."

"Was yers," Elliott said. "It's now part of our collection. We have the brooch, and ye have our protection."

She gasped. "Is this a continuation of your bad mood or a new one?" She licked her lips again and steeled her spine. "Maybe I don't need a brooch. Maybe there's a way to find the light without going inside the cave."

"Ensley!" David snapped. "Do *not* mess with the light. We don't know enough about it yet. I'm president of MacCorp, and I order ye to stay away from the cave."

"You're not in a position to do that," she said. "Erik—" All eyes turned toward her, and she realized she had spoken more sharply than she meant to.

"This isn't about Erik," David said. "It's about yer safety and that of the clan. The Illuminati might know about the light and are already waiting for someone to walk through it. For God's sake, don't do something that could bring us all down."

Austin rolled his tongue around his cheek and raised his eyebrows, the equivalent of rolling his eyes behind her back, and she turned her fury on him.

"So…what? You're on their side?"

"There's only one side here, Ensley," Austin said. "And for what it's worth, I've been on the receiving end of David's dictates, and it only stings for a few minutes. He doesn't throw his title around unless it's important."

Silence descended on the room for a moment. Then, realizing this wasn't a battle she wanted to fight, she said, "Okay. I'll stay away from the cave."

Meredith put her arm around Ensley and hugged her. "It means a lot to me that you're willing to take on Elliott to get what you want. He won't invite you, but I will. You and Austin are more than welcome to join us. But the trip won't be easy, and it might be too much on your hip."

Ensley snugged against Meredith's shoulder. "Nothing I've done lately has been easy, and my hip pain is part of my life. I'll deal with it, but I can't go to the Himalayas dressed like this. I have to go shopping. Is there a store nearby?"

"There's a women's clothes closet at the house packed with outfits for different sizes, seasons, and circumstances. You're welcome to use whatever you find."

"You're the same size as JL and Sophia," Charlotte said. "And it'll be warm and humid in Bhutan, so look for cotton pants, cotton shirts, soft-soled shoes, maybe a lightweight wool sweater. Oh, and yoga pants to wear on the plane. You'll want to be comfortable."

"I don't have any money with me." She looked at Austin. "Will you float me a loan?"

Charlotte chuckled. "We don't want your money. The next time you're here, you can leave something behind to replace what you borrowed."

"Which will be an improvement over the clothes you'll find in the closet," Meredith said, giving Ensley a level look. "You're a New York City editor. The women who leave things in the closet are all moms with young children, so don't expect runway fashions."

Ensley didn't think Meredith realized how condescending she sounded, so she gave Meredith a break instead of letting her feelings get ruffled.

"You won't find runway fashion in my apartment, either," Ensley said. "I have work clothes, jeans, and running outfits from Lululemon."

"If you ever leave anything behind from Lulu, you'll see a MacKlenna mom wearing it before you can get out the door," Kenzie said.

"That's funny," Ensley said. "Next time I'm here, I'll be sure to leave a pair of yoga pants."

"I'll notify the flight crew and then contact the Bridge to Bhutan Tour Company to arrange visas, a tour guide, and hotel reservations," David said. "I've done this for both Jack and James Cullen, so I have connections to make it happen quickly. Just to confirm, seven of ye are going. Elliott, Meredith, JC, Paul, Charlotte, Austin, and Ensley. Right?"

"Should be eight," Remy grumbled from his bed.

Charlotte's lip twitched. "If you're expecting pain meds, Remy, then you should be a good patient and rest for a while."

Remy made a snoring sound, and that did make Charlotte smile.

Kenzie put her hands on Ensley's back and pushed her toward the door. "I'm taking you upstairs. You have just enough time to pick through the closet, take a shower, and be at the door on time. Elliott's known for leaving people behind."

Before they reached the door, Paul emerged from the locker room wearing khakis and a green MacCorp polo shirt, looking like a classic leading man—magnificently tall, muscular, and handsome, with a warm brown sugar skin tone. He smelled like ginger, amber, and cedar with a top note of orange blossom, and his thick black hair was perfectly styled.

"Wow, Paul!" Ensley said, shaking and blowing her hand as if she'd burned it. "Lookin' good!"

He shot the rolled cuffs of his long sleeve shirt as if he was wearing a dress shirt. "That suit I was wearing came from the wardrobe collection at George Washington University's theater department. It was too tight, too short, and too uncomfortable to wear any longer, and the hairstyle was grotesque."

Ensley laughed. "I agree you looked pretty rough, but you've more than made up for it now."

He surprised her by kissing her cheek. "You're sweet for saying that, Ensley."

"Hell, Brodie. Leave my girl alone," Austin said, winking at her.

Paul's black brows lifted, smiling. "O'Grady, you don't have to worry about me."

Austin held up his fist, Paul bumped it, and then they gave each other a dude-hug.

"I know I don't, and I got your back."

"Thanks, bro," Paul said, then headed toward JC's bed, reshooting his sleeves.

Ensley didn't have an opinion about Paul before, but now she saw something in his eyes that told her he'd been walking on a tightrope and had finally made it to the other side. Now she had an opinion of him—a favorable one—and she trusted him to care for JC.

After a moment to let those thoughts settle in her heart, she turned back to Austin. "What are you going to do?"

"I'll come with you. If you think a cleaned-up Paul looks good, wait till you see me."

Kenzie cracked up. "You know, Austin. I haven't seen your scruffy face in anything except a basketball uniform, running shorts, or jeans with boots that lost their shine back in the '90s since Rick and Penny's wedding. I better be sitting down when you get spruced up again. I might faint when I see how gorgeous you are."

He put his arm around her and squeezed. "I'll be sure to remind you. It would suck to bend all the way down to pick you up off the floor."

"Austin," David hollered. "Ye have to call JL and Pops before ye leave town again."

"Okay, I'll call them."

"Now!" David said.

Ensley stood on tiptoe and tugged on Austin's shirt to get him to lean down so she could kiss him. "I'll see you later. After I shower, I want to call Barb and George. They've been worrying long enough."

"Remember to blame it all on me." He kissed her back. "I'll see you in about thirty minutes."

Ensley left the cleanroom with Kenzie, walked through a game room, and climbed the stairs to the mansion's main floor. She'd been to the McCabes' Southern plantation-style home before but hadn't been in the guest wing, set apart by an oak door with a keypad.

Kenzie punched in a code.

"Why's the door locked?"

Kenzie held the door for Ensley. "There are six suites here, plus the men's and women's clothes closets and a well-stocked kitchenette. Everything down this hallway is an adult-only space. That keeps it quiet for—shall I say—afternoon naps. Each bedroom has a private garden."

"Sounds like Charlotte is serious about keeping it a restful retreat."

"We all are. So, after several years of trying to keep the kids out, we finally voted on installing a lock. The code is 6423, and it changes on the first of every month. Braham sends out text messages with the new code."

"How'd the kids react?"

"Braham tried to explain that it was a lesson in respecting boundaries. They didn't buy it. So in return, they demanded a place of their own. They now have a pool house, and no one over eighteen can enter. But for everyone's safety, Braham has security cameras in there so he can see everything that goes on."

Ensley walked through the door and sighed. "This has a spa feel, and the pastel color scheme immediately lowers your blood pressure."

"The guys say it's too feminine, but as soon as they enter a bedroom and strip down, they don't think about anything but sex."

"Thanks for the warning." If that's how the men reacted, Ensley had better stay away from Austin for now. "Who keeps your kids when you're gone?"

"Granny Alice, David's mom. She's lived with us since Robbie and Henry were born. She's a godsend."

"You're lucky to have her."

Kenzie entered the first room on the right and picked up a clipboard. "This is the kitchenette, and this is the list of available rooms. Pick one and sign and date next to the suite number. It's yours as long as you're here unless Meredith and Elliott need a room, and then the youngest couple gets booted out."

"How democratic. If you get booted out, do you have to sleep in a tent?"

"No. The Kellys, Bairds, and Grants all have extra rooms, or you can ask for the Cabin. But Charlotte is particular about who stays there. I don't know why. But if you get the key, you know you're special." She handed the clipboard to Ensley. "Pick a room and sign your name. And before you ask, they all have the same layout and the same furniture but are all decorated differently. And they all open up to a Monet-style garden. I recommend you start at Room One and work your way around each time you're here. David and I like Room Three best, and if it's available, we always stay there. It's got the McCabe tartan flair to it that he likes."

"Okay, I'll take Room One." Ensley signed and dated the form and then looked around the kitchenette. "I'm dying for some chocolate mint ice cream."

"There's ice cream in there, but I don't know what kind. You can check after I give you the tour." She crossed the room and opened another door. "This is the women's closet. If you can't find what you need, I'll ask Charlotte. We raid her closet in emergencies, like when Elliott demands we dress for dinner."

"I'd never feel comfortable invading her personal space." Ensley stood in front of a rack of hanging dresses, shirts, and jackets and slowly swiped through them, checking sizes.

"I'll leave you here," Kenzie said. "Room One is across the hall. You'll find visitors' bags in the bathroom closet. The bags contain all the toiletries you'll need. After you finish shopping in the women's closet, take a long shower, and don't worry about depleting the hot water tank. You can't. David and I tried one night. Call me on the desk phone if you need me. Just dial 0-3."

Ensley hugged her. "Thanks for everything."

"I was new here once and know how it feels. Just make yourself at home."

Kenzie left her to pick through the neatly folded running clothes, jog bras, shorts, and leggings. Ensley pulled out items to try on and found a drawer full of panties from Victoria's Secret with the price tags still attached. "Man, what a closet." There were also racks of shoes and boots, and she found running shoes and hiking boots to fit. Then she gathered up what she planned to wear on the airplane and crossed the hallway to Room One.

The white and pale green suite smelled like hyacinths. Double doors led to a private garden with a lily pond, and natural light filled the room with warmth.

I might never leave.

The tension she didn't realize she was carrying in her neck and shoulders seeped out like a squirrelly balloon losing air.

The bathroom was just as calming. She found the visitors' bags in the closet and helped herself to one of them. The bag held travel sizes of everything she needed, from shampoo to a toothbrush.

She stripped out of the Victorian day dress and walked into the marbled shower, where she stayed until her mental timer rang, forcing her to turn off the blissfully hot water.

After moisturizing, she slipped into a blue cotton robe, wrapped her hair in a towel, and walked out to find Austin in a yoga cobra pose on the floor, wearing only a pair of boxer briefs.

Her heart swelled, and she couldn't take her eyes off him, but she somehow managed to squeak out a question, "How often do you do yoga?" Of course, that wasn't the question she wanted to ask, and it sounded so stupid.

What she wanted to ask was if he'd like to have sex. His answer would be yes, the same as hers, and they'd be late, and Elliott would leave them behind.

"I start every day with a few poses to loosen up. If I didn't, I'd only be able to limp to the shower." From the cobra pose, he moved into the bow pose.

"Damn, you put me to shame." She stood in front of the French door, looking out at the lily pond while watching his reflection in the glass. "Did you talk to Pops and JL?"

He pushed onto his hands and knees and up into a downward dog pose. "I did, and JL can't wait to talk to you."

She glanced back over her shoulder. After a good stretch, Austin walked his hands to his feet and slowly rolled up into a standing position. She had to look away again, gulping at the size of his package. Damn, he was huge.

He walked into the bathroom and turned on the water. "Everybody is excited to meet the woman who changed my life."

She followed him, stopping at the open door. "I didn't change anything. Your family just didn't know how happy you were before you went back in time. I hope you'll tell them about your project so I won't have to live a lie."

He shucked his briefs, and she tried to look away, but it was impossible. The scars on his leg, knee, and up to his hip were blemishes on a perfectly sculpted body and did nothing to distract from his…arousal.

"I wouldn't say I was happy, but I wasn't unhappy…if that makes sense," he said, stepping into the shower.

"It does to me."

The shower door closed, and she walked out to the enclosed lily pond and sat on a stone bench, hoping the breeze would cool her off. She unwrapped her hair and ran her fingers through the damp strands, unable to get the sight of him out of her mind. He had been so gentle with her for days now, and she was no longer afraid of his size or how they would fit together. Instead, she knew exploring would be fun and exciting.

Fifteen minutes later, Austin walked out with a towel wrapped around his waist.

She slapped her hand over her eyes. "Are you having fun parading around me only half-dressed?"

He pulled her hand away. "I'm hoping that you'll get used to seeing me half-dressed, and I won't seem so intimidating."

She grinned. "It's working!"

"Good." He headed toward the locked door. "I'm going to the clothes closet to find something to wear. Unless…you want me to watch so *I* won't be intimidated."

She burst out laughing. "All five feet, two inches of me."

He just stood there, folded his arms, and his gaze traveled up her body, slowly, leisurely, pausing for a moment on her covered breasts. But even before he got there, her breathing was disordered, agitated, her nipples were tight, and her breasts were quivering slightly.

"You might only be five two, but, man, that's five feet, two inches of honor, courage, and commitment."

As soon as she stopped laughing, she said, "I sure do have you fooled."

"There's nothing about you that would fool anyone who took the time to look beyond how damn cute you are."

"Cute? Really?"

His smile reached his eyes, and they were brighter, livelier than she'd ever seen them. "You're beautiful, Ensley. Inside out and all around."

"I wasn't fishing for compliments."

"And I'm not handing them out lightly." He kissed the top of her head. "I'll be back after I get dressed."

"Are there pants in the men's closet to fit you?"

"Yep. We always leave dirty clothes behind."

"And somebody cleans them?"

"We pay into a guest wing account every time we stay here, which pays for cleaning, meals, and alcohol. Since family members are here almost daily, Elliott had a guest wing account set up. It pays for a full-time housekeeper and keeps the kitchenette stocked."

"You'll have to float me another loan."

"I can afford it, but if I had sold my manuscript, I'd have money to pay for both of our airfares to Bhutan."

"Oh, I hadn't thought of that. I can write an IOU."

Austin laughed. "Everyone who went on this adventure has a stake in the treasure we found."

"But we can't sell any of it."

"We'll find something to sell. If we didn't make money on adventures, we couldn't keep having them. The last one the family went on, Sophia sketched what she saw, and when she came home, she painted pictures of Andrew Jackson and the Battle of New Orleans. She made millions from her Andrew Jackson exhibit. The adventure before that, Sophia attended a dinner with Thomas Jefferson, Alexander Hamilton, and James Madison. She had sketches for a Founding Fathers exhibit from that dinner alone, along with enough firsthand information for Jack to write a Broadway play. The exhibit and play made millions."

"He wrote *Dinner on Maiden Lane* from firsthand information? Damn. No wonder it seemed so realistic."

Austin picked up the T-shirt she'd picked out to wear on the plane with yoga pants. "I saw a picture of JL wearing this. It's a good color for you, too."

Ensley laughed. "It's a blue T-shirt. It looks good on everybody."

Austin gave her a cocky grin. "I thought it would sound dumb if I told my girlfriend that JL's T-shirt would look good on her. Forget I said anything."

"Girlfriend? I can't believe you just called me your girl...*friend*. Last time you just called me your girl."

"Well, aren't you?"

"I haven't thought about a name for what's going on here. But as long as it doesn't mean I've been demoted, it's fine."

He tightened the towel around his waist. "If I had clothes on, I'd hug you."

"If you had clothes on, I'd hug *you*. Go get dressed while I dry my hair."

"No," he said, "That's my job."

She flicked her damp hair over her shoulder. "Is this a thing you do with the women you date?"

He picked up a few strands of hair and sniffed them. "Hmmm. Other than my cousins, I've never combed, much less dried a woman's hair."

"Never?"

He shook his head, grinning, and let the strands fall gently over her shoulder. "You're the one and only."

"Okay." She managed to walk back into the bathroom without her suddenly weak knees collapsing. She dropped onto a stool and held out the hairdryer. "Have at it."

"Hand me the brush." He turned on the hairdryer and, using the round brush, began to blow out her hair.

"I can't believe you enjoy this."

"It turns me on."

"Well, I'm not sure what to say about that. So, to change the subject, why do you call JL by her nickname instead of Mom?"

He stood there a moment, looking at Ensley in the mirror. "To me, my mom is Maggie O'Grady. I was just a baby when she died. But when anyone mentioned her in my presence, which was often, they'd say they were sorry that I never knew my mom. As I grew older, I told people my mom died, but JL took care of me.

"When I discovered JL was my mother and not my sister, I was pissed as hell. I eventually got over the betrayal, but the word 'mom' still belongs to Maggie."

He paused, as if he was struggling with it all, and then continued, "I think I felt guilty that maybe having me had hastened her death. But honestly, Jeff, Shane, Connor, and Rick were my idols, and I didn't want to be different from them. And then it got to the point that it didn't matter. I mean, my real dad is Chris Dalton, and I call him Chris, and Pops will always be Pops. Does that make sense?"

"It does to me. I have Erik, and I'll never call him Dad. Plus, I have these weird proclamations and a legacy I don't understand."

She gazed back at Austin in the mirror and let her eyes drift down his chest, but that's as far as she could see, missing the evidence of his arousal. He had a cheeky little quirk in the corner of his mouth, and she wanted to kiss it. He must have known how sexy he looked because his expression didn't change while he methodically moved from one section of her head to another. The warm air and gentle tugging on her head almost lulled her to sleep.

"It's not completely dry, but if you want to call your cousin, you should go ahead and make the call." He turned off the hairdryer, rolled up the cord, and put it away in the cabinet.

She eased up out of the chair and was tempted to turn around and kiss him but restrained herself. If she kissed him now, they wouldn't stop with one kiss, and she refused to start something they couldn't finish.

"Go get dressed," she said, stepping away from the temptation.

"I'll be back in five minutes. There's an iPad on the desk if you want to FaceTime with your cousin and your friend."

Guilt tightened her lungs, and she cleared her throat. "I'm not sure what to tell them. I'm a terrible liar, and they'll see right through any attempt to obfuscate."

"If you get tongue-tied over a lie, leave it to me. I've gotten pretty good at it lately."

"I hope that doesn't mean you've been lying to me."

"Never. But you know I've been lying to the family. And I plan to use you to keep them from staying pissed at me."

"So I'm your easy way out?"

"Not at all. You're my redemption, and everyone will be happy for us." Austin kissed the top of her head again before leaving the room, still wearing a towel and nothing else. It was a good thing the wing was a certified adult-only area.

She hurriedly dressed in yoga pants and a T-shirt, then sat on the floor, stretching and breathing deeply, visualizing her phone call with George.

The next few minutes would be hell. She could wait for Austin, but she needed to do this herself or at least try. If she muddled it up, then she'd let him straighten it out.

She sat at the desk and FaceTimed George. He answered the call immediately. When he saw her, his jaw unhinged.

"Ensley! Where the hell are you?" He reached out as if he could drag her through the screen. "God, I've been going nuts for three days."

The thought of lying made her throat constrict, and she'd likely choke on what she said next. "I'm sorry you've been so worried. I'm at MacKlenna Ranch outside of Denver," she said, making it up on the fly. "And I'm fine."

"Why'd you wait so long to call? The entire family has been worried sick."

"The bottom line is that I'm in love with Austin O'Grady." She didn't choke on that, even though it surprised the hell out of her. But it seemed so right, so perfect, so natural.

A moment of silence before George's jaw unhinged again, and then his entire countenance turned into a big-ass pissed-off face. She hadn't seen that expression since she bested him in a Medora shooting contest.

"O'Grady? JC's cousin? In only three days in Colorado?"

Austin walked in just in time to hear George's questions. "Yep, George, that's me. I kidnapped your cousin. I was pissed as hell that she rejected my manuscript, so I secretly brought her here and held her against her will until she admitted she made a mistake. In the process of shredding my book word by word, she discovered she'd fallen in love with the author, and I fell in love with the editor."

Ensley couldn't tell if George was buying this explanation or not, but when his pissed-off faced didn't change, she had her answer.

"Where's JC? He should have told me."

"He doesn't know about us. We went hunting the other day. I'm surprised Austin gave me a gun, but he did. A grizzly came out of the woods, and I didn't have the gun nearby. Austin shot it, or I'd be dead."

"No, you wouldn't. You'd be safe in New York City."

"George, I know it's hard to understand, but Austin wouldn't let me near a phone until I explained every objection I had to his manuscript. We talked for three straight days, and at the end of it, we realized our perceived differences didn't hold up in light of how much we have in common."

"You have never wanted to be around athletes. What happened?"

"Austin happened, and I discovered he had more than a pair of talented hands that could effortlessly nail a silky three-pointer from anywhere on the court."

"Well, it sounds like you talked about more than his manuscript. I've never heard you say anything about a three-pointer." He sighed. "I can't forgive you yet, nor can I spare you the discomfort of explaining your absence to your uncle. So call Dad after we hang up."

"It's hard enough telling you. There's no way I can call your dad."

"Too bad, Ensley. You owe him an explanation. And I'm not letting you off the hook with Dad or Barb."

"Gee, thanks, George. Don't do me any favors."

"What the hell, Ensley? After what you've put us through, it will be a hell of a long time before anyone does you any favors."

Austin slapped his hand on the top of the desk. "That's enough, George. You can be pissed off all you want, but what's important here is Ensley's happiness. And if she's found it, then how she got there doesn't mean shit. You can get over it, or you can become a distant relative. You decide."

"Get off the phone, O'Grady. I don't want to look at your face while I talk to my cousin."

"George, look, I'm so sorry," she said.

"The asshole kidnapped you, and I'll have it out with JC."

"He's going back to the monastery for a while. You'll have to wait."

"He's going again? Well, I'll call him right now."

"He can't take your call, George. He's not talking to anyone, and he's flying out within the hour."

"What the hell's going on with you two? You're both losing it."

She took it as a rhetorical question and didn't answer him. George had always been an unmovable object when it came to disagreements. But he was carrying it to an extreme right now. The best thing to do was to change the subject.

"What about Barb? Where is she?" Ensley asked.

"She just left to meet a couple of friends. They plan to canvas another neighborhood close to the university. She's going to be so pissed."

"I'll call her now."

"The police might want to talk to you, too."

"If they call me, I'll answer their questions. But I need to get my stuff out of the Cambridge house."

"Barb took everything to your apartment."

"Oh, good. Well…okay. I'll call you when I get back to the city."

"Don't you have to get back to work?"

"I got laid off Thursday. I don't have a job right now."

"Why didn't you tell me?" he asked, almost sounding sympathetic, and if she was only listening to him, she could believe it, but his scowl had deepened.

"The truth is that I didn't know until I arrived in Cambridge. And why aren't you happy for me?"

"Happy? Are you kidding? Asking that question just shows how selfish you are. We've gone through hell because of you."

"I'm sorry about that, George," Austin said. "Next time you see me, I'll give you a free swing. You can knock the shit out of me."

Ensley gasped. "Please don't hit him. I've already given Austin a hard enough time over what he did."

George's phone rang. "That's Barb. I'm hanging up so you can call her."

He disconnected, and Ensley slumped in the chair. "I knew he'd be pissed, but it's way worse than I thought. I guess I was a little naïve. But I hate putting all this blame on you."

"I've got big enough shoulders to carry it. Seriously, don't worry about it. I'd rather they blame me than you or JC."

While Ensley debated her next move—call Barb or her uncle—a call came in. "That's Barb's number."

"Take it," Austin said.

She clicked on the FaceTime button. "Hi, Barb."

Angry lines had formed around Barb's mouth, but it was the circles under her eyes that bothered Ensley more. Barb hadn't slept much, and Ensley was responsible for that. And it was something else to feel guilty about.

"What the hell? I've been scared to death. Where are you now?"

"Didn't George tell you?"

Barb shook her head. "No, he only said he just got off the phone with you and that you weren't dead!"

"He's pissed."

"You betcha. So where'd you go?"

Ensley glanced up at Austin. "Austin O'Grady kidnapped me, and I'm at his ranch in Colorado."

Barb drew back, but her eyes remained fixed on Ensley. "He whaaat?"

"He was furious that I turned down his manuscript, and he wasn't going to let me go until I understood what he'd written."

"Austin O'Grady? The basketball player?"

"Yep."

"When'd he let you go?"

Ensley beckoned for Austin to come back into view.

"Hi, Barb. I'm Austin O'Grady."

Barb nearly jumped out of her chair. "OMG! How'd you even convince her to talk to you? Athletes drive her nuts."

"She thought I was an asshole, but she discovered I'm also a nice guy."

Barb was looking at Austin with dreamy eyes, and Ensley almost laughed.

"So what do you think of my friend?" Barb asked.

Without missing a beat, he said, "I'm in love with her."

"Whaaat? Did I hear you right? You're in love with her? That's impossible. She'd never be nice enough for an athlete to fall in love with her."

"Well, she discovered I'm not all brawn, that I have brains and beauty, too."

"So you like her?"

"No, I'm in love with her, Barb. She's one badass babe, and I don't plan to let her out of my sight."

"Wow! I'm impressed. So, Ens, are you ever coming back to the city?"

"I'll be there in a couple of days to gather up a few things, and then I'm coming back to Austin's ranch for a while."

"You're what?" Barb exclaimed.

"I'm going to live in Colorado for a while."

"That's what I thought you said, but what about your job?"

"I got laid off right before I talked to you the other night."

"And you didn't tell me?"

"I have several sins to confess." She came close to telling Barb that she was going with JC to Bhutan but stopped herself. Barb would compare stories later with George, and if she said she was going with JC, that would contradict what she told George. Lying was the pits.

Barb leaned closer to the screen. "I can't wait to meet your superstar in person."

Austin gave Barb one of his special-edition crooked grins. "I'll invite you and George over for dinner as soon as we get to the city."

"Where's your apartment?" she asked.

"I don't have one. I always stay at the house the family owns on 107th and Riverside."

Barb scratched her chin, looking up. "I think… Ensley, didn't you point that out once during a run through Riverside Park?"

"I did. JC told me about it, but I've never been inside. I look forward to dinner there."

Austin leaned over and whispered, "I hope you'll stay there."

Ensley's cheeks heated.

"I don't know what Austin just said to you, but it certainly pinked your cheeks," Barb teased. "Any man who can get that kind of reaction from you is a special guy. George and I will be there with bells on."

Ensley grimaced. "George isn't happy with me right now. He might not come."

"Oh, he'll come," Barb said with a wave. "And when I see you, I'll expect to hear the whole story."

"There's not that much to tell," Austin said.

"Bullshit," Barb said. "I've heard all about you, O'Grady. You better be good to my friend, or else…"

He stroked Ensley's shoulder, and she leaned into his hand. "Don't worry. I'll always put her interests first."

"Do you believe him, Ens?"

Ensley looked up, surprised. No, that was hardly the word she'd use. It was more like she was dumbfounded. "Yes, I do."

"That's all I need to hear. I'll see you soon. But damn, girl, get some sleep. You look exhausted, and you desperately need a haircut and facial. If I didn't know better, I'd say you'd been living outside for six weeks, but you've only been gone three days. That man's wearing you out."

"I know I'm tired but didn't realize I look *that* bad."

Austin kissed the top of her head. "We're both exhausted, but you still look gorgeous."

"Damn. If a man ever said that about me, I'd never get out of his bed."

Barb wouldn't believe Ensley hadn't jumped into bed with such a hot guy, so she changed the subject. "Before I go, tell me about you and George. I guess you missed dinner at the Polo Bar?"

"We canceled and agreed to reschedule. Most of the time, we ate what we could grab while we searched for you. Being together made worrying about you easier to handle."

"Well, I'm glad I could help you out."

"Nuh-uh. You're not getting off that easily. Austin was wrong not to let you call us. And if you had time to fall in love, then you had time to call."

"You're right. I'll talk to you soon." Ensley disconnected the call as tears welled in her eyes.

He squatted to be eye level with her. "Look. You did the best you could. No one likes the lying part. Kit lied to Emily's mother, and Charlotte lied to Abraham Lincoln. Sophia lied to Thomas Jefferson and Andrew Jackson. Penny lied to Jean Lafitte, and Kenzie lied to Alan Turing at Bletchley Park. Amber lied to a judge, and Amy lied to Baseball Hall of Famers. It's never easy, but it's necessary."

"And I lied to Theodore Roosevelt. If I have any regrets, it's that I didn't get enough time with him. But thank you for taking the blame today. It made it easier, although I'm not sure they completely bought the story."

"We'll have to fine-tune it before we have dinner with them." Austin's phone beeped, and he checked his message. "Elliott's ready."

"Let me just pull a bag off the shelf and pack the clothes I found to wear."

"Come on. I'll get it off the shelf for you. But if you want to read on the plane, pack up that iPad."

"Are you sure? Shouldn't I ask someone?"

"Nah. They won't care. Just bring it back."

Ensley grabbed one of the toiletry bags out of the bathroom, then crossed the hall to gather up the clothes and shoes she intended to take. A small closet held handbags, beach bags, and duffels. She used a hanger to loop around the handle of the duffel and yanked it off the shelf. When she turned around, Austin was standing in the doorway, grinning.

"Why are you standing there? You could have pulled it down for me."

"You were too cute, jumping up and down with a coat hanger."

"Well, how in the hell do you expect vertically challenged individuals to reach something on a top shelf? We have to improvise."

He picked up the bag. "If you say so." His phone rang, and he looked at the caller ID. "It's Uncle Rick. I better take the call."

"Go. I have to pack."

Austin stepped out, and she folded her clothes and packed everything in the duffel. She was zipping up the bag when he returned.

"Ready."

She slung the strap over her shoulder, but Austin took it from her. "My uncles Rick, Connor, Jeff, and Shane had a bet going. They heard we were back in town and wanted to know who fell in love with you."

"Why'd they expect me to fall in love?"

"That's part of brooch lore. Didn't Kenzie tell you?"

She shook her head. "I don't think so."

"Brooches bring soul mates together. And my uncles had a bet on who your mate would be—JC, Tavis, Remy, or me."

"Who won?"

"Nobody thought it would be me. But Shane drew my name and won the pot."

"How much did he win?"

"Five grand."

"Grand! Like five thousand dollars? Damn. Remind me never to bet with them."

"They'll catch you sooner or later and offer a bet you can't refuse."

"God, I hope not. But what'd your uncle say?"

"He's happy for me and looks forward to seeing you again."

Ensley followed Austin out into the hallway, mentally reviewing the items she packed and wondering if she missed anything. Underwear and socks? Check. Toiletries? Check. Hiking boots? Check. Jacket? Check. Pajamas? Check.

"Did you pack a gown or PJs? David made hotel reservations, but I don't know if he bunked you with Charlotte or with me."

"Either way, I'd need PJs," she teased. "And yes, I packed them. I found two pairs in the closet. One was sexy, and the other was practical."

"My brother Connor's wife, Olivia, would have left the sexy ones, and Sophia would have left the practical ones."

"How do you know something that personal?"

"The guys talk, and I know the women do, too. I've been around this family since I was sixteen, except for the past couple of years. Even when I was playing ball, I had a cheering section at every game. It feels great to be back in the fold. I've missed them."

"They can be overwhelming," she said.

"That's because everybody has their noses in everyone else's business. The older generation believes their experiences have more value, but if you can get past that, they're damn good people."

He escorted her to the front door, where Meredith was waiting. "Where's everybody else?" he asked.

"Braham and Paul rolled JC out and put him in a van with Charlotte, and Elliott went to get the car for us. We'll see the others on the plane." Then she looked at Ensley. "Did you find what you wanted in the closet?"

"That room is incredible. I found everything I need, from PJs to sandals."

"It's like a five-star hotel around here." Meredith opened the door. "Let's wait outside. If the kids see Austin, they'll get so excited we'll have to leave you two behind. He's a hero to them, and he won't be able to break loose."

Ensley looked up at him. "A hero, huh?"

He grinned. "The kids are all student-athletes and want me to play with them. It's fun."

"Maybe when we come back, we can challenge them to a game."

"*You* play basketball?"

She laughed. "Yeah, on a midget team." Ensley followed Meredith out to the circular drive in front of the mansion just as a black Mercedes-Maybach SUV pulled up.

"You want me to drive, Elliott?" Austin asked through the open window.

"Meredith doesn't let me drive her car very often. So, no, I don't."

Austin opened the front and rear doors simultaneously to let Ensley and Meredith climb in, then lifted the tailgate and dropped the bags in the back before climbing in next to Ensley.

"Ye got enough room back there?" Elliott asked.

"I never have enough room in a car, but I'm okay for now. But I want to claim one of the single seats, so I'll have plenty of space to stretch out on the plane. And Ensley will want one of the foldout sofas. She'll sleep through most of the flight."

"That sounds wonderful, but will we have time to go inside the airport to get something to eat before we board?"

Meredith turned around in her seat. "On long-haul flights, we always have Michelin star dining. I'm sure you'll find something you like on the menu."

Ensley always knew JC was wealthy, but a private jet with exceptional cuisine was more in line with billionaires than millionaires. She might not sleep through the entire flight after all. And then she remembered JC and had that I-feel-guilty flutter in her belly. This trip wasn't about her creature comforts but JC's mental health.

"I'm sure I will," Ensley said. "But a hot dog is fine with me."

Austin took her hand and kissed the back of it. "Hot dogs work for me, too, but there's always salmon, and it's outstanding."

"I'll give it a try." But as she envisioned climbing aboard a private jet, she realized she had a problem. "Wait a minute! I can't go. I don't have my passport."

"David took care of it," Elliott said. "He has a counterfeit operation in the cleanroom. He made ye a new one."

"Isn't that like…illegal?"

"Ye'll learn, lass, that sometimes we wander into the gray zone to do what we do. Ye needed a passport, so he made ye one with yer name, address, birthday. He didn't create a new identity for ye. He just made a duplicate."

She decided not to point out that making a forgery wasn't just stepping into the gray zone. It was committing a felony. At least she thought so, but in the past few days, she'd discovered she was the daughter of a twelfth-century Viking and that he had left behind what could be a billion-dollar treasure.

She leaned back in the exquisite leather seat and closed her eyes. The next thing she knew, Austin was carrying her onboard. "Sleep as long as you want." He kissed her on the lips and covered her with a blanket.

And as she fell into a deep sleep, the plane was wheels-up and on its way to Bhutan.

67

MacCorp Jet—Elliott

J AMES CULLEN SLEPT in the MacCorp jet's VIP bedroom with ensuite bathroom located in the aft section of the aircraft while Elliott, Meredith, and Paul took shifts to sit at his bedside. Charlotte wanted one, but Elliott wouldn't let her sit up with her patient, insisting that she rest as much as possible. If there was an emergency, she needed to be at the top of her game.

James Cullen woke during the refueling stop in London Luton Airport and scooted back till he was in a sitting position, asking in a groggy voice, "Why are we on the plane, Dad? Why am I in your bed? Why are you sleeping over there?"

Elliott didn't know how James Cullen would react to the plan, but he couldn't keep it from him. "Yer mom and I thought ye'd like to spend a few weeks at Tiger's Nest. We're about a third of the way to Bhutan now."

Uncertainty flickered in James Cullen's eyes. "Why'd you think that?"

Telling James Cullen that Erik suggested he go there might set him off, so Elliott dodged the question. "It means a lot to ye to be there, and ye haven't visited in a while."

James Cullen gave him a scared, wounded look, and Elliott worried that his son was about to give voice to his terrors and frighten the flight crew. If he lost control again, Charlotte would give him another injection. At least that was the plan. Or Elliott would give it to him. God knows he'd given himself plenty of them in the past.

"You're right. It's been a while." James Cullen straightened the red cloak that had tangled around him while he slept. "I don't remember when I was there last. Everything's a blur."

"What do ye remember?" As soon as Elliott asked the question, he cringed, knowing he'd made a mistake.

James Cullen's expression didn't change. "The last thing I remember was leaving Ensley with Roosevelt and taking the train to Kentucky." He stopped and looked around the room. "I think I saw her...earlier, I mean. But I don't remember where."

"She was in the cleanroom with ye. She's also on the plane with us."

"She is?" He seemed genuinely happy about that. "I went shopping for her in Chicago. Maybe she's wearing something I purchased for her."

James Cullen had the past and present confused, so Elliott had to tread carefully.

"She said the clothes are beautiful. Ye can ask her about them later. But yer mother is taking credit for yer good taste."

A sheepish, almost childlike grin split James Cullen's face. "She took credit for my taste in decorating my bedroom. She might as well take credit for my good taste in women's clothing." Then his expression changed to one of surprise. "Ensley's shirt and jeans are too dirty. They'll never get clean again. I hope she threw them away."

When James Cullen's eyes glazed over, Elliott reached out and touched his son's leg to anchor him in the present. "I'm glad ye bought her new clothes, lad, and I assure ye, she's not wearing dirty clothes right now."

Elliott hoped his tone calmed James Cullen's frantic, chaotic mind. It didn't do much to help Elliott's anxieties or the stress on his body. Right now, he couldn't hurt more if he'd been in a major car wreck. Trainer Ted would kick his ass the next time Elliott made it to the training room—which he planned to put off as long as possible.

After a long pause, James Cullen said, "I don't remember what happened after I went shopping for Ensley. It's like a black curtain drops and blocks everything that happened afterward."

He slowly slid back down the headboard until he was lying flat. "I try to lift the curtain, but when I do, my skin burns so bad I drop it and run away." James Cullen rolled over and folded into the fetal position, pulling the cloak over his head. "I don't think it's important. Do you?"

"No, lad, I don't think it's important."

James Cullen fell asleep again. It wasn't a drugged sleep, but if his vitals hadn't been so strong, Charlotte might have worried because he couldn't stay awake.

But Elliott worried, and his hatred for the scum who tortured James Cullen grew so intense that if Elliott didn't find a way to confront it, the higher stress hormone levels and heart rate could lead to a stroke.

For the longest time, he couldn't even close his eyes. He was afraid that if he did, the gift Erik gave him—his son's life—might disappear permanently.

68

MacCorp Jet—Elliott

THE MACCORP JET was airborne again after a refueling stop in England and on its way to Turkey when Meredith came into the bedroom to relieve Elliott.

He hadn't been able to sleep since they departed from Richmond, even though his body needed it. His damn brain just wouldn't shut down and give him a break from the rage and fear.

"Any change?" Meredith whispered.

"Some," he said, trying to hold his temper in check, using a soft voice, erasing the anger from it as best he could.

He eased up out of the chaise lounge, his bones cracking, and he stretched. However, it did little to relieve the tightness in his neck and shoulders or the numbness in his lower leg and foot. He hadn't mentioned the symptoms to Charlotte yet, or anyone else. He knew he was getting claudication from the stenosing graph, which would require a new graph. And while it wasn't heart surgery, it wasn't minor surgery either.

"James Cullen woke up and asked why he was on the plane."

Meredith hissed in a breath. "Uh-oh."

"I told him we were taking him to Tiger's Nest, and he seemed okay with that."

"Anything else?"

"He said he didn't remember much but did recall shopping for Ensley in Chicago. Then he curled up in the cloak like he is now and fell asleep again."

"Did he ask about the cloak?"

"No," Elliott whispered. "But he seems to know he needs it."

Meredith kissed him. "Get some sleep. I'll wake you up if there's a problem."

Elliott pulled her into his arms. "I love ye." Then he returned her kiss and left the room, passing Charlotte sleeping on one of the easy-to-berth divans and Ensley on the other. When he reached his central club seat, Aubrey, one of their two flight attendants, had already converted it into a flatbed, complete with a mint on his pillow.

"Everything okay?" Austin asked.

Elliott sat down on his bed across the aisle from Austin and removed his shoes. "Aye. The lad's calm. He can relapse, but for now, he's good. I told him we were taking him to Tiger's Nest, and he was fine with that."

"That's good, glad to hear it. But I've been thinking about what happened. Do you think the Illuminati knows about him spending time at the monastery? If so, they could find him there."

"Erik killed the connection to the Illuminati before, and he did it again in Chicago."

"But we left those other assholes alive when we escaped the train."

Elliott glanced at Austin, the overhead light illuminating his grimacing face. "When Erik left MacKlenna Farm, he said his work wasn't over." Elliott considered Austin's concern and had to admit it was alarming.

"Maybe," Elliott said, "Erik stopped in Chicago to eliminate the men on the train, and that's what detained him."

"But here's the thing, Elliott. Would Erik risk getting to Ensley too late to save her? I don't think so. I'd like to believe the assholes on the train are dead, but I don't think they are."

Aubrey stopped at Elliott's chair and picked up his shoes. "Can I get you anything, Dr. Fraser?"

"A glass of juice, please."

"How about you, Mr. O'Grady?"

"I'm good. Thanks, Aubrey."

After Aubrey returned with Elliott's juice, Austin continued, "If the assholes survived, they would likely go after JC or even Ensley. We might be setting JC up for the Illuminati to get to him again. If JC can live at the monastery to study, what's to stop someone in the Illuminati from doing the same?"

"James Cullen needs to be there. I won't let the slight possibility of danger keep him from getting the help only the monastery can provide. But I'll warn Paul to be suspicious of anyone showing special attention to James Cullen."

"But do you trust Paul to spot trouble in time?"

"Paul is a chameleon. Don't underestimate him."

"I never have. I just wanted to be sure you were on the same page."

"James Cullen and Paul have a tight bond. As the saying goes, 'Paul is the best brother from another mother.' He won't fail James Cullen."

"We should tell the entire family that the Illuminati might take a while to regroup after losing Sten, but they'll hit us again."

"I'll take care of Paul. As for the rest of us, we'll have a family meeting next week and discuss it." Elliott finished his juice and handed the glass to Aubrey when she returned with a pair of slippers. "What are ye looking at so intently on the iPad?" he asked Austin.

Austin turned around the screen for Elliott to see. "The cave photographs and videos are all uploaded, and David sent out the link. Kenzie's already at work trying to identify some of the pieces. She says it's a slog."

"I saw the link but haven't looked at the pictures yet, other than the ones Braham and I looked over before we left MacKlenna Farm."

"I've never seen anything like this," Austin said.

"After we secure the treasure, David can sell a few pieces on the black market and then anonymously donate a few pieces to the National Roman Museum. Honestly, I wouldn't mind if the treasure and the light disappeared. I have a feeling both will cause trouble for the family."

"Let's hope not."

Elliott pulled back the covers and climbed into bed. "Ye should get some sleep. The trek up the mountain won't be easy." Elliott wasn't sure he'd make it to the top, thanks to the numbness in his lower leg. And if he didn't, Charlotte would figure out why and have him in the hospital by the end of the week. He knew he wasn't in immediate danger, but she watched over his medical care like a neurotic stage mother.

"Ensley will only make it halfway. She tries to hide the pain in her hip, but I've learned the signs. If she wants to go back for Tavis, she'll have to spend time training. To do that, she has to be smart.

Climbing up the mountain to the monastery is one thing, but climbing those eight hundred steps to the entrance will be an impossible feat. But to her, quitting is synonymous with failure."

"I may have a solution," Elliott said.

"What's that?"

"I'll tell ye later. But as for Tavis, I was hoping she wouldn't want to go."

"Good luck with that. Tavis came for her, so she won't let anything get in the way of going back for him."

"Ye care for the lass. Don't ye?"

Austin turned off the iPad and put it away in the seat pocket. "It happened so fast, but what I feel for her is unlike anything I've ever experienced. I've heard stories of the weekend JL and Kevin met and what happened after the cartel kidnapped me. Our story is similar." Austin chuckled. "Although, Kevin and JL acted on their feelings immediately. That part's different."

"As her adopted father, I'm glad. But I have to admit I'm surprised it's ye she picked. If I'd participated in yer uncles' betting pool, I wouldn't have picked ye."

"Who would you have matched her with? Tavis? JC? Remy?"

"Not James Cullen. If it had been a match, they'd have hooked up years ago. But if I'd analyzed it carefully, it had to be ye."

"Why?" Austin asked. "Not that I'm objecting, but I am curious."

"Ye have a nurturing soul, lad. Ensley's drawn to that. JL has one, too, but she tries to hide behind her tough-girl persona."

"JL's a *ragazza tosta* all right." Austin pulled up the covers and adjusted his pillow.

"Ye've got yer own *ragazza tosta* now. But ye won't have the problems Kevin had. Ye and Ensley were both brought up with guns. Kevin wasn't, and he couldn't live on the edge like JL was used to living. And Ensley will like Colorado, with all its outdoor sports and hunting seasons."

"When this is over, Elliott, I want to talk about the ranch—"

"Ye want to buy it so ye can operate yer therapeutic riding center from there instead of Denver?"

Austin threw his pillow at Elliott. "Damn it! Is there anything you don't know?"

"Did ye honestly think I'd ignore ye, lad?" Elliott tossed back the pillow. "Or the ranch?"

Austin shoved the pillow under his head. "I guess not, but who else knows?"

"If anyone else knows, they didn't learn about it from me."

"Why didn't you say something before now?"

"I wasn't sure about yer motivation or yer drug use. Once I had all my facts, I would have said something to ye." Elliott slipped on an eye mask and settled down to sleep for a while, chuckling softly.

They'll make a hell of a match.

69

MacCorp Jet—Elliott

I T SEEMED TO Elliott that he'd just put on his eye mask and fallen asleep when Aubrey woke him with a gentle nudge.

"Dr. Fraser, we're an hour out from Bhutan. If you want to shower, you should do that now."

"Damn. I slept straight through the stop in Turkey. Must have been a smooth landing and takeoff." He raised his seat, yawning. "Give me a few minutes, then wake Meredith."

He went to the midcabin bathroom, took a quick shower, and as he stood at the sink shaving, he stared at himself. James Cullen had his eyes, his nose, his cheekbones, and his chin. Right now, that was all they had in common. James Cullen didn't even share his hatred for the men who tortured him.

But only because he didn't remember.

What worried Elliott most was what would happen when James Cullen's memory returned. Would his hatred for those men consume him?

Elliott gave himself one long, last look, accepting blame for all he'd done wrong, and turned away from the mirror—brokenhearted.

Meredith was waiting at the door when he walked out. "Good morning. Did ye get any sleep?"

"Not much, but enough to get me through the day." They switched places in the narrow hallway. "Tell Aubrey I'd like my regular breakfast in ten minutes."

He kissed her. "Anything for my bride." They hadn't shared a bed in days, and he missed having her naked body next to him. She turned him on as much after almost thirty years of marriage as she had when they first met. And he desperately needed that closeness now. Their intimate life had a way of removing the inevitable chill between them caused by their intense, controlling personalities. And when they shortchanged that part of their lives, the chill turned frigid rather quickly.

Right now, their relationship wasn't chilly or even frigid, but it wasn't warm either. The only cure would be uninterrupted time together to talk, make love, share a meal, or saddle up and go for a long ride.

By the time he returned to his seat, Ensley and Charlotte were digging through their carry-on bags, and Austin had covered his head with a quilt. He might as well sleep a few minutes longer since the women would keep the bathroom occupied for a while.

Elliott's breakfast and coffee were waiting for him, and he sighed at the first sip of the hot brew. He quickly ate a bowl of oatmeal and scrolled through his emails while enjoying a dish of fresh fruit. When he finished, he went back to the bedroom to check on James Cullen.

Meredith was sitting on the divan where Ensley had slept, lacing up a pair of hiking boots. She held up her leg to block him from entering the bedroom. "Remain calm. Do not react."

He stepped over her leg. "React to what?"

"I'm not saying. I want you to experience the same shock I got." She flicked her hand. "Go on in."

What could shock him at this point? "Thanks for the warning." But he did steel himself for the unknown. When it came to his son, it could be anything from making a million dollars overnight to giving away a million. He was often unpredictable but never destructive or vengeful.

Elliott knocked and opened the door without waiting for a polite "Come in." His feet froze to the threshold. He couldn't move forward, and he couldn't retreat, which was what he wanted to do. But he managed to eke out a "Good morning."

James Cullen sat on the end of the bed, wrapped in the red cloak, a short, white jacket underneath it, stockings, and handmade boots. Paul had shopped for both of them during the plane's refueling stop at Luton. They were dressed identically, except Paul's cotton cloak was multi-colored.

What shocked Elliott was not their clothes. It was their shaved faces and heads.

Elliott looked away, overwhelmed by the grief that crashed upon him. The absence of his son's thick, dark brown hair was symbolic of the loss he was experiencing, and he came close to throwing up.

"We'll be landing soon," was all Elliott managed to say.

"Aubrey told us when she brought our breakfast," Paul said.

"Good. Ye've eaten. Well… See ye on the ground, then." Elliott returned to his seat across from Meredith. "Ye should have told me he shaved his head."

"And deprive you of the shock? No way. But I didn't hear you yelling."

"I think I bit my tongue in half." He opened his mouth and wagged his tongue. "Is it all still there?"

Meredith grinned. "I'm glad you didn't lose your sense of humor."

"I don't have one anymore. The brooches have destroyed what little I had."

"Trust me. You still have one, and it's usually quite charming," she teased. "At least *I* think so."

"So what was yer reaction?"

"I had to sit down, but you know, his shaved head goes well with the red cloak. He looks the part."

"I'd rather see him at a gala wearing a tux. He always looked the part of a dashing entrepreneur."

"I don't think we'll see *that* James Cullen for a long time."

Elliott sighed. "Let's give him six months. If he's not better, or at least on the road to recovery—"

"We can't bring him back to see a psychiatrist. What would he say? 'I was tortured by the Illuminati and would have died if not for a twelfth-century Viking.' They wouldn't treat him. They'd lock him up."

"We can consider other options."

"Like what?" she asked. "Go back and try to undo what happened to him? We've already talked about this, and I'll never agree to the plan. So don't bring it up again, or—"

"Or? What? Don't give me an ultimatum, Meredith. If I think it's best for James Cullen and the family…" He'd made his point, so he let the sentence die away.

Her brows slanted down like an angry eagle and her left cheek quivered with fury. "Is that a threat?"

He carefully chose a one-word response and the tone in which he delivered it. "Aye."

She gripped the arms of the chair until her knuckles turned

white. "I can't believe we're having this discussion after what we've been through."

"Then let's not have it!"

Elliott took deep breaths while his muscles knotted and every part of him fumed. He craved vengeance for what the Illuminati did to his family.

But taking it out on Meredith was wrong, and he damn well knew it.

70

Bhutan—Elliott

MacCorp's pilots were certified to make the manual by-daylight-only approach between 18,000-foot peaks, through a long, winding valley, and onto a runway that was only visible moments before landing.

Welcome to Bhutan's Paro International Airport, frequently featured on lists of the world's most dangerous airports. It seemed appropriate that they landed here today. The aura of danger around the people inside the plane matched the threat outside.

As soon as the engines shut down, lap belts came off. *Click! Click! Click!*

James Cullen and Paul were the first to deplane, and Elliott followed close behind. But as soon as he stepped out of the plane, the altitude and humidity hit him with a *wallop*. He almost turned around and went back into the plane, but he couldn't—or wouldn't—do that.

"Dad, you don't have to go up the mountain. Paul and I can manage."

Elliott hadn't even said anything, yet his son sensed his distress. "Yer mother and I want to go. We've heard of Tiger's Nest for years and want to visit the monastery. We'll adjust to the higher altitude quickly." Elliott lightly touched James Cullen's shoulder. "Do ye mind?"

James Cullen shucked off his hand, hissing. "Don't touch me!"

Elliott's rejected hand dropped to his side. "I'm sorry, lad. I didn't mean to hurt ye. Is it just yer arms and shoulders?"

"My chest too," James Cullen said, moving farther away from Elliott.

Guilt ravaged Elliott's soul. The damn brooches had broken his son's spirit and almost killed him, and while he knew one day James Cullen would find happiness, his search might well be another challenging journey.

Meredith and Charlotte followed Elliott across the tarmac toward the customs counter, where they would meet their guide, who had their visas.

"It sounds like James Cullen doesn't want us along," Meredith said.

Elliott watched James Cullen and Paul approach the customs counter through an open door. "I don't think he objects or cares one way or the other. If Paul isn't nearby, he gets anxious, but if we're out of sight, he doesn't even notice."

"I noticed Paul touched his arm briefly before James Cullen shook it off. The same as he did to you," Charlotte said. "I think his skin is like that of a burn victim. It's extremely sensitive, but it should get better over time."

"That's good to hear." Meredith brushed past him, but he caught her arm. "Excuse us, Charlotte. Meredith and I need a minute."

"Sure." Charlotte left them on the tarmac, following Paul and James Cullen into the airport.

Elliott raked his fingers through his hair. "I'm sorry. I was out of line. There's no way in hell I would ever go anywhere without consulting ye. This situation is almost more than I can handle, and I'm taking it out on ye. It's not right. It's not fair. It makes me look like an asshole."

"You are an asshole, Elliott. We've gone through a hell of a lot together, but this time you seem determined not to share it with me. At first, I thought you blamed me for what happened, but now I know you're pushing me away intentionally."

Meredith stepped closer and gripped his hand. "You probably aren't even aware of why you're doing it. But I am. You know if I get mad enough, I'll walk, and if I'm not around you, I can't be an unintended consequence. You're afraid the Illuminati will hurt me to get at you. Well, let me tell you something, Mr. Keeper. I'm not going anywhere. So go ahead and be an asshole. I don't care."

She pushed past him and joined the others at the customs counter, where they were talking to a man wearing traditional Bhutan clothing, just like James Cullen and Paul.

"Well, I'll be damned." He always knew she was a hell of a lot smarter than he was, and she just proved it. If he wanted to get on her right side again, he had to do something drastic, like buy her that Australian winery she'd been eyeing that would bring her out of retirement. Not to pay her off, but to show her how much he loved her. Buying another winery said just that. Everyone knew he hated wine and thought investing in more wineries was a waste of money!

Elliott glanced back over his shoulder to make sure Austin and Ensley were coming. She had slept pretty much the entire trip, waking only briefly during fueling stops to go to the bathroom. About an hour outside of Paro, she cleaned up, put on hiking clothes, and ate a high-carb breakfast. Today was the first time Elliott had seen her recently without dark circles under her eyes or tightness around her mouth. After years of living with leg pain, he recognized the signs. Her hip pain had lessened, but after today's hike, it would be worse.

He went through customs and then joined Meredith and Charlotte outside, where the guide told them to wait while he picked up the van.

"Have ye talked to Ensley about her hip?" Elliott asked Charlotte.

"She had a hip replacement ten years ago. They can last fifteen to twenty years, but results vary. I told her that I highly recommend she schedule an appointment with an orthopedist. She said she doesn't want to go through another replacement."

"She can't live with that constant pain. It'll interfere with her quality of life," Meredith said.

Charlotte slipped on a pair of sunglasses. "I told her that. I also told her that robots are now assisting surgeons to achieve more precise implant positioning. I hope she'll consider it before she gets pregnant."

"Children? You think she and Austin are *that* serious?" Then Meredith answered her question. "Of course they are."

"And if you have any doubt, look at them, watch their eyes. They're always aware of where the other one is, but I don't think they've slept together."

Meredith looked over her shoulder. "How can you tell?"

"Body language," Charlotte said. "They stand close together, but there isn't an invisible piece of string pulling them together. She isn't touching him like a woman familiar with his body. There is still some hesitation. Austin is protective, but he didn't stop Paul from kissing her yesterday. They're still curious about each other, but it won't be that long. She's good for him."

"And what does he give her?" Meredith asked.

"Family. Protection. Unconditional love. And what woman wouldn't want to be part of the O'Grady family?"

"A woman who doesn't want to live on the edge with a family of former cops who still carry guns," Meredith said.

Elliott dropped his carry-on next to the other bags stacked near the curb. "Ensley's lived on the edge most of her life. She's a former bull rider."

"And look at the damage that did to her hip," Charlotte said.

An eight-passenger van pulled up to the curb, and Elliott waved. "There's our guide, but I didn't catch his name."

"It's Gangchu," Meredith said. "He's been a guide for ten years. Be nice, okay?"

"Am I that awful that ye naturally assume I'll be an ass?"

"Lately, yes."

Gangchu loaded the bags in the back of the van. "We will stop at the hotel to drop off the bags, then go directly to the car park. It's located at the entrance to the trail to Tiger's Nest and opens at eight o'clock. We have thirty minutes."

"That works," Elliott said.

As they drove away from the airport, Gangchu asked, "Are you familiar with our country's history?"

"I'll listen to your spiel," Ensley said.

Please, no! Not today!

Gangchu smiled as he looked at Ensley in the rearview mirror. "The Kingdom of Bhutan is one of the most forward-thinking countries on Earth and is located on the ancient trade route known as the Silk Road."

"Really? That's cool. I edited a book about foreigners on the Silk Road who excavated the region's abandoned cities and absconded with some of the greatest art and treasures. The countries holding the treasures should return them."

"I won't argue about that," Gangchu said.

It makes me wonder where Erik's treasures came from.

Ensley glanced out one side of the van and then the other. "It's so beautiful here. I could stay for days and do nothing but look out the window."

I don't want to look out the window. I want to get in and get out. And I don't care about the Silk Road or the landscapes.

Gangchu pulled up in front of a hotel that faced the sheer, rocky cliffs surrounding Tiger's Nest. "This hotel was built in the classic Bhutanese style with tapered stone walls and fine, hand-painted façade details. The main building and the three-story cottages hold their own against the soaring peaks."

I don't care. It's a damn hotel.

"It's beautiful," Meredith breathed.

Of course, it is. It's a five-star palace.

"I'll arrange for the bellhop to take the bags, and we can leave immediately," Gangchu walked toward the front door and met the bellhop coming out. They chatted a minute, then came back to the van for the bags.

"Your bags will be waiting at the front desk, Dr. Fraser," Gangchu said as he climbed back into the driver's seat.

"Do you have any dining advice?" Austin asked.

Damn it. Let's get this done in silence. Can we?

"Avoid the Indian menu," Gangchu said, pulling the van back out to the road. "An unidentifiable brown sauce pervades every Indian meal."

"I'll keep that in mind," Austin said.

"Where can I get a massage?" Ensley asked.

Lass, I'm coming close to kicking ye out of the van.

"The hotel offers the traditional outdoor hot-stone bath, and the therapists blend Swedish and Thai kneading techniques to work out the kinks. They're used to working on mountain climbers."

"How far to the car park?" Austin asked.

"Ten miles," Gangchu said. "The car park is at the bottom of the mountain, where the hike begins. You cannot drive or take a cable car. You have to trek for several hours on foot or horseback. The trek is not extremely difficult, but it's not easy, either. You need to be relatively fit to get there. And the oxygen gets thinner at the higher altitude."

Elliott had already caught glimpses of the monastery from the city. It was so high up that it looked from the ground like white dots.

Gangchu looked at Ensley through the rearview mirror. "Do you want to hear my spiel about the hike and the monastery?"

"Sure," Ensley said.

God, Ensley. Stop it. We're not tourists.

"The monastery sits three thousand meters above the Paro valley," Gangchu began. "It was built in the late 17ᵗʰ century on the site of a cave set into the cliff. It's called Tiger's Nest Monastery in English, but Taktsang more accurately translates to 'tigress's lair.'

"According to the legend," he continued, "in the eighth century, a disciple carried a Buddhist master up the mountain on her back. The process transformed her into a tigress. Once they arrived, the master spent three years, three months, three days, and three hours meditating in the cave. After the master finished, it became a holy place known as Paro Taktsang."

"How long does it take to get up there? Two or three hours?" Austin asked.

Not ye, too, lad.

"It depends on your physical condition." Gangchu looked at Austin in the rearview mirror. "Two or three hours for you and the gentlemen in the back. The rest will take five to seven hours, plus a couple of hours to tour the monastery, or extra time if you want to stop at the café going up or coming down."

"Dad, you don't have to go," James Cullen said. "You're in good condition, but it's a difficult hike."

"I'll be fine, James Cullen."

I just want everybody to shut the hell up.

Gangchu pulled into the parking lot. "The vendors sell crafts and walking sticks, and the horses I've reserved are over there," he said, pointing.

"If those are horses, I'll eat a day's worth of hay," Austin said quietly.

"They will only take you about two-thirds of the way up. Once you clear the trees surrounding this parking lot, you will get your first glimpse of Tiger's Nest, hanging on a precarious cliff."

I've already had a glimpse. And if I had a choice, I'd wait right here.

"You're not going?" Meredith asked.

"No, I will wait here to take you back to the hotel. You won't need me on the trail. It only goes to the monastery." Gangchu parked the van, and they all piled out.

"I'll go buy walking sticks for everyone," Austin said.

"Paul and I are going on ahead," James Cullen said. "If we don't see you on the trail, we'll meet you at the monastery."

Elliott wanted to stand at the trailhead and block James Cullen, but he couldn't do it. He caught Paul's eye, and Paul gave him a nod, then the two of them took off toward the path.

I'm counting on ye, Paul. Don't let me down.

"He sounds the same, but he's so different," Ensley said to Elliott.

"What?" Elliott asked.

"He's different from when he left me at Elkhorn Ranch. The light's gone from his eyes, and he seems driven or singularly focused, I guess. Something is pulling on him."

"I wish I knew what it was."

They followed Gangchu to a clearing where the horses were grazing. Only they weren't horses. They were mules. A handler matched each of them to a suitable mule based on height and weight. They shook their heads at Austin and put him on the biggest one they had, but his legs were still almost dragging on the ground.

"The horses are well-disciplined and focus on the road ahead," Gangchu said.

"And they don't stop to graze on the bushes along the trail. You'll stop about a third of the way up for the horses to rest, and you can pop into the Taktsang Cafeteria for tea and biscuits. The trail is quite wide and can easily accommodate two horses side by side, but they tend to walk close to the edge of the cliffs."

"Okay, that does it. I'm walking," Austin said. "Heights don't bother me unless I believe there's a good chance I might fall off a cliff."

"Just don't look down," Ensley said. "Didn't you ever ride the mules to the bottom of the Grand Canyon?"

"No!" Austin said.

"Come on," Meredith said. "Look at it as an adventure."

Ensley cracked up. "If this is an adventure, I'll take it any day over the last one I had."

"I'd take it, too, lass," Elliott commiserated.

"I'll see you when you return," Gangchu said. "Good luck."

They began their trek through the forest with Meredith and Charlotte leading, Ensley and Austin behind them, and Elliott bringing up the rear, riding a damn mule. The numbness in his leg and foot was manageable right now, but God knows what would happen once he started climbing all those steps to reach the gate at the top.

After two hours, they stopped at the only café for tea and biscuits. The owner said two young men who matched James Cullen's and Paul's descriptions had been there but left about thirty minutes earlier.

They mounted up again and rode up a steep incline on a wide dirt path, passing shrines with multicolored flags strung from all the trees.

"What's with the flags?" Ensley asked.

I don't care. Let's just get to the top.

"They're prayer flags," Meredith said. "They symbolize protection from evil forces, plus prayers for positive energy, vitality, and good luck."

"We could use some of that," Ensley said. "But how do you know?"

"I did my research."

They reached the second stop, billed as the last official photo opportunity. But the trees obstructed a full view of the monastery, and Elliott had no desire to pose for or take any pictures. He did sit for a while and drank a bottle of water.

Ensley sat down beside him. "You don't feel good, do you?"

"Well enough. I just want to see James Cullen safely ensconced in the monastery."

"I'm not talking about emotional pain. I'm talking about your leg."

"Nothing's wrong with my leg."

"Bullshit. You're talking to someone who has constant pain from a prior injury. Your leg hurts. I don't know why, but I remember JC talking about all the surgeries you had years ago. Has the problem come back?"

He looked at her and growled. "I don't want to worry Meredith, and if Charlotte knows, she'll think it's her problem to solve."

Ensley shrugged. "Meredith is already worried."

"Because her heart is breaking over James Cullen."

"That's true, but she's worried about you, too. I can see it in her eyes when she looks at you. And before you deny it again, her gaze goes to your leg. She knows it's bothering you."

"If she did, she'd have said something."

Ensley laughed. "Why would she? You'd just deny it, and it would start another fight."

Meredith walked up to them. "We have to leave the horses here and walk the rest of the way."

"Really?" Ensley asked. "I was just getting used to Eeyore."

"Leave it to ye to give that critter an identity, but Eeyore is a donkey's name."

"But it's the best fit for the cute mule I was riding." Ensley stood and stretched. "In all your research, did you find out how many steps we have to climb?"

"Eight hundred and fifty, all cut into the rock," Meredith said.

I'll never make it.

"The entrance is at the top of the steps," Meredith continued. "If we tour the monastery, we have to leave our shoes, phones, cameras, and backpacks at the gate."

"You did do your research," Ensley said. "Did you read anything about a zip line at the top? We could get back down in under five minutes."

"Don't you think it would destroy the spiritual element?" Meredith asked.

"It wouldn't matter to me. I can do a one-way spiritual thing."

Elliott chuckled. "I believe ye could."

"I'm going to the bathroom," Meredith said.

"It's dirty, so I went behind the bushes. I got sorta used to it while trekking through the Badlands."

"I've been running races for years, and squatting in the bushes is part of racing. I'll see you two on the trail," Meredith returned to the trail in search of a private bush.

Ensley linked arms with Elliott. "Come on. Let's hit the trail. If it gets too bad for you, you can use me as an excuse to stay behind."

"Thanks, lass. But I have to make it to the top. James Cullen might not care if we're here, but if everyone makes it to the gate and I don't, he'll be alarmed, and I don't want to be the cause of any distress."

"Okay, but the offer stands."

Austin returned from taking pictures. "How are you two feeling?"

"We'll survive to fight another day." She squished up next to Elliott. "Take our picture." She glanced over her shoulder. "Can you see the monastery?"

"No, but the forest is beautiful. Smile." He took the picture. "Honestly, neither one of you looks good. You're both in pain. Why don't you stay here?" He glanced at Elliott. "I'll take care of your girl if you'll take care of mine."

"I'd appreciate it if ye'd go with Meredith and Charlotte. They haven't stopped talking since they started up the mountain, and they aren't paying attention to their surroundings. I don't want them caught off guard."

"Okay, but Ensley, be careful and don't go off on your own."

"If we decide to sit it out, I'll send ye a text," Elliott said.

"You've got service out here?" she asked.

"We carry satellite phones," Austin said. "We always have reception."

"If Charlotte and Meredith ask, tell them we're talking and taking our time." Elliott stood and leaned on his walking stick as Ensley walked with Austin over to the trail. Then he chuckled when Ensley pushed on Austin's back and yelled, "Go!"

Austin walked away but kept looking back until he was too far ahead and couldn't see them anymore.

Elliott took her arm. "Let's get this done."

Over the next hour, there was a constant stream of curses from him and grunts from Ensley. Elliott stumbled a few times, but Ensley had his arm, and along with the aid of the walking stick, he didn't fall.

They reached the final approach to the monastery, which was over a bridge across a waterfall. It dropped at least two hundred feet to a pool below. Prayer flags were hung in every direction, flapping in the breeze.

"Look," Ensley pointed. "What are those pointy things crammed into crevices in the rock?"

"They're reliquaries containing ashes of the dead."

"Oh, well…that's probably better than illegally sprinkling ashes in the deceased's favorite park or lake or ocean or someplace else. But the flags are beautiful," Ensley said. "I wonder if anyone can hang them?"

"In Bhutan, people are allowed to hang prayer flags anywhere they like. And this is a place where they believe their prayers are most likely to be answered."

The wind lifted Ensley's hair, blowing it forward and covering her face. She smoothed it back into a low ponytail, twisted it, tucked the tail into the twist, creating a bun to hold her hair back.

"At least there's a breeze. I guess it carries the prayers on the wind."

"I wish the wind would blow us up to the top," Elliott said.

Ensley smiled. "Is that humor I hear in your voice?"

"I still have some left." They stood at the bottom of the steps.

Talk about being intimidated by a bunch of rocks. He offered her his elbow. "Ready?" The numbness was worse now, but as annoying as it was, it wasn't sharp pain like Ensley was experiencing. For her, each step came with a grunt or a hiss.

One last, brutal flight of steep steps hewn out of rock delivered them to the monastery, which was blanketed in low-hanging clouds, adding an aura of heaven to the place.

James Cullen and Paul were waiting at the entrance, drinking water with Meredith, Charlotte, and Austin. Austin leaned down and whispered something to Ensley, and she nodded, and then he looked at Elliott. Elliott assumed he was silently asking if he was okay, and Elliott somehow managed to muster a grin.

"Are you coming in for a tour?" James Cullen asked.

"Of course," Meredith said.

Elliott glanced at Ensley, and she shook her head. "Ensley wants to rest, so I'll stay with her."

"I can stay," Austin said.

"No, lad. Ye go with Meredith and Charlotte and take yer time."

"Then, this is goodbye." James Cullen kissed Elliott's cheek.

Elliott wanted to hug him but knew he couldn't, so he let his arms hang loosely at his side, crushing his soul that he couldn't do what his heart demanded of him. He couldn't feel his son's bones and muscles and sinew. He could only feel his son's pain sparking off him, pinging Elliott's heart.

"If ye need anything, lad, send word, and I'll see that ye get it."

"Thanks, Dad. And thanks for making it up here. I know it was difficult."

"I'd come up here every day if it would help ye."

"I'm sorry for not coming to you when I discovered Ensley had disappeared."

Elliott bit back tears. "If anyone should apologize, it's me. I should never have given ye the impression that ye couldn't talk to me about anything. I mean *anything*. I'm so proud of ye."

"I was going to ask Mom, but there is one thing you can do for me. I have a Power of Attorney granting Kevin the authority to manage my estate."

"I can do it for ye."

"I know you can, and I don't want to argue about it, but Kevin isn't as conservative as you are with your investments. He'll manage my portfolio more to my liking."

"Ye're right. He's a good choice." For a moment, James Cullen sounded almost like his old self, but his jittery hands and feet and the vacant look in his eyes told Elliott the truth. "Where's the document?"

"In my desk drawer. I also want Kevin to call Becky in my office to be sure she has everything she needs to manage the business. Paul and I both left letters of resignation from the CIA on the bedroom desk on the plane. Give those to Kevin, too, and he can forward them to the appropriate people."

That did it for Elliott, and a tear slid down his cheek. "Consider it done."

James Cullen glanced away for a minute, then looked back again. "Then that's it."

Elliott cupped his son's face and kissed his cheek. "I love ye, lad."

"I love you, Dad."

The lump in Elliott's throat nearly cut off his air as James Cullen turned and walked away with Paul, but then he stopped and looked back at Ensley for a moment. Neither one of them said anything, and then James Cullen and Paul disappeared behind the gate.

Elliott's heart was cracking, but for his son's sake, and Meredith's too, he found the composure to survive the moment without breaking down. Elliott reached for Meredith and pulled her into his arms.

"Take yer time," he said.

Meredith kissed him. "We'll be back in about an hour."

Ensley and Elliott sat on a rock bench near the gate. He was so exhausted and emotional that he just buried his face in his hands.

Ensley put her arm around his shoulders. "JC is anxious about his future, but part of that anxiety is worrying about you. I assured him that I would have your back, so you better behave yourself."

He looked up at her. "I didn't see ye talking to him."

"That's because..." She shrugged. "Well... This sounds weird, but JC and I can communicate telepathically."

"Ye can? He never mentioned it."

"I think we always knew it, but it wasn't until we were in the Badlands that it became more pronounced. It only works if we're near each other. I mean, by now, he's too far away."

"Does he believe he'll recover?"

"He doesn't know what's wrong with him. He knows something

deadly happened that he can't remember, and, honestly, he doesn't want to. I just hope he can find his way back through prayer and meditation."

Elliott straightened, put his arm around Ensley, and hugged her. "Erik must have had this all planned years ago. He knew I would lose my son for a while and brought me a daughter to fill the emptiness."

She chuckled. "I don't think you got the best end of the deal. I can be rather stubborn."

He kissed her forehead. "I'm okay with that, lass. It means ye can get yerself up, dust yerself off, and keep moving forward. That's all I can ask of my children."

71

Mallory Plantation, VA—Ensley

B Y THE TIME Charlotte, Meredith, Elliott, Austin, and Ensley returned to the car park to meet Gangchu, the group had voted to go straight home and not tour Bhutan. Since everyone was exhausted or in pain, all they would do was sleep anyway, so why not do it on the plane?

But overall, there was a profound sense of relief mixed with a coating of sadness. JC was safe now. They had to believe that.

Twenty hours later, they arrived back at Mallory Plantation.

Ensley planned to go to New York for a couple of days to see Barb and George and close up her apartment.

Austin decided it made more sense to return to Colorado to handle several business concerns before Ensley moved in. Later in the summer, they'd invite Barb and George to the ranch for a long weekend.

Charlotte planned to take both Ensley and Elliott to see specialists at the hospital.

Meredith planned to research Australian wineries to find one for Elliott to buy.

And Elliott planned to go to Scotland for a few weeks to get away from Charlotte.

But after JL discovered Braham, David, and Kenzie had arrived at the farm to relocate a treasure found in a cave, she pitched a fit and demanded they all meet to discuss the plan. She didn't want the Illuminati anywhere near the farm and insisted that moving the treasure would trigger the evil force and endanger her family.

So nobody got what they wanted—except JL. Funny how that happened.

Austin and Ensley returned to the mansion last because Ensley wanted to stop by the mall to shop for a few outfits instead of depending on the women's closet.

Mostly she wanted a sexy nightie to wear when she went to bed with Austin for the first time. Nothing like that was in the closet, and even if it had been, she wouldn't feel sexy wearing another woman's nightgown for their big night.

They headed toward the adult wing to shower before figuring out what to do for dinner and stopped by the kitchenette to see which rooms were available. Kenzie and David were in Room Three, and Meredith and Elliott had already checked into Room Four. Ensley decided on a return visit to Room One and signed her name.

"You don't want to check out the *décor* in another room?" Austin asked. "That's sort of a tradition."

"Not tonight. I want familiarity. But, if you have a favorite room"—she shrugged—"it's no big deal."

"Makes no difference to me. I just want a bed and a bathroom that accommodates people taller than six feet."

She opened the door and dropped her duffel on the upholstered bench at the end of the bed. "Why don't you shower first?"

"Sure. It won't take me long. I'll hurry up and get out of your way." He sat at the desk to untie his athletic shoes with the built-in support for his dropped foot, and his phone blasted a drum beat ringtone. "That's Remy."

"Oh, good. Find out how he's doing. I haven't heard anything new."

"Since Charlotte left him in charge of his care, he's probably in Lexington warming up for his gig."

"Not exactly. Emily was with him until this morning."

"Yeah, but Emily doesn't have Charlotte's take-no-prisoner bedside manner. If he wanted to leave, Emily couldn't stop him."

Austin answered the call. "Yeah… How're you feeling… Really… I'd thought for sure you'd be back in Lexington… Well, good for you… When… Hold on. Let me ask Ensley." Austin muted the phone. "Remy's grilling steaks, Penny's making appetizers, and Amber's cooking side dishes. Do you want to go out back and eat with them? If you don't feel like socializing, we can raid the fridge or order in."

"Are you kidding? I'll eat anything Remy cooks."

Austin unmuted the phone. "Count us in. You want me to get some beer... No... Okay... We'll be there in about forty-five minutes."

He put down the phone and finished taking off his shoes and socks. Then he sat there and cocked his head, looking at her as if he wanted to say something. She gazed into his eyes and found herself immersed in the same hot, green depths she always found there, and she fell into them again, growing breathless as somewhere out in the yard, the crooning sounds of Frank Sinatra's "Fly Me To The Moon" breezed in through the open garden door.

And Austin sang over Sinatra...

"Fly me to the moon / Let me play among the stars / Let me see what spring is like / On Jupiter and Mars / In other words, hold my hand / In other words, baby, kiss me..."

Ensley walked toward him, mesmerized by his eyes and his voice. And when she reached him, he pulled her close until she straddled his lap while he sang to her.

"Why don't you fill my heart with song? / Let me sing for evermore / Because you are all I worship / All I long for and adore / In other words, please be true / In other words / In other words / I love you..."

Then, with one hand on her ass, he pulled her even closer. "Can you feel how much I want you?"

She rubbed against his erection. "Hmmm. You want me a *lot!*"

He pushed his fingers up into the roots of her hair and kissed her. His lips were demanding, and his sandpaper whiskers rasped her chin. She fisted great wads of his shirt in her hands and clung to him, kissing him back with pent-up desire and longing. Their clashing lips and tongues stirred passion so thoroughly hot that it was a wonder she didn't spontaneously combust.

He nibbled on her bottom lip. "I want you more than I've ever wanted a woman, and if we don't stop, we won't leave this room for forty-eight hours."

"I don't want to stop." There wasn't an ounce of fear in her soul. Austin was just what she wanted. All of him. Every inch of him. And she wanted him—now!

But her stomach had a funny way of competing with her desire. The memory of living off dandelion coffee and walleye fillets was still so fresh in her mind that she was able to put everything else aside in favor of a decent meal, especially a Remy-grilled steak.

His lips twitched in a slight smile. "Should I call Remy back and tell him we're a no-show?"

She shook her head. "Do you mind if we eat first? I'd hate to faint on you. I probably will anyway, but I'd hate to faint from hunger instead of ecstasy."

His grin widened. "I might be offended if you faint from hunger instead of what I plan to do to you. But sex would be better if our stomachs didn't growl."

"Why are we so hungry? The food on the plane was haute cuisine."

He kissed the tip of her nose, her eyelids, her forehead, her cheeks. "Because it was height cuisine, not haute cuisine."

"A joke, huh?" She nipped his earlobe. "You're a snob. For us mere mortals who fly economy, anything not wrapped in a plastic container is haute cuisine."

"You're right. Since I was seventeen, I've been a spoiled traveler, but airplane food isn't a home-cooked meal, and it leaves me wanting something more substantial. And you"—he planted a quick kiss on her lips—"lost weight during your trek across the Badlands, and you can't afford to lose another pound, or I'll be able to palm you like I do a basketball."

"That doesn't sound very romantic."

He held his hand out flat. "I don't know. Holding your ass in my hand sounds erotic."

He kissed her again, and the hot, unfettered sensations stunned her into place, turning her breath into a soft gasp and her nipples into aching peaks, and she rocked back and forth on his erection. He stripped off her T-shirt, unhooked her bra, and his thumbs swiped her pebbled nipples.

She dropped her head back. "Oh, dear Lord!"

Something surreal was happening, something beyond her understanding, and she didn't want him to stop. Ever. He nuzzled between her breasts, then turned his attention to one stiff nipple, drawing it into his mouth until the tip tightened even more against his gentle suction.

And her sex ached for contact.

He moved to her other breast, repeating the action, and she arched forward, hungry to be against him. She threaded her fingers into his hair, clutching with the motion of his lips, mouth, and tongue. And he teased her until heat awakened within her, a delectable feeling both intoxicating and addictive.

He reached his hand into the waistband of her running tights, and his thumb homed in on her clit, already begging for his attention. A slow pulse started deep within her, and she knew he would drive her straight toward an explosion.

He growled electrifying words as he lifted and turned her so the pad of his thumb could torture her clit while his fingers speared her to a frantic edge. She arched against him, and her muscles clenched, spasmed, and she cried out as she unraveled.

She squeezed her eyes shut, gasping, and she heard him in her mind saying, "I love you." And when she opened them again, raw male hunger gazed back at her, almost making her climax a second time.

He stilled his hand while he kissed her shoulder and neck. "Watching you come turned me the hell on."

"I'm…glad," she managed to say.

He removed his hand, and then he picked her up and carried her to the bed, where he spooned with her. "Do you want more? As responsive as you are, I'm sure I can pull a few more orgasms out of you before dinner." He slipped his hand back into her tights and massaged her hip.

"But it's your turn."

"I'll wait until I have more time to explore you and taste you and make you come until you can't move."

His warm breath rippled across her skin, tickling her, exciting her, driving her where she wanted to go. His large hand encompassed her entire hip, and his fingers dug into the tight muscles, kneading the knots over and over. She didn't want him to stop.

"Oh, my God! That feels so good."

"Now I know how to turn you into liquid fire. You're so wet right now you could easily take all of me."

"Yeah, I was kinda wondering about that."

"Don't worry. We'll take our time."

"You should know I'm not on any birth control right now."

"That's okay. I always use a condom." He continued massaging her hip while he rained a trail of kisses down her neck and shoulder.

"Always?"

"Always, and that should answer the question about my sexual health."

"My two prior sexual partners always used them as well."

"Two?" He nibbled on her neck. "I've never been with such a

promiscuous woman before."

She turned around to face him. "And it's been almost a year since I've had sex."

He rolled over and pulled her on top of him. "I heard a year's abstinence turns a woman into a virgin again. Man, how'd I get so lucky?" He squeezed her ass and pressed her against his erection.

She rocked seductively against him while a hot blush hit her cheeks at how wanton she'd become. And she loved it. "You sure you want to wait?"

"Well, we've used twenty-four of our forty-five minutes. You decide. Sex? Or steak and beer and family."

"How do you know how long it's been? I haven't seen you once look at the time."

"NBA games are played in four twelve-minute quarters, so when I was a kid, I always practiced hard in twelve-minute increments and developed a pretty good internal clock. But I've been rather distracted. So I might be wrong."

"Okay, that's weird."

"Remy will call at exactly the forty-six-minute mark. And if I don't answer, he'll call back again and again until I do. Now that I'm back in the fold, I can't ignore calls and messages, especially from Elliott."

"But it won't be from Elliott. He's spent the last four days with you."

"Doesn't matter. There's too much going on right now to ignore a call, even if I think it's Remy telling us to get our asses down to the pavilion."

She rolled off him. "Then let's not give Remy a reason to call." She crossed the room to pick up her T-shirt and slipped it on. "Don't get me wrong. My preference is to stay right here with you. But Remy is such a fabulous cook, and my mouth is already watering."

"It's not watering in anticipation of eating me up?"

"It's hard to tell the difference right now—you or steak. My salivary glands are in overdrive."

Austin unbuckled his belt, unzipped his trousers, and pushed the khakis down over his hips. She licked her lips and just kept licking, waiting for the black boxer briefs to hit the floor. But he surprised her by wearing them to the bathroom.

"If you want to see more, you have to come in here with me."

She followed him but stopped at the door. "We'd save time if we showered together. Right?"

He turned on the water and dropped his briefs. "We could try."

She slapped her hand over her eyes. "I can't unsee that. How am I going to sit still through dinner now?"

He stepped into the stream of water, whistling, but paused long enough to say, "The same way I will. Uncomfortably."

He was in and out in ten minutes, but her turn took much longer.

Thirty minutes later, Ensley was wearing her new black fit-and-flare sundress and strappy four-inch sandals, her hair falling halfway down her back. She left the bathroom feeling like the brooch gods had—this time—dropped her into the middle of paradise.

And, man, she was thrilled to be here.

Austin was sitting at the desk, scrolling through his phone. He cocked his head and gazed at her. "Wow! You look gorgeous, rested, and happy."

She glided toward him, doing her best runway sashay. "We're late for dinner."

His sun-kissed hair was still damp, and he'd cropped his beard stubble close. Sexy in a way she couldn't ignore and didn't want to. And although they didn't have time, she delighted in teasing him and watching his pupils dilate.

He put his phone away. "I sent Remy a text and told him we'd be there in ten minutes and not to overcook our steaks."

She stopped and did a pivot turn, her full skirt swinging around her legs. "So we have a few extra minutes."

"Shit!" he said under his breath. "Ten minutes, ten hours, ten days, ten years—still not enough time to do what I want to do." He leaned forward and put his elbows on his knees, and his gaze traveled the length of her body. "With those killer sandals, you've got legs up the wazoo!"

She struck a practiced pose that accentuated the legs he kept ogling.

"Come closer."

She did but stayed out of reach and twirled again. This time, the dress swung higher.

"Man! When I saw you in the locker room without anything on, it blew my mind, and that mental picture has fueled my fantasies. But the way you look when you twirl and your dress teases your upper thighs, and your hair swirls around you, makes me want to use your hair in ways nature didn't intend."

"So you're saying you want to replace a mental image of a naked me with one that only hints at possibilities?"

He ducked his head and then shot her a shy look. "My mind does continue to play the naked picture."

"It does, huh?"

"Yep! On a continuous loop."

"Well... I'm not sure what to say about that."

He reached out, put his hands on her hips, and pulled her close enough to stand between his legs. "You've got an amazing body, and right now you look like a MacKlenna woman, all hot and sexy and loving"—he moved his hands to span her belly—"and I can easily see you pregnant."

She cupped the sides of his face. "Is that good or bad?"

"For me, it's good, but I don't know how you feel about kids."

She fingered the longer hair on the front of his head, sweeping it off his forehead. "I grew up as an only child with only a few cousins I saw once a year. I always said that when I married, I'd have four or five kids. How about you?"

"Five. I'd want a full team."

"Shouldn't you have substitute players?"

"They'll have to depend on a cousin or two."

"We haven't had sex, you haven't proposed, and we're talking about how many kids we're going to have. Isn't that putting the cart before the horse?"

"This was all foreordained by the brooches."

"Don't we get a say?"

"I don't think so. Do you want one?"

"One what? A say or a proposal?"

"Either one."

"Well, then. I want a proposal, but not tonight."

"Why not?"

"Because I want a real one. A down-on-your-knee proposal. One that you have to think about, and find the perfect words for, and write them down, and scratch through them, and write them again and again until they say just what's in your heart. And I don't think you know that yet."

"Okay. But I won't let you edit it."

"Well, I hope not. Ask Jack Mallory. He planned and executed the perfect proposal on the pitcher's mound at Yankee Stadium."

Austin smiled. "You want me to propose at Yankee Stadium?"

"No. I want it to happen at a place that's special to us. And we don't know where that is yet. I think we're doing this all ass-backward and inside out."

"Maybe, but I don't think there are any rules written in stone. How about we continue this conversation between our lovemaking sessions later tonight?"

"Why?"

"Because we're getting close to using up our extra ten minutes?"

"You won't forget?"

"Excuse me? Forget? I'm like an elephant. I never forget anything. I can tell you how many points I scored in the last game of my senior year in high school."

"I can tell you how long my last bull ride was. Some things are too memorable to forget. Now let's go to dinner. We'll be sociable, and when we can't stand it another minute, we can rush back up here and figure out how to make this work."

He kissed the top of her head, and she wrapped her arms around him, around his steel-cut muscles. He smelled masculine and familiar and sexy, and being with him was such a turn-on that she trembled.

It was almost impossible to wrap her mind around the fact that a few weeks ago, he was only a name on a manuscript. Then he graduated to an asshole on a warhorse. And now they were talking about spending the rest of their lives together.

"I don't have to figure out how to make this work," he said. "I already know."

She looked up at him. "I already know, too. I think!"

"By the time this night is over, there won't be any thinking about it. You'll know in your heart, the same as me."

She took his hand. "Then let's hustle."

He swooped her up in his arms and kissed her. "I said three magic words to you in my mind a few minutes ago, but now I want to say them out loud."

"Okay, but you don't have to. I heard you the first time. And I love you too, Austin Klenna O'Grady."

"Shit! That sounds better than hearing the announcer say, 'O'Grady hits three from the corner,' and I thought those were the best threes in the English language. I was wrong. Saying I love you and hearing you say it back has to be the best threes in the world."

72

Mallory Plantation, VA—Ensley

Ensley and Austin hurried down the mansion's back stairs and headed toward the covered entertainment center. She'd been here before, during late spring, when the emerging fragrance of the flowering dogwoods and cherry trees filled the air, and falling petals danced in the wind like spring snow blanketing the ground in color. She read that description somewhere, and it was so fitting for this landscape.

The sky over the James River caught the last red-orange rays of the setting sun, and it was the most romantic setting she'd ever seen. Maybe it had something to do with the man walking beside her, and if that was the case, she could look forward to years of gorgeous sunsets.

The sound of laughter and jazz music set the evening to a humming beat, and they eagerly followed the mouthwatering aromas of grilling beef and Cajun seasoning.

"Where are Charlotte and Braham, and Meredith and Elliott?"

"They're all having dinner with Matt and Elizabeth Kelly and Philippe and Rhona Baird over at the Bairds' house."

"How'd you know all that?"

"I read my text messages."

"Oh. I should get my phone, so I can keep up with what's going on."

"David should have a new phone for you tonight."

"One of those encrypted phones so everything is private?"

"Yep, so if we get separated for the night, you can send me nude pictures."

She waggled her eyebrows. "That works both ways, buster."

Although Austin told her he was going to Colorado while she went to New York City, she didn't think he would. The thought of spending nights apart pained her. They'd been together since the first day of the roundup, and while she'd lost track of time, it seemed like he'd been a part of her life forever.

"Will that happen often? I mean, do you think we'll spend many nights apart? I've gotten so used to looking up…and up…and up, and seeing you there. The thought of you not being nearby scares me. What if another bear comes along?"

He made a choked sound that could have passed for a laugh, but when she looked at him, she knew it wasn't. He remembered the horror, and it terrified him as much as it did her. The next time it might not be a bear, but he would have her back, and she would have his. How exactly that would work when he was fourteen inches taller, and almost a hundred pounds heavier wasn't entirely clear.

Austin stopped walking, and she paused and turned. "If we're ever apart, it will depend on Elliott."

"Why would it depend on him?"

"Because he's going to be a bigger part of your life than you might want him to be."

"I'll deal with him if his demands become a problem for us."

Austin chuckled. "I can hardly wait."

The jazz music and laughter grew louder the closer they got to a sprawling wood pavilion that overlooked the river. The pavilion had a wood-plank ceiling with recessed lighting and a floor of neutral-tone stone pavers.

The L-shaped, chef-grade outdoor kitchen had stainless steel appliances and countertop seating, and a grill with range hood and travertine-tile backsplash completed the grilling portion of the kitchen. A teak dining table large enough to accommodate alfresco dining for twelve, a sofa, and several comfy chairs filled a seating area in front of a see-through stone fireplace with built-in television. The fireplace added ambiance without blocking the view of the river.

Remy was standing in front of the grill, fork in one hand, beer in the other. He was dressed casually in Nike sandals, gym shorts, and a T-shirt with drumsticks and the words Weapons of Mass Percussion across the front. He looked sexy and fun and much less stressed, and Ensley was surprised he didn't have a girlfriend there for support.

Ensley went right over to him and kissed his cheek. "It's so good to see you up. How're you feeling?"

He turned his face and pointed to his other cheek, and Ensley kissed him again. "I doan know, but the beer helps." He gave her a once-over. "Man, you're hot, and those are killer shoes."

She glanced down at her feet, surprised that he noticed. "With these on, I almost reach Austin's waist."

"Doan go there. It sends my mind off in all sorts of weird directions."

"Ensley!" Kenzie waved. "Bring your *ragazza tosta* ass over here."

Patting her butt, Ensley strutted over to Kenzie, standing across the counter from two other women. "My ass is here, but why'd you call me that?"

"Because Austin does."

"How'd you know?"

"Sweetie, there aren't any secrets in this family, or very few." She pointed to a beautiful, dark-haired, pregnant woman. "This is Penny O'Grady, Rick's wife. You haven't met her, but you have met Amber Grant. She's married to Daniel."

Amber was a hazel-eyed beauty with a braid halfway down her back.

"The Pinkerton agent."

"He's over there with David," Amber said.

Ensley glanced over at the fireplace where the men were standing watching TV, and she remembered Daniel as soon as she saw him. "Two handsome Scotsmen."

"Yes, they are," Kenzie said.

"Amber, I love your outie braid, by the way. But I've never figured out how to do them."

"I'll teach you. My daughter Heather is eight, and she braids her hair beautifully every day."

"That's encouraging. If an eight-year-old can do it, surely I can."

Kenzie patted the stool next to her, and Ensley sat down. "Love the dress and shoes. They didn't come out of the women's closet. So feel free to leave them behind."

"But only Sophia and JL are small enough to wear them," Amber said.

"I can't leave this dress behind. Austin rented a car at the airport so we could stop at the mall on the way back. He wasn't happy about it, but I wanted something special for tonight. If I leave it here, it'll make him think I didn't appreciate the effort he made."

"You hit your mark. You look incredible, and I agree with you.

Our men go out of their way to make us happy, and sometimes we don't thank them enough." Kenzie swiveled around on her barstool and grinned at Austin. "I bet he thinks you look hot."

Ensley smiled at him, too. "Yeah, he does."

Kenzie turned Ensley's stool back around. "I got a brief update about JC from Elliott, but I know he didn't tell me everything. How do you think he is?"

"Elliott or JC?"

"Start with JC, then you can tell me about Elliott. He looks worse than I've ever seen him, and that includes after his mini-stroke."

Ensley knew Elliott looked tired but hadn't realized he looked *that* bad. "JC is in a great deal of emotional pain and doesn't know why. It's going to take him a while to recover."

"How long is a while?" Amber asked. "Six months? A year? Five years?"

"Hard to tell, but I wouldn't expect him back for at least a year, if not longer."

Penny pointed toward the river. "Look who's here. Are they eating with us?"

"I don't know," Kenzie said.

Two attractive, physically fit, and seemingly ageless men walked up to join the party. They kissed the women and fist-bumped the men. And then one of them said, "You're Ensley. I've heard all about you. I'm Ted Jenkins, but everybody calls me Trainer Ted."

Ensley smiled. "Your reputation precedes you."

"I'm glad. That means when we meet at seven in the morning, I won't have to introduce myself and explain what I do for the family."

"And I'm Laurence," the other man said. "I'm Ted's husband, and you and I have an appointment after Ted puts you through your paces in the morning."

"Huh? Seven o'clock? In the morning? Not going to happen. I plan to sleep in and then spend the rest of the day by the pool doing nothing but eating and sunning myself."

Trainer Ted shook his head. "I'll expect you in the gym by seven. We know your hip hurts, so we're going to work on that, plus build your upper body strength. I heard there's a ten-pound battle-ax you want to swing effectively, and that's not going to happen overnight." He rubbed her upper arm and shoulder. Then he turned to look at his partner. "She needs a deep-tissue massage. Her arms and shoulders are so tight they might snap."

Ensley's jaw dropped at Ted's inappropriate touching. "Seriously? Who the hell *are* you?"

"He's God!" Kenzie, Amber, and Penny exclaimed in unison.

"You can't escape him or ignore him," Amber said. "He'll find you wherever you are."

Ensley put her hands on her hips. "Look, you might have them fooled, but you're not the boss of me."

Austin came over and kissed the top of her head. "He's the boss of all of us. Elliott has given him godlike status in the family. He has everyone on fitness and diet plans, so we're always ready for whatever comes along."

She looked up at Austin. "Even you?"

"Even me. Ted and Laurence work directly with my trainer, coach, massage therapist, physical therapist, and nutritionist, except for the past six months. I cut them off when everyone started bugging me."

"So, how do you keep up with everybody?" she asked the two men, swinging her attention from one to the other.

Laurence put his arm around Ted's shoulder. "Doesn't matter where you are. We can schedule Zoom sessions."

These two fitness gurus were putting a damper on her evening. "Here's the deal. I need at least a day to let my body recover. It's been stretched on the rack, and I have to rest."

Ted shook his head. "Sorry. *Here's* the deal. I won't push you too hard. We'll do yoga, get you loosened up, and then you'll finish with a massage."

"Just yoga? No cardio?"

"Not tomorrow. We'll give you a break," Ted said. "But if there's a group run, you'll feel guilty if you don't go."

"Trust me. I won't feel guilty. I'll wave goodbye and go back to sleep or float in the pool. But I'll agree to yoga and a massage, but not until after nine o'clock."

Ted glanced at Laurence, and they had some kind of silent communication going on between them. "We can make some adjustments to the schedule and work you in at eight thirty. How's that sound?"

"Horrible." Ensley glanced up at Austin again. "Can I have a beer? This is stressing me out."

"Hey, Ted," Remy said. "Are you and Laurence staying for dinner? I'll throw on a couple more steaks."

"No, thanks, Remy. We have dinner plans—"

"—with friends—" Laurence said.

"—across town," Ted added. "We just wanted to stop by—"

"—and meet Ensley."

"Right," Ted said.

Ted and Laurence were funny the way they completed each other's sentences.

"Well, it would have been nice if you'd waited another day, but I'll be there in the morning." Then it occurred to her that they would report directly to Elliott about her overall physical condition. If they gave him a negative report, he would use it as an excuse to leave her behind when he put a rescue team together to go after Tavis. She couldn't allow that to happen.

Ted and Laurence walked away, chatting with each other, and Ensley wondered what they were saying. They were probably conspiring about how best to torture her in the morning.

"Do they live here, or are they on the traveling team?" she asked.

"They have a house here on the plantation, another one on MacKlenna Farm, and an apartment in Napa. Ted has Elliott on such a strict diet and exercise program that he goes wherever Elliott goes. But Laurence usually stays here." Kenzie walked around to the other side of the bar and opened the refrigerator. "I bet you're a Corona gal."

"I'll be whatever kind of gal I have to be tonight because tomorrow I'm going to die!"

Kenzie uncapped two bottles of Corona and handed one to Ensley. "You have a self-deprecating sense of humor, don't you?"

Ensley tipped back her beer, took a long pull, and then lifted it to signal her thanks to Kenzie. "I used to watch TV reruns and old movies with my mom. She didn't like to watch anything current. She was weird like that. But one of her favorite comedians was Bob Newhart. I got infected by his wry, self-deprecating humor."

"Have you heard the story about the cop who called his captain to tell him a giant ape was climbing the Empire State Building?" Kenzie asked.

"No. Was it one of Newhart's jokes?"

Kenzie rolled her eyes, but a suspicious tug at her lips told Ensley she was having difficulty not laughing. "No, it wasn't, but have you heard the story?"

Ensley took another swig of her Corona. "Nope."

"Well," Kenzie said, straight-faced. "The captain asked what floor the ape had reached, and the cop answered, 'He's on the eighteenth or nineteenth, depending on whether the building has a thirteenth floor or not.'"

Ensley burst out laughing, spraying Kenzie with a mouthful of beer.

Kenzie calmly grabbed a handful of napkins and wiped the beer off her arm. "Nobody's spat on me since the twins were two years old. Thanks a lot."

Ensley kept laughing. "That's the dumbest joke I've ever heard."

"Oh, sweetie. I'm just getting started." And for the next ten minutes, while Ensley finished one beer and opened another, Kenzie went through her repertoire of dumbest jokes of all time, and Ensley couldn't stop laughing. It wasn't that any of them were funny. They weren't. They were stupid. But the lighthearted moment stood in stark contrast to the confusing and often painful weeks Ensley just endured.

Austin came up behind her, kissed the top of her head, and whispered, "I love hearing you laugh. Don't stop." Then he left her to flip channels with the guys, looking for what else but basketball playoff games, of course. But now, oddly enough, she saw athletes in a different light, and if Austin wanted to drink beer and watch games, he had her full support. Well, he did as long as he slipped away every once in a while to pay attention to her.

Amber removed a plate of sliced tomatoes from the refrigerator, placed them on the bar, and then grabbed a casserole dish off the oven's bottom rack. "Look at the way Ensley is staring at Austin. She's got it bad. Don't you think?"

"What? Me?" Ensley asked. "Nah."

Kenzie took a swig of her beer. "You know what, girls? I don't think they've done the deed yet. Ensley doesn't have that look that says they did it and can't wait to do it again."

Penny took the potholders from Amber and pulled out a pan of buttermilk biscuits from the top rack. "Don't pay any attention to Kenzie. You take your time and do it when you're ready. But you're in for a wild ride. O'Grady men are passionate, protective, giving, and very romantic. But mostly, they're respectful. Their late mother was an incredible woman, and she and Pops raised those boys right.

And"—Penny rubbed her very pregnant belly—"they're great fathers."

Kenzie transferred the biscuits from the cookie sheet to a basket. "All our men are great fathers. If they weren't, David would kick the shit out of them. He had a difficult father, and he won't put up with men being assholes around their kids or disrespecting their women."

"Usually, men who have difficult fathers become difficult fathers themselves," Ensley said. "I was lucky. I had a great dad growing up."

Kenzie gave her a sympathetic look, and Ensley shook it off. Right now, she didn't want to think about her parents and Erik. She opened her mouth to change the subject, but Remy did it for her.

"Steaks are ready," he announced, setting the platter on the bar along with a dish of grilled sweet corn mixed with zucchini and mushrooms.

"Grab that covered casserole dish out of the warming oven," Amber said. "It's Austin's favorite mac and cheese."

"Gosh, I didn't bring anything." Ensley felt guilty for coming to a party without a gift or dessert or even a bottle of wine. "And you all even made my guy his favorite dish."

"Don't worry about it," Kenzie said. "You just spent a week with Elliott in a pissed-off mood. That earns you a huge credit. You don't have to cook or wash dishes for the next six months."

"The guys usually wash dishes anyway," Penny said. "They get lucky when they do household chores or give kids baths without being asked."

"That's funny," Ensley said. "I'll have to remember that, but as for cooking, I don't. In New York, it's easier to order out than buy groceries to rot in my refrigerator."

They all gathered at the table, except for Remy, who stood up at the counter to eat since he couldn't sit down. And dinner went off without a hitch. They talked, laughed, and kidded each other with spicy stories that turned mellow and bittersweet, funny, and at times raunchy. Ensley had never enjoyed a group of people more in her life. They were warm and accepting and genuinely cared for each other.

Watching Austin with Rick was heartwarming. Their relationship was one of mutual respect and love. Their mannerisms were twin-like, and while Rick's eyes were brown, not green like Austin's, the shape and long lashes were identical.

When Remy complained that Tavis wasn't there to harass him about getting shot in the ass, no one said anything, and Ensley couldn't figure out why. But they didn't talk about the treasure, either. There must be some unspoken agreement to put a lid on both.

Remy broke into the silence. "It's time to get the band together. Bring your beers, and let's do it."

"Great idea," Rick said. "But how are you going to play drums? You can't even sit down."

"Not a problem. I can improvise." Remy crossed the pavilion to a raised platform covered with tarps. "I could use some help over here."

David and Rick excused themselves to help Remy pull tarps off a drum kit, an electric keyboard, a sax, a multi-guitar rack with two guitars, and a banjo, plus microphones and speakers.

"Wow! It's a real band. Who plays all those instruments?" Ensley asked.

"David on sax. Rick on vocals, keyboard, guitar. Amber on vocals, guitar, banjo. And Remy on drums."

"He's a serious drummer? I thought he just liked to play sticks."

"No, he's serious. But he's missing his gig in Lexington tonight, so everybody's pitching in so he won't feel so bad."

"That sucks, but I'm glad we get to hear him play. That's some kit he's got."

"Four cymbal stands, hi-hat stand, throne, snare, floor tom, two rack toms on the bass drum, and a DW-5000 double bass pedal," Rick said.

"McBain!" Kenzie yelled. "Your fans want to hear 'Summertime.'"

"If I play it, will ye throw your panties at me?"

"Sure will. Just do it for me, babe."

Remy picked up his sticks and started with a single-stroke roll.

"Wait till he gets going," Austin said. "I bet he starts with the two-and-a-half-minute drum solo from Iron Butterfly's album *In-A-Gadda-Da-Vida*. It was cutting edge when it released, and now it's one of the top-ten drum solos of all time and Remy's favorite."

"How do you know?"

"What? That he's going to play it, or that it's one of the best all-time drum solos?"

"Both."

"I've heard Remy play it too many times. You'll recognize it. He was playing it on the train with his sticks and the tabletop."

"Austin," Daniel said. "Help me turn the sofa and chairs around."

They rearranged the furniture and pulled in more chairs for a second row while Remy warmed up and the others got their instruments ready. Ensley assumed that once the music started, the kids would pour out of the house. Austin grabbed five beers and a bottle of water from the fridge and gave water to Penny, who stretched out on a chaise lounge, and beers to Daniel, Amber, Ensley, Kenzie, and kept one for himself.

He sat on the sofa and patted the cushion beside him. "Come keep me warm," he said to Ensley.

"Warm? Your body is like a furnace. You can keep me warm." She snuggled up against him, and her mind immediately went to those intimate moments they shared before they ran out of time. She squeezed her legs together as a delightful shiver ran up her body, instantly hardening her nipples.

He whispered, "I'm thinking about us, too. I hope I don't embarrass you." He crossed his good leg over his bad one at the knee in an attempt to hide his hard-on. "Damn. I want you."

His warm breath tickled her neck. "I want you more."

"That's impossible, but I like hearing it anyway."

While Remy finished his drum solo, David attached the reed to the mouthpiece, the strap to the sax, and looped it around his neck. Kenzie leaned forward in her seat, excitement flashing across her face. If David played the sax with the expertise he did everything else, Ensley knew she was in for a treat.

He blew air through the sax and then winked at Kenzie as he curled his fingers around the keys. Rick played the intro on the keyboard, then David and Remy joined in. Remy used brushes instead of sticks, creating a swooshing sound on his snare drum. And the music they produced was soulful, sexy, and breathtaking.

Austin wrapped his arm tighter around Ensley. "If you want to attack my bones while he plays, that works for me."

The seductive sounds brought all conversation to a halt, and even the crickets stopped chirping. David didn't just play with lips and fingers, but with his entire body, and he moved with the music as he played to an audience of one—Kenzie.

Kenzie came out of her chair and swayed. And Ensley watched

them as they made love from twenty feet apart. The same thing was happening between Penny and Rick.

Then Amber started singing in a breathy alto voice, and Daniel had the same reaction as Penny and Kenzie.

The quartet was a razor-sharp performance of musical textures that captivated everyone. And as the last notes hung in the air, Ensley didn't think they could ever top it.

Then Rick and Amber sang "Island in The Stream," the timeless, genre-spanning love song. Rick crooned...

"Baby, when I met you there was peace unknown / I set out to get you with a fine tooth comb / I was soft inside / There was something going on..."

And seconds later, Amber joined in...

"You do something to me that I can't explain / Hold me closer and I feel no pain / Every beat of my heart / We got something going on."

Their harmony was a mixture of fierce and soft, and the two voices' push and pull was spellbinding. That number was followed by five more until Rick announced, "For our last number, we're debuting a new song. We hope you like it."

Amber opened with a mellow acoustic guitar riff, and Kenzie said, "Oh, my God! They're finally doing it."

David added the sax, and Rick began to sing...

"Tell me somethin', girl / Are you happy in this modern world? / Or do you need more? / Is there somethin' else you're searchin' for?"

And then they sang the chorus...

"I'm off the deep end, watch as I dive in / I'll never meet the ground / Crash through the surface, where they can't hurt us / We're far from the shallow now."

As the song drew to a close, Remy added the bass drums, kicking in with crashing cymbals...

"Crash through the surface / where they can't hurt us / We're far from the shallow now..."

Ensley was dazzled by their rendition that transformed music into raw emotion, and her heart thudded in time with the beats. The electrified air zipped and zapped around her and Austin, pushing them closer until she was almost in his lap.

When the last note faded, Austin said, "Let's go to the room."

When she didn't move, he picked her up. "If I don't have you on top of me in thirty seconds, I might have a heart attack." He carried her through the house to the adult wing, and Ensley punched in the code. Before he opened the door to their suite, he told her to close her eyes.

"And don't open them until I tell you." The door swung open, and he carried her into their room where it smelled like a rose garden and logs crackled in the fireplace. She'd never had turn-down service start a roaring fire or bring roses.

He set her on the bed. "Now, open your eyes."

Someone sneaked into their room, sprinkled red rose petals all over the floor, and left a bottle of champagne chilling in a silver bucket. Lighted candles burned on every surface, and soft jazz played on invisible speakers.

"How? When? Who?"

Austin chuckled. "When Rick heard we were on our way back, he sent me a text and asked if we were ready for our big night. I told him yes, and he took it from there. All of this"—he swept his arm to encompass the room—"is a tradition."

"It's a great tradition, but Rick was singing, so he had to have cohorts. Who are they? I'll thank them tomorrow."

Austin picked up the bottle, popped the cork as smoothly and silently as a sommelier, and filled two glasses. "When you see them at eight thirty tomorrow morning, you can do just that."

"What? Ted and Laurence did this?" She glanced around the room to check out all the details to be sure she hadn't missed anything. "My, God! This has reset my opinion of them. So going to dinner in Richmond was a ruse?"

Austin handed her a glass. "They were out by the pool listening to the concert. 'Island in the Stream' was their signal to go light the candles."

"What if we had left after David played 'Summertime?'"

"I would have encouraged you to stay."

"And how would you have done that?"

"I would have gone up on stage and sung to you. Rick and I have several duets we used to sing. I could have revived them to give Ted and Laurence enough time to get the job done."

"Really? Well, I'm sorry I missed that." She sipped, and the bubbles felt like pearls on her palate, exploding with flavors that stood out against a rich background of ripe fruit and exotic wood. One of the things JC taught her all those years ago was how to describe sparkling wine. And she lifted her glass, pausing for a moment to offer a silent toast to him.

Drink to th' hearts so loving and true, and never may we be ungrateful.

"Tomorrow, I'll show Ted and Laurence the respect and appreciation they deserve." She scooted off the bed and took her glass to the bathroom. "Don't let the candles burn out while I get ready."

She stripped out of the dress and shoes and jumped into the shower. It was crazy to take another one, but after weeks of being dirty, she might never feel clean enough again. After moisturizing her skin until it was silky to the touch, she brushed her hair and teeth and slipped on the sexy nightie she also bought at the mall. As aroused as they were, she doubted she'd wear it very long.

When she walked out of the bathroom, Austin was lying on the bed, propped up on his elbow while he scrolled through messages on his phone. His hair was wet, and he had a towel wrapped around his waist.

"Did you take a shower?"

"If you were going to smell fresh, so was I. I went next door." He dropped his phone on the bedside table, sat on the edge of the bed, and gazed at her with adoring eyes. "I want to go slowly, but I'm not sure I can."

She strolled toward him with her lips slightly twitching. "I'm so ready for this. I might not want you to go slow."

"This first time, we should. I don't want to hurt you. But slowing down will be tough. I've wanted you since the very first time I saw you on horseback holding your rifle, ready to shoot us if we gave you any trouble."

"And I would have."

"I don't doubt it. My first thought was, 'What a woman!' And I couldn't wait to get my hands on you."

She reached the foot of the bed and dropped the lacy bordello jacket she wore over a long, white silk gown with a V front and back, thin shoulder straps, and four-inch feathered bedroom slippers.

"I'm glad you didn't try anything. I would have run in the opposite direction." But right now, there was only one direction she wanted to go. Straight to him.

"You can thank Remy for that. He warned me if I touched you, he'd beat the shit out of me."

She stopped in front of Austin. "I believe he meant that."

Austin put his hands on her hips. "He did, but part of it was retribution for being such an ass to him."

"It took me a little bit longer to react to you because you were acting like a jerk."

"How much longer?"

"Until you dunked the pillow. It was a brilliant way to let everyone know you're an okay guy, and while you might not be able to herd cattle as well as the cowboys, you could do other things, like ride a bronc. You garnered their respect."

"There wasn't a day, an hour, a minute, a second that I didn't worry about you. But I knew if I hovered, you'd bust my balls, so I had to find another way to keep you safe. I didn't do such a good job. You almost got killed by a bear."

She pressed her finger against his lips. "Shhh. Nobody could have seen that coming, and I'd been warned about the bear and still went off without my rifle. I'll never do that again. My stupidity cost Erik his life."

Austin stroked his hands up and down her legs and over her hips. "That grizzly was supposed to be miles away. Plus, you'd been alone in the wilderness for days without a rifle, and that probably did give you a false sense of security. But Erik knew what was going to happen, and he didn't back down. He was saving his daughter, and what father wouldn't?"

"Not one I know."

"Me neither. Pops went on the warpath after the cartel shot JL, and he didn't get off it until he brought everyone involved to justice."

"How old were you?"

Austin pressed his forehead against her belly, and she ran her fingers through his damp hair. "A teenager. I remember wanting a handgun. I wanted to find those bastards and shoot every one of them. Rick caught me trying to sneak his service revolver out of the house. Instead of telling Pops, who would have grounded me for months, if not years, he sat me down, and we had a long talk about vengeance. I knew then, even if I never had a basketball career, that I could never be a cop."

"Then what would you have done?"

"Probably auditioned for a Broadway show. Rick has a stronger voice and can dance better, but I can hold my own, even as tall as I am."

"Broadway, huh?"

He nodded as he slowly slipped one thin strap off her shoulder. "I have a musical theater voice. Rick has a Top 40 voice. If he ever decided to cut a record, it would hit the charts."

"Now that I've heard him sing, I don't doubt it."

Austin slipped the other thin strap off her shoulder and pulled the gown down until it puddled on the floor. She stepped out of it and stood there, wearing only her heels. There was no shyness, no hesitation, no reservation. She was coming to him because she loved his gentle heart and his need to protect her even though he knew how capable she was.

"You have no idea how beautiful you are, do you? Your body is absolute perfection. It's sculpted and toned, with visible muscles in all the right places, and your breasts are high, full, and natural. Your nipples are sensitive to my mouth and hand, and they respond when I caress and suck on them, and you wiggle your hips when you walk, and it's sexy as hell."

He lifted her, and she straddled his legs. "I don't want to hurt you, so you take the lead, take as much as you want. If it gets uncomfortable, we'll use lube, but keep talking to me and tell me what feels good and what doesn't. It might take a while, but we can do this."

She kissed him. "You're a big guy, but you're not as big as those five babies we hope to have."

His deep dimples framed his face, making him even sexier. "Since I've never before been with a woman I wanted to have a baby with, I never thought of that." He lay back and pulled her down on top of him, kissing her mouth with unfulfilled hunger. Then he released her lips to rain kisses on her brow, her closed eyelids, her cheekbones. "You have grabbed hold of my spinning world and stopped it cold."

"Is that a good thing?"

"It's a damn good thing."

Ensley sat up and started untucking the end of Austin's towel in slow, giddy anticipation. Her fingertips vibrated with the urge just to yank it off, but her goal was to torture him and unwrap his package like it was a Christmas gift. Even though she desperately wanted to see him, touch him, taste him, she took her time, letting the tension build.

And when he was finally gloriously naked, she took his erection—full and flat against his belly—in both hands and stroked him, and with each stroke, he gasped. And she loved the impatience flashing in his eyes, and maybe there was a little bit of fear there, too.

Fear that she would jump off him and run away.

No way was she going to chicken out now. If a thousand-pound bull couldn't scare her off its back, a larger-than-normal erection wasn't going to either. But as they say in the bull-riding business, "If you're not nervous every time you ride, something's wrong with you."

She was nervous for sure, but she was ready for the chute gate to open, ready for Austin, and ready for the most incredible ride of her life.

He shoved another pillow behind his head so he'd have a better view of what she was doing. And his pecs, biceps, and abs rippled with every move he made. "Do you like what you see?" she asked.

"Of course. Do you like what you see?" he asked.

"Of course."

"Are you going to ride me the way you did in your bull-riding days?"

She gave him her best mischievous smile. "I was thinking about it."

"Don't think. Just do it!"

"Before every bull ride, I'd do an air ride as a warm-up. That's like playing air guitar. I'd go through the motions of how I would move, what I would do. I would imagine the hot flesh between my legs."

His erection twitched in her hand at either her touch or her word art, probably both. And he gave her one of his specialty grins. "Did you do an air ride while you were in the shower?"

She matched his grin and did a little wiggle for him, getting up close to his erection. "A mental one. But you want to know the last move I always made before the chute opened?"

"Sure," he said, hitching a breath.

"I'd reach way up on the railing, like this"—she reached for the bedpost with her right hand, her breast just barely out of reach of his mouth, and with her left hand, she held the base of his erection— "and then I'd pull my lady gooch to my pinkie and slide and ride."

When Austin realized what she intended to do, he had to stop her, even though it almost killed him. But he wasn't wearing a condom, and the ride would be over in less than eight seconds if she rode him right now.

And besides, he had a better plan than hers. He intended to hold her close. Hold her open. Kiss and suck her. One finger. Two fingers. In and out until she trembled.

He flipped her over onto her back and stretched out beside her. "Your slide and ride does sound sexy, but it'll have to wait."

She pushed on his chest, and when he didn't budge, she pounded him with her fists. "That's cheating. Let me back on. I want my eight seconds."

A fire burned in her eyes, and for the first time, Austin understood how she could take her life for granted and do something dangerous that could change everything in a flash. The more people told her not to ride a bull, the more she had to prove she could.

"If you ride me the way you planned, this round would be over in less than eight seconds, and I want it to be memorable. I don't want to be the butt of jokes. 'Hey, did you hear Austin only lasted eight seconds when Ensley rode him the first time?'"

Ensley cracked up, laughing so hard she cried. Through her tears, she finally said, "For years, all I wanted was a ride to last eight seconds. That's a perfect ride."

He used a corner of the bedsheet to wipe her tears away. "I want it to be a perfect ride for you, a perfect night, a perfect everything."

She kissed his lips, chin, chest, and then his nipples, gently sucking one into her mouth. He groaned, and she released it. "Hurt?"

He shook his head. "Hell, no."

She took her time with the other one and looked up at him while she licked it. "If eight seconds is a perfect ride, what's a perfect basketball game?"

"A five-by-five. Five points, five rebounds, five assists, five steals, and five blocked shots in a single game. And it's never been done." He stroked her face and neck and then skimmed his finger down to her breasts, teasing her nipples as she had his. His mouth replaced his finger, and he sucked the tip hard, raking his teeth over it until she began to murmur more nonsense about being cheated out of her eight seconds.

"You'll have to wait your turn, *ragazza tosta*."

"What's with that expression? It's Italian, and all I've met around here are lads from Ireland and Scotland. Kenzie even called me that tonight."

"Pete Parrino, JL's former partner, started calling her that early in her career, along with a few other choice Italian names, but that one stuck. And like her, you're one tough girl."

She pushed on his chest again, but it was as hard as trying to budge a damn bull. "Let me prove it."

"What? That you're tough? You don't have to prove it to me." He continued his assault on her nipples, and she gave up trying to get her way. Especially since maybe—just maybe—his way might be even more fun. And besides, there was always later.

Lie back and enjoy it. I have nothing to prove.

It was just the two of them now, suspended in time. Nothing existed except her body—soft and receptive—and his, hard as hell and hungry. His green eyes didn't blink as he watched her, teased her, and turned her furnace up as high as it would go.

He gave her a lazy grin. "You're licking your lips like I'm an ice cream cone."

She covered her ears. "Don't mention ice cream. I've been craving chocolate mint for weeks. If you put a bowl in front of me, I'll shovel it in."

"I'll get you some after we get to know each other better."

"I thought we already knew each other pretty well."

"Maybe, but you haven't screamed my name yet."

"I'll probably forget your name and call you Tornado, or Oscar, or Red Rock, or maybe Bodacious."

"Are those famous bulls?"

She did a slow-moving once-over, starting at his toes and stopping at his hairline. "Yeah, and from what I see, I think you could give them a buck for their money."

"Ha, ha." He glanced down at his leg. "I'm all scarred and beat up."

"So am I. And you like what you see. Right?"

He put her hand on his erection. "What do *you* think?"

He was hard and jerked when she touched him. "Hmm. I think you do."

While she stroked him, he gathered her hair and spread it over her breasts and belly. "The first time I ran my fingers through your hair, I thought I'd come on the spot. It's so silky and soft, and I wanted to spread it all over my chest and groin."

"Is that why you always kiss the top of my head? You like the feel of my hair?"

His eyes twinkled. "Damn. Now you know my secret."

"So the real reason you like to dry my hair is to indulge your crazy fantasies."

"Guilty as charged."

"I had an appointment to get my hair cut the day I went to Cambridge but had to cancel it when my client wanted to meet with me."

He rubbed the hank of hair across his face. "Why cut it?"

"It takes forever to wash and dry."

"But now you have someone to dry it for you. I love your hair, but it's yours to do with as you want. I'll continue to dry it, even if it grows to the floor." He splayed the silky strands over her breasts and nipped at her nipple through her hair.

She squirmed. "That tickles. Maybe I should cut it short and give you a long ponytail to use for whatever turns you on."

"*You*...turn me on, and you could be bald for all I care. It won't change how I feel about you." He rolled over and held himself above her, and his erection poked her belly.

She lifted her head to get a better look. "Um...something is looking for a place to go. Does it need directions? I could help."

"He'll have to wait his turn. I have other ideas."

"You do? Like what?"

"You'll have to wait and find out." He scooted her butt to the edge of the bed and bent her knees. She knew where this was going, and she couldn't catch her breath, knowing this was the beginning of exquisite madness.

He hovered above her, and before he did anything else, he adjusted her hair to cover her breasts and belly. "When we get to the ranch, I'm going to put you on a horse bareback and watch you gallop naked around the meadow with only your hair as a covering. And then I'll have a painting commissioned."

"So you want me to be Lady Godiva?"

"No, I want you to be you. No one else." He thumbed the slope of her neck until a sigh drifted into the rose-scented air and hung between them. Shivers erupted under his touch, raising the tiny hairs. He caressed her neck again until she released another sigh and then another.

He put his pinkie on her injured hip bone, splayed his hand, and put his thumb on her other hip bone.

"Your hand is huge, or I'm really small."

"My hand *is* huge, and you *are* really small."

"Too small for you?"

"Am I too big for you?"

"When I wear four-inch heels, you're less than a foot taller. That's not too big at all."

He cupped her breast, and his thumb toyed with her nipple, sending another whirlwind of sensations cycling from the tip to the farthest reaches of her nervous system. Then he took a nipple into his mouth, sucked it, released it, and trailed a path of kisses down her body, lower and lower, inching toward her clit.

He stroked her thighs, her knees, her calves, her ankles, and then he knelt on the floor and brought his shoulders between her legs, spreading her apart. And she loved being so vulnerable to him. He molded his lips and tongue against her heat. The flick of his tongue shocked her senses, and she burst out with a curse.

"Damn it! Don't stop."

He chuckled. "I won't."

She opened her thighs wider to encourage him to penetrate more deeply, and when a slow pulse started deep within her, she knew he would drive her straight to an explosion. He growled erotic words against her while his fingers speared into her tightness, stretching her, preparing her to accept him, and she rocked closer in welcome.

The more she moved, the harder he loved her with his tongue, sending shivers cascading down her shoulders to her nipples until she lost herself in the sensations, gasping and thrashing as she neared orgasm.

She shrieked his name while she bucked against him, her back arching up off the mattress. But he held her in place, riding her climax to the end.

AUSTIN WAS FINALLY living the fantasy that had stolen his mind that day in the Badlands when he first met her, and it had only grown more insistent.

He waited until she stilled, and then he gently lifted her and moved her farther up on the bed, tucking a pillow under her head before he lay down beside her.

"I liked that. Could you tell?" she asked softly.

"Could I tell?" He rubbed his nose. "I don't think it's broken, but it might be sprained. What do you think?"

She giggled. "You can't sprain your nose."

"You can't? Hmm. Sure feels like I did." He rolled her over on top of him while all the blood in his body returned to his shaft. And it was throbbing and craving her. He reached for a condom on the nightstand and ripped it open.

She sat up, straddled him, and took the condom. "That's my job."

She placed it on the tip and slowly rolled it down his erection as a fine mist of sweat coated his skin. Then an eruption of goose bumps trailed down his spine to the small of his back as more blood rushed to his groin.

Her slow, meticulous pace was driving him crazy. "Are you torturing me on purpose?"

"Yep. Just like you did to me. I'm glad to know it's working."

Once he was covered, she inched the crown of his shaft to her opening with agonizing deliberation. He struggled to restrain himself and not start thrusting. He had to let her do her thing and take only as much as she wanted. But what he wanted was his entire shaft sheathed inside her, welcoming him like a snug glove.

She eased herself down him, inch by agonizing inch until he had full penetration, and the soft, spongy tissue enveloped his shaft with a warm sensation. He began to thrust, and it was heaven—smooth, enveloping, embracing.

He had to let her ride at her pace, but the intense sensation short-circuited his brain until all he could think, see, and believe in were Ensley and his love for her.

HE LIFTED her and withdrew to the tip of his erection while she gasped for breath, praying for his return. Her hips flexed. The need for him to fill her again was overwhelming.

He released his hold on her hips, and she slid down him again. The up and down motion continued while a tornado of sensations exploded from her core and spread out along her spine to her fingers, toes, nipples, and scalp, triggering the unmistakable buildup she craved.

HE ROLLED her over and pulled her to the edge of the bed again. She wrapped her legs around his waist, and he thrust deeper, reaching where he hadn't touched her before.

She came alive for him, and her building ripple of muscles tightened around him. She cried out, and he thrust again. Her orgasm exploded. Her body quivered, every muscle clenching and releasing around him.

Through one wave and then the next, each as blissfully brutal and sweetly demanding, he loved her within an inch of her life, promising without a damn word that he'd give her everything she ever wanted and more.

HIS ERECTION twitched inside her, stroked her inner walls, and waves of pleasure tickled her spine yet again. Her muscles tightened, and vibrations buzzed across her skin. She rocked her hips, rubbing herself against him, reveling in every thrust, and drowning in his scent.

She embraced another incoming climax, wanting nothing more than for him to come with her. She felt the rhythm of their perfect dance down to her bones, and she thrashed for more, needing his strength to push her to climactic heaven, and then she combusted again, rippling over him while extraordinary flashes of satisfaction blew through her.

HIS EYES closed as a tsunami of sensations engulfed him, and she called his name, loud and guttural. Her muscles swallowed him, squeezing hard and sending shockwaves of shivers down his shaft and up to his spine. They darted through every part of his body, sensations such as he'd never felt before. His hips surged, and, with almost manic thrusts, he shuddered, holding her to him. And his mind shattered in ecstasy.

And then, somewhere in the dark recesses of his mind, he heard again what his mom, Maggie O'Grady, said when he nearly died…

Stay alive. The love of your life is coming.

A HEAVENLY second of watching him, seeing him lost in her, was all Ensley needed to come again, and she mouthed his name while his emerald eyes locked on to hers.

Her heart swelled with every second that passed until it encompassed the entire universe.

And then she remembered what Erik told her the day she fell off the bull and almost died…

Always remember you have the handprints of your ancestors on your heart. And when you are ready, your true love will find you.

73

Mallory Plantation, VA—Austin

AUSTIN WOKE UP with the sun shining in his eyes. He hadn't closed the drapes during the night because he and Ensley had enjoyed watching the stars during their all-night romp in the king-size bed.

There were several condom wrappers on the bedside table and dirty dishes scattered all over the room. Ted had stocked the kitchenette with peanut butter protein smoothies, chocolate milk, bananas, and apples with almond butter. Without the protein to restore his energy and muscles, Austin couldn't have kept up with Ensley. She was insatiable, or else she missed her bull-riding days.

Damn! He loved his woman.

He rolled over and pulled her close, whispering in her ear, "I love you, cowgirl."

She perked up, lifting her head slightly. "Back atcha, cowboy."

He rubbed her bare ass and gave her a little swat. "It's eight fifteen. If we're going to the gym, we need to roll."

"What if I promise a blow job or something? Can we stay in bed?"

"I'd take you up on it, then swat your ass. We promised to be at the gym, and MacCorp's position is if you say you'll do something or be somewhere, you do it or get docked."

"What does that mean?"

"The going rate is a thousand bucks for a missed meeting or missed gym appointment. If you miss Thanksgiving or Christmas after saying you'll be wherever the family is gathering, it'll cost you two grand. Other holidays are less."

"Sounds like the family expects you to spend every holiday together. I don't think I like that. What if you want to go skiing or to the beach?"

"Oh, you can go, just don't RSVP that you're coming and then be a no-show. That'll cost you."

"Then RSVP that you won't be there, and then come at the last minute."

"That'll cost you as well."

"God, Elliott is a control freak."

"It seems that way, but with all that's going on, we have to depend on each other. If there's a weak link, we could all get killed."

"Wait a minute. If you were isolating yourself from the family, why'd they want to send you on a rescue mission? You weren't at all dependable and could have gotten everyone killed."

"Shock therapy, I guess, or else Pops knew something no one else knew. I haven't had a one-on-one with him yet. I'll find out."

"So, how much do you owe MacCorp for not showing up?"

"Probably twenty grand."

She sucked in a quick breath. "Twenty grand! Are you insane? I couldn't sleep if I owed that much money." She shook her head. "I guess that's the difference between growing up wealthy and growing up on a small ranch in North Dakota."

"I didn't grow up wealthy. Pops was Deputy Chief of Police with the NYPD, and JL, Shane, Connor, Rick, and Jeff were all cops. We were comfortable but not at all wealthy. When JL married Kevin and everybody joined MacCorp, their lives changed. They started flying on private planes, staying in five-star hotels, and driving expensive cars. For me, I went to the University of Kentucky, and then I was drafted by the Cavs and made my own money."

"So you've never worked for MacCorp?"

"I did an internship at Montgomery Winery when I was in high school, but that's it. That was my exposure to wealthy people."

"And you wanted to be like them?"

"No, I only wanted to play basketball, but I was happy for my family." Austin chuckled. "I thought they'd all be safer working for MacCorp than they would be working for the NYPD. Boy, I was wrong about that."

Both his phone and Ensley's beeped with incoming text messages. Austin reached for his phone, but Ensley covered her head with the sheet.

"I'm not here, and you haven't seen me," she said, burrowing into him.

"Everybody knows where we are. And in ten minutes Ted and Laurence will know where we aren't."

"I thought this whole retreat theme Charlotte has going on with these luxurious suites and gorgeous landscaping might be an illusion, but I thought it would last a little longer than twenty-four hours."

Austin read his message. "Elliott's called a family meeting at eleven thirty. JL, Kevin, and the kids arrive in an hour." He yanked back the sheet, tilted her chin toward him, and kissed her. "I'll shower first, but be ready to jump in as soon as I finish." He rolled out of bed and stood to stretch.

"How do you do it? I mean, I know how you do the other thing"—she twirled her finger as she pointed at his semi-erect dick—"but where does the motivation come from to get up and work out? I'm not a morning person."

"From almost thirty years of bouncing a basketball and working on skills, timing, and precision. If I'm going to make a comeback, I have to work harder, smarter, and longer."

"And that's what you want to do? Make a comeback?"

"Yeah. That's what I want. My stupidity took me out of the game. I'm hoping my perseverance will get me back in."

"Is that realistic?"

"I have to keep trying until it becomes clear to me that it'll never happen, and I'm not there yet."

She rolled over and sat on the edge of the bed, clutching the sheet to her breasts. "Then what can I do to help you?"

"Trust in me. Have faith in me. And love me, but leave dishing out the tough love to Pops. He knows how to do that to get my attention."

"Trust, faith, and love. I can handle that."

The sheet dropped to her waist as she reached for the robe on the floor, and Austin's heart went to his throat, and all ten pints of his blood went straight to his dick.

He backed away from her. "You're doing that on purpose, aren't you?"

She blinked with feigned innocence, and he almost laughed.

"Doing what?" she asked.

"That!" He wagged his finger at her just as she'd done to him. "Sitting there with your nipples peeking out between strands of hair. Do you have any idea how much I want you?"

She gathered up her hair and swept it back over her shoulders, giving him a full-frontal view as a tease. Then she pulled up her legs, put her feet on the mattress, and hugged her knees with her legs slightly parted. And the view was even better. He licked his bottom lip and licked it again, remembering everything he'd done to her during the night.

"I can see how much you want me. So what does that mean? Are you coming back to bed?"

"I will in two hours," he said.

"But not right now?"

"Didn't you just ask me what you could do to help me have a comeback?"

Now she licked *her* lips. "I must have misunderstood the meaning of comeback."

"Oh, hell!" He fell back on the bed and pulled her over on top of him. "You're going to pay for this."

She squealed. "Just put it on my bill."

An hour later, they walked into Ted's domain—a state-of-the-art fitness and wellness complex—drinking from insulated bottles filled with a mixture of water and electrolyte powder. They'd had too little sleep and too much alcohol, and they were both dehydrated.

The main area was a weight and equipment room with a bank of TVs mounted on the wall. Splintering off the weight room were studios for dance, yoga, and massage, as well as a breakroom, men's and women's showers, offices, and a regulation basketball court.

Ted glanced up at the clock. "An hour late?"

Austin shrugged. "My fault."

Laurence leaned his elbow on Ted's shoulder. "I told him you wouldn't show up until this afternoon. But he reminded me you haven't worked out in almost a week. He was confident you'd get here within the hour. And you made it."

"I don't know how hard I can work, but I'm here. I'll shoot around in the gym, then lift, and call it a day. Is anyone in the gym?"

"Alicyn and Rebecca are in there working on their shooting skills."

"Good. I'll send a WhatsApp message to let all the kids know I'll be in the gym for a while."

"Tell them to enter through the gym door," Ted said. "I don't want a dozen kids running through here while I'm working with Ensley for the first time."

"Sure. No problem." Austin sent the message, and almost instantly, his phone beeped, beeped, beeped until he turned it to vibrate.

"Sounds like you're a hit," Ensley joked.

A sliver of emotion flicked in Ted's eyes. "The kids have always loved Austin. When he was playing, they ranked going to one of his games as the most fun event on their schedules. Remember, these are busy kids who study hard, travel extensively, and have opportunities other kids only dream about. So yeah, he's a hit."

Ted's observations choked Austin up. Ted had trained all the MacKlenna women during their pregnancies and afterward set up "Mommy and Me" exercise programs. He loved all the kids as if they were his own. And after Austin's accident, he'd spent extra time with all of them, explaining what happened to their favorite cousin and helping them manage their grief. Austin didn't know anything about it at the time. But since then, he'd donated new exercise equipment to the gym and a sauna as a thank you.

"But you," Ted continued, his forehead puckered as he eyed Ensley, "don't want to play basketball."

"You're right, and I don't want to lift, either." She yawned. "I just want to go back to sleep."

"You can sleep this afternoon," Austin said.

"Is that a promise?"

He winked. "It's whatever you want it to be."

"Like we said last night, we'll assess your physical fitness, go to the yoga studio and stretch for about thirty minutes."

"The best part is if you survive your first session with Ted, a massage and a few minutes in the sauna will be your reward," Laurence said.

"Okay, you sold me. But first, I want to tell you both how much Austin and I appreciate what you did last night. The roses, champagne, and romantic music made a wonderful evening even more spectacular." She kissed Ted's cheek and then Laurence's. "It was an incredible surprise. Thank you."

Laurence gave her a lopsided grin as he nodded in Austin's direction. "He told us not to upstage him too much. The evening needed to be memorable because of him, not the ambiance. We hope he did *his* part."

Her penetrating blue eyes flickered, and Austin knew he was about to get busted. "Well, I had a plan to show him how I rode bulls, but—"

Austin tilted her face up with a gentle tug on the silky braid hanging down her back and hushed her with a kiss as promising as he could make it.

She broke the kiss and looked up at him. "Well, now. That demonstration proves kissing isn't a dying art."

Laurence clapped Ted's shoulder, laughing. "I think Austin's found a woman as ballsy as JL."

"I don't know," Ted said. "Let's see how hard she'll work when she's hungover and exhausted."

That'll hit a nerve.

A red patch burned over Ensley's cheekbones. "I'll show you how hard North Dakotans are willing to work when facing adversity. Let's get this done!"

That's my girl.

"The yoga studio's empty since all the women are running or walking in a 10K in Richmond," Ted said. "Let's go there for an evaluation and then yoga."

"Why didn't anybody tell me?" she asked, holding up her hands in faux disappointment. "I missed a chance to bond with them. *Day-um.*"

"I can tell how disappointed you are," Ted said, deadpan.

Austin watched her closely. He was pretty good at detecting when she was in pain or when she was pissed—or his personal favorite—when he had her so turned on she could come with a flick of his tongue. And right now, her hip ached more than usual. If she'd gone on a run, she'd have finished the race in a respectable time but afterward wouldn't have been able to walk to the car to go home.

Austin turned his back to Ted and Laurence and kissed her again, and the soft sounds they made together became a love song. He rarely let anything get in the way of a workout, but right now, he'd rather be in bed with her. What he wanted didn't matter, though. The two men standing behind him would bar the door and sound the alarm if either he or Ensley tried to leave the building. It was Ted and Laurence's job to keep them healthy and sound.

"If you finish before I do, I'll see you back in the room. Don't forget Elliott's meeting at eleven thirty."

"Why do we have to be responsible?" she whispered against his lips.

"Because that's the kind of people we are." He kissed her once more and then left for the gym before Ted shooed him out of the way.

He followed the sound of bouncing basketballs from the recently constructed full-size gym on the opposite end of the fitness center. The next generation of MacKlennas had more basketball players than soccer players these days. And because of that, it was only a matter of time before they demanded a state-of-the-art facility, and their Second-Gen Arena opened the prior year. He remembered thinking that one day he might have a son or daughter playing on the court.

That idea seemed more possible today than it ever had. He glanced through the glass hallway at Ensley sitting on a yoga mat, and his heart was so full of love for her that he nearly wept.

Alicyn and Rebecca burst through the arena and almost ran into Austin.

"Whoa!" Austin said. "Where's the fire?"

"There's no fire. We're just going to the fridge to get water," Alicyn said. "We've been working on our shooting technique."

"Will you give us some pointers?" Rebecca asked.

"Sure. Let's see what you've got."

Within minutes eight more kids showed up ready to play, and for the next hour, Austin held a basketball clinic. He didn't work as hard as the kids, but they didn't let up, and the McBain girls even challenged him at the basket. His height didn't intimidate any of them. MacCorp's second generation was full of kids with guts and determination, and they accepted praise as more of a challenge to do better than a reason to rest on their accomplishments.

Toward the end of the session, Austin's half brothers Blane and Lance bounded into the gym, tore across the floor, and ran straight to him. He knelt to gather both boys into his arms.

"Austin! When'd you get here?" Blane demanded. "Why didn't you tell us?"

Lance's big brown eyes opened wide. "Yeah, Austin. Why didn't you tell us?"

"My bad." Austin released his hold but stayed on the floor to be at eye level with them. "Sorry, I've been busy, but I was already planning to call you today."

"You don't have to call us now cause we're here," Lance said. "Have you been adventuring with that girl? What's her name?"

Lance looked up at his big brother Blane. "Do you remember?"

"Ensley. Right, Austin?"

"You got it, bro. Ensley MacAndrew Williams. She's from North Dakota. Do you know where that is?"

"I do," Lance said. "It's above South Dakota. But it's colder there because it's in the north instead of the south."

"That makes sense," Austin said.

"We met her before. She was here for a Fourth of July celebration, and we talked about polo. She's cool. Does she play basketball, too, like your other *girlll*...friends?"

Austin laughed. "I don't know how good she is with a basketball, but she used to ride bulls."

"Bulls?" Lance exclaimed. "I saw bull riders on TV. They bounce up and down"—he demonstrated by jumping around in a circle—"and then they fall off"—he dropped on the floor, laughing. "A girl bull rider. That's funny. I bet her boobies bounce up and down."

"I doubt it," Blane said. "She probably wears one of those sports bras like JL wears when she runs."

"Oh. Makes sense." Lance picked up the ball, dribbled toward the basket, and threw it up, hitting the rim. "Fraser missed the layup, rebounds, and"—he shot again—"scores!"

Austin clapped. "Good job, buddy."

"We haven't told anybody our secret that we FaceTime with you every day," Blane said. "JL complains that you won't talk to anybody, but we know that's not true. 'Cause you talk to us."

"I'll always talk to you. You're my guys. But when did you start calling her JL? She's our mom."

"Because you call her JL, and you've known her for a long time. If it's good enough for you, it's good enough for us," Lance said. "When people ask about my mom, I tell them I don't have one. I have a JL."

"I bet she loves that," Austin said.

"No, she hates it," Blane said.

The other kids had left the gym, so Austin had his brothers to himself, and for the next hour, he worked with them on their shooting and dribbling skills. And it was a pure pleasure because not only were they both naturally athletic, they were also above average in height.

And right then, Austin pledged to stay involved in their lives. He had so much to teach them, and he refused to let his skills and passion for the game lessen in any way. If he couldn't play—and he wasn't ready to concede that—he'd help his brothers become the best ballplayers they could be.

At eleven o'clock, Austin said he had to go to a meeting, and he would catch up with them later. The boys hugged him goodbye and ran off to do whatever little boys eight and eleven did with their excess energy.

Austin took a quick shower and grabbed a protein drink from the break room before looking for Ensley. He figured she'd probably gone back to their suite, but he found her, limp and sweaty, resting on a mat in the yoga studio.

He sat on the floor beside her, leaned against the mirrored wall, and stretched out his legs. "So, how'd it go?"

"I've sweated all the toxins out of my body, and my arms are killing me. The last thing we did before my massage and sauna were ten minutes of kettlebells."

"I didn't think you were going to lift."

"I didn't, either, but you know Ted. I think he was trying to show me how much work I need to do if I wanted to swing that battle-ax. But man, both Ted and Laurence are worth their weight in gold. They're amazing. They knew exactly how hard to push, what to look for, and ways to relieve the stress on my hip. I got a lecture about wearing high heels and had to promise not to wear them for a while." She sighed. "So I guess I'll be stuck hanging out with your navel for a while."

Austin chuckled. "Sounds like you enjoyed working with them?"

"I wouldn't go that far. Ted lost favorability points when he recommended I schedule a titanium hip replacement in three months."

"Why three?"

"Because, he said, 'you need plenty of time to recover before you go through the stress of planning a wedding.' I told him our wedding would be a small family affair in Charlotte's backyard."

Austin burst out laughing. "Ask JL and Penny how that worked for them."

"What does that mean?"

"Meredith can be overwhelming at times."

"You don't have to tell me that. She kidnapped me, remember? But a wedding isn't in the mix for right now. We have too much to do. Right?"

"I'll get married whenever you want, and if you'd like to know what I think of your surgery, I'd say schedule it as soon as possible."

"Why? Do you know how long I'll have to rehab?"

"Six weeks post-op, you'll be able to participate in all regular activities, and it'll take three months to regain the strength and endurance you have now."

"Somebody has done their research."

He grinned. "A lazy man's research. I asked Charlotte. And besides, I've been putting off surgery on my leg. We can get cut on at the same time and rehab together."

"Oh, doesn't that sound romantic?"

"It could be," he said, smiling.

"I don't like that idea. I wouldn't be able to take care of you."

"Trust me. You wouldn't want to. Ask Remy. I can be an asshole."

"Sounds like we'll have to rehab in different places. I don't take my frustration out on others. I just beat myself up. But what bugged me about the conversation was that I felt Charlotte or Meredith had influenced Ted to tell me I need surgery soon. But I could be wrong."

"Ted's pretty independent. He wouldn't have told you something based on someone else's opinion, even Charlotte's. That's why Elliott has kept him employed for almost thirty years. He's like JL—one of the few people who can get in Elliott's face and speak truth to power. You can do that, too."

"And the rest of you can't?"

"It's not that we can't. It's that we choose not to. JL and Ted, and to some extent Kenzie and Charlotte, are our designated apple-cart-upsetters. As long as they continue to challenge Elliott, the family stays on an even keel."

"JC thought he couldn't challenge his dad," Ensley said. "That's why he didn't tell him about finding my brooch."

"That's not why he didn't tell him. JC thought the knowledge would endanger the family. He didn't want anyone hurt because of what he'd done in Asia."

"What'd he do?" she asked.

"I'm not sure. When Elliott wants to tell us, he will."

"So does that make me an apple-cart-upsetter?"

"'Fraid so. And when Elliott adopts you, you'll have even more privileges."

"He's not legally adopting me."

"Yes, he is. It's a gesture of his commitment to the pledge he made to Erik. Kevin and Kenzie are revising his estate plan to include you."

"Shit! I'm twenty-eight years old. He should have asked me— and besides, I don't want his money."

"It's not like he's going to stand on a street corner and tell the world he adopted you. If you want anyone to know, you can tell them. Otherwise, it'll just be a paper deal. But honestly, it's not just his money, but his protection."

"Like a mafia don?"

Austin stood and held out his hand to help her up. "The evil we're facing is centuries old. We don't know how far its tentacles stretch. If it ever becomes known that you're Erik's biological daughter, you'll be in even more danger than the rest of us."

She grabbed a towel from a rack in the corner where Ted also kept mats, blocks, bolsters, rugs, blankets, and straps and wiped away the sweat. "Do Ted and Laurence have any idea what's going on?"

"They don't know why we all live on a high wire. I think they believe we're up to something, but not anything illegal. They have a great life here. MacCorp pays all their living expenses, and they make six-figure incomes. They work hard and have a large staff to manage."

"So I'll be working with someone on their staff?"

"I'm sure Ted will manage your training until you've recovered from surgery. But eventually, he'll switch you over to someone else on his team."

"That makes sense."

"You need a shower, and I have phone calls to make before Elliott's meeting."

"Will everybody be there?"

"JL and Kevin are here if that's who you're wondering about."

"Have you seen them?"

"Not yet, but I just finished playing basketball with Blane and Lance."

"Oh, I've met them before. They probably don't remember me, though."

"We'll catch up with them after the meeting"—he checked the

time on his watch—"that starts in twenty-five minutes."

"Are you coming back to the room with me?"

"No, I'm going over to the resource center to use the guest office. The conference room is there, too."

"Wish I'd brought a change of clothes. Then I could have showered here."

"I didn't think we'd be this long." He kissed her. "Take one of the golf carts parked outside."

She reached up, clasped his shoulders, and drew him close. "I wish we could go back to the room. I have a feeling this meeting is going to lead to more stress, and the rest of the day will be one long, grueling planning session."

"I think you're right, but we've known for days where this thing was going."

"Are you talking about us or rescuing Tavis?"

He grinned. "I've known since the first time I saw you that I'd have you on top of me before my birthday."

"And when's your birthday?"

"Tomorrow."

74

Mallory Plantation, VA—Ensley

Ensley entered the conference room in the Resource Center on somewhat shaky legs. She wasn't sure if it was from her workout, nerves, or sex. If she had to rank them, she'd put a bad case of the nerves at the top of the list.

Everyone smiled or waved, acknowledging her presence without overwhelming her. JL was here, and while Ensley had met Austin's mom before, the situation was completely different now. Ensley was sleeping with her son.

The extra-large oval conference table had seating for fourteen on each side. She'd never seen such a huge table. The room's outer wall was all tinted glass and faced a flowering garden and the river. The rear wall had a TV almost the size of a movie theater screen. Extra swivel chairs lined another wall while credenzas loaded with trays of salads, sandwiches, iced tea, and lemonade filled the last.

Some of the family were already sitting at the table eating, while others were filling their plates. Ensley's stomach growled in anticipation of biting into one of Charlotte's famous egg salad sandwiches.

Ensley headed straight to the food, Austin behind her. "There are a few people I haven't met before," she said.

"They're all first-gens," Austin said. "You probably haven't met Matt and Elizabeth Kelly. They're the couple in their late sixties sitting on the other side of the table, and next to them are Philippe and Rhona Baird. Pops is over there filling his plate. Pete and Sophia, and my brother, Connor, and his wife Olivia are sitting opposite each other at this end."

"Connor and Oliva have the daughter whose hair you brush.

Right?"

"Right. They named her Betsy after her grandmother," Austin said.

"I've heard all the names but haven't put them together with faces yet."

"You've met all the other people here."

Ensley searched the room and put couples together in her mind. Daniel and Amber, Braham and Charlotte, David and Kenzie, Kevin and JL, Cullen and Kit, Rick and Penny, Elliott and Meredith.

"I see Jack Mallory, but I haven't met his wife."

"Amy," Austin said. "She's an ESPN sports analyst. You've probably seen her in the broadcasting booth during baseball games."

"Oh, yeah, right. I'm such a big baseball fan, but I don't recognize her. Sorry."

"If it weren't for kids and grandkids, most of the women here would believe an event involving a ball required glamorous clothes and expensive jewelry."

She glanced up at him and rolled her eyes. "I fit in that category, you know."

"Yeah, but you're coming around to the dark side, and soon you'll know all the players and their stats."

"I doubt it, but I'm open to learning, which is saying a hell of a lot. So, who's not here?"

"Shane's in Australia, Gabe's in Italy, and Jeff and his wife Julie rarely make meetings in person. Jeff and his staff handle mergers and acquisitions, and he's usually traveling. With five kids and six grandkids, Julie has very little extra time."

"You're the only kid here," she said.

"The second-gens in college, grad school, med school, and law school join the Zoom call if they have the time."

"How do you know all this when you've been out of the loop for so long?"

"I got updates from Connor, and Meredith sends out summaries."

Ensley watched JL trek through the crowd at the food tables. If her eyes were any indication, JL was on a mission. Ensley steeled herself.

When JL reached Austin, she hugged him around his waist. "Don't be mad at me."

"For what?" he asked.

"For helping Tavis and Remy kidnap you."

"Oh, that." He gave a dismissive wave. "I'm over it."

Ensley caught an unmistakable ripple of guilt surge across JL's face and in her green eyes before it vanished, leaving her expression cold and distant. "I find that hard to believe," she huffed.

"We're cool, JL. I told you that on the phone. Don't worry about it."

"Excuse me for asking again, but the whiplash is hard to handle. You went from not wanting to see any of us to 'Here I am. How's everybody doing?'"

Austin's breathing quickened, and his nostrils flared. He glanced away for a moment before returning his gaze to JL. "Look. We've moved on. It's time for you to do the same."

JL's brows snapped together, and she grimaced. "After dealing with your attitude the past twelve months, I'm struggling to believe that."

Austin picked up a plate and loaded it with sandwiches. "I enjoyed playing with Lance and Blane. Their basketball skills are improving."

JL snapped her hand to her hip like she had a pistol strapped there and intended to draw it to emphasize her point. "How would you know? You haven't seen them in months."

Austin continued loading his plate with spoonfuls of potato salad and egg salad while the back of his neck turned an angry red. What the hell was wrong with JL? Austin was doing everything he could to stay calm, but Ensley didn't think he'd keep his cool much longer.

Trust me. Love me.

"JL, did you hear about the grizzly Austin shot?"

"I heard three different versions—and not one of them from Austin."

Ensley let out a harsh breath. Enough was enough. She looked around for an escape. Kenzie was standing across the room and gave her a nod, which Ensley interpreted to mean, "If you need to run, come this way."

"Excuse me," Ensley said. "I have to ask Kenzie a question." She all but darted across the room. "What in the hell is wrong with JL? I can't believe the way she's talking to Austin."

"JL's in a snit. And Kevin won't call her out on it, so no one else will, either."

"A snit must be a Southern thing. In North Dakota, we just come right out and call someone a bitch when they're acting like one."

"You know Charlotte, so what can I say? But yeah, JL is acting like a bitch. She wigs out like this hours before she flies to Richmond, and it takes her a few hours to calm down once she gets here."

"If she hates the place so much, why come for a visit?"

"She loves it here, but she hates flying. Kevin was piloting his Cessna from Lexington to Chesterfield County Airport right outside of Richmond eight years ago. The landing gear collapsed, and the impact caused JL's placenta to abrupt, and she went into premature labor. Lance almost died and spent months in the NICU, so I understand why she turns into the Wicked Witch of the West. But that doesn't mean I have to be nice to her when she does."

"Why doesn't she drive?"

"Nobody will ride with her, and she doesn't want to travel alone."

"Why not?"

"Would you ride in a car for six hours when you could fly here in forty-five minutes?"

"No, so why don't they put her on a damn bus?"

"Yeah, right."

"Well, I don't care about her travel plans. I only care about the way she treats Austin. He might end up taking the leading role in another disappearing act."

"She's complaining about everything today. She's also pissed about the treasure. If we vote to haul it out of the cave, I don't know what she'll do."

"She can't get much worse...can she?"

"This is about the worst I've seen her, but she's premenopausal, so there's no telling how bad she *can* get."

"She needs a pharmaceutical intervention." Ensley watched JL and Austin another minute before deciding it was time to bail him out. "It looks like they're wrapping up their conversation. I'll head back over there."

"Hey, wait! Not until you tell me about last night."

Ensley toyed with a lock of her hair, remembering how involved her hair had been in last night's lovemaking marathon, and her cheeks heated. "Fantastic. He's a sensitive, gentle, and highly erotic lover. He knows how to use his body to enhance a woman's pleasure. Anything else you want to know?"

"So everything…fits…together?"

"Perfectly."

Kenzie gave her a side hug. "I'm so glad."

When Ensley reached Austin, JL was still scolding him for something, which pissed Ensley off again. She didn't care about JL's phobias, but Ensley pressed her fingers to her mouth out of fear the words forming on her tongue would jump out and attack JL and her shitty attitude.

Thankfully Pops came to the rescue. Austin set down his plate and hugged him.

"Good to see you, son. I haven't seen you this happy since the championship a few years ago."

"That's because I haven't been." Austin cupped Ensley's shoulder, pulling her close. "She's changed my life, Pops."

Pops winked at her. "Austin had a one in four chance of winning your heart, and I had a feeling you'd choose him over JC, Tavis, and Remy."

"That's some serious competition. All four are loving, intelligent, talented men worthy of a *GQ* or *Men's Health* cover. So why'd you think I'd fall for Austin?"

Pops cocked his head, then fixed her with a gaze that caused a squirt of adrenaline to pump into her veins. She knew exactly how one of his subordinates must have felt when on the receiving end of a reprimand by the former NYPD Deputy Police Chief. Then his gaze softened, but before he answered her question, he cleared his throat, which sent another squirt into her veins.

"The brooches have a way of finding young men when they're most in need of being found. Remy's not lost, JC's not looking for a forever love, and Tavis isn't emotionally available."

"Wow! You've got them pegged," she said. "But that doesn't—"

"—Let me finish, Ensley. Austin was lost but emotionally available"—Pops stopped and held up his finger—"but only for the right woman. Your background, growing up on a ranch, your passion for literature, and your total disinterest in sports meant you would see the whole man without being distracted by his star power, which he has in spades—even off the court."

Ensley blinked as if blinking blew away the dust, the haze, the fog that kept her from connecting to what Pops was saying. "I still don't get it. We've never met."

"I'm a cop, Ensley, and while I'm mostly a grandfather now, I do help Braham with security around here. The first time you and your cousin came to Mallory Plantation with JC, I did a background check, and I've kept up with you because you remind me of my late wife, Maggie."

Pops shoved his hand in his pants pocket and moved his fingers around, clicking something that sounded like rosary beads. "In the interest of full disclosure, I consulted with David about agents and publishing companies and called in a favor to get Austin's manuscript in front of you."

Her mouth fell open. "I'll be damned. I ruined your plan."

"No, you didn't, my dear. Even though you didn't accept Austin's manuscript, you saw the heart laid bare in the story, and your mind wanted to know the ending. So when you met him, you didn't see the asshole. You saw the unfinished man and fell in love with him, warts and all."

A tear streaked down Ensley's face, and she gazed up at her man, the love of her life. "That's exactly right, sir."

Austin wiped away the tear and hugged her. "I didn't know any of this."

"I know you didn't."

"Maggie loved Austin," Pops continued. "And even though he was only a baby when she died, our last conversations were about him. She made me promise to guide and protect him until he found the love of his life. Nobody else thought he was in any condition to be part of a rescue team. But Maggie knew, and at the planning meeting, she tugged on my heart until I had to overrule my children and give my grandson the toughest love of his life."

Austin looked heavenward for a second, then back at Pops before hugging him. "Thank you for knowing me better than I knew myself. And thank you for Ensley."

Pops reached in his pocket for a handkerchief and blew his nose. "I spent more time with you than I did with the others because I made the time. I did it for Maggie at first, but then I discovered how much you were like her. You have her gentle soul, and I knew I just couldn't fail you."

"You didn't fail me, Pops. You did everything right. And I'm sorry for the trouble I've caused."

"You didn't cause any more trouble than the others."

JL had tears in her eyes, too. "You always know just the right time to pull out a Maggie story, Pops. Thank you." She looked at her dad and then her son. "I love you both, and I'm sorry that I can be such a bitch at times."

Austin hugged her. "You know, don't you, that I talk to Blane and Lance every day and have for the last year?"

She knuckled away a tear. "They disappeared about the same time every morning, and I couldn't figure out what they were up to. Then several months ago, I overheard a conversation between them about keeping their secret with you. I didn't want to do anything to interfere, so I kept quiet."

"I'm glad you did."

"Did you know they call me JL?"

Austin nodded. "If you don't stop it now, they won't ever make the switch."

"They want to do everything you do."

Austin massaged the back of his neck, obviously struggling with something. "When I'm around them, I'll call you Mom. That might help."

More tears leaked from the corners of JL's eyes. "It would make a huge difference. It just kills me when Lance tells people he doesn't have a mom. He has a JL. It's just what you used to say."

The pain in JL's voice made it clear how much it had hurt her to be unable to claim Austin as her child. And when Blane and Lance didn't call her mom, it brought that pain front and center again.

Kenzie whispered to Ensley. "I can't take all this soul-wringing." She took Ensley's arm and dragged her out of hearing range. "There's a girls' outing at two o'clock. We're taking the pontoon out for a couple of hours, and you *have* to come. We'll drink some beer, gossip about everybody who's not there, and soak up the sun. What do you say?"

Ensley looked over at Austin. JL and Pops had left him for the food tables, and he was coming toward her. "What are you two cooking up?" he asked.

"Are you okay? That was a rough conversation."

"Whenever I've veered off course, Pops has always reminded me of what he promised Mom, and it always makes me feel cheated because she died before I knew her. But you know what? JL, Jeff, Shane, Connor, and Rick loved her and lost her, and her death broke their hearts. I got to love her through their eyes without the grief of losing her. Maybe I wasn't cheated after all."

"I wish I had someone around to tell me stories about Erik. I feel cheated."

"Maybe Tavis knows more about him," Kenzie said.

"Maybe."

"So what were you two talking about when I walked up?" Austin asked. "It looked like you were plotting something."

"We want to take Ensley out on Charlotte's pontoon this afternoon," Kenzie said.

"You should go. You'll have a blast. From what I hear, there's lots of beer, nude sunbathing, and gossiping about sex."

"I don't know about the nude sunbathing, but beer and gossiping works for me. But what are you going to do?"

"The guys are planning to go fishing, drink beer, and talk about sports."

"Are you going?" Ensley asked.

"Only if you're going with the girls."

"Geez," Kenzie said. "You should hear yourselves. You've spent way too much time together lately. Take a break. When you see each other again, it'll be twice as hot."

Matt Kelly approached them and introduced himself to Ensley. "I heard you spent a few weeks with Teddy Roosevelt. I'm a huge Roosevelt fan, so I hope you'll share your experiences with me."

"I'll be thrilled, Mr. Kelly—"

"Matt," he said.

"Okay, Matt. I have lots of notes you can read, plus I'll tell you everything I remember about the time I spent with him."

"You grew up close to the Theodore Roosevelt National Park in North Dakota."

"I did, and I get the stories mixed up. Some of them I can't remember if TR told me or a park ranger did. But he's an incredible man. We talked for hours, or rather he talked, and I listened. Most of our conversations were about literature, even when JC, Austin, and I played chess with him. But Austin played with TR the most, so he's got a few stories of his own."

"You did?" Matt asked.

"I enjoyed it," Austin said. "He's a very competitive chess player."

"He wouldn't talk about politics or his late wife," Ensley said. "Those two topics were off-limits, but everything else—from travel to the classics—he expounded on ad infinitum. I'd love to go back and spend more time with him. I don't think I could ever get enough."

"If you do, count me in," Matt said.

Elliott knocked on the table. "Let's get this meeting started, so we can get out of here and go fishing."

If only it were that easy. If only they could just drink beer and go fishing for the day.

But the danger was still out there.

Tavis was still gone.

And a billion-dollar treasure was still gathering dust in a cave.

75

Mallory Plantation, VA—Ensley

WHEN ELLIOTT CALLED everyone to the table, Ensley hung back, waiting to see what seats remained open after all the others sat down. The only two seats were on Elliott's right.

Austin whispered. "Looks like Grandpa wants you next to him."

"Terrific."

Elliott sat near the center of the table with Meredith, Kevin, JL, Connor, Olivia, Pete, and Sophia on his left. On his right were the two empty seats, then Pops, Rick, Penny, and Remy.

Directly across the table from Elliott were Kenzie and David, with Charlotte, Braham, Jack, and Amy on one side. Kit, Cullen, Daniel, Amber, Matt, Elizabeth, Philippe, and Rhona were on the other.

"Maria's not here," Austin said. "She's probably babysitting. She'd rather be with the kids than sit through one of these meetings."

"I don't blame her," Ensley said, strolling toward the empty chairs, mentally circling the table a couple of times in her mind, cementing names and faces together. At first, she thought there was a seating chart, arranging people in order of seniority, but then she and Austin would be sitting against the wall. Maybe no one other than Meredith wanted to sit next to Elliott, and Ensley was again the victim of the day. That made more sense than a seniority seating chart.

David typed on his laptop, and the Zoom login page appeared on the gigantic TV screen. After he logged in, he accepted everyone waiting to join the meeting. Six faces appeared in individual boxes. Other than Emily, Ensley didn't recognize any of them.

Braham picked up a remote and clicked a button. A small door in the tabletop opened in front of every seat and a video camera popped up. Within seconds, all the people at the table joined the first six on the TV screen in separate boxes.

"Each camera is voice-activated," Braham said. "As soon as ye speak, the camera will pick up yer voice so those on the call can hear ye. As a reminder, ye don't need to yell."

"Has everybody had a chance to get acquainted with Ensley? If ye haven't, be sure to catch up with her after the meeting," David said.

"The women are taking the pontoon out this afternoon, so we'll give her a huge MacKlenna welcome," Kenzie said.

"I'm sorry I can't be there," Emily said. "A day on the river with you gals would be so much fun."

"Next time," Kenzie said.

"Let's get this meeting started," Elliott said. "Ye all know that Erik the Viking saved James Cullen's life, and our son is now at the monastery recovering from his trauma. The last time I saw Erik, he asked me to take care of his daughter, Ensley. With that in mind, I asked Kevin and Kenzie to update my estate plan to include Ensley as my heir, to share equally with Kevin and James Cullen."

Ensley's hand shot up. "And I objected! I inherited my parents' farm, and after I sold it, I invested the proceeds. I'm not uber-rich, but I'm comfortable, and I don't need Elliott's money."

"Feel free to object," Kevin said. "But from what I hear, you'll soon be my daughter-in-law, so it'll all stay in the family anyway. And based on the treasure in the cave, which we all believe was collected and stashed there by Erik, you're richer than our combined wealth. You should be able to take care of us in our old age."

Chuckles rippled around the room until Connor asked, "What's the plan for retrieving the treasure, and where can we sell it?"

Everyone looked at Elliott, but before he could say anything, JL blurted out, "We're leaving it alone for now. After what happened to JC, we don't dare recover it, and there's not one piece in the collection we could legitimately sell."

"We sold the treasure we found in California," Connor said.

"That was different," JL said. "We could explain the gold and artifacts. We can't explain how a Roman treasure ended up in a cave in Lexington, Kentucky."

"But we don't have to," Ensley said. "That's what experts do. All we have to do is notify Sotheby's or Christie's. They'll send experts to evaluate and appraise the items. Then they'll schedule an auction."

"They'll never believe it," Connor said.

"Yes, they will," Robbie piped up from his Zoom square. His background was a mishmash of male and female soccer players, including a woman who resembled Penny kicking a soccer ball into the net. "Tell them what you found, Henry."

"In 2016," Henry said, "a metal detectorist from Lexington searched a pasture on a Central Kentucky farm for Civil War artifacts. His metal detector started pinging, indicating he'd found gold items. He dug up two Roman coins and kept poking around. Eventually, he unearthed a cache of jewelry, bowls, vases, carvings, and coins worth millions. The radiocarbon dating indicated some of the organic material near the items unearthed dated between 500 BC and 200 AD and matched the dates on the coins."

"Where'd you find that article?" Kenzie asked while opening her laptop.

"I googled 'Roman artifacts found in America.' It was at the top of the list," Henry said.

Except for the clicking of Kenzie's nails against her laptop keys, there was silence in the room. Then she looked up and slapped her hands on the table. "Robbie and Henry McBain, next time I see you, I'm giving you both the ass-kicking of your practical-joker lives."

Robbie and Henry started laughing hysterically.

Kenzie turned her computer around. "The last line of the article Henry was referring to says, 'April Fools, everyone! Have fun!'"

"It's a joke?" The muscles in Elliott's jaw twitched.

Kenzie nodded. "Your grandsons just pulled a late April Fool's joke on us."

"Kick them out of the meeting," Elliott said to David calmly, but with a bite that could chop off a head or two.

"Wait! Don't do that—" Robbie said seconds before the twins' squares disappeared.

Silence pervaded the room until snickers slipped out around the table, and then they all burst out laughing.

When Elliott pulled himself together, he said, "Let the lads back in."

When Robbie and Henry appeared again, Robbie said, "I'm sorry, Grandpa. I know this is a serious meeting"—another laugh bubbled up, and Robbie turned away from the camera to get himself under control. He turned back around, sucking in his cheeks until he'd composed himself, and started again. "We found another article, and this one is legit."

"Let me, Robbie. You'll just start laughing again," Henry said.

Although they were identical twins, Henry's background was a bulletin board full of polo players. The picture in the center was of the twins riding Thoroughbreds as large as Austin's, looking like warlords swinging their mallets. They looked fierce in the photograph. But at the moment, the eighteen-year-olds studying at Cambridge looked more like jokesters. Ensley had a hard time reconciling the two—or four—personalities.

"A smaller cache," Henry began, "was discovered in a cave in the North Dakota Badlands—"

Ensley gasped. "Where?"

"It doesn't say, but a reporter digging into the story reported that the current owners bought the ranch two months ago."

"Holy shit!" Ensley said. "That could be mine! We only closed on the deal a couple of weeks ago, but it was under contract for two months. The buyers rented the property until the closing."

"But if they found a treasure, wouldn't they have kept it a secret until they owned the property?" Robbie asked.

"You're right. It couldn't be mine. So what'd they find in the cave?" Ensley asked.

"The owners shipped the entire cache to the National Roman Museum in Rome, and the museum put a lid on the story. So no one knows," Henry said.

"Someone knows," David said. "I'll see what I can find."

"Don't you think it's weird they found a treasure on my ranch?"

"We don't know that for sure, Ensley," Austin said. "It could be a cave on a neighbor's ranch."

"Maybe," Elliott said. "But ye all know what I think of coincidences."

"It goes something like this," Penny said. "'If fate or mystery or God...or even brooches...can cause coincidences, then the cause is known, and there are no coincidences.' Do I have that right?"

"Yer memory is correct, lass."

"So Erik parked a treasure on MacKlenna Farm and another one on Ensley's ranch in North Dakota, knowing someday she would find at least one of them?" Meredith asked.

Everything seemed to rush past Ensley like a hum in the cottonwood trees, and she wanted to run away before the hum turned into a screech.

"Maybe Erik hid the first treasure, traveled into the future, and discovered the loot was found and returned to Rome, and he couldn't get it back," Ensley said. "So he collected an even bigger treasure and hid it inside a cave on MacKlenna Farm. If it's not there now—I mean in the present—we'll have to look in Colorado."

"Why Colorado?" Henry asked.

Ensley looked up at Austin, hoping he would answer Henry's question.

"Because Ensley's moving in with me."

"Oh, that's cool," Henry said. "Then if Erik knew your future, there might be a treasure there, too."

"It's possible," Elliott said. "The members of the Illuminati are often a step ahead of us."

"Then they could attack one of us again if they discover the cave on the farm," Robbie said.

"Well, thank God somebody agrees with me that the danger is real," JL said.

"There's no disagreement, JL," David said. "But we still have to get inside the cave to inventory the contents, secure the premises, and set up twenty-four-hour surveillance."

"I agree with David," Kenzie said. "We must make sure the treasure is still there and secure it. I think everybody agrees with that."

"I don't," JL said. "And it's too dangerous right now to relocate all that stuff. And really, how much more secure can you make it? To even get inside the treasure room, you have to have a brooch, and it's not like you can buy one of those at your local Target store."

"The Illuminati has a collection of brooches," David said. "If they know about the cave, they can get to the treasure."

"Let's put this to a vote," Meredith said.

"Good idea. We've had enough debate. So what's the question?" Kevin asked.

"Should we allow David and his team to enter the treasure cave, determine if any items have been added or removed, secure the premises, and set up video surveillance?" Braham asked. "And if nothing has changed inside the cave, then they should develop a plan to relocate the entire treasure to a different secure facility."

"I know I'm pissing in the wind," JL said, "but I want to go on the record with my professional opinion. I firmly believe we should stay the hell away from that cave. Putting even one foot inside will open Pandora's box and set loose an evil we're not prepared to fight and possibly can't win. And proving I'm right will bring no satisfaction because we'll probably all be dead."

"Well, aren't you the queen of gloom," Pete said. "And I thought you were a *ragazza tosta*."

"I am," JL said, "but my kids aren't, and if you do this, you'll put all the second-gens in danger."

"I disagree," Pete said. "Doing this will secure a safe future for them."

Elliott knocked on the table. "Enough. Time to move on. Everyone in favor of David inventorying the contents of the cave and establishing video surveillance, raise your hand."

Everyone except JL raised their hands.

"Kevin, bring yer family here for the summer," Elliott said.

"Why should we have to leave our home?" JL asked.

"Because it might be dangerous, JL. Stop acting like a bitch," Rick said. "We're all a little testy right now, so let up, will you? And besides, if you're here, you'll be able to see our twins right after they're born."

JL sat back in her chair and crossed her arms.

"Do it for Mom, JL. She can't be here, but you can," Rick added.

"Okay," JL said. "We'll stay, and I'll try to be my cheerful self."

Connor choked on his drink and slapped his chest. Olivia looked at him with concern. "Are you all right?"

Connor cleared his throat. "I was swallowing a drink when JL said something about being cheerful. She hasn't been cheerful in months, maybe years."

Kenzie winked at Ensley. "That's because JL needs a pharmaceutical intervention."

"Cute, Kenzie," JL snapped. "If you're talking about hormones, I have an OB-GYN appointment next week, but since you're forcing me to stay here, I'll miss it."

"I'll get you one in Richmond," Charlotte said.

Elliott knocked on the table again. "Let's move on. We don't need this family drama, even though I recognize it as the family default in times of stress. This time we're picking on JL. Last time it was Rick."

"I think a share of that pickin'-on goes to Austin," Remy said.

"He was the asshole."

"I hope I've redeemed myself by now."

Ensley kissed him. "You most definitely have."

"David, how long will it take to put a team together and organize the equipment?" Elliott asked.

"A day or two. I'll take Kenzie, Ensley, Austin, and Braham with me."

"I want to go, too," Sophia said. "I know I can look at the photographs, but I want to see the wall paintings and the contents of the treasure room in person so I can get a real sense of what's there and how it looks today."

"Fine," David said. "I guess that means Pete's going, too. Good. Ye can do the security design outside. Braham and I'll do the inside."

"That's settled, then." Elliott walked over to the food tables, poured another glass of iced tea, and filled a bowl with fruit.

"What's the plan for Tavis?" Ensley asked.

Elliott returned to his chair. "Rescuing him isn't going to be so easy. Ensley, what are yer thoughts about why he hasn't returned?"

"Erik was dying when he told me Tavis should take him home. Erik said it was time for his heir to take the empty seat at the table. But that doesn't make sense. Why didn't he ask me to take him?"

"Maybe in their culture, women can't hold positions on the Council," Kenzie said.

"If Tavis is Erik's son, I could understand the Council wanting him to stay. But he's not—" Ensley stopped, suddenly struck by the possibility that her mother wasn't the only woman Erik impregnated. She glared at Elliott. "Is Tavis Erik's son? Is Tavis my half brother?"

Elliott clasped his hands on the table and stared at them as his knuckles turned white. Ensley squeezed Elliott's tanned forearm, and the muscles bunched under her fingers. She sensed the dilemma torturing him. If Tavis was Erik's son and didn't know it, telling the family first was disrespectful.

"Never mind," Ensley said. "For whatever reason, the Council won't allow Tavis to come home."

"There's another possibility," Kenzie said. "Maybe he doesn't want to leave."

"Why would he want to live in the twelfth century?" David asked.

"Because he has a family," Remy said. "I know it sounds weird, but no one has ever seen Tavis with a date."

"We hang out," Emily said from her square on the TV screen. "We go to shows, dinner, concerts."

"But as friends, Emily. Right?" Remy asked.

She nodded.

"If Tavis had a family, he'd have brought them here. If he had a choice, I don't see him raising a kid in the twelfth century," Remy said. "Maybe the Council won't let him leave with his family."

"There's also the possibility he's dead," Kenzie said. "He could have tried to leave, gotten into a fight, and was killed."

"I believe he's alive," Elliott said. "And I'm going back to get him."

"If we do that, Elliott, the Council could be expecting us, and we could be walking into a hostile environment," Remy said.

Kenzie jumped to her feet. "Goddamn it!" She stepped away from the table and paced.

"What is it, lass? What'd ye see?" Elliott asked.

She shook her head. "I didn't see anything." She put her hands on David's shoulders. "But David saw it in his vision the day Penny disappeared from her hotel room in New Orleans. Do you remember?"

"I remember," Sophia said. "I sketched everything David described."

David typed on his laptop, and a moment later, Sophia's sketch appeared in a square on the Zoom call.

"Walk us through the sketch," Elliott said.

"There are several," Sophia said. "Will you pull the others up, too?"

More squares with sketches appeared on the screen.

"The first sketch shows several warriors with dark blue tattoos running from their fingertips to their necks. The designs vary from mythical creatures to divine symbols. The next sketch shows warriors spread out on a slanting, rocky field with blood on their arms. The next sketch shows a man on the ground who was beheaded. I compared David's description of him with a sketch I made of a man I met in Richmond in 1790. We think the man on the ground resembles James MacKlenna."

"We know the family buried James MacKlenna at Chapel Yard in Inverness," Meredith said. "But since you did that sketch three years ago, my genealogy team uncovered rumors about an older brother named Andrew. The rumor is that Andrew left home under mysterious circumstances, was disinherited, and never heard from again. I just put the information in my rumor file."

"Do ye think he could have joined the Illuminati?" Elliott asked.

"Who knows?" Meredith said.

"What's the last sketch?" Austin asked.

"David saw only one woman in his vision. She carried a tall longbow made of yew and was aiming at a target he couldn't see. He didn't know who she was but thought she resembled JL."

"I can confirm right now that I've never been to Jarlshof and never intend to go," JL said.

"I don't remember David mentioning any landmark that would identify the location as Jarlshof, and I feel confident that had he, I would have sketched it," Sophia said.

"Whatever," JL said.

Ensley shot a glance at Kenzie and mouthed, "The battle of the bitches. Bring it on."

"We need all our oars in the water and pulling in the same direction," David said. "It's apparent that we're going back for Tavis, and we must be very strategic. That means we have to be prepared and ready to fight."

"Then we'll wear black Battle Dress Uniforms with full-face balaclavas and night vision," Connor said.

"That's the only way to go," Remy said. "But we'll look like space aliens to the people there, and they could use Tavis as a hostage. I doan want him to come home with missing body parts or missing family members."

"What do you want to wear, then? Kilts?" Matt asked. "They didn't work out so well for the lads at Culloden."

"There have been several statements using the pronoun—we. I want to be clear that only Remy and I are going. I'll wear a kilt and the torc, and Remy can go as a space alien. But I'm not involving anyone else in this and risk David's vision coming true," Elliott said.

"My vision is already true," David said. "The question is, how will *our* presence change the outcome?"

"We have to go armed to the teeth. A show of force with AK-47s," Connor said.

Elliott glared at Connor. "What did I just say?"

"I don't know," Connor said. "I didn't hear you say anything."

"When do we leave?" Remy asked. "There's another gig in Lexington I'd like to play before I go fight with twelfth-century Vikings."

"David, prepare a battle plan for me. I don't intend to use it, but I should be ready for the unexpected."

"I'm going with you," Ensley said.

"No, ye're not."

"I'm going, too," Kenzie said.

"No, ye're not."

Kevin stood. "If the Frasers are going, that includes me."

David stood. "The McBains are going, and that includes Kenzie, Robbie, and Henry."

Daniel stood. "The Grants are going, and that includes Noah."

Pete stood. "The Parrinos are going, and that includes Sophia and Churchill."

Braham stood. "The McCabes are going, and that includes Lincoln."

Jack stood. "The Mallorys are going, and that includes Patrick."

Cullen stood. "One Montgomery is going."

Remy stood. "One Benoit is going."

Philippe stood. "One Baird is going."

"Philippe, yer gout flareup prevents ye from going. I'm sorry. And Matt, ye're needed here," Elliott said.

Austin stood. "Ensley and I are going. If you're keeping a scorecard, that's one O'Grady and one MacAndrew Williams."

Rick stood, and Elliott said, "Sit down, lad. Ye'll not leave yer bride's side right now."

Pops stood, and Elliott said, "Sit down, Pops. Ye're needed here."

Then Elliott sat back in his chair, rubbing his forehead. After a moment, he said, "That makes eleven men, three women, and six second-gens. Catch the next flight out, lads, then gather yer plaids, body armor, and weapons. We'll leave in a week."

76

Mallory Plantation, VA—Ensley

ONE WEEK LATER, Ensley stood in her suite's walk-in closet staring into the mirror. She looked like a space alien. Since David was leading an untrained team, he ordered everyone to wear black Battle Dress Uniforms (BDUs), body armor, helmets, combat boots, and carry M4 carbine rifles.

Elliott, however, nixed the automatic rifles in favor of M18 SIG Sauers. They were confronting twelfth-century Vikings, not twenty-first-century enemy combatants.

Rick, Pete, and Connor had worked with each member of the MacKlenna voluntary corps, providing personalized instructions on wearing BDUs with armor and how to use night-vision goggles (NVGs). Target practice with the M18 turned competitive, and Robbie lost to Austin in the shooting contest when his final shot didn't match his called shot.

Robbie took the loss well, and David immediately took his son to the target and gave him some constructive criticism. It was evident to Ensley, while watching their body language from a distance, that while Robbie was slightly taller than David, David was figuratively a head taller.

He was, she'd discovered, a man who stood out among all others, and she believed the rumor that he could perform miracles with one hand tied behind his back. After discovering David was claustrophobic yet functioned so well inside the cave, she decided the rumor had to be true.

How in the world did Kenzie live with a man like that?

I guess she sees warts that others don't.

Ensley left the closet doing her best model strut for Austin, sitting at the desk working on a laptop. She cleared her throat, and his head shot up.

"Shit, Ens. You look sexy as hell."

She managed a clumsy faux pirouette using both legs. "So do you. I feel like ripping off your ninja turtle suit and having my way with you."

He held up his hands. "I surrender. But keep in mind, ripping off turtle suits goes both ways."

"If I didn't have to put this crap back on again, I'd consider it." She looked over his shoulder. "What are you working on?"

"I'm watching the live cam of the inside of the cave, and David's right about the light. There's a pattern, but God knows what it is. Kenzie says she's ruled out a connection to the solar system."

"Meaning…it's not like the moon controlling the tides."

"Something like that. But it never comes on at the same time of day. So it remains unpredictable, at least to us."

"Maybe it's triggered by an object inside the cave."

"Like what?"

"I don't know. Maybe that sundial." She pointed to an object on top of an open chest full of third-century gold coins. "Why put it on top of the coins? It looks out of place there."

"If we stare at a picture of the entire treasure, we could find dozens of objects out of place."

"Like a 'what's wrong with this picture?' puzzle."

"Yeah. David wants to go back with the robot he and the twins built to set sensors in the light to see if he finds out anything new."

"If the robot goes in when the light is on, won't it disappear?"

"Seems logical. So I guess he'll only use it when the light is off. But once David sets the sensors, they'll continuously collect data. Connor and Rick plan to set up sensors above ground to find out if there are any fluctuations in atmospheric conditions when the light goes on."

"I thought Rick was spending all of his time lobbying the National Junior Golf Association to include tournaments for kids under five."

"He's obsessed with that idea right now since he can't go rescue Tavis and can't hurry the birth of his twins. But if anyone can successfully petition the NJGA, he can. He's got a Rolodex full of names of influential people in the winery business, politics, and Thoroughbred breeding who'll always take his call. Rick is the only person in the family besides Elliott and Kevin who has an international reputation."

A message came in on their phones, and Austin reached for his. Ensley had buried hers in one of her many pockets and couldn't get to it.

"It's go time," Austin said.

"Hallelujah!" She reached for her helmet with the NVGs flipped up, ready to use if they landed in the dark. "I hope I remember everything Rick, Pete, and Connor taught me."

"If you don't, ask me. I've got a cheat sheet."

"Geez." She laughed her way to the door. "You slay me. Like you'll have time to refer to it when the battle-axes and arrows start whizzing by."

"Oh, I'll have plenty of time because I'll be hiding behind one of those stone walls at Jarlshof."

She opened the door and walked out into the hallway, feeling more like the Hulk wearing a turtle suit instead of shredded clothes. "I doubt there's a wall there high enough to hide you."

"Thanks for that unwelcome information."

"Well, you could be short like me and worry about getting lost in the shuffle."

"I plan to stick to you like superglue, so don't worry about anyone running over you."

She glanced up at him and batted her eyelashes. "Getting stuck together sounds so romantic."

"Hold that thought. We'll be back in a few hours and can spend the rest of the day in bed."

She opened the oak door and entered the foyer, which was surprisingly quiet for a change. "If we spend a week or longer in the cold Shetland Islands weather, I'll be spending the rest of this afternoon at the pool, enjoying the sun."

"We can take the pontoon out, and you can sunbathe in the nude again."

"That sounds like a great plan. I wonder if we can get away with it."

Austin thumbed through his text messages. "Emily sent a message earlier wishing us all good luck."

Ensley reached the mansion's front door and opened it to a gorgeous spring morning, flowers blooming in every direction with their delicious scent permeating the air.

"That was sweet. So who sent the go-time message?"

"Elliott. Why?"

"Just curious to see who's gathering the troops, the general or his second-in-command. I was hoping Charlotte would talk some sense into Elliott and encourage him to stay home."

"Good luck with that. But I did hear from Rick, who heard from Penny, who heard from Kenzie, who heard from David, who heard from Elliott himself, that he had an appointment with his cardiovascular surgeon. The doc said he wasn't in immediate danger, but he wants to do a peripheral artery bypass in the next few weeks."

"Charlotte won't let him put it off, but at least he's seen his doctor. I wonder why Kenzie didn't tell me."

"That's the way things happen around here. You snooze, you lose."

"Meaning?"

Austin pointed to a golf cart parked on the drive, and they walked toward it. "Penny was with Kenzie right after she heard it from David."

"How in the world do you keep up with the gossip train?"

"It's a character trait I developed while growing up in a house full of gossipy, high-testosterone cops. The trick is to give away little in exchange for a lot. It's a talent."

Ensley hopped into the driver's seat and pushed the start button. "Thanks for telling me. Are you an expert at back-channeling, too?"

Austin buckled his seat belt and grabbed the canopy frame. "We only do that when we believe Elliott is wrong and no one has the guts to tell him."

"Cowards." She pushed the pedal, and the cart jerked forward. She didn't have good foot control because of the damn combat boots. After jerking a few more times, she figured out how much pressure to apply and drove the cart toward the barn, their dedicated staging area.

"The whole lot are cowards," she continued. "If I know he's wrong about something, I'll tell him. He's quick to anger, but it doesn't last. Look at the way he treated the twins last week. He kicked them out of the meeting, laughed, and then let them right back in."

"Speaking of the twins, I'm sorry I missed you playing polo with them yesterday. It's all the buzz in the second-gens' chat room this morning. You should have called me."

"Why? You would have told me to stop, and you couldn't do anything about it since you were in Denver."

"I go out of town, and you put your health in danger."

"Now you know it's not safe to leave me behind."

"Oh, I already knew that. But I had work that I couldn't delegate. The pictures posted in our chat room almost gave me heart failure. Have you seen them? In one, you were half out of the saddle."

"I don't have to see the picture. I remember hanging on, but I was determined to beat Henry to the ball. His reach is twice mine, but what he had in height advantage, I had in speed. Mercury is a perfect polo pony—fearless and fast, with a heart for the game."

"I'm not even going to ask how you got interested in polo. It doesn't seem to fit with a North Dakota rancher's daughter."

"Well, aren't you the snob? I'll have you know, Harvard's had a polo team since the early 1880s. During my freshman year, I made the trek from Cambridge's loud urbanity to the quiet suburbs of South Hamilton four times a week. Then I fell and broke my wrist again and didn't go back. I even sold my horse so the sport wouldn't tempt me."

"You went to Harvard. I went to an SEC school. So who's the snob?"

"You know you shouldn't talk to me like that." She patted the side of her leg. "I'm strapped!"

"Yep, and so am I. But we're not talking guns right now. We're talking about you participating in a high-risk sport."

"Let's see"—she stopped the cart and held up her hands like she was weighing something in each one—"In one hand I have a polo game, and in the other, I have an attack on a twelfth-century Viking community. Which one has the highest risk?"

Austin frowned and shook his head. "This uniform is only to make a statement that we're there for business. We don't intend to hurt anyone. A polo game with Robbie and Henry is far more dangerous. You were galloping across the field, hanging half out of your saddle. Powwowing with some Vikings isn't the same, and you know it."

She sped up again and made a sharper turn onto the road to the barn than she should have made, and Austin grabbed the canopy frame with both hands.

"In my defense," she said, "I didn't know they were going to play at a pro-level. I thought it was just a friendly game to whack the ball through the goalposts. But your cousins are vicious."

"We all play rough, regardless of the game. Don't expect a break because you're female. To us, you're a competitor, fully capable of kicking our asses. We understand the difference between chivalry and deference but opt for courtesy and respect. We have the whole gender thing figured out. We'll beat your butt in a game if we can, but we'll be the first ones at your side or covering your back in times of trouble."

Ensley parked the cart outside the barn and hopped out. "That must be the second-gens' mantra—we'll kick your ass if we can but will always have your back."

"I guess it is."

They were the last to arrive at the staging area the rescue party had used during their training sessions. The same tables they used for seating during lectures now held rucksacks packed with emergency supplies, handheld radios, and stacks of fly tartans. The team captains—Remy, David, Connor, and Pete—stood in corners with a hand in the air, trying to collect their team members.

Sophia, Churchill, Jack, and Patrick were on Pete's team. Elliott, Kevin, Austin, and Ensley were on Remy's team. Kenzie, Robbie, Henry, and Cullen were on David's team. And Daniel, Noah, Braham, and Lincoln were on Connor's team.

It was a strange attack force, a mix of young and old, vets of wars both foreign and domestic, and a few semi-invalids, all with a single-minded purpose—rescue Tavis.

"The fly tartans are spread out on the tables and separated by clans," David announced. "Ye'll find tartans for the Digbys, Frasers, Grants, MacKlennas, McCabes, McBains, MacAndrews, and Montgomerys. Austin, there is a MacAndrew *and* a MacKlenna tartan for ye. Ye can decide which one ye want to wear."

"MacAndrew," he said, walking over to the designated table.

"I hope somebody's going to show us how to wear this," Ensley said.

"Ye got instructions in yer packet. Did ye read it?" David asked.

"I missed that page," she said.

"Okay. Pay attention," David said, holding a corner of a tartan. "Remove the clan brooch then take the gathered corner of yer tartan and thread it over yer left shoulder"—he demonstrated—"and through the loop on yer jacket, put there just for this purpose. Now pull it down to yer breast and pin it to yer jacket with yer clan brooch." He pinned his tartan then turned his back to them. "See where mine falls? Yers should fall to the back of yer knee."

"If we get into a fight, this could get in the way," Austin said.

"It could, or you could swing it over your opponent and trap him," Pete said.

Austin gathered the side of the tartan and swung it out until it covered Ensley, and he pulled her to him. "Now we're talkin'!"

She flung out her turtle arms. "Let me out."

Austin untangled her. "If I see you in danger, I might do that to you."

"Great. I'll be so discombobulated. I'll probably get myself killed."

"There you go again, using your ten-dollar words." Austin shivered. "And damn, it makes me hot!"

Ensley swung her tartan, but he sidestepped, and she missed him completely. She blew him the raspberry, but he snagged her tongue with his teeth and kissed her.

Kenzie laughed and took their picture with her phone. "You two look like mating turtles."

"Braham, do ye have the brooches?" David asked.

Braham opened one of the two boxes. "David, ye take the diamond. Connor, ye take the amber. Pete, ye take the pearl, and Elliott, take the topaz"—Braham opened a flat box and removed the torc—"and this, but I wouldn't advise putting them together unless we need a distraction."

Elliott put the torc around his neck and slipped the topaz into his shirt pocket. "I'll take yer advice. I don't want to see the sparks unless it's necessary."

"Are we traveling in our groups or all together?" Ensley asked.

"We'll link arms just as we always do," Elliott said.

"Put the weakest between the strongest," David said. "Henry, ye and Robbie bookend Elliott."

"Are ye saying I'm the weak link?"

"Henry, ye and Robbie bookend our *general*," David restated. "We lose him, and the battle will be over before the winner is determined."

The twins strutted across the barn, blowing on their fingernails and buffing them on their shirts.

"Watch yer attitude, lads. Ye're assigned to protect the Keeper.

It's an honor and a responsibility."

"We know, Da. We won't let anything happen to Grandpa. We'll be his secret service agents and take a bullet for him."

"If you're taking a bullet, it'll be coming from one of us since the Vikings don't have guns," Kenzie said.

Robbie clapped Henry on the shoulder. "I'll take the right side. You take the left."

"Is that a strategy or a statement?" Henry asked.

"It's a strategy, dumbass. Grandpa's right-handed. That makes it his strongest side and easier to defend."

"Fine!" Henry said. "I'm the strongest and therefore the best warrior to defend his weak side."

Robbie glared at him, but the beeping of a dozen golf carts interrupted the moment, and everyone turned toward the doorway. The rest of the family bounded out of their carts and moved quickly toward the interior of the barn, waving small squares of tartans that matched the ones the team members wore.

"We've come for the send-off," Meredith announced. "And to bring this." She held up a duffel. "You forgot Tavis's utilities."

"Fuck!" Remy said, taking the duffel and adding it to the one containing his medical battle kit. He'd already given everyone an overview of what was in the kit in case there were multiple injuries, and he needed help.

"That's bad luck to forget his utilities. If he's lost weight, he'll be okay. But if he's gained twenty pounds, he might have a problem getting into them."

"Tavis wouldn't put on weight. He'd stay lean and mean," Austin said. "He'd want to be ready when his rescue team arrives."

"But what if it's been years?" Kevin asked. "He might have given up hope."

"The lad will never give up, and neither would any of ye. He knows how the brooches work, and we'll arrive when we're meant to arrive," Elliott said. "Not sooner. Not later."

Meredith, Kit, Charlotte, Amber, Olivia, Amy, JL, and the children kissed their husbands and fathers, but two boys broke from the group and ran up to Austin, hugging his legs.

"Ensley, these are my brothers Blane and Lance. They've grown since you saw them last."

"I remember you," Lance said. "You were the chick with JC."

"The chick? Don't you think that's a rude name to call a woman…to call me?"

He ducked his head. "I was just trying to be cool like Austin."

"Cool people use respectful names, don't you think?"

"Yes, ma'am. Sorry. A bull rider should be treated with respect. That's a real ball-buster." He slapped his hand over his mouth. "I messed up again, didn't I?"

"Ball-buster's okay. But I don't ride bulls anymore. I broke too many bones and decided that if I kept riding, I might get hurt so bad the doctors couldn't fix me."

"Like Austin got hurt bad."

"Sort of like that. If you want to see me ride, there are videos of me on YouTube. I'll show them to you when we get back."

"You'll only be gone a few minutes. You'll go *poof*! And then you'll be back before the stinky fog even disappears," Lance said. "I know all about traveling through the vortex because Robbie and Henry told me."

"Well, they should know," Ensley said. "Their job on this adventure is to protect your grandpa."

"Wow! That's an important job. Why aren't you protecting him, Austin? You're the biggest."

"'Cause I'm protecting Ensley."

"She doesn't need protecting. I watched her play polo yesterday. She's a better rider than Granny Mere. And that's saying a lot."

"Blane! Lance! Come back here," JL called. "They're leaving, and I don't want you two sucked up into the fog."

"Mom's calling," Austin said. "You better go. I'll catch up with you guys when we get back. Maybe we can shoot some hoops."

"You just called her 'Mom,'" Lance said. "How come?"

"Because it makes her happy."

"Well, I want to make her happy, too." Lance ran toward JL, yelling, "Mom!"

Blane high-fived Austin and took off after his brother.

"That was an awesome big brother thing to do," Ensley said. "Look how happy it made JL—and the boys, too."

Austin's expression barely changed, but something in his green eyes did, a change in his pupils maybe, or a slight movement in the corner of his mouth. But something subtle changed. Perhaps it was the realization that a simple act could make JL so happy.

"Yeah, well, it looks like I'm in the make-people-happy business now."

"It's not such a bad business to be in, is it?"

"I just want to make you happy."

"You do. Every minute. Every day."

He leaned over and kissed her. "Let's get this show on the road. We have lots to do when we get back."

She moved into her spot between Austin and Kevin. "I can't believe I'm making another trip through the vortex. I hope this is the last one for a while."

"I never planned to make another trip after that disastrous adventure back to 1909 New York City," Kevin said.

"It turned out okay for you, Kevin. I mean, you married JL," Austin said.

"Yeah," he smiled. "The best thing I ever did."

Remy walked over to her, carrying something wrapped in a large piece of felt. "I had it shined up for you." He reverently unwrapped Erik's battle-ax as if it was a living, breathing extension of the man who once carried it. "I did it myself…well, Braham and Daniel watched over my shoulders and offered suggestions while they smoked cigars and drank whisky. Vikings made their axes from wrought iron with a steel cutting edge. Erik could have swung or thrown this with head-splitting force."

Ensley glanced over at the two men. They were watching to see how she reacted to the gleaming steel and the polished, two-foot wood handle. "You should have warned me. I'm going to get all teary-eyed now. It's gorgeous."

"I had a sleeve made for it so you can sling it over your shoulder." He slipped the ax into the leather sleeve and showed her how to carry it on her right side. "I know you didn't have time to train on using this, so if you have to swing it, use both hands."

"Do you think the Council will recognize it as Erik's?"

"I doan know." He shrugged. "Maybe they'll recognize the designs on the handle. They're pretty weird."

"Let's go, Remy," Elliott said.

Remy took his place on the other side of Henry. "Let's rock and roll."

Ensley linked arms with Kevin and Austin, and the rest of the family members linked up, forming one large circle.

"We all have maps of Jarlshof. If we get separated, retreat to the current airport location. We'll move forward from there," David said.

"And if we arrive during the battle described in David's vision, don't rush in to help. We need to stay together and work out our battle plan," Connor said.

"I don't have a map," Henry said.

Kenzie snatched a document off the table that held extra copies of daily assignments, maps, and various instruction sheets and smacked it against Henry's chest. "What other instructions did you miss?"

Henry gave her a subtle wink. "Well, Mom, until I don't know something, I won't know what instructions I missed."

"*Errr.* You're just messing with me, right?"

"Don't worry, Kenz. I got my shit together," Henry said.

"Don't believe him, Mom," Robbie said. "I saw a pile of it in the pasture."

Elliott sighed—a small one, barely audible. The sound of a surprisingly patient man summoning up his reserves. He steepled his index fingers and pressed them against the bridge of his nose.

"Watch Elliott," Ensley whispered to Austin. "He's trying to be patient because the alternative is to tell everyone to leave the barn so he can go by himself."

"That'll never happen."

Ensley whispered to Robbie. "Tell your grandpa it'll be okay."

Robbie looked at her like she had two heads. "He knows that, Ensley. If he didn't, he'd be yelling at Henry and me."

He had a point, so Ensley decided to forget about Elliott and focused on going through the vortex again. She'd be going farther this time. Would it be bumpier? Have a few extra loops and dips? Or would it be a smooth flight? With this many people, would they bump into each other?

"One more thing, if ye're in a tight spot and out of options, use yer brooch and go home," Elliott said.

"It's time. Everyone picture Tavis in yer mind and say, 'Take me to Tavis.'" David opened the diamond brooch and recited the chant...

"*Chan ann le tìm no àite a bhios sinn a' tomhais an' gaol ach 's ann le neart anama.*"

Unlike the other trips, Ensley relaxed as the fog engulfed her, and she let it carry her away while images of Tavis flashed through her mind.

We're coming, Tavis. We're coming to bring you home.

77

Jarlshof (1128)—Tavis

TAVIS AND JOSEPH, his three-year-old son, were climbing up the high rocky spur capped by the Sumburgh Head—the name used in the future—when the watchman sounded the Gjallarhorn. The wind and the pounding surf almost drowned out the deep, stirring bellow.

The settlement used the horn for warnings, celebrations, and wakes. There was nothing to celebrate, and no one had died recently, which meant trouble had reached their shores.

He hadn't seen any longboats on the eastern side of the Shetland mainland's southern tip, nor had he seen any tracks from possible invaders. So if longboats had arrived, they'd be at anchor in the cove on the western side.

The cliffs he and Joseph climbed were home to flocks of sea-birds, mostly puffins. Tavis had caught three in his net for Helga, Erik's widowed sister, to prepare fresh, salted in brine for the evening meal. He slung the net holding the captured birds over his shoulder and adjusted his ax so it'd be handy.

"Hurry, Joseph. Something's happening at the settlement."

"I fight, too, Dad."

"Let's see what the problem is before you draw your dagger."

Joseph climbed ahead of Tavis with unusual agility and balance, far more advanced than the other children living in the settlement. Joseph wasn't bigger or taller than other children his age, but from the time he was six months old, Tavis carried him around on his broad back, taught him how to swim before he could walk, and how to climb before he could run. And Joseph's agility extended to sailing. He had just gained his sea legs, and Tavis loved their days sailing in the cove when he would let his mind wander, remembering his days at the Naval Academy.

But his kid was his life, and he loved Joseph more than he thought it was possible to love another person. And if they had to spend the rest of their lives on this goddamn island, Tavis would make the best of it—for Joseph's sake, if not for his own.

Joseph stopped climbing and looked over his shoulder. "Dad, maybe the horn is announcing Grandpa Elliott has come for us."

"One day, he will come. We must be ready."

"That's why we climb the cliffs. To be strong."

"Yes, buddy. To be strong and catch birds in our nets."

"But not to fight, to talk first. Right, Dad? That's why I learned English, too. But what if the Council doesn't let me leave when the Keeper comes?"

"Then we will grow old here together. And when you take your place on the Council and wear Erik's brooch, you can go to Grandpa Elliott's time to meet him. But you must never tell anyone what you intend to do."

"If I tell, the Council will never trust me with a brooch."

They reached the top of the cliffs and took off in a run toward the settlement, but when they were still a hundred yards away, Tavis pulled Joseph to the ground, and they stretched out flat in the grass.

"Be still, ignore the sound of the wind, and tell me what you hear."

Joseph closed his eyes. "Flapping like large birds. Sails. Iron against iron. Swords and axes. Voices of angry men. Warriors. Am I right, Dad?"

"Yes. It's dangerous. You can't go to the longhouse yet." Tavis couldn't take Joseph anywhere near the fighting because he'd take out his little dagger and attack. His son was fearless. "We must go back to the cliffs. You'll be safe there."

"I'm safe with you, Dad. Where you go, I go."

"Not this time."

They ran back to the cliff, but Tavis pulled his son to the ground again when a large cloud rose from the ground. He'd watched Arne disappear into the fog too many times not to know that travelers were coming. It could be Arne or Bjørn, Birger, or Forde, but he'd been at the last Council meeting, and they said nothing about a new brooch. The members had only told him recently that Erik's brooch heated when another brooch was activated. When that happened, a

Council member went forward in time to find the traveler and be sure a guardian was watching over them. If there was no guardian, the Council member stayed with the brooch until it found its way to the Keeper.

"What is it, Dad? Is it the fog that will bring Grandpa Elliott?" he whispered.

"It might be, son. But it could also be the other side—the bad men. Let's wait. If I tell you to run, you know where to go."

"To the cave."

They'd found a small cave while climbing the cliffs and kept supplies there in case they needed to hide one day.

"Yes, to the cave. Get ready." Tavis rested his hand on his son's back, which was tensing under his touch. "Don't be afraid." He reminded himself not to tense up. He was battle-hardened. He knew what to do, how to respond, and how to control the rush of adrenaline.

Could it be Elliott?

When the fog faded, seven SEALS wearing utilities with body armor stood near the edge of the cliff.

"Who are they, Dad? Should I go to the cave?" Joseph coiled for action while he kept his head flat to the ground.

"No, son." Tavis wiped beads of sweat off his upper lip and swallowed hard, trying to shove down the pinpricks of emotions hanging in his throat. They'd finally come for him, and if he didn't get himself under control, he'd turn into a blubbering idiot. When he started shaking, he had to stay flat on the ground, unsure if his legs would even support him.

"They look like turtles, Dad. Should we talk to them?"

To justify stalling, he identified the people for Joseph and, in a way, reinforced the truth that Elliott had come. "The man in the middle is Grandpa Elliott."

"He doesn't look so old," Joseph said.

"He'll like hearing that. The tallest one is your cousin Austin."

Joseph's head popped up with a look of surprise on his face. "The man who shot the grizzly bear?"

"Yes."

Joseph's hand was shaking with excitement as he pointed at the group. "Who is the short man?"

"That's not a man, that's Ensley, and she's carrying Erik's ax." The tightness in Tavis's neck and shoulders released in a shudder of relief. He'd left home all those years ago to rescue her, and now she was here for him.

"Your...sister?" Joseph asked in a low, awed voice.

"Yes."

"Who is the man next to her?"

"Elliott's son."

"J...C?"

"No, Kevin."

Joseph made a surprised O with his mouth.

"And the other man is Remy."

Joseph rolled over onto his back and kicked his feet. "Everybody's here, Dad! They came for us!" Then he put his hands on his chest. "My heart is beating faster and faster." He looked up at Tavis, his eyes glistening. "Remy is your friend from New Or...leans? Is your brother here, too?"

"No. Mark doesn't know about time traveling, remember?"

"Yes." Joseph rolled back over onto his stomach and studied the travelers. "Who are the two who look alike?"

"Your cousins Robbie and Henry McBain."

"The funny ones?"

"Yes."

"Where's Granny Mere?"

"She must be home with JC."

Tavis had stopped shaking and was finally sure his legs wouldn't collapse under him. He got to his feet, sure and steady with the knowledge that his son would now have the future Tavis wanted for him.

"Come on, son." He took Joseph's hand and made the twenty-yard trek, stopping several feet away, watching Elliott. There was no recognition in his eyes, and his hand, like the others, rested on his holster.

"Grandpa Elliott!" Joseph shouted. "What took you so long to get here?"

Elliott's jaw dropped as his gaze traveled from Joseph to Tavis, and the hand that hovered above his holster reached out. "Tavis!"

Tavis clasped Elliot's hand, and Elliott pulled him in for a hug. "I knew you would come. I never gave up hope." The warm embrace was nearly Tavis's undoing. Elliott's arms were like a vise around him, and then they started to tremble. Except for Astrid and his grandfather, Tavis had never been so warmly received.

"Lad—" Elliott swallowed hard, clapping Tavis on the back. "It's so good to see ye. We were worried about ye."

Before Elliott even let go of him, Remy grabbed Tavis in a head-lock. "Damn, you fucker. We've been so worried. How long have you been here?"

"Three years," Tavis said through the knot in his throat.

"Three fucking years." Remy released the headlock, clasped both sides of Tavis's face, and damn if he didn't kiss him. "When I see that mother-fucking Arne, I'm going to shoot his fucking head off for stealing three of your goddamn years. It pisses me the hell off."

Joseph slipped his hand into Tavis's. "Dad, why is Remy going to shoot off Arne's head?"

"He's not, son. That's just the way he talks. Granny Mere and Aunt Charlotte want him to clean up his language, but it doesn't sound like he's gotten any better."

"And who's this little guy?" Ensley asked, stepping into a hug from Tavis.

Tavis reached out to Joseph, but before introducing his son, Joseph said, "I'm Joseph Stuart, ma'am. Mom died when she had my sister. She died, too. It's just Dad and me now, but the Council won't let me leave. Dad can go, but not me."

The knot in Tavis's throat tightened, almost strangling him, if that was even possible.

"I wouldn't leave you, either," Ensley said. "How old are you? You look like you're ten."

"I'm three, ma'am. How old are you?"

"I'm twenty-eight."

"Dad's older," Joseph said.

Tavis cringed. He hadn't aged well, spending so much time out-doors in the cold and wet climate, and now he looked at least ten years older than he was.

Elliott clasped Tavis's shoulder. "I'm sorry we didn't arrive earlier. We might have been able to save your family."

Tavis glanced out over the sea, just as he always did when he talked about his wife and daughter. "Even if you'd arrived in time, Astrid wouldn't have left here. She'd heard too many stories growing up about wars and famines in the future, and nothing I could say assuaged her fears."

"That had to be frustrating," Ensley said. "How long ago did you lose her?"

"Two months. Not long, but yet a lifetime ago. Especially around here, where the wind blows constantly, and you rarely get a moment of silence."

No one said anything, as if pausing to pay their respects. Then Remy plowed ahead, giving the conversation a restart. "I guess you haven't seen the other teams."

Tavis had compressed his lips in remembrance and now opened his mouth in surprise. "No. How many are there?"

"Four teams. Twenty of us. David is Six Alpha. Connor is Six Bravo, and Pete is Six Charlie."

"What's Elliott?"

"I'm Six," Elliott said.

"Radio Six Alpha and tell him there's a commotion down at the cove. We heard clashing weapons and flapping sails. I didn't want Joseph to go back to the settlement until I knew what was happening."

"Robbie and I'll go see what's up," Henry said.

"No. Stay right here until we find the others." Remy handed Tavis a duffel. "If you'd rather wear utilities, I brought a uniform for you. You're more muscular than you were, but it should fit."

"Thanks. Now tell me about JC," Tavis said, addressing Elliott. "The last word I got was that you and Meredith were returning with him. What happened?" The pain in Elliott's eyes startled Tavis, and he backed off immediately. "Never mind. It can wait."

"Ye should know. It could influence what happens here. Erik's brother found James Cullen in Chicago. He tortured him, but thankfully, Erik arrived in time to save James Cullen's life. The cloak healed his body, but he's struggling emotionally. We took him and Paul to the monastery, where they'll remain for a while."

Damn. The hits kept coming. Knowing Viking culture as Tavis did, the torture would have been horrific and not survivable. "I didn't know Erik had a brother. Where is he now?"

"Erik killed him. His name was Sten. Their father kicked him out of the settlement years ago, and he'd become an influential member of the Illuminati."

"Fuck!" A slow burn exploded, and Tavis threw his helmet. "God *damn* it. Why didn't Erik tell me? I could have helped."

Ensley reached out to touch Tavis's arm but withdrew it when he looked at her with the remnants of his fury.

"He should have," she said. "He traveled back and forth between the Badlands, Chicago, and no telling how many other places, cutting it razor-thin with both James Cullen and me. A minute here or there, and we both could have died."

Joseph crossed his arms in front of his chest until Tavis picked up his helmet and brushed off the dirt. "Are you done, Dad?"

"Yeah, I'm done, Joseph."

"Sometimes Dad gets so mad that it has to come out. He never gets mad at me like that. He gets mad because Mom and my sister died. And he gets mad at Arne because he won't let us go to Grandpa Elliott. But then we go hunting, and he smiles."

Tavis tossed Joseph's unkempt black hair. "Joseph has never had the chance to be a little boy and kick a soccer ball. Life is harsh, but he's adapted like a true SEAL. I couldn't be prouder of him. And"— Tavis pulled in a deep breath to slow the burn in his gut—"he's the only one who gets to call me out on my behavior."

Tavis gave Ensley a slight nod before stripping off his shirt, and she turned her back to him. "Joseph likes to look at the pictures in the books I brought here for Astrid. He knows the world as it exists in the future and what little of it is known now. He wants to fly to Scotland and see Fraser Castle. He wants—"

"—to go to the Kentucky Derby," Joseph interrupted. "And I want to drink wine in Napa and watch Austin play basketball."

Austin laughed. "I'd like to see that, too, buddy."

"I'll take ye to the Derby next year." Elliott grinned. "It's looking like we might have another winner."

Tavis finished dressing and took the SIG Sauer from Remy, automatically doing a pistol press check before holstering the weapon. For the first time in three years, Tavis Stuart—Navy SEAL—was back.

"Dad, you look funny, but you look like the drawing you made for me. Are you going to your time and leave me here?"

Before Tavis could pick up his son, Elliott did. "I don't leave my kids behind. Ever. It took me time to get here, but the brooches control when we arrive. In our time, we left only two weeks after yer da disappeared. So we arrived when we were meant to arrive."

Tavis took Joseph from Elliott and hugged him before setting him down. "If the Council won't let us both go, then we'll stay here. I will *never* leave you behind. *Never!* Now stay close to me. You must do whatever these people tell you to do, or anyone dressed like them. Tell them you're Joseph Stuart, son of Tavis."

"And Keeper Elliott Fraser is my grandpa."

"Yes, you can tell them that."

"But Erik is my real grandpa."

Tavis cupped his son's cheek. "There are no real or unreal grandpas. Only loving ones."

Ensley took Joseph's hand. "Erik was my father, too. That makes you my nephew."

"Dad told me you were his sister, and you would come for me. Did you and Austin fall in love? He said you would because he had a vision of Austin carrying you in the snow."

"He did?" Ensley winked at Tavis. "He's right. We're very much in love."

"Did Erik tell ye about Ensley?" Elliott asked.

"Arne told me when I brought Erik's body home. I don't know why Erik didn't tell me himself."

"He didn't tell me, either," Ensley said.

They all started walking, but Elliott pulled Tavis aside. "Just so ye know. We're not leaving without *both* of ye."

"Arne won't allow it."

Elliott put his hand on Tavis's shoulder. "Arne might push us to the edge, but I have a card to play."

"If we leave with you, he'll find us. He'll bide his time, and he'll take Joseph away from me."

"I've heard that when God leads ye to the edge of a cliff, ye should trust Him and let go. One of two things will happen, Tavis. Either He'll catch ye when ye fall, or He'll teach ye how to fly!"

78

Jarlshof (1128)—David

DAVID STEPPED OUT of the fog and into the battering wind—
alone.

He was a dozen or so yards from the edge of a cliff that overlooked an unspoiled coastline, which was astonishingly beautiful,
raw, and uncivilized. The coastline looked very different from the
Jarlshof of the twenty-first century. Rising seas and coastal erosion
had destroyed much of the settlement.

He reached for his Panoscan MK-3 panoramic camera and
snapped several pictures to compare to the future landscape while
doing a quick gut check. Surprisingly, he wasn't worried about being
separated from the others. He'd expected the teams to arrive
separately. That's why they had maps and a meetup point.

Usually, there was a purpose for dispersing the travelers. But not
this time. His gut told him the separation was a deliberate move to
put their experience and firepower at a disadvantage.

But why?

Only one reason he could think of—the Keeper was a threat to
the Council, and they decided to neutralize the threat. Not that they
would kill Elliott, but they needed to limit his power. But what made
him more powerful today than he was the last time they met?

Tavis and Ensley.

The Council knew the Keeper would come for Tavis. And although Elliott was coy when Ensley asked if Tavis was Erik's son,
David believed the answer was yes. The similarities in their eyes,
cheekbones, chins, and their muscular bodies, were evident to
anyone willing to ask the question—are they related?

He was surprised Sophia hadn't already suggested it based on her sketches of Erik and the other Council members.

Now, with the allegiance of Erik's two children, Elliott's position was far more powerful. Could he demand Erik's brooch? Had that been Erik's plan decades ago, when he impregnated two twenty-first-century women? He could have fathered others, and if so, were they all on the "good" side now? Or had they turned evil, like Sten and Andrew MacKlenna? Assuming the rumors about Andrew were true.

This intrigue went much deeper than it seemed on the surface.

David continued scanning the area, wishing he'd thought to bring a drone. Directly across from where he stood, smoke rose from thatched-roof structures. He duck-walked to the edge, where he lay down on his belly and unpacked his handheld radio and binoculars.

It was time to get answers.

Without the binoculars, he would have missed the speck on the horizon. Was it a ship full of raiders, or did the vessel belong to the settlement?

A horn blew, and the wind carried its bellow across the cove. Was it a welcome or a call to arms? He pushed the talk button on the handheld radio. "Six, come in."

"Six Alpha, we have the package," Henry said.

David chuckled at how professional Henry sounded. "Six, have ye seen the rest of my team?"

"You lost 'em?" Henry asked.

David made a mental note to remind his son to always answer a question before asking one. "Separated for now. Have ye seen Six Bravo or Six Charlie?"

"That's a negative."

David zoomed in again on the ship, but it was still too far away to get any specifics. "I need a situation report."

"We're east of the settlement. Near the airport. Where are you?"

"I'm on the west side of the cove. Stay where ye are. I'll come to ye."

"Copy that, Six Alpha," Henry said.

The twins and their cousins had played war games since they were wee lads and lassies. He'd taught them to take every game seriously because the day might come when their lives depended on their skills.

David crawled away from the edge until he couldn't see the

beach below and stood. Dressed as he was, he'd stand out like a black monolith against the sun. He picked a landmark in the direction he intended to go and took off in a run across the rocky terrain, aiming to run wide of the settlement and circle back to the meetup point on the east side of the mainland.

After thirty minutes, he pressed the talk button. "Six, I need a sitrep." He waited a moment until his device beeped.

"I have eyes on you, Six Alpha. Turn left," Henry said.

David jogged left until he spotted Henry lying on his belly. He rapped on the top of his son's helmet. "Stay where ye are and stay sharp."

The rest of the team was a few feet away, sitting on the ground drinking water from their canteens.

When David saw Tavis, his heart nearly jumped out of his chest. He dropped his rucksack and rifle and grabbed Tavis, and they wrestled on the ground like kids.

"Ye son of a bitch," David said, rolling over on Tavis. "Don't ever leave again without talking it over first."

Tavis flipped David. "I didn't have a choice, bro."

They flipped each other a few more times until their game was over, and they sat up, laughing and knocking heads.

"I know ye didn't." David brushed off the dirt he'd picked up while rolling around in the grass. "How long has it been?"

"Since I brought Erik's body home?" Tavis looked David in the eye, and David almost dropped his gaze to hide from the pain he saw there. "Three years."

David's stomach roiled. "Shit! We came as soon as we could."

"I know," Tavis said.

The Bairds were stuck for seven years in New Orleans in the early 1800s before anyone even knew they were missing. But the family knew about Tavis, so why was he stranded here so long? Another goddamn question for the Council. And if he heard "Wait till ye get to the other side" again, he'd punch them all out and rip Erik's brooch out of their grubby, violent hands.

Yeah, he saw the irony there.

A child sleeping under a mylar blanket woke up and climbed onto Tavis's lap.

"Who's the lad?" David asked.

Tavis hugged him. "My son, Joseph."

"I'm three," Joseph said.

That shocked the shit out of David and added another layer of anger. Joseph wasn't an adopted child. He was a miniature Tavis, and even in the lad, David recognized Erik's features. But what pissed David off more than anything was the realization that Tavis had been to the settlement before the family met him in Gothenburg.

A boatload of questions pinged in David's brain. He wouldn't demand answers yet—but he would soon, and he'd get them.

"I look forward to meeting the woman who stole"—Ensley shot David a warning look, but he was too far into what he was saying to stop—"yer...heart."

"She died." Joseph rested his head on Tavis's chest. "And so did my baby sister, Erin."

David was a softie when it came to kids, and the loss Tavis and Joseph suffered was heartbreaking. "I'm sorry for yer loss." Kenzie was much better at this than he was, and he wished she was here to take the lead on handling the situation. The best he could do was squeeze Tavis's shoulder and pat Joseph's.

Then he waited for a beat before looking around at his companions and saying, "Bring me up to speed."

"We haven't heard from anyone else," Ensley said. "Tavis says a longboat arrived, and he heard battle sounds."

David nodded. "I spotted a vessel, but it was some distance out, and nothing was happening on the beach. I did hear a horn but didn't know if it was a warning or a welcome. It could be a warning that we're here."

"There's a settlement south of us that has sent raiders up here before. But nothing has happened in the past year or so. Maybe they're coming back," Tavis said. "But someone could have seen us and passed along a warning to the Council."

"When'd ye hear battle sounds?"

Tavis nodded toward Elliott. "Shortly before these guys arrived."

"We need to find the other teams," Elliott said. "It sounds like Tavis had a warning that trouble was coming, and David had a sighting. We have to assume the ship might be carrying the enemy. Let's find the others and get the hell out of here."

"This is the meeting point. Everyone is supposed to gather here. We shouldn't leave." Ensley opened her map and pointed to their location. "Where did you land, David?"

He pointed to where he landed. "I skirted the settlement and came in behind it. Didn't even see any locals."

A call came in on their handheld radios. "Command Post, this is Six Bravo," Connor said.

"This is Six Alpha," David said. "I'm with Six at CP. We have the package. I need a sitrep."

"We're a couple of miles from CP. Traveling down the eastern side of the mainland. All members accounted for."

"Be on the lookout for Dead-Eye, Oregon, and Six Charlie."

"Over and out."

"Seven missing souls," Robbie said.

"Maybe Aunt Sophia wanted to sketch, and that's slowed them down," Henry said.

"Pete wouldn't let her stop until we're all together. If Six Bravo is two miles away, the rest could be even farther."

"Mom and Uncle Cullen could be anywhere," Robbie said.

"Why'd we get scattered around?" Henry asked.

"To slow us down," David said.

"For what reason?" Robbie asked.

"They've got us outnumbered, but our weapons give us the advantage. What better way to change the odds than to separate us? Our superior force could take Erik's brooch and any others they have. Once we have Erik's brooch, we'll have the power," David said.

"But they must have known we'd come for Tavis," Henry said. "They should have a plan."

"Last time we met with the Council, there were only five of us," David said. "Maybe they thought we would come with another small contingent they could control. What do ye think, Tavis?"

"If they planned to separate us, then that implies the Council has control over the brooches and caused the separation to begin with," Tavis said. "I don't know if that's true, but if it is, they have more power than even I thought they had."

"So instead of brooch gods, there's only the Council pulling strings? That reminds me of the 'man behind the curtain.' I don't like them having that much power, and honestly, I don't want us to have it, either," Kevin said.

"Where is Erik's brooch now?" Elliott asked.

"I surrendered it to Arne as soon as I arrived. If I hadn't done it voluntarily, he would have taken it by force and probably thrown me on Erik's funeral pyre. Then he gave me a seat on the Council but didn't share any information about the brooches. Every question I asked went unanswered.

"He didn't come right out and say it," Tavis continued, "but I got the impression I was only there temporarily, and once Joseph was old enough, I'd get booted to the curb. Arne knew I didn't want to be here. He told me I could take his daughter, Astrid, and we could leave, but we couldn't take Joseph. That was a nonstarter."

Another call came in. "CP, Six Charlie is three miles north on the west side of the island. I've been trying to call, but the high cliffs were interfering with the signal."

"Do ye have yer entire team?"

"All accounted for," Pete said.

"All teams have reported in, but Dead-Eye and Oregon are MIA. We're at CP and have the package."

"See you in an hour. Over and out."

"Nothing to do now except rest." David still wasn't worried. Kenzie—code name Dead-Eye—was a top-notch warrior, and even though she spent most of her time in meetings or court, she kept up with her training. Except for JC disarming her recently, she hadn't lost her edge in the field.

Cullen—code name Oregon—was an excellent tracker and hunter and was calm and levelheaded in a crisis. They had a combination of skills needed to get them back on course, although he didn't believe they were lost. Their whereabouts were just unknown.

David closed his eyes and rested, and the next thing he knew, Robbie was shaking his shoulder. "It's been an hour, Da. Mom still hasn't called. Something's wrong. We have to find her."

David stretched. "We can't leave, Robbie. She knows the CP location. She'll get here."

"You lost her before, and she almost got killed," Robbie said with a tinge of fear in his voice.

Robbie's accusation would have gotten anyone else a broken nose. "I haven't lost her. She'll be here. Let's trust her."

"How long do you plan to wait?" Robbie looked right into David's soul and twisted it into a thousand knots.

"Yer mother's a soldier, lad. She knows what she's doing."

"If you'd waited for her in London, she wouldn't have come back," Henry added. "You have to go find her, Da."

David unfolded his map again. "Look. We're here"—he pointed—"at the southernmost point of the islands. Muckle Flugga off the coast of Unst is the northernmost point. That's a distance of seventy miles. The Shetland Islands cover an area of over five hundred and fifty square miles. Where do ye want to start looking?"

"You're the miracle worker, Da. Tell us where to look, where to go." Robbie folded his arms across his chest and glared at David with alternating expressions of fear and helplessness.

David rubbed his forehead. He had to stay patient with them. They'd never experienced being afraid for someone else's life before. They'd learned patience and how to control emotions during times of crisis, but they'd never been fearful for someone they loved. They didn't know how to handle that, and it would be easy for them to do something rash—like go off on their own to search for her.

"As soon as Pete and Connor get here, we'll develop a search plan to find her and Cullen. Do not go off by yerselves. That would compound the problem. Yer job right now is to rest, to prepare"— he tapped his forehead—"up here."

The twins returned to their spot to sulk, and David stared at the map, willing Kenzie's position to pop up like a symbol on a radar display. He mentally placed all the teams on the map, looking for a missing piece.

"What'd the ship you saw look like?" Tavis asked.

"It wasn't close enough to see. What should it look like?"

"If it's ours, long and narrow with a shallow draft, a snake decorating the prow. It has one large, square sail and a steering oar at the stern. It left three weeks ago and could be on its way back."

"Ye're a trained sailor. Why didn't ye go with them?" David asked.

"My fighting and strategic skills are needed here more than on a trading mission."

Joseph's watchful gaze moved from David to Tavis, and he looked up at his dad with curiosity. David knew then that Tavis's real reason was fear of leaving his son behind, knowing that any minute Arne could order Tavis's death. With Tavis out of the way, Arne would have control over Joseph.

"How many men does a longboat carry?" David asked.

"Forty oarsmen and one coxswain."

If they had to fight forty Vikings—high-powered rifles vs. battle-axes—it would all be over in minutes unless hostages were involved. But the clan didn't come here to kill off the settlement. They didn't come here to die, either.

Remy picked up Tavis's net with the dead birds. "How do you usually eat these?"

"Fresh, salted in brine, or smoked and dried," Tavis said.

"I'll just fry 'em up with some of my special seasonings." He flicked his BIC lighter. "The wind is blowing out to sea, and the breeze will carry away the aroma. I don't want any uninvited guests for dinner."

"You going to cook?" Tavis asked.

"You know me. If I can't watch basketball, I'd rather be cooking."

Tavis laughed. "You'd rather be bangin' your sticks or watching women's curling than do anything else except cook some Cajun delicacy, and that includes sex."

"What's sex, Dad?"

"Well…" Tavis said.

"It's when your parents kiss and hug each other," Robbie said. "At least that's what they told us when we were growing up."

Henry teasingly tapped Joseph's chin with his knuckles. "Don't believe him. It's one of the four big lies, along with Santa Claus, the Easter Bunny, and the tooth fairy."

"Who are they?" Joseph asked.

"Ways to control kids' behavior when they can't think of any other way," Robbie said.

"Well, you sure are cynical," Ensley said. "I'm glad you weren't around when I was growing up."

"I don't understand what they're talking about, Dad."

"For once, I'm glad, Joseph. Robbie and Henry are mad because they can't go search for their mom."

"If I could search for Mom, I'd go. I have my knife, and I would fight to protect her."

"There you go, see?" Robbie said, glaring at David. "At least somebody around here understands how Henry and I feel."

"Everybody knows how ye feel, lad," Elliott said. "We also know we have a chain of command, and ye're standing on the bottom rung. Ye'll stay put until ye receive an order."

Elliott did more in three sentences to curb the twins' urges than David could have accomplished in an hour.

"Just before actor W. C. Fields's death," Austin said, "a friend visited Fields's hospital room and was surprised to find him thumbing through a Bible. When the friend asked what Fields was doing with a Bible, Fields replied, 'Lookin' for the loopholes.'"

"So, what's your point, cuz?" Henry mumbled.

"If you can't search for Kenzie, what *can* you do? Where's the loophole in what Grandpa said? What can you do from the bottom rung?"

Henry's chin shot up, and he looked at his brother. Their eyes had a conversation—a blink, a double blink, double-double blink—and then the twins switched to hand signals before Robbie said. "Remy needs more birds to cook. He only has a few, and he can eat those all by himself."

David nodded. "Ye have a twenty-yard radius. If the Vikings capture ye, it might get dicey."

The twins had another hand-signal conversation before synchronizing their watches. Then they calmly press-checked their SIGs and gathered their gear.

"Take the net," Tavis said.

Robbie grabbed it, and they disappeared like phantoms in the night.

David stared at the spot where he'd last seen them, wishing they'd return so he could protect them, but they had wings, and he had to let them fly. At least that's what Kenz said when Cambridge accepted the lads into the freshman class.

"I'm not sure looking for loopholes was a good idea, but I enjoyed watching the lads communicate with each other. I haven't seen that for a while."

With the twins gone, now David could worry about his entire family.

The handheld radio beeped. "CP, this is Six Bravo. We're close. Can you see us?"

Austin stood with binoculars in hand and searched the beach. "I see them. Tell Connor we're at his two o'clock. He should be able to see me." Austin waved both arms, sending birds flying. After a few seconds, Connor waved back. "He can see me now."

Ten minutes later, Connor, Daniel, Noah, Braham, and Lincoln joined them at their temporary campsite. It took another ten minutes to bring them all up to speed, and just as David finished, Pete called.

"Six Charlie, calling CP," Pete said. "We're bisecting the island. We weren't as far away as I thought. Should be there in about twenty minutes."

"Six Charlie, Six Bravo just arrived. Still missing two souls."

David sat apart from the others while Remy cooked the birds. He didn't know how the Council captured Kenzie and Cullen, but now he was convinced they had.

Pete and his team arrived, along with the twins carrying a string of birds, sniffing the delicious aroma coming from Remy's skillet. It took twice as long to give the new arrivals a status update because they wanted to hear all about the other three teams.

Braham sent Patrick, Lincoln, Churchill, and Noah to guard the perimeter while the rest of them ate Remy's Cajun-spiced puffins as if they were having a picnic under the old oak tree behind Mallory Plantation.

Except for David, who was alone with his thoughts, and they weren't happy ones. He walked away from the group and stood at the cliff's edge, gazing out over the ocean, remembering the last time he was here. They'd come to investigate a murder and discovered much more. If they all got out of here in one piece again, he'd never venture back.

Elliott joined him, clasping his shoulder. "There's only one explanation for why Kenzie and Cullen aren't here."

Mounting fear and anger kept David from responding until he managed to swallow both emotions, holding them at bay temporarily. "The Council has them."

"Aye. But I don't believe the Council will risk harming them."

"I disagree. They're violent bastards," David said, "and we know personally what a butcher Arne is. He'd want us to be scared of the Council. It's how they maintain power."

"They have Erik's brooch. That's how they maintain power," Elliott argued. "They also have institutional knowledge. That's worth a hell of a lot. They know the hows and whys."

"I don't care about the brooch—or its power—right now. Finding Kenzie and Cullen and getting the hell out of here should be our only priorities."

"We can wait until dark and send the lads in with Tavis to search the settlement. They've gone through training similar to Navy SEALS."

"It's a good suggestion, but Kenzie wouldn't want us to put the lads in danger to rescue her. She'd rather die than lose one of them, and so would I. It makes more sense for Tavis and me to do a search and rescue."

"This isn't yer battle, David. It's mine," Elliott said. "And I've known it since I unpinned the ruby brooch from Kit's gown all those years ago. I'll go by myself."

David kicked at a stack of sand pebbles. As they tumbled over the cliff's edge, they sparkled in the lingering light from the sun slowly disappearing behind darkening clouds.

"That's not going to happen."

He kicked at more pebbles, and they clicked and clanked and clacked as they tumbled down, rock on rock, toward the beach. And it reminded him that they didn't have time for debate. The ship was coming. It was time to rock and roll.

"From what little I know, I believe we have power over the Council, and it lies in ye, as Keeper, along with Erik's children. The Council has his brooch, but it doesn't belong to them, and they know it."

"Then it's to their advantage to kill us—Tavis, Ensley, and me."

"They can't. If the Council had that authority, they'd have killed Tavis already."

"Then why the hell are they holding Kenzie and Cullen?"

"*If* they have them, then they want an exchange. The Council doesn't care about Tavis. They know he'll never be one of them, but Joseph is young enough to be raised to think as they do."

"No one will agree to deliver Joseph to the Council, and no one will abandon Tavis."

"If it comes down to a swap, Tavis will agree to go back."

"Then we'll leave him a brooch so he and Joseph can come forward when they're able. But I won't suggest or encourage Tavis to do that and risk his and Joseph's lives."

"We have to go as soon as it's dark. We'll start with the settlement and move out from there."

David heard footsteps behind him and turned to find Tavis walking his way. "I think you two have come to the same conclusion I have," Tavis said.

"What's that?" Elliott asked.

"Arne has Kenzie and Cullen, and he wants to offer an exchange—them for Joseph and me. Although it's not me he wants, but Joseph. Arne would never hurt my son, but he'll bide his time and eventually get rid of me."

"We have to confirm whether or not Arne has them first. Ye know the people and the land. How should we deploy our troops?"

Before Tavis could answer, a call came in. "This is Dead-Eye. I need a sitrep," Kenzie said.

David clenched his hands. It was the strangest feeling he'd ever had. The person he loved most in the world was on the other side of the handheld radio. He had no idea if she had a knife at her throat, although if her hands were free, good luck with that. But he had no idea if she'd make it out or if they'd ever see each other again.

He unclenched his hands, trying hard not to show the anger and fear taking control of him since hearing his bride's voice. It was thick, like someone with a plugged nose or someone punched in the nose. His anger snapped, hardening, intractable. He'd kill the son of a bitch who touched her. He'd kill with his hands. He'd kill slowly like the Council killed the Colonel—finger by finger, toe by toe. He'd rip the asshole apart.

He snatched up his handheld radio and took a deep breath, another one, and then another one. "This is Six Alpha at Command Post. I need a sitrep."

"Six Alpha, we're at Arne's longhouse. He'll exchange us for Tavis and Joseph. Be here in an hour, or he'll stake us out on the ground, and…"

Tavis started stripping off his uniform. "Tell Kenzie that I'm on my way."

Robbie's eyes bored into David. "If you'd looked for her earlier, Da, she wouldn't have been captured. You did the same stupid thing you did the first time. I'm going with Tavis and Joseph."

"So am I!" Henry said, almost snarling. "Whoever this Arne is, he doesn't know who he's dealing with. My mom is a supernova."

David signaled Connor, then Pete. They approached the twins from behind. Before the boys knew what was happening, Connor took Robbie down. Pete took Henry down, and the former cops had both lads cuffed within seconds.

"Shut the hell up!" Pete said. "Acting like this could get Kenzie and Cullen killed. Is that what you're trying to do, you assholes? I've never been so embarrassed for anyone in my life."

"You're not acting like a McBain," Connor said. "It's time to grow the hell up! Both of you."

The lads glared at David with the same eyes that gazed at him in moments of passion, in fits of anger, or during a romantic tango. And then their look softened and was replaced with helplessness, and it nearly broke David's heart. But right now, he was at a loss for words to give them hope. Whatever words he could dredge up, he was keeping for himself.

Then from somewhere outside his consciousness, the words came, "I've been here before—when I was much younger. Ye must trust me."

David signaled Elliott, and they huddled with Tavis, "I need a hiding place for the brooch," David said. "I plan to get us out of here without leaving ye and Joseph behind, but just in case, we need a backup plan."

Tavis wrapped his cloak around him and tied it with a leather strap. "Joseph and I have a secret cave."

"That won't do," David said. "Arne's smart. He'll figure we left a brooch to bring ye both home later, and he could trick Joseph into revealing the location. It needs to be a place he doesn't know about."

"There's another cave on the cliff, maybe twenty feet east of the one Joseph and I have used before. It's harder to access, so I've never taken him there. I'll draw a map."

David gave Tavis his map of the area and a pencil, and Tavis marked the locations. "I can't promise I'll ever use the brooch, and leaving one behind will mean it'll take you longer to fill the slots around the door at the castle. Are you sure you want to do this?"

"There's no choice to make," Elliott said. "If we never have enough brooches, so be it. We want ye and Joseph to have every opportunity to come home."

"There's something else," Tavis said. "Arne will demand a pledge from me that I will stay for the rest of my life. If I give my word, I can't go back on it."

"Aye. I can see that would be a problem for ye," Elliott said. "But it's bullshit. No one can hold ye to that promise. It's like a POW promising never to attempt an escape. Ye have a son, so any agreement ye make to stay here and raise him in the twelfth century is one ye can break without dishonor."

Tavis's jaw tightened, but then he nodded.

The handheld radio beeped. "This is Dead-Eye. Tell Guardian to bring Six."

Kenzie. Tavis. Elliott.

Elliott started stripping off his plated body armor. "I'm not going to meet with the Council dressed as a warrior. I'm the Keeper, protector of the stones, but not a warrior."

David grabbed Elliott's arm. "Damn it. We have to go in with our strongest hand, and that's *as* warriors."

Elliott glared at David's whitening fingers as if his eyes alone had the power to release the grip, and David slowly released one hot finger, two fingers, and then the rest.

"I'm the Keeper, lad, and that comes with rights, responsibilities, *and* protections. I don't know what they are, but I'm about to find out. Let me handle this."

What Elliott said awakened a memory. It was a portion of his vision, previously too elusive to see or hear or comprehend. It was trying to break through now, to come into focus, and he knew from experience he couldn't rush it. It would come in time, yet he'd gotten a whiff of it before. But when? Ah. It happened the moment he entered the cave on MacKlenna Farm and even earlier in another cave, in a much earlier time, but he'd been dealing with his claustrophobia, and if there was a message, he blocked it out.

And here it was back again. What did the situations have in common? His mind didn't have time to sort it out.

"I'm not going to escalate the situation," Elliott said. "I have the torc and the topaz. We know what happens when we join the two. If the sparks go off, come running."

"Ye can't do that," David said. "It was a twenty-minute shit show in a ten-foot radius. It could kill ye."

"Wait a minute," Ensley said. "I don't know what the shit show is about, but this situation involves me, and you're not leaving me behind."

David was losing control of the situation, and he couldn't allow that to happen. Not at the cost of losing the love of his life.

Elliott pulled a long skirt made out of the MacAndrew plaid from his duffel and tossed it to Ensley. "Strip down to yer T-shirt and shorts. Wear this with yer fly tartan, and strap yer weapon to yer leg."

"Ye knew this was going to happen," David said in an accusatorial tone.

"I suspected it," Elliott said.

"Where's mine?" Austin demanded.

Elliott jabbed Austin with his finger. "Sit yer ass down. The Council won't hurt her, at least not until she produces Erik's grandson. And then all bets are off. But ye could make this worse. Think, Austin, and trust us to take care of it."

David fully understood the emotions thundering through Austin's blood. If they didn't let him go with Ensley, he'd go on his own, and that could screw up the rescue and give Arne a chance to kill someone—like Tavis.

"Elliott, if ye insist on going in naked," David said, "then Austin and I will go as yer escorts," David said.

"Fuck that!" Pete said. "It makes more sense if Connor and I go. Austin doesn't have battle experience."

"I need ye and Connor to mount a defense of the beach. I don't want forty men to come ashore and interfere with whatever is about to go down at Arne's longhouse. Plus, ye need to guard Joseph until we reach an agreement."

"I'm going with you, Dad," Joseph said, his lip quivering. "You can't leave me behind."

Tavis hugged his son. "Let me talk to Arne first, and then you can come."

Elliott stripped down to his briefs and a black T-shirt—a man in his late seventies with the body of a forty-year-old.

"Stay with the others," Elliott said, buttoning his kilt. "Let us work this out, and then we'll come for ye." After adjusting his fly tartan, he strapped a Sig to his thigh.

David pushed the talk button on his handheld radio. "This is Six Alpha. We're coming in." David put on his rucksack and picked up his rifle. "Pete, Connor. Ye have any questions?"

"We'll have the beach covered," Connor said.

Pete pressed his flat hand against Austin's chest above his heart. "Don't do anything stupid. If you do, JL will hang my ass from the shortest tree so she can beat it every day. Be smart, and if David tells you to do something, you do it. You don't think about it. You just do it like you shoot threes or shoot goddamn bears."

Austin hugged his godfather. "I'll make you proud."

"I've always been proud of you," Pete said.

David was watching Robbie and Henry communicate with each other with blinks and nods. When they were younger, David could interpret their silent language. But by the time they turned twelve or thirteen, they had turned it into an art form. He had a feeling Kenzie could read it, but he'd never asked. Since David had never shared the hand signals he and Elliott used, he let the twins keep their secrets.

Since he was watching his sons, only his peripheral vision was on the rest of the group, so he missed the windup to Joseph's decision to bolt.

"Joseph, stop!" Tavis yelled.

Joseph ignored Tavis and ran as if someone had their hands under his armpits, lifting him above the large rocks in his path. Others he dodged like the best wide receiver in the NFL.

"Damn!" David took off right behind Tavis. He looked over his shoulder to see Elliott, Ensley, and Austin running behind him. A mad race toward the enemy wasn't the way he wanted this to go.

So deal with it.

Joseph ran as if his life depended on how far and how fast he could run. Tavis grabbed him just as he reached the settlement. By the time David arrived, men were rushing out of their longhouses, holding battle-axes and bows with quivers of arrows hanging from their belts. This wasn't the way David wanted the confrontation to go down, so he had to pivot and go in with a show of force.

"Arne! Show yerself!" David demanded. "Kenzie! I'm here for ye, lass!"

"Arne! Release my family!" Elliott shouted his demand.

"Which one is Arne's longhouse?" David whispered to Tavis.

"Second on the left. But close your eyes when you can to speed up dark adaptation. It's dark and smoky inside."

David took the lead and marched down the narrow pathway between the stone structures, squinting, and halted outside Arne's longhouse. He stood in front of Tavis, Ensley, and Elliott, and Austin towered over all of them from the rear.

Arne threw open the door. "There's no cause for violence. Lower your weapons."

David didn't.

"Lower your weapon." He walked up to David and stood inches from the barrel of his rifle. "You are the Keeper's *vængr*."

Vængr? What is that?

"You are the Keeper's wing, young David. You enable him to pass with the least possible resistance. You are there to help him escape predators, to take advantage of all resources, and to make his path easier. The Keeper cannot survive without his wing."

"Aye. I am Elliott's wing."

"You were Erik's first assignment, and he chose wisely. You have always been the Keeper's trusted confidant," Arne said.

Erik's assignment.

Aye, young David. I chose you, and I chose your bride. You needed a warrior more than you needed a doctor.

"Why'd ye capture my wife and brother?" To David, Cullen *was* his brother, the same as all the men in the clan—brothers in battle, brothers by different mothers—and he'd fight to the death for each one of them, as they would for him.

"It was the most efficient course of action to bring the Keeper and Erik's children to meet with the Council. You would not have all come at once." Arne didn't ask David and Austin to lower their weapons a second time. Instead, he turned and walked back into his longhouse, holding the door open for them.

"Leave your weapons here, or you will not be allowed to go any farther." Arne reached for the sling holding Erik's ax. "I'll take this," he said with greedy eyes.

Ensley turned away from him. "It's mine. You can't have it."

"It is not yours. It belongs to the Council and was only loaned to Erik."

"He gave it to me. You can take my guns, but not this."

Arne reached for it again but jerked back his hand. "Keep it, then."

David surrendered his rifle and sidearm, and so did Austin. But Ensley and Elliott kept theirs hidden beneath their clothes.

Do not be distracted, young David. Be the vængr I have guided you to be.

Erik?

I will not abandon you today. I will give you wisdom.

David breathed in the smoky air but didn't cough. He didn't want the enemy to know it bothered him.

Where are ye, Kenz? I canna see ye, but I feel ye near me.

Three women sat on the dirt floor, weaving cloth on weighted looms. The *click, click, click* of the stone weights was a rhythmic sound, but underneath it was another kind of click or tap of metal against stone.

It was second nature to him to match taps to letters. He waited for the letters to repeat. --. ..- -.

GUN.

And then he knew Kenzie was tapping her West Point ring against the stone wall. Someone had a gun. Did she? No. They would have disarmed her, and she carried only one. That meant someone had hers. A Council member?

He cleared his throat, hoping to let her know he got her message. She continued spelling GUN again. He cleared his throat a second time. "The smoke takes getting used to," he said, and the tapping ceased.

Bjørn, Birger, and Forde, the other Council members David met three years ago, sat on a bench against the wall.

"Where are my wife and brother? Produce them now," David demanded.

"You are in no position to demand anything," Arne said.

Arne's condescending-as-shit tone sent a bitter taste to David's mouth, and he pivoted to face the asshole full-on, his hands turning to fists at his sides.

Have patience, young David.

"If ye continue with an attitude like that, negotiations won't go very well," David replied. "Let's start over. Before we talk specifics, I want to see my family."

Arne nodded to a man standing behind David. He left, and a couple of minutes later, he and another Viking dragged a trussed-up Kenzie and Cullen into the room and dropped them at the Council's feet. Kenzie's face was cut and bruised, and her nose probably broken. Her hair was hanging loose, and there was matted blood above her ear. The body armor was gone, and all she wore were her utility pants and T-shirt, both ripped. No socks. No boots. And Cullen had similar injuries. But anger burned in both their eyes. If they were free, the fight would start all over.

David had flashes of finding her naked, battered, and bruised in the London Cage, and he almost erupted.

Do not be distracted, young David. Do not. You will all die. Be the væmgr.

It took every bit of training to ignore Kenzie and Cullen and focus entirely on Arne, all the while remaining open to Erik's wisdom.

"Why have ye kept Tavis here against his will?" Elliott demanded.

"He's Erik's heir and a Council member. He belongs here, as does Erik's grandson."

"Do ye for one moment believe that's why Erik planted his seed in two twenty-first-century women? So his heirs would live in the twelfth century? No, he intended for them to live in the future. He planned to move the Council."

"That was never his plan," Arne said. "He intended to bring new blood to the Council here in this time."

"If that's the case, why haven't ye brought Tavis into Council business and shared the history of the brooches with him?" David asked. "Ye're keeping him out. Why?"

"He has to *earn* the privilege to receive the secrets," Arne bellowed.

Tavis screwed up his face and stepped forward with clenched fists, but David blocked him, and Joseph clung to Tavis's leg to hold him back.

"There are no big secrets," David said. "There's nothing on the other side of the door except an easier way to travel. The only thing ye have is Erik's brooch, and without that, ye have nothing. Ye *are* nothing, and ye have no right to it. The brooch belongs to Erik's children. It's time to give it back."

Arne laughed. "None of that is true."

Tavis raised his clenched fists again, and this time Ensley stepped in front of him. "Erik drew the Yggdrasil on my forehead. It represents the cycle of life, death, and rebirth. I am the chosen one, and I demand you return our brooch."

"We have the torc. We have eight brooches. Elliott is the Keeper." David sent a hand signal to Elliott, telling him to prepare to insert the topaz into the torc.

"I am the legitimate Keeper of the stones. The brooch ye have belongs to Erik's heirs."

The other three Council members joined Arne. "We stand in solidarity and demand you leave Jarlshof, but Joseph must stay here."

David gripped Tavis's arm, holding him in place.

"As Keeper, I can make one request of the Council." Elliott's voice didn't waver. There were no hints of emotion slipping through the cracks in his tough façade. He went chin up. "And it has to be honored."

"You have the privilege of making one request in your lifetime. That is correct," Arne said. "Choose wisely. You cannot take it back and choose another."

It was clear to David that Elliott had two choices. If he chose Tavis, Joseph, Kenzie, and Cullen, they could all leave and never return. Or Elliott could choose Erik's brooch and assume the Council's power that came along with it.

You are the Keeper's wing, young David. Choose what you know to be right. Do not choose with your heart. Choose with your wisdom.

Aye. I am Elliott's wing.

David knew what the decision had to be for the future of the clan. He knew the advice he had to give Elliott.

I have given you wisdom. You must use it now.

David gazed at Kenzie and then at Cullen, and he willed them to know he would protect them. He signaled Elliott, and Elliott jerked as if the signal had been a cattle prod, and Elliott signaled David to confirm, which he did.

Elliott straightened his shoulders. "This is my request—"

"We grant it," Arne said.

"I haven't asked yet," Elliott said.

"We know what you want—Tavis and Joseph."

"Ye're wrong. My request is for Erik's brooch." Elliott held out his hand.

David balanced on the balls of his feet, prepared to lunge at Arne if he reached for Kenzie's SIG. Time slowed. His mind slowed. Now it was all about muscle memory.

Instead of the brooch, Arne pulled out Kenzie's gun.

Using the bullet speed that made Austin's ball delivery famous, he brought down his powerful shooting arm, snapping the bones in Arne's hand. The gun fell to the dirt floor. Ensley kicked it out of the way, and Tavis swooped it up and pointed it at Arne.

Elliott reached inside Arne's robe and unpinned Erik's brooch. "Erik and his family have had this for centuries. It isn't yers."

"You cannot keep it," Arne said. "If you take it from here, it will lose its power. And we will never tell you the secrets."

"The only thing that will lose power is this Council. Erik's family will create a new Council in the twenty-first century," Elliott said.

"And as for the secrets," David said, "you've used that line of bullshit to maintain control over the Keeper." He knelt beside Kenzie, pulled the cloth out of her mouth, and kissed her before cutting the ropes that bound both her and Cullen's hands and feet. "Can ye walk?"

"Aye," Cullen said, pushing to his feet.

"I'm not so sure," Kenzie said. "But let's try."

David helped her stand, then gently pulled her into his arms. "Let's get this hellish adventure finished."

They gathered their weapons and left Arne's longhouse. As soon as they were away from the settlement, David pushed the talk button on his handheld radio. "This is Six Alpha. All our packages are ready to go home. Return to CP."

Ensley jumped up into Austin's arms, straddling his waist, and kissed him. "Man, those moves were just like the ones you used when you killed the bear. You're amazing."

Austin laughed. "At least my shooting arm is good for something these days."

"How'd ye know Arne had a gun?" David asked.

Austin grinned. "You're not the only person who knows Morse code. I heard Kenzie's tapping as soon as we walked inside the longhouse. JC and I played games in the cave. One of them was deciphering Morse code messages. We did it fast and only had one chance to guess right. The loser had to sneak a bottle of whisky out of the house the next time we escaped to the cave."

"Who won the most games?"

"After I got the hang of it, we tied mostly."

Remy was the first to make it back to the CP. When he saw Kenzie and Cullen, he went right to work patching them up.

David sat beside Kenzie and held her hand while Remy tended to her cuts. "Why'd Arne do this to ye? I should have killed him when I had a chance."

"You should see his men." She tried for a smile but grimaced instead while patting her busted lip. "Cullen and I took down the first four, but the replacements weren't so easy. We got a bit roughed up, but we did a lot of damage, didn't we?"

Cullen wiped the blood off his cheek with his handkerchief. "Aye."

Braham and Lincoln returned to the command post, and when they saw Cullen on the ground, hurried to his side. "Let me do that."

Cullen gave Braham the handkerchief. "I heard Kenzie took down Rick and JC, and I never could figure out how that could happen. Now I know, and I never want to be on the receiving end."

The twins arrived and rushed to their mother. "Oh, god. What happened?" Henry asked, taking her other hand. "Is your nose broken?"

"I doan think so," Remy said, "but her face is going to be swollen for a while."

Robbie sat down next to Henry. "Did that Arne guy do this to you?"

"No. Arne's men captured us without a fight, but Cullen and I didn't like the idea of making it easy on them, so the first chance we got, we went for it. You should have seen Cullen. He used several Tai Chi moves Sophia taught him. I was very impressed."

"So Arne didn't threaten ye?"

"No. His men took us to his longhouse, removed our armor and boots, and tied us up."

Remy gave Braham a handful of supplies. "Use these instead of the handkerchief."

Braham opened a cleaning cloth and started washing Cullen's face.

"Give me one of those," Lincoln said. "I know how to do this. I've seen Mom do it enough times." He went to work on Cullen's hands as meticulously as a manicurist.

"Did you have a knife at your throat during the first call?" Robbie asked.

Kenzie shook her head.

Churchill, Patrick, and Noah sat down with the twins. "Does it hurt bad?" Churchill asked. "You're the first bloody warrior I've seen since the Battle of New Orleans."

"Let's hope you never have to see anyone else beat up like this," Kenzie said, holding an ice pack against the side of her head.

Joseph sat down between the twins and mimicked their body language, with his elbows on his knees. "Grandpa Elliott," he asked, gazing up at Elliott. "Am I going home with you now?"

Robbie picked Joseph up and put the boy in his lap. "You're going home with all of us, and you'll have lots of cousins to play with. There won't be a moment of free time."

"When will I work?"

"Work?" Robbie asked. "School is work."

"In this society, children are just younger people with responsibilities to contribute to the community. There's no playtime," Tavis said.

"That's all about to change," Noah said. "It was a big adjustment for Patrick, Churchill, and me because we came from the past like you. We'll teach you what you need to know, and so will our brothers and sisters who're closer to your age."

Sophia sat nearby, sketchbook and pencils in hand, watching the tableau while she sketched.

Remy finished with Kenzie and Cullen. "That's all I can do right now. Let's get you two home so Charlotte can have a go at you."

"Do ye feel okay to travel?" David asked.

Kenzie sat up, and her head wobbled a bit. "Yeah, but you better hold on to me."

"We'll hold on to you instead of Grandpa Elliott," Robbie said.

"Yeah," Henry said. "We landed tight as tigers. We'll take care of you, Mom."

David watched his sons, surprised by their transformation from the jerks they were earlier to the obedient, loving lads they were now. Was it stress and worry that caused their bad behavior? Or had Kenzie's vulnerability been a shock to their youthful sense of invincibility? Whatever it was, when they returned home at the end of the summer, he'd take them camping and have a heart-to-heart about the chain of command and personal responsibility.

"Are you ready to go, Joseph?" Tavis asked.

"Wait a minute," Kenzie said. "I've missed something. This little guy is Tavis's son?"

"Aye," David said. "Joseph is three. It looks like Tavis spent time here before we met him in Gothenburg. He's got some explaining to do."

"Well, I'm waiting with bated breath."

"Dad, I hid Mom's amber necklace in the cave. Can I take it with me?"

"I'll go get it."

"No," Joseph jumped up and ran toward the cliff. "I'll get it."

David grabbed the tike before he reached the edge. "Whoa there, wee laddie. Ye take a tumble off that cliff, and even yer aunt Charlotte couldn't put ye back together again."

"Like Humpty Dumpty? Dad told me about him."

"I'll climb down with you, son, and you can go into the cave by yourself."

Tavis and Joseph slid over the edge. Then they disappeared as if climbing down a ladder instead of a rocky cliff.

"He's fearless," Robbie said. "Uncle Tavis will have his hands full."

"I want to teach him how to use the bathroom," Noah said, laughing. "Dad called the shower a glass waterfall, and the first time he shaved, we squirted shaving cream all over the place. I'll never forget it."

"I won't, either," Patrick snickered.

Churchill laughed. "Dad was so patient with me. I'll never forget that."

"At least Tavis already knows how to pee in a toilet, so he doesn't have to figure it out like Pa and I did," Noah said.

"We didn't do so bad, did we, lad?" Daniel asked.

"We did okay," Noah said. "Now it's hard to believe I ever lived in another century."

Twenty minutes later, Joseph and Tavis returned. Joseph held up a small leather pouch. "I got it. I can go see Grandpa Elliott's horses now."

Elliott picked him up and kissed his cheek. "Granny Mere will be so happy to have a wee laddie around again. Let's go home."

79

MacKlenna Ranch, CO (a few months later)—Austin

AUSTIN LAY SPRAWLED on their bed in the master bedroom while Ensley let her three-month-old Goldendoodle out to potty. He gave the puppy to her last week to celebrate the end of physical therapy following her hip replacement. But all that meant was Ted took over her daily exercise and diet regime, and he was much harder on her than the PT had been on his best days.

Thank god she didn't give him a puppy when his orthopedist released him to normal activities following surgery to repair his drop foot. He'd put it off because the surgery came with risks. It could either worsen the condition or fix it, and up until now, he hadn't been willing to take the risk. But since falling in love with Ensley, being healthy for her was more important than reclaiming his basketball career. By giving up what he thought he wanted, he was able to reclaim what he had. Nothing stood in the way now of returning to the NBA.

He loved the game, and if he could have a few more years, he should go for it. At least that's what Ensley told him. But the thought of leaving her alone on the ranch while he played forty-one away games every season scared him. Granted, they had security up the wazoo, but that wouldn't matter if the Illuminati wanted Erik's daughter.

The sitting room's French doors leading to the garden opened and closed. "Maddie, sit. Let's wipe your feet," Ensley said to her puppy.

It sounded like the dog got into the wet mulch again. Austin was a more disciplined dog walker than Ensley. He didn't allow Maddie to run around the garden off-leash, at least in part because the puppy loved to dig in the mulch and would dig up every shrub if she could.

"Good girl. Here, take your ball and go find Austin."

Seconds later, the puppy bounded into the bedroom and jumped up on the bed, tail wagging like she hadn't seen him in days instead of minutes.

"Come here, you mutt." He reached for the dog, and Maddie licked his hands and face. "Ensley, this puppy will never learn not to dig in the flower beds if you don't train her to stay out of them."

"I know, but she gets so excited when she has the freedom to run. I want to enjoy all those little moments of bliss with her now as she explores her world. Maybe we should move the deer fence back so she'll have more room, and then she'll leave the plants alone."

"Call the fence company and tell them what you want. Or call the garden center and ask them to plant prickly and fibrous foliage that deer don't like, so then you can remove the deer fence altogeth-"

"She'll run all over the ranch, then. I'll never find her."

"Call the fence company and tell them you want an invisible fence. That'll keep her contained."

"That makes sense. I'll call both companies later." She dropped her robe and climbed back into bed naked. "Isn't she precious?"

"Yes, you are," he said, breathing in the sweet scent of the roses on Ensley's skin. Maybe chasing the dog in and out of the garden wasn't so bad after all.

She kissed him, and the kiss turned greedy, which he loved. Every taste of her made him want the next one more. She pushed past his lips, and he teased her, opening just briefly to let her lick her way into his mouth, dominating the kiss once she was where he wanted her.

When she came up for air, she said, "Thank you for everything. I didn't know I could ever be so happy."

"Yeah, I've heard that from lots of hip replacement patients."

"HRPs have to stick together."

"Is that a patient code?" He stroked and caressed her curves, and she arched into him as he gently massaged her breast the way she liked it and then teased his thumb over the taut peak.

"If it's not, it should be... The code, I mean."

She wrapped her hand around his shaft, mimicking the way he stroked her, clearly trying to torture him. His head dropped back as she stunned him into stillness.

"…because we never know when we'll need to borrow a walker…"

His pulse knocked so hard against his throat that all he could do was lie there.

"…to get to the kitchen for energy treats."

And he listened while she continued, muttering about walkers and kitchens while her melodic voice and teasing fingers pinned him in place. As much as it turned him on to let her take the lead and have her way with him, he could only take so much.

Maddie jumped off the bed, jumped up, jumped down a third, fourth, fifth time as if playing with an invisible playmate. Austin threw the tennis ball across the room. It bounced out into the hall, and, as he predicted, Maddie chased after it.

"O'Grady hits two from the corner," Ensley said, humming against his neck.

"Three from the corner."

"Oh, my bad."

While the dog was out of the room, he took advantage of the time alone and moved Ensley's hand off his shaft. The stroking was short-circuiting his brain, and all he could think about was being inside of her.

She frowned. "You're stopping me?"

"This time, yes. I want to last a little bit longer because this is *your* day." He pulled her over on top of him, and his shaft inched into her tight, hugging entrance agonizingly slowly, in what he now referred to as her torture move. All the while, he struggled not to let his erection take control and thrust into her, rushing toward the end before she was ready.

She leaned forward and teased his nipples. "Why do you wax the hairs on your chest?"

He gave her his what-the-fuck look that he usually reserved for the basketball court. "Seriously? You're sitting on my cock and thinking about my chest hair or lack thereof?"

She got on her knees and eased back down on him—slowly. "I've thought of it before, but when I do, I'm usually not clicking on very many cylinders."

"For inquiring minds, I'll share a secret. NBA regulation jerseys have small holes in them, and sometimes hairs get caught in the holes, and it pulls and hurts. I eliminated the problem after my first year."

"You're making that up."

"Nope. It's true." He palmed her ass, lifted her, and withdrew to the tip of his erection. "I liked the look—"

She gasped and flexed her hips until her core gripped his entire length. "What look?"

He chuckled. "A shaved chest." He lifted her and tortured her with a slow withdrawal, then brought her hips down so he could plunge into her again. Torture worked both ways.

"Oh, now I remember," she moaned.

"You get distracted when I do this"—he palmed her ass again and took control of the rhythm—"I'd gotten so used to the look that after I stopped playing, I kept having it done and eventually manscaped the rest of my body hair."

"You're all neat and tidy. I like that."

Ensley moaned again as she fought for control of the rhythm, and since she wanted to ride him faster, he dropped his hands and folded them behind his head to watch her breasts bounce. Damn, she was sexy.

She stopped. "Wait a minute. Back up. I got distracted. Why is this *my* day?"

The pause nearly killed him, so he gripped her ass again, urging her to keep riding him. "You don't remember"—he gasped—"do you?"

"Nope. Nothing comes to mind."

"Okay, we'll talk later." He was done talking and wanted to get on with the business at hand. He gripped her hips tighter, sliding her faster...

"Is this an anniversary?"

When she was on top, he was all hers. Those were the rules, but it was time to add a new one about interrupting the flow with senseless chatter, unless it was erotic, provocative, or a request to do something different, and he was always ready for that.

"We met five months ago today, sweetheart. And this is agony, so can we—"

"Okay." She began to ride him again but not fast enough to suit him. "How can you remember that?"

"Blessed Jesus, Ensley. You're driving me nuts. I've trained my mind to remember numbers, dates, stats, and how many eggs go in a cake."

"Oh, you have not."

Maddie returned with the tennis ball, jumped up on the bed, and dropped it on Austin's chest. He picked up the soggy ball. "The entire world is conspiring against me right now."

He threw it again, and the puppy ran off to chase it. "Call the fence company this afternoon and a construction company. She needs a fucking doggie door." He swiped his thumbs across Ensley's pink, pebbled tips, and her bottom lip quivered. Hallelujah, now they were getting somewhere.

His mind raced as he wanted more of everything—her rose-scented skin, her kiss, the taste of orange juice on her tongue, and the warm, wet channel between her legs. And he struggled to stay in the moment and not come while she called for more and more.

Everything became violently sensitive. Shudders ripped through his muscles. He thrust harder, deeper, triggering the unmistakable buildup she craved. She cried and clenched, panting, and he loved giving her what she demanded.

Maddie returned with the ball. "Shit!"

Ensley's climax started, and he threw the goddamn ball, hitting a lamp that crashed to the floor. He didn't care. The entire house could come down around him as burning breaths rushed in and out of his lungs.

Ensley tightened as she got closer. Her gasps said she needed more of him. She arched and pulsed, and he'd never been so intent watching and feeling her come. Her pouty, reddened lips parted, and her muscles tightened around him, and a wet ball hit his chest just as Ensley cried out. He threw the ball again with such force it could have taken out a window. He couldn't think past the moment, and if the act of breathing wasn't part of his autonomic nervous system, he wouldn't even be doing that.

Her orgasm exploded, and her body vibrated, every muscle taking its turn, clenching and releasing around him, and his body jackknifed into an ocean of ecstasy. Ensley dropped onto his chest, and he held her there, not wanting her to move. Ever.

Minutes ticked by, and reality trickled back in. Every time they made love took him to another dimension, like stepping into the vortex and never knowing what to expect on the other side.

"Did I hear a crash?"

"I broke something. A lamp, I think. I need to sweep up the glass before Maddie steps in it. It's been an expensive morning—a new garden, fence, doggie door, and now a lamp. If she walks all over the glass, the vet bill could break the bank."

"I'll pay for it."

"Which one? The new garden plantings? The fence? The doggie door? The lamp? The vet bill?"

"All of the above, if Elliott would let me sell something from the cave. But in the meantime," she laughed, "I'll buy a new lamp."

Money wasn't a problem for either of them. The proceeds from her New York City apartment sale went into her investment portfolio, which Kevin was now managing. And pieces of the Roman treasure would eventually sell, and she'd receive an equal share. Plus, as soon as they were married, Kevin would start moving portions of Austin's estate into their joint account.

Maddie returned with the ball, and this time when he threw it, the ball sailed through the door, down the hallway, and hopefully landed near her bowl, where she'd forget about playing and eat her breakfast.

"I forgot to tell you that Olivia called while I was outside. She and Connor want us to come to dinner tonight. Matt and Elizabeth are visiting, and Matt wants to talk about TR. Are you up for it?"

"Sure. What'd you tell Olivia?"

"That we'd be there at seven."

Austin had arranged that phone call in advance, asking Olivia to host a celebratory dinner, but he didn't tell her what he wanted to celebrate. Knowing Olivia, she probably suspected what was going on and invited the whole damn family. "So you think you know me so well that I'd agree?"

"We go to their ranch twice a week. When have you ever said no? Besides, the kids want you there to cut the ribbon for their new outdoor basketball court."

"Hmm. That might be more tempting than talking about TR. Matt should be talking to you, not me. Does he know about your book?"

"So far, you're the only one."

"You should tell him. He's a historian and will be a great resource."

"I'll probably finish the second draft in few weeks. I'll talk to him then."

Austin pushed onto his elbow, pivoted onto his side, and twirled strands of her hair around his finger. "Elliott sent you a surprise. It arrived last night."

"I didn't hear a delivery truck."

I planned it that way.

"You were reading and sipping wine in the bathtub."

"But you told me you were going to your office. So I was only going to read a chapter. I assumed you were going down the hall."

He tugged on the curl, pulling her head closer, and gave her a leisurely kiss. "I have several offices."

"So that means I should ask which one?"

"You could."

"But you might not tell me the truth?"

Maddie returned carrying her ball. "Here comes your one-trick wonder." Austin threw the ball again. "JL and my family lied to me, and the truth nearly killed me. So I promise that never, ever will I lie to you."

She sat up and wrapped her ar   und her legs, giving him a very distracting view. "Does th   clude lies of omission?"

"Does what?"

"Your promise."

He licked his lips. "I can't promise that, and neither can you. We're too protective of each other."

"So that means if either one of us gets caught in a lie of omission, we should just get over it because neither one of us will commit to never doing it."

He slipped his hand between her legs and teased her with his fingers. "If the goal is to protect one of us, I'd say yes."

"Yes, what?"

He inserted one finger, two fingers, and teased her relentlessly. Maybe he could crush another climax out of her, and she'd forget this conversation.

"We should write this down...because one of us...will deny ever agreeing to it."

Maddie returned with her ball. Enough of this. He picked Ensley up. "Put me inside you. We're going to the garden."

He carried her outside, hands on her ass, controlling every move she made. He sat down on a chaise lounge, and she rode him hard. The sounds of their gasps mingled in the rose-scented air, and electricity arrowed down his spine, drawing his balls tight.

Goddamn it. He loved her. And, for the third time, they made love without a condom. Her orgasm hit them both—its intensity blinding. Her body milked his pulsing cock, and their orgasms slammed together. She went limp in his arms while Maddie dug up the goddamn garden, and he couldn't give a shit.

He dropped his head back and stretched out while she lolled on top of him, gasping. He might never move again, but then he remembered Elliott's surprise. Austin knew Elliott would be waiting impatiently for Ensley to call.

When their breathing returned to normal, he gave her ass a gentle smack. "We're going to the barn. Put on boots and jeans."

"Do I have to muck stalls before I get to climb back on my favorite stud?"

He carried Ensley back into the house and left Maddie in the garden to wreak havoc on the roses. "Something like that." He walked into the shower, carrying her, and turned on both showerheads.

She sat down on the built-in bench. "You'll have to give me a few minutes. You've reduced my body to jelly."

"Take your time." He finished his second shower of the morning, dressed in jeans, T-shirt, and boots, and returned to the garden to assess the damage. "Maddie O'Grady. How in the hell could you do that much damage in the time it took me to fuck and shower? Since Ensley will never discipline you, you're going to go live with a dog trainer for a few weeks. God knows what will happen when the kids come."

"I heard that," she hollered. "I'll be a much better disciplinarian with kids, and since you've decided not to use condoms, it might not be that long before we find out if it's true." She joined him in the garden and shrieked. "Maddie!"

"You've got some calls to make later today." He found Maddie's leash, and they walked around to the driveway where they parked their modified golf carts. "Do you want to drive?"

"Hell, no. That stinky dog isn't going to put even one grubby paw in mine."

"Yeah, how come I'm not surprised?"

They climbed into Austin's larger golf cart, and he drove down to the barn with Maddie riding in the back. He stopped at the door and handed Ensley a blindfold. "You have to wear this until I tell you to take it off—and no cheating." He drove down the center aisle of the thirty-stall barn and stopped at the end.

"Okay, you can take it off now."

He hopped out and went to the stall's door, and she walked up beside him. "Did you get a new horse?"

He unlatched the door. "No, you did."

She pushed it ajar and stood there in shock. "Oh, my God. Where'd you find him?"

"Elliott found him in England. He's a two-year-old purebred Akhal-Teke."

She entered the stall and slowly approached the horse. "And he looks exactly like Tesoro." She smiled at Austin with tears in her eyes.

"God, I love the feeling I get, the butterflies I get, when I see you smiling like that. I think it's the eighth wonder of the world."

She kissed Austin and then kissed the horse. "Can I ride him?"

"He's your horse. I did check with Ted. He said no trotting or galloping today. It could set back your full recovery."

"Okay, I'll just walk him around." She led the horse out of the stall. "What should I name him?"

"You don't have to do that today. You can think about it."

"It has to be special. Maybe TeddyR? Or Roosevelt? Or—"

"—or Tesoro," Austin said. "Who knows? He could have come from Tesoro's sire."

"Give me a leg up."

"I will, but remember, go easy."

Maddie returned from her brief exploration of the barn and jumped up on a hay bale to watch Austin put his hands under Ensley's bent leg and pop her up onto the horse's back. He thought his heart would stop when he stepped back and saw her sitting so proudly on her Akhal-Teke.

"You look like you belong there—my Viking Princess." He swallowed the lump in his throat. "Go easy."

Austin picked up Maddie, put her in the golf cart's front seat, and followed Ensley out of the barn. As soon as she cleared the door, she squeezed her legs, and the horse took off in a trot that turned into a gallop, and she raced across the open pasture, her hair trailing behind her.

He took a few pictures with his iPhone, chuckling. He hadn't said a word to Ted about her riding a horse. He already knew what Ted would say, and at this point, Ensley wouldn't listen anyway.

Maddie climbed into his lap with her dirty paws, and together they watched Ensley ride. Maddie looked up at him with her big brown eyes. "If you're asking for forgiveness, forget it. I broke a lamp, and you dug up the garden." Maddie didn't look away. "Are you worried about Ensley?" The dog just kept staring at him. "I know she shouldn't be riding that fast, but what's a man or his best friend supposed to do?"

Thirty minutes later, Ensley returned with rosy cheeks, a huge smile, and bright eyes. "It's like Tesoro was reborn in this stallion."

Austin climbed out of the cart. *Showtime!* He lifted her off the horse and set her down.

Then he took a knee.

"Ensley MacAndrew Williams, daughter of Erik the Viking, I fell in love with you the day you confronted three men with your finger on the trigger. So here's your down-on-my-knee proposal, with words I've written and rewritten a dozen times. Words that express what's in my heart."

She gasped and patted her chest. "Is this for real?"

"It's for real. Now for once in your life, be quiet." He cleared his throat. "You are fearless and a force of nature. You are passionate about life, and I have to up my game every day to come close to what you give me."

And then he sang to her...

"Cause all of me, loves all of you / Love your curves and all your edges / all your perfect imperfections. / Give your all to me / I'll give my all to you."

And then he said, "I promise to work harder, smarter, better each day to be the man you deserve. Will you marry me?"

She smiled and sniffed, her voice shaky when she said, "That was perfect. Yes! I'll marry you and give birth to an entire team of basketball players if that's what you want."

He slipped a ring on her finger. "This is a fourth-century garnet inlaid quintuple gold ring. I found it in a small wooden jewelry chest the first time we went to the treasure cave. The box was at my eye level, so there was no way I could miss it. I asked David if I could give it to you as an engagement ring."

Tears streaked down her face. "Do you think Erik put it there for you to find?"

"I believe he did. He has watched over you for your entire life. Making sure you had the perfect engagement ring might have been one of his last acts of love."

They returned Tesoro to his stall, brushed him, gave him fresh water and hay, and took a few pictures to send to Elliott. Austin would come back later and turn the horse out in a designated one-acre paddock, and later in the day, he'd meet with his ranch manager to discuss Tesoro's individual needs.

Maddie jumped up on the driver's seat. "No, you don't. Get in the back." Austin pointed, and—surprise, surprise—she did just that, wagging her tail.

Austin's mother and uncles kidnapped him all those months ago and sent him to the past from this barn. At the time, only one person believed it was the right thing to do—Pops. And only one person knew it was the right thing to do—Erik.

Austin drove back to the house with his Viking princess and her destroyer puppy.

Damn! Life couldn't get any better than this...

Well, maybe hearing... "O'Grady scores three from the corner to tie the game" one more time might be the cherry on top.

80

MacKlenna Ranch, CO (Christmas)—Elliott

ELLIOTT STOOD ON the deck of the ranch house overlooking the snow-covered ground and distant mountaintops. He'd always thought sunsets in Scotland looked like heaven on earth, but the beauty of a Colorado winter had Scotland beat.

And with all the skiers and snowmobilers, the ranch looked like a ski resort.

He'd lost track of how many kids were here. It could be fifty, or it could be a hundred. The MacKlennas were a prolific bunch.

Ensley had requested a virgin mimosa at brunch, but there was so much confusion at the time that Elliott didn't think anyone else noticed. A baby and a new contract with the Denver Nuggets. They were living their dream. Elliott's prayer was that they got to enjoy it for a few years before another brooch forced the family to face conflict, tension, and fear again.

Tavis, still wearing his ski jacket and pants, strode out to join Elliott at the railing. "I snuck a cigar out for you."

Elliott glanced around. "Where's Meredith? Have ye seen her? She knows I smoke one now and again, but if she catches me, she'll demand that I put it out."

Tavis handed him a cigar and unwrapped one for himself. "You're safe. She bundled Joseph up and took him snowmobiling about thirty minutes ago. I warned her if she went fast and scared my kid, she'd lose her grandma privileges."

Elliott unwrapped the cigar and gently pinched it between thumb and index finger—part of his meticulous ritual—working the entire length, searching for hard or soft spots. Then, fully satisfied there would be no draw problems, he passed the cigar beneath his nose—one final step in the ritual—to take in the sweet aroma.

"I wouldn't worry about Meredith. Joseph goes rock climbing, for Christ's sake. And ye think a fast ride will scare him? He's three and already an adrenaline junkie. What'd Meredith say, 'Mind yer own business?'"

"She told me to remember this the next time we went climbing."

Tavis flicked his lighter and held the flame for Elliott to light his cigar. Elliott drew deeply until the red ember crawled up the paper, and smoke hazed the air between them. Then Elliott leaned against the railing, folded his arms across his chest, and enjoyed his insane love affair with cigars.

"How much do ye want to bet Joseph is driving on the way back?"

"So that's her plan? Not to scare the kids but to terrorize the parents?"

Elliott laughed. "That's about it." Then he stopped laughing when he saw Austin carrying Ensley toward the house with her skis dangling, George and Barb traipsing beside them, throwing a ball for Maddie to chase, and the sun setting behind them. "Oh, dear God. What happened now?"

"Not a damn thing, except she's pregnant, and Austin is hovering over her like she's a China doll, not a Viking princess."

"I didn't think anybody knew she was pregnant."

"She ordered a virgin mimosa this morning."

"I noticed, but I didn't think anyone else did."

"It's my job to notice." Tavis tapped his cigar against the railing, and the ash fell to the ground and sizzled in the snow. "By the way, Braham told me to let you know we aren't required to write a review. These are Christmas presents."

"I hate writing those damn things, but I'd hate losing my privileges more, so I do it. But since we're talking about Christmas presents, have ye given any more thought to where ye want to build yer house? Ye can't live in a guest suite indefinitely, although Charlotte wouldn't mind. But Joseph needs more stability. So is it Mallory Plantation, MacKlenna Farm, Napa, Florence, New South Wales?"

"Right now, I'm not sure. Kevin and I had a long chat last night about the housing situation. He asked if I'd be interested in living in JC's house in Georgetown. He worries about it being empty. It's got good security, but you never know. Staying there would keep Joseph and me close to Mark and his family and the plantation, but Jean and Joseph have decided they're twins and should live together. They don't like being apart. So maybe Napa."

"I've heard them talk about being twin brothers."

"They can't figure out why their eyes aren't the same color."

"Joseph's are an unusual blue."

"The same shade as Erik's."

"Aye. At some point, we'll have to bring Mark into the fold. He's Erik's son, too, and I promised to protect all his children."

"I don't think we should bring Mark in out of the cold yet. He's happy and content. Worrying about the Illuminati would bring unnecessary stress into his life, and I don't want that for him." Tavis waved his cigar, leaving a trail of smoke in the air. "I've set up a college fund for his son, but if he follows Mark and me, he'll end up at one of the academies and won't need the money for tuition."

"Let's revisit it annually. I'd like to add to the college fund."

"Sure. But if you drop a bunch of money in there at one time, Mark will think we're both dealing drugs."

"I'll tell Kevin to be conservative."

"I heard Paul sent a message. Anything you want to share?"

"James Cullen's outbursts are less frequent, but he's still troubled. Paul says they have a routine that gives them time for meditation, study, and exercise, and he doesn't anticipate coming home for a while."

"Did he say how long that was?"

"No, but he gave me the impression it could be eighteen to twenty-four months. If living in the Georgetown house works for ye, I think it's a great idea." Elliott pointed with his cigar. "Here comes Meredith—and look who's driving."

Tavis waved at his son, and the cigar left a trail of smoke in the air. "At least Meredith's hands are on the controls, too."

"They probably did a switcheroo when they got closer."

They watched Meredith park the snowmobile, then she and Joseph entered through the mudroom to strip out of their winter gear. Elliott glanced at his cigar, using how much he'd smoked of it as a measure of time. Meredith would be calling him in to change clothes soon.

"I still owe you an explanation about his mother."

"When ye're ready. No rush."

"I know everybody's curious but polite enough not to ask. So here's the deal."

Elliott held up his hand. "If ye feel like ye need to get a load off yer chest, then I'll listen to anything ye want to say. But don't do this for me."

"I'm doing it for both of us." Tavis flicked the ash again. "I was betrothed to Astrid when she was fourteen, but I refused to sleep with her until she turned eighteen, which was late for her culture, and she missed several of her best childbearing years. I think about that a lot. Maybe she was too old to have another healthy delivery."

"Maternal mortality doesn't occur in the majority of deliveries," Elliott said. "Most women who get pregnant and get past the first trimester deliver a live baby."

"Thanks, Dr. Fraser, for that bit of information. I thought your specialty was Thoroughbreds."

"When JL had a placental abruption and delivered Lance early, I learned more about pregnancy, childbirth, and neonatal care than I ever wanted to know."

"And I didn't know enough."

"Even if ye'd known what to do, ye couldn't have saved her. Astrid needed to be in the hospital."

"I know. I wanted to bring her home, but she wouldn't even consider coming for a short visit."

"I wished ye'd told me. I would have given ye a brooch to come and go as ye pleased."

"But that would have come with the expectation that I spy on them. I didn't want to do that. I regret not demanding answers from Erik. The Council meetings I attended never gave me any insight into the brooches. After a while, I got the impression Erik was the only one who knew the history in any detail, and I suspected the other Council members were afraid of him."

Tavis took a short draw, then removed the cigar from his mouth and studied it. "Erik was brilliant and knowledgeable in every subject. It's no telling how many colleges and universities he attended. Once he hinted that he'd been far into the future but never gave any specifics. It occurred to me that he might have taken JC to another time when skin harvesting is more advanced and doesn't depend on cadaver skin or autografts."

"That makes more sense than believing in a magic cloak. I wonder if James Cullen will ever remember what happened to him." Elliott shifted the cigar from one corner of his mouth to the other.

"How many times did ye see Erik?"

"I couldn't count them. He'd randomly show up, mostly during my years at Annapolis. He'd say, 'Let's go,' and we'd pop off to another century. Sometimes we were gone for days, sometimes weeks, and several times we were gone for months. But when I returned home, I'd only been gone less than a minute. I went to classes at universities all over the world. We ate exquisite meals prepared by world-renowned chefs, drank expensive wine, slept with beautiful women, and saw some of the great wonders of the world that no longer exist. Places like the Pink and White Terraces of Lake Rotomahana in New Zealand, the Porcelain Tower of Nanjing, the New York Hippodrome, London's Crystal Palace, Rotbav Fortified Church in Romania. I could go on and on."

Tavis looked down at his cigar, then pulled his Swiss Army knife cigar cutter out of his pocket and used it to trim the ash evenly. Then his gaze lifted. "I've never discussed so many esoteric topics with anyone else. I felt like Peter Pan. I never wanted to grow up.

"After I graduated, I reported to my ship for my first tour of duty that lasted twenty-four months. I only saw him a handful of times during those two years, and each year after that, I saw him less often."

"He gave ye an education ye couldn't have gotten anywhere else."

"Yes, he did. Then I got so busy I didn't think about him. In hindsight, I believe he planned it that way. He gave me what no one else could."

"Why do ye think he didn't want to talk about the brooches with ye? Any ideas?"

"I once believed he was ashamed or regretted something in his life. Every time I asked a question about his brooch, he dropped his eyes and quickly changed the subject."

"We'll never know now. But ye never traveled through the light or another cave door?"

"Never. But I like the theory that the light transports you to another location in the same year, maybe even the same month and date, and the door will take you to another century. As of yet, David and Kenzie haven't figured out when or how the light turns on."

"Maybe they should try 'open sesame.'"

"I think Kenzie tried that," Tavis said, laughing. "But here's another problem we have to solve. Once you go through the light or the door, how the hell do you get back?"

"That's not a problem. Ye just have to use a brooch for the return trip. But the bigger problem is how will we ever find out? Who wants to be the first to walk into that light?"

"Not me," Tavis said.

Meredith poked her head out the door. "We need to change, Elliott. I told Joseph we have a surprise for him tonight, so we can't mess it up."

Elliott threw his cigar into the firepit below. "Have I ever screwed up my role?"

"The jury's still out." Meredith closed the door to the large family room, took Joseph's hand, and led him away.

"Emily's flying in about now," Elliott said. "When ye see the lights at the heliport come on, will ye drive down to get her?"

"She texted earlier. She won't be here for another hour, but I'll go down as soon as the landing lights go on."

"She's a good match for ye."

"Don't start, Elliott. Astrid hasn't even been gone a year."

"Nothing says a man has to wait a year."

"That's true. But a man needs to wait until he's ready, and that's different with every man who loses his wife. I'm on the slower side."

"Just don't be like those birds who mate for life."

"If you lost Meredith, you'd never date again."

"I'm a lot older than ye are, and besides, no other woman would put up with me. On my good days, I still piss her off."

"Don't give me that shit. You two are a perfect example of those birds who mate for life. You have a strong, honest marriage. A few months ago, you put it through the wringer, but you worked it out. And I'd say you're more in love today than you were this time last year."

"Ye think ye know the inner workings of our marriage?"

"I don't have to know. I see it in the way you treat each other, the joy on your faces when one of you walks into a room, the attention to each other's needs. Yeah, you two mated for life."

"Our marriage didn't heal overnight, but we were determined to move past what happened, learn from it, and make sure we never made those mistakes again." Elliott clasped Tavis's shoulder. "Don't forget Emily."

He left Tavis alone on the deck to finish his cigar and relive his memories with Erik. Tavis wouldn't admit it, but Elliott knew the lad was still angry because Erik never told him the truth. Who wouldn't be pissed as hell?

Elliott entered the house and walked straight into a gaggle of women camped out in front of the fireplace, drinking wine and laughing. Penny sat nestled in a bunch of pillows and blankets, discreetly nursing one of the twins.

"Hurry up, Elliott," she said. "The kids are all downstairs waiting for their surprise."

He removed his jacket and cap and hung them on the hat stand near the door. "I'm sure they figured out what it is by now."

"The ones who know pretend they don't, and the ones who don't pretend they do," Kenzie said. "Try saying that five times. I bet you can't do it."

And that led to all the women trying out the tongue twister at the same time and laughing when they couldn't. Elliott wondered if any of them, other than Penny, were sober.

Rick walked in carrying the other twin. "Want to switch?"

"Sure. This little guy is done for now." They switched babies, and Rick left the room, carrying the wee laddie like a football. The guys were probably all hanging out in the billiards room, drinking beer, shooting pool, and watching ballgames.

These warrior men and women were extraordinary people, full of grit and resolve, love and friendship, compassion and passion, and he loved every one of them.

He returned to the suite he shared with the love of his life to dress for one more performance. Maybe next year, he and Meredith could retire and hand their costumes down to another couple. He entered the room and closed the door.

"Do ye know how many people are here?" he asked. "I'm just curious."

Meredith was stripping out of her warm-weather clothes, dropping pieces on the floor on her way to her closet. "I tried counting but gave up. Amber and Penny know the count for meals, and that's all that matters."

"What about the presents?"

She walked out of the closet, tying the belt to her robe. "They're all in the bags with each person's picture taped to the gift. You won't get confused."

"It's just the young McBain twins who confuse me, and I think they do that on purpose."

Meredith stood in front of the dresser and removed her earrings and necklace. "You may be right."

"So what'd ye get them this year?"

"They all went through the Roman treasure catalog Sophia put together and picked out one piece they wanted for their private collections."

Elliott picked up her clothes and his and dumped them all in his dirty clothes basket. Littering the floor with her discarded clothes was her way of saying he should pick up his without telling him to do so, and he always took the hint, especially after all they'd been through this year.

"Is that the same collection that has ticket stubs from Austin's championship games?" he asked.

"A collection is anything you have seven of, and they've all been collecting items from Italy since we bought the winery near Florence."

"Just don't tell me someone wanted the chariot."

She smiled at him and patted his cheek. "Robbie did. But he's not getting it."

"Well, I should hope not."

They stood together in front of the window and gazed out over the pasture. "This is a beautiful ranch. I'm glad you decided to give it to Austin and Ensley."

"He wanted to buy it, but I told him it was a gift, and if they divorced, the ranch would belong to the kids. That was okay with him."

"You know, about every three years, we add new couples and new babies to the family. If we keep growing at this rate, we won't have a house big enough to sleep everybody at one time."

"We'll heat the horse trailers."

"Ha, ha. You're getting a sense of humor in your old age."

"I'm working on it."

Meredith poured a glass of red wine and sat down in one of the two matching chairs next to the crackling fire. "You should have seen Joseph on the snowmobile. He was so excited." She took a sip and continued, "I think he's the most loving of all the kids, and he's curious about everything. He reminds me a lot of James Cullen, but he's more sociable. I hope Tavis doesn't move too far away."

"He has several options, but right now, Joseph and Jean believe they're twins and don't want to be separated. So it looks like Tavis might end up in Napa."

"That's fine. Tavis and Joseph can live in the guesthouse. No one stays there since Rick and Penny moved into their new home."

"Ye mean mansion?"

"It's a beautiful place, and it looks like it's always been there. The architect did a phenomenal job of incorporating it into the landscape, the vineyards, and the winery's history. I couldn't be more pleased."

"And ye stayed out of the process."

A line appeared between her brows, and she studied the crystal glass in her hand. "Well, they think I did, and that's all that matters. But the truth is, I had several conversations—off the record—with the architect and guided her in a specific direction. Just for aesthetic purposes."

He shook his head as he poured a glass of whisky. He should have known she couldn't stay out of it, but at least he never got a panicky call from Penny or Rick about his bride causing trouble.

Meredith opened the drawer in the table next to her chair and removed a folder. "After the year we've had, I decided to give you something you didn't have or couldn't get for yourself—answers." She held out the folder. "You can read this now or later."

"What's it about?"

"Erik, the brooches, murder, intrigue, family. All sorts of things. It would make a great Netflix series."

"That's all the temptation I need." He sat in the other chair next to the fire, but when he saw the single-spaced, typed, multi-page document, he closed it. "Give me the synopsis, and I'll read this tomorrow."

"Are you sure?"

"Whatever it is, just tell me."

She put her feet up on the ottoman. "I've researched the MacKlennas and Frasers in the National Records of Scotland dozens of times, and I've never seen the information in that folder. I should have found it before now. My researchers definitely should have found it. But it slipped through the cracks."

He tapped his finger on the folder. "So this is the reason ye stopped in Scotland on the way back from Florence."

"I wanted to shop in Edinburgh for kilts for Jean and Joseph, and while I was there, I went to the Archives out of habit." She sipped her drink. "This is complicated. If you get confused, stop me.

It took me half a dozen times to reread the information and put the pieces together."

"Stop explaining and just tell me what ye found."

"Your Grandfather Fraser had a brother named Malcolm, who disappeared before the start of World War I and was never heard from again."

"That's impossible. I know the Fraser history top to bottom, and I've never heard of him. Are ye sure?"

"I'm positive. Malcolm was a suspect in a brutal murder. The articles I found had pictures and physical descriptions of him, and he looked familiar." She pointed to the folder he'd set aside. "Turn to the second page and look at the photographs."

Elliott turned to the page she indicated and studied the pictures. The man looked familiar. "I must be imagining this, but he resembles Erik."

"No, it's not your overactive imagination. I compared those pictures to Sophia's sketches. This man's forehead is higher, the nose more pronounced, the chin more pointed. They're two different men, but it's obvious they're related."

"Sophia has never seen Erik or his photograph. She could be wrong."

"That's true, but three years ago, she sat down with everyone who met Erik at Jarlshof and sketched a picture based on their descriptions, and that included yours. Then earlier this summer, with Ensley, Remy, and Austin's help, she updated her sketch. The final step was incorporating Tavis's changes. She says the final painting is as accurate as any photograph could be."

"Okay, so my previously unknown great-uncle Malcolm, who resembled Erik the Viking, was a suspect in a murder case and disappeared?"

"That's right, and there's more. I found newspaper articles that described the injuries to the body of the man he's suspecting of killing. The man was skinned alive."

"Shit!"

"The police never found a motive for the murder, but in another article, I found a vague reference to a piece of jewelry Malcolm had wanted to buy, but the victim wouldn't sell it."

"Jewelry? Like a brooch?"

"Possibly."

"Ye have this all figured out. I can see it in yer eyes. So just tell me what ye think."

"The police believed Malcolm escaped to the Shetland Islands, but with the outbreak of World War I, the investigators didn't have time to follow up, and the Frasers were just thankful he was gone. The family buried Malcolm under the proverbial rug."

"Did you find a death record in the Shetland Islands?"

"There's no record of him living there or a death certificate, but he wouldn't have used his real name anyway."

"What do ye think happened to him?"

"This is all conjecture, but I believe he went back in time."

"To Jarlshof?"

"If we match up what we know, what we think we know, and then use our imaginations, I believe Malcolm used the brooch and found his soul mate—a Viking woman, and they had at least two sons—"

"—Erik and Sten."

"We can't prove any of this, and before you ask, I haven't mentioned this to Tavis or David or anyone else."

"Tavis might have heard something, even a rumor." Elliott thought back through his life, and the first questions that came to mind were—had his mother heard the rumors? Had Elliott's father's violent outbursts frightened her into leaving him before he...pulled a Malcolm?

"Who'd Malcolm kill?"

"This piece of information makes Malcolm's story more believable. The newspaper article identified the victim as Robert Stuart, Tavis's paternal great-grandfather."

"But Tavis isn't a biological Stuart since Erik fathered him."

"If Malcolm Fraser was Erik's biological father, that would make Tavis a Fraser."

"Holy shit! If everything ye're saying is true, my great-uncle Malcolm traveled back in time, had two sons—one of whom tried to kill James Cullen—and the other fathered Ensley, Tavis, and Mark. So Erik's brooch belongs to Tavis and Mark."

"Technically, the Stuarts were guardians, so the brooch should go to the Keeper."

"How could ye have not found this before?"

"I don't have an explanation."

"Tavis told me tonight that he made several trips with Erik, visiting different centuries, different cities, and staying for weeks and months at a time. If Erik traveled that much, he could have searched the archives or even planted documents so ye would find them."

"But why would he want us to know?"

"Tavis said he got the impression that Erik was embarrassed or ashamed of something. If he was aware of what his father did, he might want the Keeper to know what happened to Robert Stuart's brooches, or at least one of them."

"James MacKlenna told Sophia that an ancient tribe living in Caledonia made the brooches from a rock that fell from the sky. The gemstones came from trading with Vikings. After many centuries, a small group of survivors traveled south to the Highlands and intermarried with Clan MacKlenna. When the clan leader discovered the brooches possessed unusual powers, he took precautions to protect them, and he became known as the Keeper. When the Keeper uncovered a threat to the brooches' security, he appointed twelve guards to protect them. No one except the Keeper knew how many brooches there were or the identities of those chosen to guard them. Generations of MacKlennas have passed that knowledge down through their children."

"Let's unwind this pretzel if we can," Elliott said. "If Mr. Stuart confessed to Malcolm under torture that he was a guardian and originally had possession of four brooches, but when he sensed trouble, he gave three of them away, Malcolm would have wanted to find those three to go with one he stole from Robert Stuart."

"Maybe Malcolm was the original threat that caused the Keeper to disperse the brooches in the first place."

"And he killed the Keeper, which sent all the guardians into hiding, and every time Malcolm got close to one of them, the guardians gave away their brooches."

"That had to be frustrating for him." Meredith sipped her wine. "Maybe…Malcolm hired spies to let him know if they heard of a guardian or a brooch. But how would they communicate?"

Elliott finished his drink and set the glass on the table with the folder. "Malcolm could have given his spies access to a brooch or brooches, and they started an evil organization that's still in existence today."

"There's no way to prove any of this." Someone knocked on their door, and Meredith said, "Come in."

Ensley stuck her head inside the room, and Maddie burst in carrying a ball in her mouth and jumped up into Elliott's lap.

"Maddie!" Ensley yelled. "Get back here."

Maddie turned and looked at Ensley, cocked her head, then dropped the ball in Elliott's lap.

"With all the kids around ye pick me to play with ye? What's wrong with this picture?"

"Everything," Ensley said. "How much longer will it take you two to get ready? The kids are getting tired and cranky."

Elliott said, "Heads up!" He tossed the ball to Ensley. "Good catch. We'll be ready in fifteen minutes."

Ensley tossed the ball into the hallway, and Maddie raced after it. "I'll let everybody know. Your elves are waiting at the top of the stairs." Ensley closed the door.

Meredith walked toward her closet. "You'll have to share this news with the family."

"Ye're right, but let's not tell them tonight. It'll ruin the celebration."

Fifteen minutes later, Meredith and Elliott met Robbie and Henry—each holding two giant bags—at the top of the stairs, and at their feet were two smaller ones.

"It's about time," Robbie said.

Elliott picked up the smaller bags. "Ring yer bells, and let's go."

"How are we supposed to do that, Grandpa? We have our hands full."

"Give me the bells," Meredith said, holding up the strips of fabric with small bells attached. "These look like doggie doorbells."

"They are," Henry said, "but Maddie refuses to use them, so just ring 'em, and let's get this show on the road."

Meredith rang the bells as they all thundered down the stairs. "Merry Christmas! Merry Christmas!"

By the time Santa and Mrs. Claus reached the bottom step, the kids were screaming, "Santa's here! Santa's here!"

Positioned in front of the Christmas tree were two comfy chairs with a table between them. A glass of whisky and a glass of wine sat on a tray with appetizers. The nearby fire was blazing, Christmas music played in the background, and glowing faces filled the room.

Santa belly-laughed, "Ho! Ho! Ho!"

Blane patted the seat of one of the chairs. "Sit here, Santa. The fire's warmed it up for you."

"Yeah, it's your chair. Nobody else can sit there," Lance said. "I tried, but Blane pulled me out and dropped my ass on the floor."

"Lance, watch your language," Kevin said.

"Sure, Dad. But tell him"—Lance pointed at Remy. "And him"—he pointed at Austin. "And him"—he pointed at David—"to watch their language, too. They say ass all the time."

"And him"—Kevin pointed at his son. "Sit your ass down, or you're not going to get any presents."

"Jesus, Dad. Watch your language," Blane said.

"It's pres...*sent!*" Lance said. "This Santa has"—he held up his finger—"only one for us."

Kevin put his hands on his hips and tapped his fingers. "Sit down, son. We'll talk about this later."

Elliott stroked his fluffy white beard. Kevin was a wonderful father and husband, and Elliott was so proud of him. Because of Kevin's financial acumen, Elliott had him evaluate all business decisions, and he'd made millions for the family.

"Okay, who's first?" Elliott asked.

"You have to pull a present out of the bag and call out whose picture is on the present," Jack's daughter Margaret Ann said.

"So that's how it's done? Well, what if I don't know who it is?"

"That's impossible. You know all the children," Jean said.

For the next two hours, gifts were given and received. The volume in the room got louder and louder, and wrapping paper littered the floor. Joseph looked ready to cry.

Elliott whispered to Meredith. "Mrs. Claus needs to comfort the wee lad."

Meredith got Joseph's attention and patted her lap. "Come sit with me."

Joseph glanced up at his dad, and Tavis winked at Meredith. "Go on, buddy. She's a nice lady, just like Granny Mere."

Joseph plodded toward Meredith, sidestepping the kids, presents, and wrapping paper. When he reached Meredith, he grabbed her hand and climbed up into her lap.

"Jean told me about Santa and Mrs. Claus and presents, and all, but I couldn't... I mean... I don't understand. Robbie and Henry told me you aren't real."

"They did?" Meredith asked, giving Robbie and Henry pointed looks.

"They said parents tell kids four big lies about Santa Claus, the Easter Bunny, the tooth fairy, and where babies come from. But you're real."

Meredith looked at Elliott. "Yes, Joseph. Santa and Mrs. Claus are here to help you celebrate Christmas because we love you."

Elliott watched Jean's reaction to the attention Joseph was getting from Mrs. Claus. What would he do now? It took about thirty seconds before Jean approached Meredith.

"Mrs. Claus, Joseph and I are twins. We do everything together. Can I sit on your lap, too?"

"You certainly can, young man."

Jean climbed up, and as soon as he got settled, Maddie jumped up into Elliott's lap, and the kids rolled on the floor laughing. "Maddie's sitting on Santa's lap."

Cameras flashed while Maddie sat still, wearing her Christmas bandana, acting like the princess she thought she was. Elliott glanced over at Ensley and Austin cuddled up on the sofa with his arm around her, his hand rubbing her belly. George and Barb sat on the floor with the kids, calmly taking it all in. The couple had only flown in yesterday to celebrate Christmas and help plan a spring wedding.

"Jean, see that package by Mrs. Claus's foot?" Elliott pointed to the package with Maddie's picture on it. "Would ye get that for me?" Jean picked up the box, and Elliott asked him to open it.

"Tennis balls!" Jean said. "Are they for Maddie?"

"They sure are," Elliott said. "Do ye want to give her one of them?" Instead of pulling one out, Jean dumped all twelve on the floor, and they bounced and rolled everywhere. Maddie jumped down and dove into a stack of wrapping paper, chasing one of the balls.

Two hours later, when the excitement had worn off, Maddie was sleeping at Austin's feet, and the younger kids were rubbing their eyes.

"It's time to go, Santa," Mrs. Claus said. "You have a long night ahead."

"Ho! Ho! Ho!" Santa said. "I have to go to work now."

Santa and Mrs. Claus walked to the door that led to the pool, outdoor kitchen, and entertainment center. "Merry Christmas to all!"

"Good night, Santa," all the kids yelled.

Elliott and Meredith planned to walk around to the front of the house, sneak inside, and change their clothes before rejoining the celebration for more of Penny and Amber's appetizers. But they stopped a minute to gaze into the window and watch all the people they loved, laughing and hugging each other.

Elliott put his arm around Meredith. "All in all, it's been an okay year."

She gazed up at him. "I miss James Cullen too, Elliott. My heart breaks for what he's been through, and I'm scared to death he'll always suffer from what happened to him."

"Ye're normally the optimistic one, not me, but I believe it'll all work out." Elliott put his hand on the glass, and Meredith put hers on top of his.

"Bless the family, Elliott, then let's enjoy a private celebration for a while."

He smiled. "Good night, lads and lassies. May God hold each of ye in the palm of his hand."

THE END

AUTHOR NOTES

"We have unleashed monsters that will commit atrocities. I am responsible, and so is my son—the last MacKlenna." – Dr. Elliott Fraser, Keeper of the Brooches.

When I started plotting *The Sunstone Brooch*, I intended to go to Medora and the Theodore Roosevelt National Park, but then the COVID-19 pandemic hit, and my plans changed. So, Ensley's "follow the water" trek across the Badlands is based on Google Maps.

All mistakes in mileage, distances, and towns are my own.

In nearly forty years in public and private life, the cowboy image remained an essential element of Teddy Roosevelt's persona. He took the cowboy off the pages of western lore and turned him into a flesh and blood character. By 1885, TR was still a restless and easily influenced young man searching for himself, seeking direction, and renewed purpose.

I read several books and spent many hours with my TR expert Dr. Tom Appleton. Tom was always available to answer questions, but I couldn't pin him down about how TR would have reacted to Ensley. TR supported women's suffrage and became a champion of women's rights, so I believe he would have enjoyed her company. Their interactions are strictly my imagination at work, except for the book discussions. Those were all based on TR's reading preferences.

The fall into the ice pond, the cattle arriving on the train, the stampede, and the roundup were all actual events during TR's time in the Badlands.

In future books, we'll see him again when he becomes police commissioner in New York City, then as a Rough Rider, and finally as president. And with each of these "visits," Tavis, Remy, and

James Cullen will find their soul mates.

The Sunstone Brooch started as a love story set during TR's time at Elkhorn Ranch, but once James Cullen left Ensley behind, the story took off in another direction. But that's what usually happens when brooches are activated, and a short book became an extra-long one.

When I sit down to write, I rarely have a plan, and I'm often shocked by the turn of events. From the beginning, I didn't even know the identity of Ensley's soul mate. But of the four men, Austin was the only one ready for love.

While visiting my daughter during the 2019 Christmas holiday, I asked my son-in-law for an accident that could end a professional basketball player's career. We tossed around some ideas, and then he suggested I google Jay Williams. Williams's basketball career ended when he had a motorcycle accident. Williams has since turned his successful basketball career into a successful sportscasting career on ESPN. But in the Celtic brooch world, Austin gets a second chance to play the game he loved.

Paul Brodie was a complete surprise, and I didn't know what role he would play when he first showed up on the page. And I didn't know about Tavis's secret life until he went into the fog with Erik's body.

And Erik, wow! What a surprise he was. If you were shocked…well, so was I. Hopefully, we're finished with the Vikings, although the Illuminati will probably show up again.

As for what happened to JC in Asia, I don't have any idea. He was unable to talk about it before he went to the monastery, and by the time he gets home, it might not matter.

It was hard writing through a pandemic, and my focus suffered. Since I couldn't visit my children and grandchildren, I brought home an eight-week-old Goldendoodle named Maddie, and yes, she loves to play ball, and of course, she had to show up in the book.

It was fun to see the clan back together for a songfest and to hear David's sax again. Check out *The Sunstone Brooch* playlist on Spotify.

If you want to travel to Bhutan, it's not as easy as the MacKlennas made it seem. Independent travel isn't allowed. All travelers must make travel arrangements through an authorized tour operator on a preplanned, prepaid, and escorted all-inclusive tour package. The tour operators take care of all land arrangements, including in-country travel/road permits, temple permits, and special permits.

It takes a village to write and produce one of these big books. And I couldn't do it without the assistance of a lot of people. If you're reading the print version, check out the Author Notes for The Sunstone Brooch for links.

- Chief Editor and Content Editor: Faith Freewoman
- Virtual Assistant, Fact Checker, Researcher, and Keeper of the MacKlenna Clan Series Bible: Annette Glahn
- Freelance Proofreader: Elaini Caruso
- Beta Readers: Lori Seiderman, Paula Retelsdorf, and Jen Coleman
- Marine Advisor: John Retelsdorf
- Medical Advisor: Dr. Ken Muse
- Historical/Theodore Roosevelt Expert: Dr. Tom Appleton
- Cover Design by Damonza
- Interior Design by BB eBooks
- Cover image by photographer Jerry Blank

Some sites you might want to check out:

- Theodore Roosevelt Presidential Library
- Theodore Roosevelt's Reading List
- Elkhorn Ranch
- Bill Sewall & Wilmot Dow
- Theodore Roosevelt's Elkhorn Ranch House Plan
- The layout of the house at Elkhorn Ranch
- Theodore Roosevelt and Conservation
- Roosevelt Island
- The early years of Chicago's Palmer House
- Chicago—Passage of Time 1880s
- The Rarest Horse on Earth (Akhal-Teke)
- Jarlshof from Above
- Tiger's Next Trek
- What It's Like To Visit Taktsang Monastery (Tiger's Nest) In Bhutan
- Dresses of Bhutan – Traditional Dress of The Himalayan Kingdom

- Official railroad map of Dakota issued by the railroad commissioners, November 1st, 1886.
- No flint? No problem. How to find a rock that will spark like flint
- Clovis Point
- How to make a survival spear
- Making birch bark bowls
- Becky's thimble
- Yggdrasil: The Sacred Ash Tree of Norse Mythology

Places that inspired my imagination:

- MacKlenna Ranch in Colorado
- James Cullen's house in Washington, D.C.
- The Williams's house in Cambridge
- Flat Top Ranch
- Elliott's airplane

A few books about Theodore Roosevelt that are now part of my library:

- *Bill Sewall's Story of Theodore Roosevelt* by William Sewall
- *Hunting Trips of a Ranchman: Sketches of Sport on the Northern Cattle Plains* by Theodore Roosevelt
- *Roosevelt in the Bad Lands* by Hermann Hagedorn
- *Roosevelt's Ranch Life In North Dakota* by Albert Tangeman Vollweiler
- *The Naturalist: Theodore Roosevelt, A Lifetime of Exploration, and the Triumph of American Natural History* by Darrin Lunde
- *The Rise of Theodore Roosevelt* by Edmund Morris
- *The Strenuous Life: Theodore Roosevelt and the Making of the American Athlete* by Ryan Swanson
- *Theodore Roosevelt: An Autobiography*
- *Theodore Roosevelt: A Literary Life* by Thomas Bailey
- *Theodore Roosevelt in the Badlands: A Young Politician's Quest for Recovery in the American West* by Roger I. Silvestro

What's next? *The Bloodstone Brooch* is set in 1896 New York City with

Tavis, Remy, and Austin. When will it be out? It takes a year to research and to write a brooch book—the length of three regular-sized romance novels. I wish I could write faster.

How many brooch books will there be? I don't know. I turn 71 this year, and as long as I can keep writing and readers still want to read them, I'll keep doing what I love doing—writing in the MacKlenna World!

Blessings,

Katherine

THE CELTIC BROOCH SERIES

THE RUBY BROOCH (Book 1)
Kitherina MacKlenna and Cullen Montgomery's love story

THE LAST MACKLENNA (Book 2 – not a time travel story)
Meredith Montgomery and Elliott Fraser's love story

THE SAPPHIRE BROOCH (Book 3)
Charlotte Mallory and Braham McCabe's love story

THE EMERALD BROOCH (Book 4)
Kenzie Wallis-Manning and David McBain's love story

THE BROKEN BROOCH (Book 5 – not a time travel story)
JL O'Grady and Kevin Allen's love story

THE THREE BROOCHES (Book 6)
A reunion with Kit and Cullen Montgomery

THE DIAMOND BROOCH (Book 7)
Amy Spalding and Jack Mallory's love story

THE AMBER BROOCH (Book 8)
Amber Kelly and Daniel Grant's love story
Olivia Kelly and Connor O'Grady's love story

THE PEARL BROOCH (Book 9)
Sophia Orsini and Pete Parrino's love story

THE TOPAZ BROOCH (Book 10)
Wilhelmina "Billie" Penelope Malone and Rick O'Grady's love story

There are many more Brooch Books to come.
To read about the next few books, visit
www.katherinellogan.com/whats-next-2

ABOUT THE AUTHOR

Author Katherine Lowry Logan couples her psychology degree with lots of hands-on research when creating new settings and characters for her blockbuster Celtic Brooch series.

These cross-genre stories have elements of time travel, sci-fi, fantasy adventure, mystery, suspense, historical, and romance and focus on events in American history.

A few of her favorite research adventures include:

- attending the Battle of Cedar Creek reenactment and visiting Civil War sites in Richmond, Virginia (*Sapphire Brooch*),
- riding in a B-17 Flying Fortress bomber, and visiting Bletchley Park and the beaches at Normandy (*Emerald Brooch*),
- research in Paris, France, and Florence, Italy, with an art lesson in Florence (*Pearl Brooch*),
- a tour of New York's Yankee Stadium and several hours with their historian (*Diamond Brooch*),
- wine tours in Napa (*The Last MacKlenna*),
- and following the Oregon Trail for the first book in the series (*Ruby Brooch*).

Katherine is the mother of two daughters and grandmother of five—Charlotte, Lincoln, James Cullen, Henry, and Meredith. She is also a marathoner and lives in Lexington, Kentucky, with her fluffy Goldendoodle, Maddie the Marauder.

Website
www.katherinellogan.com

Facebook
facebook.com/katherine.l.logan

Twitter
twitter.com/KathyLLogan

I'm A Runner (Runner's World Magazine Interview)
www.runnersworld.com/celebrity-runners/im-a-runner-katherine-lowry-logan

If you would like to receive notification of future releases sign up today at KatherineLLogan.com or

send an email to KatherineLLogan@gmail.com and put "New Release" in the subject line. And if you are on Facebook, join the Celtic Brooch Series for ongoing book and character discussions.

*　*　*

Thank you for reading THE SUNSTONE BROOCH.
I hope you enjoyed reading this story as much as I enjoyed writing it.

Made in the USA
Coppell, TX
22 May 2022

78062686R10430